P9-DDY-624

DEAR READER,

There's nothing I find more fascinating to write about than the relationship between men and women. To me it's a grand mystery that can be solved time and time again in an endless variety of ways. Over the years it's given me tremendous pleasure to mix and match strong men and strong women, to watch them clash and spark. To see them discover their own hearts and fall in love.

The three stories that follow are very dear to my heart. They were written many years ago, and I'm delighted to present them to you once again. Hopefully, a new generation of readers will be entertained by them. Romance, after all, is timeless. Love never goes out of fashion, and what comes from the heart is the most basic of truths.

For those who have read my books before, and those who are reading me for the first time, I hope these stories, these people, these loves that came from my heart find a place in yours.

BEST,

Nora Roberts

From the Heart

THREE CLASSIC LOVE STORIES FROM
NEW YORK TIMES BESTSELLING AUTHOR

NORA ROBERTS...

Tonight and Always

When a renowned anthropologist agreed to help a writer research his new novel, she wasn't prepared for the passion their collaboration would spark . . .

A Matter of Choice

An international smuggling ring traps a beautiful antiques dealer and a New York City cop in a web of danger and desire . . .

Endings and Beginnings

Two Washington television reporters try to protect their love from their own professional rivalry—and the hazards of their celebrity . . .

Nora Roberts

HOT ICE
SACRED SINS
BRAZEN VIRTUE
SWEET REVENGE
PUBLIC SECRETS
GENUINE LIES
CARNAL INNOCENCE
DIVINE EVIL
HONEST ILLUSIONS
PRIVATE SCANDALS
HIDDEN RICHES
TRUE BETRAYALS
MONTANA SKY
SANCTUARY
HOMEPORT

THE REEF
RIVER'S END
CAROLINA MOON
THE VILLA
MIDNIGHT BAYOU
THREE FATES
BIRTHRIGHT
NORTHERN LIGHTS
BLUE SMOKE
ANGELS FALL
HIGH NOON
TRIBUTE
BLACK HILLS
THE SEARCH

Series

Irish Born Trilogy
BORN IN FIRE
BORN IN ICE
BORN IN SHAME

Key Trilogy
KEY OF LIGHT
KEY OF KNOWLEDGE
KEY OF VALOR

Dream Trilogy
DARING TO DREAM
HOLDING THE DREAM
FINDING THE DREAM

In The Garden Trilogy
BLUE DAHLIA
BLACK ROSE
RED LILY

Chesapeake Bay Saga
SEA SWEPT
RISING TIDES
INNER HARBOR
CHESAPEAKE BLUE

Circle Trilogy
MORRIGAN'S CROSS
DANCE OF THE GODS
VALLEY OF SILENCE

Gallaghers of Ardmore Trilogy
JEWELS OF THE SUN
TEARS OF THE MOON
HEART OF THE SEA

Sign of Seven Trilogy
BLOOD BROTHERS
THE HOLLOW
THE PAGAN STONE

Three Sisters Island Trilogy
DANCE UPON THE AIR
HEAVEN AND EARTH
FACE THE FIRE

Bride Quartet
VISION IN WHITE
BED OF ROSES
SAVOR THE MOMENT
HAPPY EVER AFTER

Nora Roberts & J. D. Robb

REMEMBER WHEN

J. D. Robb

NAKED IN DEATH
GLORY IN DEATH
IMMORTAL IN DEATH
RAPTURE IN DEATH
CEREMONY IN DEATH
VENGEANCE IN DEATH
HOLIDAY IN DEATH
CONSPIRACY IN DEATH
LOYALTY IN DEATH
WITNESS IN DEATH
JUDGMENT IN DEATH
BETRAYAL IN DEATH
SEDUCTION IN DEATH
REUNION IN DEATH
PURITY IN DEATH
PORTRAIT IN DEATH
IMITATION IN DEATH
DIVIDED IN DEATH
VISIONS IN DEATH
SURVIVOR IN DEATH
ORIGIN IN DEATH
MEMORY IN DEATH
BORN IN DEATH
INNOCENT IN DEATH
CREATION IN DEATH
STRANGERS IN DEATH
SALVATION IN DEATH
PROMISES IN DEATH
KINDRED IN DEATH
FANTASY IN DEATH
INDULGENCE IN DEATH

Anthologies

FROM THE HEART
A LITTLE MAGIC
A LITTLE FATE

MOON SHADOWS
(with Jill Gregory, Ruth Ryan Langan, and Marianne Willman)

The Once Upon Series
(with Jill Gregory, Ruth Ryan Langan, and Marianne Willman)

ONCE UPON A CASTLE
ONCE UPON A STAR
ONCE UPON A KISS
ONCE UPON A ROSE
ONCE UPON A DREAM
ONCE UPON A MIDNIGHT

* * *

SILENT NIGHT
(with Susan Plunkett, Dee Holmes, and Claire Cross)

OUT OF THIS WORLD
(with Laurell K. Hamilton, Susan Krinard, and Maggie Shayne)

BUMP IN THE NIGHT
(with Mary Blayney, Ruth Ryan Langan, and Mary Kay McComas)

DEAD OF NIGHT
(with Mary Blayney, Ruth Ryan Langan, and Mary Kay McComas)

THREE IN DEATH

SUITE 606
(with Mary Blayney, Ruth Ryan Langan, and Mary Kay McComas)

THE LOST
(with Patricia Gaffney, Mary Blayney, and Ruth Ryan Langan)

THE OTHER SIDE
(with Mary Blayney, Patricia Gaffney, Ruth Ryan Langan,
and Mary Kay McComas)

Also available . . .

THE OFFICIAL NORA ROBERTS COMPANION
(edited by Denise Little and Laura Hayden)

NORA ROBERTS

FROM *the* HEART

JOVE BOOKS, NEW YORK

THE BERKLEY PUBLISHING GROUP
Published by the Penguin Group
Penguin Group (USA) Inc.
375 Hudson Street, New York, New York 10014, USA
Penguin Group (Canada), 90 Eglinton Avenue East, Suite 700, Toronto, Ontario M4P 2Y3, Canada
(a division of Pearson Penguin Canada Inc.)
Penguin Books Ltd., 80 Strand, London WC2R 0RL, England
Penguin Group Ireland, 25 St. Stephen's Green, Dublin 2, Ireland (a division of Penguin Books Ltd.)
Penguin Group (Australia), 250 Camberwell Road, Camberwell, Victoria 3124, Australia
(a division of Pearson Australia Group Pty. Ltd.)
Penguin Books India Pvt. Ltd., 11 Community Centre, Panchsheel Park, New Delhi—110 017, India
Penguin Group (NZ), 67 Apollo Drive, Rosedale, North Shore 0632, New Zealand
(a division of Pearson New Zealand Ltd.)
Penguin Books (South Africa) (Pty.) Ltd., 24 Sturdee Avenue, Rosebank, Johannesburg 2196,
South Africa

Penguin Books Ltd., Registered Offices: 80 Strand, London WC2R 0RL, England

This is a work of fiction. Names, characters, places, and incidents either are the product of the author's imagination or are used fictitiously, and any resemblance to actual persons, living or dead, business establishments, events, or locales is entirely coincidental. The publisher does not have any control over and does not assume any responsibility for author or third-party websites or their content.

FROM THE HEART

A Jove Book / published by arrangement with the author

PRINTING HISTORY
Tonight and Always Silhouette Books edition / July 1983
A Matter of Choice Silhouette Books edition / May 1984
Endings and Beginnings Silhouette Books edition / January 1984
First Jove Books one-volume edition / November 1996

From the Heart compilation copyright © 1996 by Nora Roberts.
Tonight and Always copyright © 1983 by Nora Roberts.
A Matter of Choice copyright © 1984 by Nora Roberts.
Endings and Beginnings copyright © 1984 by Nora Roberts.
Excerpt from *Naked in Death* by J. D. Robb copyright © by Nora Roberts.
Cover art direction and design by Rita Frangie.

ISBN: 978-0-515-14918-0

JOVE®
Jove Books are published by The Berkley Publishing Group,
a division of Penguin Group (USA) Inc.,
375 Hudson Street, New York, New York 10014.
JOVE® is a registered trademark of Penguin Group (USA) Inc.
The "J" design is a trademark of Penguin Group (USA) Inc.

PRINTED IN THE UNITED STATES OF AMERICA

35 34 33 32 31 30 29 28

*To my parents, who've proven
through sixty years of marriage
that love never goes out of style.
Thanks for being mine.*

Contents

Tonight and Always

1

It was dusk, that strange, almost mystical interlude when light and dark are perfectly balanced. Within moments the soft blue would be transformed by the fiery colors of sunset. Shadows were lengthening; birds were quieting.

Kasey stood at the foot of the steps leading to the Taylor mansion. She glanced up at the massive white pillars and old rose brick with huge expanses of plate glass. Three stories. Here and there lights shone dimly through drawn drapes. There was a monied dignity about the place. Old money, inherent dignity.

Intimidating, she thought, letting her eyes roam up and down again. But it did have a certain style. Under the cover of dusk the house looked serene.

Lifting a large brass knocker, she thudded it against the thick oak door. The noise boomed into the twilight. She smiled at the sound, then turned to watch the colors bleed slowly into the sky. Already it was more night than day. Behind her the door opened. Turning back, Kasey saw a small, dark woman dressed in a black uniform and white apron.

Just like the movies, she decided, and smiled again. This just might be an adventure after all.

"Hello."

"Good evening, ma'am." The maid spoke politely and stood in the center of the doorway like a palace guard.

"Good evening," Kasey said, amused. "I believe Mr. Taylor's expecting me."

"Miss Wyatt?" Dubiously, the maid scanned her. She made no move to admit her. "I believe Mr. Taylor is expecting you tomorrow."

"Yes, well, I'm here tonight." Still smiling, she strode past the maid and into the main hall. "You might want to let him know I'm here," she suggested and turned to stare at a three-tiered chandelier that dripped light onto the carpet.

Watching Kasey warily, the maid shut the door. "If you would just wait here." She indicated a Louis XVI chair. "I'll inform Mr. Taylor of your arrival."

"Thank you." Her attention was already caught by a Rembrandt self-portrait. The maid moved soundlessly away.

Kasey studied the Rembrandt and went on to the next painting. Renoir. The place is like a museum, she decided, then continued to move idly down the hall, viewing paintings as she would in an art gallery. To Kasey, such works of art were public property—to be respected, admired and most of all, seen. I wonder if anybody really lives here, she thought and flicked a finger over a thick, gold frame.

The murmur of voices caught her attention. Instinctively, she drifted toward the sound.

"She is one of the leading authorities on American Indian culture, Jordan. Her last paper was highly acclaimed. Being only twenty-five, she's rather a phenomenon in anthropological circles."

"I'm well aware of that, Harry, or I wouldn't have agreed with your suggestion that she collaborate with me on this book." Jordan Taylor swirled a pre-dinner martini. He drank slowly, contemplatively. The drink was dry and perfect, with only a hint of vermouth. "I do find myself wondering how we're going to get on over the next few months. Professional spinsters are intimidating, and not my favorite companions."

"You're not looking for a companion, Jordan," the other man reminded him and plucked the olive from his own glass. "You're looking for an expert on American Indian culture. That's what you're getting." He swallowed the olive. "Companions can be distracting."

With a grimace, Jordan Taylor set down his glass. He was

restless without knowing why. "I hardly think I'll find your Miss Wyatt a distraction." He slipped his hands into the pockets of his perfectly tailored slacks and watched his companion polish off the martini. "I have a composite picture: mud-colored hair scraped back from a bony face, thick glasses with three-inch lenses perched on a prominent nose. Sensible suits to accent her lack of shape, and size ten orthopedic shoes."

"Size six."

Both men turned to the doorway and stared.

"Hello, Mr. Taylor." Kasey entered. Crossing the room, she extended her hand to Jordan. "And you must be Dr. Rhodes. We've done quite a bit of corresponding over the past weeks, haven't we? I'm glad to meet you."

"Yes, well. I . . ." Harry's thick brows lowered.

"I'm Kathleen Wyatt." She gave him a dazzling smile before turning back to Jordan. "As you can see, I don't scrape back my hair. It probably wouldn't stay scraped back if I tried." She tugged on one of the loose curls that surrounded her face.

"And rather than mud-colored," she continued smoothly, "this shade is generally known as strawberry blond. My face isn't particularly bony, though I do have rather nice cheekbones. Have you got a light?"

She rummaged through her purse for a cigarette, then looked expectantly at Harry Rhodes. He fumbled in his pocket and found his lighter. "Thanks. Where was I? Oh, yes," she continued before either man could speak. "I do wear glasses for reading—when I can find them—but I doubt that's quite what you meant, is it? Let's see, what else can I tell you? Can I sit down? My feet are killing me." Without waiting for a reply, she chose a gold brocade chair. She paused and flicked her cigarette in a crystal ashtray. "You already know my shoe size." Sitting back in the chair, she regarded Jordan Taylor with direct green eyes.

"Well, Miss Wyatt," he said at length. "I don't know whether to apologize or applaud."

"I'd rather have a drink. Do you have any tequila?"

With a nod, he moved to the bar. "I don't believe we do; would vermouth do?"

"That would do fine, thank you."

Kasey surveyed the room. It was large and perfectly square with rich paneling and heavily brocaded furnishings. An intricately carved marble fireplace dominated one wall. Dresden porcelain reflected in a wide, mahogany-framed mirror above it. The carpet was thick, the drapes heavy.

Too formal, she thought, observing the structured elegance. She would have preferred the drapes opened wide, or better yet, removed completely and replaced with something a bit less somber. There was probably a beautiful hardwood floor under the carpeting.

"Miss Wyatt." Jordan brought her attention back to him as he handed her a glass. Each one curious about the other, their eyes met, then a movement in the doorway distracted their attention.

"Jordan, Millicent tells me that Miss Wyatt has arrived, but she must have wandered—oh." The woman who glided into the room halted as she spotted Kasey. "You're Kathleen Wyatt?" With the same wariness the maid had shown, she surveyed the woman dressed in gray trousers and a brilliant peacock blue blouse.

Kasey sipped and smiled. "Yes, I am." She made her own survey of the elegantly groomed society matron. Jordan Taylor's mother, Beatrice Taylor, was carefully made up, impeccably groomed and stylishly attired. Beatrice Taylor knew who and what she was, Kasey thought.

"You must forgive the confusion, Miss Wyatt. We weren't expecting you until sometime tomorrow."

"I got things organized more quickly than I expected," Kasey said and sipped at her drink. "I caught an earlier flight." She smiled again. "I didn't see any point in wasting time."

"Of course." Beatrice's face creased for a moment in a frown. "Your room's prepared." She turned her eyes to her son. "I've put Miss Wyatt in the Regency Room."

"Adjoining Alison?" Jordan paused in the act of lighting a thin cigar and glanced at his mother.

"Yes, I thought perhaps Miss Wyatt would enjoy the company. Alison is my granddaughter," she explained to Kasey. "She's been with us since my son and his wife were killed three years ago. She was only eight, poor dear." Her attention shifted back to Jordan. "If you'll excuse me, I'll see about your bags."

"Well." Jordan took a seat on the sofa when his mother slipped from the room. "Perhaps we should discuss business for a moment."

"Of course." Kasey finished off the vermouth and set the glass on the table beside her. "Do you like a strict routine— you know, designated hours? Nine to two, eight to ten. Or do you just like to flow?"

"Flow?" Jordan repeated and glanced up at Harry.

"You know. Flow." She made a descriptive gesture with her hands.

"Ah, flow." Jordan nodded, amused. This was definitely not the straight-laced, low-key scientist of his imagination. "Why don't we try a little of both?"

"Good. I'd like to go over your outline tomorrow and get a better feel for what you have in mind. You can let me know what you want to concentrate on first."

Kasey studied Jordan for a moment as Harry fixed himself another martini. Very attractive, she decided, in a smooth, Wall Street sort of manner. Nice hair; warm brown with just a few light touches. He must get out of this museum now and then to get sunstreaked, she thought, but she doubted whether he was much of a beachcomber. She had always liked blue eyes in a man, and Jordan's were very dark. And, she thought, very shrewd. A lean face. Good bones. She wondered if he had any Cheyenne blood in him. The skull structure was very similar. The sophisticated clothes and manners were offset by a certain sensuousness around the mouth. She liked the contrast. He was built like a tennis player, she mused. Good shoulders, trim, strong hands. His tailor was obviously exclusive and conservative. Too bad, she thought again.

But watch out, she told herself, there's a bit more here than meets the eye. She had a feeling there was a temper under the cool sophistication. She knew, from reading his books, that he was intelligent. The only fault she had found with his work was a certain coldness.

"I'm sure we'll work very well together, Mr. Taylor," she

said aloud. "I'm looking forward to getting started. You're a fine writer."

"Thank you."

"Don't thank me, I didn't have anything to do with it." She smiled.

Jordan's lips curved in instinctive response even as he wondered what he had gotten himself into.

"I'm very pleased to have the opportunity to help you with your research," she went on. "I suppose I really should thank you, Dr. Rhodes, for suggesting my name." Her gaze shifted and locked on Harry.

"Well, you, ah—your credentials—were impeccable." Harry stammered as he tried to connect the Kathleen Wyatt whose papers he had read with the slim, curly haired whirlwind who was smiling at him. "You graduated magna cum laude from Maryland University?"

"That's right. I majored in anthropology at Maryland, then took my masters at Columbia. I worked with Dr. Spalding on his Colorado expedition. I believe it was my paper on that which brought me to your attention."

"Excuse me, sir." The dark maid hovered in the doorway. "Miss Wyatt's baggage has been taken to her room. Mrs. Taylor suggested that perhaps she would like to freshen up before dinner."

"I'll skip dinner, thanks." Kasey spoke to the maid directly, then turned back to Dr. Rhodes. "I will go up, though. Traveling tires me out. Good night, Dr. Rhodes. I suppose we'll be seeing each other over the next few months. I'll see you in the morning, Mr. Taylor."

She swept out as she had swept in, leaving both men staring after her.

"Well, Harry." Jordan thought he could all but feel the room settle back into order. "What was it you were saying about distractions?"

After following the maid up the stairs, Kasey stood in the doorway of her room. Pale pinks and golds dominated the color scheme. Pink drapes hung against oyster white walls; pink and gold cushions graced ornately carved Regency chairs. There was a gold skirted vanity table and a large, plush-covered lounge in a deeper shade of rose. The bed was huge and canopied, complete with bed curtains and a pink satin spread.

"Good grief," she murmured and stepped across the threshold.

"I beg your pardon, miss?"

Kasey turned to the maid and smiled. "Nothing. This is quite a room."

"The bath is through here, Miss Wyatt. Would you care to have me draw you one now?"

"Draw my—no." Kasey grinned, unable to do otherwise. "No, thank you—Millicent, right?"

"Yes, miss. Very well, miss. If you require anything, just press nine on the house phone." Millicent slipped noiselessly out the door, closing it carefully behind her.

Kasey dropped her purse on the bed and began to explore the room.

To her mind, it was entirely too proper and pink. She decided she would ignore it and spend as little time within its walls as possible. Besides, she was too tired from planes and taxis to care where she slept now. She began to search for the nightgown that Millicent had apparently tucked away in a bureau.

"Come on in," she called as a knock sounded on the door. She continued to rummage through the carefully folded lingerie. She lifted her eyes to the mirror. "Hello. You must be Alison."

She saw a tall, thin child in a simply cut, expensive dress. Her long blond hair was carefully groomed, pulled neatly back with a headband. Her eyes were large and dark, but their expression was neither happy nor unhappy. Kasey felt a stirring of pity.

"Good evening, Miss Wyatt." Alison broke the silence but came no further into the room. "I thought I should introduce myself, as we'll be sharing a bath for the next few months."

"Good idea." Kasey turned from the mirror and faced Alison directly. "Though I imagine we'd have run across each other in the shower before too long."

"If you have a preference for your bath time, Miss Wyatt, I would be happy to accommodate you."

Kasey moved to the bed to drop her nightgown. "I'm not

fussy. I've shared bathrooms before." She sat gingerly on the edge of the bed and glanced up dubiously at the canopy. "I'll try to stay out of your way in the mornings. You go to school, I imagine."

"Yes, I'm attending school this year. Last year I had a tutor. I'm very high-strung."

"Is that so?" Kasey lifted her brows and struggled with a smile. "I'm low-strung, myself."

Alison frowned at this. Unable to decide whether to advance or retreat, she hesitated on the threshold.

Kasey noted the uncertainty, the trained manners, the hands that were neatly folded at the waist of the expensive dress. She remembered the child was only eleven. "Tell me, Alison, what do you do around here for fun?"

"Fun?" Fascinated, Alison stepped into the room.

"Yes, fun. You can't go to school all the time." She pushed a stray curl out of her eyes. "And I'm definitely not going to be working twenty-four hours a day."

"There's a tennis court." Alison came a bit closer. "And the pool, of course."

Kasey nodded. "I like to swim," she went on before Alison could comment. "But I'm not too good at tennis. Do you play?"

"Yes, I—"

"Terrific. Maybe you can give me some lessons." Her eyes swept the room again. "Tell me, is your room pink?"

Alison stared a moment, trying to understand the change in topic. "No, it's done in blues and greens."

"Hmmm, good choice." Kasey made a face at the drapes. "I painted my room purple once when I was fifteen. I had nightmares for two months." She caught Alison's unblinking stare. "Something wrong?"

"You don't look like an anthropologist," Alison blurted out, then caught her breath at her lack of manners.

"No?" Kasey thought of Jordan and lifted her brows. "Why?"

"You're pretty." A blush rushed into Alison's cheeks.

"You think so?" Kasey rose to peer at herself in the mirror. She narrowed her eyes. "Sometimes I think so, but mostly I think my nose is too small."

Alison was staring at Kasey's reflection. As their eyes met in the glass, Kasey's lit with a smile. It was slow, warm and all-encompassing. Alison's lips, so much like her uncle's, curved in unconscious response.

"I have to go down to dinner now." She backed out of the door, unwilling to lose sight of the smile. "Good night, Miss Wyatt."

"Good night, Alison."

Turning as the door shut, Kasey sighed. An interesting group, she decided. Her mind turned toward Jordan again. Very interesting.

She walked over and picked up the nightgown again, then ran it idly through her hands. And where, she wondered, does Kasey Wyatt fit into all of this? With a sigh, she sat on the lounge chair. The conversation between Jordan and Dr. Rhodes which she had walked in on had been more amusing than annoying. But still . . . Kasey let Jordan's description of her run through her mind again.

Typical, she decided. A typical layman's view of a scientist who happens to be a woman. Kasey was perfectly aware that she had unsettled Harry Rhodes. A smile tugged at her mouth. She thought she would like him. He was rather staid and pompous and, she reflected, probably very sweet. Beatrice Taylor was another matter. Kasey leaned back in the lounge chair and ordered herself to relax. There would be no common ground between herself and the older woman, but, Kasey thought, if they were lucky, there would be no animosity. As for the child . . .

Kasey closed her eyes and began to unbutton her blouse as she lay there. Alison. Mature for her age—maybe too mature. Kasey knew what it was like to lose parents in childhood. There were feelings of confusion, betrayal, guilt. It was a lot for a young person to cope with. Who mothers her now? she wondered. Beatrice? Kasey shook her head. Somehow, she couldn't picture the elegant matron mothering an eleven-year-old girl. She would see that Alison was well-dressed, well-fed and well-mannered. Kasey felt a second stir of pity.

Then there's Jordan. With another sigh, Kasey roused herself enough to pull off her blouse and slip off her shoes.

He wouldn't be an easy man to get close to. Kasey wasn't at all certain she wanted to.

Standing, she unbuckled her trousers and headed for the bath. What she wanted was to put her education and her experience to work on his book. She wanted to see the information she gave him utilized in the best possible manner. What she wanted, she thought and turned the hot water on full, was a bath. The hours on the plane, preceded by a week of lecturing in New York, had left her as close to exhaustion as she ever came. Thinking of Jordan Taylor would simply have to wait.

Tomorrow, she thought as she lowered herself into the tub, would be here soon enough.

2

The sun glittered over the pool's surface as Jordan completed his tenth lap. He cut through the water with strong, sure strokes. When he swam, he didn't think but simply let his body take over. As a novelist, he found his mind too often crowded with characters, with places. With words. He started off the day by clearing it with something physical.

That morning there had been one more character intruding into his brain. Kathleen Wyatt. He had found her fascinating. He wasn't at all certain he wanted to be fascinated by a collaborator. His work was important to him, and the novel he was currently working on might be the most important in his career. He thought perhaps it would have been better if Kathleen Wyatt had been closer to the woman of his imagination. The reality of her was entirely too unsettling.

As he reached the pool edge and made to turn for another lap, a movement caught his attention. Jordan glanced up to see a vague face surrounded by red-gold curls.

"Hi."

Shaking water from his eyes, Jordan narrowed them against the sun. He focused on his collaborator. Kasey sat cross-legged at the pool's edge. Her cutoffs and T-shirt exposed skin still pale from October in New York. Her eyes were bright with amusement as she smiled at him. Entirely too unsettling, he thought again.

"Good morning, Miss Wyatt. You're up early."

"I suppose I haven't adjusted to the time change." Her voice, he realized all at once, wasn't eastern but had the slightest hint of the south. "I went for a run."

"A run?" he repeated, distracted from trying to place the vague accent.

"Yes, I'm into running." She lifted her face and studied the perfect sky. "Actually, I was into running before it was something to get into. Even though I resent being part of a trend, I can't stop. Do you swim every morning?"

"Whenever I can."

"Maybe I'll try that instead. Swimming uses more muscles, and you don't sweat."

"I never thought about it quite that way." After pulling himself from the water, he reached for a towel.

Kasey watched as he briskly rubbed his hair. His body, glistening with droplets of water, was lean and hard and brown. There were ropings of muscles in his arms and shoulders. The hair on his chest was blond, like the lighter streaks on his head that the sun had bleached. The brief suit clung to his hips. Kasey discovered she had been right about the athletic body beneath the conservative suit. She felt a flutter of desire and ignored it. This was not a man to become involved with, and now was not the time.

"Swimming's certainly kept you in shape," she observed.

He paused for a moment. "Thank you, Miss Wyatt." He shook his head and picked up a short terry robe.

Kasey stood in one swift, fluid motion. Her head was level with his chin. "Would you like to get started after breakfast? If you've something else to do, I can just go over your outline and notes myself."

"No, I'd like very much to get started. The idea of picking your brain becomes more intriguing by the minute."

"Really?" Her smile flashed over her face. "I hope you won't be disappointed, Jordan. I'm going to call you Jordan now. We'd have gotten to it sooner or later."

He nodded in agreement. "Do I call you Kathleen?"

"I certainly hope not." She grinned. "No one else does."

It took him a moment to understand. "Kasey, then."

He was looking at her again in that deep, searching manner

that left her slightly disconcerted. Jordan watched a frown come and go in her eyes.

"Can we eat?" she demanded. It would be simpler, she decided, if they got down to more practical matters. "I've been hungry for hours."

Kasey and Jordan closed themselves in the study immediately after breakfast. The room was large, its walls lined with books. Here a scent of old leather and new polish mixed with tobacco. Kasey much preferred it to the other parts of the house she had seen. Here she could detect signs of production, though it was scrupulously organized production. There were no scattered papers, no precariously piled books.

Large, dark-framed glasses perched on her nose, Kasey sat by the window reading Jordan's notes. Her feet were bare, and one swung idly in the air as she scanned the pages.

She wasn't beautiful, Jordan decided. Not in the classic sense, at any rate. But her face was arresting. When she smiled, it seemed she lit from the inside out. Her eyes seemed to hold some private joke. She was tall and boyishly slim, narrow-hipped and long-legged. A man, he thought, would find angles rather than curves when he got into her bed. He frowned, annoyed with the turn of his mind.

There was a coltishness in her moves—an excitement and vibrancy which raced through her conversation as well. Now it was as though she had turned down the power. She was silent. Her features were tranquil. Her only movement was the carelessly swinging bare foot.

Kasey had been perfectly aware of Jordan's survey. "You have a fascinating story in the works here," she said, rupturing the silence and the sudden hum of sexual tension that had begun between them.

"Thank you." He cocked a brow. He had felt the tension, too, and was as wary of it as she.

Pulling up her legs, Kasey picked up a cigarette. She held it absently while she continued to meet his eyes. "It would seem you're dealing mainly with the Plains Indian. They do seem to most typify our image of the American Indian, though they're the least typical of all."

"Are they?" He rose to light the cigarette she still held

between her fingers. "I leave it to you to clear up the misconception and give me an accurate picture."

"You could do the same with a few well-selected reference books." She settled back in the chair. "Why do you need me?"

Sitting back, he gave her a considering look. His eyes made a slow, complete survey. It was calculated to disconcert.

"You didn't have to send to New York for that, either," she commented dryly. "You're not going to get maidenly blushes, Jordan." She smiled and watched his lips curve in response. "I'll tell you what," she decided on impulse. "I'll put an end to your curiosity, then you put an end to mine. I'm a professional anthropologist, not a professional virgin. Now, what, precisely, do you want from me as regards your current novel?"

"Are you always so frank?"

"Not always," she said evasively. It wouldn't be smart to get too frank with him. "Now, about your book."

"Facts; details on customs, clothing, village life; when, where and how." He paused and lit a thin cigar, then regarded Kasey through a screen of smoke. "Those are things I can get from reference books. But I want more. I want *why*."

Kasey crushed out the cigarette he had lit for her. Jordan noted that she had taken no more than two halfhearted puffs. There were more nerves in her than she let show.

"You want me to supply you with theories as to why a culture developed a certain way and why it survived or succumbed to outside pressures."

"Exactly."

With the storyline he was developing and the right slant, it could be a marvelous book, Kasey thought.

"Okay," she said suddenly. With a flashing smile, she dropped her eyes to Jordan's. "I'll give you a general outline. We can pick up specifics as we move along."

Three hours later Jordan stood at his window and gazed down at the pool. Kasey swam alone. She wore a one-piece suit that clung to her. He watched her dive beneath the surface and streak along the mosaic bottom.

She swam, he decided, as she did everything else—with

quick bursts of energy interspersed with moments of calm. She was a sprinter, not a long-distance runner.

Kasey surfaced, rolled to her back, then floated. She thought about Jordan Taylor as she watched a few stringy white clouds work their way across the sky. He's brilliant, conservative, successful. Incredibly sexy. Why does that worry me? She narrowed her eyes against the sun and let her mind and body drift. I should be very pleased with myself to have been asked to work with him. I was. It's probably the house, she decided and closed her eyes completely. There's no dust in it. How do people live without dust?

He must belong to some very exclusive country club. I imagine there are some very classy women in his life. Kasey swore at herself and rolled over.

She must have men in her life, Jordan thought. Other scientists, professors, probably a struggling artist or two. He cursed at himself and turned away from the window.

Kasey pulled herself from the pool and shook the water from her hair. Well, she thought and glanced at a lounge chair, if I'm going to live with the wealthy for a while, I might as well enjoy it. She flopped down and let the sun bake the chill from her damp skin. There was something to be said for all this. Private pool, private tennis court. She let her gaze sweep the huge expanse of lawn bordered by lush, green hedges and a stone wall. She wrinkled her nose. Privacy we've got. I wonder how often he gets out of here. Her mind settled back on Jordan. With a sigh, Kasey accepted the fact that he would probably continue to intrude in her thoughts. Closing her eyes, she gave into jet lag and slept.

"You could broil out here."

Kasey opened her eyes slowly and focused. "Hi." She gave Jordan a sleepy smile.

"You're very fair. You'll burn easily."

The hint of annoyance in his voice registered, and she studied him. "You're right, I suppose." She tested her skin by pressing a finger against her shoulder. "Not yet." She gave him another direct look. "Is something wrong?"

"No." He didn't want to admit, even to himself, that he had

had a difficult time concentrating on his work knowing she was there within view of his window.

"I'll be a bit more up to standard tomorrow," she told him, thinking perhaps he was irritated that she had given him only a few hours. "Planes wear me out. It must be the altitude." Her hair was almost dry, and she pushed a hand through it absently. It appeared almost copper in the sunlight. "Do you want me?"

He looked at her thoughtfully. "Yes, I believe I do."

Kasey caught the double entendre and thought it wise to stand up. "I don't think we meant the same thing." She smiled but kept out of reach.

He took a step toward her, surprising both of them. On impulse, he reached out to touch her hair. "You're a very attractive woman."

"And you're a very attractive man," she said smoothly. "And we're going to be working in close quarters for some time. I don't think we should—complicate things. I'm not being coy, Jordan. I'm being practical. I very much want to see this book through. It could mean every bit as much to me as it will to you."

"We'll make love sooner or later, you know."

"Oh, really?" She tilted her head.

"Yes, really." Turning, he left her alone by the pool.

Well, she thought, placing her hands on her hips. Is that so? I suppose he always gets his way. She stretched out on the lounger again. Though his high-handedness irritated her, Kasey admired his directness. He could drop the polished manners and elegance when he chose to. He might be more difficult than she had anticipated.

It would be foolish to deny she was attracted to him and equally foolish to act on the attraction. Kasey frowned and twisted a curl around her finger. What did Kathleen Wyatt have in common with Jordan Taylor? Nothing. She would not, could not, involve herself emotionally or physically with a man unless there was a firm base. Attraction wasn't enough, nor was respect. There was a need for affection, for friendship. Kasey wasn't at all certain she could be friends with Jordan Taylor. Time would tell, she told herself and settled back again. Then a movement caught her eye.

Looking over, Kasey smiled and raised her hand in a wave. Alison seemed to hesitate for a moment, then walked over to join her.

"Hi, Alison. Did you just get out of school?"

"Yes, I just got home."

"I'm playing hookey." Kasey leaned back against the cushions again. "Ever played hookey?"

Alison looked horrified. "No, of course not."

"Too bad, it can be fun." A sweet child, Kasey thought, and much too lonely. She shot the young girl a grin. "What are you studying?"

"American poets."

"Have a favorite?"

"I like Robert Frost."

"I always liked Frost." Kasey smiled as lines flitted through her mind. "His poems always remind me of my grandfather."

"Your grandfather?"

"He's a doctor in a remote section of West Virginia. Blue mountains, forest, streams. Last time I went home, he was still making house calls." He'll be making them when he's a hundred, she thought, and missed him suddenly, acutely. It had been too long since she'd been home. "He's an incredible man—big and strapping with white hair and a big, booming voice. Gentle hands."

"It would be nice to have a grandfather," Alison murmured, trying to picture him. "Did you see him often when you were growing up?"

"Every day." Kasey recognized the wistfulness. She reached out to touch Alison's hair. "My parents were killed when I was eight. He raised me."

Alison's eyes were very intense. "Did you miss them?"

"Sometimes I still do." She's still hurting, Kasey thought. I wonder if any of them know it. "To me, they'll always be young and happy together. It makes it easier."

"They used to laugh," Alison murmured. "I can remember them laughing."

"That's a good memory. You'll always have it." There's not enough laughter here, Kasey decided and felt a quick flash of anger for Jordan. Not nearly enough. "Alison." She broke into the child's thoughts. "I bet you dress for dinner."

"Yes, ma'am."

"Please." Kasey grinned and shook her head. "Don't call me that. It makes me feel a million years old. Call me Kasey."

"Grandmother wouldn't approve if I called an adult by her first name."

"Call me Kasey anyway and I'll deal with your grandmother if necessary. Why don't you come up and help me find something to wear? I don't want to disgrace the Taylor name."

Alison stared at her. "You want me to help you pick out a dress?"

"You probably know more about it than I do." Kasey smiled as she tucked Alison's arm in hers.

A few hours later Kasey stood at the doorway of the drawing room observing its occupants.

Beatrice Taylor sat in the gold brocade chair. She wore black silk and diamonds. Jewels glittered at her ears and throat. Alison was at the piano, dutifully practicing a selection from Brahms. Jordan stood at the bar mixing a batch of pre-dinner martinis.

The family hour. Kasey grimaced. She thought of the dinners she had shared with her grandfather—the laughter, the arguments. She thought of the noisy meals at college, with conversations ranging from the intellectual to the bizarre. She thought of the often inedible meals on various digs. Did money box you in this way? she wondered. Or was it a matter of choice?

Kasey waited until Alison had struggled through the last notes before entering the room. "Hi. You know, a person could wander around this place for days and not see another living soul."

"Miss Wyatt. You had only to ring for one of the staff. You would have been directed to the drawing room."

"Oh, that's all right. I finally made it. I hope I'm not late."

"Not at all," Jordan said. "I have only just begun to make a cocktail. How about a martini? Or perhaps you'll tell me what you want done with this tequila?"

"You got some?" Smiling, she moved to join him. "That was a nice thing to do. May I fix it?" She took the bottle from Jordan. "Watch carefully. I'm about to trust you with an old, closely guarded secret."

"Kasey's grandfather is a doctor," Alison announced suddenly. Beatrice shifted her attention from the couple at the bar to her granddaughter.

"Who is Kasey, dear?" Her tone was mildly annoyed. "One of your friends at school?"

Kasey glanced over to see Alison blush. "I'm Kasey, Mrs. Taylor," she answered easily. "You have to give it a good squeeze of lemon," she told Jordan and demonstrated. "I asked Alison to call me by my first name, Mrs. Taylor. Are you going to have one of these, Jordan?" She poured two glasses without waiting for his answer. She smiled at Beatrice, sipped, then turned back to Jordan. "What do you think?" she asked him. "Has a nice kick, doesn't it?"

He sipped, watching her. "Delicious," he murmured. "And unexpected."

She gave a quiet laugh, knowing he spoke of her and not the drink.

He found himself once more having to control the desire to touch her hair. "Don't you like knowing where your life's leading?"

"Oh, good grief, no!" she said immediately. "I want to be surprised. Don't you like surprises, Jordan?"

"I'm not at all sure," he murmured. He touched the rim of his glass to hers. "To the unexpected, then. For the time being."

Kasey wasn't at all certain what she was agreeing to, but she lifted her glass. "For the time being," she repeated.

Over the following days Jordan resigned himself to working seriously with Kasey. Harry had been right about one thing: She was unquestionably an expert in her field. She was also unsettling. There was a vibrant sexuality about her which she did nothing to accentuate. She rarely wore anything but the most casual of clothes and almost never bothered with even the most basic cosmetics.

He watched her as she sat on the window sill in his study.

The sun streamed onto her hair. It was Titian in this light. She wore running shorts and was again without shoes. On the third finger of her right hand she wore a very thin gold band. He had noticed it before and wondered who had given it to her and why. He doubted she would buy jewelry of any kind for herself. She wouldn't think of it.

With an effort, he pulled himself away from the woman and concentrated on her words.

"The sun dance was important to the ceremonial life of many of the Plains tribes." She had a quiet, low-key voice when she spoke like this. "Some practiced self-torture to induce trances and to aid in receiving visions. The dancer would thrust sharpened sticks through the folds of the flesh on his chest and attach the sticks to a post. He would dance, sing and pray for a vision until he tore himself free. It was also a sign of courage and endurance. A warrior had to prove himself—to himself and to his tribe. It was their way."

"You approve?"

She shot him a look that was both amused and patient. "It's not my place to approve or disapprove. I study. I observe. As a writer, I suppose you have a different viewpoint. But if you're going to write about it, you'd better try to understand the motivations." Pushing a couple of books out of her way, she sat on the table. "If a man could endure that kind of pain, self-inflicted pain, wouldn't he be fearless in battle? Ruthless? The survival of the tribe was the first priority."

"Cultural necessity," he said and nodded. "Yes, I see what you mean."

"Visions and dreams were an essential part of their culture. Men who had strong visions often became shamans." Turning, she began rummaging through the books on the desk. "There's a rather good picture . . . Blackfoot tribe . . . if I can remember which book."

"You're left-handed," he observed.

"*Hmm?* No, actually, I'm ambidextrous."

"That could account for it," he said wryly.

"For what?" she asked, raising an eyebrow.

"For the unexpected."

Kasey laughed. Her laughter touched something off inside him. "You should do that more often."

"Do what?"

"Laugh. You have a wonderful laugh."

He was still smiling, and it pulled at her. For days, she had been able to keep her feelings regulated. Picking up a cigarette, she searched for matches. "Of course, if we laugh too much in here, your mother's going to camp on the threshold."

He watched her pushing through books and papers. "Why would she do that?"

"Come on, Jordan. You know she thinks I plan to seduce you and abscond with half your fortune. Do you have a light?"

"You're not interested in either project?"

"We're business associates," she said curtly. She moved over to the desk, still searching for matches. She could feel the lightest flutter of nerves beginning. She sought to settle them before they grew. "And though you're very attractive, the money is a strike against you."

"Is that so?" Jordan rose and joined her. "Why? People are normally attracted to money."

Hearing the annoyance, Kasey sighed and turned to face him. She thought it best for both of them if she made her position perfectly clear. "Normality is relative, Jordan."

"So speaks the anthropologist."

"Your eyes get very dark when you're angry; did you know that? Money is very nice, Jordan. I often use it myself. But it tends to cloud reality."

"Whose reality?"

"My point exactly." She leaned back on the desk. "People with your kind of money never really see life as it is for the majority—day-to-day struggles, budgets, creditors, coupon clipping. You're removed from all that."

"You see that as a defect?"

"I didn't say that."

"Not your place to approve or disapprove?"

She blew the curls out of her eyes. How had she gotten into all this? "I'll admit it makes me nervous, but that's a personal problem. Don't you think that money tends to isolate the individual from everyday emotions?"

"All right." He pulled her against him. "Let's test your theory."

His mouth came to hers. It was not the kiss she had expected from him. It was hungry and possessive and demanded a complete, unquestioned response. For a moment she resisted it. Her mind was set firmly against surrendering. But her body began to heat. She heard herself moan as she drew him closer.

There was something almost savage in the way his mouth took hers. There was no gentleness, no seduction. He sought her response, thrived on it and demanded more. She gave. Her own needs left her no choice.

His lips left hers a moment, and she drew back, trying to clear her thoughts. "Oh, no." He kept her tight against him. "Not yet. I'm not nearly finished yet."

He exploited, he ravaged, he possessed. He was pulling something from her that she was not yet ready to give. She wanted to regain herself, break free, but her arms were around him. Her mouth was determined to have more.

His hand was rough when he took her breast. His fingers were long and lean and made her skin burn at the touch. It was more than pleasure, more than passion. Those she had felt before. Here was something beyond her experience. It frightened her, made her ache, made her answer his demand with more fervor. Then, when she knew the border of sanity would be crossed, he released her.

She stared up at him. Thoughts and emotions shuddered through her. She could still feel the needs. His flavor still lingered on her lips.

"This is the first time I've seen you at a loss for words," Jordan murmured. He slipped his hand around the back of her neck. His fingers caressed. Kasey felt a new surge of desire shoot through her.

"You took me by surprise." She slid out of his grasp and moved away from him. She was going to have to give this a great deal of thought, but now wasn't the time. She needed to find her balance again.

He watched her. It pleased him to note that he had unsettled her. But then, she had unsettled him as well. He hadn't been prepared for the intensity of the desire he had felt at the first taste of her.

"I'll have to make a habit of surprising you." She turned and faced him.

"I don't surprise easily, Jordan. And I don't plan to have an affair with you."

"Good. That should make things more interesting. I plan to have one with you."

I miscalculated, she thought to herself. He isn't as bound by social conventions as I thought. There is a strong ruthlessness under that social veneer. She would have to be more careful. She forced her voice to sound calm as she asked, "Wasn't I about to show you a picture of a shaman?"

He took the book from her hand and closed it firmly. "First things first. How would you like to take tomorrow off and go sailing?"

"Sailing?" Her tone was wary. "Just you and me?"

"That's what I had in mind."

The offer of freedom after days of being stifled in the house—the chance to be with him away from the work—was tempting. Too tempting. She shook her head. "I don't think it would be wise."

"You don't strike me as a woman who always does what's wise." His hand slipped up over her cheek into her hair.

"I'm making an exception. I really wish you wouldn't do that." She could feel her pulse beginning to hammer.

He kissed her gently on the temple. "Come with me, Kasey. I need a day away from this room, away from these books."

Perhaps just this once, she thought.

The boat was everything she had expected: sleek, luxurious and expensive. It had pleased her to watch Jordan handle the fifteen-foot sailing yacht with an ease that spoke of long experience. She sat at the bow so she could watch the boat slice through the ocean. This is his escape when that world he's locked himself into becomes too much for him, she mused.

Kasey watched him at the tiller. He was stripped to the waist. There was power in his arms and in his eyes. What would it be like to make love with him? She curled her legs under her on the padded bench and studied him carefully. He had marvelous hands. Even as she sat with the wind whipping around her, she could feel the touch. He would be a demanding lover, she decided, remembering the aggression of his kiss. Exciting. But . . . there's a but, and I'm not sure yet why it's there. I'm not sure I want to know.

Jordan looked over and caught her eye. "What are you thinking?"

"Just working out a hypothetical problem," she said, coloring. "Oh, look!" Over his shoulder she could see a school of dolphin. They leaped and dove and leaped again. "Aren't they marvelous?" She uncurled herself to go to the stern. She balanced herself by putting her hand on his shoulder, then leaned further out. "If I were a mermaid, I'd swim with them."

"Do you believe in mermaids, Kasey?"

"Of course." She smiled at him now. "Don't you?"

"Is this the scientist asking the question?" He lifted a hand to her hip.

"Next you'll be telling me there's no Santa Claus. For a writer, you have a faulty imagination." She took a deep breath of sea air. She started to move aside, but he caught her arm. The boat listed a bit, and his fingers tightened to hold her steady. Keep it light, she told herself, trying not to respond to his touch. "You can think about it over lunch."

"Hungry?" He smiled and rose. His hands moved up her sides to rest on her shoulders.

"I usually am. I'd like to see what Francois packed in that hamper."

"In a minute." He lowered his mouth to taste hers.

It was a different sort of kiss than they had shared the day before. His lips were still confident, but today they were gentle, slower. She could feel the heat from the sun, the ribbons of wind as they whipped around her. The scent of salt was in the air. Over their heads the sails flapped and billowed.

She was losing herself again. This wasn't what she wanted, this loss of power. Very carefully she drew herself out of his arms. "Jordan," she began, then blew out a breath to steady herself. He was smiling at her, and the hands on her shoulders lightened to a caress. "You're very pleased with yourself, aren't you?" she observed.

"As a matter of fact, I am."

He turned away and remained busy for some moments dropping sail. Kasey leaned against the rail without offering assistance. "Jordan, perhaps I've given you the wrong impression." Her tone was lighter again, more at ease. "I told you I wasn't a professional virgin. But I don't go to bed with just anybody."

He didn't even glance at her. "I'm not just anybody."

She tossed back her hair. "You don't have an ego problem, do you?"

"Not that I've noticed. Where did you get that ring you wear?"

Kasey glanced down at her hand. "It was my mother's. Why?"

"Just curious." He picked up the hamper. "Shall we see now what Francois has packed for us?"

3

The days were green and golden in the perpetual summer of Palm Springs. The sky was cloudless, the desert air dry and warm. To Kasey, the sameness was both inescapable and stifling. Routines were a necessary part of life which she characteristically rebelled against. The Taylor household moved smoothly—too smoothly. There were no curves to negotiate, no bumps. If anything could make Kasey nervous, it was a perfection of organization. The human condition included flaws. These Kasey understood and accepted. But flaws were scarce in the Taylor residence.

She worked with Jordan daily, and though she was aware that her lack of regimentation frustrated him, she was confident he could find no fault with her information. Kasey knew her field. She learned more of him. He was an exacting, disciplined writer and a demanding, meticulous man. He was able to extrapolate precisely what he wanted from the flood of facts and theories she provided. And Kasey, a tough critic, grew to respect and admire his mind. It was simpler for her to focus on his intelligence and talent than to dwell on him as a man, an individual who both attracted and unsettled her. Kasey wasn't accustomed to being unsettled.

She wasn't at all certain she liked him. They were opposites in many ways. He was pragmatic, she voluble. He was reserved, she extroverted. He ran on intellect, Kasey ran on emotion. Both, however, were used to being in control. It disturbed her that she was not able to master her attraction for him.

Kasey would never have considered herself idealistic. Yet she had always thought that when she became deeply involved with a man, it would be with someone who would fit neatly into the packet of her requirements. He would be strong, intelligent, with a well of emotions she could easily tap. They would understand each other. She was quite certain Jordan didn't understand her any more than she understood him. Their lifestyles were at complete variance. Still, she continued to think of him, to watch him, to wonder. He was crowding her mind.

As she sat in his study, reading over a draft of a new chapter, Kasey recognized that on this level, at least, they were reaching a firm compatibility. He was capturing the feelings she was trying to project to him, then intermingling them with dry facts and data. It was proof of her own usefulness. Being of use was essential to her.

Kasey laid the papers back in her lap and looked over at him. "It's wonderful, Jordan."

He stopped typing and, lifting a brow, met her eyes. "You sound surprised."

"Pleased," she corrected. "There's more empathy in this than I expected."

"Really?" The statement seemed to interest him as he leaned back in his chair and studied her.

It made Kasey uncomfortable. She felt that he was intuitive enough to see through her if he chose to. That, she wouldn't care for. She rose and walked to the window.

"I think you might delve deeper into the two subcultures of Plains life. The semiagricultural tribes of the eastern plains lived in villages and had traits of the Plains as well as the eastern and southeastern cultural areas. They consisted of——"

"Kasey."

"Yes, what?" She stuck her hands in her pockets and turned back to him.

"Are you nervous?"

"Of course not. Why should I be?" She began to search for her pack of cigarettes.

"When you're nervous, you go to the window or," he paused and picked up her cigarettes, "go for these."

"I go to the window to see what's outside," she countered, irritated with his perception. She held out her hand for her cigarettes, but he put them down on the desk and rose.

"When you're nervous," he went on as he crossed to her, "you have a difficult time keeping still. Something has to move—your hands, your shoulders."

"That's fascinating, I'm sure, Jordan." She kept her hands firmly in her pockets. "Did you take a course in psychology from Dr. Rhodes? I believe we were discussing the subcultures of the Plains Indians."

"No." He reached over and twined one of her curls around his finger. "I was asking you why you were nervous."

"I'm not nervous." She struggled to keep her body perfectly still. "I'm never nervous." A smile moved over his face. "What are you grinning at?"

"It's very rewarding to unnerve you, Kasey."

"Look, Jordan—"

"I don't believe I've seen you angry before," he commented, then took his other hand to her throat. Her pulse was beginning to hammer. Desire stirred inside him as it played under his palm.

"You wouldn't like it if you did."

"I'm not at all sure," he murmured. He wanted her. Standing there, he could all but feel the movement of her body under his. He wanted to touch her, to explore the sharp angles of her body and the softness of her skin. He wanted her to give herself to him with the enthusiasm that was so much a part of her. If he had ever wanted a woman as much before, he couldn't remember. "It's always interesting to watch a strong person lose control," he told her, still caressing her throat. "You're a very strong woman, and very soft. It's an arousing combination."

"I'm not here to arouse you, Jordan." Her body yearned for him. "I'm here to work with you."

"You do both very well. Tell me . . ." His voice slid over her skin as gently as his fingers. "Do you think of me when you're alone at night, in your room?"

"No."

He smiled again. Though he drew her no closer, Kasey felt the needs battering inside her. She was unaccustomed to restraining passion, unused to feeling it necessary.

"You don't lie well."

"Your arrogance is showing again, Jordan."

"I think of you." His fingers roamed to the back of her neck and tightened. "Too much."

"I don't want you to." Her voice was weak, and that frightened her. "No, I don't want you to." Shaking her head, she pulled away from him. "It wouldn't work."

"Why?"

"Because . . ." She fumbled and became more frightened. No one had been able to do this to her before. "Because we're looking for different things. I need more than you'd be able to give me." She ran a hand through her hair and knew she had to escape. "I'm going to take a break. We can pick up after lunch."

Jordan watched her dash from the room.

She's right, of course, he thought, frowning at the closed door. Everything she says makes perfect sense. *Why can't I stop thinking about her?* He walked around his desk and sat back down at the typewriter. She shouldn't appeal to me. Leaning back, he tried to dissect what he felt for her and why. Was it simply a physical attraction? If it was, why was he suddenly drawn toward a woman who was nothing like any other woman he had desired? And why did he find himself thinking of her at odd moments—when he was shaving, when he was in the middle of structuring a paragraph? It would be best if he simply accepted his feelings as desire and left it at that. There wasn't room for anything else. She was right, he decided. It wouldn't work.

He turned back to his notes, typed two sentences and swore.

Dashing through the parlor on her way to her room, Kasey spotted Alison sitting primly on the sofa reading. The girl looked up, and her eyes lit.

"Hi." Kasey could feel nerves and longings still running through her. "Playing hookey?"

"It's Saturday," Alison told her. She gave Kasey a hesitant smile.

"Oh." She would have had to be blind not to see the needs in the child's eyes. Setting aside her own problems, she sat next to Alison. "What're you reading?"

"*Wuthering Heights.*"

"Heavy stuff," Kasey commented, flipping a few pages and losing Alison's place. "I was reading Superman comic books at your age." She smiled and ran a hand down Alison's hair. "Still do, sometimes."

The child was staring at her with a mixture of awe and longing. Kasey bent down to kiss the top of her head. "Alison." She swept her eyes down the girl's blue linen pants suit. "Are you attached to that outfit?"

Alison looked down and stammered. "I—I don't know."

"Do you have any grubbies?"

"Grubbies?" Alison repeated, experimentally rolling the word around on her tongue.

"You know, old jeans, something with a hole in it, a chocolate stain."

"No. I don't think—"

"Never mind." Kasey grinned at her and set the book aside. "With all the clothes you have, one outfit shouldn't be missed. Come on." Rising, she took Alison's hand and pulled her to the patio door.

"Where are we going?"

Kasey glanced down at Alison. "We're going to borrow the gardener's hose and make mud sculptures. I want to see if you can get dirty." They stepped outside.

"Mud sculptures?" Alison repeated as they wound their way around to the garden.

"Think about it as an art project," Kasey suggested. "An educational experiment."

"I don't know if Haverson will let you have a hose," Alison warned.

"Oh, yeah?" Kasey grinned in anticipation as they approached the gardener. "We'll see."

"Good day, miss." Haverson tipped the brim of his cap and paused in his pruning.

"Hello, Mr. Haverson." Kasey gave him a flash of a smile. "I wanted to tell you how much I admire your garden. Particularly the azaleas. This." She touched a funnel-shaped blossom. "Tell me, do you use oak leaves as mulch?"

Fifteen minutes later Kasey had her hose and was busily manufacturing mud behind a clump of rhododendron bushes.

"How did you know all of that?" Alison asked her.

"All of what?"

"How did you know so much about the flowers? You're an anthropologist."

"Do you think a plumber only knows about pipes and grouting sinks?" She smiled over at Alison, amused by the concentration on the child's face. "Education is marvelous, Alison. There's nothing you can't know if you want to." She turned off the hose and crouched down. "What would you like to make?"

Gingerly Alison sat beside her and poked at the mud with a fingertip. "I don't know how."

Kasey laughed. "It's not acid, love." She plunged in, wrist deep. "Who's to say Michelangelo didn't get his start this way? I think I'll do a bust of Jordan." She sighed, wishing he hadn't popped into her head. "He's got a fascinating face, don't you think?"

"I suppose so. But he's rather old." Alison, still cautious, began to work the mud into a pile.

"Oh." Kasey wrinkled her nose. "He's only a few years older than I am, and I'm barely out of adolescence."

"You're not old, Kasey." Alison looked up again. Her eyes were suddenly intense. "You're not old enough to be my mother, are you?"

Kasey fell in love. Her heart was lost, and there was no turning back. She was needed. "No, Alison, I'm not old enough to be your mother." Her voice was soft, understanding. When the girl dropped her eyes, Kasey lifted her chin with a fingertip. "But I'm old enough to be your friend. I could use one, too."

"Really?"

The child was crying out to be loved, to be touched. Kasey felt a wave of anger for Jordan as she cupped Alison's face in her hands. "Really." She watched the smile start slowly until it bloomed over the child's face.

"Will you show me how to make a dog?" Alison demanded and stuck her hands into mud.

When they walked back to the house an hour later, they were giggling. Each carried a pair of mud-caked shoes. Kasey's mind was clearer than it had been for days. I need her as much as she needs me, she thought and glanced down at Alison. She laughed and stopped to lift the child's streaked face.

"You're beautiful," Kasey told her. Bending, she kissed her nose. "However, your grandmother might disagree, so you'd better get upstairs and into a tub."

"She's at a committee meeting," Alison commented and giggled again, seeing the mud on Kasey's cheek. "She's always at meetings."

"Then we won't have to bother her, will we?" Kasey took Alison's hand and began to walk again. "Of course, you're not to lie to her. If your grandmother asks you if you were building mud sculptures behind the rhododendrons, you have to confess."

Alison pushed her untidy hair behind her ear. "But she'd never ask me anything like that."

"That simplifies things, doesn't it?" She pushed open the patio door. "I liked the dog you made. I believe you have artistic talent." As they walked through the brocaded parlor, Kasey began to search her pockets for a match. The room jangled her nerves.

"I liked your bust better. It looked just like—*Uncle Jordan!*"

"Yes, it was rather good." Kasey stopped at the foot of the stairs and dug in her back pockets. "You know, I never seem to have a match when I need one. I wonder why that is." Then, noting Alison's stunned expression, she glanced up. "Oh, hello, Jordan." She smiled amiably. "Have you got a light?"

He came down the steps slowly, looking from girl to woman. Alison's linen pants suit was splattered with dirt. Her hair had escaped from its band and had traces of mud clinging to it. Her eyes stared out at him from a thoroughly dirty face.

Her hands were brown past the wrist. So were Kasey's. A dozen reasonable explanations coursed in and out of his mind and were discarded. If he had learned nothing else during the past days with Kasey, it was to explore the unreasonable first.

"What the hell have you been doing?"

"We've been engaged in art appreciation," she returned easily. "Very educational." Kasey gave Alison's hand a squeeze. "You'd better go see about that bath, love."

Alison's eyes flew from her uncle's to Kasey's. She scurried up the stairs and disappeared.

"Art appreciation?" Jordan repeated, staring after his niece. He frowned back at Kasey. "You look as if you'd been wallowing in mud."

"Not wallowing, Jordan. Creating." She pushed her own untidy hair out of her eyes. "We've been building mud sculptures. Alison's very good."

"Mud sculptures? You were playing in mud? We don't even have any mud."

"We made some. It's really very easy. You just take some water—"

"For God's sake, Kasey, I know the formula for mud."

"Of course you do, Jordan." Her voice was soothing and calm, but he caught the laughter in her eyes. "You're an intelligent man."

He could feel his patience ebbing. "Would you stay on the point?"

"What point was that?" She gave him a guileless smile that nearly turned into a grin as he heaved a deep breath.

"Mud, Kasey. The point was mud."

"Well, there's little else I can tell you about that. You said you knew how it was made."

He swore as his fingers tightened. "Kasey, don't you think it's a bit juvenile for a grown woman to take an eleven-year-old girl and spend the afternoon in a mud pile?"

So you know how old she is, Kasey thought and gave him a long look. "Well, Jordan, that depends."

"On what?"

"On whether you want an eleven-year-old girl for a niece or a forty-year-old midget."

"What the hell are you talking about? Even for you, that's hard to follow."

"The child is bordering on middle age, and you're so wrapped up in Jordan Taylor, you don't see it. She reads *Wuthering Heights* and plays Brahms. She's neat and quiet and doesn't intrude on your life."

"Just a minute. Back up a bit."

"Back up a bit!" Her anger had a habit of springing quickly. She pushed at her hair again. "She's just a little girl. She needs you, needs someone. When's the last time you talked to her?"

"Don't be ridiculous. I talk to her every day."

"You *speak* to her," Kasey countered furiously. "There's a wealth of difference."

"Are you trying to tell me I'm neglecting her?"

"I'm not *trying* to tell you anything. I *am* telling you. If you didn't want to hear it, you shouldn't have asked."

"She's never complained."

"Oh, *damn*!" She whirled away, then spun back again. "How can such an intelligent man make such a ridiculous statement? Are you really so insensitive?"

"Be careful, Kasey," he warned.

"If you don't like being told you're a fool, you shouldn't behave as one." She was past caring how angry he became. Her own temper—her own sense of justice—ruled her words. "Do you think that being housed, fed and groomed are enough? Alison's not a pet, and even a pet merits affection. She's starving right in front of your eyes. Now, if you'll excuse me, I'd like to wash this mud off."

Jordan took her arm before she could walk by him. Turning her around, he propelled her into a powder room down the hall. Without speaking, she turned on the water and began to scrub. Jordan said nothing as her words played back in his mind. In silence, Kasey cursed herself steadily.

She hadn't meant to lose her temper. Though she had planned to speak to him about Alison, she had intended to broach the subject diplomatically, calmly. The last thing she had wanted to do was pour out her thoughts in a torrent of abuse. It had always been her opinion that the more you shouted, the less you were heard. She continually told herself not to become emotional when dealing with Jordan Taylor. She continued to do so. Now she took the towel he held out to her and carefully dried her hands.

"Jordan, I apologize."

His eyes were steady. "For what, precisely?"

"Precisely, for shouting at you."

He nodded slowly. "For the delivery but not the content," he commented, and Kasey sighed. He was not an easy man.

"Exactly. I have a tendency to be tactless."

He noted the way she was running the towel through her hands. She was ill at ease, he observed, but she wasn't going to back down. He felt a stir of reluctant admiration. "Why don't you start again?" he suggested. "Without the shouting."

"All right." Kasey took a moment to organize her approach. "Alison came to introduce herself to me the night I arrived. I saw an impeccably groomed young girl with shiny hair and beautiful manners. And bored eyes." Her sympathies were freshly aroused at the memory. "I can't accept boredom, Jordan, not in a child with her whole life ahead of her. It broke my heart."

Passion was back in her voice, but it was passion of a different kind. It wasn't anger this time. She was pleading with him to see as she saw. Jordan doubted she was even aware of the intensity of her eyes. She was thinking of the child only. Her compassion moved him. It was one more surprise.

"Go on," he told her when Kasey paused. "Say it all."

"It's none of my business." Kasey pulled the towel through her hands again. "You're perfectly free to tell me so, but it won't make any difference in how I feel. I know what it's like to lose parents—the rejection, the terrible confusion. You need someone to help you make sense of it, to fill the holes you don't even understand. There's nothing as devastating as the death of people you love and depend on." She took a deep breath. She was telling him more than she had intended to but couldn't seem to stop. "It isn't something you get over in a day or a week."

"I'm aware of that, Kasey. He was my brother."

Her eyes searched his and found something unexpected. He had loved deeply, too. All of her guards dropped away.

She reached out to touch his hand. "She needs you. Jordan, there's nothing like the love of a child. They don't put conditions on their emotions. They simply give. There's a purity to it we lose when we grow up. Alison's waiting to love someone again."

He looked down at the hand that lay on his. Thoughtfully, he turned it over and studied her palm. "Do you put conditions on your emotions?"

Kasey's gaze remained level. "Once I give them, no."

He studied her a moment with a small frown of concentration in his eyes. "You really care about Alison, don't you?"

"Yes, of course I do."

"Why?"

Kasey stared at him in honest confusion. "Why?" she repeated. "She's a child, a human being. How could I not care?"

"She's my brother's child," he returned quietly. "And it would seem I haven't cared nearly enough."

Touched, she lifted her hands to his shoulders. "No. Not understanding and not caring are totally different."

The simple gesture moved him. "Do you always forgive so easily?"

Something in his eyes had warnings hammering in her brain. He was coming too close to the core of her again. Once he was there, Kasey knew she'd never be free of him. "Don't canonize me, Jordan," she said glibly. It was her most successful defense. "I'd make a dreadful saint."

"You're not comfortable with compliments, are you?" She started to drop her hands, but he placed his on top of them to keep them on his shoulders.

"I love them," she countered. "Tell me I'm brilliant, and I turn to putty."

"Oh, compliments on your intelligence. You're used to them, I imagine." He smiled. "On the other hand, if I were to tell you that you were a very warm, very generous person whom I find difficult to resist, you'd reject that."

"Don't do this, Jordan." He was too close, and the door shut them off from the rest of the house. "I'm vulnerable."

"Yes." He gave her an odd look. "That, too, is a surprise."

He lowered his mouth to taste her. At the first touch, he felt her fingers tighten on his shoulders. Then she relaxed and gave. For the second time that day, Kasey fell in love. She felt the loss of her heart as a physical sensation, painful this time. *He'll hurt you,* her mind warned, but it was already too late.

"You smell of soap," he murmured as his mouth roamed over her face. "And there are a dozen freckles on your nose. I want you more than I've ever wanted another woman." His voice grew husky. "Damn you, I can't understand it."

When his mouth came back to hers, Kasey could taste the flavor of anger. His tongue probed deep as he pulled her closer. For the first time in her life, Kasey gave all—body, heart, mind.

When his hands reached for her, she offered no resistance but let them roam. Reason, she knew, would return all too swiftly. She pulled him closer, wanting to fill herself with the taste of him. Her fingers combed through his hair, then wandered down to the muscles of his shoulders and back. She wanted his strength—a strength to match her own.

He slipped both hands under her shirt to cup her breasts. Her skin was impossibly soft—as soft and warm as the inside of her mouth. He heard her moan as his thumbs brushed over her nipples. It was madness, he knew, but he wanted nothing else but to have her. Desire was pushing him as it never had before. There was a temptation to pull her to the floor and take her, quickly, fiercely, and be done with it. Would sanity return then? Would his life become his own again?

He pulled her away abruptly and stared down at her. Her breathing was quick, and the vulnerability she had claimed was all too apparent in her eyes.

"I need you," he said tersely. "And I don't like it."

"No." She nodded, understanding the feeling all too well. "Neither do I."

"And if I come to your room tonight?"

"Don't." Kasey pushed her hair back from her face with both hands. She had to think, yet thinking was impossible when she could only feel. "We're not ready, either of us."

"I'm not sure we have a choice anymore."

"Maybe not." She took a deep breath and felt her balance begin to return. "But for a while, why don't we stay out of bathrooms together?"

He laughed and caught her face in his hand. He had never known anyone else who could so easily make him laugh. "Do you really think that's going to help?"

Kasey shook her head. "No, I'm afraid it isn't, but it's the best I can do at the moment."

4

Alison sat on the pink satin spread and watched Kasey apply her makeup. The pots and tubes of color which were scattered over the vanity table fascinated her. Approaching, she began to finger them hesitantly.

"When do you think I'll be old enough to wear makeup?" Alison picked up a pot of eyeshadow for closer study.

"Not for a few years," Kasey murmured as she darkened her lashes. "But with that face of yours, you won't need illusions."

Alison leaned over to peer at both faces in the glass. "But you use it, and you're much prettier than I am. You have green eyes."

"So do cats," Kasey commented and grinned. "Brown eyes are very effective, especially on a blonde. Nothing devastates the human male more than soulful brown eyes and long lashes. You'll have boys eating out of your hand when you're fifteen." She watched Alison smile and blush. "Just don't turn on the charm too early," she warned and gave Alison's hair a tug. "And no fluttering eyelashes tonight. I don't think Dr. Rhodes could handle it."

With a giggle, Alison sat down on the edge of the lounger. "Grandmother says Dr. Rhodes is a distinguished man and a social asset."

I'll bet she does, Kasey mused to herself and picked up her lipstick. "I thought of him more as a teddy bear, myself."

Alison covered her mouth and rolled her eyes. "Kasey, you say the strangest things."

"Do you think so?" She began to search for a misplaced brush. "I thought it an accurate description. He's all round and kind of cuddly. Winnie the Pooh with glasses. I've always been fond of Winnie the Pooh. He's rather sweet and helpless and wise all at once. Have you seen my brush?"

Alison picked it up from the lounge chair and handed it to her. "He pats me on the head," she said with a sigh.

Stifling a grin, Kasey tried to convince her hair to come to order. "He can't help it. Older men who are confirmed bachelors have a tendency to pat children on the head. They really don't know what else to do with them." Kasey picked up her perfume bottle and aimed a squirt at Alison. She liked hearing the child laugh. "Let's go see if Pooh's here yet."

They entered the parlor together. Spotting Harry Rhodes across the room, Kasey looked down at Alison and sent her a conspirator's wink.

Standing beside Harry, Jordan noted the exchange. He lost the thread of his friend's conversation. When was the last time he had seen Alison smile that way? When was the last time he had taken the time to look? He felt a quick pang of guilt. As a guardian, he realized, he couldn't be faulted. But as a surrogate father, he had failed completely. It was time to make it up to her—and to himself.

He laid a hand on Harry's arm to stop his dissertation, then crossed the room to his niece. "Well, I wasn't prepared for two beautiful females." He lifted Alison's chin with his hand and studied her. She was quite beautiful, he realized with a start. And more grown up than he had thought. "I'll have to lock you up before long if I want to keep you to myself."

Alison's eyes widened in surprise. The look alone had him berating himself for having taken her for granted. How could he have lived with her for so long and not have noticed? As he watched, Alison glanced up at Kasey in confusion. Jordan felt a moment of panic as she looked at him again. Was it too late?

"Oh, Uncle Jordan." He saw Alison's heart leap into her eyes.

Love without restrictions. He felt something open inside of

him. "Oh, yes," he said quietly and touched Alison's cheek. "I believe I'll keep you."

"Alison," Beatrice called from across the room. "Where are your manners? Come say good evening to Dr. Rhodes."

Alison flashed a grin at Kasey and went to do her grandmother's bidding.

"Well, Jordan." Kasey swallowed hard and cleared her throat. "You're quite a man."

He looked back at her and smiled. "Tears, Kasey?"

"Don't." She shook her head and swallowed again. "I'll disgrace myself."

Briefly, his eyes swept to Alison. "I have you to thank for that."

"Oh, no. Please." Kasey shook her head more fiercely.

He took her hand and lifted it to his lips. "Yes. I have a feeling it's going to be a difficult debt to pay. I had love staring me in the face and didn't see it."

She studied him and let out a deep breath. *You still do,* she thought. It's just a bit more complicated. "Jordan, unless you want to send Dr. Rhodes and your mother into fits and soil that perfectly beautiful handkerchief you have tucked in your pocket, you'll change the subject and fix me a drink."

"All right." He kissed her fingers again. "For now."

Through courses of onion soup, rack of lamb and chef's salad, Harry Rhodes prompted Kasey with questions about the science of anthropology. He was unable, even with this second meeting, to equate the Kathleen Wyatt whose work he had read and admired with the quick-witted woman who sat across from him. She bounced from one subject to the next, occasionally making statements that left him completely baffled. Because he knew Jordan well, he was easily able to see that his friend's interest in her was not strictly academic. And because Kasey had come into the Taylor household on his recommendation, he worried. Had he, in fact, saddled Jordan with a problem rather than a solution?

Her knowledge in her field, however, was all-encompassing. By the time the peach flambé was served, Harry began to relax.

"Anthropology is not psychology," Kasey answered to one

of his comments. "As a psychologist, Dr. Rhodes, you attempt to hold culture constant and explore mind and psyche. As an anthropologist, I attempt to hold mind and psyche constant and explore culture. I have a good book on the subject. Perhaps you'd like to borrow it."

"Yes." Her conversation seemed lucid and relieved his mind. "I'd very much appreciate that, Miss Wyatt."

"Fine. If I can dig it up, you can take it with you tonight." She took another scoop of dessert.

"I'm afraid all this is far above my head," Beatrice put in. She sent Harry a warm smile. She ignored Kasey completely. "You psychologists and anthropologists fascinate me with your theories and philosophies on life."

"Now, Beatrice, I'd hardly consider my theories fascinating," Harry put in modestly.

"I wonder what Kasey's philosophy on life might be," Jordan mused. He sent her one of his engaging smiles. "I'm sure we'd all be fascinated."

Kasey licked the back of her spoon. "From this anthropologist's point of view, Jordan . . ." She paused to pick up her wineglass. "Life is like a moustache. It can be wonderful or terrible. But it always tickles."

Jordan laughed as Harry took a rather deep swallow of wine.

Thirty minutes later the two men were closed off in the game room. Jordan racked the balls on the pool table and listened to Harry's uneasy comments on Kasey.

"Harry, there's no need to be concerned." He indicated for the doctor to break. "Kasey's giving me everything I need, and more. I'm finding the store of knowledge in that strange brain of hers incredible."

"That's precisely the point." Harry broke and frowned. "She is strange."

"Perhaps it's the rest of us who are strange," Jordan murmured. Since she had walked into his life, he was no longer certain. "In any case, she knows her field like most people know the alphabet." He moved into position for a shot. "I'd never be able to get the depth I want without her." He shot, made his ball and moved into the next position. "What's more, she's the most intriguing woman I've ever met."

"You're not getting personally involved with her?"

"I'm doing my damnedest." Jordan frowned as the five ball missed the pocket.

"Jordan, a personal involvement with her could interfere with your work. I told you before when I read your outline, it's Pulitzer potential. You already have the reputation."

"It might be wiser to finish the book before we start thinking about Pulitzers. Your shot, Harry," Jordan reminded him.

Harry made two balls and missed a third. As he shot, he thought over his next words carefully. "Jordan, I had noticed you'd been a bit restless lately. I was going to suggest a vacation when the book was finished."

Jordan grinned and leaned over the table. He positioned his cue. "Are you trying to protect me from Kasey, Harry?"

"I wouldn't put it that way—exactly." Harry blustered and leaned against his stick. "I realize Miss Wyatt is quite attractive, in a rather unusual fashion. She's also unsettling."

"*Hmm. Unsettling,*" Jordan murmured. "She does take over. There's nothing I could do about it if I was sure I wanted to. The one thing I am sure of is that she's opened a few doors for me I hadn't known I had closed."

"You're not becoming emotionally. . . " Harry searched around for the proper phrase. "Entangled?"

"Am I in love with her?" Jordan frowned. He sunk the nine ball and scratched. "I haven't the faintest idea. I know I want her."

"My dear boy," Harry began, "sex is . . ." He faltered and cleared his throat.

"Yes?" Jordan prompted, failing to suppress a grin.

"A necessary part of life," Harry finished stiffly.

"Harry, you surprise me." His grin widened. "Your shot."

Both men glanced over as the door burst open.

"God, Jordan, you really should post road maps." Kasey strolled in carrying a thick book. "I've never seen so many corridors. Your book, Dr. Rhodes." She set it on a table and blew her bangs from her eyes. "Have I trod on sacred ground?"

Jordan leaned on his stick. Why was it that a room seemed

to come to life when she walked into it? "Would it matter?" he asked her and smiled.

"Of course not. I'm always treading on sacred ground. Can I have a drink?"

"Vermouth? I haven't stocked tequila down here."

"Yes, thanks." She was already involved with a survey of the room.

It was large and open with a gratifying absence of silks or brocades. The wood-planked floor she had imagined in the parlor was in evidence, and there were simple bamboo shades at the windows. It was scrupulously clean, but there were signs of living. A fat candle had been burnt down halfway in its pewter holder. A collection of record albums were stacked on a shelf, one or two of them at odd angles.

"I like this room," she said and walked to a glass table that held a few pieces of primitive pottery. "Very much," she added as she turned to accept the glass of vermouth from Jordan. "Thank you."

He wasn't sure why her approval pleased him, but he knew it did. She tilted her head as if trying to see him from a new angle.

"This is your room," she murmured. "Like the study."

"I suppose you could put it that way."

"Good." She sipped at her drink. "I'm beginning to like you, Jordan. I almost wish I didn't."

"We seem to have the same problem."

With a nod, she moved away. "Pool, huh? Don't let me interrupt you. I'll just finish my drink before I head back into the maze." She glanced around the room again. It was the only room in the house, other than the study, where she felt comfortable. "I'd like to talk to you about the book when you've finished it, Dr. Rhodes."

"Of course." Her smile, he thought, was indeed very appealing. "Perhaps you'd like to join us for a game, Miss Wyatt," he offered, surprising himself.

"That's very nice of you." She smiled again and watched with affection as he straightened his shoulders. "I'm sure you're betting, though, aren't you?"

"That's not necessary," Harry said.

"Oh, but I wouldn't want you to change the rules for me."

Kasey sipped again and eyed a pool stick. "What are the stakes? Perhaps they're in my range."

"I'm sure we can accommodate you, Kasey." Jordan paused to light a cigar. "How about a dollar a ball?"

"A dollar a ball," she repeated and approached the table. "Let's see, how many are there?" She frowned and counted. "Fifteen. I suppose I can handle that. How do you play?"

"Rotation might be simplest," Jordan commented and glanced at Harry.

"Fine." The older man began to chalk his cue.

"Rotation," Kasey repeated, then smiled as Harry handed her his cue. "What are the rules?"

"The object is to sink the balls into the pockets in chronological order," Jordan explained. She was wearing earrings tonight, he noticed. Small silver hoops that caught the light. Even across the table, her scent reached out to him. He brought himself back. "Or hit the next ball in order into another and sink that one, or as many as possible. Hit the cue ball, the white one, knocking it into the other balls from the lowest number to the highest. The object is to clear all the numbered balls from the table."

"I see." Kasey frowned down at the green baize and nodded. "It certainly sounds simple enough, doesn't it?"

"You'll catch on, Miss Wyatt," Harry told her gallantly. "Would you like to practice first?"

"No, why don't we dive right in?" She sent him another smile. "Who goes first?"

"Perhaps you'd care to break," Harry continued, feeling expansive as Jordan racked the balls again. "Just hit the cue ball into the rack. Whatever drops in is yours."

"Why, thank you, Dr. Rhodes." Kasey walked down to the end of the table.

"Hold the cue this way," Jordan instructed, positioning her fingers. "Keep it steady, but let it slide through. See?"

"Yes." She glanced over her shoulder at him. "I'm to smack it into the ball marked one, right?"

"That's one way to put it." He could kiss her now, he thought, right now, and send Harry into apoplexy. He could smell her hair as he stood over her, feel the smooth skin of her shoulder under his hand.

"I won't be able to hit anything on the table if you keep looking at me like that," she murmured. "And Dr. Rhodes is beginning to blush."

He stepped away. Kasey took a moment to steady herself, then bent over the table and shot.

She sank three balls on the break. Moving around the table, Kasey positioned and shot again. And again. She leaned over, narrowed her eyes to figure the angle and neatly sank the next ball. She stopped to chalk her cue while letting her eyes sweep the table to analyze the best strategy. The room was completely quiet.

She picked up her drink, took a quick sip and went back to work. There was a clatter and the thud of balls, then Harry's bluster as she executed a three-bank shot. Jordan watched her as she concentrated on the next quarry. Leaning on his stick, he enjoyed the view as she stretched out over the table in front of him and nipped the next ball into the pocket. She cleared the table, sending two balls into opposing corner pockets. Straightening, she rubbed her nose with the back of her hand and smiled at her opponents.

"Let's see, that's fifteen dollars each, isn't it? Would you like to break this time, Harry?"

Jordan threw back his head and laughed. "Harry," he said and patted the other man's shoulder. "We've just been hustled."

5

*J*ordan studied her. Kasey was reading over a portion of his notes in silence. She had been quiet for more than twenty minutes. There was something inexplicable about the way she could switch the power off and on. She was teasing his mind as no other woman had ever done. When he asked her a direct question about herself, she answered, rambling agreeably but more often than not avoiding the real question. She revealed very little about Kasey Wyatt.

What secrets roamed around in that brain of hers? he wondered. What is it she's not telling me when she seems to be saying everything that comes to her mind? And why am I obsessed with learning it all? Jordan frowned at her and thought of the changes she had already brought into his life.

A child lived in the house now. There was laughter and noise and excitement. How long had he let things drift? For the three years Alison had been with him? And how long before that?

He had left the running of the household—and the responsibility of his niece—almost exclusively in his mother's hands. It had been simpler. Simpler, he reflected. His life, on a whole, had been simpler before Kasey had strolled through the front door. He had been content. And, he realized, like Alison, he had been bored. Harry had called it restlessness. There was little difference. No one in the household had been unaffected by her arrival.

His mother. Jordan frowned again and pulled out a cigar. Beatrice had already dropped a few subtle complaints. But then, he had learned to block out his mother's comments years before. For as long as he could remember, Beatrice had been involved in her committees, her designers, her luncheons. Both he and his brother had been turned over to a variety of nannies and tutors. Jordan had accepted it. Now, however, he wondered if he had been wise to put Alison's upbringing into her hands. Simpler, he thought again. But simple was often far from right. Apparently the time had come to take another look at things. He studied Kasey again. Quite a number of things.

"You're very perceptive, Jordan," Kasey commented and pushed her glasses back up on her nose.

"Do you think so?" he asked. Once he would have agreed. Now he was beginning to wonder how much he had allowed to slip by him.

"You've explained your character's motivation very well here. It's beautifully done. I envy you."

"Envy me?" Jordan took a long drag. "Why?"

"Words, Jordan." She glanced up at him and smiled. "I envy you your words."

"I've noticed you have a supply of your own."

"Barrels of them," she agreed. "But I could never make them play like this. Jordan watched her eyes dart about the pages as she continued reading the manuscript.

"You should understand, you get deeper into this section, the interaction between relatives in Indian culture," she pointed out.

"Families," Jordan murmured, thinking of his own.

"Yes. In many tribes, relatives administered public rebuke. Offenders were often exiled. That was tantamount to execution, as enemy tribes would more than likely kill an exiled Indian on sight."

"A father would send a son to his death?"

"Honor, Jordan. These were a people of honor and pride. Don't forget that." She folded her legs under her and interlaced her fingers. "Murder was regarded as harmful to the entire tribe. Exile was the standard punishment. Not so different from what we do today. Behavior between relatives was often regulated by a strict code of rules."

"Kasey?"

"Yes?"

"May I ask you a personal question?"

She lifted her shoulders. She brought up her guard. "As long as I'm not required to answer it."

He studied the ash on the end of his cigar a moment. "Why did you become an anthropologist?"

She grinned. "Do you consider that a personal question? It's very simple, really. It was either that or the roller derby."

He sighed. She was going to take him on another detour. "God knows why, but I'm going to ask. What does the roller derby have to do with anthropology?"

"Did I say it did?" She took off her glasses and swung them idly by the frame. "I don't think so. I simply gave you my two career choices. I decided against the roller derby because it's a hazardous profession. All those bodies ramming into each other, and the floors are quite hard. I don't deal well with pain."

"And anthropology was a logical alternative."

"It was mine." She studied him a moment. "Did you know the creases in your cheek deepen when you smile? It's terribly attractive."

"I want you, Kasey."

The glasses stopped on the upswing. "Yes, Jordan, I know you do."

"And you want me."

She felt the thud of desire clearly, as if she were in his arms, his mouth on hers. "Perhaps I do." She dropped her eyes to his notes again and began to tidy them.

"Kasey." She brought her eyes back to his. "When?"

She knew what he was asking. She rose then, unable to sit. "It's not as simple as you make it sound, Jordan."

"Why?"

Turning, she stared out the window. *Because I'm in love with you,* she thought. Because you're going to hurt me. Because I'm terrified I won't be able to walk away when it's finished. Once I let you in, there'll be no turning back.

"Jordan," she said quietly, "I told you I don't deal well with pain."

"Do you think I'll hurt you?"

She heard the surprise in his voice and laid her forehead against the glass. "Oh, God, I know you will."

When his hands came to her shoulders, he felt her muscles tense. "Kasey." He brushed his lips over the top of her head. "I have no intention of hurting you."

The ache was already growing, already spreading. "Intent, Jordan?" Her voice was thickening; he could hear the tears. "No, I don't think there'd be intent, but that wouldn't stop it." His fingers moved up to caress her neck. She could feel her control slipping away. "Jordan, please, don't." She started to pull away, but he turned her to face him.

He studied her carefully, brows lowered. Lifting his thumb, he brushed a tear from her lashes. "Why are you crying?"

"Jordan, please." Kasey shook her head. She knew she was losing. "I can't bear to make a fool of myself." Her own emotions were too strong for her, pressuring her. And his eyes were too direct and too demanding. She could feel the ground slipping out from under her. Longing, needs, fears were crashing down on her. The moment was fast approaching when she would have no choice but to give her emotions to him—without restrictions. "Let me go," she told him, struggling to compose herself. "I've given you enough this morning."

"No." His grip tightened. "Not enough. Not until you explain to me why you're falling apart in front of my eyes."

"Explain to you!" She threw back her head in sudden anger. "I don't have to explain anything to you. Why should I?"

"I think," he said slowly, "a more valid question is: Why shouldn't you?"

She was hurting, and her temper rose to protect her. "How could I have said you were perceptive? How could I have thought that, when you don't see what's staring you in the face? I'm in love with you!" Her breath caught on a gasp of shock and dismay. They stared at each other, both rocked by the words.

"I didn't mean to say that." Kasey shook her head and tried

to push away. "I lost my temper. I didn't mean to say that. Let me go, Jordan."

"No." He shook her once to stop her struggles. His eyes, as they stared into hers, were dark and intense. "Do you think you can tell me that, then walk out of here? No, you didn't mean to say it," he said slowly. "But did you mean it?"

There were no tears now. Her desperation had dried them. "If I said no?"

"I wouldn't believe you."

"Then it's academic, isn't it?" She tried to draw away again, but he held her still.

"Don't pull that on me now. It won't work."

"Jordan." Kasey's voice was steady again. "What do you want from me?"

"I'm not sure." He loosened his grip, abruptly aware that he must be hurting her. "Are you in love with me, Kasey?" She started to back away, but he shook his head. "No. Look at me and tell me."

She took a long breath. "I love you, Jordan. There're no strings attached. I know some people are uncomfortable being loved. I don't understand it."

"As simple as that?" he murmured.

"As simple as that," she agreed and smiled. The weight of holding back was gone. "Don't frown, Jordan," she told him. "Being loved is easy. It's the loving that's difficult."

"Kasey." He hesitated. She had moved him, unsettled him, until he was no longer certain what he was feeling. "I don't know what to say to you."

"Then it's best not to say anything." This isn't easy on either of us, she thought and tried to smooth the path a bit. "Jordan, I'd like to explain myself to you. I'd do it better if you weren't touching me." After a moment he released her and she stepped back. The absence of contact helped steady her nerves. "I told you I loved you. That might have been a mistake, but it's done. I'd like you to accept it as it's given."

Kasey could see he didn't understand. Emotions, given freely, were always difficult to understand. How could she explain to him something that her heart had accepted over the objection of her mind?

"All of my life," she continued, "I've been taught that to

give love, to express love, isn't so much a choice but an obligation. Please, just take it and don't ask me any more questions now."

"I don't even know what questions to ask." He wanted to touch her again, to hold her, but the expression in her eyes stopped him. He didn't want to hurt her, didn't want her to be right about that, too. "Kasey, don't you want anything from me?"

"No." She answered him quickly, as though she had anticipated the question. "I told you there were no strings, Jordan. I meant it. I don't think we can work together any more today, and I certainly don't think we can talk rationally about this right now. It's late, in any case. I told Alison I'd let her beat me at tennis before dinner." She was already heading for the door.

"Kasey."

It cost her a great deal to turn back around. "Yes?"

His mind had gone from crowded to blank. He felt like a fool. "Thank you."

"You're welcome, Jordan."

She managed to get through the door before the pain started.

It was completely dark before Kasey found a moment to be alone. From the window in her room, she could watch the moon rise. It was full, with an orange tint that had her thinking of fields being harvested and haystacks. *What was happening in the world out there?* she wondered. I've been in this house too long, trapped by a love that's going to lead me nowhere. What have I done to myself? It's taken me a month to lose something I've valued more than anything else in all of my life: my freedom.

Kasey wrapped her arms around herself and turned back into the room. Even when I walk away from here, from him, I won't be free again. Love binds you—I knew that.

And what's he feeling now? What will we say to each other tomorrow? Can I continue to be casual, to hand out wisecracks as though nothing's changed? She laughed a little and shook her head. I have to, she reminded herself. Always finish what you start—isn't that Kasey's first rule? I came to do a job, and the job has to be done. I gave him my love without strings, and I have to follow through. Oh, God, she thought and hugged herself tighter. How I hate to hurt. What a coward I am.

Pressing a hand against her temple, she walked into the bath to search out her aspirin. It'll help the headache, she decided, if nothing else. As she reached for a cup, she heard a sound from Alison's room. Frowning, Kasey paused to listen.

It was quiet and muffled, but the sound of weeping was unmistakable. Kasey set down the aspirin bottle and went next door. Alison was bundled under the blankets, sobbing into her pillow. Everything but the child fled from Kasey's mind.

"Alison." She sat on the edge of the bed and touched the tangled blond hair. "What's wrong?"

"I had a nightmare." She threw her arms around Kasey's neck and clung. "It was horrible. There were spiders everywhere." She burrowed deeper as Kasey's arms came around her. "Crawling all over the bed."

"Spiders." Kasey squeezed and stroked. "Terrible. Nobody should have to handle them alone. Why didn't you call me?"

Alison could hear the steady beat of Kasey's heart under her ear and felt the comfort. "Grandmother says it's rude to disturb someone when they're sleeping."

Kasey controlled a swift, powerful wave of fury and kept her hands gentle. "Not if you have a nightmare. I used to yell like crazy when I had them."

"Did you really?" Alison lifted her face. "Have nightmares, I mean."

"The worst. Pop used to say it was the price of a creative imagination. He made me almost proud of them." She brushed the hair away from Alison's cheeks. "One more thing," she added. "You could never disturb me, Alison."

With a sigh, Alison laid her head back on Kasey's breast. "They were big spiders. Black ones."

"They're gone now. You should try kangaroos. Thinking about kangaroos is much better than thinking about spiders."

"Kangaroos?" She could hear the sleepy smile in the child's voice.

"Absolutely. Snuggle down." When Alison obeyed, Kasey slipped into bed beside her.

"Are you going to stay with me?" Her voice was small and amazed.

"For a little while." She drew the child against her and felt warm. "About those kangaroos."

"Kasey."

"*Hmm?*" She looked down to find Alison's solemn brown eyes on her.

"I love you."

Here it was, Kasey realized. Without condition, without demand. Pure love. Until that moment she hadn't known just how much she had needed it. "I love you, Alison. Close your eyes."

Jordan stood in the doorway and looked down on the two sleeping figures. Alison's head rested in the crook of Kasey's shoulder. He had lost track of the time as he stood there, captivated by the picture they made. Each was turned into the other as if they had found something they had been looking for.

They both belong to me, he thought, surprised by the warmth that flooded through him. They had both loved him, and he had been blind to it. Now that he knew, what was his next move? Love wasn't as simple as Kasey had told him. He thought about the way they had looked at him—Alison, stunned and hoping; Kasey, exposed and frightened. Walking over to the bed, he watched them sleep.

Bending over, he moved Alison gently. She stirred once and then was still, deep in a child's sleep. Carefully he lifted Kasey into his arms. She murmured something, wrapped her arms around his neck and settled into his shoulder. There was something in the trust of the gesture which aroused him more than a planned seduction. He turned to carry her through the connecting doors. Kasey's eyes opened slowly to stare at him.

"Jordan?" She was disoriented, and her voice was thick with sleep.

"Kasey." He kissed her brow. How could she go from innocent to striking by merely opening her eyes?

"What are you doing?"

"Trying to decide whether to take you to your room or

mine." He paused at the doorway of her room. "Why were you in Alison's bed?"

"Spiders." Kasey remembered and tried to clear her head.

"I beg your pardon?"

"She had a nightmare." She sighed. Kasey had never been one to wake up on a bounce. "What were you doing in there?"

"I've started to look in on her at night. Something I should have been doing long ago."

With a smile, Kasey touched his cheek. "You're a nice man, Jordan. I wasn't certain." She yawned and rested against his shoulder again. "You can put me down anytime." With barely any effort at all, she could have been fast asleep again.

"Kasey." He noticed the pillow and blankets on the lounge chair. "Why don't you sleep in the bed?"

"Claustrophobia," she told him drowsily. "Between the canopy and those bed curtains, I feel like I'm in a coffin. I'm going to be cremated."

"It's a simple matter to change your room." She snuggled against him and sent a shaft of desire through him.

"No, it doesn't matter. The lounge is fine, and the staff already think I'm eccentric."

"I can't imagine why." Jordan put her down on the lounge and sat beside her. "You always smell of violets," he murmured. His mouth sought hers and found it soft and warm and giving. He knew the exact moment when sleep cleared from her brain.

"Jordan." Kasey was wide awake and throbbing. "You have me at a disadvantage." She put her hands to his chest and held them firm.

"Yes, I know. I wondered if I ever would." He took one of her hands and pressed his lips to the palm. "I intend to take advantage of it, Kasey." He trailed a finger over her shoulder, down her breast. He could feel the nipple strain against the thin material. "Tonight," he murmured. "Now."

"Jordan." The needs were churning, demanding satisfaction. "I told you before, there's a matter of choice."

"You also told me, only a few hours ago, that you loved me." He lowered his mouth to hers again. Good God, he wanted her. No woman had ever made him ache like this. The desire was in his blood, in his bones. She might have a choice, but she left him none.

"I told you I loved you." Kasey called out the last ounce of strength. "I didn't tell you I would make love with you. You've got to leave me something, Jordan."

She couldn't allow it to happen. She knew that once she shared herself with him, once she gave, she would tie herself to him completely. It wasn't a simple matter of wanting to be touched or feel pleasure, it was a matter of needing to belong.

Jordan studied her in silence, still holding her hand in his. She was defenseless again, as she had been when sleeping with the child. He wouldn't hurt her; he swore to himself that he wouldn't hurt her. But he couldn't leave her. When he released her hand and rose to go to the door that adjoined Alison's room, Kasey let out a quiet sigh. But he closed it and turned back to her. She sprang up, prepared to send him away.

"Kasey." He crossed to her but kept his hands by his sides. "Let me love you tonight. I need you. It's the first time in my life I've needed someone else."

There was no sending him away. She might have resisted a seduction. She would have refused a demand. She was powerless against a need. Kasey drew him into her arms.

His mouth was instantly desperate, crushing down on hers until they were both reeling. He held her close—tightly, as though he feared she would spring away from him. But what she had offered she would never take back. He tugged the nightgown from her shoulders, anxious to feel her skin. He thought again how thin she was, how he had to take care lest he snap her in two. But his hands refused to be gentle.

Kasey felt no pain, only rocketing pleasure. She could sense the urgency bursting from him. She wanted him to need her. For now, it was enough. She pulled him toward the bed.

And he was on top of her. She wanted his weight; she was impatient with the clothes that separated them. Her mouth hungered. She poured herself into him through the kiss. It grew long, deep, totally involved until his hands stopped searching for her. It calmed them both.

Slowly, with care, he began to undress her. There was no longer a pressing drive for quick release. He wanted to savor her. He took his lips to her throat, and her sigh of pleasure rippled through him. Still seeking but no longer desperate, he moved to her breast. Kasey pushed at his robe until she could feel his skin under her hands. She found the strength she wanted.

She let him take her deeper, slowly, with not so much tenderness as thoroughness; neither of them looked for tenderness now. That was for later, perhaps, when the heat was less intense and the strength was sapped. He nibbled at her breast, experimenting with textures and flavors. She slipped the robe from his arms, and then he was as naked as she. He flicked his tongue over her nipple, then made a leisurely journey back to her neck. The flavor there was dark and heated, drawing him.

She let her hands roam where they pleased, testing muscles, exploring the outline of ribs, skimming over hard, narrow hips. She was lost in the feel of him. He was everything she had wanted, and his lips on her neck were sending her into a delirium of pleasure. Wanting his taste again, she murmured to him so that he brought his mouth back to hers.

A storm was building. She could feel it in the texture of the kiss. Her body was already answering, moving under him, agreeing, demanding. The breath moaned out of her lips and into his. He slid his hand over her breast, down to her hip. Her thighs were slim and strong. Her fingers gripped his shoulders, her body ached with passion. She opened for him, already shuddering.

She was hot and moist. He wanted to see her without control. His own was ebbing quickly. Too quickly. He didn't want to end it. He wanted to keep touching her, tasting her. He wanted to keep hearing her moan his name. It aroused him to near madness. His blood was pounding, but still he lingered, letting his lips brush over her hip, his tongue trace over her stomach. He could hear her breathing—quick and short. She moved under him with complete abandon. She was totally his. He needed to know it and didn't question the reason.

When he brought his mouth back to hers, he knew she had lost all restraint, all control. He felt a surge of power knowing that he and he alone held the key to her. Then she took him and drew him inside her. His thoughts shattered. He was hers.

*   *   *

Kasey curled up against him and drifted in the afterglow of drugged contentment. She felt no regrets. She loved. She knew only that she had found the man she had waited for her whole life. She would have him for as long as she would be allowed. Tomorrows could be dealt with when they came. Tonight she had everything she wanted.

Jordan lay quiet in the darkness. His body was relaxed. He hadn't realized the tension he had subjected it to over the past weeks. But his mind . . .

It's never been like that before, he thought, a bit dazed by the knowledge. I can't say that to her. She'd never believe it. I'm not sure I do myself. She pulls at me; I shouldn't let her. He closed his eyes and tried to sweep his mind clear. But she was warm and soft against him, and her hand was on his heart. Sweet Lord, I've just had her, and I want her again. She's like a narcotic. He wanted to be angry, to resent what she was doing to him, but he couldn't fight his way past the simple need for her. He heard her sigh and felt her head move as she looked up at him.

"Jordan?"

"Yes?" Before he could prevent himself, his hand reached down to stroke her.

"I completely forgot about the canopy. Isn't that odd?"

Glancing down, he saw the shine of laughter in her eyes. All the doubts and strain slipped out of his mind as he smiled. There was no resisting her. "A cure for claustrophobia?"

"Definitely." She rolled on top of him. "But a scientist always tests her theory several times. Would you be willing to donate your body to the experiment?"

"Definitely." He pulled her mouth down to his.

6

"The Nomadic tribes of the high plains lived almost completely on the buffalo. They had no agriculture and did little fishing." Kasey yawned and sat back in her chair. "Sorry." She smiled over at Jordan. "I had a late night."

Her casualness this morning wasn't a pretense. She was at ease. She had told him she loved him, she had acted on that love and she had no regrets. The tension she had felt before had come from fighting her own instincts and concealing the truth. "I wonder, Jordan, if I could momentarily abandon my values and ring for some more coffee." She yawned again.

He studied her as she took a long, luxurious stretch. "You don't like servants, do you?"

"Of course I do." Kasey leaned her elbows on her folded legs. "What I don't like is having them. About that coffee, Jordan. I'd make it myself, but Francois doesn't like anybody mucking about in his kitchen."

"Why don't you like having them?"

"Jordan, I can't philosophize properly on three hours sleep." She sighed when he only continued to study her. "What color are Millicent's eyes?"

"What the hell does that have to do with anything?"

"Only to point out that people rarely notice the people who serve them. I waited tables in college, and—"

"You were a waitress?"

"Yes, does that surprise you?"

"It flabbergasts me." He grinned at her. "I can't picture you balancing trays and scribbling orders."

"I was a terrific waitress." She frowned and pushed her glasses up on her nose. "What was I trying to say?"

"When?"

"How is it you can be so clear-eyed and annoying this morning when you didn't have any more sleep than I did?"

He smiled at that as he rose and walked to her. "Because I've been sitting here listening to you spout information on the Arapaho and various Plains tribes and thinking that the thing I want most to do is make love to you again." He pulled her to her feet. "Right now."

She accepted the kiss with a murmur of agreement. If she had one disappointment, it was that she had been unable to wake beside him that morning. But there had been Alison to think of. Last night, she thought now as her mouth heated under his, had been much too short. And the night to come was too far away.

"I don't think we're going to get much work done this way," she murmured.

"We're not going to get any done." Jordan slipped the glasses from her face and put them behind him on the desk. "Come on."

"Where?"

"Upstairs." He was already pulling her to the door.

"Jordan." Kasey laughed and tugged on her hand. "It's eleven o'clock in the morning."

"Ten minutes of," he corrected, glancing at the clock as they passed through the parlor.

"Jordan, you're not serious about this."

"Tell me that in half an hour." He was propelling her up the stairs. "Alison's in school, my mother is at one of her famous committees and I want you." He opened the door to his room. "In my bed."

She was inside and locked in his arms. There was no denying his hunger. She was already dizzy from it. His mouth was ravaging hers as if he had been starved for the taste.

"Jordan." Kasey managed to breathe when his lips sought her throat. "We're hardly alone here."

"I don't see anyone else," he murmured as his lips trailed up to her ear.

She moaned and tried to keep her balance. "There are servants all over the house this time of morning." He pulled her to him for a brief, hard kiss, then released her. Kasey felt the earth tilt.

In two strides, Jordan was beside the phone. He lifted the receiver and pressed a button without taking his eyes from her. "John, give the staff the day off. Yes, the entire staff. Right now. You're welcome." Jordan replaced the phone and smiled at her. "Fifteen people are about to be very grateful to me."

"Sixteen," Kasey corrected. "Thank you, Jordan."

He crossed back to her. "For what?"

"For understanding that I needed to be alone with you. Really alone. It's important to me."

He lifted a hand to her cheek. She was becoming important to him, he realized. Very important. "You will have to make your own coffee, now," he murmured.

"What coffee?" With a smile, Kasey began to unbutton his shirt. "Would you like to hear my opinion of coffee?"

"Not now." Jordan felt the need pushing at him as she moved to the second button.

"Well, I suppose I might bore you with it," she mused, loosening the third button.

"The one thing I don't think you could possibly do is bore me."

Kasey's fingers stopped, and her smile spread slowly. "Thank you, Jordan. That's a very nice thing to say."

Deliberately, he took his fingers to the top button of her own shirt. "But if I were to tell you that you were the most generous, the most genuine, person I've ever known, you'd change the subject."

The warmth filled her and clouded her brain. She didn't know how to answer, was terrified she would overreact and spoil the moment. Being in love, she discovered, made it more difficult to harness the emotions—and more necessary. "Yes, I imagine I would. I'd probably say something like, 'Where do you get your shirts? This material is really marvelous.'"

"Kasey." Her eyes came back to his. "You're beautiful."

She laughed at that, instantly more at ease. "No, I'm not."

"You have a dimple at the right corner of your mouth when you smile. When you're aroused, your eyes darken and cloud so that the gold in them vanishes."

She could feel her pulse start to hammer, her skin flush with heat. "Are you trying to unnerve me, Jordan?"

"Oh, yes." He slipped her shirt from her shoulders. Then he took his hands down her breasts to her waist. "Am I?"

She was trembling. It stunned her. He had barely touched her, and her body was throbbing for him. He had too much power over her, in every aspect—heart, body and mind. She resisted it. She had given him her love but refused to surrender her strength. He had to want her every bit as much as she wanted him. Kasey loosened his last button.

"You unnerve me, Jordan," she whispered and ran her hands up, slowly, over his stomach, ribs and chest. She could feel his muscles go taut under her palms. As she drew off his shirt, she pressed her lips to his shoulder. "You make me ache." She trailed her fingertips back down his sides and took her lips to his throat. "You make me want." She unhooked his slacks and let her fingers guide them over his hips. As her lips traveled down his throat, she heard his low moan of pleasure. She pulled him to the floor.

Passion had tastes. His skin was hot and moist from it where she kissed him. She could feel the thud of his heart under her tongue. It was like a dream. Her body was drugged, but her mind was active. She wanted to know all of him—what pleased, what aroused. She followed instinct, letting her hands roam; when she felt a response, she let them linger. His body was well-muscled and lean, and it excited her. His needs excited her. She could feel them pouring out of him. For this one moment of time he was as vulnerable as she.

She left a slow, lingering trail of kisses as she journeyed back to his throat. His breathing roared in her ears. Tangling his fingers in her hair, he groaned her name and pulled her mouth to his. Passion exploded in the kiss. She felt it whipping at her—an incredible mixture of pain and delight. His teeth dug into her lip, and she moaned. This was no dream, but shattering reality. His hands were suddenly rough and bruising as he pushed her on her back. He entered her swiftly, violently, and plunged her over the edge of reason. She went with him, clinging, helpless, strong. She knew she had stopped breathing. They were fused together by damp skin and desire. They rose and crested, again and again, until there were only drained bodies and empty minds.

He lay on top of her, his face buried in her hair, unable to move, though he knew she was too slight for his weight. Her body was still trembling lightly under his. Jordan lifted his head. He wanted to see her in the full light of day, after his loving.

Her face was soft, her eyes still misted. He felt a pain, both unexpected and sharp, slam into his stomach. She smiled, and the pain grew. Could he want her again? So quickly? Surely that would explain the ache he felt by just looking at her. He lowered his mouth to hers, but it was tenderness that greeted him, not passion.

"Kasey." He kissed her cheek, not certain what he was about to say. The emotions he felt were utterly new to him. There was a bruise on her shoulder, and he lifted his head again to look at it. It was small and faint and fit the pattern of his finger. It horrified him. To his knowledge, he had never marked a woman before.

"What's wrong?" Kasey saw the shock in his eyes and followed their direction. She smiled a little when she noted the bruise. "You have strong hands," she commented.

His eyes came to hers. It was difficult for him; his feelings about bruising a woman were very defined. He found no excuse for it. Abruptly, he remembered the look on her face when she had told him he would hurt her. "Kasey." He shook his head. "I don't want to hurt you."

"Jordan." She recognized the deeper meaning in his words and lifted her hand to his cheek. "I know you don't." When he rolled over on his back, she went with him to rest her head against his shoulder. "Don't think about tomorrow now," she murmured. "Let's take today. It's enough."

He pulled her closer, drawing her into the curve of his body. Today, he thought, and closed his eyes. "You're tired." He had heard the fatigue in her voice.

"You did say something about a bed," she returned, but she was content to stay where she was. Close to him.

He rose, and before her protest was complete, he lifted her into his arms. "You need to sleep awhile." When he laid her on the bed, Kasey reached out to him.

"Sleep with me."

Jordan pulled back the covers and drew her into his arms.

It was late afternoon when Kasey woke. She remembered when Jordan had left her, urging her to stay and sleep. She had pulled him back for a kiss that had led to another storm of loving. A glance at his clock told her he had left more than an hour before.

Lazy, she told herself and stretched. If he had still been with her, Kasey would have found it no effort to roll over and go back to sleep. She pictured him down in the study working. She still had a job, she reminded herself. She pulled herself from bed and dressed.

Halfway down the stairs, she heard Alison practicing the piano. Beethoven this time. A lovely piece played without interest. She paused in the doorway and watched. She's doing her duty, Kasey thought with a stir of sympathy.

"Did you know Beethoven was considered quite a revolutionary in his day?" Alison's head shot up at Kasey's voice. She'd been waiting to hear it since she'd returned from school. Kasey smiled and crossed to her. "His music is so full of power."

Alison glanced down at her fingers. "Not when I play it. Uncle Jordan said you were sleeping."

"I was." Kasey stroked a hand down Alison's hair. "You play very well, Alison, but you don't put yourself into it."

"It's important to have a firm basis in the classics," Alison stated. Kasey could hear Beatrice in the words and bit back a sigh.

"Music is one of the greatest pleasures in life."

Alison shrugged and frowned at the notes. "I don't think I like music. I might be tone deaf."

This time Kasey struggled with a grin. "That could be a problem." An idea shot into her head. "Hang on a minute."

She bounded from the room. Alison heaved a sigh and

went back to Beethoven. She was still fighting with the notes when Kasey returned.

"This is a good friend of mine," Kasey informed her and set down a guitar case. "He's good company," she went on as she pulled the battered instrument from the case. "He travels well. I don't." She smiled at Alison and was satisfied that she had caught the child's interest. "I can take him with me on a dig or on a lecture tour which makes him more practical for me than a piano. I need music." She began to tune the guitar as she spoke. Alison rose from the piano stool to take a closer look. "It relaxes me, pleases me, soothes my nerves. It's also nice to play and do the same for someone else."

"I never thought about it that way." Alison reached out to touch the neck of the guitar. "You can't play Beethoven on this."

"Oh, no?" Drawing on memory, Kasey began to play the movement Alison had been practicing.

Alison's eyes widened. She knelt down to watch more carefully. "It doesn't sound the same."

"Different instrument." Kasey stopped to cup the child's chin. "Different feeling. Music comes in all forms, Alison, but it's still music." *Why doesn't anyone take the time to talk with this child?* Kasey wondered. *She soaks up words like a sponge.*

"Will you play something else?" Alison settled down at Kasey's feet. "It sounds beautiful."

"Maybe you're not tone deaf after all." Kasey smiled at her as she began to play again.

Jordan stood in the doorway and watched them. Would she ever stop surprising him? he thought. It wasn't her playing that surprised him. If he had learned she had conducted an orchestra, he wouldn't have batted an eye. He doubted there was anything she couldn't do. But her capacity to give and draw love overwhelmed him. Was she born with it? Did she learn it? Was she even aware of the power she had?

Alison loved her. He could see it in her eyes. She simply accepted Kasey for what she was and loved. There were no questions, no doubts. And Kasey gave it back to her in the same way. *But I have doubts,* he mused. *And questions.* She's right again. When we grow up, we lose the talent for loving without restrictions.

Kasey glanced up and saw him. A smile moved across her face. "Hello, Jordan. This is the music appreciation hour."

He returned the smile. "Am I invited?"

"Uncle Jordan." Alison scrambled up and forgot to brush out the creases in her skirt. "You should hear Kasey play. She's wonderful."

"I did." He glanced at Kasey again. "You are."

"Alison was having a little difficulty with Beethoven," Kasey explained. "So I went upstairs for my friend. He's been helping me."

"He?" Jordan shot Alison a look as he sat on the sofa. He pulled her down on his lap. "Don't you think it's rather odd to call a guitar 'he'?"

Alison giggled and looked up at him. "I did, but I didn't like to say so."

"Very discreet." He nuzzled her neck.

Alison responded by flinging her arms around him and clinging. The depth of his reaction shook him. Kasey had told him there was nothing comparable to a child's love, but he hadn't fully understood. Now, with the small girl hugging him, he felt the total power of it. How had he missed it before? How had he ignored it? Closing his eyes, he held her close and let the sheer pleasure of unconditional love run through him. She smelled of powder and shampoo, and her hair was fine and soft against his cheek. His brother's child. His, now. And he'd already wasted too much time.

"I love you, Alison," he murmured.

He felt her grip tighten. "Really?" Her voice was muffled against his neck.

"Yes." He kissed her hair. "Really."

He heard her sigh and relax. She kept her face buried against his neck. He opened his eyes and met Kasey's.

She was weeping silently. When he looked at her, she shook her head violently as if to deny the tears. She rose, but he stopped her before she could dart from the room.

"Don't go" was all he said.

She turned back to look at him, then began to fumble for a

cigarette. For the first time, he heard her swear at the lack of a match. She walked to the window and stared out.

I love them both, she thought and rested her forehead against the glass. Much too much. To see them together like this, to watch them find each other—the joy of it filled her. She sighed and let the tears run their course. He had looked so stunned when she had put her arms around him. Kasey could see each emotion move through him.

How much time do I have before I lose them both? Taking a deep breath, she worked to bring herself under control. I won't think about it now. I can't think about it now. When I opened the door, I knew it was going to shut in my face sooner or later. She felt the pain ebbing. Kasey brushed the drying tears from her cheeks. She turned back just as Beatrice glided into the room.

"Jordan, I'll be leaving now. The Conway party." Seeing Alison on his lap, she frowned. "Is Alison ill?"

"No." He felt the child straighten and kept his arm around her. "Allison's fine. Enjoy yourself."

She lifted a brow. "You should be attending yourself. You shouldn't neglect your social duties."

"I'll have to neglect them awhile longer. Give my best to the Conways."

Beatrice sighed. As she turned to leave, she spotted Kasey's guitar. "What is this?"

"That's a guitar, Mrs. Taylor." Kasey stepped back into the center of the room.

"I'm aware of that, Miss Wyatt." Beatrice sent her an arched look. "What is it doing here?"

"It's Kasey's," Alison put in. She felt protected and secure in Jordan's arms. "She's going to teach me to play." She glanced up at Kasey, having taken this for granted.

"Is that so?" Beatrice's voice was clipped and frosty. "And what possible use would it be for you to learn such an instrument?"

"It's essential that a child develop an interest in music at an early age, don't you agree, Mrs. Taylor?" Kasey smiled and cut off the cold response Jordan had on the tip of his tongue. He saw his mother's brow crease and relaxed again.

"Naturally."

"I'm an advocate of introducing children to the classics, and all forms of music, in infancy. There have been some very interesting studies on the subject."

"I'm quite sure there have." Beatrice's eyes swept back to the guitar. "But——"

"The Spanish guitar, such as this one, was developed from Oriental models during the seventeenth century." Kasey had on her lecturing voice, and Jordan was struggling with a grin. His mother was definitely outmatched. "During the nineteenth and twentieth centuries a succession of Spanish virtuosos, including, as I'm sure you know, Andrés Segovia, have proven the guitar to be an important artistic instrument. I'm sure you'll agree that broadening Alison's musical abilities will be a tremendous asset to her when she takes her place in adult society."

Beatrice was still frowning but looked a trifle dazed. Kasey gave her a friendly smile. "That's a lovely dress, Mrs. Taylor," she added.

Beatrice glanced down at the mauve silk. "Thank you." She brushed absently at the skirt. "I had planned to wear my white voile, but it's rather cool tonight. One doesn't wear white when it's cool."

"Really?" Kasey's brows lifted curiously. "That dress doesn't appear very warm."

Beatrice sent her a disparaging glance. "I have a mink to wear over it." She turned and left the room, not at all certain how she had lost the upper hand.

"My, my, my," Kasey muttered. "Aren't I a fool?"

"A very cagey one," Jordan remarked. His mother had annoyed her, that was clear enough. But she had kept her temper much more under control than he would have. And there was still a trace of humor in her eyes. He laughed suddenly.

"Your grandmother has just been confused by a master," he told Alison. "Oriental guitars and seventeenth century." He shook his head. "Is there anything you don't carry around in that encyclopedia you have for a brain?"

Kasey was thoughtful for a moment. "No, I don't think so. Is there something you'd like to know?"

He tilted his head, amused at the challenge. "What's the capital of Arkansas?"

Alison giggled and whispered in his ear.

"Arkansas," Kasey murmured. Her gaze wandered to the ceiling. "Arkansas . . . south central United States. North boundary, Missouri; east boundary, Mississippi and Tennessee; south, Louisiana; west, Texas and Okalahoma. Twenty-fifth state as of June, eighteen-thirty-six. Arkansas has soil favorable to agriculture, numerous mineral deposits that include the only diamond mine in the United States and extensive forest areas. The name comes from a Siouan tribe, the Quapaw. There are no natural lakes of importance, and it has a relatively mild climate. Oh, yes." She held up a finger. "Little Rock is the capital as well as the largest city."

She dropped her eyes from the ceiling and smiled guilelessly at Jordan. "Would anyone like to take a walk before dinner?"

7

The climate in Palm Springs was dry and warm and sunny. The servants in the Taylor household were well-trained, solicitous. The food was invariably superb. And the monotony of it all was driving her crazy.

If Kasey could have loved Jordan less, she could have escaped. But as each day passed, she knew she was adding links to the chain that kept her there. The time she spent with Jordan on research was a stimulant, as was the time she shared with Alison. But there were long hours with only idleness, and she had never been able to cope with idleness.

In the night, in Jordan's arms, she could let herself forget everything else. But their hours together as man and woman were all too brief. When he would leave her bed, she was left with too much time to think. It was difficult for her to admit that for all her sophisticated education and free-thinking ideas, she was uncomfortable in an affair. Perhaps if the relationship could have been more open, she would have had less doubt. But there was a child to think of.

It was already December. For Kasey, time was running out. In another month, perhaps six weeks, her usefulness would be at an end. And what then? she asked herself as she stepped outside. How much longer could she put off thinking about the future? She should have been booking another lecture tour for January. She should have found out if the Patterson dig was going on schedule in March.

She stuck her hands in her pockets and stared at a palm tree. She needed to get away, she decided. She needed to start thinking about herself again. She had to write her doctorate. She shut her eyes against the glare of the sun.

If she didn't start to make the break soon, it would hurt much, much more when the time came. How would Jordan feel when she left? Kasey stepped from the patio onto the lawn. Would he feel as though he'd lost something? Or would he simply remember their time together as one pleasant autumn?

As someone who made it a habit to pick apart the human brain, she found it strange that she couldn't fully understand Jordan's. Perhaps it was because he was more important than anyone else had ever been. Emotions clouded her intuition, and she couldn't see clearly. She was only certain of Alison.

She had the child's love. It was simple, open. At eleven, a child had no masks. *How many does he have?* she wondered, thinking of Jordan. How many do I have? Why do we insist on wearing them? She looked around again at the smooth, even lawn, the perfectly groomed trees and organized flowers. I have to get away from here, she thought again. I can't stand the spotlessness much longer.

"Kasey!"

She turned to watch Alison dart toward her a few steps ahead of Jordan.

And when I do go, she reflected, they'll have each other. That much I can take with me.

"We couldn't find you." Alison grabbed her hand and smiled up at her. "We wanted you to go swimming with us."

The simple request set off a chain of emotional reactions. *They don't belong to you,* she reminded herself as her heart reached out for them. You've got to stop pretending they do. She kept her eyes on the child, unwilling to deal with one of Jordan's intuitive looks.

"Not today, love. I was just going for a run."

"Swimming uses more muscles," Jordan commented. "And you don't sweat."

Kasey lifted her eyes to his. She watched Jordan's narrow immediately and recognized that he sensed something of her mood. She wasn't willing to be seen so clearly.

Smiling, she gave Alison's hand a quick squeeze. "I still think I'd rather run." She turned and streaked away.

"Something's wrong with Kasey." Alison looked up at her uncle, but he was watching Kasey dash for the wall that bordered the estate. "Her eyes looked sad."

Jordan glanced down at Alison. Her words had mirrored his thoughts. "Yes, they did."

"Have we made her sad, Uncle Jordan?"

The question struck him, and he looked up in time to see Kasey disappear through the side gate. *Have we?* Her capacity to feel was beyond anyone else's he had known. Didn't it follow that her capacity to hurt was just as great? Jordan shook his head. Perhaps he was reading something more into a simple mood.

"Everyone has moods, Alison," he murmured. "Even Kasey's entitled to them." When he glanced down at the child again, her eyes were still on the side gate. Jordan swung her up over his shoulder to hear her laugh.

"Don't throw me in!" She laughed and wiggled.

"Throw you in?" Jordan countered as if the thought had never occurred to him. He mounted the steps to the pool. "What makes you think I'd do a thing like that?"

"You did yesterday."

"Did I?" He glanced over his shoulder at the hedges and wall. Kasey was on the other side. It gave him an uncomfortable feeling. With an effort, he brought his attention back to Alison. "I hate to repeat myself," he said and tossed her in.

An hour later he found Kasey in the drawing room. The run hadn't helped her mood. He watched as she paced from window to window. He felt her restlessness.

"Thinking of making a break for it?"

Kasey whirled around at his voice. "I didn't hear you come in." She searched for an ease she couldn't find, then turned away again. "I've changed my mind," she told him. "This place isn't a museum, it's a mausoleum."

Jordan lifted a brow, then took a seat on the sofa. "Why don't you tell me what's wrong, Kasey?"

When she turned back, there was a flare of anger in her eyes. It was easier to feel anger than despair. "How can you stand it?" she threw out at him. "Doesn't the everlasting sunshine ever get to you?"

He studied her a moment, then leaned back against the cushions. "Are you telling me you're upset about the weather?"

"It isn't weather," she corrected. "Weather changes." Kasey pushed her hair away from her face with both hands. She felt a dull, throbbing ache at the base of her neck.

"Kasey." Jordan's voice was quiet and reasonable. "Sit down and talk to me."

She shook her head. She had no desire to be reasonable just yet. "It amazes me," she continued, "absolutely amazes me that you can write the way you do when you've cut yourself off from everything."

His brow went up again. "Do you think that's an accurate statement? I live in a favorable climate, so I've cut myself off?"

"You're so damn smug." She spun back away as her hands balled inside her pockets. "You sit here in your sanitized little world without an idea as to how people struggle through life. You don't have to worry if your refrigerator breaks down."

"Kasey." Jordan struggled to keep his patience. "You're veering off again."

She turned back and stared at him. Why couldn't he understand? Why couldn't he see what was underneath it all? "Not everyone can rest on his laurels and bask in the sun."

"Oh, we're back to that." Jordan rose and crossed to her. "Why is it you consider my money a black mark on my character?"

"I have no idea how many black marks you have on your character," she retorted. "My objection to your money is that you use it to insulate yourself."

"From your viewpoint."

"All right." She nodded. "In my view, this entire section of California is an outrage: golf, furs, parties, Jacuzzis—"

"Excuse me." Alison stood in the doorway and stared at both of them. It was the first time she had seen either of them angry. Jordan stifled a reply and turned to her.

"Is it important, Alison?" His voice was calm, but his eyes weren't. "Kasey and I are having a discussion."

"We're having an argument," Kasey corrected. "People have arguments, and I never shout during a discussion."

"All right." He nodded at Kasey, then looked back at his niece. "We're having an argument. Would you mind giving us a few minutes to finish it?"

Alison took a step back but hesitated. "Are you going to yell at each other and everything?" There was more fascination than concern in the question, and Jordan held back a smile.

"Yes," Kasey told her. Alison took a long, last look, then darted for the stairs.

Jordan laughed before he turned back to Kasey. "She's apparently pleased at the prospect of a rip-roaring fight."

"She's not alone."

He studied Kasey a moment. "No, I can see she's not. Maybe you'd like to throw something. That's always a nice touch."

"Which do you want to lose?" she shot back, hating that he was controlled and she was not. "The Ming vase or the Fabergé box?"

"Kasey." He put his hands on her shoulders. Enough, he thought, was enough. "Why don't you sit down and tell me what this is really about?"

"Don't patronize me, Jordan." She stepped away from him, temper snapping. "I get enough of that from your mother."

There was little he could say to that, as he knew the truth of it. What he hadn't known was that Kasey had been touched by Beatrice's attitude in any way. Perhaps there were many things he still had to learn about Kasey. And perhaps the time to learn them was when she was upset enough to lower her guard.

"My mother has nothing to do with you and me, Kasey." His voice had softened, but he didn't reach out to her.

"Doesn't she?" Kasey shook her head. How could it be that he didn't notice it or understand how difficult it was to make love with him in a house in which she had to deal with constant disapproval? "Well, that's one small point of disagreement. We have several others."

"Which are?"

"Doesn't it worry you that the most important thought in Alison's head in five years will be what dress she wears?"

"Good God, Kasey, what are you talking about?" Frustration made his voice as hot as anger made hers. "Will you come to the point of all this?"

"Point?" She shouted at him now, enraged by her inability to express her feelings and his inability to understand what she was trying to say. "What point is there when you've absolutely no concept of how I feel or what I need?" She shook her head again. "There is no point, Jordan. No point at all." With this, she fled through the patio doors.

Ten minutes later Kasey sat under an oak tree in the north corner of the lawn trying to gain control of her emotions. She detested losing her temper. Nothing she had said to Jordan had made sense—to him and, barely, to herself. Honesty forced her to admit that it was basic fear that prevented her from speaking what was in her heart. She loved him too much for her own peace of mind.

Heart or intellect—which should she listen to? Her intellect told her she shouldn't love him. He didn't love her. Wanted her, needed her, perhaps, cared for her. All mild, pale words compared to love. Intellect reminded her that there were too many essential differences between them to make anything but the most transitory relationship possible. Intellect stated it was time to remember her priorities—her doctorate, her work in the field. It was time to pull up stakes and get back to it.

But her heart thrust the love on her. She was caught between the two—heart and intellect—and she was unable, for perhaps the first time in her life, to make a clear decision.

She pulled up her legs and rested her brow on her knees. When she heard Jordan sit down beside her, Kasey didn't move. She needed another moment, and he, sensing it, said nothing. They sat together, close but not close enough to touch, while a bird began to sing in the leaves directly above their heads. She sighed.

"I'm sorry, Jordan."

"For the delivery but not the content?" he returned, remembering the other time she had apologized.

She gave a quick laugh but kept her head on her knees. "I'm not really sure."

"I don't think I'd mind being shouted at if I knew why."

"Blame it on the waning of the moon," she murmured, but he slipped a hand under her chin and lifted it.

"Kasey, talk to me." She opened her mouth, but he cut her off before she could speak. "Really talk to me," he added quietly. "Without the clever evasions. If I don't know you, or what you need, it might be because you do your best to keep me from finding out."

Her eyes were very clear and directly on his. "I'm afraid to let you in any more than I already have."

Her candor unbalanced him. After a moment he leaned back against the trunk of the tree and drew her to his side. Perhaps the easiest place to begin to learn of her was through her background. "Tell me about your grandfather," Jordan requested. "Alison said he was a doctor."

"My grandfather?" Kasey stayed in the circle of his arm and tried to relax. The subject seemed safe enough. "He lives in West Virginia. In the mountains." She looked out at the even, cropped lawn. There wasn't a rock in sight. "He's been practicing for nearly fifty years. Every spring he plants a vegetable garden, and in the fall he chops his own wood. In the winter the house smells of wood smoke." She closed her eyes, and leaning against Jordan, let herself remember. "In the summer there are geraniums in the window box outside the kitchen."

"What about your parents?" He felt the tension seeping out of her as the bird continued to sing out overhead.

"I was eight when they were killed." Kasey sighed again. Each time she thought of them, the needlessness for their death swept over her. "They were taking a weekend together. I was with my grandfather. They were coming back for me when another car crossed a divider and hit them head on. The other driver had been drinking. He walked away with a broken arm. They didn't walk away at all." Her grief had dulled with time but remained grief nonetheless. "I've always been glad they had those two days alone together first."

Jordan let the silence drift a moment. He began to see why

she had understood Alison so quickly. "You lived with your grandfather afterward?"

"Yes, after the first year."

"What happened the first year?"

Kasey hesitated. She hadn't meant to go into all of this, but the lack of demand in his questions had eased the telling. With a shrug, she continued. "I had an aunt, my father's sister. She was a good deal older than he—ten, fifteen years, I think."

"You lived with her the first year?"

"I lived between her and my grandfather that year. There was a dispute over custody. My aunt objected to a Wyatt living in the wilderness. That was how she termed my grandfather's home. She was from Georgetown, in D.C."

A memory stirred. "Was your father Robert Wyatt?"

"Yes."

Jordan was silent as he let bits and pieces fall into order. The Wyatts of Georgetown—an old, established family. Money and politics. Samuel Wyatt would have been her paternal grandfather. He'd made his fortune in banking, then had gone on to become a top presidential advisor. Robert Wyatt had been the youngest son. Two older brothers had found a place in the Senate. The sister would be Alice Wyatt Longstream, congressional wife and political hostess. A very wealthy, very conservative family. As he remembered, there had been talk of grooming the youngest son for the top office in Washington.

He'd been a brilliant young lawyer. There had been a great deal of press when he was killed. And his wife. . . . Jordan frowned as he tried to remember things he had read and heard seventeen years before. His wife had been an attorney as well. They had opened a law clinic together, something his family had not wholeheartedly approved of.

"I remember reading about the accident," Jordan murmured. "Then a bit now and again about the custody suit. My mother and father discussed it occasionally. She's acquainted with your aunt. There was a good deal of publicity."

"Of course." Kasey lifted a shoulder. "Wealthy political family squabbles with backwoods country doctor over child. What makes better press?"

Jordan heard the hint of bitterness slip into the careless words. "Tell me about it, Kasey."

"What's there to tell?" She would have risen then, but his arm kept her beside him. His hold was gentle but firm. "Custody suits are ugly, and hideous for the child caught in the middle."

"Both your parents were lawyers," Jordan put in. "Surely they had clearly defined wills giving you a legal guardian."

"Of course they did. My grandfather." Kasey shook her head. How was he able to pull so much out of her with only a few words? She never discussed this part of her life with anyone. "Wills can be contested, particularly if you have a great deal of money and a great deal of power. She wanted me, not for me, but because my name was Wyatt. I understood that even when I was eight years old. It wasn't difficult; she had never approved of my mother. My parents met while they were in law school. It was one of those instant attractions. They were married within two weeks. My aunt never forgave him for marrying an unknown law student who was only at Georgetown University because of a scholarship."

"You said you lived between your grandfather and aunt the first year. What did you mean?"

"Jordan, this was all very long ago—"

"Kasey." He interrupted her, turning her face to his. "Talk to me."

She settled back in his shoulder again and shut her eyes. The tension was back in her muscles. "When my aunt filed suit, things began to get ugly. There were reporters. They came to school, to my grandfather's house. My aunt hired a firm of detectives to prove he wasn't caring for me properly. In any case, I was having a difficult time dealing with it. My grandfather thought it might be easier for me if I lived with my aunt for a while. It would take some of the pressure off, and I might find that I wanted to live with her. At the time, I hated him for sending me away. I thought he didn't want me. I didn't stop to think that it was the hardest thing he'd ever done. I was all he had left of my mother."

Jordan watched her run her thumb over the gold band she wore. "My aunt had a beautiful row house in Georgetown.

Thirty-fifth Street. It had high ceilings and fireplaces in every room. Fabulous antiques and Sevrès china. She had a collection of porcelain dolls and a black butler she called Lawrence." Kasey started to rise again. She needed to move.

"No." Jordan kept her against him. "Sit." He knew that if she stood she'd find a way to avoid telling him any more. "What happened?"

"She bought me organdy dresses and Mary Janes and paraded me around. I was enrolled in a private school and given piano lessons. It was the most miserable time in my life. I hadn't gotten over my parents' death yet, and my aunt was far from maternal. She wanted a symbol—a nice, quiet child she could dress up and show to her friends. My uncle was away most of the time. He was nice enough, I suppose, but self-absorbed. Or perhaps that's not fair; he had a great deal of responsibility. Neither of them could give me what I needed, and I couldn't give them what they were looking for. I asked obnoxious questions."

He laughed a little and kissed her temple. "I'll bet you did."

"She wanted to mold me, and I refused to be molded. It's really that simple. I was surrounded by beautiful things I wasn't supposed to touch. Fascinating people came to the house whom I wasn't supposed to speak to, except to answer, 'Yes, sir,' or, 'No, ma'am,' when I was addressed. It was like being caged."

"Your aunt dropped the suit."

"It took her three months to realize she couldn't live with me. She told me if there was any Wyatt in me it was well-hidden, and sent me back to my grandfather. It was like being able to breathe again."

Jordan frowned out over the lawn. From where they sat, he could just see the top story of the house. Is she feeling caged here? He remembered the way she had walked from window to window in the drawing room. He wanted a little time to digest the things he had just learned about her. "You're very close to your grandfather," he murmured.

"He was my anchor when I was growing up. And my kite." She smiled and plucked at a blade of grass. "He's a caring, intelligent man who can argue three viewpoints at once and believe all of them. He knows me, accepts me for what I am and loves me anyway." She brought her knees up and again rested her forehead on them. "He's seventy, and I haven't been home in nearly a year. In three weeks it'll be Christmas. There'll be snow, and someone will give him a tree in lieu of payment. His patients will be flooding into the house all day, bringing him everything from home-baked bread to home-brewed whiskey."

She's thinking of leaving, he realized and felt a quick, unexpected panic. He watched the sun filter through the leaves and fall on her hair. Not yet, he thought. Not yet. "Kasey." He touched her hair. "I've no right to ask you to stay. Stay anyway."

She gave a rippling sigh. For how much longer? she wondered. I should go home until I recover from this, from him. Kasey lifted her head, prepared to say what she felt had to be said.

Jordan's eyes were on her. They were clear and seeking. He wouldn't ask her again; he wouldn't insist. Kasey realized he didn't have to. His silence—his eyes—were doing it for him.

"Hold me," she murmured and held her arms out to him.

There would be no leaving him, she thought as she pressed against him. Not until she no longer had a choice. She had opened herself to him, offered. She couldn't take herself back now.

Then he was kissing her softly, without demand. He'd not been this gentle before, holding her as if she were something fragile. No, there would be no leaving him now. Kasey's heart had more power over her life than her intellect. Where she loved, she was vulnerable, and where she was vulnerable, her mind had no sway. She pulled him closer.

The kiss grew deep, still tender, but intimate and weakening. His hand went to her cheek to stroke her skin. It was soft, so soft, and had needs hammering inside him. He murmured her name and traced his lips down to her throat. There was warmth there and a taste he had grown to crave.

How was it she could give him so much and ask for nothing? But there was something he could give her, give both of them. "Kasey, I have to go to New York this weekend. Some business with my publisher." He didn't add that he had been putting the trip off for weeks. "Come with me."

"New York?" Her brows came together. "You haven't said anything before."

"No. It depended on the progress of the book. Kasey." He kissed her again. He didn't want her to ask questions. "Come with me. I want some time with you, alone. I want more than a few hours at night. I want to sleep with you. I want to wake up with you."

She wanted it too. To be with him, away from the house. To be able to spend the night with him in complete freedom. Kasey could feel some of the weight beginning to lift. "What about Alison?"

"As it happens, she asked me just this afternoon if she could spend the weekend with a school friend." Jordan smiled and brushed a curl from Kasey's cheek. "Let's consider it fate, Kasey, and take advantage of it."

"Fate." Her lips curved into a smile, and Jordan watched as it finally reached her eyes. "I'm a very strong believer in fate."

8

New York. The plane had landed in a miserable sleeting rain that was rapidly turning to snow. The streets were a sloshy, slippery mess, packed tight with cars. The sidewalks were crowded with people hurrying. Nothing could have delighted Kasey more. New Yorkers, she mused, were always hurrying. She loved them for it. And there wasn't a city she knew that appreciated the Christmas season more. Everywhere she looked there were decorations—trees, lights and glittering tinsel. And there were Santa Clauses everywhere.

She had tried to draw it all in on the cab ride from the airport to the hotel. Now, in the bedroom of the suite she would share with Jordan, she pressed her nose to the window glass and continued to look. There were lights and people and the muffled hum of traffic. It struck her how completely she had been starved for the sights and smells of humanity. She had needed the noise and the motion.

Jordan hadn't expected her to have this sort of enthusiasm for the city. From what she had told him of her childhood, he had thought she would prefer a rural setting. But she hadn't been able to see enough. She had been bubbling over in the taxi, pointing at this, laughing at that. Anyone would have taken her for a first-time visitor, but he knew she had spent several weeks in Manhattan in early fall.

"You act as though you'd never been here before," he commented.

She turned to smile at him. The glow was there again. He could almost forget the unhappiness he had seen in her eyes only a few days before. "It's a wonderful place, isn't it? So many people, so much life. And it's snowing. I don't know if I could have made it through December without seeing snow."

"Is that why you came?" He crossed to her to run a hand through her hair. "To see snow?"

"Naturally." She lifted her face to brush his mouth with hers. "I can't think of any other reason. Can you?"

"One or two occur to me," he murmured.

She slipped out of his arms to wander around the room. "Nice place," she commented and ran a finger over the dresser top. The faint smell of rich polish hung in the air. "Not my usual working conditions."

"We're not working."

She looked back at him over her shoulder. "No?"

"A party, a few meetings." He came to her again and turned her to face him fully. "I could have skipped the party and handled the meetings by phone if work had been the only purpose of our trip."

"Jordan, I know you did this for me." She covered his hands with hers. "I'm grateful."

"I did it for me, too." He drew her into his arms. What was she doing to him? He had known her two months, and she was rapidly becoming the most important thing in his life.

"Are we really alone?" she murmured. She felt the relief wash through her. "God, are we really alone?"

"Alone," he agreed and lured her mouth to his.

"How soon is that party?" She pushed the jacket from his shoulders and began to work on his shirt.

"An hour or so." His hands slipped up under her sweater.

"Tell me . . ." She nipped at his lip and felt his shudder of response. "Do you consider being late rude or fashionable?"

"Rude." He ran his fingers down to unbuckle the thin belt she wore. "Very rude."

"Let's be rude, Jordan." She opened his shirt and sighed when her hands slid around him. "Let's be terribly rude."

When they were naked on the bed, he took his time. They had time now for slow loving. Kasey slipped into a cloud of pleasure. Where he touched, she heated; where he kissed, she ached. He was careful to keep his hands gentle, remembering the bruises he had given her before. Her strength, her drive, made it difficult to remember her fragility.

Her skin was smooth and pale, with barely a trace of a tan line. Though she spent many of her free hours outdoors, she didn't tan easily. He could see the contrast of the bronzed color of his hand against the milky whiteness of her breast. He took his mouth to it and heard her moan. She was more responsive than any woman he had known. There were no inhibitions in her. She loved freely.

Very gently, he caught her nipple between his teeth and felt her arch beneath him as she catapulted from contentment into passion. He used his tongue to kept her trembling until she was breathless and spent. Her fingers dug into his shoulders. Her murmurs urged him to hurry. But he moved without rush to her other breast.

"Jordan." She could barely speak, for waves of need were pressing down on her. "I want you now."

"Too soon." He trailed his lips down her ribcage. "Much too soon."

His mouth roamed, and she continued to shudder. He slipped his fingers inside her, taking her to a violent peak.

Delirium. Kasey knew she had passed all reason. Pleasure could give no more, passion could take no more from her. Yet he continued to drive her. Every cell of her body was alive, humming. She was nearly panicked to have him and clutched at him, willing him to be as desperate as she. His hands seared over her and had her quivering.

Then his mouth was on hers again—hungry, urgent. He took it to her throat with his teeth digging into her skin. He had forgotten his vow to be gentle. He had forgotten everything but the feel of her thin, agile body beneath his—and his own desperation.

Need sparked need, and he was inside her. There was no longer time for slow loving.

Jordan decided he didn't get used to Kasey as time passed but only became more intrigued by her. The elegant co-op overlooking Central Park was crowded with members of the book world: writers, editors, literary agents and scions of publishing. But she was the vortex of it. Other women glittered in jewels, diamonds, sapphires, emeralds. She required none.

She sat on the arm of a chair, sipping champagne and laughing with Simon Germaine, the head of one of the top publishing houses in the country. J. R. Richards hung over her shoulder. He was on his fourth in a string of best-selling novels, each of which had made the transition to the screen successfully. Beside her was Agnes Greenfield, one of the toughest agents in the business. She had represented Jordan for ten years, and he decided this was the first time he had seen her grin. She'd smiled, sneered, and snarled, but never grinned. As he watched, Kasey laid a hand on Germaine's shoulder and said something that made him throw back his head and roar.

Kasey's eyes lifted and found Jordan's through the crowd. She smiled slowly as she brought up her glass for another sip. A shaft of desire shot straight through him, nearly settling him back on his heels. *How does she do it?* he demanded of himself. How can she make me want her when I'm still warm from having her? When am I going to get enough? He pushed the questions aside and wondered how long it would be before they could slip away and he could have her to himself again.

"The widening schism between elitist and popular literature has made it difficult for the average person to enjoy light, entertaining reading without feeling guilty."

Kasey lifted her brow at J.R. as Jordan approached. "I've read all of your books, and my conscience is clear." She sipped her champagne and smiled at Jordan.

It took J.R. a moment before he began to chuckle. "I think I've just been put in my place. I'm tempted to begin collaborating, Jordan, if I can find a partner like this."

"I've been trying to convince Kasey to write a book of her own." Germaine gulped down his straight scotch without a blink. He had a wide, florid face and a stone-gray moustache above his lip. Kasey thought he looked a bit like a children's TV show host she remembered from her own girlhood.

"I appreciate that, Simon." Kasey pushed her curls behind

her ears and crossed her legs. "But I've always felt that being a writer meant being frugal with words. I'm very lavish with mine."

"You tell a hell of a story, Kasey." He patted her knee companionably, and she caught Jordan's lifted brow. "I've got editors to deal with the excess."

"And I'm temperamental." Kasey finished off her champagne and was immediately handed a fresh glass. "Thanks." She gave J.R. a friendly smile.

"What writer isn't?" Germaine huffed and pulled out a thick cigar. "Are you temperamental, Jordan?"

"Periodically."

"I'm difficult to work with all the time, which at least makes me predictable," Kasey put in.

"The one thing I've found you are not, is predictable." Jordan lifted his own champagne.

"The perfect compliment. Jordan, there's some fantastic looking caviar over there. I wouldn't feel right if I didn't stuff myself."

They moved across the room to a sumptuously prepared buffet. He watched Kasey heap beluga caviar on a thin cracker. "You and Germaine seem to have hit it off nicely."

"He's sweet," Kasey said with her mouth full. She was already reaching for another cracker. "God, I'm starving. Do you realize what time it is, according to west coast time? Did we eat on the plane? I can never remember anything that happens at thirty thousand feet."

"Sweet?" Jordan repeated, ignoring the rest. The adjective, applied to Germaine, was enough to arrest his attention. "I don't believe I've ever heard him described quite that way before."

"Oh, I've heard the stories." Kasey began to forage for something else and found a bowl of iced cocktail shrimp. "Heaven," she muttered, spearing one with a toothpick. "He's supposed to be tough as old leather and mean as a starved dog. What is this?" She pointed toward another platter.

"Beef tongue."

"We'll just skip over that," she decided. She helped herself to another shrimp. "I like him."

"Apparently, the feeling's mutual."

Kasey smiled and paused long enough to drink some champagne. "Your sensibilities were offended when he put his hand on my knee. You're terribly cute when you're reserved and conventional, Jordan. Would it embarrass you terribly if I kissed you right now?"

She was baiting him, and he knew it. Firmly, he put his hand behind her neck and pulled her close. Her eyes laughed at him before he gave her a long, hard kiss. She carried the strong, exotic flavors of the buffet. When he drew her away, she was still smiling.

"Caviar's good, huh?"

"It seems I have a taste for it."

She turned and piled another cracker high. "Have some more," she invited with a grin. "I can't ever get enough of it myself."

He took a bite of the cracker she held up to his mouth. "I want you out of here," he told her quietly. "I want you alone, where I can take those clothes off you piece by piece."

"An interesting proposition," Kasey murmured, touching a finger to his tie. "Am I allowed to do the same to you?"

"Required."

"Jordan!" A woman glided up to them—sturdy, fortyish and unashamedly blond and busty. Kasey flipped through her memory file and drew out a newspaper picture of Serena Newport, highly successful novelist who wrote books stacked with swashbuckle and sex.

Serena kissed Jordan heartily on both cheeks. "You don't show up at these things often enough," she complained. "I like to be seen with classy men."

"Serena. It's good to see you."

"And who's this?" She gave Kasey a strong look. "Good God, thin as a rail and positively stunning. If I stand here for too long, I'll wind up looking like an albino elephant. Are you a writer, dear? And who colors your hair?"

"A fan, Miss Newport, and I was born with it."

"God, it's disgusting." She put her hand on an ample hip and shook her head. "Not the fan part, dear, the hair. Born with it? Dreadfully unfair. And whose fan are you, Jordan's or mine?"

"Both." Kasey was liking her more with each passing minute.

Serena laughed in one short boom. "That's unusual. Not too many people read both *Last Abstinence* and *Passion's Victory*, do they, Jordan?"

"Kasey's unusual, Serena. Serena Newport, Kathleen Wyatt."

"And what do you do? I know." She held up a hand before Kasey could speak. "Don't tell me—you model."

"Model what?" Kasey asked, enjoying herself.

"Clothes. No—an actress," she stated, changing her mind. "That's a very expressive face."

"Thank you, but I don't act professionally. Only in day-to-day encounters."

"Quick, too," Serena murmured. "You're not an agent trying to lure Jordan away from Agnes?"

"Not if I value my life," Kasey replied.

"Well, my dear, I'm fascinated and totally baffled." Serena hailed a passing waiter and grabbed a glass of champagne. There were chunks of precious stones on her fingers, and her nails were a brilliant red. "What are you?"

"I'm an anthropologist."

"You're joking." Serena looked at Jordan for confirmation. "Is she joking?"

"You wouldn't ask if you questioned her on the tribal rituals of the Sioux," Jordan replied and finished off his drink.

"You don't say." Serena drew out the words.

"Kasey's collaborating with me on a book."

"*Hmm.*" Serena took a healthy swallow of champagne. "You don't happen to know anything interesting about the Algonquins, do you, dear?"

"Originally a North American tribe who were dispersed by the Iroquois in the seventeenth century. Most found new settlements in Quebec and Ontario," Kasey countered.

"Fate!" Serena exclaimed and grabbed Kasey's arm. "Do you believe in fate, dear?"

Kasey shot a look at Jordan and grinned. "As a matter of fact, I do."

"I've just started a new book. The first half is in England, but the second half has my now-penniless aristocrat off to the colonies. He's half-starved and all but beaten to death when he comes upon a party of Algonquins. They wouldn't have scalped him or anything dreadful like that, would they?"

Kasey grinned. "Many of the Algonquins were friendly to white settlers for some time. It depends upon which tribe you are talking about. However—"

"Perfect. Wonderful." Serena folded Kasey's arm through her thick one. "I'm stealing her for an hour, Jordan. It's too good to miss. Have some more champagne." She gave his cheek a motherly pat. "I'll send her back to you when I'm done."

Kasey looked over her shoulder and shrugged as she was propelled away.

"It's the first time," Kasey said later, "that I've met anyone who can outtalk me." She leaned against the back seat of the cab, tucked into the curve of Jordan's arm. "I'm suitably humbled."

"I gave serious consideration to strangling her after the first hour." She was close, and the scent of her hair wafted over him. She was warm and a little sleepy, a little high on champagne. He wanted her. "She drilled you for two hours and ten minutes."

Kasey laughed softly. "She's a marvelous person."

"I've always thought so, until tonight."

"She's very fond of you." Kasey smiled up at him. "She told me you were a wonderful writer, a marvelous man, particularly when you forget to be polite." She laughed at his lifted brow. "I had to agree with her."

"If Serena's books are a barometer, she prefers a more— earthy type."

"Oh, Jordan, I just love it when you're dignified." She took a nip at his ear. "Why don't you kiss me again the way you did at the party? Sort of macho and domineering."

"Damn you, Kasey." He was laughing as he pressed his lips to hers.

"*Mmm*, swear at me and I'm yours," she murmured.

"Be careful," he warned, finding his hunger growing despite her teasing. "I ran out of patience an hour ago."

Kasey laughed again and laid her spinning head on his shoulder. "And he burned for her, burned with a white-hot heat that only she could satisfy." She sighed and snuggled. "Serena Newport, *Chesterfield's Woman*."

She was more than high on champagne, Jordan realized. She was three-quarters drunk. "Kasey, you're smashed," he said, amused.

"Well put," she agreed. "You writers have a way with words." She lifted her mouth to just beneath his. "Are you going to take advantage of my condition?"

"Absolutely."

"Oh, good." She wrapped her arms around his neck. "Start now."

The cab pulled over to the curb, and Jordan untangled himself. "Why don't I pay off the cab first?"

"Details." Kasey stepped onto the sidewalk with the help of the doorman. The cold air, still smelling of snow, whipped over her cheeks. It did nothing to clear her head. "Jordan." She tucked her arm into his when he joined her. "It's just occurred to me, something you said in the cab about Serena's barometer. Does that mean you read her books?"

"Of course I read her books." He steered Kasey through the doors and across the lobby. "Does that surprise you?"

"I stand astonished."

"It's astonishing that you can stand at all," he countered, pressing the button for the elevator.

"But Jordan, I have a difficult time picturing you reading *Chesterfield's Woman*." Kasey allowed herself to be drawn inside the elevator.

"Why?" He pushed the button for their floor, then pulled Kasey into his arms. "To quote Germaine, she tells a hell of a story."

Then he was kissing her with a quick, desperate hunger that had her rocking on her feet. She would have been dizzy without the help of champagne. The silk pressed cool against her skin as his hand ran down her back. The heat kindled in her slowly, until she was utterly pliant in his arms. Passion licked by wine simmered under his touch. Her mouth was soft under his, and his tongue moved inside to seek hers. Her thighs throbbed with need, and her head swam. She was reeling and heating and floating all at once. She could no longer cling to him but went limp in her first total surrender.

"God, Kasey, I've never known an elevator to take so long." He buried his face in her hair and tried to draw back his own sanity. She was so fluid, so totally willing to have him love her; he felt incredibly strong. He hadn't known he would find even her weakness an excitement when it had been her strength that had drawn him to her.

The elevator door slid open, and he guided her out into the hall.

"Jordan." Kasey turned to him again, leaning against him with her face lifted to his. Her eyes were misted, but the smile reached them.

"What?"

"Do you remember what Chesterfield does to Melanie in Chapter Eight right before the ship is attacked by the British frigate?"

He grinned, remembering very well. "Yes, as it happens, I do. Why?"

"Well." She put her arms around his neck again. "I was wondering—a purely academic thought—if fiction could be translated to fact. I'm thinking of doing a paper on the subject."

"And you'd like me to help you test your theory?"

"Exactly." She ran her hand through his hair. "Would you mind?"

"In the interest of academia, I might be persuaded." He swept her into his arms. "Didn't it start something like this?" He slipped the key into the lock and carried her inside.

9

She was still asleep when he woke. Jordan immediately felt her warmth and the light tickle of her hair on his shoulder. The room was still dim, with the heavy curtains drawn over the windows, but a glance at his watch told him it was morning. He had a meeting scheduled in just over an hour. With a sigh, he looked down at Kasey.

He'd never known anyone who slept so deeply. He brushed the hair away from her forehead. She didn't even stir.

He thought of how she had been the night before—the sleepy sexuality, the husky laugh, the heavy eyes. If he had been a fanciful man, he would have thought her a witch. There was something other-worldly about her. Every time he thought he had power over her, he found himself caught in hers.

But now, as she slept, she might be any woman. Now she was just a woman sleeping off a night of champagne and loving. So how was it, he wondered, that she still pulled at him? As she slept, she couldn't dispense her cockeyed charm or send out those looks that both invited and challenged him. And yet he was drawn to her, even as she lay there. He lowered his mouth to hers.

Jordan kept his lips gentle, and Kasey didn't stir. He had wanted this—to wake beside her. To wake her. Her lips were so soft, he felt he could sink into them. He murmured her name and kissed her again. Her face was pale without makeup, and there was a light sprinkling of freckles over her nose. He kissed her cheek, and his hand sought her breast. She didn't wake, didn't stir, but sighed in sleep as though she dreamed of him. He found the pulse in her throat with his lips and felt it beat slowly. His own was already beginning to race.

He stroked gently, feeling his passion build. Knowing the thrill of possession, he ran his hand down the length of her. The skin on the inside of her thighs was water-soft. He moaned, shattered by his need for her.

He took his mouth to her ear, to her temple, then back to hers to part her lips urgently. Her response was slow as he pulled her from the dream, then her lips moved under his with a quiet moan. Her heart was suddenly pounding under his hand. He entered her before she was fully awake, spinning her into passion as delirious as his own.

She was curled against him again, her arms tight, her head resting in its favored spot in the curve of his shoulder. She sighed and kissed where her lips could reach easily. "Good morning," she murmured.

She brought out something primitive in him which he wasn't certain he was comfortable with. He'd never experienced the degree of passion she could draw from him. The laughter in her voice was irresistible. "Good morning. How do you feel?"

"*Mmm*, wonderful." She snuggled closer. "And you?"

"Fine, but *I* wasn't teetering on my feet last night." He shifted away just far enough to look at her. Her eyes were clear. The dimple at the corner of her mouth appeared as her lips curved. "No hangover? You're entitled to one."

"I never have hangovers." Kasey kissed him lightly. "I refuse to believe in them." She rolled over until she was leaning on his chest looking down at him. "Do you realize how much trouble could be avoided if we simply didn't believe it?"

"An interesting theory."

"I have dozens of them."

"I've noticed." He smiled and ran a finger down her cheek. "Your theory last night was particularly interesting."

Kasey laughed and dropped her forehead onto his chest. "It worked."

"Beautifully."

"Shall we tell Serena?" She lifted her head again, and her eyes were bright with humor.

"I think not."

She kissed him again, lingering. "Do you remember I once told you that you had a terrific body?"

"Yes. I recall being surprised at the time. But I didn't know you as well then."

She sighed as she felt his hands lower to her hips. "I still think so." Kasey rested her cheek on his chest. There was a contentment in her she had never felt before. "You have meetings today, don't you?"

"Yes. I've one in . . ." He lifted his arm to glance at his watch. ". . . in about half an hour. I'm going to be late."

"If we were in Fiji," she murmured, "we could stay like this all day, and you wouldn't need that watch."

"If we were in Fiji," he countered, "you wouldn't have had your snow."

Kasey sighed again and closed her eyes. "You're so logical, Jordan. It's one of the things I love most about you."

He said nothing for a moment. She hadn't mentioned love to him since the first day she had confessed it. He had wanted to hear it again so that he could explore his own reaction. Now he could feel her beginning to drift back to sleep.

"I don't like to leave you alone," he murmured.

"There're a million people out there." She yawned and snuggled down. "I'll hardly be alone."

"I'd rather be with you."

"Don't worry about me, Jordan. I'm going to look for a sweatshirt and some jeans for Alison. Something cheap and symbolic that she can grub around in."

"For making mud sculptures?" He felt the smile tugging at his mouth again.

"Mmm-hmm." She smiled, remembering the expression on his face the first day she and Alison had made them. "And I want to see all the Christmas decorations. I'm going to have a lot more fun than you are."

"Can you break off from your busy schedule to meet me for lunch?"

"Hmm, maybe. Where?"

"Where would you like?" He knew he should be up and dressing, but he found it impossible to move.

"Rajah," she said drowsily. "West Forty-eighth Street."

"Two o'clock, then."

"Okay. Did I bring my watch?" she asked him.

"I've never seen you wear one."

"I keep it in my purse so it doesn't intimidate me."

He kissed the top of her head. "I have to get up. If I stay much longer, I'll have to make love with you again."

She lifted her face, and her eyes were half-closed. "Promise?"

He drew her back to him.

"Twenty minutes late." Agnes gave her watch a hard look. "That's not like you, Jordan."

"Sorry, Agnes." He settled back in a leather chair. Agnes sat behind a six-foot desk. It was piled with manuscripts and memos. Jordan had always felt that sitting behind that desk, she looked like a general waging battle.

"Well." She saw the humor in his eyes and leaned back, a pencil tapping on her lip. "I hope it was worth it."

Jordan lifted a brow and said nothing. Agnes had expected nothing else. She had never been able to bait him. A very cool character, she thought, not for the first time. She remembered the animated woman he had brought with him the night before. An interesting combination.

"About your collaborator," Agnes began, pushing a few papers aside. "Is she as good as you were led to believe?"

"Better," he told her.

She nodded. "Then it's money well-spent."

"I want her to have a percentage of the royalties."

"A percentage of the royalties?" Agnes scowled and shifted in her chair. "You contracted her for a flat fee."

"She's to have that as well." Jordan sat back and laced his fingers.

"Jordan, the fee you're paying her is very generous." Her voice was patient. "Your personal life is one thing, but business is business."

"This is business," he countered. Jordan's voice was patient, too, but firm. Agnes recognized the tone and stifled a sigh. As well as being cool and cautious, he was stubborn, and she knew it. "I never expected, when we wrote up the original agreement, that I'd be able to draw so much out of her. Agnes, the book's nearly as much hers as it is mine. She's entitled to benefit from it."

"Ethics." Agnes sighed. "You have such a sterling character, Jordan."

"So do you, Agnes." He smiled at her. "Or you wouldn't be my agent."

Agnes shrugged. "What percentage did you have in mind?"

Kasey fought her way through Gimbel's and loved every minute of it. She'd run into a sale and had three sweatshirts and two pairs of jeans tucked into her shopping bag. Shopping was something she did rarely, but when she did, she did it passionately. She could spend three hundred dollars on a dress without a qualm and haggle furiously over a five-dollar sweater. She pushed her way through the crowds and scrambled happily through racks of bargains as she shot from store to store.

Passing a window, she spied an inch-high pewter unicorn and rushed inside to dicker over the asking price. A pang of hunger reminded her of the time, and she began to search through her purse for her watch.

"Six-twenty-seven," she muttered, frowning at it. "I don't think so." She tossed it back into her purse and smiled at the clerk who was boxing her unicorn. "Do you know what time it is?"

"One-fifty." He responded to the smile.

Deciding she could make twenty blocks in ten minutes at an easy jog, she took off without hailing a cab. When she arrived at Rajah, her cheeks were flushed and her eyes were brilliant. She passed through the elaborate entranceway and stepped inside.

The heat rushed to meet her. It felt wonderful after the stinging cold, and she pulled off her gloves to stuff them into her bag.

"Madam."

She turned her smile on the mâitre d'. "Jordan Taylor."

"Mr. Taylor just arrived." He bowed in her direction. "This way, please."

Three hours of shopping and no breakfast had left her famished. Jordan watched her coming toward him and rose.

"Hi." She kissed him, then let him help her off with her coat.

"You were serious about the shopping, I see," he commented, glancing at the bag before she tucked it under the table.

"Deadly," she agreed as she accepted a chair. "I bought you a present. You can have it after I see the menu. I'm starving."

"Some wine first?" He gave the order to the captain at his elbow while Kasey buried her face behind the menu.

"The Crab Goa's always good. And the Barra Kabab." She put the menu down and grinned. "I think I'll have both. Shopping gives me an appetite."

"Everything seems to," Jordan commented wryly. He took her hand, needing to touch her. "I've watched you eat. It's amazing." He brought her hand to his lips. "Did you really buy me a present?"

"Yes. It's in the bag with Alison's sweatshirts." Kasey reached down to forage and brought up the box. "You can open it if you promise to order immediately afterward."

"Agreed." He lifted the top of the box and uncovered the unicorn.

"It's for luck," Kasey told him as the captain brought their wine. "You can't go wrong with a unicorn. I almost bought you a bumper sticker with a lewd saying, but I didn't think it would look quite right on your Mercedes."

"Kasey." Touched, he took her hand again. "You're outrageously sweet." Jordan tasted the wine and nodded to the captain. "The lady will have the Crab Goa and Barra Kabab. I'll have the Fish Curry."

"How hungry are you?" she asked when the captain withdrew.

"Hungry enough, why?"

"I was wondering if I'd get any of your fish." She smiled when he laughed and slipped the small box into his pocket.

"So you bought me a unicorn and Alison sweatshirts. Did you buy anything for yourself?"

"No." She tossed her hair out of her eyes, then settled her elbows on the table and cradled her chin on her hands. "There were some earrings in the shop where I got the unicorn, flashy little drops in scrolled gold, but they wouldn't bargain with me. I was in the bargaining mood. And I got hungry." She grinned and reached for her wine. "How was your meeting?"

"Fine." He had debated discussing the royalties with her and had decided against it. She might object, citing Agnes's argument about the original agreement, and in any case, he didn't want business to intrude on their time together. They had only one night left. "I've another one at four with Germaine. He'll probably ask me to use my influence to talk you into writing that book."

Kasey laughed and shook her head. "I think the writing's safer in your hands. But give him my best."

"What would you like to do tonight?" A basket of bread was placed before them, and Kasey dove into it immediately. "Would you like to see a play?"

"*Mmm*, a musical." She buttered the bread lavishly and offered him some. Jordan shook his head, smiling as she took a hefty bite. "Something with a lot of flash and a happy ending."

"I'll meet you back at the hotel at six?"

Kasey nodded, then reached for more bread. "Okay." Narrowing her eyes, she calculated the time between six and curtain. She smiled over the rim of her glass. "We'd better plan on having a late supper."

Kasey was dreaming. It was a familiar dream, too familiar, and her mind struggled to reject it before it took hold. She was alone, abruptly dropped down into a pure white sea in a small boat. She knew what would happen next and tried to push the image aside. But she wasn't strong enough.

The boat began to rock as the wind picked up, but she had no sail, no oars to guide herself. The water stretched as far as she could see. There would be no swimming for land. She was lost and alone and afraid. She was only a child.

When she saw the ship coming toward her, she shouted for it, steeped in relief. Her grandfather was at the helm, and raising a hand, he tossed out a life line. Before she could reach it, another ship floated up to her right. The wake of the two ships set her small boat rocking dangerously. Water hurled into her face and was soon ankle-deep on the deck. She was caught in the middle as each ship tried to draw her aboard.

She couldn't reach her grandfather's life line. The waves were knocking her around the boat until she screamed in frustration and begged him to come for her. He shook his head and drew the line away. She was sucked closer to the second ship. And the waves grew high until they tossed her into the sea. Water closed over her head, cutting off her air, her light.

"*No!*"

She shot straight up in bed, covering her face with her hands.

"Kasey." Her cry had roused Jordan from sleep. He reached for her and found her cold and quivering. "What is it? What's wrong?"

"Just a dream." She fought for control. "I'm all right, it's nothing."

Her voice was shaking as desperately as her body, and though she resisted, he pulled her closer. "You're not all right. You're like ice. Hold onto me."

She wanted to do as he said but was afraid. Already she depended on him too much. She'd handled the dream alone before, she would handle it again. "No, I'm all right."

Her voice sharpened as she pulled out of his arms. She struggled out of bed and drew on her robe. When Jordan switched on the bedside lamp, she began to hunt for her cigarettes. He watched her as he reached for his own robe. There was no color in her face, and her eyes were dark with fright. She was shaking from head to foot, and her breath was still trembling.

Finding her cigarettes, she fumbled to pull one out. "I'm a scientist; I know what a dream is." She covered her mouth with her hand a moment hearing the jerkiness of her own voice. Her teeth were chattering. "A sequence of sensations, images or thoughts passing through a sleeping person's mind.

It's not real." She picked up Jordan's lighter, but her hand shook and she couldn't work it.

Quietly he crossed to her. Taking the cigarette and lighter from her hand, he set them back on the table. "Kasey." He put his hands on her shoulders, feeling her shudder convulsively under his palms. "Stop this. Let me help you."

"I'll be all right in a minute." She stiffened when he drew her close again. "Jordan, please. I can't stand to fall apart this way. I hate it."

"Do you have to handle everything by yourself?" He was stroking her back, trying to warm her. "Does needing comfort make you weak? If I needed to be held, would you turn away from me? Kasey, let me help you."

With a sob, she was clinging to him, her face pressed against his throat. "Oh, Jordan, it frightens me as much as it did the first time."

Without speaking, he picked her up and carried her back to bed. Keeping his arm tight around her, he drew her against his side. "You've had it before?"

"Since I was a child." Her voice was muffled against his chest. He could feel the racing of her heart. "I don't have it often anymore. Sometimes years." She closed her eyes and tried to steady her breathing. "When I have it, it's always the same, always so vivid."

Her trembling had lessened, but he kept her tight in the circle of his arms. She was bringing out something new in him: the need to protect. "Tell me about it."

She shook her head. "It's just foolish."

"Tell me anyway."

She was quiet a moment, then, with a sigh, she began. Her description was short and her words were unemotional, but he could sense the feeling beneath them. It was childishly simple to understand, but then, it had been the dream of a child.

"I never told my grandfather about it," she went on. "I knew it would upset him. I only had the dream twice the whole time I was in college." Her voice had grown steadier and her hold on Jordan less desperate. "I had it once when I read a rehash of the custody case by some enterprising reporter who'd picked up on it when one of my uncles had been running for re-election. And again the night before graduation. I'd put that down to too much beer and the pressure of delivering the valedictorian address." She sighed now and felt her body relax.

"And since then?" He had felt the fear and tension pour out of her. Her body was warming.

"A couple of times. Once when Pop was in the hospital with pneumonia. It scared me to death; he's always bursting with health. Once on a dig. We'd had to shoot a rabid dog. It broke my heart." She felt safe and grew sleepy again. Now she'd given him her trust as well as her love. She was content, for the moment, to be cared for. "That was two years ago. I don't know what set me off tonight."

He heard her voice thickening and said nothing. She'll sleep now, he thought and stared up at the ceiling. He wouldn't. His mind was too crowded with Kasey Wyatt.

When he had first met her, he had thought her a tough eccentric with a great deal of charisma. Now he realized there was far more to her than that.

Her breathing was even now, and quiet. Tomorrow they would return to Palm Springs and complete their work on the book. In another few weeks, Kasey would be finished with her work. Then it would be up to him.

Reaching beside him, Jordan found his cigars and matches. He lit one and smoked in silence while he listened to Kasey breathing deeply in sleep.

10

In two weeks it would be Christmas. Kasey could feel the time rushing by her. The brief interlude in New York had done much to settle her. She felt in control again—of her nerves, of her situation. What she had with Jordan, she was able to accept again without all the doubts and discomfort which had been piling up. She loved him, needed to be with him. When the time came to pay the price, she'd pay it. Still, she wished time wouldn't move so fast.

For Alison's sake, she would have liked Christmas to come quickly, but for her own, she could wait. She would have drawn out each day, each hour. After Christmas would come the new year. With the new year would come the time for her to go.

Watching the child's simple pleasure helped to keep Kasey's mind off herself. For two short weeks she could spend her free time making the holiday come alive for the girl. The elegant red garland and silver bells that Kasey had seen the staff unpacking weren't really Christmas. She had spent one stiff, formal Christmas in her life. That was enough for her.

"Jordan!" Kasey dashed down the stairs and burst into Jordan's study. "You've got to see this. Come upstairs." She was pulling on his arm and laughing.

"Kasey, I'm in the middle of something here."

"Put it down," she ordered. "You work too hard." She

leaned over and gave him a quick, hard kiss. "It's really terrific. You're going to love it," she promised. "Come on, Jordan, you can be back at work before your typewriter knows you're gone."

She was difficult to refuse under any circumstances, but when she was pulling on his arm and laughing like this, it was impossible. "All right." He rose and allowed her to drag him toward the stairs. "What is it?"

"A surprise, of course. I'm crazy about surprises." Upstairs she pushed open the door to her room and motioned for him to enter. He did, then studied the room in silence.

Red and green paper chains hung everywhere, criss-crossing and draping from wall to wall. They wound down the bedposts and framed the windows. Cardboard angels, Santas and elves hung from doorknobs and balanced on dresser tops, and a red felt stocking overflowed with candy canes. There was a bright gold star suspended from the center of the ceiling.

Jordan took a turn around and faced Kasey again. "Re-decorating?"

"I didn't do it." She rose on her toes and kissed him again. He delighted her when he used that dry tone. "Alison did. Isn't it wonderful?"

"I can certainly say I'm surprised." Shaking his head, he looked around again. "And I can honestly say I've never seen anything quite like it."

"You should see the bathroom," Kasey told him. "It's spectacular!"

He smiled at Kasey and sent an elf spinning on its string. "And, of course, you told her you loved it."

"I do love it," Kasey countered. "It's one of the nicest things anyone's ever done for me. She wanted me to feel at home for Christmas. And now I do."

Jordan reached out to touch her hair. "If I had known paper chains would make you happy, I'd have made some myself."

Kasey grinned and threw her arms around him. "Do you know how?"

"I think I could manage it."

"Can you string popcorn?"

"Can I what?" He was distracted from kissing her hair.

"String popcorn," Kasey repeated, linking her hands around his neck. "What I'd really like to do on Christmas Eve is string popcorn for the tree. And I want to get Alison a puppy."

"Wait a minute." Jordan drew her away. "Sometimes it takes me just a minute to catch up."

"Just say yes to both and think of the trouble we'll save. I can't bear a tree without popcorn strings, Jordan. It's positively naked. And Alison needs a puppy."

"Why?"

"Why what?"

Jordan sighed and rubbed the bridge of his nose between his thumb and forefinger. How did she manage to do this so often? "Why does Alison need a puppy?"

"Because she wants one, first of all. That's a good reason." She smiled at him. "And a puppy would be a companion and a responsibility for her. What do you think about cocker spaniels?"

Jordan leaned back against the door. "I'm forced to admit I've never given them much thought."

"Give it a minute, then," she suggested. "It's a gentle breed, good with children. A pet is very important in childhood, Jordan. Owning one teaches a variety of valuable—"

"Wait." Jordan held up a hand to stop her. "It would be simpler if I just said yes and saved us both a lot of time."

"I told you that you were logical." Kasey smiled, pleased with herself.

Jordan put his hands on her shoulders. "I also think it's very thoughtful of you."

"So do I," she said lightly. "I'm a very thoughtful person."

"You are," he said and drew her closer. "Whether you like to hear it or not. You've made quite a difference in Alison's life—and in mine."

She couldn't speak but only laid her head on his chest. *I love you both*, she thought and shut her eyes tight.

"Does this mean yes to the popcorn, too?" she asked him. It was so warm in his arms, so secure. It was impossible to believe that one day soon she'd have to leave them.

"I don't suppose I could face a naked Christmas tree."

She squeezed him. "Thank you."

"Now I've something to ask you."

She tilted her face back to his and smiled. "Your timing's exceptional," she decided. "I'm obliged to say yes to almost anything."

He kissed her nose. "Perhaps you'll remember that at a more opportune time, but for now you've probably noticed my mother doing quite a bit of sighing because I haven't attended any of the holiday parties."

"As a matter of fact, I have." Kasey kept her voice light. "I've also noticed," she said, "how expertly you ignore her."

"I've had a lifetime of practice," Jordan said dryly. "But there's a club dance at the end of the week. I should go. Come with me."

"Are you asking me for a date, Jordan?"

"It sounded like it." He laughed suddenly and shook his head. "Kasey, you make me feel as though I were sixteen. Will you come with me?"

"I like to dance." She slid her hands up behind his neck and linked them. "I'd like to dance with you." She gave him a kiss and let it slowly deepen until she heard his quiet sound of pleasure. "I believe I'll buy a new dress," she murmured. "Do you have a favorite color?"

"Green." His mouth roamed to her neck. "Like your eyes."

She laughed a little and pressed closer. "Jordan, there's one more thing I should tell you."

"*Hmm.* What?" His mouth was back on hers.

"Alison," Kasey began, accepting the kiss. "When she finished in here, she went to do your room."

"Do what?" he murmured, steeped in Kasey's taste.

"Your room."

"My room?" Jordan drew away a bit to look at her. "My room?" He glanced over her head at the paper chains and cardboard figures. Incredulity spread over his face as he looked back at Kasey. "*My* room?"

"Jordan, you're repeating yourself." Kasey laughed as he let out a long breath. Slipping her arms around his waist, she hugged him tightly. "You're going to love it," she promised. "You're getting a foam snowman."

The next afternoon, Kasey looked on as Alison strummed her guitar. The technique was still clumsy, but she made up for it with enthusiasm. Kasey thought back to the first time she had watched Alison sit stiffly at the piano, playing Brahms with precision and disinterest.

No more empty eyes, she thought and reached out to touch the girl's hair. What would it be like to have a child of her own? she wondered. She shook her head. She was becoming too sentimental and much, much too attached.

"Terrific," she told Alison when she had finished. "You learn quickly."

"Will I ever play as well as you?"

"Better, soon." Kasey smiled and packed the guitar in its case. "I've an affection for music. You've affection and skill."

"I didn't think so before." Alison sat down at the piano and began to finger the keys. "I can play things on the piano and the guitar now."

Kasey grinned. "Alison, I have to go shopping. Want to come with me?"

"Shopping?" Alison's attention was arrested. "Christmas shopping? I've finished mine, but I'd like to help you with what you have left."

"Have left? I haven't started yet."

"None at all?" Alison's eyes widened. "But there are only ten days left."

"That many?" Kasey rose and stretched. "Well, I suppose I can start early. I usually wait until Christmas Eve. I love the confusion."

"But what if you can't find what you want?"

How like Jordan she was, Kasey thought. "That's the challenge," Kasey told her. "I drive the sales clerks crazy." The thought made her grin. "In any case, I need a dress. We can grab a hamburger, too. There must be a McFarden's around somewhere."

"McFarden's?" Alison brought her brows together. She was intrigued and cautious. So like Jordan, Kasey thought again. "I've never been to McFarden's."

"Never been to McFarden's?" Kasey gave her a look of exaggerated astonishment. "That," she said, "is positively un-American." Grabbing Alison's hand, she pulled her to her feet. "You need a lesson in patriotism."

Some time later, Kasey eased into a parking space. "I told you I'd find one." Switching off the ignition, she dropped the keys into her pocket. Alison climbed out, and Kasey locked up carefully.

"I hope Uncle Jordan won't mind that we borrowed his car."

"He told me I could use it whenever I liked." Kasey skirted around the Mercedes's hood.

"But Charles usually drives everyone except Uncle Jordan."

"Why should we drag poor Charles around?" Kasey countered. "We must have gone to a hundred and thirty-seven stores." She pushed through the glass doors. "I'm starving. Do you realize how long it's been since I had a hamburger?"

Alison looked around her and became caught up in the crowd and the noise. "It smells wonderful."

Kasey laughed and pulled her into line. "Smelling's not eating. I have a craving for French fries."

Alison stared up at the menu that hung above the counter and zeroed in on a picture of a hamburger. "I'd like one of those. Is it good?"

"Fantastic." Kasey laughed. "You have big eyes, Alison. Let's hope you have an appetite to match."

"It *is* big," Alison stated when they found a table. She took a bite and grinned. "And it's good."

"You have very discerning taste." Kasey dug into her own. She closed her eyes and sighed. "It's been too long. Do you think we can talk Francois into trying his hand at one of these?"

"You could," Alison stated and wolfed down a French fry.

"Why do you say that?"

"You could talk anybody into anything."

Kasey laughed and shook her head. "Perceptive little squirt, aren't you?"

Alison grinned and sampled her milk shake. "I've never seen anything like the present you got for Uncle Jordan."

"The shaman's rattle?" Kasey chewed thoughtfully on a French fry. "It was quite a find." It had been elegantly carved and painted. Apache. Kasey had been thrilled enough to come across it that she hadn't even thought to bargain. "It'll help him ward off evil spirits."

Alison was bulldozing her way through the hamburger. "I liked the dress you bought, too. Green looks beautiful on you."

"I don't usually wear it. It's so obvious with my coloring." She sat back with her own milk shake. "Then, I don't mind being obvious now and again."

"It's very stylish," Alison told her and took another bite of her hamburger. "And slinky."

Kasey grinned. "I did like that other one, though. You know, the smashed velvet."

"Crushed velvet," Alison corrected and giggled.

"Whatever. Would you like an apple pie?"

Alison sat back and took a deep breath. "I don't think so. Would you?"

"Not if I want to get into that dress. What did you get me for Christmas?"

"It's a—Kasey!" Alison exclaimed.

"I thought I might catch you off guard."

"It's supposed to be a secret." Alison wiped her hands primly. "Telling would spoil it."

"Really?" Kasey gave her a guileless smile. "Is that why you've been creeping around the house and searching through closets?"

Alison blushed,then giggled again. "I only thought I might shake some boxes."

"That's an old story."

"Christmas is more fun with you here, Kasey." Her eyes were serious again. "Will you stay forever?"

Kasey felt the first crack in her heart. How could she explain to the girl what she didn't want to think of herself? "Forever is a long time, Alison." She kept her voice quiet and her eyes level. "I'll have to leave when my job's finished."

"But can't you stay and keep working for Uncle Jordan?"

"He doesn't need a resident anthropologist, Alison. And I've work of my own." She watched the child's gaze falter and drop. "Friends stay friends, Alison, no matter how far apart they are. I love you." She reached out to lay her hand over Alison's. "That's not going to change."

"Will you come back?" Alison lifted her eyes again. "And visit me?"

I can't, she wanted to say. How can you ask me? Can't you understand how it would hurt me? "You could visit me," she said instead. "Would you like that?"

"Really?" Alison's smile bloomed again. "And your grandfather?"

"Sure. Pop would love it." She began to pile things back on the tray. "You're much better behaved than I ever was. Why don't you dump all this stuff in the trash?"

Kasey took a moment when she was alone at the table to pull herself together. It was better this way. Alison was already being prepared. *And what about me?* She shut her eyes a moment. I've said I'll pay the price when the time comes. I have to stick to that.

"Ready?" she said and gave Alison a smile when she came back to the table. "Now we have to find a post office so I can mail off those things to my grandfather. Do you think he'll like that little gnome with the buck teeth?"

When they entered the house, Alison was laughing, struggling to balance her share of Kasey's purchases. "I'll help you wrap them," she said, grabbing at a sliding box.

"We'd better get them upstairs first." Kasey rescued the box and glanced up as Beatrice came down the stairs.

"Alison, what have you been doing?" She frowned at the child's windblown hair.

"Alison helped me with my Christmas shopping, Mrs. Taylor."

Beatrice shifted her gaze and met Kasey's eyes. "I don't approve of you taking Alison from the house without discussing it with me first." She turned to her granddaughter again. "Go up and brush your hair, Alison. You look a sight."

"Yes, ma'am."

Kasey watched her walk obediently up the stairs. She turned back to Beatrice and spoke calmly. "I'm sorry if you were concerned, Mrs. Taylor. You were out when we left, and I did tell Millicent what our plans were."

Beatrice lifted a brow. "I dislike being informed by a servant of the whereabouts of my grandchild."

"It didn't occur to me you'd notice she wasn't here."

Beatrice's color flared. "Are you criticizing me, Miss Wyatt?"

"Of course not, Mrs. Taylor." Kasey fought to keep the conversation in perspective. "I enjoy Alison's company, she enjoys mine. We spent an afternoon together. I'm sorry if you were worried."

"I find your attitude impertinent."

"I can only repeat, I'm sorry," Kasey replied evenly. "Now, if you'll excuse me, I'd like to go put these things away."

"You'd be wise to remember your position in this house, Miss Wyatt." Kasey stopped, then set down her packages. It seemed they weren't through just yet. "You're a paid servant and can very easily be replaced."

"I'm here on a job, Mrs. Taylor, and no one's servant unless I choose to be." She paused a moment. "Is that all you have to say to me?"

"I won't tolerate your insubordination." Beatrice's knuckles whitened on the post of the banister. She wasn't accustomed to being looked at so directly by someone she considered an employee. "I won't tolerate your disruptive influence on my granddaughter."

"I was under the impression that Alison was Jordan's ward." *What am I doing?* Kasey thought abruptly. I'm putting Alison right between us. I'm putting her right in the middle. "Mrs. Taylor," she began, searching for a way to ease the tension for the child's sake.

"What's going on?" Jordan came through the drawing room doorway. He'd heard the argument the moment he'd stepped out of his study.

"This woman," his mother began, turning to him, "is insufferably rude."

Jordan lifted a brow. "Kasey?" he asked turning to her.

"Probably," she agreed and tried to relax her muscles.

"Miss Wyatt took it upon herself to disappear with Alison for the entire afternoon, then had the effrontery to criticize me when I expressed concern."

Jordan, caught between amusement and annoyance, studied Kasey again. "Been busy, have you?"

"We only went Christmas shopping, Uncle Jordan." Alison

came down half the stairs in a rush, then stopped when her grandmother turned to her.

"This is none of your concern, Alison. Go back up to your room."

"I don't think that's necessary." Jordan stepped around his mother and held out a hand to Alison. She dashed down the rest of the stairs. "Well, you appear relatively unharmed. Did you have a good time?"

"It was wonderful." Alison grinned up at him. "We went to McFarden's."

"Really?" Jordan shot a look at Kasey. He knew her well enough to see beyond the careless front. She was raging inside and, he thought curiously, hurting. What had been said, he wondered, before he had come upon them? He smiled at her, wanting to soothe her. "You might have asked me to go along."

Kasey was working to control her temper. She knew very well anger wasn't the way to handle Beatrice Taylor. And handling Beatrice Taylor would be necessary if she wanted to keep things smooth for Alison. It helped to see Alison standing under Jordan's arm.

"You were working," she returned. "And I didn't think the idea of tramping through shops would appeal to you."

"Kasey bought you a present, Uncle Jordan."

"Did she?" He drew the child to his side, but his eyes were on Kasey's.

"Chocolate cookies," Kasey told him. "Alison thought they were pretty."

"Obviously you intend to treat this matter lightly." Beatrice spoke again.

"Mother. There's nothing here to be concerned about. Alison's fine."

"Very well." She nodded, then brushed by him to mount the stairs.

Kasey looked down at Alison, who was watching her grandmother's retreating back. "I'm sorry, Uncle Jordan. I didn't know Grandmother would be upset. She wasn't here when we left, and we told Millicent, in case you wondered where we were."

"You haven't done anything." He bent and kissed her

cheek. "Your grandmother's probably a bit tired after her luncheon today, that's all. She needs to rest awhile. Why don't you take these packages up for Kasey?"

Alison gathered up boxes. "I'll bring wrapping paper to your room."

"Thanks." Children spring back quickly, she noted. Alison was already more concerned with the presents than with her grandmother's annoyance.

Jordan put his hands on Kasey's shoulders as Alison disappeared up the steps. "Shall I apologize, too?" he asked quietly as he soothed the remaining tension from her muscles.

Kasey shook her head. "No." She sighed. She was aware that it was Beatrice's dislike of her which had caused the confrontation. She felt responsible. "I've put you in a bad position. Alison, too. I never meant to, Jordan."

"Let me handle my mother," he told her. "I've been doing it for a long time. And next time you go off for an afternoon," he added, "invite me. I might have found tramping through shops and a hamburger appealing."

"All right." She smiled, steadying. "Next time I will."

He started to pull her close, then stopped. His brows drew together. "Chocolate cookies?"

11

*K*asey paused in the drawing room doorway. She'd taken her time dressing for the dance at Jordan's club, wanting to be certain Beatrice was gone before she came downstairs.

Standing there, she had a moment to study Jordan unobserved as he mixed drinks at the bar. Formal dress—the stark black and white, the perfect tailoring—suited him. He moves well, she thought, a man used to elegant clothes and elegant rooms. Yet there's so much more to him than I realized that first night I walked in here. More depth, more character, more strength. If I could have chosen a man to fall in love with, I couldn't have chosen any better.

Taking a deep breath, she walked into the room. "It seems my timing's perfect."

Jordan turned to watch her. The dress was dark green and clinging with a deep slash of a neckline. It was caught at the side of her waist and fell straight, leaving a slit that opened and closed as she walked.

"I thought once you were a witch," Jordan murmured. "Now I'm sure of it."

Kasey took the glass from his hand. "Like it?" She smiled and sipped. "Jordan, you've picked up the knack for mixing these. You could make a living from it."

"Yes, I like it." He took the glass from her, set it down, and then drew her into his arms. He gave her a long, deep, satisfying kiss that begged for more. "The thought comes into my mind," he said as his lips grazed her cheekbone, "of locking those doors over there and staying right where I am."

"Oh, no." Kasey smiled and shook her head. "You asked me for a date. I'm holding you to it."

"We could be late." He kissed her again, lingeringly. They hadn't had nearly enough time together since they had returned from New York. "We've been late before."

But not here, she thought, floating under the kiss. We're not alone here.

She drew herself carefully out of his arms. "Someone once told me that being late was rude. Besides," she picked up her glass again, "you promised to dance with me. I should think you dance very well."

It occurred to him that he wasn't going to like sharing her. He shook off the notion. Jealousy was foreign to him. "All right," he agreed. "A date's a date."

Kasey took his hand as they walked to the door. "Can we go parking afterward?" she asked.

"Love to." He grinned and nudged her outside.

Jordan slipped two glasses from the tray of a roving waiter. "Champagne?" he asked her.

"Absolutely." Kasey took the glass and sipped. "It's beautiful here. I'm glad you asked me to come."

He touched the rim of his glass to hers. "To anthropology," he murmured. "A fascinating science."

Kasey gave a low laugh and raised her glass to her lips. She turned to watch a slim brunette in a filmy white dress weave through the crowd toward them. Reaching Jordan, she rose on her toes to kiss his cheek.

"Jordan. You've finally come out of hibernation."

"Hello, Liz. You look lovely, as always."

"I'm surprised you remember what I look like after all this time. It's been months." She smiled and turned to Kasey. She had round, fawn's eyes and creamy skin. There was a single, perfect diamond on a chain at her throat.

"Kathleen Wyatt." Jordan touched Kasey's shoulder lightly. "Elizabeth Bentley."

"Kathleen Wyatt?" Liz repeated. "The name's very familiar, but we haven't met before, have we?"

"No, Miss Bentley, we haven't met." Kasey gave her a friendly smile, appreciating the frank interest in her eyes. "Would you like some champagne?" she asked, slipping a glass from another tray. "It's really very good."

"Thank you." Liz glanced down at the glass, then back at Kasey.

"Kasey's been working with me on my novel," Jordan explained. He could see Liz was both confused and intrigued.

"Oh, yes." A piece fell into place. "Harry Rhodes mentioned your name at dinner the other night." She hesitated a moment. "He said you were extraordinarily intelligent."

"That's because I hustled him at pool." Kasey's eyes gleamed with laughter over the rim of her glass as she lifted it again. "Do you play?"

"Play—pool?" Liz shook her head, and a faint line of concentration appeared between her brows. "No. You're an archaeologist?"

"No, an anthropologist." Kasey smiled and couldn't resist. "An archaeologist is one who studies the life and culture of ancient peoples by excavating ancient cities, relics, artifacts. An anthropologist is one who studies the races, physical and mental characteristics, distributions, customs, social relationships of mankind." She took another sip of champagne. "That's a terrific dress," she commented, nodding at Liz. "French?"

"You did a fine job of confusing Liz," Jordan stated when he had Kasey in his arms on the dance floor.

"Really?" Kasey lifted her cheek from his. She laughed at the wry look he gave her. "She's a very pretty lady, Jordan, and a very nice one. I like her."

"You make up your mind quickly."

"Usually it saves time." She smiled as he whirled her around the floor. "I decided you were a marvelous dancer," she pointed out. "And I was right."

"If I told you I'd never enjoyed a waltz more, would you believe me?"

"I might." She laughed up at him.

"I'm going to have to let you dance with the men here who can't keep their eyes off you. I'm not going to like it."

Her brows lifted. "Are there many?" she asked, teasing him while she tried to sort out how she felt about his statement.

"Too many. You walk into a room, and every eye rests on you. Including mine."

Kasey laughed and shook her head. "You've a writer's imagination, Jordan."

"And a man's," he murmured. "I can't get you out of my mind."

She was staring up at him, forgetting the music they moved to, the people who moved with them. "Do you want to?"

He couldn't look away from her. "I don't know." He couldn't think straight when she was in his arms, pressed close. "I wish I did. Is it enough to tell you there's never been another woman who's been as important to me as you are?"

It was a cautious step, and Kasey took it no further. She touched his cheek with her fingers. "It's enough, Jordan."

Throughout the evening Kasey was never alone. She sparked interest everywhere she went. She enjoyed answering the questions put to her and fielding flirtations. She enjoyed the elegance, the glamour, just as she enjoyed a trip to the corner movie. Buttered popcorn or champagne, it was all part of life.

"Miss Wyatt."

Kasey turned away from a discussion with a yachting enthusiast and his wife and smiled at Harry Rhodes. "Hello, Harry. It's good to see you."

"It's nice seeing you again. You look lovely."

"So do you." She touched the lapel of his dinner jacket. He cleared his throat.

"I wanted to tell you how much I enjoyed reading the book you loaned me."

"Anytime, Harry." He had a nice face, she thought. Jordan was fortunate to have him for a friend.

"I've been practicing, you know. I'm going to challenge you to another game of pool."

"I'd like that." She grinned now. "We'll have to try eight ball this time."

"Miss Wyatt . . . Kathleen . . . Kasey," he decided, as her smile warmed for him. "That's what Jordan calls you, isn't it?"

"All my friends do."

He fiddled with his glasses and smiled. His eyes were kind, she thought, like the wise little bear he reminded her of.

"Kasey, I don't suppose you'd care to risk the dance floor with a doddering old professor."

"I don't see one." Kasey set down her glass and offered her hand. "But I'd love to dance with you, Harry."

"Jordan's a very fortunate man to have found you," he told her as they headed for the dance floor.

"But it was *you* who found me, wasn't it, Harry?"

"Then I should pat myself on the back." He liked the dimple at the corner of her mouth, the way her hair curled without design around her face. She seemed a little of the waif, a little of the siren. "I hope Jordan appreciates you."

"He's a very kind man, isn't he? Kind, loving, and gentle."

"He loved his brother very much, you know." Harry gave a sigh. "They were close. Allen, his father, was a dear friend of mine. He died several years before, and Beatrice has never been a maternal woman. Best hostess I know," he added. "But simply not cut for mothering. The boys were quite a pair. A bit wild now and then, but—"

"Wild?" Kasey interrupted with a surprised laugh. "Jordan?"

"He had his moments, my dear." Recalling a few, Harry decided it would be more discreet not to detail them. "It was very difficult for Jordan when he lost his brother. They were twins."

"I didn't know." Losing a brother would be hard enough, she mused, but losing a twin would be losing part of yourself. "He's never talked about it with me."

"He closed himself in after that. It hasn't been until recently that I've noticed the door opening again." Harry looked down at Kasey. "That's your doing. You care for him very much, don't you?"

Kasey met his eyes directly. "I'm in love with him."

Harry nodded. He was no longer surprised by her frankness. "He's needed someone like you to snap the life back in him. If he's not careful, he could turn out to be a crusty old bachelor like me."

"You're a beautiful man, Harry." The music stopped, and Kasey kissed his cheek, holding him a moment.

"What's this?" Jordan crossed over to them and slipped an arm around Kasey's shoulders. "Turn my back for a moment and you're nuzzling up to my date. I thought I could trust you, Harry."

Harry colored and harrumphed. "Not with this lady, my boy. I'm part of the competition. And I haven't lost my touch yet," he announced before he strolled away.

"What did you do to him?" Bemused, Jordan watched Harry's swagger. "I believe he meant that."

"I certainly hope so." Kasey drew Jordan's eyes back to her. "Would you be jealous? That would be a marvelous Christmas present, Jordan."

"It's not Christmas yet," he countered. "Let's go outside before I have to compete with someone else."

"Competition's very healthy," Kasey stated as they slipped through the terrace doors. "In studies with white mice—"

He kissed her firmly, cutting off the impending lecture. "I'm damned if I'm going to compete with white mice," he muttered, pulling her closer.

His hand was in her hair, and his mouth demanded. Kasey yielded, sensing it was what he needed. Her mouth was soft, and her arms lifted to wind around his neck. A submission of the moment; later there would be time for challenge, for aggression, for equal strength. He needed something different from her now. It was simple to surrender to him when she knew her own power. She could feel his heart pound as he kept her molded against him.

Jordan drew her away to stare down at her. "Who are you?" he muttered. "I never know who you are."

"You're closer to knowing than most," she murmured and turned to lean on the rail. "It's lovely here, Jordan. The air's soft, and I can smell—verbena, I think." Kasey lifted her face. "The stars are close." She sighed and scanned them. "Back at home I used to sit outside for hours and pick out constellations. Pop bought me a telescope one year. I was going to be the first woman on the moon."

"What changed your mind?" There was a click from his lighter, then the scent of tobacco on the air.

Kasey shrugged her shoulders. She would remember that scent for the rest of her life. "I tried to live on dehydrated food for a week. It's terrible." He laughed, and she pointed skyward. "There's Pegasus. See? He flies straight up. Andromeda's head touches his wing." She brought her hand down and sighed. She felt pleasantly sleepy. "Marvelous, isn't it? All the pictures up there. It's comforting knowing they'll be there tomorrow."

Jordan came closer to touch her shoulder. Her skin was smooth and just a bit cool from the night air. "Is that why you dig into the past? Because it's a link with the future?"

She gave another restless shrug. "Maybe."

He tossed aside the cigar and pulled her close again. She rested her head on his shoulder. "Dance with me again, Jordan," she murmured. "The night's almost over."

12

Christmas Eve. Magic. Kasey was ready for magic. She had palm trees rather than snow, but she'd lived through Christmases without snow before. This time she had something of more value. She would have the day with the man she loved and with a child who was burning with excitement. That was magic enough for her.

She was aware that her job was finished, or at least nearly so. Jordan spent more and more time working without her. What she filled in now could be done by a letter or a simple phone call. She was procrastinating, and she knew, whether Jordan realized it or not, that so was he. The break had to come—but not on Christmas. Kasey was taking that for herself. When the holidays were over, she'd make her plans, pack, then tell him. In that order. It would be better if everything was set before the words were said.

With a firm plan in mind, Kasey felt better. She told herself she was entitled to a week. The first of the year, she would take the step away from him, away from Alison, and begin again. She was strong; she'd lived through losses before. But now it was Christmas, and she had a family, if only for another week.

She sat on the rug in the drawing room and watched Alison poke at the stacks of presents under the tree. She chattered like a magpie. What might this be? What that *had* to be. How many hours were left?

"Not quite one less than the last time you asked," Jordan told her and pulled her up on his lap. "Why don't we open everything now?"

"Oh, no, Uncle Jordan, we couldn't!" She glanced at Kasey, waiting to be overruled.

"No, we couldn't. Santa would be very annoyed."

Alison laughed and snuggled into the curve of Jordan's arm. "Kasey, you know there isn't really a Santa Claus."

"I know nothing of the sort. You, Miss Taylor, are a cynic."

"I am?" Alison digested the word. Reaching over, she picked up a small glass ball that held a miniature forest scene. Turning it upside down, she let the snow fall. "I haven't seen this before."

"No." Jordan had wondered when she would notice it. "I found it in the attic this morning. It was your father's when we were boys."

"Really?"

"Yes. Really. I thought you might like to have it."

"To keep?" She curled her fingers around the glass and looked up at him.

"To keep."

Alison looked back at the glass and watched the snow drift. "He liked the snow," she mused. "When we lived in Chicago, we had snow fights. He'd let me win." She leaned back against Jordan's chest and tilted the ball again.

Kasey watched them and kept silent. He'd gone searching for that to give Alison something of her father for Christmas. If she hadn't loved him before, she would have fallen in love with him at that moment. He's a good man, she thought. Above everything else he is, he's a good man.

She rose, wanting to give them time alone.

"Kasey?" Jordan's eyes lifted to hers, and she stopped.

"I think I still have a few things to wrap," she told him. He smiled, seeing through her.

"Didn't someone mention something about stringing popcorn?"

"Popcorn?" Alison's eyes lit up. "For the tree?"

"Kasey told me a tree wasn't suitably dressed unless it wore popcorn," Jordan stated. "What do you think?"

"May we do it now?"

"I'm all for it, but Kasey seems to have something else to do." Jordan kept his eyes on her, still smiling.

"I'm flexible," Kasey returned, then looked at Alison. "We'll need several miles of string and three needles. Can you handle it?"

"Are we going to eat some, too?"

"Absolutely."

Alison scrambled up and, taking the glass ball with her, shot out of the room.

"Sometimes you're transparent, Kasey." Jordan rose and went to her. "You were going to cry and didn't want to do it in front of Alison. Or in front of me."

"That was a marvelous thing you did."

"Alison was with me last Christmas, and it never occurred to me." He lifted Kasey's chin a bit higher and kissed her.

"Don't make me cry, Jordan. It's Christmas Eve."

"I've got them!" Alison came to the doorway at a full run. She held up a packet of needles and a thick ball of string.

"Half the battle." Kasey crossed to her, then turned back to Jordan. "Coming?"

"I wouldn't miss it."

As they approached the kitchen door, Jordan said, "You know, I'm not sure how Francois is going to take this. His kitchen's sacred."

"Piece of cake," Kasey murmured as they entered.

Francois turned and bowed. He didn't wear the white hat Kasey had hoped for all those weeks ago, but he did have the moustache. "*Monsieur.*" He bowed at Jordan. "May I assist you?"

"Francois." Jordan took a moment. He'd witnessed more than one tantrum over the years. "We have a need to make something for the Christmas tree."

"*Oui, monsieur?*"

"We're going to string popcorn."

"Popcorn? You want to make this popcorn in my kitchen?" Before Jordan could answer, Francois was off on a stream of indignant French.

"Francois?"

He turned and gave a stiff bow. "*Mademoiselle?*"

Kasey smiled at him. "*Vôtre cuisine est magnifique,*" she

began, then continued in flawless French. She praised his food, his stove, his counters, sampled the stock pot he had simmering while he joined the discussion with passion. She was enthusiastic about the perfection of his cookware and impressed with his cutlery.

When she had finished, he kissed her hand cordially, bowed to Jordan again and strolled from the room.

"Well." Jordan glanced at the closed door, then back at Kasey. He watched as she took down a pan and placed it on the stove. "Where did you learn to speak French like that?"

"My roommate at college was a language major. Where's the popcorn?"

He walked to her, ignoring the question. "What did you say to him? I always thought my French was good, but the two of you went well beyond me."

"Just this and that." Kasey smiled. "I did tell him you wanted him and the rest of the kitchen staff to have the night off. You do have popcorn, don't you?"

Jordan laughed and reached into a bottom cabinet. "I smuggled it in at great personal risk."

"You're a tough guy, Taylor." She took the can from him. "I'll need some oil." He gestured for Alison to get it, then leaned close and whispered a quick French phrase in Kasey's ear. Her mouth turned up. "I'm shocked," she murmured. "Interested, but shocked. I don't think I'll ask you where you learned that."

In moments the kitchen was noisy with the popping of the corn. Alison sat at the butcher block table, ankles crossed, carefully cutting lengths of string. Jordan settled across from her and watched. When was the last time he had sat listening to that sound? he wondered. In college? No, at his brother's house, five, perhaps six, years ago. Perhaps Kasey had been right. He had insulated himself.

"Another masterpiece," Kasey declared, turning the popcorn into a bowl. "No duds."

He dipped his hand into the bowl. "Where's the butter?" he demanded. Alison's hand brushed his as she dug in.

"Grab a needle," Kasey instructed each of them.

They worked in anything but silence. Alison chattered continually between mouthfuls. Her string of popcorn grew longer by the minute. It seemed to Kasey that they had sat like this before on other Christmas Eves, that they would sit like this again. But she knew better and shivered.

"Cold?" Jordan asked her.

"No." She tried to shake off the feeling. "A goat ran over my grave."

"That's a goose," he said and smiled at her.

"Goose, goat." She shrugged. She stuffed a piece of popcorn into her mouth. "You're not doing so well there, Jordan," she observed.

"I need incentive."

"Mine's going to be the longest," Alison declared. "It's going to be a hundred miles long."

"Don't count your chickens before they cross the road," Kasey advised. "How do you do that, Jordan?" she asked, studying him. "Did it come naturally, or did you practice?"

Jordan shook his head in amused confusion.

"I mean lift one eyebrow," Kasey explained. "It's marvelous. I'd love to be able to do it, but both of mine work at the same time. Let's have some hot chocolate." She sprang up and began to rummage through cupboards. Jordan abandoned his string and watched her.

"Kasey, come here a minute."

"Jordan, preparing hot chocolate requires concentration and care." She measured in the milk. Crossing the room, he took her arm and pulled her under the doorway. He pointed above their heads with one finger. Kasey smiled at the mistletoe. "Is it real?" she asked.

"It's real," he assured her.

"Well, in that case . . ." She touched her mouth lightly to his.

"That's not how they kiss in the movies," Alison commented and plucked another piece of popcorn.

"Absolutely right," Jordan agreed before Kasey could comment. He drew her back into his arms and covered her mouth with his. The kiss lengthened, and the sweetness of it made Kasey's throat ache. She held him close. She would remember that kiss before all the others, she knew.

"That was much better," Alison stated when Kasey drew away. "My string's finished."

Later they sat in the drawing room again. Alison was curled next to Jordan on the sofa with Kasey's guitar in her lap. Kasey watched the colors from the lights on the tree play across her face as she drifted into sleep.

"She's had a long day," Kasey murmured.

"I'm looking forward to seeing her face when she gets her presents tomorrow." He slipped the guitar from Alison's limp arms and handed it to Kasey. "Your little gift is safely tucked away?"

"Charles is guarding my little gift in the garage. I'm not sure he's going to part with it easily." She rose. "I'll take Alison up and put her to bed."

"I'll do it." Jordan shifted his niece into his arms and stood. "Why don't you put some music on?"

When he had gone, Kasey went to the cabinet that held the stereo. Chopin, she decided, shifting through the albums. It was a night for romance.

The house was quiet. The servants were settled in their wing. Beatrice was at a party. It might have been only the three of them in the house. Kasey sighed as she slipped the record onto the turntable. For tonight she could pretend it was true. Wandering to the window, she parted the curtains and looked out. The moon was high and full, the night clear. She found Pegasus again and mused over it. When she heard the doors shut quietly, she turned. Kasey watched Jordan lock them.

"Did you settle her in all right?" Her heart began to skip rapidly. Silly, she thought. I act as though it's the first time I've been with him.

"She's fine. She never even woke up. You sleep like that." He crossed the room and set the bottle of wine he carried on the bar. "Deep, like a child." He opened the wine, then moved to the fireplace. Kneeling, he set gas flames burning over the logs. "Now you can pretend it's snowing." He smiled up at her.

"You do see through me, don't you?"

"At times." When he had poured two glasses, he moved back in front of the fire and sat. He held up a hand for her. Kasey took it and settled next to him. "How do you feel?" he asked when she was leaning against him.

128 NORA ROBERTS

"Like I'm snowed in," she murmured, accepting the wine he offered. "Snuggled in a log cabin in the Adirondacks, away from the world and its problems."

"Is there room in the log cabin for me?"

She tilted her head to smile at him. "Anytime."

"We'd have wood," he said quietly and he took the glass from her hand. "And wine." He bent to kiss the corner of her mouth. "And each other." Gently he lowered her to the floor. "We wouldn't need anything else."

"No." Kasey's lids lowered as she drew him closer. "Nothing else."

She lost herself in the feel of him, in the taste of him. Her mind and body were in complete harmony, and both belonged to him. From somewhere deep in the center of the house, the clock struck midnight, and it was Christmas.

How long they loved each other that night Kasey would never know. Neither of them had wanted to unlock the door and open themselves to the rest of the world. Once, when they dozed together, Jordan woke to hear the front door open and close behind his mother. Then the house was silent again. Theirs. He turned to Kasey and roused her slowly until she was quivering for him again and he for her. There was firelight and the colors from the tree and the scent of pine. The wine grew warm.

Kasey slept again and woke groggily when Jordan lifted her.

"I'll take you up," he murmured.

"I don't want to leave you." She buried her face in his neck. "The nights are too short. Hours and hours too short."

Then she was asleep again, as deeply as Alison had been when he had carried her up the stairs.

Morning came all too soon. Only her own determination and Alison's excitement kept Kasey from crawling back under the covers. The neat, formal drawing room was soon strewn with torn paper, boxes and discarded ribbons. A cocker spaniel puppy, Kasey's gift to Alison, raced around the tree while Alison sat, awestruck, with a new guitar, a gift from her uncle, on her lap.

"Shouldn't you wake your mother, Jordan?" Kasey murmured, pushing some crumpled paper aside.

"At six o'clock in the morning?" He laughed and shook his head. "Mother doesn't rise before ten, Christmas or no Christmas. We'll have a very civilized brunch later."

Kasey wrinkled her nose and grabbed for a box. "It's about time I had one," she announced, knowing the gift was from Alison. "I've heard a lot of whispering about this one," she said, unwinding the ribbon slowly. "Seen a lot of telling looks." Alison caught her bottom lip between her teeth and looked at Jordan. "Like that one," Kasey stated and ripped the paper with a flourish. Opening the box, she found a long, pale green neck scarf in soft wool.

"It's the first present I ever made," Alison said anxiously. "Rose the kitchen maid taught me. I made some mistakes."

Kasey tried to raise her eyes, tried to speak, but could do neither. She stroked the awkwardly crocheted scarf with her fingers.

"Do you like it?"

Kasey looked up and nodded helplessly. Her eyes were already brimming over.

"Women," Jordan said, tucking Alison's hair behind her ear. "Some women," he corrected, "tend to weep when they're particularly happy. Kasey's one of them."

"Really?"

"Really," Kasey managed and took a deep breath. "Alison, it's the most beautiful present I've ever had." She gathered the girl into her arms and squeezed. "Thank you."

"She really likes it," Alison said, grinning at Jordan over Kasey's shoulder. "Do you think she'll cry if you give her yours?"

"Why don't we find out?" Jordan reached under the tree for a small, square box. "Of course, maybe she's not interested in any more presents."

"Of course I am." Kasey drew out of Alison's arms. "I'm very greedy on Christmas." She took the box from him and drew a deep breath. Opening it, she felt her heart lurch for the second time that morning.

She held the gold, finely etched drop earrings, remarkably similar to those she had seen the day she had bought his unicorn. She looked up at him and shook her head. "Jordan, how did you remember something like this?"

"I haven't forgotten anything you've told me. I thought this went with it." He handed her another box, this one long and flat, then smiled as she hesitated. "I thought you were greedy on Christmas."

Kasey opened the box and found three thin gold chains ingeniously twisted together to form one. "It's beautiful," she murmured.

He took the chain from her fingers and clasped it around her neck.

Kasey swallowed, then laid her cheek against his. "Thank you, Jordan." She scrambled up. "I'm going to see about some coffee."

"She liked yours, too," Alison told him and shifted her guitar. "She was crying again."

When Millicent brought coffee and croissants into the drawing room fifteen minutes later, she stood balancing the tray and stared. In all her years in the Taylor household she'd never seen anything like it. Papers and ribbons and boxes were everywhere. And Mr. Taylor was wrestling with a puppy in the middle of it all. *Mr. Taylor!* Miss Alison and Miss Wyatt were giggling. No, she'd never seen anything like it, not in this house.

13

$\mathcal{K}$asey intended to keep herself very busy when she left Palm Springs. First she was going home. She had made her decision; New Year's Eve would mark her last full day with Jordan. All she had left to do was tell Jordan. After looking at it from every angle—from hers, from his, from Alison's—Kasey had decided to wait until the first of the year. Her flight was booked. It would hurt less if the hours between weren't heavy with the knowledge that they were the last ones. She'd cram everything she could into that final twenty-four hours.

"I'd have had you in the third game of the second set if I hadn't double-faulted." She swung her racket at the air as she and Jordan walked from the tennis court. "And if you hadn't served to my backhand in the fourth game of the second set, I would have won that one, too. You really are a vicious player, coming into the net like that."

He took her racket, a bit leery of the enthusiasm she showed in swinging it. "Look, there's Alison by the pool. She appears to be dutifully doing her homework."

Alison glanced up as they approached, waved, then settled back with a sigh. "Uncle Jordan, I don't know what to do about this assignment."

"No?" He set the rackets down on the umbrellaed table. "What is it?"

"I have to list five items typical of the nineteen-eighties.

Something I'd put into a time capsule to show future societies what our culture was like."

"Alison." He grinned and ran a finger down her nose. "Why ask a writer when you have an anthropologist?"

"Oh, I forgot." She looked up at Kasey. "What would you put in a time capsule?"

"Let's see." Kasey narrowed her eyes against the sun a moment. "A stalk of wheat, a container of petroleum, an MOS chip, a cassette of punk rock music and a pair of Gucci loafers."

Jordan laughed. "And that's your encapsulization of the eighties?"

Alison frowned as she scribbled. "What's an MOS chip?"

"It's a—"

"Oh, no." Jordan stopped Kasey's explanation cold. "Don't get her started, Alison."

"Well," Alison said, frowning at the list doubtfully, "I suppose I'd better think about this some more." She gave Kasey a look that told her she'd been little help, then left to work out her problem indoors.

"I'm not sure that Alison or her teacher is ready for your opinion on our society," Jordan commented.

"It was my educated analysis of our culture as it stands today, from technology to fashion. You know, Jordan, you really look hot after that tennis match. You should cool off."

She gave him a firm shove and sent him backwards into the pool. He surfaced, pushing his hair from his eyes. "Impulse," she claimed and grabbed her middle as she laughed. "I've never had a firm control over impulses." Saying nothing, he narrowed his eyes and swam to the edge. "Sorry, Jordan, but you really did look hot. I'm sure the water's wonderful. You're not mad, are you? I'll help you out."

She'd no more than offered her hand when she realized her mistake. He took it firmly, then grinned at her as he gave it a quick tug and sent her headlong into the water. She came up sputtering.

"I had that coming, I suppose."

"So you did. How's the water?"

"Terrific." She treaded water with one hand and pulled off a sneaker with the other. "I've always thought"—she tossed the sneaker over his head and out of the pool—"that when you find yourself in an inevitable situation, you should make the most of it." She lofted her other shoe, then, doing a surface dive, streaked along the bottom.

She jerked when Jordan's hands took her waist. He turned her, and she found herself tangled with him in an underwater kiss. Her heartbeat jumped from normal to frantic, and she clung to him. When she surfaced, her pulse was still soaring.

"I was making the most of an inevitable situation," Jordan murmured and caught the lobe of her ear in his teeth.

"You scared me." She took a deep breath. "I should never have seen that shark movie."

"We don't stock sharks in the winter." He ran a hand through her hair. "It's nearly copper when it's wet and the sun hits it. The first day you were here I stood at my window and watched you swim. I couldn't get you out of my mind even then."

She leaned her head on his shoulder. It was so difficult to be strong when he was gentle. She wanted to tell him again that she loved him, that it was breaking her heart to have to leave him. She didn't know, even then, what she would do if he asked her to stay. Or perhaps she did, and that was why she had made her plans without telling him. They couldn't go on as they were, and she saw no future for them. If he could love her. . . . But Kasey shook her head and drew away from him.

"I'll race you," she challenged. "I'm a much better swimmer than tennis player."

He smiled. "All right, I'll give you a head start."

Kasey lifted her brows. "That is an assumption of male superiority." She pushed her hair from her eyes. "I'll take it."

She was off like a rocket in a flurry of water. Even with her advantage, Jordan reached the far edge two strokes ahead of her. Kasey wrinkled her nose at him. "Of course," she began and stood in the shallow water, "if I'd grown up in a pool . . ."

She noted that he was paying no attention to her words. Following his eyes, she glanced down.

The T-shirt she had worn modestly enough on the tennis court now clung to her breasts. Rather than a cover, it was an erotic invitation. Her brief shorts were molded wetly to her hips and upper thighs. Naked, she would have been less of a temptation. Water ran slowly down the sleekness of her hair.

"I think this sort of swimming apparel belongs in deeper water," Kasey decided and pushed away from the edge.

She was in his arms before she was halfway across the pool. His mouth took hers, hungry, quickly desperate. They lowered below the surface again, tied to each other. Kasey hung on as a mixture of fear and passion ran through her. There were sensations of weightlessness, of claustrophobia, of helplessness. She might have fought against them, but the will had slipped from her, and she held him tighter. He brought them up, and air rushed into her lungs.

"You're trembling," he noticed abruptly. "Did I frighten you?"

"I don't know." She held on and let him keep them above surface. "Oh, Jordan, I want you," she breathed. The need was unexpectedly urgent and powerful.

His mouth found hers again. His excitement was doubled by the desire he felt pouring out of her. "How long can you hold your breath?" he murmured.

"Not long enough." She gave a shaky laugh and searched for his lips again. "Not nearly long enough. Will we drown?"

"Probably." His hand ran down her side, to her hip, to her thigh and back to her waist. "Do you care?"

"Not at the moment. Just kiss me again. Just kiss me and don't say anything."

She couldn't bear it. By that time the next day she would be on a plane. She wouldn't be able to reach out and touch him, to feel his hands on her. She would have the taste of him only in memory. These three months out of her life would be swallowed up by whatever was to come. How could she leave? How could she stay? Already the price she was going to have to pay seemed overwhelmingly high. Then she'd take something else for the bargain, she thought. One last night. One full, last night.

"Jordan, let's not go to that party tonight." She drew away from him, wanting to see his face. "I need to be alone with you, the way we were in New York. Can't we go someplace, just for tonight? Tomorrow's a whole new year. I want to spend the last night of this one with you. Just you."

"A suite at the Hyatt?" he murmured. "Champagne and caviar? I seem to recall you're rather fond of caviar."

"Yes." Her grip around his neck was quick and desperate as she brought her cheek to his. "Or pizza and beer at the Last Chance Motel. It doesn't matter. I love you." She couldn't stop herself from saying it. "I love you so much." Her mouth fastened on his before he could speak.

"Jordan!"

Beatrice's voice broke through the quiet. Jordan drew his mouth from Kasey's without hurry.

"Mother." He glanced up, keeping an arm around Kasey. "Back so soon?"

"What are you doing?"

"Why, I'm swimming," he told her easily. "And kissing Kasey. Was there something you wanted?"

"You're aware that we have servants who could wander out here at any time?"

"Yes. Was there something else?"

Beatrice's eyes flared, but she kept her dignity. Kasey was forced to admire her for it. "Harry Rhodes phoned. He needs to see you in an hour on business. He says it's quite important."

"All right. Thank you."

"You've made her angry, Jordan," Kasey commented when Beatrice left them.

"I'll probably make her a good deal angrier," he mused. It was time for some changes, he thought. Some definite changes. The house was his inheritance, but it might be wise to turn it over to her and take Alison elsewhere. And Kasey . . . Kasey was something else. Well, they had the whole night to talk about it, he decided and pulled her close again. "If you're ready when I get back from talking to Harry, we can start early."

"Talk fast," Kasey told him.

Kasey had just dried her hair when the knock came at her bedroom door. "Come in." She opened her closet. The green dress again tonight? she wondered and pulled it out. "Hello, Millicent."

The maid hovered in the doorway. "Miss . . ." Millicent folded her hands in front of her and looked uncomfortable. "Mrs. Taylor would like to see you—in her sitting room."

"Now?" Kasey fingered the material of the dress she held.

"Yes, please."

I might as well get it over with, she thought and hung the dress back in the closet. It was going to be unpleasant. If she hadn't known it already, the maid's face told everything.

"All right, I'll go right now."

Millicent cleared her throat. "I'm to take you."

Kasey sighed. She could hardly blame the maid. "Lead on," she invited, and followed her.

Millicent knocked on Beatrice's door, turned the knob, then hurried away. Kasey took one last deep breath and entered.

"Mrs. Taylor?"

"Come in, Miss Wyatt." Beatrice never turned from her ivory toned desk. "And shut the door."

Kasey obeyed and found herself itching for a cigarette. The room was oppressive and, she thought, as difficult to live with as the woman. "What can I do for you, Mrs. Taylor?"

"Sit down, Miss Wyatt." She waved her hand toward an Edwardian chair. "It's time we had a chat."

Kasey seated herself and awaited the inevitable.

"You've stretched your time here as far as possible." Beatrice turned to her now and folded her hands on the desk.

"Are you concerned with Jordan's research, Mrs. Taylor?" *You can't hurt me today*, she told herself. *It's my last one.* "Why don't you tell me just what's on your mind, Mrs. Taylor, and spare us both," she said aloud.

"I've checked your credentials." Beatrice tapped a gold pen against the desk. It was her only outward sign of emotion. "You seem to be considered an expert in your field."

"You checked up on me." Kasey could feel the anger rising and tried to stem it.

"In doing so, I learned you're Samuel Wyatt's granddaughter. I'm slightly acquainted with his daughter, your aunt. There was quite a scandal years back concerning you. A very unfortunate affair." She tapped the pen again. "A pity you didn't stay with your aunt rather than being raised by your grandfather."

"Please." Kasey's voice had lowered. "Don't make me angry."

Beatrice noted she had cracked Kasey's calm. That had been her first objective. "You weren't in your paternal grandfather's will."

"You have done your share of checking."

"I'm a very thorough woman, Miss Wyatt."

"But not one to quickly come to the point."

"The point, then," Beatrice agreed. "Apparently you're financially solvent but hardly . . ."

"Loaded?" Kasey suggested.

"In your vernacular," Beatrice conceded. "Your stay here has been a very lucrative arrangement for you. It's quite understandable that you would pursue the possibilities of future rewards by ingratiating yourself with Jordan and with Alison."

"Future rewards?" Kasey felt the burning start in the pit of her stomach.

"I didn't think I'd need to be graphic." Beatrice set down the pen and folded her hands again. "Jordan is a very wealthy man. Alison will come into a very healthy inheritance at maturity."

"I see." Kasey struggled to keep her hands still. "You're implying that I hope to benefit financially by developing a relationship with Jordan and Alison." She gave Beatrice a long, level look. "You're a hard lady, Mrs. Taylor. Doesn't it occur to you that I'd care about them regardless of the size of their bankbooks?"

"No." Beatrice let the word hang a moment. "I've dealt with your type before. Alison's mother was one, but my son wouldn't listen. He chose to marry her over my objections and move halfway across the country. Of course," she said as she sat back and eyed Kasey, "the problem is different in this case. Jordan has no intention of marrying you. He's satisfied with an affair. Again, in your vernacular, you overplayed your hand."

Kasey wanted to throw something. She wanted to rip some holes in the perfection of white that surrounded her. She sat rigid with control. "I'm aware of the boundaries of my relationship with Jordan, Mrs. Taylor. I always have been. You don't have anything to worry about."

"I'm not going to tolerate you under my roof any longer. Your influence on Alison will take months to repair."

"A lifetime, I hope." Kasey rose. She had to get out of that room. "You're never going to fit her into that mold again. She's outgrown it."

"Jordan has custody of Alison."

It was the tone, not the words, that halted Kasey. She felt a quick thrill of fear. "Yes."

Beatrice turned a bit in her chair so she might face Kasey directly. "If you don't leave today, this afternoon, I'll be forced, for Alison's sake, to sue him for custody of her."

"That's absurd." The fear came back, doubled in force. She felt the cold hit her skin. "No court would give you custody over Jordan."

"Perhaps, perhaps not." Beatrice moved her shoulders elegantly. "But you know how distressing a court battle can be, particularly when there's a child involved. Suing on the grounds of immoral conduct would make it particularly unpleasant."

"He's your son." The words came out as barely a whisper. "You couldn't do that to him. To Alison. Jordan's done nothing to hurt her; he never would."

"Alison requires protection." She gave Kasey a cool glance. "So does Jordan."

"Protection? You mean manipulation, don't you?" She crossed back to Beatrice. She had to be dreaming. But not even her nightmare hurt this acutely. "You wouldn't do this to them. You couldn't. She's just a child. She loves him." She wouldn't cry in front of this woman. "You don't have anything to gain from this. You don't love Alison the way Jordan does. You don't need her. If you could understand what it's like to be fought over this way, you wouldn't do it."

Beatrice took a small breath. "The choice is up to you."

It was incredible, impossible, but Kasey saw she meant every word she said. "I was going tomorrow," she said quietly. "I'm not worth it, Mrs. Taylor."

"Today, before Jordan returns. You're to say nothing of this to him."

"Today," Kasey agreed. There were tears in her voice; she couldn't prevent them. She struggled to keep them from her eyes. "Today, because I'm capable of something you're not. Of loving them both enough to give them what they need. Each other."

Beatrice turned her back again. "Millicent will have your bags packed by now, and Charles will drive you wherever you'd like to go." She opened her checkbook. "I'm willing to compensate you for your discretion and for your inconvenience, Miss Wyatt—"

Kasey's hand slammed down on the checkbook and cut her off. Beatrice looked up in surprise.

"Don't press your luck," Kasey whispered. "I gave you my word. It's free." She lifted her hand slowly and straightened. "There'll come a time when you'll have to deal with what you did today. You've lost more than I ever had, Mrs. Taylor."

She made it out the door, then nearly doubled over with the pain. She needed time, a few moments, to pull herself back together. She still had to see Alison. She wouldn't leave without saying good-bye to her. *Let me find the right words.* Kasey moved down the hall like a sleepwalker. *Don't let me cry in front of Alison.*

The sharp flash of pain had left her numb. She reached for the knob of Alison's door with nerveless fingers.

"Kasey!" Alison glanced up. The puppy was curled on the bedspread while Alison sat with him plucking at her guitar. "I learned a new song. Shall I play it for you?"

"Alison." Kasey came to sit beside her.

"What's wrong?" The child's forehead creased as she studied Kasey. "You look funny."

"Alison. You remember I told you that someday I'd have to go." She saw the look in the child's eyes and touched her cheek. "It's someday, Alison."

"No." She set the guitar aside and grabbed Kasey's hand. "You don't have to. You could stay."

"I explained it to you before. Remember? About my job?"

"You don't want to stay?" The tears were starting. Kasey felt a moment of panic.

"Alison, it's not a matter of wanting. I can't."

"You could. You could if you wanted to."

"Alison, look at me." Kasey was on the edge and knew it. But there was no leaving her this way. "Sometimes people can't do exactly what they want. I love you, Alison, but I have to go."

"What will I do?" It was almost a wail as she threw her arms around Kasey's neck.

"You have Jordan. And I'll write you, I promise. Maybe in the summer you can visit. Like we talked about before."

"The summer's months and months away."

Kasey hugged her tight, then drew her back. "Sometimes time goes quickly." She slipped the gold band from her finger and pressed it into Alison's hand. "This is for you. Whenever you think I don't love you anymore, you can look at it and remember I do." Rising, she walked to the doorway. The pain was festering, and her time was running out.

"Alison . . ." She turned back with her hand on the knob. "Tell Jordan I . . ." She shook her head and opened the door. "Just take care of him for me."

There was only one small light on in her hotel room, but even that hurt her eyes. Kasey couldn't summon the energy to walk over and switch it off. The weeping had drained her, left her sick and empty. She could hear the sounds of celebration from other rooms.

It was nearly midnight.

I should be with him now, Kasey thought. I should have had this one last night. What did he think when he came back and found me gone? Gone without a word. He'll never understand. He can't ever understand, she reminded herself. Will he be hurt or just angry? She shook her head. It was no use speculating. It was over.

She heard the rattle of a key and turned. When Jordan walked in, she said nothing. Her thoughts were drowned in pain and shock.

"You should use a chain when you want to shut someone out, Kasey." He tossed the key onto a table. "Keys are easy enough to come by. Twenty dollars and a good story buys one. You know all about good stories."

She sat exactly where she was. Beatrice's threat cut off her impulse to run into his arms. "How did you find me?"

"Charles." He turned and fastened on the chain. "Though I had to visit a few bars to find him. He had the night off."

"You seem to have put the time to good use." He'd been drinking, she noted, if not heavily, enough to show. She had to keep calm. Her hands were beginning to shake, and she curled her fingers around the edge of the dresser behind her.

Jordan glanced around the small hotel room. "You didn't choose the Hyatt, I see."

"No." There were going to be angry words, hard words. Kasey rose and reached for a cigarette. "Isn't that ridiculous? Hotels are always leaving matches everywhere, and I can't find one." She caught her breath when he gripped her arms and spun her around.

"Why did you leave?"

"I had to leave sometime, Jordan." Her voice tightened with pain as his fingers dug into her skin. "We both know the research was finished."

"Research?" If he didn't keep his fingers tight, he was afraid he'd strike her. She'd hurt him more than he had known he could be hurt. She had opened him up for the pain. He gave her a savage shake. "Is that all there is between us?"

She was beginning to tremble all over, but he didn't seem to notice. She had never seen him like this—brutal, furious. She wished he would hit her if that would bring a quick end to it.

"Damn you." He shook her again, nearly lifting her off her feet. "Couldn't you at least have faced me with it? Did you have to leave behind my back, without a word?"

Kasey gripped the dresser edge again. The sickness was rising back to her throat. "It's better this way, Jordan. I—"

"*Better?*" The word exploded from him. Kasey jumped. "For whom? If you didn't have the decency to think of me, what about Alison?"

That was almost too much to bear. Kasey closed her eyes a moment. "I thought of Alison, Jordan. You must believe I thought of Alison."

"How can I believe anything you say? She was devastated. Look at me." He took her hair and pulled her head back. "I spent an hour holding her while she cried trying to make her understand what I couldn't."

"I did what I had to do." Her head was beginning to spin. She had to make him leave, and quickly. "Jordan, you've had too much to drink." Her voice was amazingly calm now. "And you're hurting me. I want you to go."

"You said you loved me."

Kasey swallowed and straightened. "I changed my mind." She watched the color drain from his face.

"Changed your mind?" The words came slowly, with no understanding.

"That's right. Now go and leave me alone. I've a plane to catch in the morning."

"Bitch." He whispered the word as he dragged her against him. "I'll go when I'm finished. We still have a date."

"No." She struggled against him in quick panic. "No, Jordan."

"We'll finish what you started," he told her. "Here. Now."

And his mouth was on hers, cutting off her protest. Kasey pushed against him, wild with fear. Would even this be taken from her—the memories of the joy of loving him, being loved by him. He was dragging her toward the bed, and she fought, but he was strong and senseless with rage. *What are we doing to each other?* Her mind dimmed as he ripped the shirt from her shoulders. His hands were everywhere, pulling, tearing her clothes as she struggled against him.

The memory of Beatrice's calm, cool face floated behind her eyes. *I won't let you do this to us.*

Kasey stopped struggling. Under Jordan's mouth, hers softened and surrendered. *I can give you this,* she told him silently and felt her panic subside. *One last night.* She hasn't taken it from us, after all. She stopped thinking and let herself love.

14

$\mathscr{K}$asey awoke to full, blinding light. She moaned in automatic protest and rolled over. Her hand touched the emptiness beside her. She opened her eyes. He was gone. She struggled to sit up, scanning the room quickly for some sign of Jordan. When she laid her hand on the pillow beside hers, she found it cool.

When had he gone? She remembered only that they had loved each other again and again in the night, in desperation and in silence. She thought he had slept, was certain they had had a few hours of total peace together. She needed to know they had.

No one could take those last hours from her. If there hadn't been tenderness, there had been need. He won't hurt anymore. Her last hope was that the night would have purged the pain from him, if not his anger. She doubted Jordan would ever forgive her for her method of ending it. Kasey rose from the bed. She still had a plane to catch.

When she saw the note on the dresser, she stared at it. It might be better not to read it, to pretend she hadn't seen it. What could he say to her now that wouldn't bring the pain flooding back? But she reached for it before she could stop herself. She opened it and read:

Kasey,
   An apology for last night would mean little, but I have nothing else to offer. Anger is no excuse for what

happened. I can only tell you I regret it more than anything I've ever done.

I'm leaving you a check for your services of the last month. I hope you realize what you've given me, because I don't have the words to tell you.

Jordan

Kasey read the letter through once, then again. She'd been right to think it would bring pain. She crumpled it in her hand, then dropped it on the floor. *Regret it*, she thought and slowly picked up the check that had been laid beneath the note. She was cold now. She had little emotion left to spend. Briskly she scanned the amount and gave a quick laugh.

"Generous, Jordan. You're a generous man." She tore the check methodically into tiny pieces and let them drift to the floor. "That ought to drive your accountant crazy." She wasn't going to cry again. There weren't any tears left. With a shuddering sigh, Kasey reached for a cigarette.

"Montana," she decided all at once. "Montana will have six feet of snow and be cold as hell." Now wasn't the time to go home, she thought. It would be too easy to fall apart at home. Dashing to the phone, Kasey prepared to change her plans.

Dr. Edward Brennan switched off the ignition on his old Pontiac. The sun was beginning to set, and he'd put in a full day. His back let him know it. *Getting old*, he mused as he sat. There'd been a day when he could have delivered three babies, plucked out a pair of tonsils, set a broken tibia and inoculated three families against flu before lunch without slackening speed. But he was seventy and thinking it was time to slow down.

Maybe it was time to take on an associate, someone young with fresh ideas. Dr. Brennan liked fresh ideas. He smiled a moment and watched the sunset. Too bad Kasey hadn't taken to medicine. She'd have made a hell of a doctor. What a bedside manner she would have had.

There were orange streaks shooting through the trees on his mountain. He was very proprietary about his little section of land. His mountain, his sunset. He felt that way when he sat alone. It was a good feeling and kept him going.

Opening the car door, he lifted out the bundle of homemade bread and preserves that Mrs. Oates had pressed on him when he had treated her boy for chicken pox. He would enjoy his fee with a cup of coffee. After, he thought as he stretched his tired back, he might just have a glass of the illegal whiskey Mr. Oates had slipped him before he had left. Oates had the best still on the east side of the mountain.

The door to his house was never locked, and he pushed it open, already tasting the bread.

"Hello, Pop."

Dr. Brennan jolted, then stared at the woman seated behind his kitchen table. *"Kasey!"* He was stunned to find her and surprised that she hadn't jumped up to rush to him for a fierce hug and noisy kiss. It was her traditional way of greeting him, whether they had been parted for a day or a year. "I thought you were still in Tennessee."

"Nope, I'm right here." She smiled at him, then glanced at the bundle he carried. "Smells like fresh bread. Part of your fee?"

"Mrs. Oates," he answered, crossing the room to set the bundle on the table.

"Ah." Kasey grinned up at him. "Then you'll have something a little more lively from Mr. Oates, I imagine. How's your stomach lining?"

"Sturdy enough for a glass or two."

She laid a hand on his. "How are you, Pop?"

"Fine, Kasey." He was studying her face carefully with a mixture of affection and professionalism. Something was not quite right. He squeezed her hand in return. She'd tell him when she was ready, in her own way. He'd known her too long to expect anything else. "What about you? What have you been up to? I haven't had one of your six-page letters in nearly a month."

"Not too much." She gave a half shrug. "I spent a couple of weeks in Montana. I got a terrific coat there; it would keep you warm in the Aleutians. I joined the Phiefer team for a while in Utah. Molly Phiefer's just as tough as ever. She celebrated her sixty-eighth birthday in camp. I did a two-part lecture in St. Paul and fished for trout in Tennessee. And I quit smoking." Her eyes darkened. She drew in her breath. "Pop . . . I'm pregnant."

"Pregnant?" His eyes shot open. "What do you mean, pregnant?"

"Pop." Kasey reached for his hand. "You're a doctor. You know what pregnant means."

"Kasey." Dr. Brennan discovered he had to sit down. "How did it happen?"

"The traditional way," she said, attempting a smile. "Even modern methods aren't always reliable," she added, anticipating the inevitable question.

He'd let that pass for now. "How far along are you?"

"What's today?"

He was used to her casual indifference to the passing of time. "May seventeenth."

"Four months and seventeen days."

"Very specific," he noted with a nod of his head.

"I'm sure." She laced and unlaced her hands.

Observing the nervous move, he switched to professionalism. "Have you seen a doctor? Are you having any discomfort, any side effects?"

"Yes, I've seen a doctor." She smiled again, soothed by the objective questions. "No, I'm not having any discomfort, and after an unfortunate month of morning sickness, I haven't any side effects. We're disgustingly healthy."

"And the father?"

She laced her hands again. "I'm sure he's very healthy, too."

"Kasey." He cupped his hand over her fingers to stop their movement. "What are his plans about the baby? Obviously, you've decided to complete the pregnancy. You and the baby's father must have come to terms of some kind."

"No, we haven't come to terms of any kind." She looked at him directly, and some of the vulnerability seeped through. "I haven't told him."

"Haven't told him?" He was more shocked by this than anything else. It simply wasn't like her. "When do you plan to?"

"I plan not to." She reached for a cigarette and began to tear it into small pieces.

"Kasey, he has a right to know. It's his baby."

"No." Her eyes shot up again. "It's my baby. The baby has rights, I have rights. Jordan can take care of himself."

"That's not like you, Kasey," he said quietly.

"Please." She shook her head and crushed the remains of the cigarette in her hand. "Don't. I didn't make this decision overnight. I've thought about it for months. I know it's the right thing to do. My baby isn't going to be pulled apart because his father and I made mistakes. I know what would happen if I told Jordan."

Her voice was beginning to shake, and she took a moment to steady it. "He'd offer to marry me. He's an honorable man. I'd refuse because I couldn't bear . . ." Her voice broke again, and she shook her head impatiently. "I couldn't bear to have him ask me out of obligation. Then he'd want to set me up some kind of financial support. I don't need it. My baby doesn't need it. There'd have to be structured visitation rights with the baby bouncing from coast to coast, never knowing where he belonged. It's not fair. I won't have it. The baby belongs to me."

He took her hands again and gave her a long look. "Do you love the father?"

He watched her crumple before his eyes. "Oh, God, yes." Kasey laid her head on the table and wept.

Her grandfather let her cry it out. He hadn't seen this sort of grief from her since she had been a child. He kept her hands in his and waited. What sort of man was this Jordan, whose baby she carried? If she loved him, why was she weeping here alone instead of sharing the joy of impending parenthood with him?

He tried to remember the patches of information from her letters. He knew who Jordan was—the writer she had worked with during late fall and early winter of the last year. Dr. Brennan had admired his work. Kasey's letters had been enthusiastic and confusing. But he was used to both from her.

Why hadn't he read between the lines? And now, for months, she had been dealing with the most important decision in her life alone. He hated to see her this way—lost, weeping. Once he had had to send her away from him. She had been lost and weeping then, too. He had thought his own decision had been right for her, and when the dust had settled, it had been. But the time in between had had its effect on her. He was intuitive enough to know that part of her present decision stemmed from her own experiences. All he could offer her was time and support and his love. He hoped it would be enough.

Her weeping had stopped. Kasey kept her head down on the table while she rested from it. She hadn't given into tears for months. Slowly she straightened and began to speak again.

"I loved him—I do love him. That's one of the reasons I'm handling it this way." She sighed. She had needed to talk to someone since she had walked out of Beatrice's sitting room four months before. "Let me explain things to you, and maybe you'll understand."

Her voice was quiet now, without emotion, and she detailed the circumstances in the Taylor household. When she spoke of Alison, he saw the parallel immediately and kept his silence. Only when she told him of her final encounter with Beatrice did he explode.

"Are you telling me she threatened you?" He had sprung up, forgetting the strain in his back. He was ready to fight.

"Not me." Kasey reached for his hand and drew herself to her feet. "Jordan, Alison. There was nothing she could do to me, nothing that would have mattered."

"It was blackmail, Kasey. Simple, ugly blackmail." His voice was rough with temper. "You should have gone straight to Jordan and told him."

"Do you know what he would have done?" Kasey took his arm. "He would have stormed in there, just as you'd like to do right now. It would have been a horrible scene with Alison right in the middle of it. Do you think I could take a chance on there being a court battle? She's just a little girl. I know how she'd feel seeing her name and picture splashed in the papers, listening to the whispering." Her eyes were eloquent, and her tears had dried. "Put yourself in my place, Pop. You were very close to it once. If you had to change what you did all those years ago, would you?"

He sighed and drew her into his arms. "Kasey, I never thought you'd have to go through something like this again."

She had needed to come home, to feel his big, strong arms and gentle hands. She had needed a rock and had never known a sturdier one. "I love you, Pop."

"I love you, Kasey." He held her for a moment and said nothing. It struck him suddenly that she was no longer willow slim. He could feel the roundness as she pressed against him. Unprofessionally, he was shocked by the change. She wasn't his baby anymore but a woman carrying one of her own. "It just occurs to me," he said softly. "I'm going to be a great-grandfather."

"You've always been a great grandfather," Kasey murmured. "The best."

"You'll stay until the baby comes."

Kasey sighed and relaxed against him. "I'll stay."

He drew her away. "Are you taking vitamins?"

"Yes, doctor." She grinned and kissed his cheek.

"And drinking your milk?"

She kissed his other cheek. "What do you think of Bryan?" she asked him. "It could work whether the baby's a boy or a girl. I think Bryan Wyatt has a nice sound. Dignified but not stuffy."

He lifted his brows. "I can see my work's cut out for me."

"Or there's Paul," she went on as he walked to the refrigerator. "Of course, I'd have to have a boy, then." Kasey watched as he poured a tall glass of milk. "Are we going to have some of Mrs. Oates's goodies now?" She opened the bundle. "Are these damson preserves?" she asked as she held up a Mason jar. "I love damson preserves."

"Good." Dr. Brennan handed her the glass of milk and smiled. "You can have some with your milk before I examine you."

15

It was July before Kasey knew it. There were wildflowers in the woods and geraniums in the kitchen window box. At night the crickets sang incessantly. She could lie in bed late and listen to them while the baby moved restlessly inside her. He's in a hurry, she thought. Or they are. Her grandfather was all but certain there were two. She had refused his suggestion that they go down to the hospital and make certain. She wanted to be surprised.

It had been a long time since she had slept deeply. The baby wouldn't permit it. *They* wouldn't permit it. Kasey didn't need any sophisticated equipment to tell her there were two. No one baby could be so active. When one slept, the other was wide awake and kicking. And she was huge.

Kasey rested a hand on either side of her stomach. I won't go full term, she mused. Twins traditionally arrive early. Closing her eyes, she began to drift again. She liked the movements inside her, liked knowing life was growing, impatient to arrive. She could almost see how they would look. A boy and a girl, she thought, with warm, brown hair and dark blue eyes. When she looked at the eyes, she would think of Jordan.

She shifted again as she felt the distinct shove of an elbow. What was he doing now? she wondered. What time was it in California? Early enough that he might still be working? Would he have finished the book? Kasey wanted badly to find it in a bookstore, to bring it home and closet herself with it. It would bring him back, along with all the hours they had spent together in his study. She could save it for her children. They would never know it was their father who had written it, but they would learn to admire and respect him through his words. She wanted that for them and for Jordan.

And Alison. Kasey rolled from her side to her back. She had written the girl, as she had promised. Her own zig-zagging course across the country had made it impossible for Alison to answer. I should hear from her soon now, Kasey mused. I've been settled for nearly two months. I wrote nearly three weeks ago.

Kasey pulled herself from bed and walked to the window. It was hot and sultry, making sleep that much more difficult. It might be best if she did forget me. I can hardly ask her to visit me now. She stroked her hand over her stomach. There'd be no way to explain to her and no way to be certain Jordan wouldn't find out. He'll take care of her and keep her safe. And I'll do the same for our babies.

The movement inside her stopped. Kasey went back to bed and slept.

Dr. Brennan watched Kasey as she knelt on the ground between rows of vegetables and weeded. She was blooming. He had no worries about her physically. She was the picture of health, and strong. She had taken up her life again with characteristic enthusiasm. He was proud of her.

He had some doubts about the wisdom of her decision, but she was dead certain. He had plans to speak with her again about Jordan, but he would give her until she had delivered and was on her feet again. The baby was his main concern. And the baby's mother.

"I don't know why I planted lima beans," she muttered and ripped at a stubborn weed. "I hate lima beans, but I just love the way they all sit in a fat little pod. I suppose I could have them bronzed." She sat back on her heels and dusted her hands. "Some of the tomatoes are ripe. You could have them with supper tonight with the corn Lloyd Cramer gave you for his appendix." She shielded her eyes from the sun and smiled up at him.

"I got the best of the deal. His appendix was in bad shape."

"You're so mercenary." She held up a hand so he could help her to her feet, then she kissed him with her usual exuberance. "Do you think I should water the garden? It hasn't rained all week."

He glanced up at the sky. "Watering the garden's a sure way to bring it on. We could use it. The heat's keeping you up at night."

"That, among other things." She patted her stomach. "And, no, I'm not tired." She laughed, anticipating his question. "I've got enough energy for all of us."

"Did you have your milk today?"

"My carrots aren't doing well," Kasey responded. "I'm going to get the hose."

"I'll water it this evening when it cools off. Go have a glass now."

"I'll throw up," she threatened.

"That hasn't worked since you were twelve."

She narrowed her eyes, measuring him. She knew he was every bit as stubborn as she was. "I'm going to make scalloped potatoes for dinner. And vanilla custard. That's enough milk for anybody."

"You'll get fat."

"I *am* fat." She dashed into the house before he could comment.

She sat at the kitchen table and peeled. A small mountain of potatoes was growing in front of her. There was something soothing in the simple, mindless chore, and she skinned more than her grandfather and she could possibly eat in a single sitting. We'll have leftovers, she decided and glanced at the pile. All week. This is the last one, she promised herself and shook the potato in her hand. Or we'll have to invite the neighborhood. She didn't glance up as the door opened but continued wielding the peeler. "You might have to dig up a couple of starving patients," she said aloud. "I got carried away here. You know, they don't peel potatoes by hand in the army anymore, a terrible lack of tradition. They have these machines, and . . ."

She glanced up and froze.

Jordan watched the color drain slowly from her face. He

saw vivid shock in her eyes, and fear. The fear made his stomach twist. She dropped the peeler, and her hands shot under the table.

Oh, God, dear God, she thought desperately. What do I do? What do I say?

He said nothing, but his eyes were riveted on her face. Her hair was longer, he noted, almost to her shoulders now. *When had she grown beautiful?* She had been striking, alluring, unforgettable. But when had she grown beautiful? He couldn't take his eyes from her face. How long had he waited to see it again, to watch it light up for him? It wasn't lit now, it was terrified. That was his doing, but it wasn't too late. It couldn't be too late. All these months of desperation couldn't be for nothing.

Was her skin as soft as he remembered? Would she cringe if he touched her? He was afraid to test it and could only stare at her.

Kasey gripped her hands together tightly under the table. She had to do something, to say something. She waited a moment until she was certain her voice wouldn't give her away.

"Hello, Jordan." She smiled at him while her nails bit into her palms. "Passing through?"

He took a few steps toward her but kept the table between them. Without it he would have to touch her. "I've been looking for you for months." It came out as an accusation. He hadn't meant to greet her that way. He had sworn to himself he would be calm, but calmness had deserted him the moment she had looked up at him.

"Have you?" Kasey managed to keep her eyes level. "I'm sorry. I've been doing some traveling. Is it something about the book? I don't know of anything we didn't cover."

"Would you stop!" He was shouting at her. How could he be shouting at her now? he asked himself. But he couldn't stop. Everything that had kept him going since she had left had crumbled the moment he had set eyes on her again. "I've spent six months in hell. How can you sit there looking at me as though I were a neighbor dropping in for a visit?" He skirted the table before she could speak and dragged her to her feet. "Damn it, Kasey . . ." His voice trailed off as he

looked at her. "Oh, God." It was barely more than a whisper as his gaze swept down, then up to her face again. "You're pregnant."

"Yes, I am." His hold had loosened. She felt his fingers drop away one at a time. He stared at her as though he'd never seen her before.

"You . . ." He shook his head as if he were resurfacing. "You're carrying my child, and you haven't told me."

She took a step away from him. "My child, Jordan. I never said it was yours."

She was pulled back against him so quickly, she didn't have time to gasp. His eyes were no longer blank, but furious. "Look at me," he demanded between his teeth. "Look at me and say it's not mine." He saw the fear jump into her eyes again and released her. Why couldn't he stop himself from repeating the mistake that had caused him to lose her? Jordan turned away and searched for control. He hadn't been prepared for this. How could he have been prepared for this? A long, long moment passed before he could trust himself to speak again.

"In God's name, Kasey," he said quietly. "How could you keep this from me? No matter how you felt about me, I had a right to know."

"My baby has rights, Jordan." Her voice held the deadly calm of desperation. "I'm not concerned with yours."

He faced her again, ready to plead if necessary. He'd shelved his pride months before. "Don't shut me out, Kasey, please." He started to touch her, then, when she stiffened, he dropped his hand to his side. There were a hundred things he had planned to say when he finally found her, but now there was only one. "I love you."

"No!" She struck out at him in a furious slap. "Don't you say that to me! Don't you dare say that to me now." Her eyes were dry one minute and flooding the next. "I would have given anything to have heard that from you six months ago. Anything. What you gave me was a note and a check for services rendered, as though I were a—"

"No, Kasey. Please, you can't think . . ." He reached for her again, but she pushed him away.

"I haven't slept with many men. Surprised?" She drew both

hands over her cheeks to push away tears. "But you're the first who ever left payment."

"Kasey, no, it was nothing like that." Her words left him shaken. "Let me explain."

"I don't want explanations." She shook her head and walked away from him. "I want you to go. I asked you once before to leave me alone. Now I'm asking you again."

"I couldn't then, I can't now. Don't you understand?"

"I don't want to understand." She took deep breaths. "I don't need to." Her voice was calm again, but she didn't turn to him. "I'm sorry I hit you. I've never done anything like that before."

"Kasey, please." Gently he touched her shoulder. "Just sit down and listen to me. You loved me once. I can't leave this way." She didn't move. She didn't answer. Jordan felt the panic rising up and forced it down again. "Just hear me out, then I'll go if that's what you want."

"All right." She moved away from his touch and sat down. "I'll listen to you."

He didn't know where to begin or how. Where were his words? "When I woke up that last morning . . ." He hesitated. His mind was so crowded with all he wanted to say, and his emotions were hammering at him. She carried his child inside her. Right now she had her hands folded over her stomach as if she would protect what was partly his from him.

"When I woke up," he continued, "I hated myself. I remembered that I had come into your room. I remembered everything I had said to you, what I had done. You were still sleeping. I left the note because I thought you wouldn't want to see me again."

"Why did you think that?"

"Dear God, Kasey, I . . ." He had had to deal with it for half a year, and now he had to say it. "I raped you. I woke up and there were bruises on your arms that I had put there." Now it was he who turned away. He walked to a window, and his knuckles whitened on the sill. "I'll have to live with that for my entire life."

Kasey sat in silence for a moment. An honorable man, she thought and laid her hands on the arms of the chair. And an honorable man can't bear knowing he could contemplate doing something dishonorable. Perhaps if she hadn't hurt so badly herself, she could have read his pain in the note he had left her.

"Jordan." She waited until he turned to face her again. "What happened that night was a long way from rape. I could have stopped you or fought you all the way. You know I didn't."

"It wouldn't have made any difference if you had." He walked to her again. "I was drunk and crazy. I hurt you. You told me from the very beginning I would." He paused again but never took his eyes from her face. "I think you should know that I was going to ask you to marry me that night." He saw the shock fill her eyes before they closed.

"When I got back from seeing Harry and found you'd gone, I couldn't believe it. I got angry quickly; it was easier to deal with that way. You opened me up, forced me to feel again, and then when you meant everything to me, you walked away. I wanted to hurt you."

She still sat with her eyes closed, and he studied her face as he spoke. "For weeks, those first weeks after you walked into my life, I had told myself I couldn't be in love with you. It was too quick. I was just attracted, intrigued. If I hadn't been such a fool, I might not have lost you. You gave me everything freely, and I took it, but I was afraid to give too much back to you."

She opened up her eyes again and looked at him. "There's too much in the way even now, Jordan. Please don't say any more."

"You told me you'd listen. You're going to hear it all." He watched her hands slip back over the baby. Something ripped inside him, and he took a moment before continuing. "After that last night together, when you'd gone, I tried to forget. I told myself you'd lied to me. I told myself you'd been playing a game. Then I'd remember how you looked that first time you told me you loved me. I knew you had gone because I hadn't given you anything back and because when I'd had my last chance, I'd hurt you."

"Jordan, it's done," she began. "Don't—"

"I tried to live without you." He shook his head and crouched down in front of her chair so their eyes were nearly level. "There was no color. You'd taken all the color with you. I came after you."

"Came after me?" she repeated.

"Your first letter to Alison came from Montana. When I got there, you'd left three days before. Three days. It might as well have been years. You'd left no forwarding address. And because you'd rented a car, there was no way of tracing you. I started to hire detectives, but then I remembered." He stopped again and rose. "I thought how you might feel. So instead, I went back and prayed for you to write Alison again."

Jordan dragged a hand through his hair as he relived the frustration and panic. "Each time you wrote, I tried to catch you before you moved on. Once I missed you by five hours. I thought I'd go mad. I knew I couldn't keep leaving Alison that way, even for a day or two. And I began to think you'd keep moving, one step ahead of me, for the rest of my life. Then your last letter came.

"When you said you were going to be staying with your grandfather for a few months, Alison was so excited. Losing you has been hard on her."

Kasey shook her head and balled her hands into fists. "Don't."

"I'm sorry." He took one of her rigid hands into his. "As soon as she got the letter, she wanted to come out and see you. She said you told her she could."

"Yes, I had." Kasey removed her hand. She couldn't let him touch her, not now. She'd never be strong enough to send him away if he was touching her.

Jordan looked down at his empty hand a moment, then slipped it into his pocket. "I didn't want to leave her with my mother again, not even for a few days. I told her we'd both come."

"Alison's here?" Kasey felt the smile light her face. "Outside?"

"No." Jordan swallowed the envy. The smile was for Alison, but not for him. "I wanted to see you alone first. Had to see you alone. She's back at the hotel. There's a family there with a couple of kids who've taken to her. She was hoping you'd come with me when I went back to get her."

Kasey shook her head. "I can't do that. I'd love to see her if you'd bring her here."

Jordan felt a fresh flash of pain. He was losing and he was powerless to prevent it. "All right, if that's what you want. We're taking the rest of the summer to look for a new place."

"A new place?"

He had to talk about something, anything, to keep from pressuring her. To keep from begging her. "I decided some time ago, just before Christmas, actually, that Alison needed to get out of that house, away from my mother. I've already had the papers drawn up to turn the house over to her. We won't need anything so large. I told Alison we'd look together and try to be settled somewhere by the time she starts school again."

He was ready to explode. Jordan turned to her again, and the passion showed in his face. "Don't ask me to leave now that I've found you, Kasey. Don't turn away from me. You can't ask me to walk away from you, from my child."

"My child." Kasey rose now. She'd be stronger if she were standing.

"Our child," Jordan corrected quietly. "You can't change that. A child's entitled to know his father. If you can't think of me, think of the baby."

"I am thinking of the baby." She pressed her hands to her temples and pushed. Maybe it would ease the tension. "I didn't expect you to come here; I didn't expect you to love me. I knew what I had to do."

"But I did come." Jordan took her shoulders gently. "And I do love you."

"No." She stepped back, shaking her head. "Don't touch me."

She covered her eyes and didn't see the flash of emotion in Jordan's. "I knew what I had to do," she repeated. "I can't afford to think about you, about me. I have to think of my baby. I can't take chances with my baby."

"Chances?" Jordan began, but she was stumbling on.

"I won't have him shipped from coast to coast. He's going to know where he belongs. Nobody's going to pull at him. I won't have it. Not this time; this time it's my choice." She was sobbing now with her hands covering her face. He knew no way to bring comfort. "This is my baby, not a piece of property we can split down the middle. She might try to get at me through the baby. She might try to take him from me. I lost you, I lost Alison, but I can't lose this baby. It would kill me. Your mother's not going to get her hands on my baby!"

"What are you talking about?" He forgot himself and took her elbows, pulling her hands from her eyes. "What are you saying?"

Kasey didn't answer. She was breathing quickly. She didn't know what she had said.

Jordan's eyes narrowed to slits. "Did my mother have anything to do with your leaving?" Kasey started to shake her head, but his look stopped her. "You don't lie worth a damn, so don't try it. What did she say to you? What did she do?" When she didn't answer, he forced his voice into calmness. There was fear in her eyes again, but this time he knew it wasn't he who had put it there. "You're going to tell me exactly what went on between you."

"A very good idea." Dr. Brennan spoke as he came in the front door. Jordan glanced over but didn't release Kasey's arm. No one was going to stop him from learning the truth now. "No need to pick up the club, son," he told Jordan, amused. "I told her that's what she should do when she came home months ago."

"Pop, don't interfere."

"Don't interfere." He raised his brows at his granddaughter. "You always were snippy."

"Pop, please." Kasey pulled her arms away from Jordan. "You've got to stay out of this."

"The devil I do!" he boomed out at her. "This man has a right to know what went on behind his back. You just stopped playing solitaire, Kasey. I've dealt him in."

She shook her head, going to him. "Alison."

"He'll take care of Alison, Kasey. Any fool could see that. Are you going to tell him, or am I?"

"You tell me," Jordan addressed Dr. Brennan directly. "I want it straight."

"Sensible. Sit down and shut up, Kasey," her grandfather ordered.

"No, I won't—"

"Kathleen, *sit!*"

Her chin came up at the tone, but the training of a lifetime had her obeying.

"All right, Jordan," the doctor began. "This might not be easy to hear. Would you like to sit down?"

"No." Jordan bit off the word, then caught himself. "No, thank you."

"I will, I'm getting old." Dr. Brennan settled himself. "Your mother put Kasey in a position of choosing," he began. "I would conclude that she's an excellent judge of character, as she must have known what Kasey's choice would be. Her own happiness, or yours and Alison's."

"I don't understand what you're saying."

"The best way is straight up, then. Your mother threatened to sue for custody of Alison unless Kasey took her bags and left on the spot."

"Sue for . . ." Jordan pulled his hand through his hair again. "That's crazy. She doesn't want Alison, and in any case, there wouldn't be grounds for a suit."

"I said she was a good judge of character." Dr. Brennan glanced at his granddaughter. Frowning, Jordan followed his eyes. He felt the strength drain out of him.

"Oh, God." He rubbed his hands over his face in a gesture of fatigue. "I suppose she found out about Kasey's background. She should have come to me." He spoke quietly to the doctor again. "I would never have let my mother get away with a threat like that. She should have come to me."

"Yes." Dr. Brennan nodded in agreement. "But she wouldn't take the risk with two people she loved. Your mother threatened to sue on grounds of immoral conduct."

"Pop." The word was only a tired whisper.

"All of it, Kasey, all at once. And," he turned back to Jordan, "she offered to pay her. That was her only miscalculation."

There was a window above the kitchen sink which looked out over the mountains. Jordan walked to it and stared out. "I'm having a difficult time handling this." His voice was strained and raw. "I knew she was capable of a lot of things, but I wouldn't have believed this of her. I appreciate your telling me." Jordan thought he had felt all the rage he could feel, all the pain he could stand. But he'd been wrong. Now he wasn't sure which was uppermost. "I'll deal with my mother, Dr. Brennan, you can be sure of it."

"I am sure of it." After casting a last look at Kasey, her grandfather rose. "I have a garden to water." He left them, and the room dropped into silence.

Kasey took a deep breath. It was out now, all of it. There would be little more to say. "I'm going to fix some tea." Rising, she walked over to set a kettle on to boil.

"Kasey, there's nothing I can say or do that will ever make up for this."

"It wasn't your doing, Jordan, and it's not your place to make up for it." She reached above her head into a cupboard. "It's herbal tea. Pop's cut off my caffeine."

"Kasey, please, keep still a minute." She stopped and turned to face him. Jordan drew together all of his words. He had to say everything quickly and get out while he could still stand. "First, I promise you, my mother will never come anywhere near our—your baby." He felt the pain rolling around in his stomach as he relinquished his rights. "I won't make any demands. I'll give you financial support if you'll take it. I'll understand if you won't."

"Jordan—"

"No, don't say anything yet." He knew he had to get it out quickly. "The baby's yours, completely yours; I accept that. You have my word I won't ever make any claim. I know how much Alison means to you. I'll leave her with you for a few days if you like while I go back to deal with my mother."

"It doesn't matter, Jordan—"

"It matters to me!" He lifted a hand as if to stop himself from breaking free of control. "When I've found a place for us, and we're settled, I'll send your grandfather our address. All I'd like is to know when the baby comes and that you're all right."

His words were changing everything. What had made sense an hour before seemed absurd now. People who love should be together. "Jordan," she began, then made a slight sound and pressed a hand to her side.

"What is it?" Panicked, he grabbed her arms. "Are you in pain? Is it the baby? Oh, God, I should never have come. I should never have upset you this way. I'll call your grandfather."

"That's not necessary." Kasey smiled at him. "The baby's kicking, that's all. He's very active."

Jordan looked down. Slowly he brought up his hand to place his palm on the mound of her stomach. Life quivered impatiently beneath it. Simple wonder flooded through him. Part of himself was growing in there. Part of Kasey. Between them, they'd created a human being. He could almost feel the outline of a tiny foot as it pounded against his hand.

When he lifted his eyes to hers, Kasey saw the swimming emotion, the dazed awe. She smiled and laid her hand on top of his. "You should feel it when he really gets going."

The pain swept down on him immediately, stealing his color. That would be his first and last contact with his child. The last time he touched the woman he loved. Kasey saw the change before he turned to walk to the door.

Don't let him go, her heart shouted at her. Don't be a fool. *It's a risk,* her mind reminded her. For you, for all of you. *Take the risk,* her heart insisted. You're strong enough. You're all strong enough.

"Jordan." She called to him before he reached the door. "Don't go." When he turned, she was halfway across the room. "We need you." She threw her arms around his neck. "I need you."

He wanted to take what she offered but held himself back. "Kasey, you don't have to do this for me. I don't want . . ."

"Oh, shut up and kiss me. There's been too much talk. It's been so long." She found his mouth, then heard his quiet moan of relief.

"I love you." He rained kisses over her face. "You'll never go a day without hearing me say that again. I love you."

"Really kiss me," she murmured, trying to halt his roving mouth. "You won't break the babies."

He pulled her against him, losing himself in her taste. She was his—finally, completely his. "Babies?" he said suddenly and drew her away. *"Babies?"*

"Didn't I mention there were two?"

Jordan shook his head and gave a quick, astonished laugh. "No." He laughed again and crushed her against him. He could feel the lives inside of her shifting and stretching. "No, you didn't mention it. How did I live without you for more than half a year? It wasn't living." He answered his own question. "I've just started to live again." He gave her a feverish kiss as though he could fill six months of emptiness with one embrace. He drew her back again, and his eyes were intense. "Strings this time," he told her. "I want strings this time, Kasey."

"On both of us," she agreed and went into his arms.

EPILOGUE

The fire roaring in the hearth had the living room cozy with heat. Outside there was two feet of snow, and it was still falling. Kasey slipped a last-minute present under the Christmas tree, then stood back to admire it. Strings of popcorn draped and criss-crossed from top to bottom. She grinned, remembering the chaos of the kitchen the evening they had made them. Chaos remained one of her favorite things.

Bending, she toyed with a box with her name on the tag.

"Cheating?" Jordan asked from the doorway, and she quickly straightened.

"Certainly not." She waited until he had crossed the room and slipped his arms around her. "Just poking. Poking's not cheating. Poking's required at Christmas."

"Is that your educated analysis, Dr. Taylor?" He nuzzled into her neck, finding his favorite spot.

"Absolutely. How's the book coming?"

"Fine. I have a fascinating main character." He drew her away to look at her. She was glowing. Was it Christmas Eve that made her glow this way? "I love you, Kasey." He kissed her gently. "And I'm proud of you."

"What for?" She linked her hands behind his neck and smiled. "I like specific compliments."

"For earning your doctorate, raising a family, making a home."

"Of course, I did it all by myself." Smiling, she cupped his face in her hands. "Jordan, you're terribly sweet. I'm crazy about you." She drew him close until their mouths met.

It took only an instant for the kiss to heat. They were locked tight, enveloped in each other. Soft pleasure and hot passion merged.

"It's snowing," Jordan murmured.

"I noticed." Kasey sighed softly as his lips brushed her neck.

"We've got plenty of wood."

"You chop it beautifully. I'm always impressed." She drew his head back far enough so that her mouth could find his.

"There's wine in the cellar." Desire was pushing at him. The wanting never seemed to lessen. He slipped his hand under her shirt to roam her back. "Do you remember the fantasy we talked about on Christmas Eve two years ago?"

"Mmm." Kasey pressed closer. "Snowed in," she murmured. "With wood and wine and each other."

The cocker spaniel came barreling into the room just ahead of two scrambling toddlers.

Run for your life, Kasey thought, smiling as she rested her head on Jordan's shoulder.

"Bryan, Paul, you two come back here." Alison bounded into the room on their heels. "You know you're not supposed to tease Maxwell." She sighed and shook her head as the twins collapsed on the floor with the dog clutched between them.

Jordan watched as his children noisily adored the long-suffering dog. He slipped his arm more snugly around Kasey's shoulders. "They're gorgeous," he murmured. "It always astonishes me how perfectly gorgeous they are."

"And so well-mannered," Kasey observed as Bryan shoved Paul aside to ensure a better grip on the dog's neck. Alison dove in to referee.

He laughed and drew her to face him again. "About that fantasy . . ."

"I'll meet you at midnight," she whispered. "Right here."

"You bring the wine, I'll bring the wood."

"It's a deal." The children grew noisier, and Kasey knew a private conversation would soon be impossible. Besides, she wanted to get down and play, too. "One more thing," she added and gave him one of her guileless smiles.

He gave her a puzzled look, and she brought her mouth close to his. "We're going to have another baby," she told him. "Or two," she managed before his mouth crushed hers.

A Matter of Choice

PROLOGUE

James Sladerman frowned at the toe of his shoe. He'd been frowning since the summons from Commissioner Dodson had reached him in the squad room that morning. After blowing out a long stream of smoke, Slade crushed out the cigarette in the mosaic ashtray to his left. He barely shifted his body. Slade knew how to wait.

Only the night before he had waited for more than five hours in a dark, chilly car in a neighborhood where it paid to watch your back as well as your wallet. It had been a tedious, fruitless five hours, as the stakeout had produced nothing. But then, Slade knew from long experience that police work consisted of hours of endless legwork, impossible boredom, and paperwork, punctuated by moments of stark violence. Still he preferred the five-hour wait to the twenty minutes he had spent in the commissioner's carpeted, beige-walled outer office. It smelled of lemony polish and now, his own Virginia tobacco. The keys of a typewriter clattered with monotonous efficiency as the commissioner's secretary transcribed.

What the hell does he want? Slade wondered again. Throughout his career Slade had studiously avoided the politics of police work because of an inherent dislike of bureaucracy. In his climb from cadet to detective sergeant, there had been little opportunity for his path to cross Dodson's.

Slade had had brief personal contact with Dodson at his

father's funeral. Captain Thomas C. Sladerman had been buried with all the glory and honor that comes from serving on the force for twenty-eight years. And dying in the line of duty. Mulling over it, Slade recalled that the commissioner had been sympathetic to the widow and the young daughter. He'd said the right things to the son. Perhaps on some level he had been personally grieved. Early in their careers Dodson and Sladerman had been partners. They had still been young men when their paths had separated—one finding a niche in politics and administration, the other craving the action of the streets.

On only one other occasion had Slade had one-to-one contact with Dodson. Then Slade had been in the hospital, recovering from a gunshot wound. The visit of the commissioner of police to a mere detective had resulted in talk and speculation that had embarrassed Slade as much as annoyed him.

Now, he realized, it would be all over the station house that the old man had called him in. His frown became a scowl. For a moment he wondered if he had committed some breach in procedure, then became furious with himself for behaving like a kid hauled before the school principal.

The hell with it, he decided, forcing himself to relax. The chair was soft—too soft, and too short. To compensate, Slade curved his spine into the back and stretched out his long legs. His eyes half closed. When the interview was over, he had the stakeout to look forward to again. If it went down tonight, he'd have a few evenings free to spend at the typewriter. With any luck—and a solid month without interruptions—he could finish the novel. Blocking out his surroundings, he mentally reviewed the chapter he was working on.

"Sergeant Sladerman?"

Annoyed by the distraction, Slade lifted his eyes. Slowly his expression cleared. He realized he'd wasted his time staring at the floor when the commissioner's secretary provided a far more appealing view. His smile was at once appraising and charming.

"The commissioner will see you now." The secretary answered the smile, wishing he'd looked at her like that before, rather than sitting in sullen silence. He had a face any female would respond to—a bit narrow, angular, with dark coloring that came from Italian ancestors on his mother's side. The mouth had been hard in repose, but now, curved, it showed both promise and passion. Black hair and gray eyes were an irresistible combination, especially, she thought, when the hair was thick and a bit unruly and the eyes were smoky and mysterious. He was an interesting prospect, she thought as she watched Slade unfold his long, rangy frame from the chair.

As he followed her to the oak door he noted that the ring finger of her left hand was bare. Idly, he considered getting her phone number on the way out. The thought slipped to the back of his mind as she ushered him into the commissioner's office.

There was a Perillo lithograph on the right wall—a lone cowboy astride a paint pony. The left wall was crowded with framed photos, commendations, diplomas. If Slade found it an odd combination, he gave no sign. The desk, with its back to the window, was dark oak. On it were papers in tidy stacks, a gold pen and pencil set, and a triple picture frame. Seated behind them was Dodson, a dark, tidy little man who had always reminded Slade more of a parish priest than New York's commissioner of police. His eyes were a calm, pale blue, his cheeks healthily ruddy. Thin wisps of white wove through his hair. All in all, Dodson was the picture of avuncular gentleness. But the lines in his face hadn't been etched by good humor.

"Sergeant Sladerman." Dodson motioned Slade to a chair with a gesture and a smile. Built like his father, he thought briefly as he watched Slade take his seat. "Did I keep you waiting?"

"A bit."

Like his father, Dodson thought again, managing not to smile. Except that there'd been talk that the son's real interest lay in writing, not in police work. Tom had always brushed that aside, Dodson remembered. *My boy's a cop, just like his old man. A damn good cop.* At the moment Dodson was banking on it.

"How's the family?" he asked casually while keeping those deceptive blue eyes direct.

"Fine. Thank you, sir."

"Janice is enjoying college?" He offered Slade a cigar. When it was refused, Dodson lit one for himself. Slade waited until the smoke stung the air before answering. Just how, he wondered, did Dodson know his sister was in college?

"Yes, she likes it."

"How's the writing?"

He had to call on all of his training not to reveal surprise at the question. His eyes remained as clear and steady as his voice. "Struggling."

No time for small talk, Dodson thought, tapping off cigar ash. The boy's already itching to be gone. But being commissioner gave him an advantage. He took another slow drag of the cigar, watching the smoke curl lazily toward the ceiling. "I read that short story of yours in *Mirror*," Dodson went on. "It was very good."

"Thank you." What the hell's the point? Slade wondered impatiently.

"No luck with the novel?"

Briefly, almost imperceptibly, Slade's eyes narrowed. "Not yet."

Sitting back, Dodson chewed on his cigar as he studied the man across from him. Had the look of his father, too, he mused. Slade had the same narrow face that was both intelligent and tough. He wondered if the son could smile with the same disarming charm as the father. Yet the eyes were like his mother's—dark gray and thoughtful, skilled at keeping emotions hidden. Then there was his record, Dodson mused. He might not be the flashy cop his father had been, but he was thorough. And, thank God, less impulsive. After his years on the force, the last three in homicide, Slade could be considered seasoned. If an undercover cop wasn't seasoned by thirty-two, he was dead. Slade had a reputation for being cool, perhaps a shade too cool, but his arrests were clean. Dodson didn't need a man who looked for trouble, but one who knew what to do once he found it.

"Slade . . ." He allowed a small smile to escape. "That's what you're called, isn't it?"

"Yes, sir." The familiarity made him uncomfortable; the smile made him suspicious.

"I'm sure you've heard of Justice Lawrence Winslow."

Curiosity came first, then a quick search through his mental file. "Presided over the New York Appellate Court before he was elected chief justice of the Connecticut Supreme Court about fifteen years ago. Died of a heart attack four, maybe five years ago."

Facts and figures, Dodson mused. The boy didn't waste words. "He was also a damn fine lawyer, a judge who understood the full meaning of justice. A good man. His wife remarried two years ago and lives in southern France."

So what? Slade thought with fresh impatience as Dodson gazed broodingly over his shoulder.

"I'm godfather to his daughter, Jessica." The same question zipped through Slade's mind as Dodson focused on him again. "She lives in the family home near Westport. Beautiful place—a stone's throw from the beach. It's quiet, peaceful." He drummed his fingers against the desk. "I imagine a writer would find it very appealing."

There was an uncomfortable premonition which Slade pushed aside. "Possibly." Was the old man matchmaking? Slade almost laughed out loud. No, that was too ridiculous.

"Over the last nine months there has been a rash of thefts throughout Europe."

The abrupt change of subject startled Slade so much that the surprise showed clearly on his face. Quickly he controlled it and lifted a brow, saying nothing.

"Important thefts," Dodson continued. "Mainly from museums—gems, coins, stamps. France, England, Spain, and Italy have all been hit. The investigation has led the respective authorities to believe the stolen articles have been smuggled into the States."

"Smuggling's federal," Slade said briefly. And, he thought silently, has nothing to do with a homicide detective—or some justice's spoiled daughter. Another uncomfortable thought came to him which he ignored.

"Smuggling's federal," Dodson repeated, a bit too amiably for Slade's taste. He placed the tips of his neat fingers together, watching the younger man over them. "I have a few connections in the Bureau. Because of this case's . . . delicate nature, I've been consulted." He paused a beat, long enough for Slade to comment if he chose to, then went on. "Some substantial leads in the investigation point to a small, well-respected antique shop. The Bureau knows there's an operator. From the information I have, they've narrowed down the possibilities for dump sites, and this shop is one of the . . . chosen few," he decided dryly. "It's believed someone on the inside is on the take." Pausing, he adjusted the picture frame on his desk. "They want to put an operative on it, inside, so that the head of the organization won't slip away from them this time. He's clever," Dodson mused, half to himself.

Again Dodson gave Slade a moment to question or comment, and again he went on as the other man remained silent. "Allegedly, the goods are hidden—cleverly hidden—in an antique, then exported to this shop, retrieved, and ultimately disposed of."

"It seems the Feds have things under control." Barely masking his impatience, Slade reached for a cigarette.

"There's one or two complications." Dodson waited for the hiss and flare of the match. "There's no concrete evidence, nor is the identity of the head of the organization known. A handful of accomplices, yes, but we want him . . . or her," he added softly.

The tone had Slade's eyes sharpening. Don't get interested, he warned himself. It has nothing to do with you. Swallowing the questions that had popped into his head, he drew on his cigarette and waited.

"There's also a more delicate problem." For the first time since Slade had walked into the room, he noticed Dodson's nerves. The commissioner picked up his gold pen, ran it through his fingers, then stuck it back in its slot. "The antique shop alleged to be involved is owned and operated by my goddaughter."

Dark brows lifted, but the eyes beneath them betrayed nothing. "Justice Winslow's daughter."

"It's generally believed that Jessica knows nothing of the illegal use of her shop—if indeed there is illegal use." Dodson reached for the pen again, this time holding it lengthwise between both hands. "I know she's completely innocent. Not only because she's my goddaughter," he went on, anticipating Slade's thoughts, "but because I know her. She's every bit as honest as her father was. Jessica cherishes Larry's memory. And," he added, carefully setting down the pen, "she hardly needs the money."

"Hardly," Slade muttered, picturing a spoiled heiress with too much time and money on her hands. Smuggling for kicks, he mused. A change of pace from shopping and parties and jet-setting.

"The Bureau's closing in," Dodson stated. "The next few weeks could bring the whole mess down around her ears. It might be dangerous for her." Slade controlled the snort of derision. "Even the shield of ignorance isn't going to protect her once things come to a head if her shop's involved. I've tried to convince her to come to New York for a visit, but . . ." His voice trailed off. Amused exasperation moved over his face. "Jessica's stubborn. Claims she's too busy. She tells me I should come visit her." With a shake of his head, Dodson let out what passed for a sigh. "I considered it, but my presence at this point could jeopardize the investigation. However, I feel Jessica needs protection. Discreet protection. Someone trained to deal with the situation, who can stay close to her without causing speculation." A smile touched his eyes. "Someone who could assist the investigation from the inside."

Slade frowned. He liked the conversation less and less. Taking his time, he stubbed out his cigarette. "And how do you expect me to do that?"

Dodson smiled fully. He liked the irritation in Slade's voice as much as the directness. "Jessica will do what I want—to a point." Leaning back in the overstuffed leather chair, he relaxed again. "She's been complaining lately about the mess her library's in, about not having enough time to sort through and catalog. I'm going to call her, tell her I'm sending the son of an old friend of mine and her father's. That's true, by the way," he added. "Tom and Larry knew each other some years back. Your cover's simple enough. You're a writer who needs a quiet refuge for a few weeks, and in turn, you'll sort out her library."

Slade's eyes had darkened during Dodson's casual run-down. "Jurisdiction—" he began.

"Some paperwork," Dodson interrupted easily. "It can be

taken care of. After all, it's the boys from the Bureau who'll make the collar when it's time."

"I'm supposed to play librarian and baby sitter." Slade gave a snort of disgust. "Look, Commissioner, I'm that close to wrapping up the Bitronelli murder." He brought his thumb and forefinger together. "If—"

"You'd better be," Dodson interrupted again, but with a hint of steel in his voice. "The press is having a great time making the NYPD look like fools on that one. And if you're so close," he added before Slade could toss back a furious retort, "you should be able to leave for Connecticut in a couple of days. The Bureau is interested in having a cop on the inside. A cop who knows how to keep his eyes and ears open. They've checked you out and agree with my choice."

"Terrific," Slade muttered. Standing, he prowled the room. "I'm homicide, not robbery."

"You're a cop," Dodson said shortly.

"Yeah." Baby-sitting for some snobby little heiress, Slade thought darkly, who was either smuggling for thrills or too dizzy to see what was going on under her nose. "Terrific," he muttered again.

Once Janice was out of college, he thought, he could quit the force and concentrate on his writing. He was tired of it. Tired of the misery he came in contact with almost every day of his life. Tired of the dirt, the futility, tired of the nasty little pieces of humanity his job forced him to deal with. And tired too of seeing the look of relief in his mother's eyes each time he came home. With a sigh, he resigned himself. Maybe a couple of weeks in Connecticut would be a nice change. A change anyway.

"When?" he demanded as he turned back to face Dodson.

"Day after tomorrow," Dodson said smoothly. "I'll give you a complete briefing, then I'll call Jessica and tell her to expect you."

With a shrug, Slade went back to his chair to listen.

1

Fall touched the trees and stung the air. Against a hard blue sky, the colors were vibrant, passionate. The ribbon of road cut through the hills and wound eastward toward the Atlantic. Whipping through the open car windows, the wind was chilled and fragrant. Slade wondered how long it had been since he had smelled that kind of freshness. No city smells of sweat and exhaust. When his book was accepted, perhaps he could move his mother and Janice out of the city—a home in the country maybe, or near the shore. It was always *when* or *as soon as*. He couldn't afford to think *if*.

Another year on the force—another year of scraping up tuition money—and then. . . . Shaking his head, Slade turned up the radio. It wasn't any good thinking of next year. He wasn't in Connecticut to appreciate the scenery. It was just another job—and one he resented.

Jessica Winslow, he mused, age twenty-seven. The only child of Justice Lawrence Winslow and Lorraine Nordan Winslow. Graduate of Radcliffe, senior class president. She'd probably been head cheerleader, too, he thought with a sneer. All button-downed and pony-tailed. Ralph Lauren sweaters and Gucci loafers.

Struggling to be open minded, he continued his catalog. Opened the House of Winslow four years ago. Up until two years ago she did the majority of buying herself. Good excuse to play around in Europe, he thought as he punched in the car lighter.

Michael Adams, Jessica Winslow's assistant and current buyer. Thirty-two, Yale graduate. Figures, Slade reflected, exhaling smoke that rushed out of the open window. Son of Robert and Marion Adams, another prominent Connecticut family. No firm evidence, but someone Slade was instructed to keep his eye on. He leaned his elbow on the window as he considered. As chief buyer, Adams would be in a perfect position to handle the operation from overseas.

David Ryce, shop assistant for eighteen months. Twenty-three. Son of Elizabeth Ryce, the Winslow housekeeper. Dodson had said he was often trusted with running the shop alone. That would give him the opportunity to handle the local operation.

Systematically, Slade ran through the list of the Winslow staff. Gardener, cook, housekeeper, daily maid. Good God, he thought in disgust. All that for one person. She probably wouldn't know how to boil an egg if her life depended on it.

The gates to the Winslow estate stood open, with room enough for two cars to pass easily. Slade turned into the long, macadam drive, lined with bushy, bloomless azaleas. There was a burst of birdsong, then silence. He drove nearly a quarter of a mile before pulling up in front of the house.

It was large but, he had to admit, not oppressively so. The brick was old, mellowed by sun and sea air. Smoke rose from one of the chimneys on the hipped roof. The gray shutters weren't just decorative, he noted, but could be used for practical purposes if a storm rose up off the Sound. He smelled the chrysanthemums before he saw them.

The blossoms were huge, growing near the base of the house. They were rust, gold, and copper, complimenting the violent red of bushes. It charmed him, as did the lazy odor of woodsmoke. This wasn't indolence but peace. He'd had too little of that. Shaking off the mood, Slade walked up the steps to the front door. He lifted a fist and knocked, hard. He hated doorbells.

In less than a minute the door opened. He had to look down, quite a distance down, to see a tiny, middle-aged woman with a pleasantly ugly face and gray-streaked hair. He caught a whiff of a pine-scented cleaner that reminded him of his mother's kitchen.

"May I help you?" The accent was broad New England.

"I'm James Sladerman. Miss Winslow's expecting me."

The woman scrutinized him with cautious black eyes. "You'd be the writer," she stated, obviously not overly impressed. Stepping back, she allowed him to enter.

As the door closed behind him, Slade glanced around the hall. The floor was uncarpeted, a gleaming blond oak that showed some wear under the careful polishing. A few paintings hung on the ivory-toned wallpaper. A pale green glass bowl sat on a high round table and overflowed with fall flowers. There were no overt displays of wealth, but wealth was there. He'd seen a print of the painting to his right in an art book. The blue scarf that hung negligently over the railing of the steps was silk.

Slade started to turn back to the housekeeper when a clatter at the top of the steps distracted him.

She came barrelling down the curved staircase in a flurry of swirling blond hair and flying skirts. The hammer of heels on wood disrupted the quiet of the house. Slade had a quick impression of speed, motion, and energy.

"Betsy, you make David stay in bed until that fever's broken. Don't you dare let him get up. Damn, damn, damn, I'm going to be late! Where are my keys?"

Three inches away from Slade, she came to a screeching halt, almost overbalancing. Automatically he reached for her arm to steady her. Breathless, she brought her eyes from his shirt front to stare at him.

It was an exquisite face—fair skinned, oval, delicate, with just a hint of cheekbone that added a rather primitive strength. Indian? Viking? he wondered. Celtic? Her eyes were large, the color of aged whiskey, set below brows that were lowered in curiosity. The faintest line appeared between them. A stubborn line, Slade reflected. His sister had one. She was small, he noted. The top of her head barely skimmed his shoulder. Her scent was reminiscent of fall—something musky—blossoms and smoke. The arm beneath his hand was slender under a thin wool blazer. He felt the stir inside him—man for woman—and hastily dropped his hand.

"This is Mr. Sladerman," Betsy announced. "That writer."

"Oh yes." The smile cleared away the faint line between her brows. "Uncle Charlie told me you were coming."

It took Slade a moment to connect Uncle Charlie with Dodson. Not knowing if he was smothering an oath or a laugh, he accepted her extended hand. "Charlie told me you could use some help, Miss Winslow."

"Help." She rolled her eyes and cleared her throat. "Yes, you could call it that. The library. . . . Look, I'm sorry to rush off the minute you get here, but my assistant's ill and my buyer's in France." Tilting her wrist, she grimaced at her watch. "I have a client coming to the shop ten minutes ago."

"Don't worry about it." If this frazzled lady can run a business, I'll volunteer to walk a beat, he decided, but gave her an easy smile. "It'll give me a chance to get settled in."

"Fine. I'll see you at dinner then." Glancing around, she muttered again about keys.

"In your hand," Slade told her.

"Stupid." With a sigh, Jessica uncurled her fingers and stared at the keys in her palm. "The more I have to rush, the worse it gets." Lifting amused eyes to his, she brushed her hair from her shoulders. "Please don't bother with the library today. It may shock you so much that you'll run away before I can smooth things over. Betsy . . ." As she dashed for the door Jessica looked over her shoulder. "Tell David he's fired if he gets out of bed. 'Bye."

The door slammed behind her. Betsy clucked her tongue.

Ten minutes later Slade inspected his suite of rooms. They were nearly as large as the apartment he had grown up in. There was a faded carpet on the bedroom floor that he recognized was not *old* but *antique*. In a small, black marble fireplace, wood was neatly laid for burning. Crossing to the sitting room, he saw a sturdy desk topped with a vase of the chrysanthemums, a brass paperweight, and a feather quill. Without hesitation, he cleared it off to make room for his typewriter.

If he had his way, his writing would be more than a cover. When he wasn't baby-sitting, he'd get some work done. Of course, there was the library to fool with. On an exasperated sigh, Slade turned his back on his typewriter and went back downstairs. He roamed, filing the position and layout of rooms in the cop's part of his mind, their descriptions in the writer's.

In his tour of the first floor, Slade could find no fault with Jessica's taste. It was only the nouveau riche who went in for ostentation. The Winslow woman preferred muted colors and clean lines. In her clothes, too, he mused, remembering how she had looked in the dun-colored blazer and skirt. Still, the blouse she'd worn had been a deep, almost violent green. That just might indicate something else.

Slade stopped to run his fingers over the surface of a rosewood piano. Compared to this, he mused, the battered upright his mother treasured was so much kindling. With a shrug, he wandered to the next door.

The library. He caught the scent of old leather and dust as he looked on the largest private collection of books he'd ever seen. For the first time since he had walked into Dodson's office, Slade felt a stir of pleasure. A quick study told him that the books were well read as well as carelessly filed. He crossed the room and mounted the two stairs to the second level. Not filed at all, he corrected, but simply jumbled. He ran a long finger along a row of volumes. Robert Burns tilted onto a copy of Kurt Vonnegut.

A big job, he concluded. One he might have enjoyed if it had been his only purpose. He took one long look around before absently pulling out a book. There was nothing he could do about Jessica Winslow at the moment, he thought as he settled down to read.

Jessica swerved into the parking area beside her shop, relieved to see it empty. She was late, but her client was later. Or, she thought with a frown, he'd grown tired of waiting and left. With a half-hearted oath, she hurried to unlock the front door. Quickly she went from window to window, letting the shades snap up. Without slackening pace, she headed for the back room, tossed her purse aside, then filled a small kettle with water. She gave the struggling ivy in the rear window a quick douse before setting the kettle on the stove. Halfway out of the room, she went back to turn the burner on underneath it. Satisfied, she wandered into the main shop.

It wasn't large—but then Jessica had never intended it to be. Intimate, personal. Yes, it was that, she thought, with her signature on it. The shop was more than a business to her; it was an accomplishment, and a love. The business end—invoices, filing, books—she ran meticulously. All of her organizational efforts went into the shop, which perhaps was the reason for her lack of order elsewhere.

The shop was the focus of her life, and had been since she'd conceived of it. Initially she'd needed something to give some purpose to her life after college was behind her. The idea for the shop had germinated slowly, then had grown and developed. Jessica had too much drive, too much energy, to drift. Once she had decided to start a business, she'd moved quickly. Then that same drive and energy had made it work. It turned a profit. The money itself meant little, but the fact that her shop made it, meant everything.

She'd spent six months scouring New England, then Europe, for the right pieces. A large inventory hadn't been her goal, but an exclusive one. After her opening the response had begun as a small trickle, mostly friends and friends of friends. Justice Winslow's daughter running a shop had brought out the curiosity seekers as well. Jessica hadn't minded. A client was a client, and a satisfied one, the best advertising.

For the first two years she'd run the shop alone. Indeed, she had never considered that her business would outgrow her. When it had, she'd hired Michael Adams to handle the overseas buying. He was charming, capable, and knowledgeable. The women customers adored him. Gradually their relationship had mellowed from business to friendship to easy affection.

As business had continued to thrive, Jessica had hired David Ryce. He'd been hardly more than a boy, at loose ends, bored enough to find trouble if it got in the way. Jessica had hired him because they'd grown up together; then she had come to depend on him. He was quick with figures and tireless with details. He had a streak of street sense that made him a good man to have in business.

Street sense, Jessica mused. James Sladerman. Odd that the term would bring him back to her mind. Even in that quick exchange at the foot of the stairs, she'd felt something in him. It told her he was a man who would know how to handle himself—in business, maybe. In an alley, definitely. With a half laugh, she stuck her hands in her pockets. Now why should she think that?

The fingers that had gripped her arm had been strong. His build had been wiry. But no, it had been his eyes, she thought. There was something . . . hard in his eyes. Yet she hadn't been repelled or frightened, but drawn. Even when he'd looked at her for those first three or four seconds, with that intensity that seemed to creep beneath her skin, she hadn't been afraid. Safe, she realized. He'd made her feel safe. That was odd, Jessica decided, catching her bottom lip between her teeth. Why should she suddenly feel safe when she had no need for protection?

The door of the shop jingled open. Pushing speculation aside, Jessica turned.

"Miss Winslow, I apologize. I'm very late."

"Don't give it a thought, Mr. Chambers." Jessica considered telling him that she'd also been late, then decided against it. What he didn't know wouldn't hurt him. Behind her, the kettle whistled. "I'm just making tea. Why don't you join me before we look over the new snuffboxes?"

Chambers removed a rather fussy hat from a balding head. "Wonderful. I do appreciate you calling me when you get a new shipment in." He smiled, revealing good dentures.

"You don't think I'd let anyone see the snuffboxes before you." In the kitchen Jessica poured boiling water into cups. "Michael found these in France. There are two I think you'll be particularly interested in."

He preferred the ornate, Jessica thought with a smile as she lifted the tray. He loved the foolishly gaudy little boxes that men with lace cuffs used to carry. She glanced at Chambers' stubby form and wondered if he pictured himself as a cavalier or perhaps a Regency buck. Still, his fascination with snuffboxes had made him a regular customer who had more than once recommended her shop to other people. And he was rather sweet in his fussy little way, she thought as she placed the tea tray on a table.

"Sugar?" she asked him.

"Ah, I shouldn't." Chambers patted his ample middle. "But perhaps one cube." His glance flicked briefly down to her legs as Jessica crossed them. A pity, he thought with an inward sigh, that he wasn't twenty years younger.

Later he left happily with two eighteenth-century snuffboxes. Before Jessica could file the invoice, she heard the grumble of an engine. Glancing up, she saw the large delivery truck pull in front of the shop. She read the company logo on the side of the steel doors and frowned a bit. She could have sworn the delivery that Michael was shipping wasn't due until the following day.

When she recognized the driver, Jessica waved, then walked to the front door to meet him.

"Hi, Miss Winslow."

"Hello, Don." She accepted the itemized list he handed her, muttering about not expecting him until tomorrow. He shrugged.

"Mr. Adams put a rush on it."

"Mmm." She jiggled the keys in her pocket as she scanned the list. "Well, he seems to have outdone himself this time. And another delivery on Saturday. I don't . . . oh!" Her eyes lit up with pleasure as they fixed on one item. "The writing desk. The Queen Anne. I meant to tell Michael to keep his eyes open for one, then forgot. It must be fate." Of course, she should uncart it first, at least take a look. No, impulses were the best, Jessica decided. Smiling, she looked back up at the driver. "The rest comes in here, but that goes to my home. Would you mind?"

"Well . . ."

It was easy to justify using the smile. Jessica could already see the desk in the front parlor. "If it's not too much trouble," she added.

The driver shifted to his other foot. "I guess it'll be all right. Joe won't mind." He jerked his thumb at his partner, who had opened the wide double doors of the truck.

"Thanks. I really appreciate it. That desk is just what I've been looking for."

Feeling triumphant, Jessica went to the back room for more tea.

As she had burst out hours before, Jessica burst in through the front door of the house. "Betsy!" She slung her purse over the newel post. "Did it come?" Without waiting for an answer, she dashed toward the front parlor.

"Since you were six, I've been telling you to slow down." Betsy came through the parlor doors, intercepting her. "At least then you wore sensible shoes."

"Betsy." Jessica gave her a quick, hard squeeze that held as much impatience as affection. "Did it come?"

"Yes, of course it came." The housekeeper straightened her apron with a tug. "And it's sitting in the parlor just like you told me. It'll be there whether you walk sensibly or run like a fool." The last of the sentence was wasted, as Jessica was already rushing by her.

"Oh, it's lovely!" Gently, she ran a finger over the wood, then quickly began to examine it on all sides. It was a delicate, airy little piece. A woman's desk. Jessica opened the slant top, then sighed at the unmarred interior. "Really lovely. Wait until David sees it." She opened one of the inner drawers. It slid out smoothly. "It's exactly what I've been looking for. What luck that Michael came across it." Crouching, she ran a hand down one of its slender legs.

"It's pretty," Betsy admitted, thinking that the carving would be one more thing to keep dust out of. "I bet you could have sold it for a pretty penny too."

"The advantage of owning a shop is being able to cop some of the merchandise for yourself." Rising, Jessica shut the lid again. Now all she needed was a frivolous little inkwell, or perhaps a porcelain box to set on top of it.

"Supper's nearly ready."

"Oh, supper." Shaking her head, Jessica brought herself back to the moment. "Mr. Sladerman, I've neglected him all day. Is he upstairs?"

"In the library," Betsy announced grimly. "All day. Wouldn't even come out for lunch."

"Oh boy." Jessica combed a hand through her hair. He hadn't looked like a man who would have much patience with disorganization. "I really wanted to ease him into that. Well, I'm going to go be charming so we don't lose him. What's for supper?" she asked over her shoulder.

"Stuffed pork chops and mashed potatoes."

"That should help," Jessica muttered as she headed for the library door.

She opened it slowly, enough to stick her head inside. Some things, she decided, you don't rush into. He was sitting at a long work table, surrounded by pillars and piles of books. A thick pad was in front of him, and the pencil in his hand was worked halfway down. His hair fell over his forehead, but she could see his brows drawn together in concentration. Or annoyance, she mused. She put on her best smile.

"Hi."

He looked up, eyes pinning her. Jessica could feel the little prickles of power all over her skin. She absorbed it, intrigued by the sensation. Without being aware of it, her smile had faded into a look of puzzlement.

Who is this man? she wondered. It was curiosity as much as courage that had her coming all the way into the room. The lamp on the desk slanted across his face, highlighting his mouth and putting his eyes in shadow. She didn't feel safe with him this time, but unsettled. She continued toward him.

"You've got a hell of a mess here," Slade said shortly, tossing his pencil aside. It was better to attack than let himself dwell on how beautiful she was. "If you run your shop like this"—he gestured widely—"it's a miracle you're not bankrupt."

The specific complaint eased the tension in her shoulders. There'd been nothing personal in that look, she assured herself. She'd been foolish to think there had been. "I know it's terrible," Jessica admitted, smiling again. "I hope you're not going to do the sensible thing and walk out." Gingerly, she lowered a hip to the table before lifting a book at random. "Do you like challenges, Mr. Sladerman?"

She was laughing, he noted. Or her eyes were. But he sensed very clearly that she laughed at herself. A reluctant smile tugged at his mouth as he struggled to study her objectively. Maybe she was innocent—maybe not. He didn't have the same blind faith as the commissioner. But she was beautiful, and he was attracted. Slade decided the attraction was going to be difficult to work around.

Letting out a long breath, he gazed around the room. How

much choice did he have? "I'm going to take pity on you, Miss Winslow . . . I have a fondness for books."

"So do I," she began, then had to deal with another of his cool, direct looks. "Really," she claimed with a laugh. "I'm just not neat. Do we have a deal, Mr. Sladerman?" Solemnly, she offered her hand.

He glanced at it first. Soft and elegant, he thought, like her name and her voice. With a quick curse at fate for making the commissioner her godfather, Slade took her hand in his. "We have a deal, Miss Winslow."

Jessica slid from the table, keeping his hand in hers when he would have drawn away. Somehow she'd known it would be hard and strong. "How do you feel about stuffed pork chops?"

They were tender and delicious. Slade ate three after his stomach remembered the lack of lunch. And, he thought after a slice of cheesecake, this case had some advantages over the one he'd just wrapped up. For two weeks he'd made do on cold coffee and stale sandwiches. And his partner hadn't been as easy to look at as Jessica Winslow. She'd guided the conversation expertly during the meal and had ended by tucking her arm through his to lead him back to the parlor.

"Have a seat," she invited. "I'll pour you a brandy."

As he started to cross the room the desk caught his eye. "That wasn't here this morning."

"What?" With a decanter in her hand, she glanced over her shoulder. "Oh no, it just came this afternoon. Do you know anything about antiques?"

"No." He gave the desk a cursory study before taking a chair. "I'll leave that to you, Miss Winslow."

"Jessica." She poured a second brandy before crossing to him. "Do I call you James or Jim?"

"Slade," he told her as he took a snifter. "Even my mother stopped calling me Jim when I was ten."

"You have a mother?"

The quick, unconscious surprise in her voice had him grinning. "Everybody's entitled to one."

Feeling foolish, Jessica sat across from him. "You just seem to be capable of arranging the whole business without one."

Both sipped brandy, and their eyes met over the snifters. Jessica felt the moment freeze, out of time, out of place. Do minds touch? she thought numbly. Wasn't she sensing at that moment the turbulent spin of his thoughts? Or were they hers? Brandy slipped, hot and strong down her throat, snapping her back. Talk, she ordered herself. Say something. "Do you have any other family?" she managed.

Slade stared at her, wondering if he had imagined that instant of stunning intimacy. He'd never felt that with any woman before, any lover. It was ridiculous to imagine that he'd felt it with one he barely knew. "A sister," he said at length. "She's in college."

"A sister." Jessica relaxed again and slipped out of her shoes. "That's nice. I always wanted a brother or sister when I was growing up."

"Money can't buy everything." Slade shrugged with the words. Seeing the puzzled hurt on her face, he cursed himself. If she was getting to him already, what would it be like in a week?

"You're quick with clichés," Jessica observed. "I suppose that's because you're a writer." After another sip of brandy, she set the glass aside. "What do you write?"

"Unpublished novels."

She laughed as she had in the library, drawing another smile from him. "It must be frustrating."

"Only daily," he agreed.

"Why do you do it?"

"Why do you eat?"

Jessica considered for a moment, then nodded. "Yes, I suppose it's like that, isn't it? Have you always wanted to write?"

He thought of his father, how he had bragged that his son would be the next Sladerman on the force. He thought of his teenage years, when he had written his stories in longhand in spiral notebooks late into the night. He thought of his father's eyes the first time he had seen his son in uniform. And he thought of the first time he'd had a short story accepted.

"Yes." Perhaps it was easier to admit to her what he had never been able to explain to his family. "Always."

"When you want something badly enough, and you don't give up," Jessica began slowly, "you get it."

Slade gave a short laugh before he drank. "Always?"

She touched the tip of her tongue to her top lip. "Almost always. It's all a gamble, isn't it?"

"Long odds," he murmured, frowning into his glass. "I usually play long odds." He studied the amber liquor, which was almost exactly the shade of her eyes. She shouldn't be so easy to talk to, he mused. He'd find himself saying too much.

"Ah, Ulysses, I wondered where you were."

Lifting his eyes, Slade stared at a large, loping mop of fur. It lunged, unerringly, into Jessica's lap. He heard her groan, then giggle.

"Damn it! How many times do I have to tell you you're not a lap dog. You're breaking my ribs." She twisted her head, but the wet, pink tongue found her cheek. "Stop!" she sputtered, pushing impotently. "Get down," she ordered. "Get down right this minute." Ulysses barked twice, then continued to lap his tongue all over her face.

"What," Slade asked slowly, "is that?"

Jessica gave another mighty shove, but Ulysses only rested his head on her shoulder. "A dog, of course."

"There's no 'of course' about that dog."

"He's a Great Pyrenees," she retorted, quickly running out of breath. "And he flunked obedience school three times. You mangy, soft-headed mutt, get down." Ulysses let out a long, contented breath and didn't budge. "Give me a hand, will you?" she demanded of Slade. "I'll have internal injuries this time. Once before I was stuck for two hours until Betsy got home."

Rising, Slade approached the dog with a frown. "Does he bite?"

"God, I'm suffocating and the man asks if he bites."

A grin split Slade's face as he looked down at her. "Can't be too careful about these things. He might be vicious."

Jessica narrowed her eyes. "Sic 'em, Ulysses!" Hearing his name, the dog roused himself to lick her face again, joyfully. "Satisfied?" Jessica demanded. "Now grab him somewhere and get me out."

Bending, Slade wrapped his arms around the bulk of fur.

The back of his hand brushed Jessica's breast as he shifted his grip. "Sorry," he muttered, dragging at the dog. "Good God, what does he weigh?"

"About one twenty-five, I think."

With a shake of his head, Slade put his back into it. Ulysses slid to the floor to lay adoringly at Jessica's feet. Taking a deep gulp of air, Jessica closed her eyes.

She was covered with loose white hair. Her own was disheveled and curled around her shoulders, the color, Slade observed, of sun-bleached wheat. With her face in repose, the slant of her cheekbones was more pronounced. Her lips were just parted. Their shape was utterly feminine—the classic cupid's bow but for the fullness in the lower lip. It spoke of passion—hidden, quietly simmering passion. The mouth and the cheekbones added something to the tearoom looks that had Slade's pulse responding. He couldn't want her, he told himself. That wasn't just irresponsible, it was stupid. He stared down at the dog again.

"You should do something about training him," he said shortly.

"I know." With a sigh, Jessica opened her brandy-colored eyes. Her affection for Ulysses made her forget the discomfort and the mess he usually created. "He's very sensitive really. I just haven't got the heart to subject him to obedience school again."

"That's incredibly stupid," Slade tossed back. "He's too big not to be trained."

"Want the job?" Jessica retorted. Straightening in the chair, she began to brush at stray dog hair.

"I've got one, thanks."

Why should it annoy her that he hadn't once used her name? she asked herself as she rose. Dignity had to be sacrificed as she stepped over the now sleeping dog. "I appreciate the help," she said stiffly. "And the advice is duly noted."

Slade shrugged off the sarcasm. "No problem. You struck me as more the poodle type, though."

"Really?" For a moment Jessica merely studied his eyes. Yes, they were hard, she decided. Hard and cool and cynical. "And I have the impression you don't think much of the poodle type. Help yourself to the brandy. I'm going up."

2

$\mathscr{F}$or the next two days there was an uneasy truce. Perhaps it lasted that long because Jessica made a point of staying out of Slade's way. He in turn stayed out of hers while patiently noting her routine—which, he discovered, was no routine at all. She simply never stopped. She didn't take time for the social rigamarole he had expected—luncheons, clubs, committees—but worked, apparently inexhaustibly. Most of her time was spent at the shop. At the rate he was going, he knew he would find out little in the house. His next move was the House of Winslow. It followed that he needed to make peace with Jessica to get there.

From his bedroom window, he watched her drive away. It was barely eight o'clock, a full hour before she normally left. Slade swore in frustration. How did the commissioner expect him to watch her—or protect her if that's what she needed—if she was always in one place while he was in another? It was time to improvise an excuse to pay her a visit at her place of business.

Grabbing a jacket on the way, Slade headed for the stairs. He could always claim that he wanted to do a bit of research on antique furniture for his novel. That would buy him a few hours, as well as give him a reason to poke around. Before he'd rounded the last curve in the steps he heard Betsy's voice.

". . . nothing but trouble."

"Don't fuss."

Slade stopped, waiting as the footsteps came his way. There was a tall, gangly man walking down the hall. His mop of dark blond hair was long and straight, cut rather haphazardly just below the collar of a chambray workshirt. He wore jeans and wire-rim glasses and stood hunched over a bit—either from habit or fatigue. Because he was staring down at his sneakers, he didn't see Slade. His face was pale and the eyes behind the lenses were shadowed. David Ryce, Slade concluded, and kept silent.

"I told you she said you weren't to come in today." Betsy bustled after him, a feather duster gripped in her hand.

"I'm fine. If I lie around in bed another day, I'm going to mold." He coughed violently.

"Fine, fine indeed." Betsy clucked her tongue, swinging the duster at his back.

"Mom, lay off." Exasperated, David started to turn back to her when he spotted Slade. He frowned, choking back another cough. "Oh, you must be the writer."

"That's right." Slade came down the last two steps. Just a boy, he thought, taking David's measure quickly. Who hasn't completely thrown off the youthful defiance.

"Jessie and I figured you'd be a short, stooped little guy with glasses. I don't know why." He grinned, but Slade noted that he placed a hand on the newel post for support. "Getting anywhere with the library?"

"Slowly."

"Better you than me," David murmured, wishing for a chair. "Has Jessica come down yet?"

"She's already gone," Slade told him.

"There, you see." Betsy folded her arms over her chest. "And if you go in, she'll just send you right back home. Thunder at you too."

Because his legs threatened to buckle, David gripped the newel post harder. "She's going to need help with the new shipment. Another's due in today."

"Lotta good you'd do," Betsy began. Catching the look in David's eye, Slade cut in.

"I was thinking about running down there myself. I'd like to see the place, maybe do a little research. I could give her a hand." He watched David struggle, caught between his desire to go to the shop and his need to lie down.

"She'll try to move everything herself," he muttered.

"That's the truth," Betsy agreed, apparently switching her annoyance from her son to her employer. "Nothing stops that one."

"It's my job to move in the new stock, check it off. I don't—"

"Moving furniture around shouldn't require any great knowledge of antiques," Slade put in casually. Knowing it was too perfect to let pass, he slipped into his jacket. "And since I was heading that way anyway . . ."

"There, it's settled," Betsy announced. She had her son by the elbow before he could protest. "Mr. Sladerman will go look out for Miss Jessica. You go back to bed."

"I'm not going back to bed. A chair, all I want's a chair." He sent Slade a weak smile. "Hey, thanks. Tell Jessie I'm coming back on Monday. The paperwork on the new stock can wait over the weekend. Tell her to humor the invalid and leave it for me."

Slade nodded slowly. "Sure, I'll tell her." Turning, he started out, deciding that the new stock interested him very much.

Fifteen minutes later Slade parked in the small graveled lot beside Jessica's shop. It was a small, framed building, fronted with several narrow windows. The shades were up. Through the glass, he could see her tugging on a large and obviously heavy piece of furniture. Cursing women in general, he walked to the front door and pulled it open.

At the jingle of bells she spun around. That anyone would be by the shop at that hour surprised her—that Slade stood inside the door frowning at her surprised Jessica more. "Well . . ." The physical exertion had winded her so that she struggled to even her breathing. "I didn't expect to see you here." She didn't add that she wasn't particularly pleased either.

She'd stripped off her jacket and pushed up the sleeves of her cashmere sweater. Beneath it, small high breasts rose and fell agitatedly. Slade remembered their softness against the back of his hand very clearly. He forgot he'd come to make peace with her.

"Don't you have more sense than to push this stuff around yourself?" he demanded. With a quick oath, he pulled off his jacket and tossed it over a chair. Jessica stiffened her back as well as her tone.

"Well, good morning to you too."

Her annoyance rolled off of him. After crossing to her, Slade leaned against the large piece she'd been struggling with. "Where do you want it?" he asked shortly. "And I hope to God you're not one of those women who changes her mind a half dozen times."

He watched her eyes narrow and darken as they had that night in the parlor. Oddly, he found her only more attractive when she was agitated. If it hadn't been for that, the way her chin jutted out might have amused him. "I don't believe anyone asked for your assistance." For the first time he was treated to the ice in her tone. "I'm capable of arranging my stock myself."

"Don't be any more stupid than necessary," he shot back. "You're just going to hurt yourself. Now where do you want this thing?"

"This *thing*," she began heatedly, "is a nineteenth-century French secretaire."

He gave it a negligent glance. "Yeah, so? Where do you want me to put it?"

"I'll tell you where you can put it—"

His laughter cut her off. It was very male and full of fun. It wasn't a sound she had expected from him. With an effort, she swallowed a chuckle of her own as she stepped back from him. The last thing she wanted was to find anything appealing about James Sladerman. "Over there," she said coolly, pointing. Turning away, Jessica picked up a washstand to carry it in the opposite direction. When the sounds of wood sliding over wood had stopped, she turned back to him.

"Thank you." The gratitude was short and cold. "Now, what can I do for you?"

He treated himself to a lengthy look at her. She stood very straight, her hands folded loosely, her eyes still dangerous. Two mother-of-pearl combs swept her hair back from her face. He allowed his gaze to sweep down briefly. She was very slender, with a hand-spanable waist and barely any hips. The trim flannel skirt hid most of her legs, but Slade could appreciate what was visible from the knees down. Her feet were very small. One of them tapped the floor impatiently.

"I've thought about that from time to time," he commented as his eyes roamed back to hers. "But I came by to see what I could do for you. Ryce was worried that you might do just what you were trying to do a few minutes ago."

"You've seen David?" Her cool impatience evaporated. Swiftly, Jessica crossed the room to take Slade's arm. "Was he up? How is he?"

Suddenly he wanted to touch her—her hair, her face. She'd be soft. He felt an almost desperate need for something soft and yielding. Her eyes were on his, wide with concern. "He was up," he said briefly. "And not as well as he wanted to be."

"He shouldn't have been out of bed."

"No, probably not." Did her hair carry that scent? he wondered. That autumn-woods fragrance that was driving him mad? "He wanted to come in this morning."

"Come in?" Jessica pounced on the two words. "I gave specific orders for him to stay home. Why can't he do as he's told?"

Slade's eyes were suddenly keen on her face. "Does everyone do what you tell them?"

"He's my employee," she retorted, dropping her hand from his arm. "He damn well better do what I tell him." As quickly as she had flared up, her mood shifted and she smiled. "He's hardly more than a boy really, and Betsy nags at him. It's just her way. Though I appreciate his dedication to the business, he's got to get well." Her eyes drifted to the phone on the counter. "If I call, he'll just get defensive."

"He said he wouldn't come in until Monday." Slade leaned against the secretaire. "He wanted you to leave the paperwork on the new shipments for him."

Jessica stuck her hands in her pockets, obviously still toying with the idea of phoning to lecture David. "Yes, all right. If he's going to come in on Monday, at least he'll be sitting down. I'll get the new stock situated in the meantime so he's not tempted." She smiled again. "He's nearly as obsessed with this place as I am. If I so much as move a candlestick, David knows it. Before he got sick, he was trying to talk me into a vacation." She laughed, tossing her head so that her hair swung behind her. "He just wanted the place to himself for a week or two."

"A very dedicated assistant," Slade murmured.

"Oh, David's that," Jessica agreed. "What are you doing here, Slade? I thought you'd be buried in books."

Half glad, half wary that the reserve of the last few days had vanished, he gave her a cautious smile. "I told David I'd give you a hand."

"That was very nice." The surprise in her voice had his smile widening.

"I can be nice occasionally," he returned. "Besides, I thought I might be able to get some information on antiques. Research."

"Oh." She accepted this with a nod. "All right. I wouldn't mind having some help with the heavier things. What period were you interested in?"

"Period?"

"Furniture," Jessica explained as she walked to a long, low chest. "Is there a particular century or style? Renaissance, Early American, Italian Provincial?"

"Just a general sort of lesson today to give me the feel of it," Slade improvised as he nudged Jessica away from the chest. "Where do you want this?"

He lifted and carried. Jessica arranged the lighter pieces while keeping up a running dialog on the furniture they moved. This chair was Chippendale—see the square, tapered seat and cabriole leg. This cabinet was French Baroque—in satinwood, gilded and carved. She ran over a little table with a polishing cloth, explaining about Chinese influences and tea services.

During the morning they were interrupted half a dozen times by customers. Jessica turned from antique lover to salesperson. Slade watched her show pieces, explain their background, then dicker over prices. If he hadn't been sure before, he was certain now. Her shop was no toy to her. She not only knew how to manage it, but worked harder than he'd given her credit for. Not only did she handle people with a deft skill he was forced to admire, but she made money—if the discreet price tags he'd come across were any indication.

So why, he wondered, if she was dedicated to her shop, if she turned a profit, would she risk using her business for smuggling? Now that he'd met her and spent some time with her, it wasn't as easy for Slade to dismiss it as kicks or thrills. Yet she wasn't lacking in brains. Was it plausible that an operation was going on under her nose without her knowledge?

"Slade, I hate to ask." Jessica kept her voice lowered as she came close to his side. Touching came naturally to her, it seemed, for her hand was already on his arm. Irresponsible or not, he discovered that he wanted her. Turning, he trapped her effectively between the chest and himself. Her hand remained on his arm, just below the elbow. Though they touched in no other way, he suddenly had a very clear sensation of how her body would feel pressed against his. His eyes brushed over her mouth, then came to hers.

"Ask what?"

Her mind went blank. Some sound filled her head, like an echo of surf pounding on the shore. She could have stepped back an inch and broken the contact—stepped forward an inch to consummate it. Jessica did neither. Dimly, she was aware of a pressure in her chest, as though someone were pressing hard against it to cut off her air. In that instant they both knew he had only to touch her for everything to change.

"Slade," she murmured. Half question, half invitation.

He snapped back, retreating from the edge, from an involvement he couldn't afford. "Did you want me to move something else?" His voice was cool as he stepped away from her.

Shaken, Jessica backed toward the chest. She needed distance. "Mrs. MacKenzie wants to take the chifforobe with her. She's gone out to pull her car to the front. Would you mind putting it in the back of her station wagon?"

"All right."

She indicated the piece with a silent gesture, not moving until he was out the front door with it. Alone, Jessica allowed herself a long, uneasy breath. That was not a man a woman should lose control with, she warned herself. He wouldn't be gentle, or particularly kind. She placed the flat of her palm on her chest as if to relieve the pressure that lingered there. Don't overreact the next time, she advised herself.

It's the way he looks at me, Jessica decided, as if he could see what I'm thinking. She ran an unsteady hand through her hair. I don't even know what I'm thinking when he looks at me, so how could he? And yet . . . and yet her pulse was still racing.

When the door jingled open again, she hadn't budged from her spot in front of the chest of drawers.

"I'm starved," she improvised swiftly, then started to move. As Slade watched she hurried from window to window, lowering shades. She hung a sign on the door and then locked it. "You must be too," she said when he remained silent. "It's after one, and I've had you dragging furniture around all morning. How about a sandwich and some tea?"

Slade managed to smile and sneer at the same time. "Tea?"

Her laughter eased her own tension. "No, I suppose not. Well, David keeps some beer." She hustled to the back of the shop and pulled open the door of a small refrigerator. She crouched, then rummaged. "Here. I knew I'd seen some." Straightening, Jessica turned and collided with his chest. He took her arms briefly in reflex, then as quickly dropped them. Heart hammering, she stepped away. "Sorry, I didn't know you were behind me. Will this do?" Safely at arm's length, she offered the bottle.

"Fine." His expression was bland as he took it and sat at the table. The tension had settled at the base of his neck. He'd have to be careful not to touch her again. Or to give in to the urge to taste that subtly passionate mouth of hers. Once he did, he'd never stop there. Desire tightened, a hard ball in the pit of his stomach. Almost violently, Slade twisted the cap from the beer.

"I'll fix some sandwiches." Jessica became very busy in the refrigerator. "Roast beef all right?"

"Yeah, that's fine."

What goes on in his mind? she wondered as she kept her hands busy. It's just not possible to tell what he's thinking. She sliced neatly through bread and meat, prudently keeping her back to him. Looking down at her own hands, she thought of Slade's. He had such long, lean fingers. Strong. She'd liked the look of them. Now, she caught herself wondering how they would feel on her body. Competent, experienced, demanding. The flare of desire was quick, but not unexpected this time. Fighting it, she sliced the second sandwich a bit savagely.

He watched the sunlight stream through the window onto her hair. It fell softly on the varied hues of blue in her sweater. He liked the way the material clung to her, enhancing the straight, slender back and narrow waist. But he noted too the tension in her shoulders. He wasn't going to get very far if they were both preoccupied with an attraction neither wanted. He had to make her relax and talk. Slade knew one certain way of accomplishing that.

"You've got quite a place here, Jessica."

He wasn't aware that it was the first time he'd said her name, but she was. That pleased her as much as the careful compliment.

"Thank you." Belatedly she remembered to turn the burner on under the kettle as she brought his sandwich to the table. "People have finally stopped calling it Jessica's Little Hobby."

"Is that what it started out to be?"

"Not to me." She stretched on tiptoe to reach a cup. Slade watched the hem of her skirt sneak up. "But to a lot of people it was just Justice Winslow's daughter having a fling at business. Did you want a glass for that?"

"No." Slade brought the bottle to his lips and drank. "Why antiques?"

"It was something I knew . . . something I loved. It's sensible to make a career out of something you know and appreciate, don't you think?"

He thought of the standard police-issue revolver hidden in his bedroom. "When it's possible. How'd you get started?"

"I was lucky enough to have the funds to back me up the first year while I gathered stock and renovated this place." The kettle shrilled, then sputtered when she switched off the heat. "Even with that, it was hard enough. Setting up books, getting licenses, learning about taxes." She wrinkled her nose as she brought her plate and cup to the table. "But that's a necessary part of the whole. With that, the traveling, and the selling, the first couple of years were killers." She bit into her sandwich. "I loved it."

She would have, he mused. He could sense the pent-up energy even as she sat there calmly drinking tea. "David Ryce work for you long?"

"About a year and a half. He was at that undecided point of his life I suppose we all go through when we've finished being teenagers but haven't quite grasped adulthood." She smiled across the table at Slade. "Do you know what I mean?"

"More or less."

"You probably less than most," she commented easily. "As it turned out, he resented the offer of a job and the fact that he needed one. David and I grew up together. There's nothing harder on the ego than having big sister give you a break." She sighed a bit, remembering his moodiness, his grudging acceptance, his initial lack of interest. "Anyway, within six months he stopped being resentful and became indispensable. He's very quick, particularly with figures. David considers the books his province now. And he's better with them than the selling angle."

"Oh?"

Her eyes danced. "He isn't always . . . diplomatic with customers. He's much better with bookkeeping and inventory. Michael and I can handle the buying and selling."

"Michael." Before he drank again, Slade repeated the name as though it meant nothing.

"Michael does almost all my buying, all the imports at any rate."

"You don't buy the stock yourself?"

"Not from overseas, not anymore." Jessica toyed with the last half of her sandwich. "If I'd tried to keep up with it, I wouldn't have been able to keep the shop open year round. Watching out for estate sales and auctions just in the New England area takes me away from the shop enough as it is. And Michael . . . Michael has a real genius for finding gems."

He wondered if her analogy was fact. Was Michael Adams shipping gems as well as Hepplewhites across the Atlantic?

"Michael's been handling that part of the business for nearly three years," Jessica went on. "And he's not only a good buyer, but a terrific salesman. Particularly with my female clientele." She laughed as she lifted her cup. "He's very smooth—both looks and manner."

Slade noted the affection in her voice and speculated. Just how much was between owner and buyer? he wondered. If Adams was involved in smuggling, and Jessica's lover. . . His thoughts trailed off as he looked down at her hands. She wore a thin, twisted band of gold on her right hand and a star-shaped group of opals on her left. The sun hit the stones, shooting little flames of red into the delicate blue. It suited her, he thought, taking another swig of beer.

"In any case, I've gotten spoiled." Jessica stretched her shoulders with a sigh. "It's been a long time since I've had to run the shop alone. I'll be glad to have both Michael and David back next week. I might even take Uncle Charlie up on his invitation."

"Uncle Charlie?"

Her cup paused halfway to her lips. "Uncle Charlie," Jessica repeated, puzzled. "He sent you."

Slade gave a quick silent oath as he shrugged. "The commissioner," he said blandly. "I don't think of him as Uncle Charlie."

"The commissioner's awfully formal." Still frowning at him, Jessica set down her cup.

She's not a fool, Slade concluded as he swung an arm over the back of his chair. "I always call him that. Habit. Don't you like to travel?" He changed the subject neatly, adding a quick, disarming smile. "I'd think the buying end would be half the fun."

"It can be. It can also be a giant headache. Airports and auctions and customs." The line between her brows vanished. "I have been thinking about combining a business and pleasure trip next spring. I want to visit my mother and her husband in France."

"Your mother remarried?"

"Yes, it's been wonderful for her. After my father died, she was so lost. We both were," she murmured. And after nearly five years, she mused, there was still an ache. It was dull with time, but it was still there.

"There's nothing harder than to lose someone you loved and lived with and depended on. Especially when you think that person is indestructible; then he's taken away with no warning."

Her voice had thickened, touching off a chord of response in him. "I know," he answered before he thought.

Her eyes came up and fixed on his. "Do you?"

He didn't like the emotion she stirred up in him. "My father was a cop," he answered curtly. "He was killed in action five years ago."

"Oh, Slade." Jessica reached for his hand. "How terrible— how terrible for your mother."

"Wives of cops learn to live with the risk." He moved his hand back to his beer.

Sensing withdrawal, Jessica said nothing. He wasn't a man to share emotion of any kind easily. She rose, stacking plates. "Do you want something else? I imagine there're cookies stashed around here somewhere."

She wouldn't probe, he realized, wouldn't eulogize. She'd offered him her sympathy, then had backed off when she'd seen that it wasn't wanted. Slade sighed. It was difficult enough to deal with his attraction to her without starting to like her as well.

"No." He rose to help her clear the table.

When they entered the shop, Jessica went straight to the door to snap up the shade on the glass. Slade whirled sharply as he heard her quick cry of alarm. It was immediately followed by a laugh. "Mr. Layton." Jessica flipped the lock to admit him. "You scared the wits out of me."

He was tall, well dressed, and fiftyish. His bankerish suit was offset by a gray silk tie the same color as his hair. The rather thin, stern face lightened with a smile as he took Jessica's hand. "Sorry, dear, but then, you did the same to me." Glancing past her, he gave Slade an inquiring look.

"This is James Sladerman, Mr. Layton. He's staying with us for a while. David's been ill."

"Oh, nothing serious, I hope."

"Just the flu," Jessica told him. "But a heavy dose of it."

She gave him a sudden shrewd smile. "You always manage to pop in on me when I've just gotten in a shipment. I've just managed to get this one arranged, and another's on its way."

He chuckled, a hoarse sound due to his fondness for Cuban cigars. "It's more your predictability than chance, Miss Winslow. Your Michael's been in Europe for three weeks. I'd asked him to keep an eye out for a piece or two for me before he left."

"Oh, well—" The jingle of the door interrupted her. "Mr. Chambers, I didn't expect you back so soon."

Chambers gave her a rather sheepish smile as he removed his hat. "The box with the pearl inlay," he began. "I can't resist it."

"Go on ahead, my dear." Layton gave Jessica's shoulder a pat. "I'll just browse for the moment."

Pretending an interest in a collection of pewter, Slade watched both men. Layton browsed, lingering here and there to examine a piece. Once he drew out a pair of half glasses and crouched down to study the carving on a table. Slade could hear Jessica's quiet voice as she discussed a snuffbox with Chambers. He choked back a snort of derision at the idea of a rational man buying anything as ridiculous as a snuffbox. After telling Jessica to wrap the box, Chambers turned to fuss over a curio cabinet.

It was a simple matter for Slade to mentally note both men's descriptions and names. Later he would commit them to paper and call them in. Whoever they were, they appeared to have at least a basic knowledge of antiques—at least from what he could glean from their conversation as they both discussed the cabinet. Wandering to the counter, Slade glanced down at the ticket Jessica was writing up. Her handwriting was neat, feminine, and legible.

One eighteenth-century snuffbox. French with pearl inlay.

It was the price that had him doing a double take. "Are you kidding?" he asked aloud.

"Ssh!" She glanced over at her customers, saw that they were occupied, then sent Slade a wicked grin. "Don't you have any vices, Slade?"

"Immoral, not insane," he retorted, but the grin had appealed to him. He leaned a bit closer. "Do you?"

She let the look hold, enjoying the easy humor in his eyes. It was the first time she'd seen it. "No." She gave a low laugh. "Absolutely none."

For the first time he reached out to touch her voluntarily — just the tip of her hair with the tip of his finger. The pen slipped out of Jessica's hand. "Are you corruptible?" he murmured. He was still smiling, but she no longer felt easy. Jessica found herself grateful that the counter was between them and there were customers in the shop.

"I wouldn't have thought so," she managed. Layton's hoarse chuckle distracted her. Coming around the counter, Jessica walked toward her customers, giving Slade a wide berth.

Dangerous curves ahead, her mind warned. One wrong turn with this man and you'd be through the guardrail and over the cliff. She'd been too cautious for too long to be reckless now.

"It's a lovely little piece," she said to both men. "It arrived right after you'd left the other day, Mr. Chambers." She was aware, though he made no sound, when Slade turned his attention from her and wandered to the far end of the room.

In the end Chambers bought the cabinet, while Layton chose what Jessica referred to as a fauteuil and a console from the Louis XV period. Slade saw them as a chair and a table, too ornate for the average taste. But elegant names, he imagined, equaled elegant prices.

"With customers like that," he commented when the shop was empty, "you could open a place twice this size."

"I could," she agreed as she filed the slips. "But it's not what I want. And, of course, not everyone buys as freely. Those are men who know what they like and can afford to have it. It's my good fortune that they've taken to buying it here for the past year or so."

She watched him poke around, opening a drawer here and there until he settled in front of a corner cabinet. Inside was a collection of porcelain figures.

"Lovely, aren't they?" she commented as she joined him.

He kept his back to her, though that didn't prevent her scent from creeping into his senses. "Yeah, they're nice." She caught her bottom lip between her teeth. It wasn't often

Dresden was described as *nice*. "My mother likes things like this."

"I've always thought this was the best in the collection." Jessica opened the door and drew out a small, delicate shepherdess. "I nearly whisked her away for myself."

Slade frowned at it. "She does have a birthday."

"And a thoughtful son." Her eyes were dancing when he lifted his to them.

"How much?" he said flatly.

Jessica ran her tongue over her teeth. It was bargaining time. There was nothing she liked better. "Twenty dollars," she said impulsively.

He laughed shortly. "I'm not stupid, Jessica. How much?"

When she tilted her head, the stubborn line appeared between her brows. "Twenty-two fifty. That's my last offer."

Reluctantly, he smiled. "You're crazy."

"Take it or leave it," she said with a shrug. "It's your mother's birthday after all."

"It's worth a hell of a lot more than that."

"It certainly would be to her," Jessica agreed.

Frustrated, Slade stuck his hands in his pockets and frowned at the figurine again. "Twenty-five," he said.

"Sold." Before he could change his mind, Jessica hustled over to the counter and began to box it. With a deft move, she peeled the price tag from the bottom and dropped it in the trash. "I can gift-wrap if you like," she said. "No charge."

Slowly he walked over to the counter, watching as she laid the porcelain in a bed of tissue paper. "Why?"

"Because it's her birthday. Birthday presents should be wrapped."

"That's not what I mean." He put a hand on the box to stop her movements. "Why?" he repeated.

Jessica gave him a long, considering look. He didn't like favors, she concluded, and only took this one because it was for someone he cared for. "Because I want to."

His brow lifted and his eyes were suddenly very intense. "Do you always do what you want?"

"I give it my best shot. Doesn't everyone?"

Before he could answer, the door opened again. "Delivery for you, Miss Winslow."

Slade felt a stir of excitement as the delivery was off-loaded. Maybe, just maybe, there'd be something. He wanted to tie this case up quickly, neatly, and be gone . . . while he still had some objectivity. Jessica Winslow had a way of smearing the issue. They weren't a man and woman, and he couldn't forget it. He was a cop, she was a suspect. His job was to find out what he could, even if it meant turning evidence on her. Listening to her steady stream of excitement as he uncarted boxes, Slade thought he'd never known anyone who appeared less capable of dishonesty. But that was a feeling, a hunch. He needed facts.

In his temporary position as mover and hauler, he was able to examine each piece carefully. He caught no uneasiness from Jessica, but rather her appreciation for helping her check for damage during shipping. The twinge of conscience infuriated him. He was doing his job, he reminded himself. And it was her damn Uncle Charlie that had put him there. Another year, Slade told himself again. Another year and there'd be no commissioner to hand him special assignments as a baby sitter cum spy for goddaughters with amber eyes.

He found nothing. His instinct had told him he wouldn't but Slade could have used even a crumb to justify his presence. She never stopped moving. For the two hours it took to unload the shipment, Jessica was everywhere, polishing, arranging, dragging out empty crates. When there was nothing more to do, she looked around for more.

"That's it," Slade told her before she could decide that something might be shown to a better advantage somewhere else.

"I guess you're right." Absently, she rubbed at the small of her back. "It's a good thing those three pieces are being shipped out Monday. It's a bit crowded. Hey, I'm starving." She turned to him with an apologetic smile. "I didn't mean to keep you so long, Slade. It's after five." Without giving him a chance to comment, she dashed to the back room for their jackets. "Here, I'll close up."

"How about a hamburger and a movie?" he said impulsively. I'm just keeping an eye on her, he told himself. That's what I'm here to do.

Surprised, Jessica glanced around as she pulled down the

last shade. From the look on his face, she thought, amused, he was already half regretting having asked. But that was no reason to let him off the hook. "What a romantic invitation. How can I refuse?"

"You want romance?" he countered. "We'll go to a drive-in movie."

He heard her quick gurgle of laughter as he grabbed her hand and pulled her outside.

It was late when the phone rang. The seated figure reached for it and a cigarette simultaneously. "Hello."

"Where's the desk?"

"The desk?" Frowning, he brought the flame to the tip and drew. "It's with the rest of the shipment, of course."

"You're mistaken." The voice was soft and cold. "I've been to the shop myself."

"It has to be there." A flutter of panic rose in his throat. "Jessica just hasn't unpacked it yet."

"Possibly. You'll clear this up immediately. I want the desk and its contents by Wednesday." The pause was slight. "You understand the penalty for mistakes."

3

*J*essica woke thinking of him. She took time on the lazy Sunday morning to ponder the very odd Saturday she had spent—most of it with Slade. A moody man, she mused, stretching her arms toward the ceiling. By turns she had been comfortable with him, exasperated by him, and attracted to him. No, that wasn't quite true, she amended. Even when she'd been comfortable or exasperated, she'd been attracted. There was something remote about him that made her want to pry him open a bit. She'd put quite a lot of effort into that the evening before and had come up with nothing. He wasn't a man for divulging secrets or bothering with small talk. He was an odd combination of the direct and the aloof.

He didn't flatter—not by looks or words. And yet she felt certain that he wasn't indifferent to her. It wasn't possible that she'd imagined those moments of physical pull. They'd been there, for him as well as for her. But he had guards, she thought with quick frustration. She'd never known a man with such guards. Those dark, intense eyes of his clearly said "Keep back; arm's length." While the challenge of piercing his armor appealed to her, her own instinctive awareness of what the consequences would be held her back. Jessica enjoyed a dare, but she usually figured the odds first. In this case, she decided, they were stacked against her.

A nice, cautious friendship was in order, she concluded. Anything else spelled trouble. Rising, she picked up her robe and headed for the shower. But wouldn't it be nice, she thought, to feel that rather hard mouth on hers. Just once.

Downstairs, Slade was closeted in the library. He'd been up since dawn—she was crowding his mind. What crazy impulse had prompted him to ask her out the night before? After downing his fourth cup of coffee, Slade lit a cigarette. For God's sake, he didn't have to date the woman to do his job. She was getting to him, he admitted as he pushed a pile of books aside. That low, musical laugh and all that soft blond hair. It was more than that, he thought ruefully. It was her. She was too close to possessing all the things he'd ever wanted in a woman—warmth, generosity, intelligence. And that steamy, almost primitive sexuality you could sense just under the surface. If he kept thinking of her that way, it was going to cloud his objectivity. Even now he was finding himself trying to work out a way to keep her out of the middle.

When Slade drew on the cigarette, his eyes were hard and opaque. He'd protect her when the time came, expose her if it came to that. But there was no way to keep her out of it. Still, over the mix of leather and dust and smoke, he thought he caught a lingering trace of her scent.

After evading the cook's admonishment to put something in her stomach, Jessica drank a hurried cup of coffee. "Where's David?" she called out when she spotted Betsy, armed with a rag and a bottle of silver polish.

"He took a walk down to the beach." His mother harrumphed a bit, but added, "He looks better. I guess the air'll do him good."

"I'll grab a jacket and check on him."

"Long as he doesn't know that's what you're up to."

"Betsy!" Jessica feigned offense. "I'm much too good for that." As the housekeeper snorted, the doorbell sounded. "Go ahead," Jessica told her. "I'll get it." She made a dash for the door. "Michael!" With pleasure, she threw her arms around his neck. "It's good to have you back."

Slade came into the hall in time to see Jessica embraced and kissed. With that low promising laugh, she pressed her cheek against the cheek of a slender, dark-haired man with smooth features and light green eyes. Michael Adams, Slade concluded, after conquering the urge to stride up to the couple and yank them apart. The description fit. He caught the gleam of a diamond on the man's pinky as he ran his hand through Jessica's hair. Soft hands and a sunlamp tan, Slade thought instantly.

"I've missed you, darling." Michael drew Jessica back far enough to smile into her face.

She laughed again, touching a hand to his cheek before she stepped out of his arms. "Knowing you, Michael, you were too busy with business and . . . other things to miss anyone. How many broken hearts did you leave in Europe?"

"I never break them," Michael claimed before brushing her lips again. "And I did miss you."

"Come inside and tell me everything," she ordered while tucking her arm through his. "The stock you sent back is wonderful, as always. I've already sold . . . oh, hello, Slade." The moment Jessica turned, she saw him. Quickly, potently, his eyes locked on hers. She had to use all of her strength of will not to draw in her breath. Was there a demand in them? she wondered. A question? Confused, she gave a slight shake of her head. What was it he wanted from her? And why was she ready to give it without even knowing what it was?

"Jessica." There was a faint smile on his face as he waited.

"Michael, this is James Sladerman. He's staying with us for a while and trying to make some order out of the library."

"No small job from what I've seen of it," Michael commented. "I hope you've got plenty of time."

"Enough."

Knowing the housekeeper would be close enough to eavesdrop, Jessica stepped away from Michael and called her. "Betsy, could we have coffee in the parlor? Slade, you'll join us?"

She had expected him to refuse, but he gave her a slow smile. "Sure." He didn't have to look at Michael to see the annoyance before they walked into the parlor.

"Why, Jessica, what's the Queen Anne doing here?"

"Fate," she told him, then laughed as she sat on the sofa. "I'd meant to ask you to find one for me. When I saw it on the shipping list, I wondered if you were psychic."

After studying it for a moment, he nodded. "It certainly

suits this room." He sat next to Jessica as Slade settled in an armchair. "No problem with the shipments?"

"No, they're already unpacked. As a matter of fact, three pieces go out tomorrow. David's been ill this past week. Slade helped me get things in order yesterday."

"Really?" Michael took out a wafer-thin gold case, then offered Slade a cigarette. Refusing with a shake of his head, Slade pulled out his own pack. "Do you know antiques, Mr. Sladerman?".

"No." Slade struck a match, watching Michael over the flame. "Unless we count the lesson Jessica gave me yesterday."

Michael sat back, tossing an arm casually over the back of the sofa. "What do you do?" His smooth, neat fingers toyed absently with Jessica's hair. Slade took a hard drag on his cigarette.

"I'm a writer."

"Fascinating. Would I have read any of your work?"

He gave Michael a long, steady stare. "I wouldn't think so."

"Slade is working on a novel," Jessica intervened. There were undercurrents that made her uncomfortable. "You haven't told me yet what it's about."

He caught the look in her eye, recognizing it as a plea for peace. Not yet, he decided. We'll just see what we can stir up. "Smuggling," he said flatly. There was a loud clatter of china from the doorway.

"Damn!" David took a firmer grip on the tray, then gave Jessica a sheepish smile. "I almost dropped the whole works."

"David!" She sprang up to take the coffee tray from him. "You can hardly carry yourself, much less all this." Slade watched him give her a disgruntled look before he flopped into a chair.

David was still pale—or had the loss of color come when smuggling had been mentioned? Slade wondered. There was a faint line of sweat on his brow between his mop of hair and his glasses. After setting down the tray, Jessica turned back to him.

"How do you feel?"

David scowled at her. "Don't fuss."

"All right." She leaned over until her face was level with his. "If I'd known you were going to be such a bad patient, I'd have brought you some crayons and colored paper."

Though he gave her hair a hard tug, he grinned. "Get me some coffee and shut up."

"Oh, yes, sir," she said meekly.

When she turned, David sent Slade a quick wink. "Gotta know how to handle these society types. Hi, Michael. Welcome back." Reaching in his pocket, he found a crumpled pack of cigarettes. As he searched for matches, his eyes lit on the desk. "Hey, what's this?"

"One of Michael's finds I've already laid claim to," Jessica told him as she brought him his coffee. "You can take care of the paperwork next week."

"Monday," he said firmly, eyeing the desk. "Queen Anne."

"It's lovely, isn't it?" She handed Slade a cup before crossing to it. Opening the lid, she showed off the inside.

Slade felt the back of his neck prickle. There was a rise in tension, he felt it—could nearly smell it. Shifting his eyes from Jessica, he studied both men. Michael added cream to his coffee. David found his match. With a half shrug, Slade told himself he was getting jumpy.

"And wait until you see the rest of the stock," Jessica told David as she came back to the sofa. "Michael outdid himself."

Slade let the conversation hum around him, answering briefly if he was asked a direct question. She was crazy about the kid, he concluded. It showed in the way she teased, lightly bullied, and catered to him. Slade remembered her comment about having wanted a brother or sister. David was obviously her substitute. How far would she go to protect him? he wondered. *All the way* flashed through his mind. If there was one firm impression he'd gotten from Jessica Winslow, it was loyalty.

Her relationship with Michael was less defined. If they were lovers, Slade concluded that she was very casual about it. Somehow he didn't feel Jessica would be casual about intimacy. Passion, he thought again. There was hot, vibrant passion smoldering in that slender little body. If Michael was her lover, Slade would have seen some sign of it in the kiss they had exchanged at the door.

If she had been in his arms, it would have been there, he thought as his gaze drifted to her mouth. It was soft and unpainted. From ten feet away he could all but taste it. Slowly, irresistibly, desire crept into him, and with it an ache—a dull, throbbing ache he'd never felt before. If he could have her, even once, the ache would go. Slade could almost convince himself of that. He needed to touch that butter-soft skin, experience that promise of passion, then he'd be free of her. He had to be free of her.

Glancing up, Jessica found herself trapped again. His eyes imprisoned her. She could feel herself being pulled—as physical a sensation as if he had taken her hand. She resisted. He's quicksand, her mind flashed. You'll never get away if you take that final step. And yet the risk tempted her.

"Jessica."

Michael took her hand, scattering her thoughts. "Hmm, yes?"

"How about dinner tonight? The little place up the coast you like."

His calm, familiar green eyes smiled at her. Jessica felt her pulses level. This was a man she understood. "I'd love to."

"And don't worry about getting home early," David put in. "I'm minding the shop tomorrow; you stay home."

Jessica lifted her brow at the order. "Oh, really?"

David snorted at the dry tone. "There goes Miss Radcliffe," he told Slade. "She forgets I was around when she was twelve and had braces on her teeth."

"How would you like to be flat on your back again?" she invited sweetly. "I'll be ready at seven," she told Michael, ignoring David's grin.

"Fine." Giving her a quick kiss, Michael rose. "See you tomorrow, David. Nice to meet you, Mr. Sladerman."

As he left, Jessica set down her cup and sprang up, as if she had been in one place too long. "I'm going to take Ulysses for a walk on the beach."

"Don't look at me," David drawled. "I have to conserve my energy."

"I wasn't going to ask you. Slade?"

He would have liked to steer clear of her for a while. Resigned, he rose. "Sure. I'll get a jacket."

The beach was long and rocky. From off the bay, the breeze was keen and tinged with salt. Jessica was laughing, stooping to pick up driftwood and toss it for the dog to chase. Ulysses bounded up the beach and back again, running energetic circles around them until Jessica flung another stick. To the right, water hurled itself on rocks, then rose in a misty spray. Slade watched Jessica run to another piece of driftwood.

Doesn't she ever walk? he wondered. She laughed again, holding the stick over her head as the dog leaped clumsily at it. *Don't contact us unless you have something useful.* Slade jammed his hands in his pockets as he remembered his orders. *Watch the woman.* He was watching the woman, damn it. And she was getting to him. Watch what the sunlight does to her hair. Watch how a pair of faded jeans cling to narrow hips. Watch how her mouth curves when she smiles. . . . Watch Detective Sladerman blow everything because he can't keep his mind off a skinny woman with brandy-colored eyes.

"What are you thinking?"

He snapped back to find Jessica a step in front of him searching his face. Cursing himself, he realized he was going to blow more than his cover if he wasn't careful. "That I haven't been to the beach in a long time," he improvised.

Jessica narrowed her eyes. "No, I don't think so," she murmured. "I wonder what it is about you that makes you so secretive." With an impatient gesture, she pushed back her hair. The wind immediately blew it back in her face. "But it's your business, I suppose."

Annoyed, he picked up a rock and hurled it into the breakers. "I wonder what it is about you that makes you so suspicious."

"Curious," she corrected, a bit puzzled by his choice of word. "You're an interesting man, Slade, perhaps because there's so much you don't say."

"What do you want, a biography?"

"You annoy easily," she murmured.

He whirled to her. "Don't push it, Jess."

The nickname pleased her—no one but her father had ever

used it. The fury on his face pleased her too. She'd poked the first hole in his shield. "And if I do?" she challenged.

"You'll get pushed back. I'm not polite."

She laughed. "No, you damn well aren't. Should that scare me?"

She was baiting him. Even knowing it didn't help. Slim and strong, she stood in front of him, her hair whipped around her face by the wind. Her eyes were gold and insolent. No, she wouldn't scare easily. Slade told himself it was to prove a point. Even as he yanked her into his arms, he told himself it was to prove a point. He saw it on her face: anticipation, acceptance. No fear. Cursing her, he brought his mouth down hard on hers.

It was as he thought it would be. Soft, fragrant, pliant. She melted like wax in his arms even as his lips bruised hers. A man could drown in her. The pounding of the surf seemed to echo in his head. There was a sensation of standing in the surf, having it ebb and suck the sand from under him. He dragged her closer.

Her breasts yielded against the hard line of his chest, tempting him to explore their shape with his hands. But all his power, all his concentration, was bound up in the pressure of mouth to mouth. Her hands slid under his jacket, up his back, pressing, urging him to take more. Head swimming, he drew away, struggling to separate himself. With a long, shaky breath, Jessica dropped her head on his shoulder.

"I nearly suffocated."

His arms were still around her. He'd meant to drop them. Now, with her snuggled close, her hair brushing his cheek, he wasn't certain he could. Then she tilted her face to his—she was smiling.

"You're supposed to breathe through your nose," he told her.

"I think I forgot."

So did I, he mused. "Then take a deep breath," Slade suggested. "I'm not nearly finished yet."

With no less force, with no less turbulence, his mouth returned to hers. This time she was prepared. No longer passive, Jessica made demands of her own. Her lips parted and her tongue met his, searching, teasing, tasting. His flavor was as dark and unsettling as she had imagined. Greedy, she dove deeper. She heard his moan, felt the sudden race of his heart against her own. An urgency filled her so quickly that it took total command. There was nothing but him—his arms, his lips. He was all she wanted.

She had never felt this kind of need or this kind of power. Even when his lips were brutal, she returned the same aggression. Arousal was too tame a word, excitement too bland. Jessica felt a frenzy, a burst of energy that could only be tamed by possession.

Touch me! she wanted to scream as her fingers gripped his hair desperately. Take me! It's never been like this and I can't bear to lose it. She strained against him, her gesture as much a demand as an offering. He was stronger, she knew—the sleek, hard muscles warned her—but his need could be no greater. No need could be greater than the one that throbbed in her, pounded in her. Her body felt assaulted, both helpless and invulnerable.

Oh show me, she thought dizzily. I've waited so long to really know.

A gull screamed overhead. Like a spray of ice water, it jolted Slade back. What the hell was he doing? he demanded as he pushed Jessica away. Or more to the point, what was she doing to him? He'd lost everything—his purpose, his identity, his sanity—in one heady taste of her. Now she stared at him, cheeks flushed with passion, eyes dark with it. Her mouth was moist and swollen from his, parted, with her breath coming rapidly.

"Slade." With his name husky on her lips, she reached for him.

Roughly, he caught her wrist before she could touch him. "You'd better go in."

There was nothing in his eyes now. They were opaque again, unreadable. He stared down at her with a complete lack of interest. For an instant she was too confused to understand. He'd taken her to the edge, to that thin, tenuous border, then had rudely shoved her back as though she hadn't moved him in the least. Shame flooded her face with color. Anger stole in again.

"Damn you," she whispered. Turning, she dashed for the beach steps and took them two at a time.

Jessica dressed with care. There was nothing like the feel of silk against the skin to salve wounded pride. Turning sideways in front of the full-length mirror, she gave a nod of approval. The lines of the dress were simple, except for the surprising plunge in the back that dipped just below the waist. It didn't bother her conscience that she had chosen the dress more with Slade in mind than Michael. And the color suited her mood—a deep, imperial purple. She swept her hair back from her face with two diamond-crusted pins, then let it fall as it chose. Satisfied, Jessica grabbed her evening bag and started downstairs.

She found Slade in the parlor, tightening a screw in a Chippendale commode. His hands were lean and competent. She remembered the feel of them when they'd run over her body in a quick, desperate search. "Well, aren't you handy," Jessica stated.

He glanced up, frowned, and tightened his grip on the screwdriver. Did she have to look like that? he thought darkly. The dress clung everywhere, and from the way she walked by him, he knew she was aware of it. Slade turned the screw savagely. "Betsy complained that the handle was loose," he muttered.

"Jack of all trades," she said lightly. "Drink? I'm fixing martinis."

He started to refuse, then made the mistake of looking over at her. Her back was naked and slim and smooth. The silk shifted enticingly as she reached for a bottle of vermouth. Desire was as breathtaking as a punch in the solar plexus.

"Scotch," he snapped.

She smiled over her shoulder. "Rocks?"

"Straight up."

"Drink like a man, do you, Slade?" Oh, she'd get through that damned indifference, Jessica vowed. And enjoy every minute of it. After pouring him three fingers, she brought the glass to him. He slipped the screwdriver into the back pocket of his jeans and rose. Keeping his eyes on hers, Slade took a long, slow sip of Scotch.

"Dress like a woman, do you, Jess?"

Determined to rattle him, she turned a circle. "Like it?"

"Did you wear it to stir up Adams' juices or mine?" he countered.

With a provocative smile, she turned away to finish the martinis. "Do you think women always dress to stir men up?"

"Don't they?"

"Normally I dress for myself." After pouring a drink, she turned back to regard him over the rim. "Tonight I thought I'd test a theory."

He went to her. The challenge in her eyes and his own ego made it imperative, just as she had anticipated. "What theory?"

Jessica met his angry gaze without faltering. "Do you have any weaknesses, Slade? Any Achilles' heel?"

Deliberately he set down his own glass, then took hers. He felt her stiffen, though she didn't back away. His fingers circled her neck, coaxing her lips to within an inch of his. She felt the warm rush of his breath on her skin.

"You could regret finding out, Jess. I won't treat you like a lady."

She tossed her head back. Though her heart was hammering, she met his eyes with an angry dare. "Who asked you to?"

His fingers tightened; her lashes lowered. The doorbell rang. Slade picked up his drink and downed the rest of it. "Your date," he said shortly, then stalked out of the room.

Slade pulled his car to a halt a short distance away from the restaurant, switched off the engine, pulled out a cigarette, then waited. Michael's Daimler was just being parked by the valet. Slade would have been more comfortable if he could have slipped inside to keep a closer eye on Jessica, but that was too risky.

He saw the car pull up behind him. Tension pricked at the back of his neck as the driver climbed out to approach his car. Slade slipped a hand inside his jacket and gripped the butt of his gun. A badge was pressed against the window glass. Slade relaxed as the man rounded the hood to enter by the passenger side.

"Sladerman." Agent Brewster gave a quick nod of greeting. "You follow the lady, I follow the man. Commissioner Dodson told you I'd be in touch?"

"Yeah."

"Greenhart's looking after Ryce. Not a lot of action there; the guy's been laid up for more than a week. You've got nothing yet, I take it."

"Nothing" Slade shifted to a more comfortable position. "I spent the day at her shop Saturday, helped her uncart a new shipment. If there was anything in it, I'd swear she didn't know it. I had my hands all over everything in that place. She's too damn casual to be hiding anything."

"Maybe." With a weighty sigh, Brewster pulled out a worn black pipe and began to pack it. "If that fancy little shop's the dump site, at least one of 'em's hiding something . . . maybe all three. Seems Ryce is like baby brother. As for Adams . . ." Brewster struck a match and sucked on his pipe. Slade said nothing. "Well, the lady's got the justice's name behind her and a lot of political pressure to keep her name clear, but if she's involved, it's going to hit the fan."

"She's not," he heard himself say, then flipped his cigarette out the window.

"You're in the majority," Brewster commented easily. "Even if she's as pure as a mother's heart, she's in a hell of a spot right now. Pressure's building, Sladerman. The lid's going to blow real soon, and when it does, it's going to get ugly. Winslow might find herself right in the middle. Dodson seems to think you're good enough to keep her out of the way when it goes down."

"I'll take care of her," Slade muttered. "I don't like her being alone with Adams in there."

"Well, I missed my dinner." Brewster touched his rounded stomach. "I'll just go eat on the taxpayers' money and keep an eye on your lady."

"She's not my lady," Slade mumbled.

The restaurant was quiet and candlelit. By the table where Jessica sat with Michael was a breathtaking view of the Sound. On the night-black water there was moonlight and the scattered reflection of stars. The murmur of diners was discreet—low tones, soft laughter. The scent of fresh flowers mixed with the aroma of food and candlewax. Champagne buzzed pleasantly in her head. If someone had told her she'd been working too hard lately, Jessica would have laughed. But now she was completely relaxed for the first time in over a week.

"I'm glad you thought of this, Michael."

He liked the way the light flickered over her face, throwing a mystery of shadows under her cheekbones, enhancing the odd golden hue of her eyes. Why was it she always seemed that much more beautiful when he'd been away from her? And had he, for a dozen foolish reasons, waited too long?

"Jessica." He brought her hand to his lips. "I've missed you."

The gesture and the tone of his voice surprised her. "It's good to have you back, Michael."

Odd that he'd always been known for his smooth lines and was now unable to think how to proceed. "Jessica . . . I want you to start coming with me on the buying trips."

"Come with you?" Her brow creased. "Why, Michael? You're more than capable of handling that end. I hate to admit it, but you're much better at it than I."

"I don't want to be away from you again."

Puzzled, Jessica gave a quick laugh as she squeezed his hand. "Michael, don't tell me you were lonely. I know there's nothing you like better than zipping around Europe hunting up treasures. If you were homesick, it's a first."

His fingers tightened on hers. "I wasn't homesick, Jessica, and there was only one thing I was lonely for. I want you to marry me."

Surprise was a mild term; Jessica was stunned, and her face was transparent. *Marry?* She nearly thought she had misunderstood him. She could hardly conceive of Michael wanting to be married at all, but to her? They'd been together for nearly three years, business associates, friends, but never . . .

"Jessica, you must know how I feel." He placed a hand over their joined ones. "I've loved you for years."

"Michael, I had no idea. Oh, Michael, that sounds so trite." She ran the fingers of her free hand up and down the stem of her glass. "I don't know what to say to you."

"Say yes."

"Michael, why now? Why all of a sudden?" She stopped the nervous movement of her hand and studied him. "You never even hinted that you had any feelings for me other than affection."

"Do you know how hard it's been," he asked quietly, "contenting myself with that? Jessica, you weren't ready for my feelings. You've been so wrapped up in making a success out of the shop. You needed to make a success of it. And I wanted to build up my own part of it before I asked you. We both needed to be independent."

It was true, all that he said. And yet how was she to suddenly stop seeing him as Michael, her friend, her associate, and see him as Michael, her lover, her husband? "I don't know."

He squeezed her hand, either in reassurance or frustration. "I didn't expect you would so quickly. Will you think about it?"

"Yes, of course I will." And even as she promised, the memory of a violent embrace on a windy beach ran through her mind.

In the late hours the phone rang, but it didn't wake him. He'd been expecting it.

"You've located my property?"

He moistened his lips, then dried them again with the back of his hand. "Yes . . . Jessica took the desk home. There's a small problem."

"I don't like problems."

Cold beads of sweat broke out on his forehead. "I'll get the diamonds out. It's just that Jessica's always around. There's no way I can take the desk apart and get them while she's in the house. I need some time to convince her to go away for a few days."

"Twenty-four hours."

"But that's not—"

"That's all the time you have . . . or all the time Miss Winslow will have."

Sweat coated his lip and he lifted a trembling hand to wipe it away. "Don't do anything to her. I'll get them."

"For Miss Winslow's sake, be successful. Twenty-four hours," he repeated. "If you don't have them by then, she'll be disposed of. I'll retrieve my property myself."

"No! I'll get them. Don't hurt her. You swore she'd never have to be involved."

"She involved herself. Twenty-four hours."

4

Jessica had no answers. Alone, she sat on the beach, chin on her knees, and watched the early sun spread streaks of pink above the water. Yards away, Ulysses chased the surf, bounding back to the shore each time it turned on him. He'd given up on the idea of conning Jessica into tossing sticks for him.

She'd always liked the beach at sunrise. It helped her think. The screech of gulls, the pound of water against rock, the burgeoning light, always calmed her mind so that an answer could be found. Not this time. It wasn't as if she'd never considered marriage, sharing a home, raising a family—but she'd never had a clear picture of the man. Could it be Michael?

She enjoyed being with him, talking to him. They shared interests. But . . . oh, there was a *but*, she thought as she lowered her forehead to her knees. An enormous *but*. And he loved her. She'd been blind to it. Where was her sensitivity? she wondered with a surge of guilt and frustration. How could a thing—a business—have been so important that it blocked her vision? Worse, now that she knew, what was she to do about it?

Slade came down the beach steps swearing. How the hell could he keep a rein on a woman who took off before sunrise? Gone walking on the beach, Betsy had told him. Alone on a deserted beach, Slade thought grimly, completely vulnerable to anything and anyone. Did she always have to be moving, doing? Why couldn't she have been the lazy halfwit he'd imagined her to be?

Then he spotted her—head down, shoulders slumped. If it hadn't been for the mass of wheat-colored hair, he would have sworn it was another woman. Jessica stood straight and was always heading somewhere—usually too fast. She didn't curl up in a ball of defeat. Uncomfortable, he thrust his hands in his pockets and walked toward her.

She didn't hear him, but sensed the intrusion and the identity of the intruder almost simultaneously. Slowly she straightened, then looked out at the horizon again.

"Good morning," she said when he stood beside her. "You're up early."

"So are you."

"You worked late. I heard your typewriter."

"Sorry."

"No." A fleeting smile. "I liked it. Is the book going well?"

Slade glanced up as a gull soared over their heads, white-breasted and silent. "It moved for a while last night." Something's wrong, he thought. He started to sit beside her, then changed his mind and remained standing. "What is it, Jess?"

She didn't answer immediately, but turned her head to study his face. And what would he do, she wondered, if he wanted a woman to marry him? Would he wait patiently, choose the best time, then be satisfied when she asked him to wait for an answer? A ghost of a smile touched her lips. God no.

"Have you had many lovers?" she asked.

"What!"

She didn't pay any attention to his incredulous expression but turned to stare out at the surf again. "I imagine you have," she murmured. "You're a very physical man." The clouds skimming over the water were shot through with red and gold. As she spoke Jessica watched them brighten. "I can count mine on three fingers," she continued in a tone that was more absent than confidential. "The first was in college, a relationship so brief it hardly seems fair to include it. He sent me carnations and read Shelley out loud."

She laughed a little as she settled her chin back on her knees. "Later, when I was touring Europe, there was this older man, French, very sophisticated. I fell like a ton of bricks . . . then I found out he was married and had two children." Shaking her head, Jessica gripped her knees tighter. "After that there was an advertising executive. Oh, he had a way with words. It was right after my father died, and I was . . . groping. He borrowed ten thousand dollars from me and vanished. I haven't been involved with a man since." She brooded out to sea. "I didn't want to get stung again, so I've been careful. Maybe too careful."

He wasn't overly pleased to hear about the men in her life. Forcing himself to be objective, he listened. When she fell silent, Slade dropped down beside her. For the space of a full minute, there was nothing but the sound of crashing waves and calling gulls.

"Jess, why are you telling me this?"

"Maybe because I don't know you. Maybe because it seems I've known you for years." A bit shakily, she laughed and dragged her hands through her hair. "I don't know." Taking a deep breath, she stared straight ahead. "Michael asked me to marry him."

It hit him hard—like a stunning blow to the back of the neck that leaves you disoriented just for an instant before unconsciousness. Very deliberately Slade gathered a handful of sand, then let it sift through his fingers. "And?"

"And I don't know what to do!" She turned to him then, all turbulent eyes and frustration. "I hate not knowing what to do."

Stop it now, he ordered himself. Tell her you're not interested in hearing about her problems. But the words were already slipping out. "How do you feel about him?"

"I depend on Michael," she began, talking fast. "He's part of my life. He's important to me, very important—"

"But you don't love him," Slade finished calmly. "Then you should know what to do."

"It's not that simple," she tossed back. With a sound of exasperation, she started to rise, then made herself sit still. "He's in love with me. I don't want to hurt him, and maybe . . ."

"Maybe you should marry him so he won't be hurt?" Slade gave a mirthless laugh. "Don't be such an idiot."

Anger rose quickly and was as quickly suppressed. It was difficult to argue with logic. More miserable than offended, she watched a gull swoop low over the water. "I know marrying him would only hurt both of us in the long run, especially if his feelings for me are as deep as he thinks they are."

"You're not sure he's in love with you," Slade murmured, considering the other reasons Michael might want her to marry him.

"I'm sure he thinks he is," Jessica returned. "I thought maybe if we became lovers, then—"

"Good God!" He caught her by the shoulder roughly. "Are you considering offering your body as some sort of consolation prize?"

"Don't!" She shut her eyes so she couldn't see the derision in his. "You make it sound so dirty."

"What the hell are you thinking of?" he demanded.

In an uncharacteristic gesture of futility she lifted her hands. "My track record with men has been so poor, I thought . . . well, given a little time he'd change his mind."

"Imbecile," Slade said shortly. "Just tell him no."

"Now you make it sound so easy."

"You're making it complicated, Jess."

"Am I?" For a moment she lowered her forehead to her knees again. His hand was halfway to her hair before he stopped himself. "You're so sure of yourself, Slade. Nothing makes a coward of me more than people I care about. The idea of facing him again, knowing what I have to do, makes me want to run."

He was responding to the fragility she so rarely showed. Deep inside him, something struggled to be free to comfort her. He banked it down an instant before it was too late. "He won't be the first man who's had a proposal turned down."

She sighed. Nothing she'd said had made sense once it had been spoken aloud—everything he said had. Some of the burden lifted. With a half smile, she turned to him. "Have you?"

"Have I what?"

"Had a proposal turned down."

He grinned, pleased that the lost look had left her eyes. "No . . . but then, marriage didn't figure in any of them."

She gave her quick gurgle of laughter. "What did?"

Reaching over, he grabbed a handful of her hair. "Is this color real?"

"That's an abominably rude question."

"One deserves another," he countered.

"If I answer yours will you answer mine?"

"No."

"Then I suppose we'll both have to use our imagination." Jessica laughed again and started to rise, but the hand on her hair stopped her.

The quizzical smile she gave him faded quickly. His eyes were fixed on hers, dark, intense, and for once readable. Desire. Hot, electric, restless desire. And she was drawn to him, already aroused by a look. For the first time she was afraid. He was going to take something from her she wouldn't easily get back, if she managed to get it back at all. He pulled her closer, and she resisted. In an instinctive defense against a nebulous fear, Jessica put her hands to his chest.

"No. This isn't what I want." *Yes, yes, it is,* her eyes told him even while her hands pushed him away.

In one move she was under him on the sand. "I warned you, I wouldn't treat you like a lady."

His mouth lowered, took, and enticed. Fear was buried in an avalanche of passion. At the first taste of him, response overwhelmed her, wild and free. Jessica forgot what she stood to lose and simply experienced. His tongue probed, slowly searching, expertly seducing, while his lips crushed hers in an endless, exquisite demand. She answered, mindlessly willing, desperately wanting. Then he tore his mouth from hers to move over her face, as if to absorb the texture of her skin through the sense of taste alone.

She fretted to have his lips on hers, turning her head in search. Then suddenly, fiercely, he buried his lips at her throat, wrenching a moan from her. The sand made whispering sounds as she shifted, wanting the agonized delight he was causing to go on and on.

Her hands found their way under his sweater, up the planes

and muscles of his back, down the hard line of ribs to a lean waist. The moist air smelled of salt and the sea, and faintly, of the musky scent of passion. His mouth found hers again, unerringly, as water crashed like thunder on the rocks nearby. She felt his lips move against hers, though the meaning of his murmur was lost to her. Only the tone—a hint of angry desperation—came through. Then his hands began to search, with bruising meticulousness, from her hips to her breasts, lingering there as if trapped by the softness. She was unaware of the sun beating down on her closed lids, of the coarse sand under her back. There was only his lips and hands now.

Calloused fingers ran over her skin, scraping, kindling fresh fires while feeding those already ablaze. Roughly he caught her bottom lip between his teeth, drawing it into his mouth to suck and nibble until her sighs were moans. In a sudden frenzy Jessica arched against him, center to throbbing center. Denim strained against denim in a thin, frustrating barrier.

On a groan, Slade buried his face in her hair, immersed in the scent of it as he groped for control. But there'd be no control, he knew, with the taste and scent and feel of her overpowering him.

With a muffled oath he rolled from her, springing up before she could touch him and make him forget all reason.

Slade drew air into his lungs harshly, letting it cool the heat that radiated through him. He had to be out of his mind, he thought, to have come that close to taking her. Seconds passed. He could tick them off by the sound of her unsteady breathing behind him. And his own.

"Jess—"

"No, don't say anything. I get the picture." Her voice was thick and wavering. When he turned back, she had risen to brush off the clinging sand. The glint of the morning sun haloed the crown of her head even while the breeze tossed the ends up and back. "You changed your mind. Everyone's entitled." When she started to walk by him, Slade gripped her arm. Jessica jerked against his hold, found it firm, then threw up her chin.

Hurt. Slade could see it all too well beneath the anger in her eyes. It was better that way, he told himself. Smarter. But the words came out of his mouth before he could stop them. "Would you prefer that we'd made love on the beach like a couple of teenagers?"

She'd forgotten where they'd been. Place and time hadn't mattered when the need to love had been paramount. It only cut deeper into her pride that he had remembered and had maintained enough control to stop. "I'd prefer you didn't touch me again," she returned coolly. She lowered her eyes to his restraining hand, then lifted them again, slowly. "Starting now."

Slade's grip only tightened. "I warned you once not to push me."

"Push you?" Jessica retorted. "I didn't start this, I didn't want this."

"No, you didn't start it." He took her shoulders now, giving her three hard shakes. "And I didn't want it either, so back off."

Her teeth snapped together on the final shake. If hurt had outweighed anger before, now the tide was turned. Enraged, Jessica knocked both of his hands away. "Don't you dare shout at me!" she yelled, outdoing him in volume. Behind them water hurled itself against rock, then lifted in a tumultuous spray. "And don't intimate that I've thrown myself at you because I haven't." With her arms pinned, she had to toss her head to free it of blowing hair. Her eyes glinted behind the dancing strands. "I'd have you crawling on your hands and knees if I wanted!"

His eyes became gray slits. Anger mixed with an uncomfortable certainty that she probably could. "I don't crawl for any woman, much less some snotty little twit who uses perfume as a weapon."

"Snotty little—" She broke off, sputtering. "*Twit!*" she managed after an outraged moment. "Why, you simple-minded, egotistical ass." Unable to think of a better defense, she shoved a hand against his chest. "I hope you haven't put a woman in that novel of yours because you know zip! I'm not even *wearing* any perfume. And I wouldn't need—" Breathing hard, Jessica trailed off. "What the hell are you grinning at?"

"Your face is pink," he told her. "It's cute."

Her eyes flashed, golden fury. The intent for violence was clear in the step she took toward him. Lifting his hands aloft, palms out, Slade stepped back.

"Truce?" He wasn't sure when or how, but sometime during her diatribe his anger had simply vanished. He was almost sorry. Fighting with her was nearly as stimulating as kissing her. Nearly.

Jessica hesitated. Her temper hadn't run its course, but there was something very appealing about the way he smiled at her. It was friendly and a shade admiring. She had the quick notion that it was the first absolutely sincere smile he'd given her. And it was more important than her anger.

"Maybe," she said, not willing to be too forgiving too quickly.

"State your terms."

After a moment's consideration she placed her hands on her hips. "Take back the snotty little twit."

The gleam of pure humor in his eyes pleased her. "For the simple-minded, egotistical ass."

Bargaining was her biggest vice. Jessica curled her fingers and contemplated her nails. "Just the simple-minded. The rest stands."

He hooked his thumbs in the front pockets of his jeans. "You're a tough lady."

"You got it."

When he held out his hand, they shook solemnly. "One more thing." Since they'd dealt with the anger, Slade wanted to deal with the hurt. "I didn't change my mind."

She didn't speak. After a moment he slipped an arm around her shoulders and began to lead her back toward the beach steps. Without too much effort, he blocked out the nagging voice that told him he was making a mistake.

"Slade."

He glanced down at her as they skirted the small grove at the top of the steps. "What?"

"Michael's coming to dinner tonight."

"Okay, I'll stay out of the way."

"No." She spoke too quickly, then bit her lip. "No, actually, I was wondering if you could . . ."

"Play chaperone?" he finished shortly. "Careful, Jess, you're coming close to being a twit again."

Refusing to be angry, she stopped in the center of the lawn and turned to him. "Slade, everything you said on the beach is true. I'd said the same to myself. But I love Michael— almost the same way I love David." When he only frowned at her, she sighed. "What I have to do tonight hurts. I'd just like some moral support. It would be a little easier if you were there during dinner. Afterward I'll handle it."

Reluctant and resigned, Slade let out a long breath. "Just through dinner. And you're going to owe me one."

Hours later Jessica paced the parlor. Her heels clicked on the hardwood floor, fell silent over the Persian carpet, then clicked again. She was grateful that David had a date. It would have been impossible to have hidden her mood from him, and just as impossible to have confided in him. The business relationship was bound to be strained now between her and Michael. Jessica didn't want to add more problems. Perhaps Michael would even decide to resign. She hated the thought of it.

Oh, it would always be possible to replace a buyer, she thought, but they'd been so close, such a good team. Shutting her eyes, she cursed herself. She couldn't help thinking of Michael in conjunction with the shop. It had always been that way. Maybe if they had known each other before the partnership, like she and David, her feelings would be different. Jessica clasped her hands together again. No, there simply wasn't that . . . spark. If there had been, the shop would never have interfered.

She'd felt the spark once or twice in her life—that quick jolt that says maybe, just maybe. There'd been no spark with Slade, she mused. There'd been an eruption. Annoyed, Jessica shook her head. She shouldn't be thinking of Slade now, or of the two turbulent times she'd been in his arms. It was only right that she concentrate on Michael, on how to say no without hurting him.

Before coming into the room, Slade stopped to watch her. Always moving, he thought, but this time there were nerves beneath the energy. She was wearing a very simple, very sophisticated black dress with her hair caught in a braid over one shoulder. Looking at her, Slade had a moment's sympathy for Michael. It wouldn't be easy to love a woman like that and lose. Unless Michael was a total fool, one glance at her face was going to give him her answer. She'd never have to open her mouth.

"He's going to survive, Jess." When she whirled, Slade strode over to the liquor cabinet. "There are other women, you know." He was deliberately off-hand, deliberately cynical, knowing what her reaction would be. Even with his back to her, he thought he could feel the sudden blaze of heat from her eyes.

"I hope you fall hard one day, Slade," Jessica retorted. "And I hope she thumbs her nose at you."

He poured himself a Scotch. "Not a chance," he said lightly. "Want a drink?"

"I'll have some of that." She walked over and snatched the glass from his hand, then took a long sip.

"Dutch courage?" he asked when she swallowed, controlling a grimace.

She gave him a narrow look while the liquor burned her throat. "You're being purposely horrid."

"Yeah. Don't you feel better?"

With a helpless laugh, she shoved the glass back in his hand. "You're a hard man, Slade."

"You're a beautiful woman, Jessica."

The quiet words threw her completely off balance. She'd heard them dozens of times from dozens of people, but they hadn't made the blood hum under her skin. But then, compliments wouldn't roll easily off the tongue of a man like Slade, she thought. And somehow she felt he wasn't only speaking of physical beauty. No, he was a man who'd look beyond what could be seen and into what could only be felt.

Their eyes held, a moment too long for comfort. It occurred to her that she was closer to losing something vital to him now than she had been on the beach that morning.

"You must be a very good writer," she murmured as she stepped away to pour a glass of vermouth.

"Why?"

"You're very frugal with words, and your timing with them is uncanny." Because her back was to him, she allowed herself to moisten her lips nervously. The clock on the mantel gave the melodious chime that signaled the hour. "I don't suppose you'd like to write me a speech before Michael gets here."

"I'll pass, thanks."

"Slade . . ." Hesitating only briefly, Jessica turned to him. "I shouldn't have told you everything I did out on the beach this morning. It really isn't fair to Michael for you to know, and it isn't fair to you that I dropped my life's history on you that way. You're an easy person to confide in because you listen a bit too well."

"Part of my job," he muttered and thought of the endless stream of interviews with suspects, witnesses, victims.

"I'm trying to thank you," Jessica said shortly. "Can't you take it graciously?"

"Don't be grateful until I've done something," he tossed back.

"I'd choke before I'd thank you again." She dumped a splat of vermouth in her glass as the doorbell rang.

Neither man was pleased to be sharing a meal with the other, but they made the best of it. The general conversation eased slowly toward talk of the shop.

"I'm glad you went by for a few hours, Michael." Jessica poked at the shrimp Dijon rather than eating it. "I don't think David's really up to a full day's work yet."

"He seemed well enough. And Mondays are usually slow in any case." He swirled his wine, giving his dinner little more attention than Jessica. "You worry too much, darling."

"You weren't here last week." She shredded a roll into tiny pieces.

Saying nothing, Slade passed her the butter. Glancing down, Jessica saw the mess she'd made and picked up her wine.

"He was well enough today to sell the Connecticut chest to Mrs. Donnigan," Michael commented after noting the exchange.

"David made a sale to Mrs. Donnigan?" Initial surprise turned to humor. "You'd have to know the lady, Slade. She's a died-in-the-wool Yankee who can stretch a dollar like a piece of elastic. Michael sells to her. On a rare occasion I do, but David . . ." Trailing off, she smiled. "How did he manage it?"

"By being very reluctant to part with it. When I came in he was nudging her toward the pecan hope chest, telling her he'd all but promised the other to another customer."

She gave a quick spurt of laughter. "Well, it looks like our boy's learning. I'm going to have to give in and let him go to Europe with you next time."

Briefly, Michael frowned down at his plate, then very deliberately stabbed a shrimp. "If that's what you want."

Her distress was immediate. Before Jessica could fumble for a new line of conversation, Slade intervened by asking what a Connecticut chest was. She threw him a swift glance of appreciation and let Michael take over.

Why did I say that? she demanded of herself. How could I be insensitive enough to forget that he'd asked me to go to Europe with him the next time? On an inward sigh, Jessica toyed with her dinner. I'm not going to handle this well, she thought. I'm simply not going to handle it well at all.

How different they are. It occurred to her all at once as she watched the two men talk casually. Michael, with his smooth gestures, was well groomed in voice and manner, sleekly dressed. Jessica reflected that she'd never seen him in anything more casual than a polo shirt and golf pants. He was all civilized charm and sophisticated sexuality.

Slade rarely gestured at all. It was as if he knew that body language could give his thoughts away. No, he had a strange capacity for stillness. And she wouldn't term him rugged though he favored jeans and sweaters. Not charming but disarming, she decided. And his sexuality was anything but sophisticated. Animal.

Slade asked questions on antiques when he couldn't have cared less. This would give Jessica a few moments to regain the composure she had so nearly lost. It might also give him the opportunity to form a more concrete opinion of Michael. He seemed harmless enough, Slade reflected. A pretty boy with enough brains to make it his profession. Or enough brains to be one of the rungs on the smuggling ladder. Not the top one, Slade thought instinctively. Not enough guts.

He was the type of man Slade might have matched Jessica

with. Polished, intelligent. And he was good looking enough, if you liked that type. Apparently Jessica didn't. They hadn't been lovers. Slade pondered this as he listened to Michael. What sort of man, he wondered, could be around that woman day after day and not make love to her—or go mad? Michael had managed to keep himself in check for nearly three years. Slade calculated that he hadn't been able to do so for as many days. Michael Adams was either madly in love with her or more clever than he looked. Catching the way Michael's eyes would drift to her occasionally, Slade felt a stir of sympathy. Madly in love or not, he wasn't indifferent.

Michael took another sip of wine and tried to continue a conversation he was beginning to detest. He knew Jessica. Oh yes, he thought fatalistically, he knew Jessica. He'd seen her answer in her eyes. The one woman who mattered to him was never going to be his.

All three of them were relieved when Betsy brought in the coffee tray. "Miss Jessica, if you don't start eating more than that, Cook's going to quit again."

"If she didn't quit once a month, she'd throw the entire household off schedule," Jessica said lightly. Food was something she could do without until after she had settled things with Michael.

"I'll just take a cup to the library." Slade was up and pouring his own before Betsy could object. "I've got some things to finish up tonight."

"Fine." Jessica took care not to look at him. "Let's have ours in the parlor, Michael. No, no, Betsy, I'll carry it," she continued as the housekeeper started to mutter. Slade disappeared before she could lift the tray. "Help yourself to the brandy," she told Michael as they entered the parlor. "I'll just have the coffee."

He poured a generous amount, placing the crystal stopper back in the decanter before turning. Betsy had lit the fire while they were eating. It crackled with a cheer neither Jessica nor Michael were feeling. Remaining across the room, he watched her pour coffee from the china pot into china cups. The set had a delicate pattern of violets on an ivory background. Michael counted each petal before he spoke.

"Jessica." Her fingers tightened on the handle of the

creamer and he swore silently. Strange that he'd never wanted her more than at the moment he was sure he'd never have her. He'd been too confident that when the time was right, everything would simply fall into place. "I didn't mean to make you unhappy."

Her eyes lifted to meet his. "Michael—"

"No, you don't have to say anything, it's written all over your face. The one thing you've never been able to do well is hide your feelings." He took a long swallow of brandy. "You're not going to marry me."

Say it quick, she ordered herself. "No, I can't." Rising, she walked over to stand with him. "I wish I felt differently, Michael. I wish I'd known what your feelings were sooner."

He looked into his brandy—the same color as her eyes and just as intoxicating. He set the snifter down. "Would it have made any difference if I'd asked you a year ago? Two years ago?"

"I don't know." Helplessly, she lifted her shoulders. "But as we're basically the same people we were then, I don't think so." She touched his arm, wishing she had better words, kinder words. "I care, Michael, you must know that I do. But I can't give you what you want."

Lifting a hand, he circled the back of her neck. "I can't tell you I won't try to change your mind."

"Michael—"

"No, I'm not going to pressure you now." He gave her neck a gentle squeeze. "But I have the advantage of knowing you well—what you like, what you don't like." Taking her hand, he pressed a kiss in her palm. "I also love you enough not to hound you." With a smile, he released her hand. "I'll see you at the shop tomorrow."

"Yes, all right." Jessica pressed her hands together. She'd felt nothing but regret when he'd pressed his lips to her palm. "Good night, Michael."

When the front door closed behind him, she stood where she was. She had no taste for coffee now, nor the energy to carry the tray to the kitchen and deal with Betsy or the cook. Leaving things as they were, Jessica headed for the stairs.

"Jess?" Slade stopped her with a word. He came down the hall as she paused on the second step. "Okay?"

All of a sudden she wanted badly to cry—to turn, run into his arms, and weep. Instead she snapped at him. "No, it's not okay. Why the hell should it be?"

"You did what you had to do," he said calmly. "He's not going to drive off a cliff."

"What do you know about it?" she tossed back. "You haven't got any feelings. You don't know what it's like to care for someone. You have to have a heart to be hurt." Whirling, she dashed up the stairs, making it almost halfway before she stopped. Shutting her eyes tight, Jessica slammed a fist onto the railing. After a deep breath, she turned and walked back down. He stood at the bottom, waiting.

"I'm sorry."

"Why?" Because her words had cut deeper than he liked, he shrugged. "You were on target."

"No, I wasn't." Wearily, she rubbed a hand over her forehead. "And I haven't any right to use you for a punching bag. You gave me a lot of support today, and I'm grateful."

"Save it," he advised as he turned away.

This time it was her turn to stop him. "Slade." He took two more steps, swore, then turned back to her. His eyes were dark, smolderingly angry, as if her apology had flamed his temper more than her insults. "I realize you might think differently, but you don't go to hell for being kind."

With that, she left him staring after her as she continued up the stairs.

5

TWO A.M. Jessica heard the old Seth Thomas clock in the hall strike two musical bongs. Her body was exhausted, but her mind refused to settle. Slade's spurts of stop-and-go typing had silenced over an hour before. He could sleep, she thought in disgust as she rolled to her back to stare, again, at the ceiling. But then, he wasn't in an emotional whirl.

Thoughts of Michael drifted to her and she sighed. No, let's be honest, Jessica, she ordered herself. It isn't Michael who's keeping you awake, it's the man two doors down on the left.

Alone in the dark, in the tangle of soft linen sheets, Jessica could feel the scrape of sand against her back, the heat of the sun and bite of the wind on her face. The press of his body against hers. Desire churned in her tired body, awakening pulses she struggled to calm. She felt the ache move slowly from her stomach to her breasts. Quickly she sprang out of bed and tugged on a robe. All she needed was a hot drink to settle her, she decided, almost frantically. If that didn't work, she'd switch on the television until some old movie lulled her to sleep. In the morning she'd have herself in order again. She'd go back to work, stay out of Slade's way until he finished the library and went back to where he came from.

Jessica slipped out of the room and moved on silent bare feet down the hall. She paused in front of Slade's door, even reached for the handle before she caught herself. Good God, what was she thinking of! Moving quickly, she headed for the stairs. Maybe a brandy would be a better idea than the hot drink, she decided.

Out of habit, she went quietly down the steps, avoiding the spots that creaked and groaned. Brandy and an old movie, she told herself. If that didn't put her to sleep, nothing would. Seeing that the parlor doors were closed, she frowned. Now who would have done that? she wondered. They were never closed. With a shrug, she decided Slade had shut them before coming up to write. She crossed the hall and pulled one open.

A light blinded her. It shone straight in her eyes, forcing her to throw up a hand to shield them. Shock came first. She stepped back, stunned by the glare, confused by its source. Before she could speak, Jessica froze. *A flashlight*. No one should be in the closed parlor with a flashlight in the middle of the night. Fear ran coolly over her skin, then lodged like a fist in her throat. Without a second's thought, she turned and raced back up the stairs.

Slade snapped fully awake the moment his door was flung open. A shadow darted toward his bed and instinctively he grabbed it, twisted it, and pinned it underneath him. It gave a quiet whoosh of air as it slammed onto the mattress. At the moment of contact he knew he held Jessica.

"What the hell are you doing?" he demanded as his fingers clamped over her wrists. Her scent flooded his senses; instant desire roughened his voice.

With the wind knocked out of her, Jessica struggled to speak. Fear had her body shuddering under his. "Downstairs," she managed. "Someone's downstairs."

He tensed, but schooled his voice to casualness. "A servant."

"At two o'clock in the morning?" she hissed as anger began to take over. It suddenly seeped into her that he was naked, and that her robe had parted when he had yanked her into bed. Swallowing, she struggled beneath him. "With a flashlight?"

He rolled from her quickly. "Where?"

"The parlor." Snatching her robe together, Jessica tried to pretend that she hadn't been weakened, not for a minute, by desire. She watched his shadow as he tugged on jeans. "You're not going down there?"

"Isn't that what you expected me to do when you came in here?" he countered. He opened a drawer and found his gun.

"No, I didn't think at all. The police." Reaching over, she switched on the light. "We have to call . . ." The sentence died as she saw what he held in his hand. A new bubble of terror rose in her throat. "Where did you get that?"

"Stay here."

He was nearly at the door before Jessica could propel her numb body from the bed. "*No!* You can't go down there with a gun. Slade, how—"

He stopped her with a hard, bruising grip on her shoulder. When they fixed on her, his eyes were ice cold and expressionless. "Stay put," he ordered, then closed the door firmly in her face.

Too shocked to do otherwise, Jessica stared at the blank wood. What in God's name was going on? she demanded as she pressed her hands to her cheeks. It was crazy. Someone sneaking around the parlor in the middle of the night. Slade handling a big ugly gun as if he'd been born with it in his hand. Nerves jumping, she began to pace the room. It was too quiet, she thought as her fingers laced and unlaced. Just too quiet. She couldn't just stand there.

Slade had just finished a quick, thorough tour of the first floor when the creak on the steps had him whirling. He saw Jessica stagger back against the wall, eyes wide as he turned the gun on her.

"*Goddammit!*" The word exploded at her as he lowered the gun. "I told you to stay upstairs."

She had enough time to register that she'd seen the stance he'd taken with the gun on a hundred television police shows. Then the trembling started. "I couldn't. Is he gone?"

"Looks that way." Seizing her hand, Slade dragged her into the parlor. "Stay in here. I'm going to check outside."

Jessica sank into a chair and waited. It was dark; the thin, shifting moonlight tossed wavering shadows around the room. Defensively, she curled her feet under her and cupped her elbows with her hands. Fear, she realized, was something she'd rarely dealt with. She wasn't doing a good job of it now. Shutting her eyes a moment, Jessica forced herself to take deep, even breaths.

As the shuddering calmed, her thoughts began to focus. What was a writer doing with a revolver? Why hadn't he called the police? A suspicion rose out of nowhere and she shook it off. No, that was ridiculous. . . . Wasn't it?

When Slade returned to the parlor ten minutes later, she hadn't moved from the chair.

With a flick of the wrist, he hit the switch, flooding the room with light. "Nothing," he said shortly though she hadn't spoken. "There's no sign of anyone, or any sign of a break-in."

"I saw someone," she began indignantly.

"I didn't say you didn't." Then he was gone again, leaving her next retort sputtering on her lips. He came back without the gun. "What did you see?" As he asked he began a more careful search of the room.

Brows drawn together, she watched his practiced movements. "The parlor doors were closed. When I opened them, a light hit my eyes. A flashlight. I didn't see anything."

"Anything out of place in here?"

She continued to watch his deft, professional search as he roamed around the room. No, the suspicion wasn't ridiculous, she realized as her stomach tightened. It was all too pat. He's done this before. He's used that gun before.

"Who are you?"

He heard the chill in her voice as he crouched in front of the liquor cabinet. None of the crystal had been disturbed. He didn't turn. "You know who I am, Jess."

"You're not a writer."

"Yes, I am."

"What is it?" she asked flatly. "Sergeant? Lieutenant?"

He took the brandy decanter and poured liquor into a snifter. His brain was perfectly cool. He walked to her and held out the glass. "Sergeant. Drink this."

Her eyes stayed level on his. "Go to hell."

With a shrug, Slade set the snifter beside her. A deadly calm washed over her, dulling the sting of betrayal. "I want you out of my house. But before you leave," Jessica said quietly, "I want you to tell me why you came. Uncle Charlie did send you, didn't he? Orders from the commissioner?" The last sentence was full of carefully calculated disgust.

Slade said nothing, debating just how much he'd have to tell her to satisfy her. She was pale, but not with fear now. She was spitting mad.

"Fine." Keeping her eyes on his, she rose. "Then I'll call your commissioner myself. You can pack your typewriter and your gun, Sergeant."

She was going to have to have it all, he decided and wished fleetingly for a cigarette. "Sit down, Jess." When she made no move to obey, he gave her a helpful shove back into the chair. "Just shut up and listen," he suggested as she opened her mouth to yell at him. "Your shop's suspected in connection with a major smuggling operation. It's believed that stolen goods are hidden in some of your imports, then transferred to a contact on this side, probably through the sale of the whole article." She wasn't attempting to speak now, but simply staring at him as if he'd lost his mind. "Interpol wants the head man rather than the few underlings already under observation. He's managed to slip away from them before; they don't want it to happen again. You, your shop, the people who work for you, are under observation until he's in custody or the investigation leads elsewhere. In the meantime the commissioner wants you safe."

"I don't believe a word of it."

But her voice shook. Slade thrust his hands in his pockets. "My information as well as my orders come from the commissioner."

"It's ridiculous." Her voice was stronger now, touched with scorn. "Do you think something like that could go on in my shop without my knowing about it?" Even as she reached for the brandy, she caught the look in his eyes. Jessica's hand froze on the glass, then dropped away. "I see," she said quietly. The pain was dull in her stomach. Briefly, she pressed a hand to it before linking her fingers together. "Did you bring your handcuffs along, Sergeant?"

"Cut it out, Jess." Because he couldn't handle the way she looked at him, Slade turned to prowl the room. "I said the commissioner wanted you protected."

"Was it part of your job to attract me enough so that I might be indiscreet?" When he whirled back, she sprang to her feet to meet his fury with her own. "Is making love to me all in a day's work?"

"I haven't begun to make love to you." Infuriated, he grabbed the lapels of her robe, nearly hauling her off her feet. "And I wouldn't have taken the damn assignment if I'd known you were going to tie me up in knots every time I looked at you. The Bureau thinks you're clean. Don't you understand that only puts you in a more dangerous position?"

"How can I understand anything when I'm not *told* anything?" she tossed back. "What kind of danger could I possibly be in?"

"This isn't a game, Jess." Frustrated, he shook her. "An agent was killed in London last week. He was close, too close, to finding out who's pulling the strings. His last report mentioned a quarter of a million dollars' worth of diamonds."

"What does that have to do with me!" Jessica jerked away from him. "If they think there're diamonds stashed away in one of my imports, let them come in. They can take the furniture apart piece by piece."

"And tip off the number one man," Slade returned.

"How do you know I'm not in charge?" A raging headache was added to the sickness in her stomach. Wearily, Jessica rubbed at her temple. "I run the shop."

He watched her slender fingers knead at the ache. "Not alone."

All movement stopped. Very slowly, Jessica lowered her hand. "David and Michael?" she whispered. Incredulity gave way to anger. "No! I won't have you accusing them."

"No one's accusing anyone yet."

"No, you're here to spy on us."

"I don't like it any better than you."

"Then why are you here?"

The deliberate scorn in her tone made him want to strangle her. He spoke slowly, brutally. "Because the commissioner didn't want his goddaughter to end up with her beautiful throat slit."

Her color drained at that, but she kept her eyes level. "Who would hurt me—David, Michael? Even you must see how absurd that is."

"You'd be surprised what people do to survive," he said

tersely. "In any case, there are other people involved—the kind who wouldn't think of you as any more than an expendable obstacle."

She didn't want to think about that—couldn't if she wanted to stop herself from having a bout of hysteria. Be practical, she ordered herself. Be logical. This time she lifted the brandy and drank deeply before speaking. "If you're with the NYPD. you have no jurisdiction here."

"The commissioner has a lot of clout." The hint of color that seeped back into her cheeks relieved him. She was tougher than she looked. "In any case I'm not here about the smuggling, not officially."

"Why are you here—officially?"

"To keep you out of trouble."

"Uncle Charlie should have told me."

Slade lifted his shoulders in a half shrug as he looked around the room. "Yeah, maybe. There's no way of telling if he was after something in here, or slipping through this room to another. Not with the way this house is set up." With a frown, he ran a hand absently over his bare chest. "Do you see anything out of place in here?"

Jessica followed the sweep of his eyes. "No. I don't think he could have been around very long. You didn't stop typing until one. Wouldn't it make sense for him to wait until all the lights were out before he broke in?"

He started to remind her that no one had broken in, then changed his mind. If it helped her to believe it had been a stranger, she might sleep better. He thought of David, who had a room on the east wing of the first floor. "I've got to call in my report. Go on to bed."

"No." Unwilling to admit that she couldn't bring herself to go upstairs alone, Jessica lifted the brandy again. "I'll wait."

She sat as he went out to the phone in the hall. Purposely, she tuned out his conversation, though it was carried on in such quiet tones that she would have had to strain to hear. Her shop, she thought. How was it possible for her shop to be tangled up in something as fantastic as international smuggling? If it hadn't been so frightening, she would have laughed.

Michael and David. With a brisk shake of her head, she

shut her eyes. No, that part she wouldn't believe. There was a mistake somewhere, and in time the police or the FBI or whoever was haunting her would realize it.

A burglar had been in the parlor. It was as simple as that. Hadn't Betsy grumbled a dozen times about her not using the alarm system? The image of Slade with the gun in his hand came back to her too clearly. That was something she couldn't shut out.

When he came back into the room, Jessica was sitting very still, eyes closed. There were shadows under them. What he'd just learned on the phone wasn't going to make them go away, but perhaps a good night's sleep would.

"Come on," he said briskly, trying not to soften as her eyes shot open in alarm at his voice. "You're tired. Go up and take a pill if you can't sleep. And you're not going in to the shop tomorrow."

"But I have to," she began.

"You have to do as you're told from here on," he corrected. "You'll be safer here where I can keep an eye on you. Starting now, you don't leave the house without me. Don't argue." Taking her hand, he hauled her to her feet. "You haven't got any choice at this point; you have to trust me."

She did. Jessica realized as he pulled her up the steps that if everything else was a maze of confusion, that was clear. That very quick first impression she'd gotten when she'd all but run into him at the bottom of the staircase had been viable. With him she was safe.

"I don't like knowing you're a cop," she murmured.

"Yeah, I'm not always crazy about it myself. Go to bed, Jess." He dropped her arm as they came to her door. Before he could move on, Jessica grabbed his hand.

"Slade . . ." She hated what she was going to ask, hated admitting to herself, much less him, that she was terrified of being alone. "I . . ." She looked away from the impatience in his eyes and glanced into her darkened room. "Could you stay?"

"I told you, I've got my orders from the commissioner."

"No, I don't mean . . ." She moistened her lips. "I mean with me—tonight."

She looked up at him, pale, soft, vulnerable. He felt the

blood start to pound in his chest. In defense, his voice was blunt and cold. "When I go to bed with a woman, I tend to give her my complete attention. I haven't got time for that now."

She felt a flutter that was both panic and excitement. "I'm not asking you to make love with me, just not to leave me alone."

He allowed his eyes to rake down her. Warm flesh, soft curves, and ice-blue silk. "Do you think I'd spend the night with you and not have you?"

"No." The answer came quick and quiet. The flutter became a throb.

In a quick move calculated to frighten her, Slade backed her up against the door. "You haven't the experience to deal with me, lady." Not quite gently, his hand closed over her throat. Beneath his palm he felt the wild scramble of her pulse, but her eyes . . . her eyes were tawny and unafraid. He wanted her with a desperation that threatened to drive everything else aside. "I'm not one of your polite country club men, Jess," he told her in a dangerously quiet voice. "You don't know the places I've been, the things I've done. I could show you tricks that would make your French lover look like a Boy Scout. If I decided I wanted you, you couldn't run fast enough."

She could barely hear him over the dull thud of her heart. Her eyes had misted over with desire. "Which of us is running, Slade?" Her arms were already heavy, but she lifted them. In one long slow stroke, she ran her hands up his naked back. He stiffened. The fingers on her throat tightened swiftly. She pressed her body to his.

"Damn you, Jess." On a groan, his mouth came down to savage hers.

Her senses whirled from the onslaught, but she clung. This was what she wanted—the mindless passion he could bring her on the instant of contact. The kiss wasn't loverlike; it wasn't the worshipful merging of lips, the gentle teasing of tongues. It was madness. Jessica abdicated her sanity without a second thought. Let him teach her what he would.

He ripped the robe from her where they stood, then gave into the driving need to let his hands mold every inch of her.

Softer, inconceivably softer than he imagined, her skin seemed to flow under his fingers. Within seconds he had her trembling, one wracking, convulsive shudder after another. Her thighs were slim and strong. Running a hand up them, he found her, then took her gasping to a staggering peak until she swayed helplessly in his arms.

Slade swore again, knowing he couldn't stop. He had told himself he would treat her callously and then walk away—to save her . . . to save himself. Now she was moist and warm and pliant in his arms. Her fragrance clung to the air, seducing him. He shook his head, struggling to clear it, but she pressed her lips to his throat, huskily murmuring his name.

He was with her in bed, not even aware if he had dragged or carried her there.

Jessica twisted under him, answering his kiss deliriously as his hands moved everywhere. He gave her no chance to orient herself. There was a tangle of sheets under her, the soft fabric of his jeans against her legs, but she was only aware of the hurricane. That's where he took her—all speeding wind and black sky. His ragged breathing shivered into her ear before his tongue darted inside.

In a zigzagging journey that had her mind spinning, he ran open-mouthed, nibbling kisses down her throat to the hollow between her breasts. She arched, her nipples hard with need, but he continued down and ran his tongue along the line of her ribs. Half mad, she dug her fingers into his hair, wanting him to take her before she exploded, wanting the agonizing pleasure to go on forever.

Greedily, he came back to her breast, the moist trail his tongue left causing her to shudder with fire and ice by turns. His teeth nipped into the soft swell of flesh while with a fingertip he began a slow, torturous path around the other. Lips and finger circled in until she was writhing beneath him. He drew her nipple into his mouth, catching the other arching point between his thumb and finger. Jessica cried out as the dual pleasure exploded, then was lost in wave after wave of sensation as his teasing became rampant hunger.

She was tugging at his jeans, but he shifted away from her seeking hands. Without the restriction he knew he'd take her instantly. He was far from ready. He'd sensed her passion, knew it lay smoldering, but now it was engulfing him in a heat he hadn't foreseen. She was wildly responsive, like a thoroughbred mare given her head. He wanted to drive her—drive them both—to the breaking point.

The musky, woodsy scent seemed to emanate from her skin wherever he buried his lips. Her body was slender, almost too slender, but with a seductive womanly softness that made him want to go on touching and tasting until there was no inch of her he didn't know. When his mouth brushed low over her stomach, she moaned, nails digging into his shoulders as she urged him down. He could hear his name trembling out of her lips between raw, gasping breaths. But when his tongue sought and found the center of her pleasure, he lost everything else.

He drove her to peak after peak. Exhausted, Jessica hungered for more. Her skin was fused to his, both hot and damp with desire. Her body was stunningly alive, throbbing from thousands of minute pulses he had discovered and exploited. Even his name wouldn't form on her lips any longer. Together they struggled with the last barrier of clothing that kept them apart. She found his hips, lean and long-boned; his thighs, firm and muscled.

They came together savagely, each gasping from the shock of power.

She couldn't stop the shudders. They continued to race through her long after Slade lay beside her, silent. Her body ached. And glowed. Did we make love or war? Jessica wondered dizzily. Whatever had happened between them had never happened to her before, and she knew with a certainty that it would never happen with any other man.

None of her inhibitions had surfaced—he wouldn't have allowed them to. Was there another man with his strength, his intensity, his . . . savagery? Not for her, Jessica realized, instinctively rolling to him. There had never been, nor would there ever be anyone else for her. She'd lost that vital part of herself to him long before they had ever gone to bed—her heart.

Oh, I love you, she thought, whoever, whatever you are. And the surest way to turn you away from me now is to tell you. Closing her eyes, Jessica rested her head on his shoulder.

You're already wondering how you lost control enough to take me to bed, she concluded with instinctive accuracy. Already wondering how to prevent this from happening again. *But I'm not going to lose you.* The vow formed firmly as she ran a hand over his chest. You're not getting away, Slade; struggle all you want. Lightly, she ran a trail of kisses over his shoulder to his throat.

"Jess." Slade put up a hand to stop her. He'd never be able to think clearly with her touching him. If he was going to find his way out of the quicksand he was rapidly sinking in, he had to think.

Jessica merely kissed the fingers that got in her way, then trailed her lips to his cheek. "Hold me," she murmured. "I want your arms around me."

With an effort, Slade resisted the husky demand and the soft lips that insisted on clouding his brain. "Jessica, this isn't smart. We've got—"

"I don't want to be smart, Slade," she interrupted. She shifted so that her head was just above his, her lips just above his. "Don't talk, not tonight." When her fingers ran down his side, she had the satisfaction of feeling his quick, involuntary tremor. "I want you." Her tongue traced his lips. She felt the sudden thunder of his heart against her breast. "You want me. That's all there is tonight."

In the darkness he could see the pale clouds of hair, the moonlit skin shadowed by the slash of cheekbone. He saw the amber fire of her eyes before her mouth took his and captured him.

6

Slade woke beside her. She was deep in an exhausted sleep, her breathing slow and regular. There were shadows under the sweep of lashes, dark smudges against pale skin. His arm was around her slim waist; in sleep he'd betrayed himself by wanting her close. They shared the same pillow. He spent several minutes cursing himself before he rolled out of bed. Jessica didn't even stir. He grabbed up his jeans and went to his own room and straight to the shower.

Deliberately, Slade turned the cold on full. Hadn't he saturated himself enough with her last night? he asked himself furiously as the icy spray hit his body like sharp pinpricks. Did he have to wake up wanting her? Need for her, this kind of consuming need, was going to interfere with his job. Slade had to remind himself again and again that Jessica was a job, only a job.

And in the brief phone conversation the night before, he had been told enough to make him realize that her position had become only more delicate. Someone wanted something in her house—someone she trusted. Knowing who it was wouldn't be enough. Slade had to find out what it was. Or rather the Feds had to find out what, he corrected grimly. He had to stick to her like glue until it was all over.

Why the hell don't they let me get her out of here? he thought on a fresh burst of fury. The order over the phone had been firm and unarguable. Jessica stayed. The investigation couldn't be jeopardized by letting her walk. She stayed, Slade repeated silently. And he wasn't to let her out of his sight for the next forty-eight hours. That didn't include sleeping with her, he reminded himself as he let the cold water sluice over his head. It didn't include getting so caught up in her that he forgot what he was doing there in the first place. And how the hell was he supposed to live in the same house with her now and not touch her?

He grabbed the soap and lathered himself roughly. Maybe it would wash away the woodsy scent that seemed to have crept into his own skin.

Waking, Jessica reached for him. He was gone, and so, instantly, was her peace. The few hours of sleep had left her tightly strung instead of relaxed. If he had been there, if she could have turned to him on wakening, she wouldn't have felt the sick sense of loss.

David and Michael. No, she couldn't even allow herself to think it. Covering her face with her hands, Jessica struggled to block it out. But then she could see the icy look in Slade's eyes when he had aimed the gun on her. It's madness, it's a mistake. A quarter of a million in diamonds. Interpol. *David and Michael.*

Unable to bear it, she sprang out of bed. She needed to clear her brain, to think. The house felt like an airless prison. She threw on her clothes and headed for the beach.

When he came by her room to check on her ten minutes later, Slade found the bed empty. The quick panic was as uncharacteristic as it was unprofessional. Hurriedly, he checked the bath and her sitting room before going downstairs. He didn't find Jessica in the dining room, but Betsy.

"Where is she?" he demanded.

Betsy cleared off the place she had set for Jessica, then scowled at him. "So you're in a chipper mood too."

"Where's Jessica?"

Betsy sent him a shrewd look. "Looks sick this morning, wonder if she caught David's flu. Down at the beach," she continued before he could snap at her.

"Alone?"

"Yes, alone. Didn't even take that overgrown mutt with her.

Said she's not going into work today, and . . ." Betsy placed her hands on her hips and scowled at his retreating back. "Well," she muttered and clucked her tongue.

It was cold. Concealing his shoulder holster under his jacket was simple. By the time Slade had reached the beach steps, he'd nearly run out of curses. Hadn't anything he'd said to her the night before gotten through? He spotted her standing near the breakers and tore down the steps and across the sand.

Jessica heard his approach and turned. Whatever she might have said slipped back down her throat as he grabbed her by the shoulders and shook her.

"*You idiot!* What are you doing down here alone? Don't you know the position you're in?"

Her hand swung out, connecting sharply with his cheek. The slap stunned both of them, causing angry eyes to meet angry eyes in quick surprise. His grip loosened enough for Jessica to step back. "Don't you shout at me," she ordered, automatically soothing the flesh his hands had bruised. "I don't have to take that from anyone."

"You'll take it from me," he said evenly. "I'll give you that one, Jess, but remember, I hit back. What are you doing out here?"

"I'm taking a walk," she snapped. "I arranged for David to take over the shop today, as per your orders, Sergeant."

So we're back to that, he reflected and dug his hands into his pockets. His hair whipped unheeded around his face. "Fine. My next order is that you're not to leave the house until I say so."

The fire in her eyes was suddenly misted with tears. Hugging herself, she spun away from him. She'd show him anger, she'd show him passion, but she refused to show him weakness. "House arrest?" she said thickly.

He'd rather have had her slap him again than cry. "Protective custody," he countered. With a sigh, he placed his hands on her shoulders. "Jess . . ."

Swiftly she shook her head, knowing that kind words would undermine her completely. When she felt his brow drop to the top of her head, she squeezed her eyes tight.

"Don't fall apart now," he murmured. "It won't be for very long. When it's over—"

"When it's over, what?" she interrupted in swift despair. "Will one of the people closest to me be in jail? Am I supposed to look forward to that?" On a long breath, she opened her eyes and looked out to sea. The water was choppy, white-capped and gray. A storm was coming in, she thought dispassionately. The sky was beginning to boil with it.

"You're supposed to get through today," he told her, tightening his grip. "Then you're supposed to get through tomorrow."

Life, she mused. Is that really how life's supposed to be? Is that how he felt about his? "Why did you leave me alone this morning?"

His hands dropped away from her shoulders. Without turning, Jessica knew he'd stepped back. Gathering her courage, she faced him. All the guards were back. If her body had not still ached from the fury of lovemaking, she might have thought she'd imagined all of the night before. The man staring at her showed no hint of emotion.

"You're going to tell me it was a mistake," she managed after a moment. "Something that shouldn't have happened and won't happen again." Her chin came up as love warred with pride. "Please don't bother."

He should have let her go. He intended to let her go. Before he could stop himself, Slade took her arm, carefully wrapping his fingers around it as if measuring its size and strength. "I'm going to tell you it was a mistake," he said slowly. "Something that shouldn't have happened. But I can't tell you it won't happen again. I can't be near you and not want you."

The man shifted his position in the cover of trees. With businesslike movements, he opened the briefcase and began to fit the pieces of the rifle together. For the moment he paid little attention to the two figures down on the beach. One thing at a time. That was one of the reasons for his success in his field. He'd only had the contract for four hours and was relatively pleased that it would take him little more than that to complete it.

After snapping on the sight, he pulled out a handkerchief.

The brisk wind wasn't doing his head cold any good. But then, ten thousand dollars bought a lot of antihistamines. After sneezing softly, he replaced his handkerchief, then drew a bead on the figures on the beach.

Jessica felt some of her strength returning. "Why was it a mistake then?"

Slade let out an impatient breath. *Because I'm a cop from the Lower East Side who's seen things I could never tell you about. Because I want you so much—not just now, this minute, but tomorrow, twenty years from now—and that scares me.*

"Oil and water, Jess, it's as simple as that. You wanted to walk, we'll walk." Slipping his hand from her arm, he interlaced his fingers with hers, then turned away from the shore.

He lowered his rifle as Slade blocked his clear shot of Jessica. The contract was for the woman only, and business was business. The wind fluttered at his drab-colored overcoat and snuck underneath it. Sniffling, he brought his handkerchief out again, then settled down to wait.

Jessica kicked a pebble into a clump of rocks. "You are a writer, aren't you?"

"So I tell myself."

"Then why do you do this? You don't like it—it shows."

It wasn't supposed to show. The fact that she could see what he'd successfully concealed from everyone—including himself from time to time—infuriated Slade. "Look, I do what I have to, what I know. Not everybody has a choice."

"No," she disagreed. "Everyone has a choice."

"I've got a mother waiting tables and living off a dead cop's pension." The words exploded from him, stopping her. "I've got a sister in her third year of college who's got a chance to be something. You don't pay tuition with rejection slips."

Jessica lifted both hands to his face. Her palms were cool and soft. "Then you made your choice, Slade. Not every man would have made the same one. When the time comes, and you publish, you'll have everything."

"Jess." He took her wrists, but held them a moment instead of pulling her hands from his face. Her pulse speeded instantly at his touch, drawing an unwilling response from him. "You get to me," he muttered.

"And you don't like it." She leaned toward him, lashes lowering.

He crushed her to him, devouring the willing mouth. It was as cool as her hands but heated quickly beneath his. Already frantic, he grabbed her hair, drawing her head back farther so he could plunder all the sweet, moist recesses. Her arms went around his neck, imprisoning him in the softness, the fragrance, the need.

The back of his head was caught in the crosshairs of the scope of a high-powered rifle with a sophisticated silencer.

"Jess." His lips moved against hers with the sound of her name. He broke away only to catch her close to his chest, holding her there while he tried to steady himself. "You're tired," he said when he heard her sigh. "We'll go in. You should get some more sleep."

She allowed him to shift her to his side. Patience, she told herself. This isn't a man who gives himself easily. "I'm not tired," she lied, matching her steps to his. "Why don't I give you a hand in the library?"

"That's all I need," he muttered, casting his eyes up. In his peripheral vision, he caught a quick flutter of white among the thinning leaves in the grove. He tensed, muscles tightening as he strained to see. There was nothing more than a rustling, easily caused by the wind. Then the flutter of white again.

"I'm terrific at organizing if I put my mind to it," Jessica claimed as she stepped in front of him. "And I—" The breath was knocked out of her as Slade shoved her to the ground in back of a small outcropping of rock. She heard a quick ping, as if stone had struck stone. Before she could fill her lungs with air, he'd drawn out his gun. "What is it? What's wrong?"

"Don't move." He didn't even look at her, but kept her pinned beneath him as his eyes swept the beach. Jessica's eyes were locked on his gun.

"Slade?"

"He's in the grove, about ten feet to the right of where we are now," he calculated, thinking out loud. "It's a good position; he won't move—at least for a while."

"Who?" she demanded. "What are you talking about?"

He brought his eyes to hers briefly, chilling her with the hard, cold look she'd seen before. "The man who just took a shot at you."

She went as still and stiff as a statue. "No one did, I didn't hear—"

"He's got it silenced." Slade shifted just enough to get a clearer view of the beach steps. "He's a pro, he'll wait us out."

Jessica remembered the odd sound she'd heard just as Slade had shoved her to the ground. Stone hitting stone. Bullet hitting rock. A wave of dizziness swept over her, clouding her vision until she saw nothing but a gray mist. From a distance she heard Slade's voice and struggled against the faintness. Heart pounding in her ears, she focused on him again. He was still looking beyond her to the beach steps.

". . . that we know he's there."

"What?"

Impatiently, Slade looked down at her. There wasn't a trace of color in her face. Against the pallor, her eyes were dull and unfocused. He couldn't allow her the luxury of going into shock. "Snap out of it and listen to me," he said harshly, catching her face in his hand. "Odds are he doesn't know we've made him. He probably thinks we're back here making love. If my cover was blown, he'd have taken care of me instead of waiting to get a clear shot at you. Now you've only got to do one thing, Jess, understand?"

"One thing," she repeated with a nod.

"Stay put."

She nearly gave way to a hysterical giggle. "That sounds like a good idea. How long do you think we'll have to stay here?"

"You stay until I get back."

Her arms came around him quickly and with desperate strength. "You're not going out there! He'll kill you."

"It's you he wants," Slade said flatly as he pried her arms away from his neck. "I want you to do exactly as I say."

He wriggled on top of her and managed to shrug out of his jacket, then the shoulder holster. After tugging his shirt out of his jeans, he tucked the gun in the back waistband. "I'm going to stand up, and after a minute I'll walk over to the steps. He'll either think you wouldn't play games or that we're finished and you're staying out for a while."

She didn't hold on to him because she knew it was useless. He was going to do it his own way. "What if he shoots you?" she asked dully. "A hell of a bodyguard you'd make dead."

"If he's going to, he'll do it the minute I stand up," Slade told her, cupping her face again. "Then you'll still have the gun, won't you?" He kissed her, hard and quick, before she could speak. "Stay put, Jess. I'll be back."

He rose nonchalantly, still looking down at her. Jessica counted ten long, silent seconds. Everything in her system seemed to be on slow motion. Her brain, her heart, her lungs. If she breathed at all, she was unaware of it. She lay in a vacuum of fear. Slade grinned at her, a flash of reassurance that didn't reach his eyes. Numbly she wondered if the smile was for her benefit or for the man in the grove.

"No matter what, you stay where you are." With this he turned away from her and strolled easily to the beach steps. He hooked his thumbs lazily in his pockets as if every muscle in his body wasn't tensed, waiting. A thin stream of sweat rolled down his back.

A hell of a bodyguard you'd make dead. Jessica's words played back to him as he forced himself to take the steps slowly. He knew how close that one silent bullet had come. He was taking a chance coming out in the open, not only with himself, but with Jessica.

Calculated risk, Slade reminded himself. Sometimes you played the odds. He counted the steps off. Five, six, seven. . . . It wasn't likely the gunman had the rifle trained on him now. He'd be waiting for Jessica to make a move from behind the clump of rocks. Ten, eleven, twelve. . . . Did she listen this time? he thought with a quick flash of panic. Don't look back. For God's sake don't look back. There was only one way left to keep her safe.

The moment he reached the top, Slade drew out his gun and dashed for the trees.

The carpet of dried leaves would betray him. Slade counted it a mixed blessing. It would distract the man's mind from Jessica. He took a zigzagging pattern toward the place where he had spotted the flutter of white. Just as he dashed behind an oak, he heard the dull thud. Dispassionately he saw splinters of bark fly out, inches from his shoulder.

Close, he thought. Very close. But his brain was cool now. The man would know he'd botched the contract. Just as he'd know, if Slade's luck ran out, that the police were involved. Slade's gun and his shield would tell the pro all he needed to know.

Patiently, Slade waited. Five eternal minutes became ten. The sweat was drying cold on his back. Neither man could move soundlessly, so neither moved at all, one laying seige to the other. A bird, frightened off by Slade's mad rush into the grove, came back to settle on a limb and sing joyfully. A squirrel hunted acorns not ten feet away from where he stood. Slade didn't think at all, but waited. The storm-brewing clouds closed in, completely blocking out the sun. Now the grove was cold and gloomy. Wind whipped through his loose shirt.

There was a muffled sneeze and a rustle of leaves. Instantly Slade sprang out toward the sound, hitting the ground and rolling when he caught a quick glimpse of the man and the rifle. Prone, he fired three times.

Jessica lay numbed by a fear icier than the wind off the Sound. That was all she could hear—the wind and the water. Once she had loved the sound of it, the howling wind, the passionate crash of water against rock. Staring up at the sky, she watched the clouds boil. With one hand she clutched Slade's discarded jacket. The leather was smooth and cold, but she could just smell him. She concentrated on that. If she could smell him, he was alive. If she willed it hard enough for long enough, he'd stay alive.

Too long! her mind shouted. It's been too long! Her fingers tightened on the leather. He'd said he'd be back. She was going to believe that. With her fingertips, she touched her lips and found them cold. The warmth he'd left there had long since faded.

I should have told him I love him, she thought desperately. I should have told him before he left. What if. . . No, she wouldn't let herself think it. He was coming back. Painfully, she shifted enough so that she could watch the beach steps.

She heard the three rapid shots and froze. The pain in her chest snapped her out of it. Her lungs were screaming for air. Dimly, Jessica ordered herself to breathe before she scrambled up and ran. Fear made her clumsy. Twice she stumbled on her way up the steps, only to haul herself up and force more speed into her legs. She broke into the grove, skidding on cracked leaves and branches.

Slade sprang around the moment he heard her. He was quick, but not quick enough to prevent her from seeing what he'd been determined she wouldn't see. Jessica stopped her headlong rush into his arms, relief turning to shock and shock to trembling.

Cursing, he stepped in front of her, blocking her view. "Don't you ever listen?" he demanded, then pulled her into his arms.

"Is he . . . did you . . ." Unable to finish, she shut her eyes. She wouldn't be sick, she ordered herself. She wouldn't faint. One of his shirt buttons ground into her cheek and she concentrated on the pain. "You're not hurt?"

"No," he said shortly. This aspect of his life should never have touched her, he berated himself. He should have seen to it. "Why didn't you stay on the beach?"

"I heard the shots. I thought he'd killed you."

"Then you'd have done us both a lot of good rushing in here." He pulled her away, took one look at her face, and yanked her back into his arms. "It's all right now."

For the first time his tone was gentle, loving. It broke her down as his shouting and anger would never have done. She began to weep in raw, harsh sobs, the fingers of one hand digging into his shirt, the fingers of the other still holding his jacket.

Without a word he led her to the edge of the grove. He sat on the grass, then drew her down into his lap and let her cry it out. Not knowing what else to do, he rocked, stroked, and murmured.

"I'm sorry," she managed, still weeping. "I can't stop."

"Get it all out, Jess." His lips brushed her hot temple. "You don't have to be strong this time."

Burying her face against his chest, she let the tears come until she was empty. Even when she quieted, he stroked the hair from her damp face, rocking her with a gentle rhythm. The need to protect had long since stopped being professional. If he could have found the way, Slade would have blocked the morning from her mind—taken her away somewhere, someplace where no ugliness could touch her.

"I couldn't stay on the beach when I heard the shots."

"No." He kissed her hair. "I suppose not."

"I thought you were dead."

"Ssh." He took her lips this time with a tenderness neither of them had known he possessed. "You should have more faith in the good guys."

She wanted to smile for him but threw her arms around his neck instead. The contact was another reassurance that he was whole and safe. "Oh, Slade. I'm not sure I could live through something like that again. *Why?* Why would anyone want to kill me? It just doesn't make sense."

He drew her away so that their eyes met. Hers were red and swollen from weeping, his cool and direct. "Maybe you know something and don't even realize it. The pressure's on, and whoever's in charge of this business is smart enough to know it. You've become a liability."

"But I don't *know* anything!" she insisted, pressing the heels of her hands to her temples. "Someone wants to kill me and I don't even know who it is or why. You said that . . . that man was a professional. Someone paid him to kill me."

"Let's go inside." He pulled her to her feet, but she jerked away. The helpless weeping was over and the strength was back, though it had the dangerous edge of hysteria.

"How much was I worth?" she demanded.

"That's enough, Jess." He took her by the shoulders for one quick shake. "Enough. You're going to go in and pack a bag. I'll take you to New York."

"I'm not going anywhere."

"The hell you aren't," he muttered as he started to pull her toward the house.

Jessica yanked out of his grip for the second time. "You listen to me. It's *my* life, my shop, my friends. I'm staying right here until it's over. I'll do what you tell me to a point, Slade, but I won't run."

He measured her slowly. "I've got to call this business in. You're to go straight to your room and wait for me."

She nodded, not trusting his easy acceptance. "All right."

He nodded, not trusting hers.

The moment she stepped into her room, Jessica began to peel off her clothes. It was suddenly of paramount importance that she scrub off every grain of sand, every lingering trace of the time she had spent on the beach. She turned the hot water in the tub on full until the room was misted with steam. Plunging in, she gasped at the shock of the heat against her chilled skin, but took the soap and lathered again and again until she could no longer smell the scent of salt water—the scent of her own fear.

It had been a nightmare, she told herself. This was normalcy. The cool green tile on the walls, the leafy fern at the window, the ivory towels with the pale green border she had chosen herself only the month before.

A month ago, she thought, when her life had been simple. There'd been no man then coolly attempting to kill her for a fee. David had still been the brother she'd never had. Michael had been her friend, her partner. She hadn't even heard of a man named James Sladerman.

She closed her eyes, and pressed hot, damp fingers to them. No, it wasn't a nightmare. It was real. She had lain curled behind a pile of rocks while a man she barely knew—and loved—had risked his life to protect hers. It was horribly, horribly real. And she had to face it. The time was over when she could try to pass off what Slade had told her as a mistake. While she had been blindly trusting, someone she loved had deceived her, involved her. Used her.

Which one? she asked herself. Which one could she believe it of? Would either David or Michael have stood passively by while someone arranged to have her killed? Lowering her hands, Jessica forced herself to be calm. No, whatever else she would believe, she wouldn't believe that.

Slade thought she might know something without being aware of it. If that was true, she was no closer to the solution than she had been before. Jessica slid her body down in the tub and closed her eyes again. There was nothing for her to do but wait.

Anything but satisfied with his conversation with his contact, Slade put a call through directly to the commissioner.

"Sergeant, what have you got for me?"

"Someone tried to kill Jessica this morning," he answered curtly.

For a moment there was dead silence on the wire. "Give me the details," Dodson demanded.

Briefly, emotionlessly, Slade reported while his knuckles turned white on the receiver. "She won't leave voluntarily," he finished. "I want her out, today. Now. I need you to officially give me the right to put her in protective custody. I can have her in New York in less than two hours."

"I take it you've already checked in with this."

"Your friends in the Bureau want her to stay." This time he didn't attempt to disguise the bitterness in his voice. "They don't want anything to interfere with the investigation at this delicate state," he quoted, jamming a cigarette between his lips. "As long as she's willing to cooperate, they won't move her."

"And Jessica's willing to cooperate."

"She's a stubborn, thick-headed fool who's too busy thinking about Adams and Ryce and that precious shop of hers."

"You've gotten to know her, I see," the commissioner commented. "Does she trust you?"

Slade expelled a stream of smoke. "She trusts me."

"Keep her in the house, Slade. In her room if you think it's necessary. The servants can think she's ill."

"I want—"

"What you want isn't the issue," Dodson cut him off curtly. "Or what I want," he added more calmly. "If it's gone far enough that a pro was hired, she'll be safer there, with you, than anyplace else. We've got to nail this down fast, with luck, before it's known that the contract on her is no longer operable."

"She's nothing more than bait," Slade said bitterly.

"Just make sure she isn't swallowed," Dodson retorted. "You've got your orders."

"Yeah. I've got them." Disgusted, Slade slammed down the receiver. Looking down at his hands, he realized, frustrated, that they were as good as tied. He was up against a solid wall of refusal from Jessica right on down. The investigation, the justice of it, didn't matter to him any longer. She was all that mattered. That in itself destroyed his objectivity, and by doing so, made her vulnerable. He cared too much to think logically.

His hands curled into fists. No, *cared* wasn't the right word, he admitted slowly. He was in love with her. When or how, he didn't have the faintest idea. Maybe it had started that first day she had come tearing down the steps toward him. And it was stupid.

He scraped his hands roughly over his face. Even without the mess they were in, it was stupid. They'd been born on opposite sides of the fence, had lived their entire lives on opposite sides of the fence. He didn't have any right to love her, even less to want her to love him. She needed him now, professionally as well as emotionally. That would change when it was over.

Right now he couldn't afford to think of how he would deal with his feelings once Jessica was safe again. First he had to make certain she would be. With slow, deliberate force he crushed out his cigarette, then went upstairs to her.

They came into the bedroom together, Jessica from the bath, Slade from the hall. She was wrapped in one of the ivory towels with the pale green border. Her hair fell wet around her shoulders while the clean, sharp scent of soap surrounded her. Her skin was flushed and glowing from the heat of her bath.

For a moment they stood still, watching each other. She could feel the frustration, the anger in him, as he turned to close the door behind him.

"Are you all right?"

"Yes." She sighed a little because it was nearly the truth. "I'm better. Don't be angry with me, Slade."

"Don't ask for the impossible."

"All right." Needing something to do, she went to the dresser and picked up her brush. "What do we do now?"

"We wait." Straining against impotence, he jammed his fists in his pockets. "You're to stay in the house, let the servants think you're ill or tired or just plain lazy. You're not to answer the door, or the phone, or see anyone unless I'm with you."

She slammed the brush back down, her eyes meeting his in the mirror. "I won't be jailed in my own home."

"Either that or a cell," he improvised, adding a shrug. "Either way you want it."

"You can't put me in a cell."

"Don't bet on it." Leaning back against the door, he ordered his muscles to relax. "You're going to play this my way, Jess. Starting now."

Her automatic rebellion was instantly quelled as she remembered those agonizing minutes on the beach. She wasn't only risking her own life, she realized, but his as well. "You're right," she murmured. "I'm sorry." Abruptly she whirled around. "I *hate* this! I hate all of it."

"I told Betsy you didn't want to be disturbed," he answered calmly. "She's got it into her head that you've caught a touch of David's flu. We'll let her go on thinking it. Why don't you get some sleep?"

"Don't go," she said quickly as he reached for the doorknob.

"I'll just be down in the library. You need to rest, Jess, you're worn out."

"I need you," she corrected and walked to him. "Make love to me, Slade . . . as if we were just a man and a woman who wanted to be together." Lifting her arms, she circled his neck. "Can't we believe that it's true for just a few hours? Let's give each other the rest of the morning."

He lifted the back of his hand to her cheek in a gesture they both found uncharacteristic. Slade wondered if she knew that his need was as great as hers—to touch, to lose himself in lovemaking. So close, he thought as he ran his knuckles over the line of her cheekbone. He'd come so close to losing her.

"Your eyes are shadowed." His voice was rough with emotion. "You should rest." But his lips were already lowering to seek hers.

The brush of mouth on mouth—gentle, caring, comforting. Jessica melted against him, overpowered by the tenderness she'd drawn out of him. His hand was still on her face, gliding over her features as if to memorize them. On a sigh, her lips parted, softening under his until he thought he would sink into them.

They had stood there only the night before, locked in an embrace that had been turbulent with passion, almost brutal with desire. The soothing quality of his kiss was no less arousing.

The pulse at the base of her throat beat thickly as Slade's fingertip slid down to it. She needed, he needed. Thinking only of this, he brought his hand to the loose knot of the towel to draw the material from her before he carried her to bed.

Jessica saw his eyes, dark and intense, sweep over her as she began to unbutton his shirt. Then her fingers were trapped between their bodies, his mouth fixed on hers again. The night before, he'd made her soar; now he made her float. Soft kisses, soft words, both unexpected, rained over her. His fingers combed through her damp hair, spreading it out on the pillow, lingering in its silk as if he would touch each individual strand.

Her hands were free again and, trembling, they dealt with the last buttons on his shirt. She felt a quiver race after her exploring hands, heard his incoherent murmur as she worked the rest of his clothes from him. Flesh to heated flesh, they began the journey. Rain began to patter against the windows.

He'd never been a gentle lover—intense, yes, passionate, yes, but never gentle. She unlocked something in him, something giving and tender. No less desperately than the night before, he wanted her, but with the hunger came the sweet calming breath of love. The peaceful emotion guided them both to meet the unspoken needs of the other. *Touch me here. Let me taste. Look at me.* There was no need for words when hearts and minds were attuned.

He wandered over the body he already knew so well. In the gray, gloomy light he worshiped her with hands, lips, and eyes. Naked, heavy eyed, skin flushed with desire, Jessica lay quietly as he took his gaze over her with the slow intensity she recognized. She was a willing prisoner in the thick, humming world conceived by pleasure and sensation. The rain grew loud, the room dimmer.

Lifting a hand to either side of his face, she drew him back to her. With her tongue, she slowly traced the shape of his mouth, then probed inside to drink up all the tastes of him. Flavors musky and sharp seeped into her, deep into her, until she hungered for more. Desire rose to the next plane.

Not so gentle now, nor so calmly, they sought each other. Kisses became possessive, caresses urgent. Under the sound of the rain she heard his breath shudder. Under the pressure of her hands, she felt his muscles tighten. The liquefying pleasure that had ruled her became a hot, torrid need, catapulting her beyond the gray, insular room into a place of white light and golden fire.

Searing, searching, seducing, his mouth veered down her, over her, until her skin was molten. With a strength only recently discovered, she rolled on top of him to complete a crazed journey of her own. They tangled and untangled in a wildly choreographed dance of passion. The light wasn't white now, but red; the fire flamed blue.

She heard her name rip from his lips before they crushed down on hers. Whatever madness he spoke was muffled against her in his urgency. Desire spun into delirium as they came together. There was speed and strength and desperation. Faster and faster they climbed while his mouth clung to hers, swallowing her gasps, mixing them with his own.

Spent, she lay beneath him. His mouth was pressed to her throat, his hands tangled in her hair. The rain drummed against the windows now, hurled by the wind. His body was warm and damp and heavy on hers. A feeling of security drifted over her, followed by a weariness that reached her bones. Slade lifted his head to see her eyes glazed over with fatigue.

"You'll sleep now." It wasn't a question. He tempered the command with a kiss.

"You'll stay?" The words were thick as she fought off sleep long enough to hear his answer.

"I'll start the fire." Rising, Slade walked to the white brick hearth and added paper to the kindling. The long match hissed as he struck it. Crouched, he watched the flames lick, then catch.

Minutes passed, but he remained, staring steadily at the fire without seeing it. He knew what was happening to him. No, what had happened to him, Slade corrected. He was in love with a woman he should never have touched. A woman he had no business loving. A woman, he reminded himself grimly, whose life depended on him. Until she was out of danger, he couldn't afford to think of his own feelings, or of their consequences. For her sake, the cop had to come first, the man second.

Straightening, he turned back to her. The shock of the morning had taken its toll in exhaustion, he noted. She lay on her stomach, one hand balled loosely on the pillow. Her hair fanned out, dry now, her face pale beneath its disorder. Her eyes were shadowed, her breathing heavy. The fire brought flickers of light into the room to play over her skin.

She was too small, he thought, too slender, to deal with what had happened; to deal with the threat of what could happen. And how much good would he do her? he asked himself as his eyes passed over her. Love clouded his judgment, slowed his reflexes. If he'd been an instant slower that morning. . . Shaking his head, Slade began to dress. It wouldn't happen again. He'd keep her in the house if he had to chain her. He'd see her through this, keep her safe, and then . . .

Then he'd get out of her life, he promised himself. And get her out of his.

He drew the sheet over her, allowing his hand to linger on her hair briefly before he left the room.

7

Late, late in the morning, while Jessica slept, Slade stood at the library window that faced the garden. Watery sunlight struggled through the clouds to fall on the wet shrubs and grass. Rosebushes were naked and thorny. Fall flowers hung heavy-headed and dripping, their petals scattered. The storm had stripped the leaves away from the trees so that they lay soggy and dull on the ground. The wind had died.

Someone had let Ulysses out. The dog lumbered along on the wet ground, sniffing here and there without any apparent interest. Finding a likely branch, he clamped it between his teeth, then trotted off toward the beach. Hell of a watchdog, Slade thought in disgust. But then, who could blame the dog for not barking at someone he knew—someone he'd seen in the house for years?

Scrubbing his face with his hands, Slade turned away from the window. The waiting was eating at him—another sign that he was losing his objectivity. By rights he should have taken this part of the assignment in his stride. As long as Jessica did what she was told, there was virtually no way for anyone on the outside to get to her. The man who had been in the parlor the night before was running scared and for that reason wouldn't test his luck during the day in a house full of active servants. If everything went according to plan, it was simply a matter of holding tight until the FBI made its move. *If*, Slade thought tightly, everything went according to plan.

Plans had a way of veering off course when the human element was involved.

A glance at his watch told him that Jessica had been asleep for half an hour. With luck, she'd sleep through the day. When she slept, she was safe—and every hour that she was safe brought them closer to the finish.

Idly, he picked up one of the books from a pile he'd begun to organize. She'd have to get someone to take care of this mess, he thought—once her life was settled again. Once her life was settled, he repeated silently, and he was back in New York, away from her. With an oath, he tossed the book aside. Was he ever going to get away from her? he wondered with something uncomfortably close to fear. Oh, he could put the distance between them—miles of distance. All he had to do was to get into his car and head it in the right direction. But how long would it take him to chase her out of his head? That was for tomorrow, he reminded himself and was suddenly, abominably tired. He knew better than to think of tomorrows.

"Slade?"

Turning, he saw Jessica in the doorway. It annoyed him that she was there, infuriated him that her face was still pale, her eyes still shadowed. "What are you doing up?" he demanded. "You look like hell."

Jessica managed a weak smile. "Thanks. You know how to boost a woman's morale, Sergeant."

"You're supposed to be resting," he reminded her.

"I couldn't sleep."

"Take a pill."

"I never take pills." Because her hands were clammy, she linked them together. She wouldn't tell him of the nightmare that had woken her—of the sharp, sweating fear that had had her choking back a scream as she fought off sleep. Nor would Jessica tell him how she had reached for him only to find him gone. "Are you working?"

Slade frowned, then followed her gaze to the pile of books beside him. "I might as well clear up some of this," he said with a shrug. "I've got nothing but time now."

"I could help." Uncomfortably aware that her movements were jerky, Jessica walked farther into the room. "And don't make one of those snide remarks," she continued hurriedly. "I know the library's a disgrace and the finger points at me, but I do have a knack for organizing once I get started. If nothing else I can fetch and carry for you until—"

He cut off her stream of hasty words by putting his hand over hers as she reached for a book. Her skin was ice cold. Instinctively he tightened his grip, wanting to warm her. "Jess, go back to bed. Get some sleep. I'll have Betsy bring you up a tray later."

"I'm not sick!" The words erupted from her as she yanked her hand away.

"You're going to be," Slade returned evenly, "if you don't take care of yourself."

"Stop treating me like a child," she ordered, enunciating each word carefully. "I don't need a baby sitter."

"No?" He gave a quick laugh, remembering his early conception of his assignment. "Then tell me, how much sleep have you had in the last two days? When's the last time you've had a meal?"

"I had dinner last night," she began.

"You pushed your dinner around your plate last night," he corrected. "Keep it up. You'll pass out and make my job easier."

"I'm not going to pass out," she said quietly. Her eyes had darkened, that much more of a contrast to her skin.

Because he wanted to rage at her, Slade withdrew. "I wouldn't count on it but suit yourself," he said carelessly. "Overall it doesn't matter whether you're conscious or unconscious." In dismissal, he turned back to the stack of books.

"I'm sorry I'm not as accustomed to this sort of thing as you are," Jessica began in a tone that started off calm, then became more and more agitated. "It isn't every day I'm investigated by the FBI and shot at by a professional gunman. The next time I'm sure I'll be able to enjoy a banquet after I see a dead body on my property. All in a day's work for you, isn't it, Slade? Killing a man?"

A hard knot lodged in his stomach, another in his chest. Casually, he pulled out a cigarette and lit it.

Chest heaving with the emotion of her words, she watched him. "Don't you feel *anything*?" Jessica demanded.

He made himself take a long slow drag, made himself speak calmly. "What do you want me to feel? If I'd been slower, I'd be dead."

Swiftly, she turned away, then pressed her forehead to the window glass. The few clinging raindrops blurred and seemed to multiply until she shut her eyes. *And so would you*, she reminded herself. What he did, he did for you. "I'm sorry," she murmured. "I'm sorry."

"Why?" His voice was as cool as the pane she rested upon. And just as hard. "You were on target again."

Taking a deep breath, Jessica turned to face him. Yes, the guards were there, but she knew him better now. What he had done that morning hadn't been done coldly. "You hate being reminded that you're just as human as the rest of us, don't you? It infuriates you that you're haunted by feelings, emotions, needs." Slowly she walked to him. "I wonder if that's why you won't stay with me after we've made love. Are you afraid I'll find a weakness, Slade? A little crack I might be able to widen?"

"Watch how far you go," he warned softly. "You won't like the trip back."

"You hate wanting me, don't you?"

In a deliberately controlled movement, Slade crushed out his cigarette. "Yes."

As she opened her mouth to speak again, the door to the library swung open. Both she and Slade turned to see David stride in. He took a long look at Jessica, then pushed his glasses back up on his nose.

"You look like hell. Why aren't you in bed?"

"David." She couldn't control the tremor in her voice or the sudden urge that had her racing into his arms to hug him fiercely. David sent Slade a surprised look over her shoulder as he awkwardly patted her back.

"What's all this? You got a fever? Come on, Jessie."

Not him, she thought desperately. Please, God, not David. Through sheer force of will, Jessica controlled the tears that burned in her eyes.

In silence, Slade watched the exchange. Jessica clung to David's thin frame as if it were an anchor while he looked puzzled, concerned, and embarrassed all at once. Speculating, Slade dipped his hands into his pockets.

"Hey, what's all this? Is she delirious?" David tossed the question at Slade, but managed to nudge Jessica back enough to peer into her face. "You look ready to drop," he stated and tested her forehead with his palm. "Mom called me at the shop, giving me all kinds of grief about passing on my germs." Drawing her away, he grimaced at the memory. "That's what you get for coming into my room and shoving that chicken soup down my throat."

"I'm all right," she managed. "Just a little tired."

"Sure, tell that to someone who didn't spend last week flat on his back moaning."

Jessica wanted to cling to him again, to pour out everything that was inside her. Instead she took a step back, smiled, and hated herself. "I'll be fine. I'm just going to take it easy for a couple of days."

"Have you called the doctor?"

"David—"

The annoyance in her tone pleased him. "It's great having the situation reversed," he told Slade. "She did nothing but nag for two weeks. Have you?" he demanded of Jessica again.

"When I need one, I'll call one. Why aren't you at the shop?"

"Don't worry, I'm heading right back." David shot her a grin, relieved by the question and the brisk tone. That was more like Jessica. "After Mom called and read me the riot act, I wanted to check on you. The deliveries went out yesterday without any problem. Traffic's been light, but I've made enough sales to earn my keep." He gave her hair a quick tug. "I don't want to see you in the shop until next week, babe. Michael and I can handle it. In fact, you look like you could use a vacation."

"If you tell me how terrible I look again, you're not going to get that raise you've been hinting about."

"That's what happens when you work for a woman," he told Slade. Turning, David headed back for the door. "Mom says for you two to come in to lunch. This time *you're* getting the chicken soup." With a satisfied grin tossed over his shoulder, he left them.

The moment the door closed, Jessica pressed both hands to her mouth. What ran through her wasn't pain, not even an ache, but a bloodless kind of hurt that left her numb in the vital areas of heart and mind. She didn't move or make any sound. For a moment she felt that she had simply ceased to exist.

"Not David." Her own whispered words jolted her. With them came a torrent of emotion. "*Not David!*" she repeated, whirling on Slade. "I won't believe it. Nothing you can say will make me believe he'd do anything to hurt me. He isn't capable, any more than Michael is."

"In a couple of days it'll be over." Slade kept his tone neutral. "Then you'll know one way or the other."

"I know *now*!" Spinning around, she dashed for the door. Slade's hand clamped down on hers on the handle.

"You're not going after him," he said evenly. When she tried to jerk free, he took her by the shoulders with more gentleness than he was feeling. He hated to see her like this, tormented, desperate—hating knowing it was him she would turn against. But he had no choice. "You're not going after him," he said again, spacing the words precisely. "Unless I have your word, I'll cuff you to the bed and lock you in." He narrowed his eyes as her hand struggled beneath his. "I mean it, Jess."

She didn't turn against him, but to him. And that, Slade discovered, was worse. "Not David," she murmured, crumpling into his arms. "Slade, I can't bear it. I think I could stand anything but knowing either one of them was involved with what—with what happened this morning."

She seemed so fragile. He was almost afraid she would shatter if he applied the least pressure. What do I do with her now? he wondered as he laid his cheek on her hair. He knew how to handle her when she was furious. He could even manage her when she dissolved into stormy tears. But what did he do when she was simply limp and totally dependent on him? She was asking him for reassurance he couldn't give, emotion he was terrified to offer.

"Jess, don't do this to yourself. Block it out, a couple of

days." He tilted up her chin until their eyes met. He saw trust, and a plea. "Let me take care of you," he heard himself say. "I want to take care of you." He wasn't aware of moving until his lips found hers. Her vulnerability undermined him. To keep her from harm, to shield her from hurt, seemed his only purpose. "Think of me," he murmured, unconsciously speaking the thoughts that raced around in his head. "Only think of me." Slade drew her closer, changing the angle for more soft, nibbling kisses. "Tell me you want me. Let me hear you say it."

"Yes, I want you." Breathless and pliant, she allowed him to give and to take while she remained passive. For the moment Jessica had no strength to offer anything but surrender in return, but it was enough for both of them. In his arms she could almost forget the nightmare, and the reality.

He took her hands and buried his lips in the palm of one, then the other. It surprised her enough to steady rather than arouse her. Slade wasn't a man for endearments, or for typically romantic gestures. Even as the tingle ran up her arms, it occurred to Jessica that her weakness, her despair, only made his difficult job impossible. He'd been wiser than he knew to ask her to think of him. Drawing on her reserves of strength, she straightened her shoulders and smiled at him.

"Betsy has a nasty temper when she has to keep meals waiting."

Gratified, he answered the smile. "Hungry?"

"Yes," she lied.

Jessica managed to eat a little, though the food threatened to stick in her throat. Knowing Slade watched her, she made an effort to appear as though she were enjoying the meal. She talked—rambled—about anything but what was foremost on her mind. Too many topics of conversation could lead back to the shop, to David, to Michael. To the man in the grove. Jessica found herself fighting the inclination to look out the window. To look out only reminded her that she was imprisoned in her own home.

"Tell me about your family," she demanded, almost desperately.

Deciding that it would be better to go along with her

pretense than insist she eat or rest, Slade passed her cream for the coffee she was allowing to grow cold. "My mother's a quiet woman—the kind of person who talks only when she has something to say. She likes little things like the figure I bought in your shop and fussy glass. She plays the piano—started taking lessons again last year. The only thing she ever insisted on was that Janice and I learn to play."

"Do you?"

Slade heard the surprise in her voice and gave her a mild scowl. "Badly," he admitted. "She finally gave up on me."

"How does she feel about . . ." Jessica hesitated, then picked up her spoon to stir her coffee. "About what you do?"

"She doesn't say." Slade watched her move the spoon around and around until a tiny whirlpool formed in the cup. "I wouldn't think it any easier to be the mother of a cop than the wife of one. But she manages. She's always managed."

With a nod, Jessica pushed the untouched coffee aside. "And your sister, Janice . . . you said she was in college."

"She wants to be a chemist." He gave a quick mystified laugh. "She said so after her first day in high school chemistry. You should see her mixing all those potions. This tall skinny girl with soft eyes and beautiful hands—not your average mad scientist. She blew up our bathroom when she was sixteen."

Jessica laughed—perhaps her first genuine laugh in twenty-four hours. "Did she really?"

"A minor explosion." Slade passed it off, pleased to hear the low gurgle that had been so much a part of her until the day before. "The super wasn't too impressed with her explanation of unstable compounds."

"One can see his point," Jessica mused. "Where does she go to school?"

"Princeton. She got a partial scholarship."

And even with that, Jessica reflected, the cost of tuition must devour his income. How much did a cop make? she wondered. Not enough, she thought instantly. Not nearly enough to compensate for the risk. His writing takes a back seat to his sister's education. Jessica studied the cold coffee in her cup and wondered if Janice Sladerman realized how much her brother was willing to sacrifice for her.

"You must love her very much," she murmured. "And your mother."

Slade lifted a brow. It wasn't something he thought of, it simply was. "Yes, I do. Things haven't been easy on either of them. They never complain, never expect."

"And you?" Lifting her eyes, Jessica gave him a long, quiet look. "How have you managed to hide from them what you really want?" Sensing his instant withdrawal, she reached out to take his hand. "You really hate anyone knowing what a nice person you are, don't you, Slade? Doesn't suit the tough cop image." She grinned, pleased to see that she'd embarrassed him. "You can always tell me how you knock suspects around until they beg to confess."

"You've been watching too many old movies." Linking his fingers with hers, Slade drew her to her feet.

"They're one of my vices," she confessed. "I can't tell you how many times I've seen *The Big Sleep*."

"That's about a private detective, not a cop," he pointed out as he walked her back to the library.

"What's the difference?"

He shot her a look. "How much time do you have?"

"Well." She considered, glad to forget the outside world for a few moments. "It might be interesting to learn why one's called a flatfoot and the other a gumshoe."

He stopped, turning to her with an expression between amusement and exasperation. "Very old movies," he decided.

"Classics," she corrected. "I only watch them for their cultural value."

Slade only lifted a brow at that. It was a gesture Jessica had learned he used in lieu of dozens of words. "Since you want to help, you can do the cataloging." He gestured toward the pile of books littering the work table. "Your handwriting has to be better than mine."

"All right." Grateful for any task, Jessica plucked one of a neat stack of index files. "I suppose you'll want to reference and cross-reference and all that sort of thing."

"Something like that."

"Slade." She put the card back down before she turned to him. "You'd rather be working on your book than doing this. Why don't you take a couple of hours for yourself?"

He thought of the novel, nearly finished, waiting for him on the desk upstairs. Then he thought of the way Jessica had looked when she had walked through the library doors an hour before.

"This kind of mess drives me crazy," he told her. "While I'm here, I might as well point you in the right direction. How many books are in here?" he asked before she could voice another objection.

Momentarily distracted, Jessica looked around. "I don't have any idea. Most of these were my father's. He loved to read." A smile touched her lips, then her eyes. "His taste was eclectic to say the least but I think he had a preference for hard-boiled whodunits." The thought occurred to her quite suddenly. "What's your book about? Is it a detective novel?"

"The one I'm working on now?" He grinned. "No."

"Well?" She lowered a hip to the table. "What then?"

He began to make a clear space for her to work. "It's about a family, beginning in the postwar forties and working through modern day. Changes, adjustments, disappointments, victories."

"Let me read it," she demanded impulsively. His words, she knew instinctively, would reveal much of the inner man.

"It's not finished."

"I'll read what is."

Searching for a pencil, Slade stalled. He wanted his words read. It was a dream he'd lived with for too many years to count. But Jessica was different; she wasn't the nameless, faceless public. Her opinion, good or bad, held too much weight. "Maybe," he muttered. "If you're going to help, you'd better sit down."

"Slade." Wrapping her arms around his waist, Jessica rested her cheek on his back. "I'll just bother you until you say yes. It's a talent of mine."

Something about the casually intimate embrace stirred him beyond belief. Her breasts pressed lightly against his back; her hands linked loosely at his waist. In that moment, for that moment, he surrendered completely to the love he felt for her. It was deeper than need, sharper than longing.

Didn't she see that there was nothing he could refuse her? Slade thought as he brought his hands down to cover hers.

Couldn't she see that she'd become woman and dream and vulnerability, all in the space of days? If they were to pretend—for her sake—that there was no threat beyond the walls, perhaps they could pretend for his that she belonged to him.

"Bother me," he invited, turning so that he could gather her into his arms. "But I warn you, I'm no pushover."

With a low laugh, Jessica rose on her toes until her lips brushed his. "I can only hope my work's cut out for me." Deepening the kiss, she slid her hands under his shirt to run them up the firm planes of his back, along the ridge of muscle.

"That might get you a couple of pages," he murmured. "Want to try for a chapter?"

She allowed her tongue to trace his lips lazily, giving them a quick teasing nip as she slid a finger up and down his spine. She sensed his response, just as she sensed his reluctance to show it to her. "Bargaining is my forte," she told him quietly. She gave him a slow, lingering kiss, retreating just as she felt him increase the pressure. "Just how many chapters are in this book?"

Slade closed his eyes, the better to enjoy the sensation of being seduced when no seduction was necessary. "About twenty-five."

"*Hmmm.*" He felt her lips curve as they touched his again. "This could take all day."

"Count on it." Unexpectedly, he drew her away, then framed her face with his hands. "We can start negotiations right after we do some work in here."

"Oh." Catching her tongue between her teeth, Jessica looked around at the disordered books. "After?"

"After," Slade said firmly, nudging her down in a chair. "Start writing."

Jessica was hardly aware of the hours that passed—one, then two, then three. He worked quietly, systematically, and with a patience she could never hope to emulate. Slade knew the books a great deal better than she. Jessica saved reading for the rare times when her physical energy lagged behind her mental energy. She enjoyed books. He loved them. She found this small realization another step in the ladder to discovering him.

It was easier in the quiet, cluttered library to get him to talk. *Have you read this? Yes. What did you think of it?* And he would tell her, easily and in depth, without ever stopping his work. How her father would have liked him, Jessica thought. He would have admired Slade's mind, his strength, his sudden flashes of humor. He would have seen the goodness Slade took such care to keep hidden.

She doubted Slade realized that, by letting her work with him here, he was revealing his other side. The dreamer. Perhaps she'd always known it was there, even when she had recognized the streak of hard street sense. It was a complex man who could carry a gun and discuss Byron's *Don Juan* with equal ease. That afternoon she needed the dreamer. Perhaps he knew it.

The light began to fade to a soft gray. Shadows gathered in the corners of the room. Jessica had forgotten her tension and had become involved with the mindless task of copying titles and names onto the index cards. When the phone rang, she scattered two dozen of them on the floor. Quickly she began to retrieve them.

"It just startled me," she said when Slade remained silent. She cursed her trembling hands as she gathered the cards back into a pile. "It's been so quiet, that's all." Furious with herself, she let the cards fall again. "Damn it, don't sit there looking at me like that! I'd rather you swore at me."

He rose and went to her, then crouched in front of her. "You made a hell of a mess," he murmured. "If you can't do better, I'll have to get myself a new assistant."

With a sound that was part sigh, part laugh, she leaned her forehead against his. "Give me a break, it's my first day on the job."

Betsy opened the door, then lifted her brows and pursed her lips. Well, she always figured where there was smoke there was fire, and she'd smelled smoke the minute those two had set eyes on each other. She gave a quick harrumph and watched Jessica jump as though she'd been scalded.

"Mr. Adams is on the phone," Betsy said regally, then closed the door again.

Slade closed his hand over Jessica's. "Call her back," he said quietly. "Have her tell him you're resting."

"No." With a quick shake of the head, she rose. "Don't keep asking me to run, Slade, because I might do it. Then I'd hate myself." Turning, she picked up the phone. "Hello, Michael."

Slowly Slade straightened, tucked his hands in his pockets, and watched her.

"No, it's nothing really, just a little touch of the flu." Jessica spoke in quiet tones while she wrapped the phone cord around and around her fingers. "David's just feeling guilty because he thinks I caught it from him. He shouldn't have worried you. I am taking care of myself." She shut her eyes tightly a moment, but her voice remained light and steady. "No, I won't be in tomorrow." The cord of the phone dug into her skin. Carefully Jessica unwound it. "That's not necessary, Michael. . . . No, really. I promise—don't worry. I'll be—I'll be fine in a couple of days. Yes, I will. . . . Good-bye."

After replacing the receiver, Jessica stood for a moment, staring down at her empty hands. "He was concerned," she murmured. "I'm never ill. He wanted to come over and see me, but I put him off."

"Good." Sympathy wouldn't help her now, Slade decided. "We've done enough in here for today. Why don't we go upstairs?" He walked to the door, as if taking her agreement for granted. He opened it, then paused and looked back. She still hadn't moved. "Come on, Jess."

She crossed to him, but stopped at the door. "Michael would do nothing to hurt me," she said without looking at him. "I just want you to understand that."

"As long as you understand that I have to look at everyone as a potential threat," he returned evenly. "You're not to see either one of them—or anyone else—unless I'm with you." Spotting the light of defiance in her eyes, he continued. "If he and David are innocent, the next couple of days won't do them any harm. If you really believe it," he went on, shrugging off the look of fury she sent him, "you should be able to handle all this."

He wasn't going to give her an inch, Jessica concluded as

she fought both tears and rage. Perhaps it was best if he didn't. She took a long steadying breath. "You're right. And I will handle it. Are you going to work on your book now?"

Slade gave no sign that the change of subject made any difference to him. "I thought I might."

Jessica was determined to be just as practical as he—at least on the surface. "Fine. Go on up then and I'll bring some coffee for both of us. You can trust me," she went on before he could object. "I'll do exactly what you tell me to do so I can prove you wrong. I *am* going to prove you wrong, Slade," she told him with quiet, concrete determination.

"Fine, as long as you stick to the rules."

Finding herself more at ease with a goal in mind, Jessica smiled. "Then I'll bring up the coffee. While I'm reading your book, you can concentrate on finishing it. It's one sure way to keep me occupied for the rest of the day."

He pinched the lobe of her ear. "Is that a bribe?"

"If you don't know one when you hear one," she countered, "you must be a pretty lousy cop."

8

Jessica's coffee grew cold again. She sat up against the headboard of Slade's bed with a pile of manuscript on either side of her. The stack of pages she had read was rapidly outgrowing the pile she had yet to read. Engrossed, she had been able to pass off Betsy's nagging when the housekeeper had brought up a tray of soup and sandwiches. Jessica had given her an absent promise to eat which she had forgotten the moment the door was closed again. She'd forgotten, too, though he had scrawled notes and revisions in the margins, that she was reading Slade's work. The story, the people, had completely taken her over.

She traveled with an ordinary family through the postwar forties, through the simplicities and complexities of the fifties, into the sixties with their turbulence and fluctuating mores. Children grew up, values changed. There were deaths and births, the realization of some dreams and the destruction of others. Through it all, as a new generation coped with the pressures of the seventies, Jessica came to know them. They were people she might have met—undeniably people she would have cared for.

The words flowed, at times gently, at other times with a grittiness that made her stomach tighten. It wasn't an easy story—his characters were too genuine for that. He showed her things she didn't always want to be shown, but she never considered setting the pages aside.

At the end of a chapter Jessica reached automatically for the next page. Confused, she glanced down to see that there were no more. Annoyed with the interruption, she then realized she had read all he had given her. For the first time in almost three hours, the sound of Slade's typing penetrated her concentration.

There was a full moon. That, too, came to her abruptly. The light flowed into the room to vie with the stream of the bedside lamp. The fire Slade had lit when they'd come upstairs had burned down to glowing embers. Jessica stretched her cramped muscles, wanting to give herself a moment before she went into Slade.

When she had insisted on reading his work, Jessica hadn't been certain how she would feel or what she would say to him when she was finished. Knowing herself too easily influenced by emotion, she had been certain that she would find some merit in his writing. Now she wanted time to decide how much her feelings for Slade had to do with her feelings about the story she had just read.

None, she realized. Before she had completed the first chapter Jessica had forgotten why she was reading it even though her main purpose had been accomplished. She knew Slade better now.

He had a depth of perception she had only sensed, an insight into people she envied as well as admired. In his writing as well as his speech, he was frugal with words—but in the writing, his inner thoughts surfaced. He might be sparing with his own emotions, but his characters had a range to them that were rooted in their creator.

And, Jessica mused, she'd been wrong when she had once told him he didn't know women. He knew them—almost too well, she thought as she fingered the tip of a page. How much did he see, when he looked at her, that she had been confident was private? How much did he understand, when he touched her, that she had been certain she could keep hidden?

Did he know she loved him? Instinctively Jessica glanced at the doorway that separated the bedroom and the sitting room. Slade's typing continued. No, she was certain he had no idea how deep her feelings ran. Or, she thought with a small smile, that she was determined not to let him walk out of her life whenever, or however, things were resolved. If he knew, she mused, he'd put her at arm's length. A cautious man, she reflected. Slade was a very cautious man—one who saw himself suited for the solitary life. Jessica decided that he had some surprises coming. When she felt her life was her own again, she was going to deal him a few.

She rose and went to the doorway. His back was to her, the light falling on his hands as they moved over the keys. From the set of his shoulders, the angle of his head, she could tell his concentration was deep. Not wanting to disturb him, she waited, resting against the doorjamb. The ashtray at his elbow was half full, with a lit cigarette smoldering and forgotten. His coffee cup was empty, but his dinner tray hadn't been touched. She felt a Betsy-like urge to scold him for neglecting to eat.

This is how it could be, she realized abruptly, if the nightmare was behind us. He could work here, and I'd hear the sound of his typing when I came home. There'd be times he'd get up in the middle of the night and close the door so the noise wouldn't wake me. We'd walk on the beach on Sunday mornings . . . watch the fire on rainy afternoons. One day, she thought and closed her eyes. It could happen one day.

With an exasperated sigh, Slade stopped typing. One hand reached up to rub at the stiffness in his neck. Whatever impetus had driven him for three hours had suddenly dried up, and he wasn't ready. Automatically he reached for his coffee, only to find the cup empty. Maybe if he went down for some more, the flow would come back. Even as he considered it, Jessica came to him.

Wrapping her arms around his neck, she rested her cheek on top of his head. Love was coursing through her swiftly, too swiftly. She squeezed him tightly, forcing back the words she was afraid he wasn't ready to hear. There were others she wanted to say first.

"Slade, don't ever stop doing what you were meant to do."

Not sure of her meaning, he frowned down at the words he'd just written. "How much did you read?"

"All you gave me—not enough. When will you finish? Oh, Slade, it's wonderful!" Jessica continued before he could speak. "It's a beautiful piece of work. Everything: the words, the feeling, the people."

Slade turned so that he could see her face. He didn't want platitudes, not from her. Her eyes were lit with enthusiasm while his remained cool and guarded. "Why?"

"Because you told a story with depth, about people all of us have met or have been." She spread her fingers, searching for words that would satisfy him. "Because it made me cry, and cringe, and laugh. There were parts—that scene in the parking lot in the seventh chapter—I didn't want to read. It was hard, savage. But I had to read it even when it hurt. Slade, no one that reads that is going to be untouched." She laid her hands back on his shoulders. "And isn't that why a writer writes?"

His eyes never left hers. He waited, weighing what he saw there with her words. "You know," he said slowly, "I don't think I realized until just now what a chance I was taking by letting you read it."

"A chance," she repeated. "Why?"

"If you hadn't been touched, I'm not sure I could have finished it."

Nothing he could have said would have meant more. Jessica brought his hand up to her cheek, wondering if he realized how much he'd said in one sentence. "I was touched, Slade," she said quietly. "When it's published, and I read it, I'm going to remember that part of it was written right here."

"Going to erect a monument?" he asked with a smile.

"Just a discreet plaque." Leaning over, she kissed him. "I wouldn't want it to go to your head. What about an agent?" she asked suddenly. "Do you have one?"

Chuckling, he drew her down into his lap. "Yes, I have one. so far we haven't done each other much good, but he's marketed some short stories, and he's doing whatever it is agents do to sell my other novel."

"The other one." Jessica drew away as Slade began to nibble on her ear. "It's finished then?"

"Mmm-hmm. Come back here," he demanded, wanting to taste that soft, sensitive spot at the curve of her shoulder.

"What's it about?" she demanded, eluding him. "When can I read it? Is it as good as this one?"

"Has anyone ever told you that you ask too many questions?" His hand slipped under her sweater to cup her breast. With his thumb, he flicked lazily over the point, feeling it harden as her heartbeat went from steady to erratic. "I like that," he murmured, nipping at the cord of her neck. "I can feel your pulse go crazy everywhere I touch." In one long stroke, he moved down her rib cage to her waist. "You're losing weight," he said with a frown. "You're already too thin. Did you eat any dinner?"

"Has anyone ever told you that you talk too much?" Jessica asked before she pressed her lips to his.

His answer was a low sound of pleasure. She tasted warm—more pungent than sweet—as the tip of her tongue slipped to his to tantalize, then retreated to provoke. He thought he heard her laugh, low and husky, before he gripped the back of her neck in his hand and plunged deep. Her scent and her taste were the same so that he felt himself surrounded by her. Before Slade could rise to carry her to the bed, Jessica was pulling him to the floor.

There was a sudden urgency in her, a flash of fire. The habitual energy that had been lacking in her all day abruptly surfaced in a torrent of passion. She tugged at the buttons of his shirt, impatient to have his flesh against hers while her mouth was already making wild passes over his face and throat. Her aggression both unbalanced and aroused him. Because he understood that part of it came from a need to block out her fears, Slade let her lead. The pace was hers—and it was frantic.

Within moments he was too caught up in her to think at all. She was undressing him swiftly, her lips following the path of her busy hands until his mind was totally centered on her. Shivering thoughts, quick tastes, maddening touches—she gave him no time to focus on only one, but insisted he experience all in an enervating haze of sensation.

Vulnerability was something new to him, but he found himself trapped in a sultry, viscous world where he had no guards, no defense. She was driving him beyond the point of reason, but still he couldn't find the will to stop her and take command. This time there was only response. It poured from him, increasing her strength and depleting his.

When her mouth fixed on his again, he fumbled with her sweater. He, whose hands were always sure, found them damp and trembling when at last he could touch her. Though her flesh was as hot as his, she allowed him to linger nowhere, moving over him with a speed and agility that left his hands frustrated and his body throbbing. Skin slid over skin, her moist, hungry mouth ravaging, her soft hands greedy.

Knowing he was helpless excited her. This strong man, this hard man, was completely powerless under her spell. But Jessica had no spells, only needs. And love. She realized that she loved him more on finding that he could be weak. His body was firm and muscled, but it shuddered now—for her.

The light from the desk lamp slanted across his face so that she could see his eyes, opaque with passion, on hers. His mouth was tempting, and she took it, tasting all the hot, heady flavors that sprang from desire. His breath was warm and ragged as it trembled into her open mouth. With sudden clarity, she smelled the lemon and beeswax polish from the desk. In some sane portion of her mind, Jessica knew the scent would come back to her whenever she thought of the first time he fully gave himself to her. For she had him now—mind, emotion, and body. Even when he took them back, she would have had this one instant in time when he held nothing away from her.

So she gave herself to him, taking him into her on a flash of sharp silvery pleasure. Her strength soared, driving both of them fast and hard, until it crested, suspending them. When it ebbed, she seemed to dissolve into him so that they lay entwined, joined and sated.

Slade struggled to clear his mind but found that she filled it, consumed it. The power that had driven her was depleted, her body nearly weightless on his, but he discovered that she still dominated him. He wanted to draw away, perhaps to prove to both of them that he could, that he had a choice. His hands only tangled deeper into her hair until he found the soft, slender neck. Though she lay passive, hardly breathing, he could feel the hammer of her heart against his. No force of will could make his pulses level though his physical need was fully satisfied. He wanted her—but his wants were only to have her near.

"Jess." He lifted her face to his without any idea what thoughts would spill out into words. Her eyes were huge and heavy and shadowed. Her face was soft, with the afterglow of passion and with weariness. He'd had no right, he thought on a quick rage of guilt, no right to allow her to use up all her reserves of energy and strength to satisfy his needs.

"No, don't." Jessica could see the change in his face. Already, she thought, he was taking back what he had so briefly given her. "Don't shut me out," she said quietly. "Don't shut me out so soon."

Without realizing he was doing so, he traced her lips with his thumb. "Sleep with me tonight" was all he said.

Slade waited until he was certain she slept before he eased from the bed. Watching Jessica, he dressed in silence. Thin moonlight washed over her face and bare shoulders, shifting with shadows as a cloud passed over the moon. With any luck, he calculated that he could give the first floor a thorough check, stake out the parlor for a couple of hours, then be back without her ever knowing he had gone. Giving her one last look, he slipped from the room.

With the soundless efficiency that came from years of experience, Slade tested the multitude of doors and windows. He noted with disgust the simple locks that would keep out only the rankest of amateurs.

The house is full of silver and small, portable valuables, he reflected. A burglar's paradise—and she seals it off with dime-store locks. A credit card and a hairpin, Slade decided as he examined the rear kitchen door. He'd have to see that Jessica installed something less flimsy before he left.

In a mound of white fur, Ulysses slept on the cool tile floor, snoring lightly. He never stirred as Slade stepped over him. Testing, Slade rattled the knob on the back door. Ulysses' rhythm never altered.

"Wake up, you good-for-nothing mutt."

At the command, the dog opened one glazed eye, thumped his tail twice, then went back to sleep.

Rubbing the back of his neck, Slade reminded himself that

a run-of-the-mill burglar wasn't the immediate problem. He stepped over the dog again and left him snoring.

Cautiously, he moved through the servants' wing. There was a pale light under one door and the muffled laughter of a late-night talk show. The rest were silent. Glancing at his watch, he saw that it was just past midnight. Slade went back to the parlor to wait.

He sat in a wingback chair, lost in the shadows. Watch and wait. There was little more he could do. And he was itching to do something—anything to move the investigation along. Maybe the commissioner picked the wrong man after all, he mused. This time Slade wanted to look for trouble—and he wanted to find it. Whoever had hired the man in the grove was going to pay, he had little doubt of that. But he wanted to collect personally.

The woman upstairs in his bed was all that mattered. The diamonds were incidental—they were just rocks, after all, with a market value. Jessica was priceless. With a silent laugh, he stretched out his legs. Dodson could hardly have foreseen that his hand-picked bodyguard would fall in love with his assignment. Slade knew his own reputation: thorough, precise, and cool.

Well, he thought, he'd lost his cool almost from the instant he'd seen the little blond whirlwind with the Viking cheekbones. He wasn't thinking like a cop but like a man—a man who wanted revenge. And that was dangerous. As long as he remained on the force, he had to play by the rules. The first rule was no personal involvement.

Slade nearly laughed aloud at that. Rule one down the tubes, he decided as he dragged a hand through his hair. How could he be more personally involved? He was already in love with her, already her lover. If they were any more personal they'd be married and having children.

That thought stopped him cold. He couldn't permit his mind to run in that direction. He wasn't for her. They'd drift apart once the investigation was over. Naturally that's what he wanted, Slade told himself, but the frown remained in his eyes. He had his own life to deal with—the demands of his profession, his responsibilities, his writing. Even if there was room in his life for a woman, their paths ran in opposite directions. They weren't about to cross again. It was only chance that had brought them together this time, circumstances that had brought about an intimacy that had led to emotional attachment. He'd get over her. He pinched the bridge of his nose between his thumb and forefinger. The hell he would.

Wasn't a man allowed a few dreams? he demanded of himself, when he sat alone in the dark in a room that smelled of lemon wax and fall flowers. Wasn't he allowed to weave some sort of future when a woman lay soft and warm in his bed? He was entitled to some basic selfishness, wasn't he? With a half sigh, Slade settled against the back of the chair. Maybe the man was, but the cop wasn't. And, he reminded himself, Jessica needed the cop more whether she believed it or not.

Blanking out his mind, Slade waited in the dark for just under three hours. Instinct told him he was wasting his time. Some sleep was essential if he was to be alert enough to keep her safe and occupied during the daylight hours. Stiff from sitting, he absently worked out the kinks as he headed back to the stairs. Another day, he mused, two at the most—if Agent Brewster was as close as he'd led Slade to believe.

Fatigue settled over him the moment he allowed his muscles to relax. Four hours' sleep would recharge his system—he'd gotten by on less. Quietly, he turned the knob of his bedroom door.

Jessica was sitting in the middle of the bed, curled into a tight ball. She took the deep, tearing breaths of a drowning woman fighting for air. Moonlight pooled over her as she shuddered.

"Jess?"

There was a scream rising in her throat. When her head jerked up, Slade saw the wild sheen of fear in her eyes before she focused on him. She could hold back the cry by digging her teeth into her lip, but the shudders went on. Slade went to her swiftly. Her skin was clammy as he took her shoulders; her face damp with a mixture of tears and perspiration. It ran through his mind that someone had slipped past him and gotten to her, then the idea was as quickly dismissed.

"What is it?" he demanded. "What's the matter?"

"It's nothing." Desperately she fought to control the tremors. The nightmare had come back, horridly vivid, to attack all of her senses. Cold wind, the smell of salt spray, the roar of the surf—and someone's heavy footsteps as they ran after her, the shifting shadows as clouds blocked out the sun, the iron taste of her own terror. And worse, much worse, she had been afraid to turn, afraid she would see the face of someone she loved on the man who pursued her.

"I woke up," she managed. "I guess I panicked when you weren't here." It was partially true and difficult enough to confess. She couldn't bring herself to admit she could be terrorized by a dream.

"I was just downstairs." He brushed sweat-dampened hair from her cheeks. "I wanted to make sure everything was locked up."

"Professional habit?" She nearly managed a smile before she dropped her head to his shoulder.

"Yeah." Even as he gathered her close, she trembled. It wasn't the moment, he decided, to lecture her on flimsy locks and thin chains. "I'll go down and get you a brandy."

"No!" She bit her lip again as the refusal came out too forcefully. "No, please, I already feel like an idiot."

"You're entitled to be jumpy, Jess." Softly, he brushed a kiss over her hair.

She wanted to cling, to beg him not to leave her alone for an instant. She wanted to pour out every fear and fantasy and dread. But she couldn't, and the denial was as much for her own sake as his. "With a policeman in the house?" she countered. Tilting back her head, she looked up at him. A strong face, she mused. Strong arms and serious eyes. "Just come to bed; you must be tired." Making the effort, she forced away the nerves and gave him a smile. "How does one man cope with two careers, Sergeant?"

He shrugged as he kneaded her tense shoulders. "I manage. How can a woman look so beautiful at three o'clock in the morning?"

"My mother claims it's bone structure." Her smile warmed a bit as she willed herself to relax under his hands. "I prefer to think it's something less scientific . . . like being born during a lunar eclipse."

Nuzzling her neck, he chuckled. "Were you?"

"Yes. My father said that's why I had cat's eyes—to help me see in the dark."

Slade kissed her lightly before he set her away from him and rose. "If you don't get some sleep, they're going to be bloodshot."

"What a gallant thing to say." Jessica frowned at him as he undressed. "What about you?"

"I can get by on three or four hours when I have to."

She gave a quick snort. "Your machismo's surfacing, Slade."

When he turned his head, the moonlight streamed over his face, illuminating the lightning-fast grin. Jessica felt her heart flutter up to her throat. Shouldn't she be used to him by now? she wondered. The mercurial moods, the streaks of boyish good humor in the sometimes overly serious man? His body was sleek and limber, streamlined like a Channel swimmer's, muscled like a lightweight boxer's. His face mirrored both of his professions—the intellect and the action.

He'll take care of you, her mind comforted. Just trust. But there were lines of fatigue and strain that the moonlight accented as well. *And you take care of him*, her thoughts added. Smiling, she held out her arms to him.

"Come to bed," she ordered.

Lying down beside her, Slade drew her close. There was no driving physical need to possess her. Instead he felt a simple serenity, all the more precious for its rarity. For the next few hours they would be any man and woman sharing the intimacy of sleep. She curled warmly into him, as much to soothe as be soothed. There were no more words.

Jessica lay still, schooling her breathing so that it was deep and even until she felt him drift off. With her eyes open and fear threatening on the verges of her mind, she watched the moonlight play on his shoulder as it rose and fell. The light was misty with predawn before she slept.

When the phone rang, he jolted out of a restless sleep. Sweat pearled on his forehead. Afraid to answer, more afraid not to, he lifted the receiver. "Yes, hello."

"Your time's up."

"I need more," he said quickly. Knowing that weakness would never be tolerated, he swallowed the tremor in his voice. "Just a few days. . . . It isn't easy to get to them with the house full of people."

"Must I remind you that you aren't paid to do only what's easy?"

"I tried to get to them last night . . . I was nearly caught."

"Then you were careless. I've no use for carelessness."

Less for carelessness than weakness, he thought rapidly and moistened his lips. "Jessica—Jessica's not feeling well." He reached for a cigarette to steady his nerves. He had to think quickly and calmly if he wanted to stay alive. "She isn't planning on coming into the shop. In a couple of days I should be able to convince her to take a long weekend. She'll listen to me." He took a greedy drag of his cigarette, praying that he spoke the truth. "With her out of the house, I can get to the diamonds without taking any chances." Moisture beaded on his top lip and he wiped the back of his hand across it. "You'll have them this weekend. A couple of days won't matter."

A sigh breathed through the phone, chilling him. "You're mistaken again—too many mistakes, my young friend. Remember my associate in Paris? He made mistakes."

The phone slid wetly in his hand. He remembered the man found floating in the Seine. "Tonight," he said desperately. "I'll have them for you tonight."

"Ten o'clock at the shop." He paused to make certain the weapon of fear had done its work. The soft, jerky breathing pleased him. "If you fail this time, I won't be so . . . understanding. You've done very well since you started to work for me. I'd hate to lose you."

"I'll bring them. Then I—then I want out."

"We'll discuss it. Ten o'clock." With a gentle click, the connection was broken.

9

$\mathscr{S}$lade's mind and body awoke at the same instant. The luxury of drifting slowly awake was something he had forfeited years before. He had had to perfect the ability to sleep quickly and lightly and to awake just as quickly, ready to function. It was a habit he looked forward to breaking without really believing he ever would.

He saw from the slant of the sun that it was still early, but he shifted his gaze to check the mantel clock nonetheless. Just past seven. The four hours' rest had done all it needed to do.

Turning his head, he looked down at Jessica. The pale blue smudges under her eyes made him frown. Though by his calculations she had slept nearly eight hours, the smudges were deeper than they had been the day before. Today he'd make certain she rested more—if he had to slip a sleeping pill into her coffee. And ate something—if he had to force-feed her. He could all but feel the pounds slipping off her.

Though he barely shifted the mattress as he moved away from her, her hand tightened on his arm. Her eyes flew open. "Get some more sleep," he ordered, touching his lips to hers.

"What time is it?" Her voice was husky and thick, but her hand stayed firm on his arm.

"Early."

Jessica relaxed, muscle by muscle, but didn't release him. "How early?"

"Too early." He bent to give her another brief kiss before he rose, but she pulled him closer.

"Too early for what?"

She felt his lips curve against hers. "You're not even awake yet."

"Wanna bet?" Running a hand down, she trailed her fingers over his flat stomach. The sleepy kiss smoldered with burgeoning passion. "Maybe you can't get by on three or four hours' sleep after all."

Cocking his brow, he lifted his head. "Wanna bet?"

Her answering laugh was smothered by his lips.

It had never been like this for her. Each time they made love it stunned her, enticed her, then consumed her. In his arms, with his hands and lips running wild and free over her body, she could lose herself. And how she needed to lose herself.

He'd known from the first how to play her. Each time they came together he found new variations, giving her no opportunity to become familiar with a touch or to anticipate a demand. He could dominate her mind so effortlessly, plunge her back into a world that was all keen emotion and sharp sensation.

Everything would magnetize, from the bare brush of a fingertip to the bruising pressure of lips. Jessica thought she could feel the individual threads of the sheet against the naked flesh of her back. The whispering tick of the clock was like thunder. Pale sunlight danced, gray and ghostly. She could see it fall over his hair, accenting its dark confusion as she dove her hands into it.

In her ear he whispered something poetic and foolish about the texture of her skin. Though the tone was almost reverent, his hands were aggressive—arousing and drugging in turns. Murmuring, she told him what she wanted. Shifting, she offered what he needed.

When he took her, Slade took her slowly, watching the flickers of pleasure and passion on her face in the thin morning light. Savoring the sensations that rippled through him as she moved, he nibbled on her parted lips. He tasted her, and himself, before he roamed over her closed lids.

Fragile, he thought, her skin was so fragile. Yet all the while her hips urged him to take, to take quickly. With iron control he kept the rhythm easy, prolonging the ultimate delight.

"Jess." He could hardly form her name between labored breaths. "Open your eyes, Jess. I want to see your eyes." The lids fluttered, as if weighed down by the pale gold lashes. "Open your eyes, love, and look at me."

He wasn't a man for endearments. Even through the haze of needs and sensations, Jessica recognized it. A new warmth filled her—pure emotion—to double the physical ecstasy. She opened them.

The irises were opaque, rich amber filmed over with passion. As he moved inside her, the lashes flickered, threatening to lower again. "No, look at me." His voice had dropped to a rough whisper. Their lips were close so that their breath merged, shudder for shudder. Jessica saw that his eyes were dark, dark gray and intense, as if he would look into her mind and read whatever frantic thoughts raced inside. "Tell me that you need me," he demanded. "I have to hear you say it, just once."

Jessica struggled to form words as she climbed higher toward delirium. "I need you, Slade . . . you're the only one."

His lips crushed down on hers to muffle her cry as he drove her swiftly to the peak. His last rational thought was almost a prayer—that the words he had demanded would be enough for him.

Strange that his body felt more rested, more relaxed now than it had upon waking. Slade slid down to press a kiss at the hollow between her breasts before he shifted from her. "Now, get some more sleep," he ordered, but before he could rise, Jessica had her arms locked around his neck.

"I've never been more awake in my life. What're you going to do with me today, Slade? Make me fill out more of those silly cards?"

"Those silly cards," he said as he slipped a hand under her knees, "are a necessary part of any organized library."

"They're boring," she said defiantly when he lifted her.

"Spoiled," he decided, carrying her into the bathroom.

"I certainly am not." The line appeared between her brows as he switched on the shower.

"You certainly are," he corrected genially. "But that's all right, I kind of like you that way."

"Oh well, thanks a lot."

He grinned, kissed her, then set her down in the shower stall. Jessica let out one long surprised scream. "*Slade!* It's freezing!"

"Best way to get the blood moving in the morning." He stepped in with her, partially blocking the spray. "Well, second best," he amended, then cut off a stream of abuse with his lips.

"Turn on the hot water," she demanded when he let her breathe again. "I'm turning blue."

He picked up her arm, giving it a light pinch. "No, not yet," he disagreed. "Want the soap?"

"I'll go take my own shower, thanks." Huffily, she tried to climb out only to find herself tangled with him under the icy spray. "Let go! This is police brutality." She lifted her face to glare at him and got struck fully with the cold needle spray. "Slade!" Sputtering, she blinked her eyes to clear them. Her body was pressed against his, frigid and tingling. "You're going to pay for this, I swear you are."

Blinded by the water and her own streaming hair, she struggled to free herself. With one arm keeping her prisoner, Slade took his free hand over her, lavishly soaping her skin.

"Stop it!" Infuriated and aroused, Jessica fought against him. When his hand passed intimately over her bottom, she grew more desperate. Then she heard him chuckle. Temper had her head snapping back up though the spray made her vision vague and watery.

"You listen to me," she began. Soapy fingers passed over her nipple. "Slade, don't." With a moan, she arched away. His palm slipped between her thighs. "No."

But her mouth blindly sought his. Jessica no longer felt the cold.

When she left the shower, she was glowing. Some color had seeped back into her cheeks. Slade noted it with a mixture of relief and pleasure though Jessica did her best to maintain outward indignance.

"I'm going to go get dressed," she informed him as she wrapped her wet hair in a towel. Because she was still naked, Slade found it hard to be offended by her haughty tone. Refreshed, he hooked his own towel around his waist.

"Okay, I'll meet you downstairs for breakfast in ten minutes."

"I'll be there," she told him grandly as she stooped to pick up his shirt, "when I get there."

Grinning, he watched her slip into his shirt and button it. "I could get used to seeing you like that," he commented. When she sent him an arch look, his grin only widened. "Wet and half naked," he explained.

"It's that machismo again," Jessica muttered, holding back the smile. Turning, she flounced to the door.

"Ten minutes," he reminded her.

Jessica cast a baleful look over her shoulder, then slammed the door behind her. Her grin quickly escaped, then almost as quickly faded. David stood directly outside her own bedroom door, his hand already poised to knock. His head had turned at the sound of the slam, but he hadn't moved. His eyes roamed over her, taking in Slade's shirt, the damp, glowing skin and sleep-starved eyes.

"Well." His tone, like his eyes, turned cool. "I guess you're already up."

Jessica felt more color flow into her cheeks. As close as she and David had been, living in the same house, they had never chanced upon each other under these circumstances. Both had always been extremely private about that area of their lives.

We're both adults, Jessica reminded herself as she walked toward him—but they'd been children together.

"Yes, I'm up. Did you want me?" Part of her wanted to run to him as she had the day before; part of her no longer trusted so unconditionally. Guilt gave her a reserve toward him nothing else could have. Sensing it, he became only more distant and disapproving.

"Thought I'd check with you before I went in, that's all." He gave her another brief, telling look. "Since you're busy . . ."

"I'm not busy, David. Come in." Coolly polite, Jessica

opened the bedroom door, then gestured him inside. It never occurred to her that she was breaking one of Slade's rules by talking to David alone. Even if it had, she would have done no differently. "Were there any problems yesterday I should know about?"

"No . . ." His eyes rested on the bed, which hadn't been slept in. His voice tightened. "Nothing to worry about. Obviously you've got enough to keep you busy."

"Don't be sarcastic, David. It doesn't suit you." She took the towel from her hair and flung it aside. "If you have something to say to me, come out with it." She plucked up a comb and began to drag it through her hair.

"Do you know what you're doing?" he blurted out.

Jessica's hand paused in midstroke. Slowly she lowered the comb to place it back on the dresser. She caught a glimpse of herself—pale, shadow-eyed, damp—and inadequately covered in Slade's wrinkled shirt. "Be specific."

"You're sleeping with the writer." Shoving up his glasses, he took a step toward her.

"And if I am?" she countered tightly. "Why should you object?"

"What do you know about him?" David demanded with such sudden heat that she was rendered speechless. "He comes out of nowhere, probably without two nickels to rub together. It's a nice setup here, big house, free meals, a willing woman."

"Be careful, David." She stiffened as the anger in her eyes met his.

"How do you know he's not just a sponge? A couple million dollars is a hell of a target."

The angry color paled with hurt. "And, of course, what else could he be interested in, other than my money."

When she would have turned away, he took her shoulders. "Come on, Jessie." The eyes behind the glasses softened. "You know I didn't mean it that way. But he's a stranger and you're . . . well, you're just too trusting."

"Am I, David?" She swallowed the sudden rise of tears as she studied his well-known face. "Have I made a mistake by trusting?"

"I don't want you to get hurt." He squeezed her shoulders before he dropped his hands. "You know I love you." The admission seemed to make him uncomfortable. With a shrug, he stuck his hands in his pockets. "And damn it, Jessica, you must know how crazy Michael is about you. He's been in love with you for years."

"But I'm not in love with him," she said quietly. "I'm in love with Slade."

"In love with him? *Jeez*, Jessie, you hardly know the guy."

The use of the silly exclamation brought a quick laugh from her as she dragged a hand through her hair. "Oh, David, I know him better than you think."

"Look, let me check into him a little bit, maybe find out—"

"No!" Swiftly, Jessica cut him off. "No, David, I won't permit that. Slade is my business."

"So was that creep from Madison Avenue who soaked you for ten thousand," he muttered.

Turning away, she covered her face with her hands. It was funny, she thought. She should be able to laugh. Two of the most important people in her life were warning her about each other.

"Hey, Jessica, I'm sorry." Awkwardly, David patted her wet hair. "That was a dumb thing to say. I'll butt out, just . . . well, just be careful, okay?" He shifted from one foot to the other, wondering why she was suddenly so emotional. "You're not going to cry or anything, are you?"

"No." That did nudge a small laugh from her. He sounded suspiciously as he had when he'd been twelve and she'd come home after fighting with her current boyfriend. Loyalty came full circle, overlapping everything else. "David . . ." Turning, Jessica laid her hands on his shoulders, looking beyond the lenses and deep into his eyes. "If you were in trouble—if you'd gotten in over your head and made a mistake, a serious one—would you tell me?"

His eyes narrowed slightly, but she couldn't tell if it was from curiosity or guilt. "I don't know. I guess it would depend."

"It wouldn't matter what you'd done, David, I'd always be on your side."

The tone was too serious. Uncomfortable, he shrugged his thin shoulders and tried to lighten it. "I'm going to remind you of that the next time you jump me for making a mistake in the books. Jessie, you really don't look good. You ought to think about getting away for a few days."

"I'll be fine." Sensing an argument, she continued. "But I'll give it some thought."

"Good. I've got to go, I told Michael I'd open up today." He gave her a quick kiss on the cheek. "I'm sorry if I came on too strong before. I still think . . ." Hesitating, he shifted his shoulders again. "Well, we've all got to do things our own way."

"Yes," she murmured as she watched him walk to the door. "Yes, we do. David . . . if you or Michael need money . . ."

"Are we going to get a raise?" he asked with a quick grin as he turned the knob.

Forcing a smile, Jessica picked up her comb again. "We'll see about it when I come back to work."

"Hurry back," he said, then left her alone.

Jessica stared at the closed door, then down at the comb in her hand. On a sudden spurt of rage, she hurled it across the room. Look at what she'd been doing! Pumping him, half hoping he'd confess so that she could see an end to things. She'd watched him, searching for some sign of guilt. And she wouldn't be able to prevent herself from doing the same with Michael. Her own lack of trust appalled her.

Dropping onto the stool of her vanity, she stared at her reflection. It wasn't right that she should feel this way—alienated from the two people she'd felt closest to. Watching for signs, waiting for them to make a mistake. Worse, she thought, worse, wanting them to make one so that she could stop the watching and waiting.

She took a long, hard look at herself. Her hair was wet and tangled around an unnaturally pale face. The pallor only accented the smudges under her eyes. She looked frail, already half beaten. That she could put an end to with a few basic practicalities. Stiffening her spine, Jessica began to dab makeup on the smudges. If an illusion of strength was all she had left, she'd make the best of it.

When the phone rang across the room, she jolted, knocking a small china vase to the floor. Helplessly, she stared at the shattered pieces that could never be put back together.

Betsy answered the phone as Slade reached the bottom of the stairs. "Yes, he's here. May I say who's calling?" She stopped Slade with an arch look as she held out the receiver. "It's a *Mrs.* Sladerman," she said primly.

Frowning, Slade took the receiver. "Mom?" Betsy sniffed at that and walked away. "Why are you calling me here? You know I'm working. Is anything wrong?" he demanded as annoyance turned to concern. "Is Janice all right?"

"Nothing's wrong and Janice is fine," his mother put in the moment he let her speak. "And how are you?"

Annoyance returned swiftly. "Mom, you know you're not supposed to call when I'm working unless it's important. If the plumbing's gone again, just call the super."

"I could probably have figured that one out all by myself," Mrs. Sladerman considered.

"Look, I should be home in a couple of days. Just put whatever it is on hold until I get there."

"All right," she said mildly. "But you did tell me to let you know if I heard anything from your agent. We'll talk about it when you get home. Good-bye, Slade."

"Wait a minute." Letting out an impatient breath, he shifted the phone to his other hand. "You didn't have to call to pass on another rejection."

"No," she agreed. "But I thought maybe I should call with an acceptance."

He started to speak, then stopped himself. Anticipation only led to disappointment. "On the new short story for *Mirror*?"

"Now, he did mention something about that too . . ." She let the sentence trail off until Slade was ready to shout at her. "But he was so excited about selling the novel that I didn't take it all in."

Slade felt the blood pounding in his ears. "What novel?"

"Your novel, idiot," she said with a laugh. "*Second Chance* by James Sladerman, soon to be published by Fullbright and Company."

Emotion raced through him too swiftly. Resting his forehead against the receiver, he closed his eyes. He'd waited all of his life for this one moment; now nothing seemed ready to function. He tried to speak, found his throat closed, then cleared it.

"Are you sure?"

"Am I sure," she muttered. "Slade, do you think I can't understand English, even if it's fancy agent talk? He said they're working up a contract and he'll be in touch with the details. Business about film rights and serial rights and clauses with numbers. Of course," she added when her son remained silent, "it's up to you. If you don't *want* the fifty-thousand-dollar advance . . ." She waited, then gave a maternal sigh. "You always were a quiet one, Slade, but this is ridiculous. Doesn't a man say something when he finally has what he's always wanted?"

Always wanted, he thought numbly. Of course she'd known. How could he have ever deceived himself into thinking he'd concealed it from her. The money hadn't sunk in. He was still hearing the magic word *published.* "I can't think," he said finally.

"Well, when you can, get the one you're working on now together. They want to see it. Seems they think they've got a tiger by the tail. Slade . . . I wonder if I've told you often enough that I'm proud of you."

"Yeah." He let out a long breath. "You have. Thanks."

Her chuckle was warm in his ear. "That's right, darling, save your words for your stories. I have a few hundred phone calls to make now; I love to brag. Congratulations."

"Thanks," he said again, inadequately. "Mom . . ."

"Yes?"

"Buy a new piano."

She laughed. "Good-bye, Slade."

He listened to the dial tone for nearly a full minute.

"Excuse me, Mr. Sladerman, would you like your breakfast now?"

Confused, Slade turned to stare at Betsy. She stood behind him—little black eyes, wrinkled skin, and graying hair on short sturdy legs. She smelled faintly of silver polish and lavendar sachet. The smile Slade gave her had her taking a cautious step back. It looked a bit crazed.

"You're beautiful."

She backed up another step. "Sir?"

"Absolutely beautiful." Swooping her up, he spun her in a fast circle, then kissed her full on the mouth. Betsy managed one muffled shriek. Her lips tingled for the first time in ten years.

"Put me down and behave yourself," she ordered, clinging to her dignity.

"Betsy, I'm crazy about you."

"Crazy, period," she corrected, refusing to be charmed by the gleam in his eye. "Just like a writer to be nipping at the brandy before breakfast. Put me down and I'll fix you some nice black coffee."

"I'm a writer," he told her with something like wonder in his voice.

"Yes, indeed," she said soothingly. "Put me down like a good boy."

Jessica stopped halfway down the steps to stare. Was that Slade grinning like a madman and holding her housekeeper two feet off the ground? Her mouth dropped open as he planted another kiss on Betsy's staunch, unpainted lips.

"Slade?"

Taking Betsy with him, he turned. It flashed through Jessica's mind that it was the first time she had seen him fully, completely happy. "You're next," he announced as he set Betsy back on her feet.

"Pixilated," Betsy told Jessica with a knowing nod. "Before breakfast."

"Published," Slade corrected as he swung Jessica from the stairs. "Before breakfast." His mouth crushed hers before she had a chance to speak. She felt the emotion coming from him in sparks; hard, clean emotion without eddies or undercurrents. The joy transferred into her so that she was laughing even as her mouth was freed.

"Published? Your novel? When? How?"

"Yes. Yes." He kissed her again before continuing to answer her questions in turn. "I just got a call. Fullbright and Company accepted my manuscript and want to see the one

I'm working on." Something changed in his eyes as he drew her back against him. She saw it only briefly. It wasn't a loss of happiness, but a full dawning of realization. "My life's my own," he murmured. "It's finally mine."

"Oh, Slade." Jessica clung to him, needing to share the moment. "I'm so happy for you." Lifting her face, she framed his in her hands. "It's just the beginning. Nothing will stop you now, I can feel it. Betsy, we need champagne," she said as she wrapped her arms around Slade's neck again.

"At nine o'clock in the morning?" The sentence trembled with righteous shock.

"We need champagne at nine o'clock on *this* morning," Jessica told her. "Right away in the parlor. We're celebrating."

With her tongue clucking rapidly, Betsy moved down the hall. Writers, she reminded herself, were hardly better than artists. And everyone knew the sort of lives *they* led. Still, he was a charming devil. She allowed herself one undignified chuckle before she went into the kitchen to report the goings-on to the cook.

"Come inside," Jessica ordered. "Tell me everything."

"That's everything," Slade told her as she pulled him into the parlor. "They want the book, that's the important thing. I'll have to get the details from my agent." The figure of fifty thousand finally registered fully. "I'll get an advance," he added with a half laugh. "Enough to keep me going until I sell the second one."

"That won't be long—I read it, remember?" On a sudden burst of energy, she grabbed his hand. "What a movie it would make! Think of it, Slade, you could do the screenplay. You'll have to be careful with the film rights, make sure you don't sign away something you shouldn't. Or a miniseries," she decided. "Yes, that's better, then you could—"

"Ever thought about giving up antiques and opening an agency?" he asked mildly.

"Negotiating's negotiating," she countered, then smiled. "And I'm an artist."

With her face set in lines of disapproval, Betsy entered carrying a tray. "Will there be anything else, Miss Winslow?"

When Betsy used such formal address, Jessica knew she

had sunk beyond reproach. "No, nothing, thank you, Betsy." She waited until the housekeeper had disappeared before casting Slade a baleful glance. "That's your fault really," she informed him. "She'll be polite and long-suffering all day now because you molested her and I joined you in champagne depravity before breakfast."

"We could ask her to have a glass," he suggested as he worked the cork from the bottle.

"You really do want me to be in trouble." Jessica lifted both glasses as the cork popped out. "To writing 'James Sladerman' on one of those necessary cards in my library," she said when both glasses were full.

Laughing, he clinked his rim against hers. "You'll have the first copy," he promised, then drained his glass.

"How do you feel, Slade?" Sipping more cautiously, Jessica watched him refill his glass. "How do you feel really?"

He studied the bubbles in the wine as if searching for the word. "Free," he said quietly. "I feel free." Shaking his head, he began to wander the room. "After all these years of doing what I had to, I'll have the chance to do what I want to. The money just means that I won't starve doing it even after this last year's tuition is paid. But now the door's open. It's open," he repeated, "and I can walk through it."

Jessica moistened her lips and swallowed. "You'll quit the force now?"

"I intended to next year." He toyed with the wick of a candle on the piano. A restlessness crept into the other feelings—a restlessness he hadn't permitted himself to acknowledge before. "This means it can be sooner—much sooner. I'll be a civilian."

She thought of the gun he secreted somewhere in his rooms upstairs. Relief flowed through her to be immediately followed by anxiety. "I guess it'll take some getting used to."

"I'll manage."

"You'll . . . resign right away?"

"No need to wait," he considered. "I've got enough to get by on until the contract's signed. I'll need time if they want rewrites. Then there's this novel to finish and another I've been kicking around. I wonder how it'll feel to write full-time instead of grabbing snatches."

A Matter of Choice

"It's what you were meant to do," she murmured.

"As soon as this is over, I'm going to find out."

"Over?" Her eyes fixed on his, but he wasn't looking at her. "You're staying?"

"What?" Distracted, he brought his gaze back to her. The expression on her face made him frown. "What did you say?"

"I thought you'd turn over the assignment to someone else." Jessica reached for the bottle to add champagne to a glass that was already full. "You'll want to get back to New York right away."

With deliberate care, Slade set down his glass. "I don't leave things until they're finished."

"No." She set the bottle back down. "No, of course you wouldn't."

"You think I'd walk out of here and leave you?"

The anger in his voice had her taking a quick sip of champagne. "I think," she said slowly, "when someone's about to get what they've worked for, waited for, they shouldn't take any chances."

He went to her and took the glass from her hand, then set it beside the half-filled bottle. "I think you should shut the hell up." When she started to speak, he cupped her face in one strong hand. "I mean it, Jess."

"You're a fool to stay when you have a choice," she blurted out.

His eyes narrowed with temper before he brought his mouth to hers for one brief, hard kiss. "You're a fool to think I have one."

"But you do," Jessica corrected more calmly. "I told you once before, we always have a choice."

"All right." Slade nodded, never taking his eyes off hers. "Say the word and I'll go back to New York today . . . if you'll go with me," he added when she started to speak. Her answer was a quick, defiant shake of the head. "Then we're in this together until the finish."

Jessica went into his arms and clung. She needed him to stay as badly as she wanted him to go. For now, she would only think of tomorrows. "Just remember, I gave you your chance. You won't get another one." Tilting her head back, she smiled at him. "One day I'm going to remind you of it. We're in this together."

He nodded again, not noting that she had edited his phrase. "Okay, let's get some breakfast to go with this champagne before Betsy completely writes you off."

10

For Jessica, the day crawled. The confinement alone would have been torture to her. She hated seeing the sun pour through the windows while she remained trapped inside. Even the beach was off limits, so she was prevented from learning if she could walk there again without looking over her shoulder.

Thinking of her shop only brought on a dull, nagging headache. The one thing she'd conceived and built by herself had been taken out of her hands. Perhaps she would never feel the same pride in it, the same dedication to making it the best she was capable of. Worse, her own weariness was taking her to the point where she no longer cared.

Jessica detested being ill. Her usual defense against a physical weakness was to ignore it and go on. It was something she couldn't—or wouldn't—change. Now, however, she had no outlet. The quiet library and monotonous tasks Slade gave her were grating on already taut nerves. Finally she tossed her pen across the table and sprang up.

"I can't stand this anymore!" She gestured widely to encompass the library at large. "Slade, if I write one more word, I'll go crazy. Isn't there something we can do? Anything? This waiting is unbearable."

Slade leaned back in his chair, listening calmly to her complaints. He'd watched her fidget throughout the morning, fighting off boredom, tension, and exhaustion. The only surprise he felt was that she'd managed to go so long without exploding. Sitting still, he mused, was not Jess Winslow's forte. He pushed aside a pile of books.

"Gin," he stated mildly.

Jessica plunged her hands into the pockets of her trousers. "Damn it, Slade, I don't want a drink. I need to *do* something."

"Rummy," he finished as he rose.

"Rummy?" For a moment she looked puzzled, then gave a gusty sigh. "*Cards?* I'm ready to beat my head against the wall and you want to play cards?"

"Yeah. Got any?"

"I suppose." Jessica dragged a hand through her hair, holding it back from her face a moment before she dropped her arm to her side. "Is that the best you can come up with?"

"No." Slade came to her to run his thumb along the shadows under her eyes. "But I think we've given Betsy enough shocks for today."

With a half length, Jessica gave in. "All right then, cards." She went to a table and pulled open a drawer. "What stakes?" she asked as she rummaged around in the drawer.

"Your capital's a bit bigger than mine," Slade said dryly. "Half a penny a point."

"Okay, big spender." Jessica located a pack of cards, then flourished them. "Prepare to lose."

And he did—resoundingly. At Slade's suggestion, they had settled in the parlor. His thoughts had been that the sofa and a quiet fire would relax her, and a steady, boring game might put her to sleep. He'd already concluded that asleep was the only way Jessica could handle the waiting without losing her mind.

He hadn't expected her to know a great deal about the game, any more than he had expected to be trounced.

"Gin," Jessica announced again.

He looked down in disgust at the cards she spread. "I've never seen anyone with that kind of luck."

"Skill," she corrected, picking up the cards to shuffle them.

His opinion was a brief four-letter word. "I've worked vice," he told her while she dealt. "I know a hustle when I see one."

"Vice?" Jessica poked her tongue in her cheek. "I'm sure that was very interesting."

"It had its moments," he muttered, scowling at the cards she'd dealt him.

"What department are you with now?"

"Homicide."

"Oh." She swallowed, but managed to keep her voice light. "I suppose that has its moments too."

He gave her a grunt that might have been agreement as he discarded. Jessica plucked it up and slipped it into her own hand. When Slade narrowed his eyes, she only smiled.

"You must have met a lot of people in your work." She contemplated her hand, then tossed out a card. "That's why your characters have such depth."

Briefly he thought of the street people; dealers and prostitutes, petty thieves and victims. Still, she was right in her way. By the time he'd hit thirty, Slade had thought he'd seen all there was to see. He was constantly finding out there was more.

"Yeah, I meet a lot of people." He discarded again, and again Jessica plucked it up. "Busted a few professional card sharks."

Jessica sent him an innocent look. "Really?"

"One was a great-looking redhead," he improvised. "Ran a portable game in some of the best hotels in New York. Soft southern accent, white hands, and a marked deck." Experimentally, he held a card to the light before he discarded it. "She went up for three years."

"Is that so?" Jessica shook her head as she reached for the card. "Gin."

"Come on, Jess, there's no way—"

Apologetically, she spread her cards. "There seems to be."

After a quick scan of her cards, he swore. "Okay, that's it." Slade tossed in his hand. "Figure up my losses. I'm finished."

"Well, let's see." Jessica chewed on the end of a pencil as she scanned the notepad dotted with numbers from previous hands. "You got caught with a bundle that time, didn't you?" Not bothering to wait for his reply, she scribbled on the pad. "The way I figure it, you owe me eight dollars and fifty-seven and a half cents." Setting down the pad, she smiled at him. "Let's just make it eight dollars and fifty-seven, even."

"You're all heart, Jess."

"Just pay up." She held out a hand, palm up. "Unless you want to go for double or nothing."

"Not a chance." Slade reached into his pocket and drew out his wallet. He tossed a ten onto the table. "I haven't got any change. You owe me a buck forty-three."

With a smirk, Jessica rose to retrieve her purse from the hall closet. "One dollar," she said, rummaging through her billfold as she came back into the parlor. "And . . . twenty-five, thirty, forty-three." She dropped the change into his hand, then grinned. "We're even."

"Not by a long shot." Slade grabbed her and gave her a long, thorough kiss. "If you're going to fleece me," he murmured, gathering her hair in one hand, "the least you can do is make it worth my while."

"Seems reasonable," she agreed as she offered her lips again.

God, how he wanted her. Not just for a moment or a day or a year, he thought as he lost himself in the taste of her. For always. Forever. All those terms he never allowed himself to think. There was a wall between them—the thin glass wall of status he forgot when she was in his arms. He had no business feeling what he felt or asking what he wanted to ask. But she was warm and soft, and her lips moved willingly under his.

"Jess—"

"Don't talk." She wrapped her arms tighter around him. "Just kiss me again." Her mouth clung to his, smothering the words that begged to be said. And the longer the kiss went on, the thinner the wall between them became. Slade thought he could feel it crack, then shatter without a sound.

"Jess," he murmured again as he buried his face in her hair. "I want—"

She jolted and Slade swore when the doorbell rang.

"I'll get it," she said.

"No, let Betsy." He held her another minute, feeling the hammer of her heart against his chest.

More than willing, Jessica nodded. When Slade released

her, she sank into a chair. "It's silly," she began, then Michael walked into the parlor.

"Jessica." Ignoring Slade, Michael went to her to take her hand. "You're so pale—you should be in bed."

She smiled, but couldn't prevent her fingers from tightening on his. "You know I'd go crazy if I stayed in bed. I told you not to worry, Michael."

"How could I help it?" He lifted her hand to brush his fingers over the knuckles. "Especially with David muttering all afternoon about you not knowing how to take care of yourself."

"That was—" She broke off, casting a quick look at Slade. "That was just a small disagreement we had. I'm fine, really."

"You don't look fine, you look exhausted." Frowning, Michael followed the direction of her gaze until he too looked at Slade. Understanding was followed by anger, resentment, then weary acceptance. "She should be in bed," he told Slade curtly, "not entertaining guests."

Slade shrugged as he eased himself into a chair. "It's not my place to tell Jess how to run her life."

"And what exactly is your place?"

"Michael, please." Jessica cut off Slade's answer and rose hastily. "I'll be going up soon, I am tired." With a silent plea, she turned to Slade. "I've kept you from your work too long. You haven't written all day."

"No problem." He pulled out a cigarette. "I'll make it up this evening."

Michael stood between them, obviously not wanting to leave—and knowing there was no point in staying. "I'll go now," he said at length, "if you promise to go up to bed."

"Yes, I will. Michael . . ." She put her arms around him, feeling the familiar trim build, smelling the light, sea-breeze scent of his after-shave. "You and David mean so much to me. I wish I could tell you."

"David and I," he said quietly and brushed a hand down her hair. "Yes, I know." He cast Slade a last look before he drew her away. "Good night, Jessica."

"Good night, Michael."

Slade waited until he heard the front door close. "What kind of disagreement did you have with David?"

"It was nothing to do with this—it was personal."

"Nothing's personal right now."

"This was." Turning, she fixed him with weary eyes, but he saw the stubborn crease between her brows. "I have a right to some privacy, Slade."

"I told you not to see either of them alone," he reminded her.

"Book me," she snapped.

"Don't tempt me." He met her angry eyes directly. "And don't do it again."

"Yes, Sergeant." On a disgusted sigh, Jessica dragged a hand through her hair. "I'm sorry."

"Don't apologize," he told her briefly. "Just do what you're told."

"I think I will go up. I'm tired," she added, not looking at Slade.

"Good." He didn't get up, nor did he take his eyes off her. "Get some sleep."

"Yes, yes, I will. Good night, Slade."

He listened to her go up the steps, then tossed his cigarette into the fire and swore.

Upstairs, Jessica filled the tub. That was what she needed, she told herself—an aspirin for the headache, a hot tub for the tension. Then she would sleep. She had to sleep—her body was crying for it. For the first time in her life Jessica felt the near weightlessness of true exhaustion. She waited until the bathroom was steamy, then lowered herself into the tub.

She knew she hadn't deceived Slade. Jessica wasn't fool enough to believe that he'd taken her excuse of being tired at face value. He was just as cognizant of what was going on inside her head as she was. The visit from Michael had been the last straw in a day filled with unspoken fears and rippling tension.

Nothing had happened, she thought in frustration as she let the water lap over her. How much longer would she have to wait? Another day? A week? Two weeks? On a long, quiet sigh she shut her eyes. Jessica understood her own personality too well. She would be lucky to get through the night much less another week of waiting and wondering.

Take an hour at a time, she advised herself. It was seven o'clock. She'd concentrate on getting through until eight.

At twenty past eight Slade went systematically through the first floor, checking locks. He'd waited, throughout an unbearably long day, for the phone call that would tell him his assignment was over. Silently he cursed Interpol, the FBI, and Dodson. As far as he was concerned, they were all equally to blame. Jessica wouldn't be able to take much more—that had been made abundantly clear during Michael's visit.

Another thing had been made abundantly clear. Slade had found himself entirely too close to stepping over the last boundary. If the doorbell hadn't rung, he would have said things best left unsaid, asked things he had no right to ask of a vulnerable woman.

She might have said yes. Would have said yes, he corrected as he stepped past a snoring Ulysses. And would have regretted it, he reflected, when the situation changed and her life was back to normal. What if he had asked her, then they'd been married before she'd had time to readjust? A good way to mess up two lives, Slade, he told himself. It was better to make the break now, draw back until they were just cop and assignment again.

At least she was upstairs resting, not beside him, tempting him to cross the line again. When she wasn't there where he could see her, touch her, it was easier to keep things in perspective.

The servants were settled in their wing. He could hear the low murmur of a television and the settling of boards. After he'd finished checking the locks, he'd go upstairs and write. Slade rubbed a hand over the back of his neck where the tension concentrated. Then he'd sleep in his own bed, alone.

As he walked toward the kitchen door, Slade saw the knob slowly turn. Muscles tensed, he stepped back into the shadows and waited.

Eight-thirty. Jessica glanced at the clock again as she roamed her bedroom. Neither the bath nor the aspirin had relaxed her enough to bring sleep any closer. If Slade would come up, she thought, then shook her head. She was becoming too dependent, and that wasn't like her. Still, she felt that her nerves would calm somewhat if she could just hear the sound of his typewriter.

An hour at a time, she reminded herself, glancing at the clock yet again. Well, she'd made it from seven to eight, but she wasn't going to make it until nine. Giving up, Jessica started back downstairs.

If he's annoyed, she mused, she'd just have to make the best of it. Being confined in the house was bad enough without restricting herself to her rooms. She'd almost be willing to fill out some more of those silly cards—anything to keep her hands busy until . . .

Her thoughts broke off as she came to the foot of the stairs. For the second time the parlor doors were closed. A tremor ran up her back, urging her to turn around, go to her room, and pretend she'd never left it. She'd taken the first step in retreat before she stopped herself.

Hadn't she told Slade not to tell her to run? This was her home, Jessica reminded herself as she stepped forward. Whatever happened in it was hers to deal with. Taking a deep breath, she opened the parlor doors and flicked on the light switch.

Slade waited as the rear door opened quietly. At first there was only a shadow, but the build was familiar. Relaxing, he stepped forward into the moonlight. Startled, David whirled around and swore.

"You scared the hell out of me," David complained as he let the door swing shut behind him. "What're you doing standing around in the dark?"

"Just checking the locks," Slade said easily.

"Moving right in," David muttered. After turning on the lights, he went over to the stove. "Want some coffee?" he asked grudgingly.

"Thanks." Slade straddled a chair and waited for David to come out with whatever was on his mind.

The last report Slade had received from Brewster had put David in the clear. His name and face and fingerprints had been run through the most sophisticated computers. His every movement had been under surveillance for over a month.

David Ryce was exactly what he seemed—a young, faintly defiant man who had a knack for figures and an affection for antiques. He was also having what he thought was a discreet affair with a pre-med student. Slade recalled Brewster's almost paternal amusement with David's infatuation.

Though he'd felt an initial twinge of guilt at keeping the knowledge of David's clean slate from Jessica, Slade had decided she had enough trouble keeping herself under control. Better that she suspected both men than for her to be certain that Michael Adams was up to his neck in the smuggling operation.

"Michael." Jessica stared, facing the truth and not wanting to believe it.

"Jessica." He stood with pieces of the desk in his hand, frantically searching for some viable excuse for his presence and his actions. "I didn't want to disturb you. I'd hoped you'd be asleep."

"Yes, I'm sure you did." With a quiet, resigned sigh, she shut the parlor doors at her back.

"There was a problem with this piece," Michael began. "I wanted to—"

"Please don't." Jessica crossed the room, poured two fingers of brandy, and drank it down. "I know about the smuggling, Michael," she told him in a flat voice. "I know you've been using the shop."

"Smuggling? Really, Jessica—"

"I said don't!" She whirled sharply, pushed by anger and despair. "I *know*, Michael. And so do the police."

"Oh God." As his color drained, he looked around wildly. Was there anyplace left to run?

"I want to know why." Her voice was low and steady. "You owe me that."

"I was trapped." He let the pieces of the desk fall to the floor, then groped for a cigarette. "Jessica, I was trapped. He promised you wouldn't be involved—that you'd never have to know. You have to believe that I'd never have gotten you mixed up in this if there'd been any choice."

"Choice," she murmured, thinking of Slade. "We all have our choices, Michael. What was yours?"

"In Europe a couple of years ago, I . . ." He took a greedy drag of his cigarette. "I lost some money . . . a lot of money. More than I had to lose, and to the wrong person." He sent her a swift, pleading look. "He had me worked over— you might remember when I took those extra two weeks in Rome." He drew in and expelled smoke quickly. "They were pros. . . . It was days before I could walk. When he gave me an alternative to crippling me permanently, I took it."

Dragging a hand through his hair, Michael walked over to the bar. He poured bourbon neat, splattering drops, then downed it in one swallow. "He knew who I was, of course, my family, my connection with your shop—your unimpeachable reputation." The liquor gave him temporary strength. His voice steadied. "It worked beautifully for him. It wasn't for the money, Jessica, I just wanted to stay alive. And then . . . I was in too deep."

She felt something soften inside her and quickly pushed it aside. No pity, she ordered herself. He wouldn't drag pity from her now. "Who is *he*, Michael?"

"No." Shaking his head, he turned to face her. "I won't tell you that. If he found out you had his name, you'd never be safe."

"Safe?" She laughed shortly. "If you were concerned for my safety, you might have told me not to walk on the beach when someone was going to shoot at me."

"Sh-shoot . . . good God, Jessica, I didn't think he'd. . . He threatened, but I never believed he'd actually try to hurt you. I would have done something." His hand trembled, spilling ash onto the carpet. With a jerky movement of his arm, Michael tossed the cigarette into the fire. "I begged him not to involve you, swore I'd do anything he wanted if he'd leave you out of it. I love you, Jessica."

"Don't talk about loving to me." With more control than she was feeling, Jessica bent over to pick up one of the pieces he had dropped. It was part of the inner molding. "What's in the desk, Michael?"

"Diamonds," he said and swallowed. "A quarter of a million. If I don't take them to him tonight—"

"Where?" she interrupted.

"To the shop, ten o'clock."

"Let me see them."

She watched him separate one of the partitions of a cubbyhole from the space where a drawer had been. Lifting a thin piece of wood, he revealed a false bottom. He drew out a small padded bag. "It's the last time," he began, clutching the bag in his palm. "I've already told him I'm through. As soon as I deliver these, I'm going to leave the country."

"It is the last time," Jessica agreed, then held out her hand. "But you're not delivering anything. I'm taking the diamonds, Michael. They're going back where they came from, and you're going to the police."

"You might as well hold a gun to my head!" He swiped an unsteady hand over his mouth. "He'll kill me, Jessica. If he finds out I went to the police, I wouldn't even be safe in a cell. He'll kill me, and if he knows what you've done, he'll kill you too."

"Don't be a fool." Eyes glittering, she grabbed the bag from his hand. "He'll kill you anyway, and me. Is he stupid enough not to know the police are closing in?" she demanded. "Is he stupid enough to leave you alive as a liability? Think!" she ordered impatiently. "Your only chance is with the police, Michael."

Her words touched off a fear he'd buried. Deep inside his mind, Michael had always known his involvement in the operation could only end one way. That fear, much more than money, had kept him loyal. "Not the police." Again, his eyes darted around the room. "I have to get away. Don't you see, Jessica, someplace where he won't find me! Let me have the diamonds, I can use them."

"No." Her hand tightened on the bag. "You used me, no more."

"For God's sake, Jessica, do you want to see me dead?" His breathing was raw and jerky as the words tumbled out. "I don't have time to raise the money I'll need. If I leave now, I'll have a start."

She stared at him. A thin film of sweat covered his face, beading over lips that trembled. His eyes were glazed with terror. He'd used her, she thought, but that didn't kill the feelings she had for him. If he was determined to run, she'd give him what he wanted. Jessica crossed to a painting of a

French landscape and swung it out on hidden hinges, revealing a wall safe. Quickly she twirled the tumblers and opened it.

"Take this." She offered Michael a stack of bills. "It's not worth what the diamonds are, but cash should be safer in any case. It won't take you far enough, Michael," she said quietly as he reached for the money. "But you have to make your own decision."

"There's only one I can make." He slipped the bills inside his jacket, then finally met her eyes. "I'm sorry, Jessica."

Nodding, she turned away. She heard his footsteps as he crossed to the doors. "Michael, was David involved in this?"

"No, David did nothing but take what he thought were routine orders." He saw everything he'd ever wanted, everything he'd ever cared about, slipping through his hands. "Jessica—"

"Just go, Michael. When you run, you have to run fast."

She listened for the click of the doors before she opened the padded bag. A cold, sparkling stream of diamonds fell into her palm. "So this is what my life's worth," she murmured. Carefully, she replaced them, then stared at the remains of the Queen Anne desk. "All for a whim," she whispered. If she hadn't had that impulse to bring the desk home then . . .

With a fierce shake of her head, Jessica broke off the thought. There were no if's. She needed to see Slade, but she needed a moment to herself first. On a sigh, she sank into a chair, letting the bag of diamonds fall into her lap.

"I guess Jessica told you about this morning." As the coffee heated on the stove, David reached for cups.

Slade lifted a brow. What was this, he wondered. "Shouldn't she have?" he countered.

"Look, I don't have anything against you—I don't even know you." David turned, tossing back the hair that fell over his brow. "But Jessie's important to me. When I saw her come out of your room this morning, I didn't like it." He measured the man across the room and knew he was outmatched. "I still don't like it."

Slade watched the eyes behind the lenses. So this was her private disagreement. Jessica had the loyalty she expected here, he mused. "I'd say you don't have to like it," Slade said slowly, "but Jess wouldn't feel that way."

Uncomfortable under the direct stare, David shifted a bit. "I don't want her to get hurt."

"Neither do I."

David frowned. Something about the way Slade said it made him believe it. "She's a soft touch."

Temper leaped into the gray eyes so quickly, David nearly backed away. When Slade spoke, the words were soft and deadly controlled. "I'm not interested in her money."

"Okay. Sorry." Relaxing a bit, David shrugged. "It's just that she's gotten stung before. She trusts everybody. She's really smart, you know—for a scatterbrain who forgets what she's doing because she's doing twenty things at once. But with people, Jessica wears blinders." The coffee began to boil over behind him. David spun around and turned off the burner. "Look, forget I said anything. She told me this morning it was none of my business, and it isn't. Except that . . . well, I love her, you know," he mumbled. "How's she feeling?"

"She'll be better soon."

"Boy, I hope so," he said fervently as he brought the coffee to the table. "I wouldn't want her to hear me say it, but I could use her at the shop. Between getting the new stock checked in and Michael's moodiness . . ." David grimaced and dumped milk into his coffee.

"Michael?" Slade prompted casually.

"Yeah, well, I guess everybody's entitled to a few temper tantrums. Michael just never seems to have a temper at all." He flashed Slade a grin. "Jessica would call it breeding."

"Maybe he has something on his mind."

David moved his shoulders absently before he drank. "Still, I haven't seen him this unraveled since the mix-up on the Chippendale cabinet last year."

"Oh?" Some wells, Slade mused, took no priming at all.

"It was my fault," David went on, "but I didn't know he'd bought it for a specific customer. We do that sometimes, but he always lets Jessie or me know. It was a beauty," David remembered. "Dark kingwood, great marquetry decoration. Mrs. Leeman bought it the minute it was uncarted. She was standing in the shop when the shipment came in, took one look, and wrote out a check. Michael got back from Europe the day we were packing it for delivery and had a fit. He said it had already been sold, that he'd had a cash advance." David took a quick sip of his coffee, discovered it was bitter, and drank again resignedly.

"The paperwork had been mislaid, I guess," he went on. "That was odd because Jessie's a fiend for keeping the invoices in order. Mrs. Leeman wasn't too pleased about the mix-up either," he recalled with a grin. "Jessie sold her a side table at cost to soothe her feathers."

"Who bought it?" Slade demanded.

"What, the cabinet?" David adjusted his glasses. "Lord, I don't know. I don't think Michael ever told me, and with the mood he was in, I didn't like to ask."

"You have the receipt?"

"Yeah, sure." Puzzled, David focused on him again. "At the shop. Why?"

"I have to go out." Slade rose swiftly and headed for the rear stairs. "Don't go anywhere until I get back."

"What are you—" David broke off as Slade disappeared upstairs. Maybe he was a nut after all, David mused as he frowned at Slade's empty chair. You're having a casual conversation with a guy and all of a sudden he's . . .

"Make sure Jess stays put," Slade ordered as he came down again. His jacket was already zipped over his revolver.

"Stays put?"

"Don't let anyone in the house." Slade paused long enough to aim hard, direct eyes at David. "No one comes in, got it?"

Something in the eyes had David nodding without question.

Slade grabbed a napkin and scrawled a number on it. "If I'm not back in an hour, call this number. Tell the man who answers the story about the cabinet. He'll understand."

"The cabinet?" David stared dumbly at the napkin Slade thrust into his hand. "*I* don't understand."

"You don't have to, just do it." The back door slammed behind him.

"Yeah, sure," David grumbled. "Why should I understand anything?" A loony tune, he decided as he stuffed the napkin into his pocket. Maybe writers were supposed to be loony tunes. Jessica sure knew how to pick them. With a glance at his watch, he decided to check on her. Maybe the writer was a little loose upstairs, maybe not, but he'd managed to unsettle him. When David was halfway down the hall, the parlor doors opened.

"David!" Jessica closed the distance between them at a run, then launched herself into his arms.

"Hey, what gives!" He managed to struggle out of her hold and take her by the shoulders. "Is there a different strain of flu running around that affects the brain?"

"I love you, David." Close to tears, Jessica framed his face with her hands.

He flushed and shifted his weight. "Yeah, I love you too. Look, I'm sorry about this morning—"

"We'll talk about that later. There's a lot I have to tell you, but I need to see Slade first."

"He went out."

"Out?" Her fingers dug into David's thin arms. "Where?"

"I don't know." Intently, he studied her face. "Jessie, you're really sick. Let me take you upstairs."

"No, David, it's important." Her voice changed from frantic to stern—the one he always responded to. "You must have some idea where he went."

"I don't," he returned a bit indignantly. "We were sitting there talking one minute, and he was up and heading out the next."

"About what?" Impatient, Jessica gave him a quick shake. "What were you talking about?"

"Just this and that. I mentioned that Michael'd been moody—like he'd been when we'd had that mix-up on the Chippendale cabinet last year."

"The Chippendale . . ." Jessica pressed her hands to her cheeks. "Oh God, yes, of course!"

"Slade gave me some business about not letting anyone in the house and calling some number if he didn't get back in an hour. Hey, where are you going?"

Jessica had swung her purse from the newel post and was rummaging through it. "He's gone to the shop. To the shop and it's nearly ten! Where are my keys! Call—call the shop, see if he answers." In a quick move, she dumped the contents of her purse on the floor. *"Call!"* she repeated when David gaped at her.

"Okay, take it easy."

While Jessica made a frantic search through the items on the floor, David dialed the phone. "I can't find them. I can't—they're in my coat!" she remembered and dashed for the hall closet.

"He doesn't answer," David told her. "Probably hasn't had time to get there yet if that's where he was going in the first place. Which doesn't make any sense because it's closed and . . . Jessie, where are you going? He said you weren't to go out. Damn it, you forgot your coat. Will you wait a minute!"

But she was already racing down the front steps toward her car.

11

It took Slade only a few moments to pick the lock on the front door of the shop. If there was one thing he was going to see to before he left, he decided, it would be to get Jessica to a decent locksmith. A miracle she hasn't been cleaned out, he mused as he moved through the main shop into the back room. Blind luck, Slade concluded, then tossed his jacket over a chair. Moving in the dark, he passed through the kitchen into what served as an office.

There was a large mahogany desk with neat stacks of papers, a blotter with names and numbers scribbled on it, and a Tiffany lamp. Slade switched it on. He caught the boldly printed ULYSSES NEEDS FOOD on the blotter right beneath the scrawled "New mop hndl—Betsy annoyed." With a half grin, Slade shook his head. Jessica's idea of organization was beyond him. Turning away, he walked to the file cabinet set in the rear corner.

The top drawer seemed to be her personal items. He found a receipt for a blouse she had bought two years before in a file marked INSURANCE POLICIES—SHOP. Between two file folders was a wrinkled grocery list. On a sound of annoyance, he pulled out the second drawer.

It was the other side of the coin. The files were neat, legible, and in perfect order. A quick flip through them showed Slade they were receipts for the current year, arranged chronologically, delivery bills, also current and chronological, and business correspondence. Each section was a study in organized filing. He thought of the top drawer and shook his head.

In the third drawer he found what he was looking for—receipts from the previous year. Slade drew out the first file folder and took it to the desk. Methodically, he scanned each one, beginning in January. He learned nothing else, when he had completed the first quarter's receipts, other than the fact that Jessica did a thriving business.

Slade replaced the first folder and drew out the second. Time ticked away as he examined each paper. He drew out a cigarette and worked patiently from month to month. He found it in June. *One Chippendale cabinet—kingwood with marquetry decoration.* His brow rose slightly at the price.

"Not a bad deal, I imagine," he murmured. Noting the name of the purchaser, he smiled. "Everyone makes a tidy little profit." After pocketing the receipt, Slade reached for the phone. Brewster might find David's little story very interesting. Before he had punched two numbers, Slade heard the sound of a car pulling up outside. Swiftly he turned out the light. As he moved from the desk he drew out his gun.

Jessica sped along the winding back road that led to her shop. If she'd had an ounce of sense, she berated herself, she would have told David to call the number Slade had given him. Why hadn't she at least told him to keep calling the shop until he reached Slade?

Nervously, she glanced at her watch. *Ten o'clock.* Oh God, if only the man coming to meet Michael were late! Slade would be in the back room, she concluded, searching through the old receipts. What would the man do when he got to the shop and found Slade there instead of Michael? Jessica pressed down harder on the gas and flew around a turn.

The beams of approaching headlights blinded her. Over-reacting, she swerved, skidding the left rear wheel on the shoulder of the road. Heart in her throat, she fishtailed, spun on gravel, then righted the car.

That's right, she thought with her heart pumping, wreck the car. That'll do everybody a lot of good. Cursing herself, Jessica wiped a damp palm on her slacks. Don't think, she ordered herself. Just drive—it's less than a mile now. Even as she said it, the car sputtered, then bucked. Frustrated, Jessica pressed down hard on the accelerator only to have the Audi stall, then die.

"*No!*" Infuriated, she slammed both hands against the steering wheel. The needle on the gas gauge stayed stubbornly on empty. How many times! she demanded. How many times had she told herself to stop and fill up? Knowing it wasn't the time for self-lectures, she slammed out of the car, leaving it in the middle of the road, lights beaming. She started to run.

Slade stood pressed behind the doorway that led to the back room. He heard the quiet click of the doorknob, then the cheery jingle of bells. He waited, listening to the soft footsteps and gentle breathing. Then there was a coldly patient sigh.

"Don't be childish, Michael. It hardly pays to hide when you leave a car out front in plain view. And you should know," he added softly, "there's no place you can hide from me."

Slade hit the overhead lights as he turned into the room. "Chambers, isn't it?" he said mildly. "With the fetish for snuffboxes." He leveled the gun. "We're closed."

With no change of expression, Chambers removed his hat. "You're the stockboy, aren't you?" He gave a wheezy chuckle. "How foolish of Michael to send you. But then, he hasn't the stomach for violence."

"I don't have that problem. Rippeon's in the morgue." When Chambers gave him a pleasantly blank look, Slade continued, "Or don't you catch the names of the pros you hire?"

"Death is an occupational hazard," Chambers said with an elegant shrug. He never bothered to glance at the gun leveled at his chest. He knew a man was the real weapon, so he watched Slade's eyes. "What has Michael promised you, Mr. . . ."

"Sergeant," Slade corrected, "Sladerman, NYPD, temporarily attached to the FBI." Slade caught the faint flicker in Chambers' eyes. "The only deal I have with Adams is a quiet . . . talk in the near future involving Jessica Winslow." The thought gave Slade a moment's grim pleasure. "Game's up, Chambers. We've had Adams under surveillance for some time, along with a few other members of your team. You were all that was missing."

"A slight miscalculation on my part," Chambers murmured as he glanced around the shop. "Normally I don't involve myself directly with any of the transports. But then, Miss Winslow has such a charming shop, I couldn't resist. A pity." He looked back at Slade again. "You don't look to be the type who'll take a bribe . . . even a lucrative one."

"You seem to be a good judge of character." Keeping the gun steady, Slade reached for the phone on the counter.

With the breath tearing in her lungs, Jessica dashed the last yards toward the shop. She could see the lights glowing behind the drawn shades. Her thoughts centered solely on Slade, she hit the door at a full run.

At a speed unexpected in a man of his bulk, Chambers grabbed her the moment she stumbled inside. His arms slid around her throat. Before fear could register, Jessica felt cold steel against her temple. Slade's forward motion stopped with a jerk.

"Put down your gun, Sergeant. It seems the game isn't quite over after all." When Slade hesitated, Chambers merely smiled. "I assure you, though the gun is small, it works very well. And at this range . . ." He trailed off delicately.

Casting a furious look into Jessica's stunned eyes, Slade let the gun drop. "Okay." He held up empty hands. "Let her go."

Chambers gave him a mild smile. "Oh, I don't think so. It seems I need an insurance policy—momentarily."

"Mr. Chambers." Jessica put a hand to the arm that was constricting her air.

"The Sergeant doesn't appreciate your timing, Miss Winslow," he said pleasantly. "However, I do, very much. This, shall we say, puts a different aspect on things."

Slade shot a quick glance at the clock on his right. By his calculations, David should be calling his contact within moments. The name of the game now was stall. "You won't have to put a bullet in her," he commented, "if you keep choking her."

"Oh, I beg your pardon." Chambers loosened his hold

fractionally. The gun stayed lodged at her temple. Greedy for air, Jessica gasped it in. "A beautiful creature, isn't she?" he asked Slade. "I often wished I were twenty years younger. Such a woman looks her best on a man's arm, don't you agree?"

"Mr. Chambers, what are you doing here this time of night?" It was a weak ploy, but the best Jessica could think of. "Let me go and put that thing away."

"Oh, my dear, we all know I can't do that. I would like to for your sake," he continued as Jessica, too, shifted her eyes to the clock. *How much time do we have?* she wondered frantically.

"She could be useful to you," Slade commented. "You'll need a shield to get out of this."

"I have my . . . escape routes plotted, Sergeant." He smiled. "I always leave a back door open."

"You can't expect to get away, Mr. Chambers." Jessica's eyes met Slade's, then shifted meaningfully to the clock. "Slade must have told you that the police know everything."

"He mentioned it." Keeping his arm firm, he patted her shoulder. "You became a small weakness of mine. I enjoyed those pleasant chats we had, those pleasant cups of tea. I felt badly that this was to be my last shipment before moving on. Oh yes," he said to Slade, "I was aware the authorities were getting close, though I confess I miscalculated just how close. And though it would seem the diamonds are temporarily lost, I'll find Michael eventually."

"He doesn't have them," Jessica said quickly, then grabbed Chambers' arm as it cut off her breath again.

"No?" The word was soft and silky. Even as Slade anticipated moving forward, Chambers shot him a warning look. "Where are they?"

Jessica swallowed, straining to hear the sound of sirens. *Why don't they come!* "I'll show you." Perhaps she could bargain for Slade's life. If she could keep him alive, then get Chambers out of the shop, even for a little while . . .

"Oh no, that won't do." He tightened his grip again. "Tell me."

"No." Jessica managed to whisper the word. "I'll take you."

Without speaking, Chambers took the gun from her temple and aimed it at Slade.

"No, don't! I have them at home," she said frantically. "I have them in the wall safe in the parlor. Don't hurt him, please. I'll give you the combination. Thirty-five to the right, twelve to the left, five right, and left to twenty-three. They're all there, I wouldn't let Michael take them."

"Honest," Chambers commented. "And trusting. I am fond of you, my dear, so I suggest you close your eyes. When it comes to your turn, I promise to make it as painless as possible."

Even as Slade made his move, Jessica screamed in protest. *"No!"* Using all of her weight and the adrenaline of terror, she flung herself on the arm holding the gun. She heard the shot echoing in her head as she stumbled, then was shoved roughly aside.

Jessica landed in a heap. She felt the pain in her shoulder as it connected with the floor, tasted the iron flavor of blood or fear in her mouth as she scrambled up. As she pushed the hair out of her eyes she saw Slade's fist fly toward Chambers' face. The portly man seemed to crumble layer by layer on his way to the floor.

So quickly, she thought numbly. It was all over so quickly. One moment they were both at the edge of their lives, and then it was over. She'd never take her life for granted again—not a second of it. Weakly, she leaned back against a highboy.

"Slade . . ."

"Get me some rope or cord from the back room, you idiot."

She pressed her fingers between her brows and stifled a hysterical giggle. So much for romantic endings, she thought as she stumbled blindly toward the storeroom. Blinking away the haze that covered her eyes, Jessica found some packing cord. She stared at it a moment, losing track of why she needed it.

"Will you hurry up!" Slade shouted at her.

Responding automatically, she brought it out to him. Ten-fifteen, she thought as she passed the clock. How could it only be ten-fifteen? Could people come so close to death and escape all in ten minutes? Slade ripped the cord out of her hand without looking up.

"Damn it, Jess, of all the stupid things to do! What the hell do you mean by bursting in here like that? You know you weren't to leave the house." Binding the unconscious Chambers, Slade let out a steady stream of curses.

"Michael told me ten o'clock," she murmured. "And I thought—"

"If you'd had a thought in your head you would have stayed put like you were told. What did you think you could do, racing out here like this. Damn it, I had him before you came barrelling through the door. That's not even enough for you." He secured the knot, then pushed passed her on the way to the phone. "Then you throw yourself on the gun." He wrenched off the receiver and started to dial. "You could've been shot."

"Yes." In dumb fascination, Jessica stared down at the stain spreading on the arm of her sweater. "I think I was."

"What?" Annoyed, he turned back to her, then dropped the phone out of suddenly nerveless hands. "Oh my God." In two strides he was back beside her, ripping the arm of the sweater off by the seam. "Jess, you're hit!"

Brows lowered in concentration, she stared at the wound. "Yes, I am," she said in the deliberately steady voice of a drunk. "I don't feel it. Should it hurt? There's a lot of blood."

"Shut up, damn it, just shut up!" He examined the wound quickly, seeing that the bullet had gone cleanly through the flesh. *Jess's flesh*, he thought. His stomach rolled. He stripped off his shirt and tore it into a tourniquet. "Stupid fool, you're lucky it wasn't your head." His hands trembled, causing him to fumble with the knot and curse her more violently.

"It was a little gun," she managed.

He shot her a look, ripe with conflicting emotions, but her vision was blurred. "A bullet's a bullet," he muttered. Feeling the warmth of her blood on his hands, he swallowed. A line of sweat ran down his naked back. "Damn it, Jess, what were you trying to do, jumping out that way? I knew what I was doing."

"Terribly sorry." Her head lolled a bit as she tilted it back and tried to focus on him. "How rude of me to intercept a bullet with your name on it."

"Don't get cute now," he said between his teeth. "If you weren't bleeding, I swear, I'd deck you." He wanted to hold her and was terrified she'd dissolve in his arms. His throat was dry from the rawness of his own breathing as he forced himself to treat her arm as an object, not part of her. When he'd finished binding the wound, Slade held her steady with one hand. "You probably saw that move on one of your stupid movies. Is that why you threw yourself at the gun?"

"No." She felt as if she were floating as he started to lead her to a chair. "Actually, Sergeant, it was because I thought he would kill you. Since I'm in love with you, I couldn't allow that."

He stopped dead at her words and stared down at her. When he opened his mouth to speak, he found he couldn't form a sound, much less a word. His hand dropped away from her uninjured arm.

"I'm really sorry," Jessica said in a thick voice. "But I think I'm going to faint."

The last thing she heard over the buzzing in her head was a stream of curses.

Jessica floated toward consciousness to a blur of white. She felt as though her body were drifting, apart from her mind. Even the steady throb in her shoulder seemed separate from her. The white dimmed to gray, then gradually lightened again until she focused on what was a wall. Perplexed, she stared at it.

With an interest dulled by medication, she shifted her gaze. All the walls were white, she noted. There were horizontal blinds at the window that showed hints of night between their slants. The blinds were white, too, as was the bandage around the arm that didn't feel like part of her. She remembered.

Letting out a sigh, she focused on a blue plastic pitcher and a clear plastic glass. Hospital, she thought with an absent grimace. She hated hospitals. A face bent over her, obscuring her line of vision. Amber eyes studied pale blue. They were nice enough eyes, she decided, in a round smooth face with a hint of jowl. She spotted the white coat and stethoscope.

"Doctor," she said in a whispery voice that made her frown.

"Miss Winslow, how are you feeling?"

She thought about it seriously for a moment. "Like I've been shot."

He gave a pleasant chuckle as he took her pulse. "A sensible answer," he concluded. "You'll do."

"How long . . ." She moistened dry lips and tried again. "How long have I been here?"

"Just over an hour." Taking out a slim flashlight, he aimed the beam at her right eye, then her left.

"It feels like days."

"The medication makes you sluggish. Any pain?"

"Just a throb—it doesn't feel like my arm."

He smiled and patted her hand. "It's yours."

"Slade. Where's Slade?"

His brow creased, then cleared. "The sergeant? He's spent most of his time pacing the corridors like a madman. He wouldn't wait in the lounge when I ordered him to."

"He's better at giving orders." Jessica lifted her head off the pillow, letting it fall back again when the room whirled around.

"Lie still," he told her firmly. "You'll be spending a little time with us."

The line appeared between her brows. "I don't like hospitals."

He only patted her hand again. "A pity."

"Let me see Slade," she demanded in the best authoritative voice she could muster. Her eyelids threatened to droop and she forced them open. "Please," she added.

"I don't think you take orders any better than he does."

"No." She managed a smile. "I don't."

"I'll let him come in, a few minutes only." Then, he thought as he studied her eyes, you'll sleep for the next twenty-four hours.

"Thanks."

With an absent nod, he murmured something to the nurse who entered.

* * *

Slade paced up and down the hospital corridor. Dozens of thoughts, dozens of fears, raced through his mind. A headache pulsed behind his right temple. She'd been so pale—no, it was just shock, she'd be fine. She'd been unconscious through the ambulance ride. It was better that way—she might have been in pain. God, where was the doctor? If anything happened to her. . . His stomach convulsed again. Swallowing, Slade forced the muscles to relax, turned fear to anger. The headache spread to the back of his neck. If they didn't let him see her soon, he was going to . . .

"Sergeant?"

Whirling, Slade caught the doctor by the lapel of his coat. "Jess? How is she? I want to see her now. Can I take her home?"

Well versed in dealing with frantic spouses, parents, and lovers, the doctor spoke calmly without bothering to struggle out of the hold. "She's awake," he said simply. "Why don't we sit down?"

Slade's fingers tightened. "Why?"

"Because I've been on my feet since eight o'clock this morning." With a sigh, he decided it was best to treat this one standing up. "Miss Winslow is as well as can be expected."

"What the hell does that mean?"

"Exactly what it says," the doctor returned evenly. "You did a good job of emergency first aid. As to your second question, you can see her in a moment, and no, you can't take her home. Does she have any family?"

Slade felt the color drain from his face. "Family? What do you mean family? The wound wasn't that bad, the bullet went clean through. I had her here inside a half hour."

"You did very well," the doctor told him. "I simply want to keep her here for a few days under observation. I need to know who to notify."

"Observation?" Terrifying visions ran through his mind. "What's wrong with her?"

"To put it simply, exhaustion and shock. Would you like more complicated medical terms?"

Shaking his head, Slade released him and turned away. "No." He rubbed his hands over his face. "That's all it is, then? She's going to be all right?"

"With rest and care. Now, her family?"

"There isn't anyone." For lack of something to do with his hands, Slade stuck them in his pockets. A sensation of utter helplessness covered him, sapping the strength that tension and anger had given him. "I'll take the responsibility."

"I know this is a police matter, Sergeant, but what exactly is your relationship to Miss Winslow?"

Slade gave a short laugh. "Baby sitter," he muttered. "I'll take the responsibility," he repeated with more force. "Call Commissioner Dodson, NYPD—he'll verify it." Turning back, he fixed the doctor with a steady look. "I want to see her. Now."

Jessica was watching the door when Slade opened it. Her lips curved. "I knew you'd find a way to get past the guards. Can you bust me out of this place?"

Keeping his hands in his pockets, he crossed to her. She was as white as the sheets she lay on. Only her eyes gave a hint of color. He thought of the first day he had seen her—vibrant, rushing. A feeling of total inadequacy swept over him so that the hands in his pockets balled into fists.

"How do you feel?"

"I told the doctor I felt like I'd been shot." Gingerly, she touched the bandaged arm. "Actually I feel like I've drunk a half dozen martinis and fallen off a cliff." She sighed, closing her eyes briefly. "You're not going to get me out of here, are you?"

"No."

"I didn't think so." Resigned, she opened her eyes again to stare at the blue plastic pitcher. "Slade, I lied about the diamonds. I tossed them under the seat in my car. It's in the middle of the road on the way to the shop. I forgot to get gas." She looked at him then. "It's not even locked. And . . ." Jessica moistened her lips when he remained silent. "I gave Michael money to get away. That's accessory after the fact or something, isn't it? I suppose I'm in trouble."

"I'll take care of it."

Even through her drugged haze, she felt surprise. "Aren't you going to shout at me?"

"No."

Fighting to keep her eyes open, Jessica laughed. "I'll have to get shot more often." She held out a hand, not noticing his hesitation to take it. "David wasn't involved. Michael told me everything. David had no idea what was going on."

"I know."

"It seems I was half right," she murmured.

"Jess . . ." Her hand felt so fragile. "I'm sorry."

"What for?" Jessica found that it took much too much effort to keep her eyes open. The world was soft and gray when she closed them. She thought she felt his fingers lace with hers but couldn't be sure. "You didn't do anything."

"No." Slade looked down at her hand. It was limp now; he had only to release it for it to fall back on the bed. "That's what I'm sorry for."

"It's all over now, isn't it, Slade?"

Her breathing was deep and even before he answered. "It's all over now, Jess." Bending, he pressed his lips to hers, then walked away.

12

Slade banked down the uncomfortable sensation of déjà vu as he waited in the commissioner's outer office. His scowl was a bit more pronounced than it had been the first time he had sat there. Three weeks had passed since he had left Jessica's bedside.

He'd gone directly back to her home on leaving the hospital. There, he'd had to deal with a puzzled, then furious, then frantic David.

"Shot, what do you mean *shot*!" Slade could still visualize the pale, strained look on David's face, still hear the trembling, angry words. "If you're a cop, why didn't you protect her?"

He'd had no answer for that. Slade had gone up to pack even as David had dialed the number of the hospital. Then he'd driven home, taking the miles to New York in a numbed weariness.

Slade had told himself to cross Jessica off, as he crossed off what he considered the final assignment in his police career. She'd get the care and the rest she needed. When she was ready to go home, the nightmare would be behind her. And so, he told himself, would he.

Then fatigue, the bone-deep exhaustion that comes after a long, intense period of tension, did the rest for him. He collapsed into bed and slept around the clock. But she had been the first thing in his mind when he woke.

He'd called the hospital daily, telling himself he was just tying up loose ends. The reports were always the same—resting comfortably. There were days when Slade had to fight the urge to get into his car and go back to her. Then she was released. He told himself that was the end of it.

Slade had plunged into an orgy of work. The novel was finished in a marathon sixteen-hour stint while he kept his door locked and his phone off the hook. With his resignation turned in, there were only a few necessary visits to the station house. More loose ends. He signed his contract and mailed his agent a copy of his second novel.

The reports and debriefings on the smuggling case brought Jessica back too vividly. Slade filled out his papers and answered questions with a brevity that bordered on curtness. He took the professional praise for his work in stony silence. He wanted it over—completed. He reminded himself that his life was his own for the first time in thirty-three years. But she wouldn't leave him alone.

She was there at night when he lay awake and restless. She was there in the afternoon when he poured his concentration into the outline of his next novel. She was there, always there, whether he walked the streets alone or surrounded himself with people.

He could see her on the beach, laughing, the wind grabbing at her hair as she tossed driftwood for the dog to chase. He could see her in the kitchen of the shop, slicing sandwiches while the sun dappled over her skin. Though he tried to block it out, he could hear the way she murmured his name when she lay in his arms, soft and warm and eager. Then he would see her white and unconscious—and her blood was on his hands.

The guilt would overwhelm him until he threw himself into work again, using the characters he developed to dilute her memory. But they all seemed to have pieces of her—a gesture, a phrase, an expression. How could he escape someone who seemed to know where he would run, how fast, and how far?

Now, sitting again in Dodson's outer office, Slade told himself this would be the end of it. He'd known all along that Dodson would want a personal meeting. Once it was done, all ties would be severed.

"Sergeant?"

He glanced up at the secretary, oblivious this time to the slow, inviting smile she sent him. Without a word, he rose to follow her into Dodson's office.

"Slade." Dodson leaned back in his chair as Slade entered, then gave his secretary a brief nod. "No calls," he ordered. "Have a seat."

Silently, Slade obeyed while the commissioner sucked pleasurably on a cigar until the tip glowed. Smoke wafted to the ceiling in a spiraling column which Dodson watched with apparent fascination.

"So, congratulations are in order." When Slade gave him nothing but the same silent stare, Dodson continued. "On your book," he said. Absently, he fingered his small, scrolled tie pin. "We're sorry to lose you." Saying nothing, Slade waited for the pleasantries to be over. "In any event"—Dodson leaned forward to tap his cigar ash—"your last case is wrapped up, by all accounts tightly. I don't doubt we'll get a conviction. You're aware that Michael Adams had made a full confession?"

He sent Slade an arch look and got no reply. "The domino theory seems to be working very well in this case—one name leads to another. As far as Chambers himself goes, we've got enough on him to put him away. Conspiracy to commit murder, accessory to murder, attempted murder—perhaps murder one on that business in Paris—not to mention the robberies and smuggling. No . . ." Dodson regarded the tip of his cigar with interest. "I don't think we need worry about him for quite some time."

He waited for a full thirty seconds, then went on as if he were engaged in a two-way conversation. "You'll give your evidence, naturally, when the time comes, but it shouldn't interfere too much with your new career." *Stubborn young fool*, he thought as he puffed on his cigar. He decided to test the younger man's iron control by saying a name. "Jessica told me she gave Michael several thousand dollars to aid in his escape."

Watching for a reaction, he caught the faintest flicker in Slade's eyes—here then gone. It was all he needed to confirm the notion that had seeded in his mind when he had seen his goddaughter. "She felt that made her an accessory. Strange, Michael never mentioned her giving him any money—and I spoke with him myself. There's a rumor that you saw him too, right after he was brought in. . . ." Dodson let the sentence trail off suggestively. When Slade didn't rise to the bait, Dodson went on, undaunted. He'd cracked a few tough eggs in his own career, on the street and behind a desk.

"I imagine a few choice words were sufficient to keep Michael quiet, and of course, Jessica can afford to lose a few thousand. We might have a bit of trouble keeping *her* quiet, though." He smiled. "That conscience of hers, you know."

"How is she?" The words were out before Slade could stop them. Though he swore under his breath, Dodson gave no sign of hearing.

"She's looking very well." He swiveled gently in his chair. "I'll tell you, Slade, I was shaken when I visited her in the hospital. I've never known Jessica to be ill in her life, and . . . well, it was quite a shock." Slade pulled out a cigarette, lighting a match with sharp, controlled violence. "She's bounced back," the commissioner continued, pleased with the reaction. "Drove the doctor crazy until he'd let her out, then she went right back to work.

"That shop of hers." He gave Slade a quick grin. "I don't suppose the notoriety will do her business any harm." Noting the tension in the set of Slade's shoulders, Dodson paused long enough to tap out his cigar. "She speaks very highly of you."

"Really?" Slade expelled a long stream of smoke. "My assignment was to keep her safe—I did a remarkably poor job of it."

"She is safe," Dodson corrected. "And as stubborn as ever. David and I both tried to persuade her to go to Europe, take a little time off to get her bearings. She won't hear of it." He settled back in his chair as a faint smile flickered on his lips. "Says she's going to stay put."

Slade's eyes flew from the view out the window to pin Dodson's. Emotions smoldered in them, fiercely, quickly, then were suppressed. "Hard to believe," he managed. "She never did before."

"So she tells me." Dodson steeped his fingers. "She's given

me a full report—with a great many details you omitted from yours. Apparently," Dodson commented as Slade narrowed his eyes, "you had your hands full."

"Full enough," Slade returned.

Dodson pursed his lips, in speculation or agreement, Slade couldn't tell. "Jessica seems to think she handled the entire business badly."

"She handled it too well," Slade disagreed in a mutter. "If she'd fallen apart, I could have gotten her out."

"Yes, well . . . differing points of view, of course." Dodson's gaze fell on the triple-framed photos of his wife and children. He'd had a few . . . differing points of view with that lady from time to time. He remembered the look in Jessica's eyes when she'd asked for Slade. "Of course, now that it's over," he ventured, "I'm not entirely sure she won't fall apart—delayed reaction."

Slade smothered the instant urge to protect and prevent. "She'll get through the aftermath all right. There're enough people in that house to take care of her."

Dodson laughed. "That's usually the other way around. Half the time Jessica serves her staff. Of course, Betsy will cluck around her for a time until Jessica's ready to scream. And of course, Jessica won't. Betsy's been with her for twenty years. Then there's the cook, she's been there nearly as long. Makes great biscuits." He paused reminiscently. "I guess it was about three years ago that Jessica picked up all her medical bills when she had a stroke. I suppose you saw old Joe, the gardener."

Slade grunted, crushing out his cigarette. "He must be ninety years old."

"Ninety-two if memory serves me. She doesn't have the heart to let him go, so she hires a young boy during the summer to do the heavy work. The little maid, Carol, is the daughter of her father's chauffeur. Jessica took her on when the girl's father died. That's Jessica." He sighed gustily. "Loyal. Her loyalty's one of her most endearing traits and one of her most frustrating." Now, Dodson concluded, was the time to drop the bomb. "She's hired a lawyer for Michael."

This time the reaction was fast and furious. "She did *what*?"

While he lifted his hands, palms up, in a gesture of helplessness, Dodson struggled with a smile. "She tells me she feels it's her responsibility."

"Just how does she come by that?" Slade demanded. His control deserted him so that he sprang up and paced the office.

"If he hadn't been working for her, he wouldn't have gotten tangled up in this mess. . . ." Dodson shrugged. "You know how her mind works as well as I do."

"Yeah. When it works at all. Adams is the one who got her involved. He's responsible for everything that happened to her. She was nearly killed twice because he didn't have the spine to protect her."

"Yes," Dodson agreed quietly. "*He's* responsible." The emphasis on the pronoun was slight, but full of meaning. Slade turned back at that. Dodson met his eyes with a look that was too understanding and too knowledgeable. He thought Slade looked like his father for a moment—impulsive, emotional, hot-headed. But Tom, Dodson mused, would never have been able to struggle with such turbulent feelings and win. Slade turned away from him again.

"If she wants to hire a lawyer for him," he murmured, "that's her business. It's got nothing to do with me."

"No?"

"Look, Commissioner." On a spurt of fury, Slade whirled around. "I took the assignment, I finished the assignment. I've written my report and been debriefed. I've also turned in my resignation. I'm finished."

Let's see how long you can convince yourself of that, Dodson mused. Smiling, he extended his hand. "Yes, as I said, we're sorry to lose you."

The air smelled of snow when Slade climbed out of his car. He glanced up at the sky—no moon, no stars. There was a keen night wind that made low howling noises through the naked trees. He shifted his gaze to the house. Lights glowed here and there; in the parlor, in Jessica's bedroom. Even as he watched, the upstairs light winked out.

Maybe she's gone to bed, he thought, hunching his shoulders against the cold. I should go—I shouldn't even be here. Even as he told himself so, he walked up the steps to the front door. He told himself he should turn around, get back in the car, and drive away. He cursed whatever demon had prompted him to make the trip in the first place. He lifted his hand to knock.

Before Slade's fist connected with the wood, the door flew open. He heard Jessica's breezy laugh, felt the quick brush of fur against his legs, then caught her as she raced out after Ulysses and collided with his chest.

Everything, everything he had tried to forget, came back to him in that one instant—the feel of her, the scent, the taste of her skin under his lips. Then Jessica tilted back her head and looked him fully in the face.

Her eyes were bright and alive, her skin flushed with laughter. As he stood tense, her lips curved for him in a smile that made his legs weak.

"Hello, Slade. I'm sorry, we almost knocked you flat."

Her words were truer than she knew, he thought. Quickly he released her and took a step back. "You're going out?"

"Just for a run with Ulysses." Jessica looked beyond his shoulder. "And he's gone now." Looking back at Slade, Jessica offered her hand. "It's good to see you. Come in and have a drink."

Warily, Slade stepped inside, but evaded the offered hand. She turned away to fling her jacket over the newel post, shutting her eyes tightly a moment when her back was to him. "Let's go in the parlor," she said brightly when she faced him again. "There's a nice fire in there."

Without waiting for his answer, Jessica dashed away. She was moving, Slade observed, at her usual speed. And the shadows were gone from under her eyes—gone as if they had never existed. She was as she had been in the beginning—a woman with boundless energy. He followed her more slowly into the parlor. She was already pouring Scotch into a glass.

"I'm so glad you came, the house is too quiet." Jessica picked up a decanter of vermouth with no idea what was inside. As she poured she continued to talk. "It was wonderful for a few days, but now I almost regret that I sent everyone away. Of course, I had to lie to get them out of here." You're talking too fast, too fast, she told herself, but couldn't stop. "I told David and the staff I was going to Jamaica to lie in the sun for a week, then I bought them all airline tickets and shoved them out of the house."

"You shouldn't be alone." He was frowning at her when she handed him his drink.

"Why not?" With a laugh, Jessica tossed back her hair. "I couldn't stand being treated like an invalid. I got enough of that in the hospital." Sipping her drink, she turned to the fire. She wouldn't let him see the hurt. Every day that she'd been confined in that sterile white room she had waited for his call, watched the door for his visit. Nothing. He'd cut himself out of her life when she'd been too weak to prevent it. Slade stared at her slim, straight back and wondered how he could leave without touching her.

"How are you?" The question was curt and brief.

Jessica's fingers tightened on her glass. *Do you care?* she wondered. She sipped the vermouth, making the words slip back down her throat. Turning, she smiled at him. "How do I look?"

He stared at her until the need was a hard ball in his stomach. "You need to gain some weight."

She laughed shortly. "Thank you very much." Needing to do something, Jessica wandered over to toy with the keys of the piano. "Did you finish your book?"

"Yes."

"Then everything's going well for you?"

"Everything's going just dandy." He drank, willing the liquor to dull the ache.

"Your mother liked the figure?"

Confused, he drew his brows together. "Oh, yeah. Yeah, she liked it."

They lapsed into silence, accented by the crackling wood and drifting notes. There was too much to say, Slade thought. And nothing to say. Again, he cursed himself for not being strong enough to stay away.

"You've gone back to work?" he asked.

"Yes. We've had a stream of customers since the publicity. I suppose it'll taper off. Have you resigned from the force?"

"Yes."

Silence fell again, more thickly. Jessica stared down at the piano keys as if she were about to compose a symphony. "You'd want to tie up loose ends, wouldn't you?" she murmured. "Am I a loose end, Slade?"

"Something like that," he muttered.

Her head came up at that, and her eyes fixed on his once, searingly. Turning away, she walked to the window. "Well then," she whispered. With her finger, she drew a maze on the glass. "I think I've told every proper authority every proper thing. There was a steady stream of men in dark suits in my hospital room." She dropped her hand to her side. "Why didn't you come to see me . . . or call?" Her voice steadied as she stared at the reflection of the lamp in the window. "Shouldn't there have been a final interview for your report— or is that why you came tonight?"

"I don't know why the hell I came," he tossed back, then slammed down his empty glass. "I didn't come to see you because I didn't want to see you. I didn't call because I didn't want to talk to you."

"Well, that certainly clears that up."

He took a step toward her, stopped himself, then thrust his hands in his pockets. "How's your arm?"

"It's fine." Absently, she reached up to touch the wound that had healed while she thought of the one that hadn't. "The doctor says I won't even have a scar."

"Great. That's just great." Slade pulled out a pack of cigarettes, then tossed it on a table.

"I like the idea," Jessica returned calmly. "I'm not fond of scars."

"Did you mean what you said?" It rushed out of him before he could think to prevent it.

"About the scar?"

"No, not about the damn scar." Frustrated, he dragged a hand through his hair.

"I try to mean what I say," she murmured. Her heart was in her throat now, so that she forced herself to say each word carefully.

"You said you were in love with me." Every muscle in his body tensed. "Did you mean it?"

Taking a deep breath, Jessica turned back to him. Her face was composed, her eyes calm. "Yes, I meant it."

"It's your warped sense of gratitude," he told her, then paced to the fire and back again.

Something began to warm in her. Jessica felt simultaneous sensations of relief and amusement. "I think I could tell the difference," she considered. "Sometimes I'm very grateful to the butcher for a good cut of meat, but I haven't fallen in love with him . . . yet."

"Oh, you're funny." Slade shot her a furious glance. "Don't you see it was just circumstance, just the situation?"

"Was it?" Jessica smiled as she crossed to him. Slade backed away.

"I don't want any part of you," he told her heatedly. "I want you to understand that."

"I think I understand." She lifted a hand to his cheek. "I think I understand very well."

He caught her wrist, but couldn't force himself to toss it aside. "Do you know how I felt, having you unconscious—your blood on my hands? Do you know what it did to me, seeing you in that hospital bed? I've seen corpses with more color." She felt his fingers tremble lightly before they dropped her wrist. "Damn it, Jess," he breathed before he spun away to pour himself another drink.

"Slade." Jessica wrapped her arms around his waist. Why hadn't she thought of that? she demanded of herself. Why hadn't she realized that he would blame himself? "I was the one who was in the wrong place at the wrong time."

"Don't." He put his hands on hers, firmly pushing them away. "I've got nothing for you, can't you understand? Nothing. Different poles, Jess. We barely speak the same language."

If he had faced her, he would have seen the line form between her brows. "I don't know what you're talking about."

"Look at this place!" He gestured around the room as he whirled to her. "Where you live, how you live. It's got nothing to do with me."

"Oh." Pursing her lips, she considered. "I see, you're a snob."

"Damn you, can't you see anything?" Infuriated, he grabbed her shoulders. "I don't want you."

"Try again," she suggested.

He opened his mouth, then relieved his frustration by shaking her. "You've no right—no right to get inside my head this way. I want you out. Once and for all I want you out!"

"Slade," she said quietly, "why don't you stop hating it so much and give in? I'm not going anywhere."

How his hands found their way into her hair, he didn't know. But they were sunk deep, and so was he. Struggling all the way, he gave in. "I love you, damn it. I'd like to choke you for it." His eyes grew dark and stormy. "You worked on me," he accused as she gazed up at him, calm and composed. "Right from the beginning you worked on me until I can't function without you. For God's sake, I could smell you down at the station house."

Pushed as much by fury as by need, he dragged her into his arms. "I thought I'd go mad unless I could taste you again." His lips covered hers, not gently. But then Jessica wasn't looking for gentleness. Here was the hard, bruising contact she had longed to feel again. Her response came in an explosion of heart, body, and mind so that her demand met his and fulminated. They clung for one long shimmering instant, then they were tangled together on the hearth rug.

"I need you." The words shuddered from him as two pairs of hands struggled with clothes. "Now." He found her naked breast and groaned. "It's been so long."

"Too long."

Words were no longer possible. Beside them the fire sizzled, new flames licking at wood. Wind rattled at the windows. They heard nothing, felt nothing, but each other. Lips sought, then devoured; hands explored, then possessed. There was no time for a slow reacquaintance. Hungry, they came together swiftly, letting sharp pleasure cleanse all doubts. They remained close, body to body and mouth to mouth, until need drifted to contentment.

Jessica held him against her when he would have shifted to her side. "No, don't move," she murmured.

"I'm crushing you."

"Only a little."

Slade lifted his head to grin at her and found himself lost in the cloudy amber of her eyes. Slowly, he traced the slanted line of her cheekbone. "I love you, Jess."

"Still angry about it?" she asked.

Before he buried his face at her throat, she caught the grin. "Resigned."

On a small gasp, she punched his shoulder. "Resigned, huh? That's very flattering. Well, let me tell you, I didn't picture myself falling in love with a bad-tempered ex-cop who tries to order me around."

That musky, woodsy fragrance of her skin distracted him. He began to nuzzle at her neck, wallowing in it. "Who did you picture yourself falling in love with?"

"A cross between Albert Schweitzer and Clark Gable," she told him.

Slade gave a snort before raising his head again. "Yeah? Well, you came close. Are you going to marry me?"

Jessica lifted a brow. "Do I have a choice?"

Bending, he nibbled on her lips. "Aren't you the one who says a person always has a choice?"

"Mmm, so I am." She pulled him closer for one long, satisfying kiss. "I suppose we both have one to make, don't we?"

Their eyes met, then they spoke together. "You."

Endings and Beginnings

1

"*A* White House source has confirmed the imminent retirement of Secretary of State George Larkin. Secretary Larkin underwent extensive cardiac surgery last week and is currently recovering at Bethesda Naval Hospital. His health is given as the reason for his midterm retirement. Stan Richardson has an on-the-scene report from Bethesda Naval."

Liv watched the monitor switch to the location shot before she turned to her co-anchor. "Brian, this could be the biggest thing to hit since the Malloy scandal last October. There must be five viable replacements for Larkin. The scrambling's going to start."

Brian Jones flipped through his notes, running over his timing. He was a thirty-five-year-old black with a flare for clothes and ten years of television news experience. Though he had grown up in Queens, he considered himself a Washingtonian. "Nothing you love better than a good scramble."

"Nothing," Liv agreed, and turned back to the camera as control gave her her cue.

"The president had no comment today on Secretary Larkin's replacement. Speculation from a high official lists Beaumont Dell, former ambassador to France, and General Robert J. Fitzhugh as top candidates. Neither could be reached for comment."

"A twenty-five-year-old man was found slain in his apartment in Northeast Washington this afternoon." Brian took over his first segment of their anchor partnership.

Liv listened with half an ear while her mind raced with possibilities. Beaumont Dell was her choice. His aides had given her the classic runaround that afternoon, but she was determined to be parked on his doorstep the next morning. As a reporter, she was accustomed to runarounds, waiting, and having doors shut in her face. Nothing, absolutely nothing, she told herself, was going to stop her from interviewing Dell.

Hearing her next cue, Liv turned to camera three and began her lead-in. In their homes, viewers saw the head and shoulders of an elegant brunette. Her voice was low-key, her pace unhurried. They would have no idea how carefully the minute and fifteen seconds had been timed and edited. They saw sincerity and beauty. In the television news game one was often as important as the other. Liv's hair was short and sculptured around a finely boned face. Her eyes were cool blue, serious and direct. A viewer could easily believe she spoke especially for him.

Her television audience found her classy, a little remote, and accurate. Liv was satisfied with the consensus on her role as co-anchor of the local evening news. As a reporter, she wanted more, much more.

A colleague had once described her as having "that wealthy, Connecticut look." Indeed, she had come from a well-off New England family, and her degree in journalism was from Harvard. However, she had worked her way up through the ranks of television reporting.

She had started at base pay at a tiny independent station in New Jersey, reading weather and doing quick consumer spots. She had played the usual game of hopscotching from station to station, city to city—a little more money, a little more air time. She had landed a position at a CNC affiliate in Austin, working her way up in her two-year stay to an anchoring position. When she had been offered the co-anchor spot at WWBW, the CNC affiliate in Washington, D.C., Liv had jumped at it. There were no firm ties in Austin, nor, for years, anywhere else.

She had wanted to make her name in television journalism. Washington, she felt, was a perfect place to do it. She didn't mind dirty work, though her smooth, narrow hands looked as if they were accustomed to only the silks and satins of life. She had a seeking, eager, shrewd brain under the ivory skin and patrician features. She thrived on the fast, close to impossible pace of visual news, while on the surface, she was cool, remote and seemingly untouchable. For the past five years, Liv had been working hard to convince herself that the image was fact.

At twenty-eight, she told herself she was through with personal upheavals. The only roller coaster she wanted to ride on was a professional one. What friends she had made during her sixteen months in D.C. were allowed only a glimpse of her past. Liv kept a lock on her private life.

"This is Olivia Carmichael," she told the camera.

"And Brian Jones. Stay tuned for 'CNC World News.'"

The quick throb of theme music took over; then the red light on the camera facing her blinked out. Liv unclipped her mike and pushed away from the semicircular desk used by the news team.

"Tight show," the man behind camera one commented as she started past. Overhead, the hot, bright lights shut down. Liv shifted her thoughts and focused on him. She smiled. The smile transformed her cool polished beauty. She only used that particular smile when she meant it.

"Thanks, Ed. How's your girl?"

"Cramming for exams." He shrugged and pulled off his headset. "Doesn't have much time for me."

"You'll be proud of her when she gets that degree in education."

"Yeah. Ah—Liv." He stopped her again, and she lifted a brow in acknowledgment. "She wanted me to ask you . . ." He looked uncomfortable as he hesitated.

"What?"

"Who does your hair?" he blurted out, then shook his head and fiddled with his camera. "Women."

Laughing, Liv patted his arm. "Armond's on Wisconsin. Tell her to use my name."

She moved briskly from the studio, up the steps and through the winding corridors that led to the newsroom. It was noisy with the transition from day to evening shift.

Reporters sat on the corners of desks, drank coffee or typed furiously to meet the deadline for the eleven o'clock broadcast. There was a scent of tobacco, light sweat and old coffee in the air. One wall was lined with television screens, which gave the action but not the sound of every station in the metropolitan area. Already on screen one was the intro for "CNC World News." Liv headed straight through the confusion to the glass-walled office of the news director.

"Carl?" She stuck her head in his door. "Do you have a minute?"

Carl Pearson was slouched over his desk, hands folded, as he stared at a TV screen. The glasses he should have been wearing were under a pile of papers. He had a cup of cold coffee balanced on a stack of files, and a cigarette burned down between his fingers. He grunted. Liv entered, knowing the grunt was affirmative.

"Good show tonight." His eyes never left the twelve-inch screen.

Liv took a seat and waited for the commercial break. She could hear the crisp, hard-line tones of Harris McDowell, New York anchor for "CNC World News," coming from the set at her side. It was fruitless to talk to Carl when the big guns were out. Harris McDowell was a big gun.

She knew he and Carl had worked together in their early days as reporters at the same station in Kansas City, Missouri. But it had been Harris McDowell who had been assigned to cover a presidential cavalcade in Dallas in 1963. The assassination of a president, and his on-the-scene reports had rocketed McDowell from relative obscurity to national prominence. Carl Pearson had remained a big fish in a sea of little fishes in Missouri and a handful of other states until he had hung up his notebook in exchange for a desk in Washington.

He was a tough news director, exacting, excitable. If he was bitter about the different path his career had taken, he was careful not to show it. Liv respected him, and had grown steadily fonder of him during her stint at WWBW. She'd had her own share of disappointments.

"What?" It was Carl's way of telling her to speak her piece once the break had come.

"I want to follow up on Beaumont Dell," Liv began. "I've

done a lot of legwork on this already, and when he's appointed Secretary of State, I want to put it on the air first."

Carl sat back and folded his hands over his paunch. He blamed too much sitting at a desk for the extra fifteen pounds he carried around. The look he aimed at Liv was as direct and uncompromising as the look he had aimed at the television screen.

"A little ahead of the game." His voice was roughened by years of chain-smoking. As she watched, he lit another, though a cigarette still smoldered in his overfilled ashtray. "What about Fitzhugh? And Davis and Albertson? They might question your appointment of Dell. Officially, Larkin hasn't resigned."

"It's a matter of days, probably hours. You heard the doctor's statement. The acting secretary won't be appointed permanently; Boswell's not the president's favorite boy. It's going to be Dell. I know it."

Carl sniffed and rubbed a hand over his nose. He liked Carmichael's instincts. She was sharp and savvy despite the born-to-the-manor looks. And she was thorough. But he was understaffed and the budget was tight. He couldn't afford to send one of his top reporters out on a hunch when he could assign someone he could spare more. Still . . . He hesitated a moment, then leaned over the desk again.

"Might be worth it," he mumbled. "Let's hear what Thorpe has to say. His report's coming up."

Liv shifted in her chair in automatic protest, then subsided. It was pride that had her ready to object to having her assignment hinge on the words of T.C. Thorpe. But pride didn't cut weight with Carl. Instead, she rose to sit on the corner of his desk and watch.

The Washington anchor was broadcasting from the studio above her head. It was a much more stylized set than the one she had just left. But that was the difference between the local and national news—and the local and national news budgets. After his brief lead-in, the screen switched to the location shot and T.C. Thorpe's stand-up. With a frown, Liv watched him.

Though it was no more than thirty degrees with a wicked

windchill factor, he wore his coat unbuttoned and had no hat. It was typical.

He had a rugged, weather-tanned face Liv associated with a mountain climber, and the streamlined body of a long-distance runner. Both professions required endurance. So did reporting. T.C. Thorpe was all reporter. His eyes were dark and intense, locking on the viewers and holding them. His dark hair blew furiously around his face, giving his report an air of urgency. Yet his voice was clean and unhurried. The contrast worked for him more successfully than flash or gimmicks worked for others.

Liv knew his visual appeal was tremendous. He had the athletic, just-short-of-handsome looks that appealed to both men and women. His eyes were intelligent and instilled trust, as did the deep, well-pitched voice. He was accessible. She knew reporters were put into slots: remote, mystical, omnipotent, accessible. Thorpe was flesh and blood, and viewers could welcome him into their living rooms comfortably and accept his word. And there was the feeling that if the world began to collapse, T.C. Thorpe would report it without missing a beat.

In his five years as senior Washington correspondent, he had built an enviable reputation. He had the two things most essential to a reporter: credibility and sources. If T.C. Thorpe said it, it was believed. If T.C. Thorpe needed information, he knew which numbers to call.

Liv's resentment against him was instinctive. She specialized in the political beat for the local broadcast. Thorpe was her nemesis. He guarded his turf with the ferocity of a dog in a junkyard. He was rooted in Washington; she was still the new kid on the block. And he wasn't giving her any room. It seemed inevitable that when she had a hot lead, he had been there first.

Liv had spent months looking for a viable criticism of him. It wasn't accurate to call him flashy. Thorpe dressed down on the job, wearing nothing to distract the viewer's attention from his reporting. His style was straightforward. His reports had depth and bite, while he remained objective. There was no fault to find in the way he worked. All Liv could criticize him for was arrogance.

She watched him now as he stood with the White House lit in the background. He was recapping the Larkin story. It was obvious he had spoken to Larkin personally, something she had been unable to do though she had pulled all the strings available to her. That alone grated. Thorpe, too, listed prospective candidates for the position. He named Dell first.

Carl nodded behind her back as Liv scowled at the screen. He felt it put a bit more power into her hunch.

"This is T.C. Thorpe, at the White House."

"Tell the desk you have an assignment," Carl announced, and drew hard on the butt of his cigarette. Liv turned to him, but his eyes were still on the screen. "Take crew two."

"Fine." She swallowed the annoyance that it was Thorpe's influence more than her own that had gained her what she wanted. "I'll make the arrangements."

"Bring me something for the noon news," he called after her, and squinted to focus on the next segment.

Liv looked over her shoulder as she opened the door. "You'll have it."

It was eight A.M. and freezing when Liv and her two-man crew arrived at the iron gates of Beaumont Dell's home in Alexandria, Virginia. Liv had been up since five, preparing her questions. After half a dozen phone calls the evening before, she had elicited a promise from one of Dell's aides that she would be granted a ten-minute interview that morning. A good reporter could learn quite a bit in ten minutes. Sliding out of the crew van, Liv approached the guard at the gate.

"Olivia Carmichael with WWBW." She flashed her press pass. "Mr. Dell is expecting me."

The guard examined Liv's credentials, then his clip board, before nodding. Without a word, he pressed the button to open the gates.

Friendly sort, she decided as she climbed back into the van. "Okay, be ready to set up fast; we're not going to have much time." She was reaching in her purse to take out her notes for a final check as the van wound up the drive. "Bob, I'd like a pan of the house, and one of the gates when we leave."

"Already got one of the gates." He gave her a grin as she

smiled back at him. "And of your legs. You've got some great legs, Liv."

"Think so?" She crossed them and gave them a critical stare. "You're probably right."

She enjoyed his good-natured flirting. Bob was harmless, happily married with two growing children. A serious flirtation would have frozen her. She separated men into two categories: safe and dangerous. Bob was safe. She could relax with him.

"All right," she said as the van stopped in front of the three-story brick house. "Try to look like respectable members of the working press."

Grinning, Bob muttered a short expletive and climbed out of the back of the van.

At the front door, Liv was once again the cool, aloof newswoman; no one would dare to comment on her legs. Not out loud. She knocked briskly, leaving the crew to follow with their equipment.

"Olivia Carmichael," she announced to the maid who opened the door. "To see Mr. Dell."

"Yes." The maid glanced past her with the slightest moue of disapproval at the blue-jeaned crew hauling equipment up the front steps. "This way, Ms. Carmichael. Mr. Dell will be right with you."

Liv recognized the maid's disapproval. She thought little of it. Her own family and many of her childhood friends felt the same way about her profession.

The hall was an elegant, refined entrance to a wealthy home. Liv had seen the same hall in a dozen homes in a dozen styles when she was growing up. There had been hundreds of teas, stiff little parties and carefully organized outings, all of which had bored her to distraction. She never cast a glance at the Matisse on the wall on her left. She heard Bob's low whistle as he entered behind her.

"Some place," he commented as his sneakers moved soundlessly over the parquet floor.

Liv made a distracted sound of agreement as she went back over her strategy. She had grown up in a home not so very much different from this one. Her mother had preferred

Chippendale to Louis XIV, but it was all the same. Even the scent was the same—lemon oil and fresh flowers. It stirred old memories.

Before Liv had taken two steps behind the maid, she heard the sound of male laughter.

"I'll swear, T.C., you know how to tell a story. I'll have to make sure the first lady's not around when I repeat that one." Dell came lightly down the stairs, trim, handsomely sixtyish and beside Thorpe.

Liv felt her stomach muscles tighten. *Always one step ahead of me*, she thought on a swift rush of fury. *Damn!*

Briefly, potently, she met Thorpe's eyes. He smiled, but it wasn't the same smile he had given to Dell as they had begun their descent.

"Ah, Ms. Carmichael." Spotting her, Dell extended his hand as he crossed the hall. His voice was as smooth as his palm. His eyes were shrewd. "Very prompt. I hope I haven't kept you waiting."

"No, Mr. Dell. I appreciate the time." Liv let her eyes pass over Thorpe. "Mr. Thorpe."

"Ms. Carmichael."

"I know you're a busy man, Ambassador," Liv turned her eyes back to him with a smile. "I won't take much of your time." An unobtrusive move put the mike in her hand. "Would you be comfortable talking to me here?" she asked, to give the soundman a voice level.

"Fine." He made an expansive gesture and gave a generous smile. The smile was the stock-in-trade of the diplomat. From the corner of her eye, Liv watched Thorpe move out of camera range to stand by the door. The eyes she felt on the back of her neck made her uncomfortable. Turning to Dell, she started her interview.

He continued to be expansive, cooperative, genial. Liv felt like a dentist trying to pull a tooth from a patient who smiled with his mouth firmly shut.

Of course he was aware that his name was being linked with the position to be vacated by Larkin. Naturally, he was flattered to be considered—by the press. Liv noted he was careful not to mention the president's name. She was being led in circles, gently, expertly. Just as gently, she backtracked and probed from different angles. She was getting the tone she wanted, if not the firm words.

"Mr. Dell, has the president spoken to you directly about the appointment of a new Secretary of State?" She knew better than to expect a yes or no answer.

"The president and I haven't met to discuss an appointment."

"But you have met with him?" she persisted.

"I have occasion to meet with the president from time to time." At his subtle signal, the maid appeared at his elbow with his coat and hat. "I'm sorry I can't give you more time, Ms. Carmichael." He was shrugging into his coat. Liv knew she was losing him. She moved with him to the door.

"Are you seeing the president this morning, Mr. Dell?" It was a blunt question, but it wasn't the verbal answer Liv looked for as much as the reaction in the eyes of the man she asked. She saw it—the faint flicker, the briefest hesitation.

"Possibly." Dell extended his hand. "A pleasure talking to you, Ms. Carmichael. I'm afraid I have to run. Traffic is so heavy at this time of the morning."

Liv lifted a hand to signal Bob to stop the tape. "Thank you for seeing me, Mr. Dell." After passing the mike to the soundman, Liv followed Dell and Thorpe outside.

"Always a pleasure." He patted her hand and smiled with his old-world southern charm. "Now you be sure to call Anna, T.C." He turned to Thorpe and gave him a friendly slap on the shoulder. "She wants to hear from you."

"I'll do that."

Dell walked down the steps to the discreet black limo where his driver waited.

"Not bad, Carmichael," Thorpe commented as the limo pulled away. "You do a tough interview. Of course . . ." He looked down at her and smiled. "Dell's been dancing his way around tough interviews for years."

Liv gave him a cool stare. "What were you doing here?"

"Having breakfast," he answered easily. "I'm an old family friend."

She would have liked to knock the smile from his face with a good swift punch. Instead, she meticulously pulled on her gloves. "Dell's going to get that appointment."

Thorpe lifted a brow. "Is that a statement, Olivia, or a question?"

"I wouldn't ask you for the time of day, Thorpe," she retorted. "And you wouldn't give it to me if I did."

"I've always said you were a sharp lady."

Good God, she's beautiful, he thought. When he saw her on the air, it was easy to attribute the nearly impossible beauty to lighting, makeup, camera angles. But standing face to face in harsh morning light, she was quite simply the most physically beautiful woman he had ever seen. The incredible bone structure; the flawless skin. Only her eyes were hot, giving away the fury she was controlling. Thorpe smiled again. He loved to watch the ice crack.

"Is that the problem, Thorpe?" Liv demanded as she stepped aside to let the crew pass. "Don't you like reporters who happen to be women?"

He laughed and shook his head. "You know better than that, Liv. 'Reporter' is a word without sex."

His eyes weren't intense now, but filled with good humor. She didn't like them any better. More accurately, she refused to like them any better. "Why won't you cooperate with me?" The wind was tossing his hair around his face as it had the night before. Thorpe seemed untouched by the cold as Liv shivered inside her coat. "We have the same job; we work for the same people."

"My turf," he said quietly. "If you want a share, Liv, you're going to have to fight for it. It took me years to establish myself here. Don't expect to do the same in months." He saw her shudder against the cold as she continued to glare at him. "You'd better get inside the van."

"I'm going to have my share, Thorpe." It was half threat, half warning. "You're going to have a hell of a fight on your hands."

Thorpe inclined his head in acknowledgment. "I'll count on it."

It was obvious to him that Liv wasn't leaving until he did. She would stand there shivering for an hour out of sheer stubbornness. Without a word, Thorpe walked down the steps to his car.

Liv stood for another moment after he'd driven off. She

was aware—and annoyed by the fact—that she was able to breathe with more ease when he was no longer standing beside her. He had a strong personality; it was impossible to be indifferent to him. He demanded definite emotions. Liv decided hers were all unflattering.

He wasn't going to block her way. She wasn't going to put up with it. She walked down the steps to the van slowly.

Anna, she thought suddenly, remembering the name Dell had mentioned to Thorpe. Anna Dell Monroe—Dell's daughter and official hostess since the death of her mother. Anna Dell Monroe. Whatever was going on in her father's life, she'd know about it. Moving quickly now, Liv climbed in the van.

"We'll drop the tape at the station for editing; then we head for Georgetown."

2

Liv typed furiously. She had given Carl the Dell interview for the noon news; but she had more, a great deal more, for the evening show. Her hunch about Anna Monroe had paid off. Anna knew the details of her father's life. Though she had been careful during the interview, she wasn't the trained diplomat her father was. Liv had enough from her half-hour interview in the parlor of Anna Monroe's Georgetown row house to give her viewers a story with touches of glamour and suspense.

The tape was good. She had already taken a quick look at it while it was still being edited. Bob had captured the stylish elegance of the room and the gentle, privileged breeding of the woman. It would be a good contrast to the compact shrewdness of her father. Anna's respect for her father came through, as well as her taste for the finer things. Liv had worked both into the interview. It was a solid piece of reporting, and it gave a glimpse of the larger-than-life world of affluent people in politics.

Liv transcribed her notes hurriedly.

"Liv, we need you for the voice-over on the tease."

She glanced up long enough to search for Brian. The look she gave him made him sigh. He pushed away from his desk and stretched his shoulders. "All right, all right, I'll do it. But you owe me one."

"You're a prince, Brian." She went back to her typing.

Ten minutes later, Liv pulled the last sheet from her typewriter. "Carl!" she called to the director as he crossed the newsroom toward his office. "Copy for the lead story."

"Bring it in."

.As she rose, Liv checked the clock. She had an hour before air time.

The television was on, its volume low, when she entered Carl's office. Seated behind his desk, he checked copy and time allowances.

"Did you see the tape yet?" Liv handed him her pages.

"It's good." He lit a cigarette from the butt of another and gave a quick, hacking cough. "We'll run part of this morning's business with Dell, then lead into the interview with the daughter."

He read Liv's copy with a small furrow of concentration between his brows. It was a good, tidy story, giving quick bios on all top contenders for the cabinet post, and focusing in on Beaumont Dell. It gave the audience a full, open view before it brought them to Dell's doorstep.

Liv watched smoke curl toward the ceiling and waited.

"I want to flash pictures of the rest of them while you read the bios." He scribbled notes on her script. "We should have them on file. If not, we'll get them from upstairs." Upstairs was the term for CNC's Washington bureau. "Looks like you're going to have about three minutes to fill."

"I want three and a half." She waited until Carl looked up at her. "We don't replace many secretaries of state midterm, Carl. Our next biggest story is the possibility of a partial shutdown of the Potomac River filtration system. This is worth three and a half."

"Go argue with the time editor," he suggested, then held up his hand as she began to speak.

Liv saw immediately what had shifted his attention. The graphics for a special bulletin flashed across the screen. She obeyed his quick hand signal to turn up the volume. Even as she did, T.C. Thorpe stared directly into her eyes. Liv hadn't been prepared for the intensity of the look.

She felt a sexual pull—a quick, unexpected flash of desire. It left her stunned. She leaned back against Carl's desk. She hadn't felt anything like that in more than five years. Staring at the television image, she missed the first few words of Thorpe's report.

". . . has accepted Secretary of State Larkin's resignation as expected. Secretary Larkin resigned his cabinet post for reasons of poor health. He remains in Bethesda Naval Hospital recovering from extensive cardiac surgery performed last week. With the acceptance of Larkin's resignation, the president has appointed Beaumont Dell to fill the vacated post. Dell officially accepted an hour ago in a meeting in the Oval Office. Press Secretary Donaldson has scheduled a press conference tomorrow at nine A.M."

Liv felt the supports fall out from under her and leaned back heavily. She heard Thorpe recap the bulletin while she closed her eyes and took a deep breath. Carl was already swearing.

Her story was dead. The guts had just been torn out of it. *And he had known it*. Liv straightened as the scheduled program flashed back on the screen. He'd known it at eight o'clock that morning.

"Do the rewrites," Carl was telling her, grabbing for his phone as it rang. "And get somebody upstairs for Thorpe's copy. We need it to fill in. The bit with the daughter is scrubbed."

Liv grabbed her papers from Carl's desk and marched to the door.

"They need you in makeup, Liv."

She ignored the statement and continued out of the newsroom. Impatient, she paced back and forth in front of the elevator, waiting for it to make the descent.

He's not going to get away with it, she fumed. He's not going to get away with this without a scratch.

She continued to pace back and forth inside the elevator on her way to the fourth floor. It had been years—she could count the years—since anything or anyone had made her this angry. She was bursting with the need to let out her temper. And there was only one man who deserved the full force of it.

"Thorpe," she demanded curtly when she entered the fourth-floor newsroom.

A reporter glanced up and cupped her hand over the mouthpiece of her phone. "In his office."

This time Liv took the stairs. She darted up them, forgetting her carefully constructed poise and control.

"Ms. Carmichael." The receptionist outside the fifth-floor offices rose as Liv dashed through. "Ms. Carmichael!" she repeated to Liv's retreating back. "Whom did you want to see? Ms. Carmichael!"

Liv burst into Thorpe's office without a knock. "You louse."

Thorpe stopped typing and turned toward the door. He watched, more intrigued than annoyed, as the unannounced visitor crossed the room. "Olivia." He leaned back, but didn't rise. "What a nice surprise." He noted the receptionist hovering in the doorway and shook his head slightly to send her away. "Have a seat," he invited with a gesture of his hand. "I don't believe you've graced my office in over a year."

"You killed my story." Liv, her copy still in her hand, remained standing and leaned over his desk.

He noted the high color in her normally pale face, the dark fury in her normally calm eyes. Her hair was mussed from her mad scramble up the steps and she was breathing hard. Thorpe was fascinated. How far, he wondered, could he push before she really let loose? He decided to find out.

"What story?"

"You know damn well." She put her palms down on the desk and leaned over farther. "You did it deliberately."

"I do most things deliberately," he agreed easily. "If you're talking about the Dell story, Liv," he continued, sweeping his eyes back to hers, "it wasn't your story. It was mine. It *is* mine."

"You broke it forty-five minutes before my broadcast." Her voice was raised in fury, something he had never witnessed before. To his knowledge, Olivia Carmichael never spoke above her carefully modulated pitch. Her anger was usually ice, not fire.

"So?" He laced his fingers together and watched her over them. "You've got a complaint about my timing?"

"You've left me holding nothing." She held out her copy, then crumpled it and let it drop. "I've worked for two weeks putting this together, since Larkin had the heart attack. You killed it in two minutes."

"I'm not responsible for protecting your story, Carmichael; you are. Better luck next time."

"Oh!" Enraged, Liv struck both fists on the mahogany desk. "You're contemptible. I poured hours into this story, hundreds of phone calls, miles of legwork. It's because of you that I have an obstacle course to run in the first place." Her eyes narrowed, and he noted that a faint New England accent was slipping through. "Do I scare you that much, Thorpe? Are you so insecure about your sanctified piece of turf and the mundane quality of your reporting?"

"Insecure?" He was up, leaning on the desk until they were nose to nose. "Worrying about you inching onto my ground doesn't keep me up at night, Carmichael. I don't concern myself with junior reporters who try to scramble up the ladder three rungs at a time. Come back when you've paid your dues."

Liv made a low sound of fury. "Don't talk to me about paying dues, Thorpe. I started paying mine eight years ago."

"Eight years ago I was in Lebanon dodging bullets while you were at Harvard dodging football players."

"I never dodged football players," Liv retorted furiously. "And that's totally irrelevant. You knew this morning; you knew what was going down."

"And what if I did?"

"You knew I'd be spinning my wheels. Don't you feel any loyalty to the local station?"

"No."

His answer was so matter-of-fact, it threw her for a moment. "You started there."

"Would you call WTRL in Jersey and give them your exclusive because you read the weather there?" he countered. "Drop the alma mater routine, Liv; it doesn't cut it."

"You're despicable." Her voice had dropped to a dangerous level. "All you had to do was tell me you were going to break the story."

"And you'd have politely folded your hands and let me break it first?" She watched the ironical lift of his brow. "You'd have slit my throat to put that story on the air."

"Gladly."

He laughed then. "You're honest when you're mad, Liv—and gorgeous." He took some papers from his desk and held them out to her. "You'll need my notes to revise your lead. You've less than thirty minutes until air."

"I know what time it is." She ignored the outstretched papers. She had an almost irresistible urge to hurl something through the plate glass window at his back. "We're going to settle this, Thorpe—if not now, soon. I'm tired of having to crawl over your back for every one of my stories." She snatched the notes, hating to accept anything from him, but knowing she was boxed in.

"Fine." He watched her retrieve her own crumpled copy. "Meet me for drinks tonight."

"Not on your life." She turned and headed for the door.

"Afraid?"

The one softly taunting word stopped her. Liv turned and glared at him. "O'Riley's, eight o'clock."

"You're on." Thorpe grinned as she slammed the door behind her.

So, he thought when he settled back in his chair. There is flesh and blood under the silk. He'd begun to have his doubts. It appears I've made my first move. He laughed a little as he swiveled to stare out at his view of the city.

Damn but she'd made him mad. All for the best, he decided; otherwise he'd still be biding his time. One of the most important qualities a reporter had to have was patience. Thorpe had been patient for more than a year. Sixteen months, he thought, to be exact.

Since the first night he'd watched her broadcast. He remembered the low, calm voice, the cool, clean beauty. His attraction had been immediate and absolute. The moment he had met her, felt that aloof gaze on him, he had wanted her. Instinct had told him to hold off, keep a distance. There was more to Olivia Carmichael than met the eye.

He could have checked her background thoroughly. He had the talent, the contacts. Yet something had curbed his reporter's drive to know. He had fallen back on patience. Having spent time cooling his heels staking out politicians,

Thorpe knew all about patience. He sat back and lit a cigarette. It looked as though it were about to pay off.

At eight o'clock, Liv pulled into a parking space beside O'Riley's. For an instant she rested her brow against the steering wheel. All too clearly, she could picture herself storming through the newsrooms and into Thorpe's office. With perfect clarity, she heard herself shouting at him.

She detested losing her temper, detested more losing it in front of Thorpe. From the first time she had met him face to face, Liv had recognized a man she would need to keep at a distance. He was too strong, too charismatic. He fell into the "dangerous" category. Headed it, in fact.

She had wanted to keep an impersonal distance, and formality was necessary for that. A few hours before, Liv had dropped all formality. You couldn't be formal with someone when you were pressed nose to nose and shouting.

"I'm not cool and unruffled," she murmured, "no matter how hard I try to be." And, she realized with a sigh, Thorpe knew it.

When she was a child, she had been the misfit. In a family of sedate, well-mannered people, she had asked too many questions, cried too many tears, laughed too lustily. Unlike her sister, she hadn't been interested in party dresses and ribbons. She had wanted a dog to run with, not the quiet little poodle her mother had babied. She had wanted a tree house, not the tidy pristine playhouse her father had hired an architect to build. She had wanted to race, and had been constantly told to walk.

Liv had escaped from the strict rules and expectations of being a Carmichael. There had been freedom in college . . . and more. Liv had thought she had found everything she could ever want. Then, she had lost it. For the last six years, she had been dealing with a new phase in her growth. The final phase, she had determined. She had only herself to think about, and her career. She hadn't lost the thirst for freedom, but she had learned caution.

Liv straightened and shook her head. This wasn't the time to think of her past. Her present—and her future—demanded her attention. I won't lose my temper again, she promised herself as she climbed from the car. I won't give him the satisfaction.

She walked into O'Riley's to meet Thorpe.

He saw her enter. He'd been watching for her. She's slipped the veil back on, he noted. Her face was composed, her eyes serene as they scanned the room in search of him. Standing in the noise and smoke, she looked like marble— cool and smooth and exquisite. Thorpe wanted to touch her, feel her skin, watch her eyes heat. Anger wasn't the only passion he wanted to bring out in her. The desire he had banked down for months was beginning to crowd him.

How long will it take to peel away those protective layers? he mused. He was willing to take his time, enjoy the challenge, because he intended to win. Thorpe wasn't accustomed to losing. He waited until her eyes settled on him. He smiled and inclined his head, but didn't rise to lead her to the table. He liked the way she walked—smooth, fluid, with undercurrents of sensuality.

"Hello, Olivia."

"Thorpe." Liv slid into the booth opposite him.

"What'll you have?"

"Wine." She glanced up at the waiter, who was already at her elbow. "White wine, Lou."

"Sure, Ms. Carmichael. Another round, Mr. Thorpe?"

"No, thanks." He lifted his scotch. He had noted the quick smile she had given the young waiter. It had warmed her face for a brief moment. Then her eyes were back on his, and the warmth was gone.

"All right, Thorpe; if we're going to clear the air, I suggest we get to it."

"Are you always all business, Liv?" He lit a cigarette, watching her face. One of his greatest assets was his ability to study directly, endlessly. More than one high-powered politician had squirmed under his dark, patient gaze.

She didn't like the quiet power, or its effect on her. "We met here to discuss—"

"Haven't you ever heard of pleasantries?" he countered. "How are you? Nice weather we're having?"

"I don't care how you are," she returned evenly. He wasn't going to get the best of her. "And the weather's terrible."

"Such a sweet voice, such a nasty tongue." He observed the flare, quickly controlled, which leaped into her eyes. "You have the most perfect face I've ever seen."

Liv stiffened—back, shoulders, arms. Thorpe noted the involuntary movement and sipped his scotch. "I didn't come here to discuss my looks."

"No, but then looks are part of the job, aren't they?" The waiter set the wine in front of her. Liv slipped her fingers around the stem, but didn't lift the glass. "Viewers would rather invite attractive people into their living rooms. It makes the news easier to swallow. You add a little class as well; it's a nice touch."

"My looks have nothing to do with the quality of my reporting." Her voice was cold and unemotional, but her eyes were beginning to heat.

"No, but they do score you points in broadcasting." He leaned back, still studying her. "You're a damned good broadcaster, Liv, and you're picking up speed as a reporter."

She frowned at him. Was he trying to unbalance her by tossing out a compliment?

"And," he added without changing rhythm, "you're a very cautious woman."

"What are you talking about?"

"If I asked you out to dinner, what would you say?"

"No."

He acknowledged this with a quick, unoffended grin. "Why?"

Deliberately, she took a sip of wine. "Because I don't like you. I don't have dinner with men I don't like."

"Which implies that you do have dinner with men you like." Thorpe took a last, thoughtful drag, then crushed out his cigarette. "But you don't go out with anyone, do you?"

"That's none of your business." Infuriated, Liv started to rise, but his hands came down firmly on hers.

"You tend to jump and run when the button's pushed. I'm curious about you, Olivia." He was speaking quietly, below the laughter and raised voices around them.

"I don't want you to be interested in me in any way. I don't like you," she repeated, and controlled the urge to fight against his hold. His palms were hard and unexpectedly rough. It was an odd sensation on her skin. "I don't like your understated machismo or your overstated arrogance."

"Understated machismo?" He grinned, enjoying himself. "I think that's a compliment."

The grin was appealing, and she steeled herself against it. She knew she had been right to term him dangerous.

"I like your style, Liv—and your face. Iced sex," he continued, then saw that he had hit a nerve, a raw one. Her hands jumped convulsively under his. Her eyes went from angry to hurt to carefully blank.

"Let go of my hands."

He had wanted to annoy her, prod her, but not to hurt her. "I'm sorry."

The apology was simple, sincere and unexpected. It killed her urge to spring up and leave. When his hands left hers, she reached for her wine again. "If we're finished with the pleasantries now, Thorpe, perhaps we can get down to business."

"All right, Liv," he agreed. "Your turn at bat."

She set down her glass. "I want you to stop roadblocking me."

"Be specific."

"WWBW is an affiliate of CNC. There's supposed to be a certain amount of cooperation. The local broadcast is just as important as the national."

"And?"

At times he was maddeningly closemouthed. She pushed her wine aside and leaned forward on the table. "I'm not asking for your help. I don't want it. But I'm tired of the sabotage."

"Sabotage?" He picked up his drink and swirled it. She was becoming animated again, forgetting her vow to remain distant and untouchable. He liked the hint of pink under her ivory-toned skin.

"You knew I was working on the Dell story. You knew every step I took. Don't try that innocent, boyish look on me, Thorpe. I know you have contacts in the woodwork at WBW. You wanted me to make an ass of myself."

He laughed, amused at the phrase coming from her. "Sure, I knew what you were doing," he admitted with an easy shrug. "But that's your problem, not mine. I gave you my copy; that's standard procedure. The local always gets feed from upstairs."

"I wouldn't have needed your copy if you hadn't held a knife to my throat." She wasn't interested in standard procedure or the generosity of upstairs. "With the right information, I could have changed the tone of my interview with Anna Monroe and still have used it. It was a good piece of work, and it's wasted."

"Tunnel vision," he stated simply, and finished off his scotch. "A hazard in reporting. If," he continued as he lit another cigarette, "you had considered a few more possibilities, you would have asked Anna different questions, led her by the nose a bit more. Then, after I'd broken the story, the interview could have been reedited. You'd still have been able to use it. I saw the tape," he added. "It was a good piece of work; you just didn't press enough of the right buttons."

"Don't tell me how to do my job."

"Then don't tell me how to do mine." Now, he too leaned forward. "I've had the political beat for five years. I'm not handing you Capitol Hill on a platter, Carmichael. If you've got a problem with the way I work, take it up with Morrison." He tossed out the name of the head of CNC's Washington bureau.

"You're so smug." Liv had a sudden desire to choke him. "So sure of your sanctified position as keeper of the Holy Grail."

"There's nothing sanctified about the political beat in this town, Carmichael," Thorpe countered. "I'm here because I know how to play the games. Maybe you need a few lessons."

"Not from you."

"You could do worse." He paused a moment, and calculated. "Look, for the sake of professional courtesy, I'll give you this much. It takes more than a year to spread roots here. The people in this town are insecure; their jobs are always on the line. Politics is an ugly word—uglier since Watergate, Abscam. Exposing them is our job; they can't ignore us, so they try to use us the same way we use them."

"You're not telling me anything I don't know."

"Maybe not," he agreed. "But you have an advantage you're not cultivating. Your looks and your class."

"I don't see what—"

"Don't be an idiot." He cut her off with a quick, annoyed gesture. "A reporter has to use everything he can beg, borrow or steal. Your face doesn't have anything to do with your brain, but it does have something to do with the way people perceive you. Human nature." He let his words sink in.

She was digesting what he said, annoyed because she knew he was right. Charm worked for some reporters, abrasiveness for others. And class, as he put it, could work for her.

"There's an embassy party Saturday night. I'll take you."

Her attention came full circle back to him. Astonished, she stared. "You'll—"

"You want to get in the door, take the one that's most accessible." The incredulity in her eyes amused him. "A lot of interesting gossip goes on in the ladies' room after a few glasses of champagne."

"You'd know all about that, of course," Liv said dryly.

"You'd be surprised."

She was cautious, uneasy, tempted. "Why would you do this?"

He pushed her wine glass back in front of her. "There's a saying about gift horses, Liv."

"There's one about Trojan horses, too."

He laughed and sat back. "A good reporter would have opened the gates and had a scoop."

He was right, of course, but she didn't like it. She knew that if it had been anyone else but Thorpe, she wouldn't have hesitated. That gives him too much importance, she told herself, and gathered up her purse. "All right. What embassy?"

"Canadian." It had amused him to watch her work out the decision.

"What time should I meet you?"

"I'll pick you up."

She had started to rise, but now stopped. "No."

"My party, my terms. Take it or leave it."

She didn't like it. To have met him would have kept the evening professional and relatively safe. Though she doubted that a woman was ever really safe with Thorpe. He was boxing her into a corner. If she refused now, she'd look, and feel, like a fool. "All right." Liv reached for her notebook. "I'll give you my address."

"I know your address." He watched her eyes fly back to his, wary and suspicious. Thorpe smiled. "I'm a reporter, Liv; I deal in information." He slid from the booth. "I'll walk you out."

Taking her arm, he led her to the door. Liv kept silent. She wasn't certain if she had won a point or taken two steps backward. In any case, she thought it better than standing still.

"You don't have to come out," she began, as he steered her toward the parking lot. "You haven't got your coat."

"Worried about me?"

"Not in the least." Annoyed, she reached for her keys.

"Have we finished conducting business for the evening?" he asked her as she stuck the key in the door lock.

"Yes."

"Completely?"

"Completely."

"Good."

He turned her to face him, kept his hands firmly on her shoulders, and took her mouth with his. Liv was too stunned to protest. She hadn't been prepared for that kind of move from Thorpe. She hadn't expected that hard, uncompromising mouth to be soft and gentle. He drew her closer, and she was pressed against him.

His body was hard, firm and arousing. Her blood began to heat. Liv lifted her hands, not certain whether she would draw him closer or push him away. She ended by curling her fingers into the material of his shirt.

Thorpe made no attempt to deepen the kiss or seek quick intimacy. He could sense her struggle against responding, and knew he would simply wait her out. He blocked out his own needs and concentrated on hers.

Slowly, her lips softened, yielded. She could feel the world slip out of focus, as if a new lens had been placed on a camera and hadn't yet been adjusted. "No," she murmured against his mouth, and uncurled her hands to push him away. "No."

When he released her, Liv leaned back against the car. Feelings she had thought completely dead had begun to flicker into life. She didn't want them, didn't want Thorpe to be the man to revitalize them. She stared at him while he watched the emotion, the vulnerability, run over her face. He felt something more complex than desire move through him.

"That—" Liv swallowed and tried to speak again. "That was—"

"Very enjoyable, Olivia, for both of us." He kept his voice light for himself as well as for her. "Though it would appear that you're a bit out of practice."

Her eyes flared and the cloudiness vanished. "You're insufferable."

"Be ready at eight on Saturday, Liv," he told her, and walked back into O'Riley's.

3

She chose a plain black dress. It fit her closely from neck to hem, with no glitter, no flounces to spoil the line. Against the unrelieved black, her skin glowed like marble. Liv hesitated over jewelry, then decided on the pearl studs she had received on her twenty-first birthday.

For a moment, she only held the earrings in her hand. They brought memories, bittersweet. Twenty-one. She had thought nothing could mar her life, her happiness. Hardly more than a year later, her world had started to crumble. At twenty-three, she hadn't been able to remember what it had been like to feel happy.

She tried to recall what Doug had said when he had given her the pearls. Liv shut her eyes a moment. It had been something about their being like her skin, pale and smooth. Doug, she mused. My husband. She looked down at her ringless hands. Ex-husband. We loved each other then, I think. For the four years we were together; for at least part of them. Before . . .

Feeling the pain well up, she shut her eyes again. She couldn't think of what she had lost. It was too enormous, too irreplaceable.

Seven years had passed since he had given her the earrings. She had been a different woman then, in a different life. It was time for this woman to wear them again, in the life she had now.

Liv put the earrings on and went to find her shoes. It was nearly eight o'clock.

She was nervous, and tried to convince herself that she wasn't. She hadn't been on a date in years. It's not a date, she reminded herself. It's business. A professional courtesy. And why was Thorpe suddenly showing her courtesy of any kind?

Liv sat with one shoe on and the other in her hand. He wasn't a man she should trust, personally or professionally. On the job, he was ruthless and proprietary. She'd known that from the outset. And now . . .

The way he had kissed her. Just like that. Just as if he had the right to. She chewed on her bottom lip and stared into space. He hadn't led up to it. She would have thrown up the barricades if he had. She knew the signs to look for: the smiles, the soft, promising words. Thorpe hadn't spared any of those. It was an impulse, she decided, and shrugged it off. There hadn't been anything desperate or even particularly loverlike in the kiss. He hadn't been rough; he hadn't tried a seduction. She was making too much of it. She had wanted to kiss him. She had wanted to go on kissing him. To be held close, to be needed, desired. Why? He meant nothing to her, she told herself firmly.

"What do you want?" she whispered to herself. "And why don't you know?"

To be the best, she thought. To win. To be Olivia Carmichael without having to lose pieces of myself along the way. I want to be whole again.

The doorbell rang. Business, she reminded herself. I'm going to be the best reporter in Washington. If I have to socialize with T.C. Thorpe to do it, then I'll socialize with T.C. Thorpe.

She glanced at the perfume on her dresser, then turned away from it. There was no point in giving him any ideas. She felt sure he had enough of his own. She moved through the apartment without hurry. It gave her a small touch of satisfaction to keep him waiting. But when Liv opened the door, Thorpe didn't appear annoyed. There was approval and simple male appreciation for a woman in his eyes.

"You look lovely." Thorpe handed her a single rosebud,

long-stemmed and white. "It suits you," he said, as she accepted it without a word. "Red's too obvious; pink's too sweet."

Liv stared down at the flower and forgot everything she had just told herself. She hadn't counted on being moved by him again so quickly. She lifted serious eyes to his. "Thank you."

Thorpe smiled, but his tone was as serious as hers. "You're welcome. Are you going to let me in?"

I'd be smarter not to, she thought abruptly, but stepped back. "I'll go put this in water."

Thorpe scanned the living room as she walked away. It was neat, tastefully furnished. No decorator, he thought. She had taken her time here, choosing precisely what she wanted. He noted that there were no photographs, no mementos. Liv wasn't putting any parts of herself on display. Very careful, very private. The vague hint of secrecy had aroused his reporter's instincts.

It might be time, he considered, for a bit of gentle probing. He walked into the kitchen and leaned on the door as Liv added water to a crystal bud vase.

"Nice place," he said conversationally. "You have a good view of the city."

"Yes."

"Washington's a far cry from Connecticut. What part are you from?"

Liv raised her eyes. They were cool again, cautious. "Westport."

Westport—Carmichael. Thorpe had no trouble with the connection. "Tyler Carmichael's your father?"

Liv lifted the vase from the sink and turned to him. "Yes."

Tyler Carmichael—real estate, staunch conservative, roots straight back to the Mayflower. There had been two daughters, Thorpe remembered suddenly. He'd forgotten because one had simply slipped from notice a decade before, while the other had struck out on the debutante circuit. Five-thousand-dollar dresses and a pink Rolls. Her daddy's darling. When she had graduated from Radcliffe and snapped up her first husband, a playwright, Carmichael had given her a fifteen-acre estate as a wedding present. Melinda Carmichael Howard LeClare was now on husband number two. She was a nervous, spoiled woman with a desperate sort of beauty and a taste for the expensive.

"I've met your sister," Thorpe commented, studying Liv's face. "You're nothing like her."

"No," Liv agreed simply, and moved past him into the living room. She set the rose down on a small glass table. "I'll get my coat."

A good reporter, Thorpe mused, makes the worst interview subject. They know how to answer questions with a yes or no, and without inflection. Olivia Carmichael was a good reporter. So was he.

"You don't get along with your family?"

"I didn't say that." Liv chose a hip-length fox fur from her closet.

"You didn't have to." Smoothly, Thorpe took the coat and held it out. Liv slipped her arms into the sleeves. She wore no scent, he noted, just the light lingering fragrance from her bath, and the clean faintly citrus scent from shampoo. The lack of artifice aroused him. He turned her so that she faced him. "Why don't you get along with them?"

Liv let out an annoyed breath. "Look, Thorpe—"

"Aren't you ever going to call me by my first name?"

She lifted a brow and waited a beat. "Terrance?"

He grinned. "Nobody calls me that and lives to tell about it."

Liv laughed. It was the first time he'd heard her laugh and mean it. She leaned down to pick up her bag.

"You never answered my question," Thorpe pointed out, and unexpectedly took her hand as she turned back to him.

"And I'm not going to. No personal questions, Thorpe, on or off the record."

"I'm a stubborn man, Liv."

"Don't brag; it's unattractive."

He laced his fingers with hers, then lifted the joined hands and studied them thoughtfully. "They fit," he decided, giving her an odd smile. "I thought they might."

She wasn't used to this. It wasn't a seduction, though she

was feeling stirrings of desire. It wasn't a challenge, though she felt the need to fight. It wasn't even an assumption she could dispute. He had simply stated a fact.

"Aren't we going to be late?" Liv said a little desperately. She found it strange that though his eyes never left hers, she could feel their gaze through her coat, through her dress, on her skin. She would have sworn he knew precisely what she looked like right down to the small sickle-shaped birthmark under her left breast.

"Thorpe." There was a quick sense of panic at what she was feeling. "Don't."

Hurt. He saw it. He sensed it. She had been hurt. He reminded himself of his decision to move slowly. Keeping her hand in his, he walked to the door.

Light. Music. Elegance. Liv wondered how many parties she had been to in her life. What made this party different from hundreds of others? Politics.

It was a hard-edged, intimate little world. You were appointed or elected, but always an open target for the press, vulnerable because of their influence on the public. One group habitually accused the other of staging the news. Sometimes it was true. Whether at a social event or an official one, there were images to project. Liv understood images.

The senator nibbling pâté was a liberal; his hair was boyishly styled around an open, ingenuous face. Liv knew he was sharp as a tack and viciously ambitious. A veteran congressman told a slightly off-color story about marlin fishing. He was lobbying furiously against a pending tax proposal.

Liv spotted a reporter for an influential Washington paper drinking steadily. By her count, he had downed five bourbons without showing a flicker. But his fingers were curled around the glass as though it were a life preserver and he were drowning. She recognized the signs and felt a stir of pity. If he wasn't already drinking his breakfast, he soon would be.

"Everybody handles pressure differently," Thorpe commented, noting where Liv's gaze had focused.

"I suppose. I had a friend on a newspaper in Austin," she

said, as she accepted the glass of wine Thorpe offered her, "who used to say newspapers gave information to the thinking public, while television put on a show."

He lit a cigarette. "What did you say to her?"

"I pointed out that the ads scattered through the *New York Times* weren't any different than commercials in a broadcast." She smiled, remembering her earnest fellow reporter. "I would say that television was more immediate; she'd say newspapers were more reflective. I'd say television allowed the viewer to see; she'd say print allowed a reader to think." Shrugging, she sipped the cool, dry wine. "We were both right, I suppose."

"I did some print reporting when I was in college." Thorpe watched Liv study the people, her surroundings. She was soaking it all up. Now, she looked back at him, curious.

"Why did you switch to broadcasting?"

"I liked the faster pace, the sense of reaching people on the spot."

She nodded, understanding perfectly. There was a glass of scotch in his hand. Unlike the reporter she had observed, Thorpe drank moderately . . . but smoked too much, she decided. She thought of Carl and his endless chain of cigarettes. "How do you deal with the pressure?"

He grinned, then surprised her by running a thumb over the pearl in her ear. "I row."

"What?" His touch had distracted her. Now she focused fully on his face again.

"Row," he repeated. "A boat, on the river. There's handball when it's too cold."

"Rowing," Liv mused. That would explain the calloused, worked feeling of his palms.

"Yes, you know: Go, Yale!"

She smiled at that—a quick smile that lit her eyes.

"That's the first time you've done that for me," he said. "Smiled with your whole face. I think I'm in love."

"You're tougher than that, Thorpe."

"A marshmallow," he corrected, and lifted her hand to his lips.

Carefully, she removed her hand from his. Her fingertips

were tingling. "No marshmallow was responsible for that exposé on misappropriation of funds in the Interior Department last November."

"That's work." He took a step closer so that their bodies nearly touched. "The man is a pathetic romantic, weakened by candlelight, devastated by a Chopin prelude. A woman could have me for the price of an open fire and a bottle of wine."

Liv lifted her glass again. It had to be the wine that was making her feel unsteady. "And thousands have."

"You told me not to brag." He grinned. "And reporting limits your time."

Liv was having a difficult time keeping her distance. She shook her head and sighed. "I don't want to like you, Thorpe. I really don't."

"Don't rush into anything," he advised genially.

"T.C." The gentleman from Virginia clapped a hand on Thorpe's shoulder. "I knew I'd find you with an attractive woman." He ran an appreciative eye over Liv. Senator Wyatt was a few pounds overweight, pink cheeked and jovial. Liv knew he was leading a campaign to kill proposed cuts in education and welfare. She had been fighting to get past his front door for two weeks.

"Senator." Thorpe took the heavy-handed greeting genially. "Olivia Carmichael."

Liv's hand was pumped in the best senatorial style. "Well now, I don't forget faces, and I've seen this one. But I'll swear you're not one of T.C.'s regulars."

Thorpe made a sound that was somewhere between throat clearing and sighing. Liv shot him a glance. "I'm with WWBW, Senator Wyatt. Mr. Thorpe and I are . . . colleagues."

"Yes, yes, of course. I remember perfectly now. T.C. fancies a different type." He leaned closer to Liv and winked. "Lots of leg, short on brains."

"Is that so?" Liv aimed a thoughtful look at Thorpe.

"You have great legs, Liv," Thorpe commented.

"So I've been told." She turned to Wyatt. "I'd very much like to speak with you, Senator, about your stand on the proposed education cuts. Perhaps you could suggest a more appropriate time?"

Wyatt hesitated a moment, then nodded. "Call my office Monday morning. You two should be dancing," he decided, and straightened his dinner jacket with a quick tug. "I'm going to see if I can find any real food at that buffet. Fish eggs and goose liver." With a grimace, he sauntered away.

Thorpe took her hand. When Liv glanced up at him, he smiled. "Just taking the senator's advice," he explained. Keeping to the edge of the dance floor, he drew her into his arms.

It was the second time she had been held against him. The second time her body had responded despite herself. Liv went rigid.

"Don't you like to dance, Olivia?" he murmured.

"Yes." She made an effort to keep her voice cool and even. "Of course."

"Then relax." His hand was light at her waist, his mouth close to her ear. Small thrills trembled along her skin. "When we make love, it won't be with members of Washington's brass looking on. I like privacy."

Because she had been struggling with the first part of his statement, it took a moment for the second part to penetrate. Liv threw her head back so that their eyes met. "What makes you think—"

"Not think, know," he corrected. "Your heart's racing just as it did when I kissed you outside of O'Riley's."

"It is not," she denied hotly. "It wasn't then; it isn't now. I told you before, Thorpe, I don't like you."

"More recently you said you didn't want to like me—a totally different thing." She was so slender. He wanted to press her closer until she melted into him. "I could find out how you feel right now if I kissed you. The federal grapevine would be buzzing about Thorpe and Carmichael fraternizing on neutral ground."

"The lead story would be Thorpe's broken jaw when Carmichael severs diplomatic relations."

"You don't have the hands for packing much of a punch," he mused. "Anyway, I prefer reporting stories, not being featured in them."

Liv drew away when the music ended. "I'm going to check

out your theory about the ladies' room," she said evenly. Her heart *was* racing. She detested him for being right.

Thorpe watched her move away. He suddenly wished the damn party were over so he could have her alone, even for a few minutes. His body still tingled from the brush of hers against it. He had never wanted a woman so badly, nor been as frustratingly certain of the uphill battle he had yet to fight. Taking out a cigarette, he flicked on his lighter and drew deeply.

He was used to pressure in his work. In truth, he thrived on it. That was his secret. He could go for days on snatches of sleep and still throb with energy. He didn't need vitamins, just a story. But this was a different sort of pressure—wanting something and knowing it was still out of reach. Not for long, he decided grimly, and drew on the cigarette again. If he had to lay siege to Olivia Carmichael, that's exactly what he'd do. She wasn't getting away from him.

"T.C., you pirate. How are you?"

Thorpe turned and clasped hands with the Canadian ambassador's press secretary. Returning the greeting, he reminded himself to relax. A successful siege took time.

Liv took her time renewing makeup which needed no renewing. She tried, as she dusted powder on her nose, to consider her response to Thorpe logically. Hadn't she termed him a charismatic man? Even attractive, she admitted reluctantly, in a purely physical, athletic way. That had nothing to do with his being difficult and frustrating.

"Of course he's a pompous old bat, but I rather like him."

Liv glanced in the glass to see the reflections of two women who entered. One was Congresswoman Amelia Thaxter, a thin, hardworking woman who had a penchant for lost causes and dowdy clothes. Her constituents loved her, proving it by electing her for a second term by a landslide.

The woman with her, who was speaking, was also fiftyish, but plumper and dressed in elegant gray silk. There was something vaguely familiar about her. Liv took out her compact a second time and listened.

"You're more tolerant than I am, Myra." Amelia sat down and tiredly took out a comb.

"Rod's not a bad sort, Amelia." Myra sat and took out a

silver case of flashy red lipstick. "If you'd use a bit of honey, you might find him a help instead of a hindrance."

"He's not concerned with the ecological problems of South Dakota," Amelia put in. She hadn't bothered to use the comb, but kept tapping it against the palm of her hand. "No matter what you or I say to him tonight, he's not going to support me when I put my proposal on the floor Monday."

"We'll see." Myra slashed on the lipstick.

Rod, Liv realized as she slipped a thin brush out of her purse, was Roderick Matte, one of the more influential men in Congress. If a vote was going to be close, he was the man to sway.

A pompous old bat, Liv thought, and suppressed a grin. Yes, he was that, as well as his party's hope for the highest office in Washington in the next election. Or so the rumors went.

The congresswoman muttered at the comb, then stuck it back in her purse. "He's a bigoted, narrow-minded pain in the—"

"My dear," Myra said sweetly, interrupting her friend's impassioned speech with a smile for Liv, "that's a perfectly stunning dress."

"Thank you."

"Didn't I see you with T.C.?" The woman took out a small vial of expensive perfume and used it lavishly.

"Yes, we came together." Liv vacillated between identifying herself and keeping silent. She decided it was both wiser and more fair to establish her credentials. "I'm Olivia Carmichael with WWBW."

Amelia made a small, unidentifiable sound, but Myra pressed on, undisturbed. "How interesting. I don't watch the local news, I'm afraid, or much news at all, except for T.C.'s reports. News tends to give Herbert indigestion."

Justice Herbert Ditmyer. Liv finally placed the face. Justice Ditmyer's wife, Myra, a woman with power and influence enough of her own to call Congressman Matte a pompous old bat without fear of repercussions.

"We're on at five-thirty, Mrs. Ditmyer," Olivia told her. "Your husband might find our broadcast easy to digest."

Myra laughed, but she was studying Liv carefully. "I know

some Carmichaels. Connecticut. You wouldn't be Tyler's younger daughter, would you?"

Liv was used to the nameless term. "Yes, I am."

Myra's face split into a smile. "Isn't that something. The last time I saw you, you were seven or eight years old. Your mother was giving a proper little tea, and you came into the parlor—a scruffy thing with a rip the size of a fist in your skirt and the buckle off your shoe. I believe you got quite a scold."

"I usually did," Liv agreed, not remembering the particular incident, but others like it.

"I remember thinking you must have had a great deal more fun that afternoon than the rest of us did." She gave a gleaming smile. "Your mother gave a stuffy party."

"Myra, really." Amelia took her mind from her pending bill long enough to give a disapproving tsh-tsh.

"It's all right, Congresswoman," Liv said smoothly. "She still does, I believe."

"I must say, I would never have recognized you." Myra rose and brushed off her skirt. "Quite an elegant young woman now. Married?"

"No."

"Are you and T.C. . . . ?" She let the sentence trail off delicately.

"No," Liv said positively.

"Do you play bridge?"

Liv lifted a brow. "Poorly. I never acquired a taste for it."

"My dear, a detestable game, but useful." She plucked a business card out of her bag and handed it to Liv. "I'm having a card party next week. Call my secretary Monday; she'll give you the details. I have a nephew I'm rather fond of."

"Mrs. Ditmyer—"

"He won't bore you—at least not too much," Myra continued smoothly. "And I think I'm going to like you. My husband will be there," she added, shrewd enough to dangle tempting bait before the reporter. "He'd love to meet you."

"Let's go back, Myra," Amelia suggested, wearily rising. "Before you're up on bribery charges. Good evening, Ms. Carmichael."

"Good evening, Congresswoman."

Alone, Liv studied the elegant little calling card for a moment, then dropped it into her purse. One didn't turn up one's nose at a direct invitation from Myra Ditmyer—even if it included bridge and a nephew.

Snapping her purse shut, Liv rejoined the party.

"I was beginning to think you were holding a press conference in there," Thorpe commented, offering her a fresh glass of wine.

She gave him an enigmatic smile. "Close."

"Want to elaborate?"

"Does accepting your invitation mean I have to share?" Liv took a careless sip of wine. She was feeling curiously buoyant. Three unexpected contacts in one evening was well worth the trip. "Actually," she continued, "I believe I'm going to be a blind date at a bridge party."

"Date?" Thorpe frowned. He had noted the women who had come out of the powder room before Liv.

"Yes, date. You know—a man and a woman finding a common interest for a certain number of hours."

"Cute. Had enough of this place?"

"As a matter of fact, yes." Liv took a last sip, then handed him back the glass.

"We'll get your coat." He took her arm and propelled her through the room.

"I do appreciate your letting me tag along, Thorpe." Liv reached for her keys as they stepped from the elevator on her floor.

"Tag along," he repeated. "That wasn't included in your definition of a date, was it?"

"This wasn't a date."

"Still." Thorpe took the keys from her and slipped one into the lock on the door. "Good manners would buy me a cup of coffee."

"Fifty cents would buy you one down the street."

"Liv." Thorpe gave her an offended look that made her smile.

"All right, manners it is. A cup's worth."

"You're incredibly generous," he told her as he opened the door.

Liv tossed her coat on a chair as she walked to the kitchen. He eyed the coat with a small smile. Now and again, she forgot the carefully created image she had built. Olivia Carmichael would never throw down a coat—much too fastidious. Much too organized. More than ever, Thorpe wanted to know the woman behind the image. There was warmth there, humor, passion—all hidden behind a thin shield. The shield had been raised for a reason. He intended—sooner or later—to find out what it was.

She liked color, he decided. He'd noted it before in the way she dressed. Now he noted it again in the furnishings of her apartment: a brilliant blue throw pillow, a persimmon-colored bowl. Small signs of fire, he thought, like the quick flare of temper. She banked it, constantly, but it was there.

"How do you take your coffee?" she called out as he walked to the kitchen.

"Black."

He wandered to the stereo and flipped through records. "Van Cliburn to Billy Joel," he commented when Liv came back into the room. "Very eclectic."

"I like variety," she answered, and set a tray with two cups and saucers on the coffee table.

"Do you?" He smiled—a bit, she thought, as if he were enjoying a private joke. Liv began to wish she hadn't agreed to the cup of coffee. "What do you do for entertainment?" Thorpe walked over and took a seat on the sofa. Liv hesitated a moment, then sat beside him. She could hardly choose a chair across the room.

"Entertainment?" she repeated, and reached for her coffee.

"That's right." He had noticed the hesitation. It pleased him to know that she wasn't indifferent toward him. If he made her nervous, it was a beginning. "You know, bowling, stamp collecting."

"I haven't had much time for hobbies lately," Liv murmured, and sipped at her coffee. She wondered why she had been at ease when she had walked out of the kitchen and was now strung tight. Thorpe lit a cigarette and kept watching her.

She struggled against an adolescent urge to move away from him.

"What have you had time for?"

"I work," she said, and moved her shoulders. Why was a simple cup of coffee and conversation making her pulse pound? "That keeps me busy enough."

"Sunday afternoons?"

"What?" She had looked up to meet his eyes before she realized the mistake. His were dark and direct and closer than she had thought.

"Sunday afternoons," he repeated. He didn't touch her. His eyes drifted slowly down to her mouth, then back. "What do you do on Sunday afternoons?"

Something was kindling inside her—something elemental and strong. Liv hadn't felt the quick tug of desire for years. But he wasn't touching her, wasn't making love to her. They were only drinking coffee and talking. She told herself she had had too much wine, and lifted her coffee again.

"I usually try to catch up on my reading." She watched a plume of smoke drift by before Thorpe crushed out his cigarette. "Murder mysteries, thrillers." Her eyes flew up again when Thorpe took the cup from her hand.

"I've always liked solving puzzles," he murmured. "Digging underneath to find something that's not on the surface. You've very thin skin." He brushed a knuckle over her cheek. "But I haven't been able to get beneath it—not yet."

She started to draw away. "I don't want you poking into my mind."

"We'll save that for later, then." He slid his arms around her. "I want to hold you. When we were dancing, I promised myself I'd hold you again when we were alone."

You don't want him to hold you, her mind insisted. But she didn't tell him, and didn't resist as he pressed her closer.

His eyes flicked briefly to her mouth. "I've wanted for days to taste you again." Lightly, his lips rubbed over hers. "Too long," he muttered.

You don't want him to kiss you, her mind insisted. But she didn't tell him, and didn't resist as he crushed her mouth with his.

Thorpe wasn't patient this time. The demand seemed to

spring up—hot, almost violent. Liv was caught in it, stunned by his lightning passion and her own instant response. She had no time to think, to reason, only to react. Her arms locked around him. Her lips parted.

Where had the urgency come from? Both of them seemed trapped by it, unable to keep to their planned routes. She couldn't stop him or herself; he couldn't adhere to the easy pace he had outlined. Desperation. They both felt it. Need. Outrageous need to taste and touch and belong. He hadn't known her mouth would become so soft in passion. He wanted to rip the black dress from her and discover her. It was madness. Control was slipping from him too quickly.

Liv moaned when his mouth went to her throat. She wanted to be touched, and heard herself telling him, then pressed against him as he caressed her breast through the thin layers of silk. She pulled his mouth back to hers.

She was starving and took from him what she had so long denied herself. She craved the intimacy of his tongue against hers, the feel of his hands roaming her body. There was strength there, and need. A need for her. And he made her need him with an intensity that frightened her. She couldn't allow herself to need anyone again. The risks were too great, the punishment too severe.

"No." Liv pushed against him in sudden panic. "No," she said again, and managed to draw back, if not away. His hands stayed firm on her shoulders. She could see the raw desire in his eyes, knew it must be mirrored in her own.

"No what?" His voice was rough, half-angry, half-aroused. He hadn't expected the brutal degree of passion she had brought out in him.

"You have to go." Liv pulled out of his hold and stood. She needed distance, needed to stand on her feet. Thorpe rose more slowly.

"I want you." It was a simple statement, almost flat, as he fought against the throbbing that beat inside him. "You want me."

It would have been absurd to deny it. Liv took a deep breath. "Yes, but I don't *want* to want you." She let the breath out again. "I won't."

Thorpe felt his control snap. He grabbed her and pulled her

against him. He saw her eyes widen as the pupils dilated. "The hell you won't," he said quietly. He released her again so quickly that she nearly tumbled back onto the sofa. He stuck his hands in his pockets to keep them off her.

"This isn't the end of it, Carmichael," he warned before he turned for the door. "It's just the beginning."

He let the door swing closed behind him as he headed for the elevator. He needed a drink.

4

"The tape on the school board meeting's still being edited." Liv glanced briefly at the clock before she sat down to review the script for the evening broadcast. I'd have more time, she thought fleetingly, if I hadn't had to do those teases.

"Know what the story count is tonight?" Brian stripped the wrapper from a chocolate bar and sat on Liv's desk.

"Hmm?"

"Eighteen." He took a generous bite. "We're packing them in. The general manager's frantic because we slipped a couple notches in the ratings. I heard he wants to change the tone of the weather forecast. Go for the chuckles. Maybe he'll hire a comedy writer."

"Or put on a ventriloquist and a magic act," Liv mumbled. Gimmicks annoyed her. Even as she spoke to Brian, she was running over her timing on the stories she would soon read on the air. "The next thing you know, we'll have the weather being given by a guy in a clown suit standing on one leg and juggling plates."

"Maybe we need the comic relief." Brian balled the candy wrapper and pitched it into Liv's wastebasket. "Lead story's the rape in the supermarket parking lot."

"So I see." She was skimming the copy, one eye on it, the other on the clock, with her attention divided between the script and her colleague. It was a skill most reporters developed early.

"Marilee did a spooky little stand-up out there. I just saw the tape." He swallowed the last of the chocolate. "My wife shops there. Damn."

"Everything in here tonight's grim." Liv glanced up, running a hand over the back of her neck. "Wholesale prices are up six percent; unemployment's following suit. Two robberies in Northeast and an arson in Anne Arundel County to add to the rape. Lovely."

"Like I said, maybe we need that comic relief."

"I want to see daffodils," she said suddenly. Weariness settled over her all at once. Was it the tone of the news? she wondered. Surely by now she was immune to it. Was it something else? Something had been nagging inside her for the last few days. Something she couldn't quite pinpoint. It had kept her awake long after Thorpe had left her apartment the night before.

Brian studied her a moment. He'd noticed the faint shadows under her eyes that morning. It was past five now, and they were deeper. "Is it something you'd like to talk about?"

Liv opened her mouth, surprised by the question. She shut it again. There was nothing she could say.

"I know something's been eating at you lately." He leaned a bit closer so other ears wouldn't overhear his words. "Look, why don't you come to dinner tonight? I'll call Kathy and tell her to add a can of water to the soup. Sometimes a few hours with friends helps."

Liv smiled and squeezed his hand. "That's the nicest invitation I've had in a long time."

"So don't turn it down."

"I have to. I've got something lined up tonight." The offer made her feel better, less isolated. "Can I have a rain check?"

"Sure." He rose, but Liv took his hand before he moved away.

"Brian, thanks." She tightened the grip a moment when he started to shrug it off. "I mean it."

"You're welcome." He pulled her to her feet. "It's nearly airtime. You'd better haul yourself into makeup and have them do something about those shadows under your eyes."

Liv lifted her fingers to them automatically. "That bad?"

"Bad enough."

With a quiet oath, Liv walked off to follow Brian's advice. The last thing she needed was to appear haggard on the air. It would be her luck to go on looking as if she hadn't slept, and then have Thorpe catch her broadcast.

So I haven't been sleeping well, Liv thought as she took her place on the set. It hasn't anything to do with Thorpe. I've just been a bit restless lately. And I was at the southwest gate of the White House at eight o'clock this morning waiting to catch comments from cabinet officials. I'm a bit tired. It has nothing to do with the night of the embassy party . . . or what happened later.

Liv clipped on her mike, then flipped through the script one last time. Timing was important as story was piled on top of story.

She'd been working too hard. That's what she told herself. The last few days had been particularly hectic—that was all. T.C. Thorpe had been the last thing on her mind. There'd been the aftermath of Dell's appointment, then that mess at the school board to cover. She frowned down at the script and told herself she hadn't given a thought to her last meeting with Thorpe. It hadn't crossed her mind since it happened. Not once. Only a thousand times.

Swearing silently, she heard the thirty-second cue. She straightened in her chair and glanced up. Thorpe stood in the back of the studio. He was watching her steadily, eyes level as he leaned back against the heavy doors.

Fifteen seconds.

What is he doing here? Liv felt her throat go dry. Ridiculous, she told herself, and tore her eyes away from his to the camera.

Ten seconds.

The monitor was flashing the opening, an aerial view of the city.

Five seconds. Four, three, two, one. Cue.

"Good evening, this is Olivia Carmichael." Her voice was cool and precise. It amazed her that her palms were damp. She read off the lead story, then never glanced toward the rear of the studio as they went to tape for the reporter's stand-up on location.

The cameras switched between Liv and Brian, keeping the pace brisk. She gave her report on the school board meeting without missing a beat, though she could feel the physical pressure of Thorpe's eyes on her face.

She gave the depressing news on the wholesale price index. To her knowledge, Thorpe never came to the studio before or during a broadcast. Why wasn't he upstairs where he belonged, polishing his own words of wisdom?

There was a buildup of tension at the base of her neck, which increased when they broke for commercial. Liv knew, without glancing over, that he was coming toward her.

"Nice style, Liv," Thorpe commented. "Sharp, cool and clean."

"Thank you." The sportscaster settled into his chair at the end of the table.

"Going to the Ditmyer card party tonight?"

There was nothing he didn't know, she decided, and folded her hands over her copy. "Yes."

"Want a lift?"

Now she met his eyes directly. "Are you going?"

"I'll pick you up at seven-thirty. We'll grab some dinner first."

"No."

He leaned a bit closer. "I can arrange for you to be my partner tonight."

"You'll lose," she told him. She had never known a set of commercials to take so long.

"No," he corrected, and smiled. "I don't intend to lose." He kissed her quickly, casually, before she could prevent it, then sauntered away.

Thirty seconds.

She scowled as the doors swung behind his back. Without turning, she could feel the speculative gazes on her. Thorpe had successfully set the ball rolling. And the tongues wagging.

Ten seconds.

Fuming, she vowed to make him pay for it.

Cue.

* * *

Liv arrived at the Ditmyers' promptly at eight. Bridge wasn't the inducement. She could remember the dry, stuffy card parties her mother had given when she was growing up. Liv remembered Myra's flashy red lipstick and careless gossip from the powder room at the embassy. She pressed the doorbell and smiled. She didn't think Myra Ditmyer gave stuffy parties. And, she reminded herself, how often does a reporter get invited to the home of a justice of the Supreme Court? Unless, of course, the reporter's name was T.C. Thorpe.

Liv frowned, then quickly smoothed out her features as the door opened.

Though it was a maid who led Liv inside, Myra herself came bustling down the hall seconds later. It was obvious, Liv thought, smiling to herself, that Myra was a woman who didn't like to miss anything.

"Olivia." Myra clasped both of her hands warmly. "So glad you could come. I like having beautiful women around. I was one myself once."

As she talked, she was pulling Liv with her down the hall. "I watched your newscast. You're good."

"Thank you."

Myra propelled Liv into a large drawing room. "You must meet Herbert," she went on. "I reminded him of the tea with your parents, and your torn dress, but he didn't remember. Herbert's mind is filled with weighty matters. He often misses details."

But you don't, Liv decided as she was pulled through the room at top speed. It was spacious, accented with splashes of vivid color and ornately patterned wallpaper. Liv decided the room suited her hostess perfectly.

"Herbert." Myra snatched her husband away from a conversation without a moment's hesitation. "You must meet lovely Ms. Carmichael. She does the newscast on . . . What is the name of that station, dear?"

"WWBW." Liv extended her hand to Justice Ditmyer. "We're the Washington affiliate of CNC."

"All those initials," Myra commented with a cluck of her

tongue. "It would be simpler if they just gave it a name. Isn't she beautiful, Herbert?"

"Yes, indeed." The justice smiled with the handshake. "A pleasure to meet you, Ms. Carmichael."

He was a small and, Liv thought, curiously unimposing man without the black robes of his office. His face was lean and lined. He looked like someone's grandfather rather than one of the top judiciary leaders of the country. The skin of his hand was soft and thin with age. He lacked the vitality of his wife, possessing instead a quiet stability.

"Myra tells me we met briefly, a number of years ago."

"A great number of years ago, Justice Ditmyer," Liv agreed. "I disgraced myself, I believe, so we're both to be forgiven for not remembering."

"And she hardly resembles that little wildcat who burst into tea that afternoon," Myra put in. She was eyeing Liv with her good-natured shrewdness. "How does your mother feel about your career in television?"

"She wishes I'd chosen something less public," Liv astonished herself by saying. It wasn't like her to be so frank with strangers. Myra Ditmyer, she decided, would have made a terrific interviewer.

"Ah, well, parents are so hard to please, aren't they?" Myra brushed it off with a smile and a pat on Liv's hand. "My children find me terribly difficult, don't they, Herbert?"

"So they tell me."

"All nicely married now," she continued, overlooking her husband's dry response. "So I've time to work on my nephew. Nice boy—a lawyer. He lives in Chicago. I believe I mentioned him."

"Yes, Mrs. Ditmyer." Liv heard the justice sigh, and tried not to echo with one of her own.

"He's here on business for a few days. I do want you to meet him." Myra scanned the room quickly, then her eyes lit. "Yes, there he is. Greg!" She lifted her voice, and her hand in a signal. "Greg, come over here a moment. I have a lovely girl for you to meet."

"She can't help it," Justice Ditmyer said in an aside to Liv. "A dyed-in-the-wool busybody."

"Romantic," Myra corrected. "Greg, you must meet Olivia. She's a newscaster."

Liv turned to meet the nephew, and stared. An avalanche of memories crashed down on her. If any words had formed in her brain, she wouldn't have been able to speak them.

Greg stared back, equally stunned. "Livvy?" He reached out a hand to touch hers, as if to reassure himself she was real. "Is it really you?"

She wasn't certain what she felt. Surprise, yes, but she couldn't separate pleasure from anxiety. The past, it seemed, refused to stay buried. "Greg." She hoped her face wasn't as pale as her voice.

"This is incredible!" He smiled now and pulled her against him for a hug. "Absolutely incredible. What has it been? Five years?"

"It appears you two know each other already," Myra said wryly.

"Livvy and I were in college together." Greg drew her away to take a long look. "My God, you're more beautiful than ever. It doesn't seem possible." He lifted his hand with the privilege of an old friend and touched her hair. "You've cut it." He glanced at his aunt. "It used to be down to her waist, straight as a dime. Every woman in Harvard envied Livvy her hair." He turned back to her. "Still, this suits you—very chic."

There were a hundred questions jumbled in her head, but she couldn't bring herself to ask them. He looked almost the same, hardly older, though the beard he had sported in college had been trimmed down to a moustache. It suited him, sandy blond like his hair, and gave his almost boyish face an air of experience. His eyes were as friendly as ever, and his smile as enthusiastic. Five years seemed to evaporate in an instant.

"Oh, Greg, it's good to see you again." This time it was she who hugged him. It didn't matter that college was a million years behind her. It mattered only that he was there for her to touch and hold on to—someone she had known in happier times. And in sadder ones.

"I'm going to steal her from you for a few minutes, Aunt Myra." Greg gave her a quick kiss on the cheek before taking Liv's hand. "We've got some catching up to do."

"Well, well." Myra beamed as she watched them walk away. "That worked out better than I planned." She glanced over and lifted a brow. "T.C. just came in." Myra smiled and ran her tongue over her teeth. "I think I'll have a word with him."

"Now, Myra." Justice Ditmyer laid a restraining hand on her arm. "Don't go stirring up trouble."

"Herb." She patted the hand before she drew away from it. "Don't spoil my fun."

Greg led Liv through a pair of corridors and into the solarium. "I just can't believe it. Running into you like this. It's fantastic."

"When we were in college, I didn't know you had such illustrious relatives."

"I didn't want comparisons," he told her. The moonlight was dim, and because he wanted to see her, Greg switched on a low light. "Living up to family expectations can be traumatic."

"I know what you mean." Liv wandered to one of the windows. It was an interesting semicircular room with cushioned benches and a light scent of flowers. She didn't sit. Seeing Greg again so unexpectedly had unnerved her. Liv thought better on her feet.

"How long have you been in Washington, Livvy?" She was slimmer now than he remembered, and more poised. Five years. Sweet Lord, he thought, it could have been yesterday.

"Almost a year and a half." She tried to remember the last time anyone had called her Livvy. That too, she realized, had been left in another life.

"Aunt Myra said you were a newscaster."

"Yes." She turned back to him. In the shadowed light, her beauty struck him like a blow. He'd never gotten used to it. "I'm co-anchor on the evening news at WWBW."

"It's what you always wanted. No more weather reports?" She smiled. "No."

There were no rings on her fingers. Greg crossed to her. Her scent was different, he noticed, more sophisticated, less artless. "Are you happy?"

She kept her eyes level as she thought over the question. "I think so."

"You used to be more definite about things."

"I used to be younger." Carefully, she moved away from him. She wanted to keep it light. "So, your aunt tells me you're single."

"She would." Greg laughed and shook his head. "Whenever I'm in town, she finds an eligible female to dangle in front of me. This is the first time I've appreciated it."

"You never married, Greg? I'd always thought you would."

"You turned me down."

She faced him again and smiled gravely. "You were never serious."

"Not enough. My mistake." He took her hand between both of his. It was still fine boned and fragile, a contrast to the strength in her eyes. "And you were too crazy about Doug to see it if I had been." He saw her expression change even as she started to turn away. "Livvy." Greg stopped her. "Doug and I are partners in Chicago."

For a moment she didn't speak. She had to fight through a wave of pain for the easy words. "That's what you both had planned. I'm glad it worked out for you."

"Those first few months after . . ." He stopped, wanting to choose his words carefully. "After you left weren't easy for him."

"Neither were the last few months before." She felt cold suddenly.

"It was a bad time. The worst kind of time for both of you."

Liv drew a deep breath. She didn't often allow herself to remember. "You were a good friend to us, Greg. I don't think I ever told you just how good. It was a difficult period of my life. You made it a bit easier." Now, she returned the pressure of his hand. "I don't think I realized that until much later."

"I hated to watch you hurting, Livvy." When she turned away, he took her shoulders and rested his head on her hair. "There's nothing that makes you feel more helpless than watching people you care about in pain. Everything that happened seemed so unjust at the time. It still does."

Liv leaned back against him. She remembered he had tried to comfort her all those years ago, but she had been beyond it then. "Doug and I didn't handle it well, did we, Greg?"

"I don't know." He hesitated a moment, wondering if he

should tell her. Perhaps it was best for her to know everything. "Livvy, Doug's married again."

She said nothing at all. Somehow she had known he would be, had been all but sure of it. *Does it matter?* she asked herself. She had loved him once, but that was over. Dead. Love was long dead. Still, she felt a wave of grief for what they had had, what they had lost. A long, shuddering sigh broke from her.

"Is he happy?"

"Yes, I think so. He's put his life back together." Greg turned Liv to face him. "Have you?"

"Yes." She went into his arms, wanting to be held by someone who understood. "Yes, most of the time. My work's important. I needed something important to keep me sane. I've put all those years behind me, into their own little box. I don't open it often. Less and less as the years pass." She closed her eyes. The grief was still there, only dulled by time. "Don't tell him you saw me." She lifted her face so that she met Greg's eyes. "He shouldn't open the box either."

"You always were strong, Livvy, stronger than Doug. I think he had a hard time accepting that."

"So did I." She sighed again and rested against him. "I wanted too much from him; he didn't want enough from me." Suddenly, she clung to him. "When the one thing that bound us together was gone, we fell apart. Picking up the pieces is hell, Greg. I'm still missing some, and I don't even know where to look for them."

"You'll find them, Livvy." She felt him kiss her hair, then lifted her face to smile at him.

"I'm awfully glad I was the female your aunt chose to dangle in front of you this trip. I've missed you."

He would like to have kissed her, as a man kisses a woman who has always held a special place in his heart. But he knew her too well. He touched her lips lightly with his.

"Excuse me."

Liv's eyes flew to the doorway. Even in the shadows, she could make out Thorpe's silhouette. Carefully, she drew out of Greg's arms, angry that Thorpe had discovered her in a weak, unguarded moment.

"Myra needs to fill in a table."

"Bridge." Greg grimaced and took Liv's arm. "This is my punishment for not making it down last Christmas. You'll have to tolerate being my partner for old times' sake, Livvy."

"You couldn't do much worse." She knew Thorpe's eyes were fastened on her face, and felt absurdly guilty. To compensate, she smiled at Greg. "If you fix me a drink, I'll try not to trump your ace."

Thorpe stepped aside as they walked through the doorway.

He stood in the shadows another moment, watching them walk away. Jealousy was a new emotion. He found he didn't care for it. Olivia Carmichael belonged in a man's arms. He was going to make damn sure they were his.

"Two clubs." Liv bid on a poor excuse for a hand. She and Greg had as opponents the head of thoracic surgery at a Baltimore hospital and his wife. They were being badly beaten. Neither of them played the game with much skill. After a particularly humiliating hand, Greg jokingly challenged the surgeon and his wife to a tennis match. He remembered well Liv's energy on the court. With a grin, the surgeon marked down the scoring.

The three other tables in the room included two senators, a five-star general and the widow of a former secretary of the treasury. Liv kept her ears tuned to the light political talk and gossip. She wouldn't learn any state secrets, but she had made contacts. A reporter couldn't afford to ignore the smallest scrap of information. You could never tell what could lead to bigger things. Liv found it ironic that a torn dress and scuffed shoes had brought her to the drawing room of a Supreme Court justice.

"Five spades." Greg took the bid, and Liv spread her cards on the table and rose.

"Sorry," she said when he gave a small sigh at what she had to offer him.

"Tennis," he muttered, and played his first ace.

"I'm going to get some air."

"Coward," he said, and shot her a grin.

With a laugh, Liv slipped out to the terrace.

It was still cool. Spring was fighting its way into Washington like a dark horse candidate. After the heat of the drawing room, Liv found the chill refreshing. There was little light as clouds drifted over a half-moon. And it was quiet. The rear of the house was shielded from the street sounds and hum of city traffic. She heard Myra's boom of a laugh as she won game point.

How strange it was, Liv thought, to meet Greg again like this—to have those bittersweet years of her life brought back. Extremes, she mused. I lived on extremes. Staggeringly happy, unbearably sad. It's better this way, without all those peaks and valleys of emotion. Safer. I've had enough of risks and failures. Smarter.

Wrapping her arms around herself, she walked to the edge of the terrace. Safer and smarter. You can't be hurt if you don't take chances.

"No wrap, Liv?"

She gasped and whirled. She hadn't heard the terrace doors open, or Thorpe's steps on the stone. What moonlight there was shone directly on her face, while his was in shadows. She felt at a disadvantage.

"It's warm enough." Her answer was stiff. She hadn't forgiven him for embarrassing her in the studio.

Thorpe moved closer and laid his hands on her arms. "You're chilled. Nobody wants to listen to a newscaster with the sniffles." He stripped off his jacket and slipped it over her shoulders.

"I don't need—"

Keeping his hands on the lapels, Thorpe pulled her against him and silenced her with a bruising kiss. Her arms were pinned between his body and her own, her mouth quickly and expertly conquered. Liv's thoughts seemed to explode, then spiral down to a small, unintelligible buzz in her head. She felt the unwanted pull of desire begin to take over just before his mouth lifted from hers.

"Maybe you didn't need that." He kept her close, still gripping the lapels of his own jacket. "But I did."

"You must be crazy." The words were strong and scathing, but husky with awakened passion.

"I must be," he agreed easily enough. "Otherwise I wouldn't have walked out of your apartment the other night."

Liv let that pass. The memories of her response to him

were too uncomfortable. "You had no right pulling that business in the studio this evening."

"Kissing you?" She watched his grin flash. "I intend to make a habit of that. You have a fantastic mouth."

"Listen, Thorpe—"

"I hear you and Myra's nephew are old friends," he interrupted.

Liv let out a frustrated breath. "I don't see what that has to do with you."

"Just weeding out the competition," he said smoothly. He liked holding her close, waiting for the slight resistance of her body to melt.

"Competition?" Liv would have drawn away, but she was trapped in the jacket. "What are you talking about?"

"I'll have to learn about the other men you let hold you so I can dispose of them." Thorpe pulled her fractionally closer. The heat of his body seemed to skim along her skin. His eyes were direct on hers. "I'm going to marry you."

Liv's mouth dropped open. She hadn't thought it was possible for Thorpe to shock her again. He was a man she had learned to expect anything of. But not this. Here was a calm, matter-of-fact statement. He might have been saying he was going to be her partner for the next round of bridge. After a close, thorough study of his face, Liv could have sworn he was completely serious.

"Now I know you're crazy," she whispered. "Really, really mad."

His brow lifted in acknowledgment, but he continued in a reasonable tone. It was the tone more than anything else that left her baffled. "I'm willing to give you six months to come around. I'm a patient man. I can afford to be; I don't lose."

"Thorpe, you're in serious trouble. You should ask for a leave of absence. Pressure does strange things to the mind."

"I think it'll be simpler if I'm straight with you." He was smiling now, amused by her reaction. Her eyes were no longer shocked, but wary. "Now you'll have time to get used to the idea."

"Thorpe," she said, "I'm not going to marry anyone. I'm certainly not going to marry you. Now, I think you should—"

She found herself cut off again as he took her mouth. Her

small sound of protest was muffled, then silenced as his tongue slowly seduced hers. She was pressed against him, her arms still pinned straight down at her sides. But he felt the resistance melt, just as he had wanted. His own desire pounded. Her mouth wasn't submissive, but active on his. She sought more, even as he did.

Clouds covered her mind and there was only sensation. She could feel the somehow soft and strong texture of his lips, the slow, sure movement of his tongue. If they had been free, she would have wrapped her arms around him and clung. Only her mouth and the pressure of her body told him that she wanted him. Just as his told her.

She was suddenly and completely a creature of the flesh. She wanted nothing more than to be touched by him. Her skin burned for it; her body ached. She murmured something neither of them could understand. Thorpe could feel her response. He wanted her desperately. The thought ran through his mind that she had been right to call him mad. He wanted her to the point of madness. If they had been alone . . . If they had been alone . . .

Gradually, he brought himself back. There would be other times, other places. Banking his desire, he lifted his mouth from hers. "What was it you were going to tell me to do?" he murmured.

Her breathing was unsteady. She struggled to remember who she was, who it was who held her, what he had just said to her. As he smiled at her, her brain began to clear. "See a doctor." She couldn't manage more than a whisper. Her body was tingling. "Quickly, before you really crack."

"Too late." Thorpe drew her back for a last, burning kiss. Stunned by her completely uninhibited response, Liv pulled out of his arms. She ran a hand through her hair.

"This is crazy." She kept the hand aloft, gesturing with it as if to make him see reason. "This is really crazy." Steadying, she took a quick breath. "Now, I'll admit I'm attracted to you, and that's bad enough; but that's the limit. I'm going to forget all of this." She slipped his jacket from her shoulders and dropped it into his hand. "I want you to do the same. I don't know how much you had to drink in there, but it must have been too much."

He was still smiling at her, a patient smile. "You wipe that grin off your face, Thorpe," she ordered. "And—and stay away from me." She stormed to the terrace doors, then turned her head to look at him a last time. "You're crazy," she added for good measure before she yanked the doors open and dashed through them.

5

There was a white rose on Liv's desk in the morning. It stood in a slender porcelain vase, a bud only, with petals tightly closed. Of course, she knew who had sent it. Baffled, she dropped into the chair behind her desk and stared at it.

When she had returned to the card table the evening before, she had promised herself she wouldn't think of her conversation with Thorpe. A sane person didn't dwell on the words of a lunatic. Yet there had been a long, quiet stretch in the night when she had lain awake in bed. Every syllable of their conversation on the terrace had played back in her head. And now he was sending her flowers.

The smart thing to do would be to dump it, vase and all, into the trash and forget it.

Liv touched a fingertip to a white petal of the rose. She couldn't bring herself to do it.

It's just a flower, after all, she reminded herself. Harmless. I just won't think about where it came from. Briskly, she pulled a sheet of copy toward her. She had a news brief to give in fifteen minutes.

"Liv, thank God you're here!"

She glanced up as the assignment editor barreled down on her desk. "Chester?" He was an excitable, usually desperate man who lived on antacids and coffee. She was accustomed to this sort of greeting from him.

"Take crew two and get out to the Livingston Apartments in Southeast. A plane just crashed into the sixth floor."

She was up, grabbing her purse and jacket. "Any details?"

"You get them. We're going live as soon as you're set up. An engineer's going with you. Everybody's scattered around town or down with the flu." His tone hinted that the flu was no excuse for being unavailable for assignment. "Go, they're in the van." He popped a small, round mint into his mouth.

"I'm gone." Liv dashed for the door.

It was worse, much worse than she could ever have imagined. The tail section of the plane protruded from the face of the building like the shaft of an arrow. It might have been taken from a scene of a movie, carefully staged. Fires, started by the impact, belched out smoke. The air radiated with waves of heat and smelled pungent. The building was surrounded by fire engines and police cars, and they were still coming. Fire fighters were geared up, going in or coming out of the building, or spraying it with the powerful force of their hoses. The lower floors were being evacuated. She could hear the weeping and the shouts above the wail of sirens and crackle of the fire.

Behind the barricades, the press was already at work. There were cameras and booms, reporters, photographers and technicians. All were moving in their special organized chaos.

"We'll stay portable," she told Bob as he hefted the camera on his shoulder. "For now, get the building on tape, a full pan of these trucks and ambulances."

"I've never seen anything like this," he muttered, already focusing in on the visible section of the plane. "Can you imagine what it's like inside there?"

Liv shook her head. She didn't want to. There were people inside there. She forced back a swell of nausea. She had a story to report.

"There's Reeder." She glanced in the direction Bob indicated. "Assistant fire chief."

"Okay. Let's see what he can tell us." Liv worked her way through the crowd. She was jostled now and again, but she was used to that. She knew how to snake through masses of people to her objective. And she knew the crew would follow behind her. Coming to the edge of the barricade, she secured her position and took the mike from her soundman.

"Chief Reeder, Olivia Carmichael with WWBW." She managed to get the mike out to him by leaning over the barricade and planting her feet. "Can you tell us what happened, and the status of the fire?"

He looked impatiently at the mike, then at Liv. "Charter plane out of National." His voice was curt, gruff and as impatient as his eyes. "We don't know the cause of the crash yet. Four floors of the building are involved. Of the six floors, three have been evacuated."

"Can you tell me how many people are on the plane?"

"Fifty-two, including crew." He turned to bark an order into his two-way.

"Has there been any contact with them?" Liv persisted.

Reeder gave her a long, silent look. "My men are working down from the roof and up from the lower floors."

"How many people are still in the building?"

"Talk to the landlord, I'm busy."

As he walked away, Liv signaled to Bob to stop the taping. "I'm going to try to find out how many people are still inside." She turned to the sound technician. "Go back to the radio; find out if the desk knows the flight number yet, the plane's destination, any clue to the cause of the crash. We'll set up for a live bulletin." She checked her watch. "Five minutes, right here."

She turned to push through the crowd again. There was a woman sitting alone on the curb. She was dressed in a worn robe and clutched a photo album to her breast. Liv backtracked from her search for the building's landlord and went to her.

"Ma'am."

The woman looked up, dry eyed, pale. Liv crouched down beside her. She recognized the look of shock.

"You shouldn't be sitting out here in the cold," Liv said gently. "Is there somewhere you can go?"

"They wouldn't let me take anything else," she told Liv, pressing the album closer. "Just my pictures. Did you hear the noise? I thought it was the end of the world." Her voice was reed thin. The sound of it pulled at Liv. "I was fixing tea," she went on. "All my china's broken. My mother's china."

"I'm sorry." The words were pitifully inadequate. Liv touched the woman's shoulder. "Why don't you come with me now. Over there. The paramedics will take care of you."

"I have friends up there." The woman's eyes shifted to the building. "Mrs. McGiver in 607, and the Dawsons in 610. They have two children. Did they get out yet?"

Liv heard another window explode from heat. "I don't know. I'll try to find out."

"The little boy had the flu and had to stay home from school." Shock was giving way to grief. Liv could see the change in the woman's eyes, hear it in her voice. "I have a picture of him in here." She began to weep—deep, tearing sobs that pulled at Liv's heart.

Sitting on the curb beside her, Liv gathered the woman into her arms. She was fragile, almost paper thin. Liv was very much afraid that the picture would be all that was left of the Dawson boy. Holding her close, Liv wept with her.

She felt a hand on her shoulder. Looking up, she saw Thorpe standing tall beside her.

"Thorpe," she managed as he stepped in front of them. Her eyes were eloquent. Thorpe lifted the old woman from the curb gently. She was still clutching the album. He slipped an arm around her, murmuring in her ear as he led her toward the paramedics. Liv let her forehead drop to her knees.

She had to pull herself back together if she was going to do her job. A reporter couldn't afford personal involvement. She could hear someone coughing violently as smoke clogged her lungs. The wind brought it still closer.

"Liv." Thorpe took her arm and drew her to her feet.

"I'm all right," she said immediately. She heard another explosion. Someone screamed. "Oh, God." Her eyes flew back to the building. "How many people are still trapped in there?"

"They haven't been able to break through to the sixth floor yet. Anybody still on it, or in that plane, is gone."

She nodded. His voice was calm and unemotional—

exactly what she needed. "Yes, I know." She took a deep, cleansing breath. "I need something to put on the air. I have a stand-up to do." She looked at him again. "What are you doing here?"

"I was on my way in to the station." There was a smear on her cheek from the smoke and ash. He rubbed it off with his thumb. He kept his voice light. "This isn't my beat, Liv. I'm not here for a story."

She looked past him to where paramedics were working frantically on a burn victim. "I wish to God I weren't," she murmured. From somewhere to the left, she heard a child screaming for her mother. "I hate this part of it—poking, prying into people's pain."

"It isn't an easy job, Liv." He didn't touch her. He wanted to, but knew that wasn't what she needed.

She looked over as her crew made their way toward her. Liv took the scribbled note from the sound technician with a nod.

"All right, we'll shoot from here with the building at the back." Drawing a breath, she faced the camera. "After I'm into it, I want you to pan the building." She took the mike again and waited for the cue that would patch her into the station. "Then focus in on the plane before you cut back to me. Keep in the background noise." In her earphone, she heard the countdown to cue.

"This is Olivia Carmichael, outside the Livingston Apartments, where at nine-thirty this morning charter flight number 527 hit the sixth floor of the building." Bob panned the building as she continued. "The cause of the crash has not yet been confirmed. Fire fighters are evacuating the building and working to gain access to the sixth floor and the plane. There were fifty-two people on board, including crew, en route to Miami." The camera came back to her. "There is no report as yet on the number of casualties. Burn and smoke-inhalation victims are being treated here by paramedics before being transported to the hospital."

Thorpe stood back and watched as Liv continued the report. Her face was composed, but for her eyes. The horror was there. Whether she knew it or not, it added to the impact of her facts and statistics. There were still traces of soot on her cheek, and her skin was dead white against it. A viewer looking beyond the words would see a woman, not just a reporter. She was good at her job, he reflected, perhaps because she constantly struggled to tamp down her emotions. The effort showed from time to time and made her more accessible.

"This is Olivia Carmichael," she concluded, "for WWBW." She waited until they were off the air, then whipped off the earphone. "All right, get some tape of the paramedics. I'll find out if they've gotten through to the sixth floor yet. Get a courier out here. They'll need whatever we've got for the noon news."

Liv felt the control slip back into place. She wasn't going to fall apart again.

"Very efficient," Thorpe commented.

Liv looked at him. He was all quiet intensity, all understated strength. It disturbed her that for just a brief moment she had needed him—simply needed to know he was there to lean on. It was a luxury she couldn't afford to allow herself.

"The trick is being good at it," Liv repeated. "Let's say we finally have a point of agreement."

He smiled and brushed a stray lock of hair from her forehead. "Want me to hang around?"

She stared at him, struck with conflicting emotions. Why was he so easily able to move her? "Don't be nice to me, Thorpe," she murmured. "Please don't be nice to me. It's simpler when you're a louse."

He bent and touched her lips with his. "I'll call you tonight."

"Don't," she returned, but he was already walking away. Swearing, Liv spun around. She couldn't worry about Thorpe. She still had information to gather and a story to finish.

Liv watched the tape on the eleven o'clock news. It was a different feeling than she had experienced during her own earlier broadcast. Sitting behind the desk, giving her report and watching herself on the monitor, she could separate her emotions from her job. Now, alone in her apartment, watching the tape as any other viewer, the tragedy washed over her again. Sixty-two people had died, and fifteen more had been hospitalized, including four fire fighters. The reports weren't official yet, but it looked as though a pilot error had been responsible.

Liv thought of the woman she had tried to comfort on the curb—the precious photo album she had clutched, the stunned grief, then the mourning. There had been no survivors from the sixth floor.

The time of day had been a blessing. Liv had said so herself in her report. Most of the apartments had been vacant. Children had been in school, adults at work. But the little Dawson boy in 610 had had the flu.

Rising, Liv snapped off the set. She couldn't think about it, couldn't dwell on it. She pushed at her temples. It was time to take a couple of aspirin and go to bed. Nothing could change what had happened in the morning hours, and it was time to find her distance again.

It occurred to her, as she crawled into bed, that she had missed dinner. Hunger might be partially responsible for the severity of her headache, but she was too weary to take anything more than the aspirin. Shutting her eyes, she lay in the darkness.

This is what she had decided she wanted. Quiet, privacy. No one to depend on—no one to answer to. What she had now was hers; what mistakes she made were hers. That was the best way.

She opened her eyes to stare at the ceiling, wondering just when she had begun to doubt that.

The phone beside her shrilled, and Liv sat straight up. She fumbled for the bedside lamp, then picked up a pencil even as she lifted the receiver. Who but the desk would call her at midnight?

"Yes, hello."

"Hello, Liv."

"Thorpe?" Liv dropped the pencil and lay back. He was incredible.

"Did I wake you?"

"Yes," she lied. "What do you want?"

"I wanted to say good night."

She sighed, then was grateful he couldn't see her smile. She didn't want to give him any encouragement. "You woke me up to say good night?"

"I've been tied up. I just got home." Thorpe yanked off his tie. If there was one thing he hated about the job, it was ties. "Want to know where I've been?"

"No," Liv returned dauntingly, and heard him chuckle. Damn it, she thought, then propped her pillow behind her. She did want to know. "All right, where were you?"

"At a meeting with Levowitz."

"Levowitz?" Her attention was caught. "The bureau chief?"

"That's the one." Thorpe pried off his shoes.

"I didn't know he was in Washington." The wheels began to turn in her head. Levowitz wouldn't make a trip from New York to D.C. without good cause. "What did he want?"

"Harris McDowell's going to retire at the end of the year. He offered me the spot."

The news wasn't nearly as surprising as his casualness. Being offered McDowell's job was nothing to take lightly. Exposure, power, money. To be considered capable of stepping into McDowell's shoes was no idle compliment. It was an accolade.

Liv searched around for something to say, and settled on, "Congratulations."

"I didn't take it."

Now she waited a full beat. "What?"

"I didn't take it." Thorpe pulled off his socks and tossed them in the direction of the hamper. "You're off this weekend—" he began.

"Wait a minute." Liv sat up straighter. "You turned down the most prestigious position in CNC or any other news organization in the country?"

"You could put it that way if you want." He lit a cigarette from his second pack that day.

"Why?"

Thorpe blew out a stream of smoke. "I like working the field. I don't want to anchor, at least not in New York. About this weekend, Olivia."

"You're a strange man, Thorpe." She settled back against

the pillows. She couldn't quite figure him out. "A very strange man. Most reporters would kill for the job."

"I'm not most reporters."

"No," she said slowly, considering. "No, you're not. You'd make a good anchor."

"Well." He smiled as he unbuttoned his shirt. "That's quite a compliment from you. Want some company?"

"Thorpe, I'm in bed."

"If that's an invitation, I accept."

Unable to do otherwise, she laughed. "No, it's not. I haven't had a conversation like this since high school."

"We can go out and neck in the back seat of my car."

"No thanks, Thorpe." Relaxed, she snuggled down into the pillows. When was the last time, she wondered, that she had had a foolish conversation in the middle of the night? "If you only called to say good night . . ."

"Actually, I called about tomorrow afternoon."

"What about it?" Liv yawned and closed her eyes.

"I've got two tickets for opening game." He stripped off his shirt and tossed it to follow the socks.

"Opening game of what?"

"Good God, Liv, baseball. Orioles against the Red Sox."

He sounded so sincerely shocked by her ignorance, she smiled. "Dick Andrews handles sports."

"Broaden your outlook," he advised. "I'll pick you up at twelve-thirty."

"Thorpe," she began, "I'm not going out with you."

"It's not a seduction, Liv; that comes later. It's a ball game. Hot dogs and beer. It's an American tradition."

Liv turned off the light and pulled the covers up over her shoulders. "I don't think I'm making myself clear," she murmured.

"Try it again tomorrow. Palmer's pitching."

"That's very exciting, I'm sure, but—"

"Twelve-thirty," he repeated. "We want to get there early enough to find a parking place."

Sleepy, she yawned again and let herself drift. It was probably simpler to agree. What harm could it do? Besides, she'd never been to a ball game.

"You're not going to wear one of those hats, are you?"

He grinned. "No, I leave that to the players."

"Twelve-thirty. Good night, Thorpe."

"Good night, Carmichael."

She was smiling as she hung up. Just before she drifted into sleep, she realized her headache had disappeared.

6

*M*emorial Stadium was packed when they arrived. Liv was to learn that Baltimore was very enthusiastic about their Orioles. There were not, as she had presupposed, only men wearing fielders' caps and clutching beers in the stands. She saw women, children, young girls, college students, white- and blue-collar workers. There must be something to it, she concluded, to draw out so many people.

"Third base dugout," Thorpe told her, gesturing down the concrete steps.

"What?"

"That's where we're sitting," he explained. "Behind the third base dugout. Come on." Taking her arm, he propelled her down. She frowned out at the field, trying to put together what she knew of the sport with the white lines, brown dirt and grass.

"Know anything about baseball?" Thorpe asked her.

Liv thought a moment, then smiled at him. "Three strikes and you're out."

He laughed and took his seat. "You'll get a crash course today. Want a beer?"

"Is it un-American to have a Coke instead?" While he signaled a roving concessionaire, Liv leaned against the railing in front of her and studied the field. "It seems simple enough," she commented. "If this is third base here, then that's first and second." She gestured out. "They throw the ball, the other guy smacks it and then runs around the bases before someone catches it."

"A simplistic analysis of the thinking man's sport." Thorpe handed her the Coke.

"What's there to think about?" she asked before she sipped.

"Strike zones, batting averages, force-outs, double play balls, switch hitters, wind velocity, ERAs, batting lineup, bull pen quality—"

"All right." She stopped him in midstream. "Maybe I do need that crash course."

"Have you ever seen a game?" Thorpe leaned back with his beer.

"Snatches on the monitor during a sportscast." She glanced around the stadium again.

The sun was bright and warm, the air cool. She could smell beer and roasted peanuts and hot dogs. From somewhere behind them, a man and woman were already arguing over the game that was yet to be played. There was a feeling of involvement she had completely missed in her occasional glimpses of a ball game on the television screen.

"This is a different perspective." She studied the scoreboard. Its initials and numbers told her little. "So, when does it start?" Liv turned to face Thorpe, to find him studying her. "What is it?" The unblinking stare made her uncomfortable. The distance she had planned on hadn't worked. Now she began to wonder if the casual friendliness she had decided upon would fare any better.

"I've told you. You have a fantastic face," he returned easily.

"You weren't looking at my face," Liv countered. "You were looking into my head."

He smiled and ran a finger down her fringe of bangs. "A man should understand the woman he's going to marry."

Her brows drew together. "Thorpe—"

Her intended lecture was cut off by the blast from the organ and the roar of the crowd.

"Opening ceremonies," Thorpe told her, and draped his arm behind her chair.

Liv subsided. *Just humor him*, she cautioned herself. The

man is obviously unstable. She settled back to watch the hoopla of the season's start.

By the end of the first inning, Liv was lost, and completely fascinated. "No one got any points," she complained, and crunched a piece of ice between her teeth.

Thorpe lit a cigarette. "Best game I've ever seen was in L.A., Dodgers and Reds. Twelve innings, one to nothing, Dodgers."

"One point in twelve innings?" Liv lifted a brow as the next batter stepped into the box. "They must have been lousy teams."

Thorpe glanced at her a moment, saw she was perfectly serious, then burst out laughing. "I'll buy you a hot dog, Carmichael."

The batter dropped a short single into left field, and she grabbed Thorpe's arm. "Oh, look, he hit one!"

"That's the wrong team, Liv," Thorpe pointed out wryly. "We're rooting for the other guys."

She accepted the hot dog and peeled off a corner on the packet of mustard. "Why?"

"Why?" he repeated, watching as she squeezed the mustard on generously. "The Orioles are from Baltimore. The Red Sox are from Boston."

"I like Boston." Liv took a healthy bite of the hot dog as Palmer whipped a mean curve by the next batter. "Shouldn't he have swung at that one?"

"Don't like Boston too loudly in this section," Thorpe advised. The crowd roared as the batter grounded into a double play.

"Why didn't the man on first just stay where he was?" she demanded, gesturing with her hot dog.

Thorpe kissed her, surprising her with a full mouth. "I think it's time for that crash course."

By the bottom of the fifth, Liv was catching on to the basics. She'd taken to leaning over the rail as if to get a closer view. The score was tied at three to three, and she was too involved to be surprised her adrenaline was pumping. In her excitement, she had forgotten Thorpe was a lunatic. Her shield was slipping.

"So, if they catch the ball in foul territory before it hits the ground, it's still an out."

"You catch on fast."

"Don't be a smart aleck, Thorpe. Why are they changing pitchers?"

"Because he's given up two runs this inning and he's behind on this batter. He's lost his stuff."

She leaned her chin on the rail as the relief pitcher took the mound to warm up. "What stuff?"

"His speed, his rhythm." He liked the way she was absorbed in what was happening on the field. "He isn't getting his change-up over, and his slider isn't working."

She gave Thorpe a narrow look. "Are you trying to confuse me?"

"Absolutely not."

"How long have you been coming to games?"

"My mother took me to my first when I was five. Washington had the Senators then."

"Washington still has plenty of senators."

"They were a ball team, Liv."

"Oh." Again, she rested her chin on the rail. He grinned at her profile. "Your mother took you? I would have thought baseball a father-son sort of thing."

"My father wasn't around. He wasn't much on kids and responsibilities."

"I'm sorry." She turned her head to look at him. "I didn't mean to pry."

"It's no secret." He shrugged. "I wasn't traumatized. My mother was a terrific lady."

Liv looked out to the field again. Strange, she mused, she hadn't thought of Thorpe as ever being a child, with a family, growing up. She tried to picture it. Her vision of him had been limited to a tough, hard-line reporter with a gift for biting exposés. Thinking of him with a childhood, perhaps a difficult one, altered the view. There were entirely too many facets of him. She had to remind herself she didn't want to explore them.

But—what had he been like as a boy? How much had the early years influenced the way he was today?

There was sensitivity in him. The rose—the damn rose.

Liv thought of it with a sigh. It made it difficult to remember that distance was necessary. And his sexuality. He knew how to arouse a woman, even a reluctant one. Arrogance, yes, but he was so blatantly at ease with it, the trait was somehow admirable. And his skill in his profession couldn't be faulted. She couldn't term him power or money hungry—not when he had casually refused a position most reporters would slit throats for.

I'd better be careful, she decided. I'm dangerously close to liking him.

Thorpe watched her profile, observing the play of emotions over her face. When she forgot her guards, he reflected, she was clear as glass. "What are you thinking?" he murmured, and cupped the back of her neck with his hand.

"No comment," Liv returned, but couldn't bring herself to discourage the familiarity. She couldn't find the will to push it away. "Look, they're ready to start again."

"The count's still three and one," Thorpe explained. "The runner on second's charged to the first pitcher. If he scores, it goes against him, not the relief."

"That seems fair," Liv commented as the batter knocked a foul tip straight at her. In automatic reflex, she reached up to protect her face and snagged the ball. As she looked down at it, stunned, the impact stung her palms.

"Nice catch," Thorpe congratulated, grinning at her astonished face.

"I caught it," she said in sudden realization, then gripped the ball tighter. "Do I have to give it back?"

"It's all yours, Carmichael."

She turned it over, rather pleased with herself. "How about that," she murmured, then suddenly giggled.

It was the first time he had heard the young, carefree sound from her. It made her seem seventeen. He had to check the urge to pull her against him and just hold her. She had never appealed to him more than she did at that moment, with the sun full on her face and a baseball clutched in her hands. Love for her was abruptly and unexpectedly painful.

He lost track of the game. It was Liv whose head shot up at the hard crack of ball on bat. Her eyes grew wide as she jumped from her seat with the rest of the stadium. She grabbed Thorpe's arm, dragging him with her.

"Oh, look! It's going all the way over the fence! That's a home run, isn't it? A home run, Thorpe!"

"Yeah." He watched the ball drop over the green barricade. "Home run. First one of the year."

"Oh, it was beautiful." She was caught in the loud blast of celebration music, the cheers of the crowd. Liv turned, giving Thorpe a quick, spontaneous kiss. It was over before she could be surprised by her own action, but he pulled her back for a deeper, lingering one. The shouts went on around her, lost in the fast, rocketing beat of her heart. She gave him pressure for pressure, taste for taste.

"Could be," Thorpe murmured as he drew his lips an inch from hers, "there'll be a whole volley of long balls."

Breathless, Liv eased out of his arms. In them, she lost everything but need. "I think one's enough," she managed. Because her legs weren't as steady as they might have been, she sat back down. She was closer to the edge than she had realized. It was time to take a few steps back. "Are you going to buy me another hot dog?" she demanded, and smiled at him. She ignored the tingling that still brushed along her skin. "I'm starving."

The rest of the game was a shrewd defensive battle. Liv had difficulty keeping her attention focused. She was too aware of Thorpe, too aware of the pulsing needs he had aroused, could arouse, so easily. She saw his hands and was reminded of the rough palms. She saw his arms and remembered there were muscles that could make her feel soft and safe. Liv didn't want to be soft. It made it too easy to be hurt. She didn't want to rely on anyone for safety again. It was too easy to be disappointed. She saw his mouth and knew how well it seduced. She told herself that to be seduced was to be weak and vulnerable. His eyes were intelligent, shrewd, saw too much. The more he saw, the greater the risk that he could gain an emotional hold on her.

She had allowed herself to be involved before. She still bore the scars. For years she had lived on the belief that the only way for her to keep her serenity was by withdrawal. She was coming to realize that Thorpe could change this. For the first time, she understood that she was afraid of him—of what he could come to mean to her.

Friendship, she reminded herself. That was all there was going to be. Just simple friendship. She spent the last two innings convincing herself it was possible.

"So we won." Liv checked out the final score on the board. "Five to three." She rubbed the foul ball between both palms.

"It's *we* now, huh?" Thorpe grinned and tugged on her hair. "I thought you liked Boston."

Liv leaned back in her seat and propped her feet on the rail as the crowd began to file out of the stands. "That was before I understood the intricacies of the game. You know, it's amazing how deceptive television can be. It's faster, more intense than I thought. Do you come often?"

He watched as she passed the ball from hand to hand and studied the field. "Are you fishing?"

"Just a casual question, Thorpe," she said coolly.

"Whenever I can," he answered, still smiling. "I'll take you to a night game next. It has a whole different feel."

"I didn't say—"

"T.C.!"

They both looked up as a man worked his way through the aisles toward them. He was short and stocky, with stone gray hair and a lived-in face. It was lined and pitted, with a square jaw and crooked nose. Thorpe rose to accept a bear hug.

"Boss, how are you?"

"Can't complain, no, can't complain." He drew back far enough to study Thorpe's face. "Good God, you look good, boy." With a meaty hand, he slapped Thorpe on the back. "Still watch you every night on the TV giving those politicians hell. You always were a sassy young pup."

Liv remained seated and watched the exchange in silence. She was fascinated to hear Thorpe referred to as a boy and a young pup. Thorpe was a good half foot taller than the man who grinned up at him.

"Someone has to keep them straight. Right, Boss?"

"You bet your—" Boss stopped himself and glanced down at Liv. He cleared his throat. "Gonna introduce me to your lady, or are you afraid I'll steal her away from you?"

"Liv, this old schemer is Boss Kawaoski, the best catcher ever to harass an umpire. Boss, Olivia Carmichael."

"Why sure!" Liv's hand was captured in the gnarled, broad one. "The lady on the news. You're even prettier face to face."

"Thank you." He was beaming at her out of eyes that seemed a trifle myopic.

"Careful, Liv." Thorpe slipped an arm around her shoulder. "Boss has a reputation as a lady-killer."

"Ah, sh—" He cleared his throat quickly again, and Liv struggled with a grin. "Shoot," he modified. "Wouldn't do to have my missus hear you talk that way. What'd you think of the game, T.C.?"

"Palmer's still dishing it out." He pulled out a cigarette and lit it. "It looks like the Birds have a tight team this year."

"Lots of new blood," Boss added, glancing wistfully out at the field. "The young left fielder has a mean bat."

"So did you, Boss." Thorpe looked back at Liv. "Boss carried a .324 average the year he retired."

Not completely certain of the meaning, Liv tried a safer angle. "Did you play for the Orioles, Mr. Kawaoski?"

"Just Boss, miss. I played for the Senators. That was twenty years ago." He shook his head at the passage of time. "This one used to hang around the clubhouse making a nuisance of himself." Jerking a thumb at Thorpe, he grinned. "Wanted to be a third baseman in those days."

"Did he?" Liv gave Thorpe a thoughtful look. Somehow, she had never considered him wanting to be anything but what he was.

"Wasn't so good with a bat," Boss reminisced. "But he had a great pair of hands."

"I still do," Thorpe said dryly, and gave Liv a broad smile which she ignored. "How are things going at the store, Boss?"

"Just fine. My wife's running it today. She didn't want me to miss opening game." He ran a hand along his squared chin. "Can't say I argued with her much. She'll be sorry she missed you. Alice still lights a candle for you every Sunday."

"Give her my best." Thorpe crushed the cigarette under his heel. "This is Liv's first game."

"Well, no fooling." Boss's attention was switched as

Thorpe had intended. Liv noted the move and filed it. Boss glanced at the baseball still clutched in her hand. "Caught yourself a foul too, first time out."

"Beginner's luck," she admitted, and held it out to him. "Would you sign it for me? I've never met a real ballplayer before."

Slowly, Boss turned the ball over in his hand. "Been a long time since I put my name on one of these." He took the pen Liv offered. "A long time," he repeated softly. He signed his name carefully around the curve of the ball.

"Thank you, Boss." Liv took the ball back from him.

"Thank *you*. Almost makes me feel like I could still pick a man off of second. I'll tell Alice I saw you." He gave Thorpe a final thump on the shoulder. "And the pretty news lady," he added. "Come by the store."

"First chance I get, Boss." Thorpe watched him move through the thinning crowd and up the steps. "That was a very nice thing you did," he murmured to Liv. "You're a perceptive woman."

Liv glanced down at the signature on the ball. "It must be hard to give up a career, a way of life, thirty years before most people have to. Was he very good?"

"Better than some." Thorpe shrugged. "That hardly matters. He loved the game, and the playing of it." Sweepers were already pushing their brooms through the narrow aisles, and Thorpe took her arm to lead her up the steps. "All the kids loved him. He never minded being hounded or catching a few pitches after a game."

"Why does his wife light a candle for you on Sundays?" She had told herself she wouldn't ask, that it was none of her business. The words were out before she could prevent them.

"She's Catholic."

Liv let that pass a moment as they walked toward the parking lot. "Don't you want to tell me?" she asked at length.

He jingled the keys impatiently in his pocket, then drew them out. "They run a small, independent sporting goods store in Northeast. A few years ago, they were having some trouble. Inflation, taxes, the building needed some repairs." He unlocked Liv's side of the door, but she didn't get in, only stood and watched him.

"And?"

"Twenty years ago ballplayers, average ballplayers like Boss, didn't make a lot of money. He didn't have much saved."

"I see." Liv slipped into the car as Thorpe rounded the hood. Leaning over, she unlocked the handle for him. "So, you lent him money."

"I made an investment," Thorpe corrected as he shut the door. "I didn't offer a loan."

Liv watched him as he started the ignition. She could see he didn't like her touching on this aspect of his life. She persisted. It was simply a reporter's habit, she told herself, to press for details. "Because you knew he wouldn't accept a loan. Or that if he did, it would put a dent in his pride."

Thorpe let the car idle and turned to her. "That's a lot of supposition on a very brief encounter."

"You just told me I was perceptive," she pointed out. "What's the matter, Thorpe?" A smile tugged at her mouth. "Don't you like people finding out you can be a nice guy?"

"Then you're expected to be nice," he told her. "I don't make a habit of it."

"Oh, yes." She was still amused, and the smile grew. "Your image. Tough, unsentimental, pragmatic."

He kissed her firmly, impatiently. Her surprise spun into longing. She felt his fingers tighten on her skin, and she opened for him. If it was a mistake, she had to make it. If it was madness, she'd find sanity later. In that moment, she only wanted to renew the pleasure he could give her.

His mouth was enough—enough to satisfy the slowly growing hunger. It wasn't the time to question why he was the one, the only one, who was able to crack the shield she had erected. She wanted only to experience again, to feel again.

His heart beat against hers, lightly, quickly, making her understand the hunger was mutual. She was wanted— desired. What would it be like to make love with him? What would it be like to feel his skin against hers? To have his hands touch her? But no—she couldn't let herself imagine. She couldn't stop herself from imagining.

He let his lips wander to the crest of her cheekbone, then on to her temple. "I'd like to continue this someplace more private. I want to touch you, Liv." His mouth came back to hers, hot, possessive. "All of you. I don't want an audience." He drew back until his eyes locked on hers. He saw desire, and his own clawed at him. "Come home with me."

Her heartbeat was echoing in her head, fast and furious. For the first time in years, it would have been so simple to say yes. She wanted him, shockingly. It overwhelmed her. How had it happened so quickly? If someone had suggested a month before that she would be tempted to make love with Thorpe, she would have laughed. Now, it didn't seem ludicrous at all. It seemed natural. It frightened her. Liv drew out of his arms and ran a hand through her hair. She needed some room, some time.

"No. No, I'm not ready for this." She told herself to take a deep breath, and did so carefully. "Thorpe, you make me nervous."

"Good." He fought back a powerful surge of need and leaned back. "I wouldn't want to bore you."

She managed a husky laugh. "You don't bore me. I don't know exactly what my feelings are toward you. I'm not even sure you're quite stable. This—this delusion you have about getting married . . ."

"I'm going to remind you of this conversation on our first anniversary." He put the car in first. If he was driving, he might keep himself from touching her again. Thorpe was discovering he wasn't as patient as he had thought.

"Thorpe, that's ridiculous."

"Think of what it's going to do for the ratings."

She wondered how he could be likable one minute, desirable the next, and then infuriating. Liv was torn between laughing and beating her head against the windshield in frustration.

"Okay, Thorpe," she began, opting for patience as he joined a stream of traffic. "I'm going to make this crystal clear in the simplest terms I can. I am not going to marry you. Ever."

"Wanna bet?" he countered smoothly. He shot her a grin. "I've got fifty says you will."

"Do you seriously expect me to bet on something like that?"

"No sporting blood." He shook his head. "I'm disappointed, Carmichael."

Liv narrowed her eyes. "Make it a hundred, Thorpe. I'll give you two-to-one odds."

He grinned again and cruised through a yellow light. "You're on."

7

$\mathscr{P}$rime Minister Summerfield's death was unexpected. The fatal stroke which ended the British official's life left his country saddened. It sent the world press into a fever of preparation. There were special reports to air, recaps of Summerfield's forty-year career in British government to assemble, reactions to gather from the heads of other countries. How would the death of one man affect the balance of power in the world?

Two days after the prime minister's death was announced, the president was in *Air Force One*, crossing the Atlantic to attend the funeral. Thorpe was with him.

As press reporter, it would be his job to stick by the president, as close as a reporter was allowed, then share his information with the other news people who took the same journey on the press plane. He had a crew, pooled from the networks, ready to film any pertinent business on the flight. The cameraman, lighting and sound technicians were settled in the rear of the plane with their equipment close at hand. Their colleagues and backups were following on the press plane. In the forward portion of *Air Force One* were the president, first lady, and their entourages—secretaries, secret service, advisors. The mood was subdued.

Behind Thorpe, members of the pool crew played a quiet game of poker. Even the swearing was low key. On most trips, he would have joined them, whiled away the hours with a few hands, a few stories . . . but he had a lot on his mind.

The job itself would keep him occupied on the plane ride. He had research and information to put together and pick apart, a loose script to outline for the day of the funeral. Then, in London, it would be up to him to keep close to the president—watch for reactions, wait for a quote. The desire to be in the field and report his own stories had been the major element in his refusal of the anchor job in New York.

Thorpe would take what tidbits he could glean from the press secretary and use his own talents for observation and assimilation not only to give his own report, but to feed information to his colleagues.

Though the assignment was a plum, he almost wished it had been handed to Carlyle or Dickson, correspondents from the competing networks. He was on *Air Force One*. Liv was on the press plane.

She had kept her distance from him during the past few days, and Thorpe had given her room. He'd had little choice with the pressures of a top news story taking up his time. Yet the same story had brought them both, with frustrating consistency, to the same locations.

She'd been cool, he recalled, each time they had run into each other—at the White House gates, at the Capitol, at the British embassy. There had been no hint of the woman he had seen eating hot dogs and cheering over a home run. The ease with which she distanced him was more frustrating than he liked to admit. Even to himself. Impatience was dangerous, he knew. But his was growing.

She wasn't indifferent to him, he thought, as he scowled out of the window. A bit of turbulence made the plane tremble slightly as he pulled out a cigarette. No matter what she said, or how she acted, she couldn't erase the way she responded to him. There was hunger, and no matter how she struggled against it, the hunger won whenever he held her in his arms. Thorpe was willing to settle for that. For now.

"Three kings!" Thorpe heard the muttered expletive from the seat behind him. "Hey, T.C., let me deal you in before this guy cleans us all out."

As he started to agree, Thorpe saw the president slip inside his office with his secretary and speech writer.

"Later," he said absently, and rose.

When was the last time I went to England? Liv wondered. As she thought back, she remembered the summer she had been sixteen. She had traveled with her parents and her sister in first class. She had been allowed to nibble caviar and Melinda had been given champagne. The trip had been Melinda's eighteenth birthday present.

Liv remembered how her sister had chattered endlessly about the parties she would go to, the balls, the teas, the theaters. Clothes had been discussed unceasingly until her father had buried himself behind a copy of the *Wall Street Journal*. Too young for balls, ambivalent about dresses, Liv had been bored to distraction. The caviar, an unwise sampling of her sister's champagne and air turbulence had proven an unfortunate combination. She'd been ill—to her sister's disgust, her mother's surprise and her father's impatience. For the rest of the journey she had been looked after by a flight attendant.

Twelve years ago, Liv thought with a sigh. Things had certainly changed. No champagne and caviar on this trip. Unlike *Air Force One*, the press plane was both crowded and noisy. The card games here were less restrained. Reporters and crew from Washington stations roamed up and down the aisles, gambled, argued, slept—finding ways to ease the tedium of a long plane flight. Still there was an air of anticipation, of energy. The Big Story.

Liv busied herself with working on notes while two correspondents across the aisle speculated on the political ramifications of Summerfield's death. He'd been a reserved, almost bookish member of Britain's Conservative party. Yet underneath, Liv mused as she scribbled down her thoughts, there'd been a fine edge of steel. He hadn't been a man to be tampered with, or intimidated by tricky diplomatic maneuvers. She made notations on three potentially volatile situations he had handled during his term as prime minister, and other legislative triumphs, small and large, during his government career.

Liv had done quite a bit of research during the past two days, boning up on parliamentary procedure and Summerfield in particular. She had needed a firm handle on British politics in order to convince Carl to send her on the story. His argument that Washington politics were her forte had been only the first stumbling block. Thorpe, as usual, had been a larger one. Pressing down hard on her pencil with this thought, Liv snapped off the point.

Thorpe was going to England. Thorpe had been assigned as the president's press reporter. Thorpe would be traveling on *Air Force One* with the presidential entourage and the crew pooled from the various networks. WWBW could use Thorpe's feed without dipping into the budget for the funds to send a reporter and crew of their own.

It had taken Liv an hour of calm, lucid reasoning, and a further hour of determined arguing, to change Carl's mind. Afterward, she had been torn between cheering or screaming in frustration. *Thorpe.* Whatever she did, wherever she went, he was always there to make things twice as difficult for her.

And not just professionally.

She couldn't stop thinking about him. During the day, with the countless pressures of the job, he would crop up—either in person or by name. Then she would remember the dance at the embassy, the embrace on the terrace, the laughter at the ball game. At night, when she was alone, he would invade her mind, sneak into her thoughts. No matter what Liv did to prevent it, he would just suddenly *be* there. The way he laughed, the ironic lift of brow, the hard, rough hands. And worse, much worse, there were times she was certain she could taste his mouth on hers. That's when the needs would grow out of nowhere—unexpected, vibrant. She was never certain whether to be angry or terrified.

He had no right to bother her this way, she thought furiously as she groped in her briefcase for another pencil. He had no right to upset the order of her life. *And that bet.* Liv closed her eyes on a sigh of frustration. How had she ever allowed him to annoy her into making that ridiculous bet?

Marriage! Could he possibly be unbalanced enough to think she would seriously consider marriage? With him? What sort of man would waltz up to a woman he knows can barely tolerate his presence and announce his intention to marry her? A foolish one, Liv decided with a shrug, then caught her bottom lip between her teeth. Or a very shrewd one. Uncomfortably, Liv felt T.C. Thorpe fell into the latter category.

Of course, it didn't matter how shrewd he was; he couldn't *trick* her into marriage, and she would never be talked into it. So, she was perfectly safe.

Liv stared down at her notes and wondered why she didn't feel that way.

"Mike." Thorpe slipped into the seat beside Press Secretary Donaldson.

"T.C." Donaldson closed a file folder and gave Thorpe a careful smile. He was a man who looked like someone's kindly uncle: a little plump, beginning to go bald. His mind, however, was sharp and disciplined.

"What have you got to give me?" Thorpe asked him, and settled himself comfortably.

Donaldson raised both brows. "What's there to give?" he countered. "A state funeral, condolences, support, some pomp and ceremony. You'll have a lot of top officials, past and present, rubbing elbows. Royalty too. Good copy, T.C." He reached in his pocket for his pipe, then slowly began to pack it. "There'll be plenty to fill your time for the next couple of days. You've got the president's itinerary."

Thorpe watched Donaldson push tobacco into the bowl with his thumb. "He's going to be busy."

"He's not going to London to sight-see," Donaldson said dryly.

"None of us are, Mike," Thorpe reminded him. "All of us have our jobs. I wouldn't want to think you were making mine tougher by holding back on me."

"Holding back, T.C.?" Donaldson gave a quick laugh. "Even if I did, you usually manage to ferret out enough to get by."

"I notice there's a couple extra secret service aboard," Thorpe put in casually.

Donaldson went right on filling his pipe. "First lady's aboard, too."

"I counted her men, too." Thorpe waited a moment before going on. "The funeral of a man like Summerfield brings diplomats from all over the world." He paused, accepting coffee from the flight attendant while Donaldson eyed him over a lighted match. "Representatives from every country in the UN, and a few more. It promises to be quite a turnout."

"Depressing business, funerals," Donaldson commented.

"Mmm. Depressing," Thorpe agreed. "And dangerous?"

"All right, T.C., we've known each other too long. What are you fishing for?"

"Vibrations," Thorpe told him with a cool smile. "Any vibrations of trouble, Donaldson? Any reason the president or any of those other high political officials should be extra careful paying their last respects?"

"What makes you think so?" Donaldson countered.

"An itch," Thorpe said amiably.

"You'd better scratch it, T.C.," Donaldson advised. "I've got nothing for you."

As if considering the matter, Thorpe sipped his coffee. "Summerfield wasn't popular with the IRA."

Donaldson gave a dry chuckle. "Or the PLO, or a dozen other radical organizations. Is that a news bulletin, T.C.?"

"Just a comment. Can I get a statement from the president?"

"Pertaining to what?"

"His views on Summerfield's policy with the Irish Republican Army, and thoughts on the new prime minister."

"The president's views on the IRA are already documented." Donaldson chewed on the stem of his pipe. "Let's get Summerfield buried before we start on the new P.M." He shot Thorpe a straight look. "It might not be wise to talk about your hunch, T.C. No use giving people ideas, is there?"

"I only give people the facts," Thorpe said carefully, and rose. "I want to get some film."

Donaldson pondered a moment. "I'll arrange it, but no sound. We're going to a funeral. Let's keep this low key."

"My thoughts exactly. You'll let me know if there are any changes?" Without waiting for an answer, Thorpe wandered back to the card game.

"I want some film as soon as Donaldson clears it," he

instructed the crew. Glancing down, he noted the cameraman held two pair. "Silent," he told the sound technician. "You can relax. Get a shot of the first lady working on her needlepoint." He grinned as the cameraman raised the bet.

"Looking for the homey touch, T.C.?"

"That's right." Leaning closer, he lowered his voice. "And see if you can get in a pan of the secret service."

The cameraman cocked his head to shoot Thorpe a look and met the cool stare. "Okay."

"Call." The lighting technician tossed in his chips. "What d'ya got you're so proud of?"

"Just a pair of eights," the cameraman said with a smirk. "And a pair of queens."

"Full house." The lighting technician spread his cards. Thorpe went back to his seat with mumbled curses following him.

He had always had an uncanny sense of intuition. The few moments with the press secretary had sharpened it. There was definitely more security on this trip than usual—enough to alert Thorpe.

Terrorism was a common word in the world today. It didn't take heavy thinking to conclude that when you brought heads of state from all over the globe together, political violence was more than a remote possibility.

A bomb threat? An assassination attempt? A kidnapping? Thorpe studied the quiet, three-piece-suited secret service agents. They'd be on the lookout, and so would he. It would be a long three days.

And the nights? he wondered. After the president's safely tucked away out of the reach of the press? He and Liv would stay at the same hotel. With luck—and a little strategy, he added thoughtfully—he could arrange to keep her close for most of the trip. At the moment, Thorpe considered proximity his biggest asset. Proximity, he amended, and determination.

Restless, Liv set aside her notes. She was unable to concentrate. She could not get Thorpe off her mind. It didn't help to be aware of how often they were going to be thrown together on this assignment. At least in Washington there were a number of stories to cover in the course of a day. This time, there would be only one. And Thorpe had the upper hand.

If she wanted a concise, thorough report, she would have to take whatever information he would give her. She would have to meet and talk with him on a scheduled basis. Of course, she reminded herself, regardless of everything else, he was a professional. That she couldn't fault him for. The information would be clear and incisive. If only it didn't have to come from him.

Kicking back her seat, Liv shut her eyes. Why was it her luck that Thorpe had been chosen as press reporter? If circumstances had been different, she would soon be three thousand miles away from him. Though she didn't like admitting it, she needed the distance. There had to be a way to stay clear of him. For the next couple of days, she would have to be on her toes just to keep up with the story and all the angles. He'd be busy too. That should solve a great deal of the problem.

When it came to free time, Liv decided she would make herself scarce. He was too thick skinned to respect her refusals or her coolness. If a no or a cold shoulder didn't work, unavailability was the next step. It was a pity they had to share the same hotel.

Nothing can be done about that, she reminded herself. But . . . she could see to it that she spent very little time in her room and very little time alone. It should be simple enough to lose herself in the crowd of press people that were about to descend on London.

With a small sound of disgust, she shifted in her chair. She didn't like playing hide-and-seek. But it's not a game, she told herself. It's more like war—a war she forgot to fight when he got too close. Yearnings, yes, she felt yearnings when he held her, when his mouth—Shaking her head, she pushed the seat straight up. It wasn't Thorpe, she insisted silently. It was simply time she started feeling again. Five years was a long time to bury yourself. Clearly, too clearly, she saw his face in her mind's eye. And his smile—the charming, self-assured smile. She was definitely going to keep her distance.

*   *   *

The landing was smooth. Thorpe had had to stick to the president for another two hours before he could set off for his hotel. He had film, plenty of film to feed back to the States, along with his commentary. As he checked his watch and adjusted for the time difference, he noted CNC would have his report for the evening broadcast. With a revamp and update at eleven, he'd done his job for the day.

He watched London whiz by. It had been a good many years since he'd been there. Six? he mused. No, seven. But he thought he could still find the pub in Soho where he had interviewed a nervous attaché from the American embassy. Then there had been that little gallery in the West End where he had met a fledgling artist with a Rubenesque body and a voice like thick cream. Fleetingly, he recalled the two very exhilarating nights they had spent together.

Seven years ago, he thought, before he had settled in Washington. Before Liv. This London assignment was going to be different. He wasn't interested in two exhilarating nights with an unknown woman; he wanted a lifetime. And one woman. *Liv.*

Stepping out of the cab, Thorpe hefted his bag himself. He'd learned long ago to travel light. There was a damp chill in the air—the result of a drizzle which had stopped only moments before. People on the sidewalk were hunched inside jackets and moving quickly. As he stepped inside the hotel lobby, Thorpe saw the crowd of reporters checking in. His hopes to get to his room for a shower before the briefing were immediately aborted.

"Thorpe."

Shifting his bag, he smiled at Liv. She nodded politely.

"What have they got set up for us?" he asked, and was told there was a temporary press room on the second floor. "Okay, let's head up and I'll brief you." Before Liv could lose herself in the crowd, he had her arm. "How was your flight?"

"Uneventful." Knowing she could hardly snatch her arm from his without causing comment, Liv answered casually. "And yours?"

"Long." He grinned at her as they squeezed into the elevator. "I missed you."

"Stop it, Thorpe," she said crisply.

"Stop missing you? I'd be glad to if you'd stop avoiding me."

"I haven't been avoiding you. I've been busy." The crush in the elevator had her pressed tight to his side. After shifting his bag to his other hand, Thorpe slid an arm around her shoulders.

"Crowded in here," he said amiably when she shot him a narrow glance. Above the smells of tobacco, old cologne and light sweat, her scent lifted, sweet and clean. He had to control a desire to bury his face in her hair and lose himself in it.

"You'll make a scene, won't you?" she said softly, under the hum of conversation.

"If you'd like me to," he agreed. "I want to kiss you, Liv," he whispered, bending close to her ear. "Right here, right now."

"Don't!" There was no room to push away from him. She could only look up and glare. It was her first mistake.

His mouth was inches from hers. His eyes, calmly amused, stared back into hers. There was a surge of need, a devastating sexual pull. Her mind went blank.

When the elevator doors opened, people began to file out around them. Liv stood still, trapped not by the arm around her shoulders but by the look of quiet, patient knowledge in his eyes.

"Come on, T.C., let's get this show on the road."

Thorpe didn't answer. He smiled at Liv and led her into the corridor. "We'll have to save it for later," he told her.

Freed of the trance, Liv stepped out of his reach. "There *is* no later," she snapped, then cursed herself as she took a place in the press room.

It took Thorpe less than thirty minutes to brief his colleagues and send them rushing off to complete their own reports. When he finally reached his own room, he had put in a twenty-hour day. Heading for the shower, he stripped on the way.

Liv walked into her room and let the bellboy bring in her bags. She waited while he fussed around the room opening drapes, checking the towel count. What she wanted was a pot of tea from room service, and her bed.

Jet lag, she thought wearily as she stuffed a pound note into the bellboy's hand. Why was it her sister never suffered from it no matter how many times she zipped here or there, country to country, party to party? If she had been Melinda, she would never have settled down with a cup of tea and a quiet room. She would have changed and rushed out to take in London's night life.

But she wasn't Melinda, Liv reminded herself as she slipped out of her suit jacket. And she had already crammed a day and a half into a scant twenty-four hours. Tomorrow, Liv mused, stepping out of her shoes, there wouldn't be a moment's rest. Glancing in the mirror, she spotted the faint shadows of fatigue. It wouldn't do to have them show up on camera. A cup of tea, then a quick glance at her notes before sleep, she decided. She was heading for the phone to order when she heard the knock on the connecting door.

She frowned at it, then gave a sigh of annoyance. If one of the other reporters wanted to party or discuss the angles of the Summerfield story, she wasn't interested.

"Who is it?"

"Just another member of the working press, Carmichael."

"Thorpe!" The word came out in a rush of indignation. Without thinking, she flicked the lock and opened the door. He was leaning against the jamb, smiling, dressed only in a worn terry cloth robe. His hair was still damp from his shower, and the scent of soap and shaving lotion clung to him. "What are you doing here?" she demanded.

"Reporting the news," he said soberly. "It's my job."

"You know very well what I mean," she tossed back between her teeth. "What are you doing in the room next to mine?"

"The luck of the draw?" he ventured.

"How much did you give the desk clerk to arrange it?"

He grinned. "Liv, I don't have to respond to a leading question. You'll have to get that corroborated and ask me again." Still grinning, he let his eyes roam down to her stocking feet. "Going out?"

"No, I am not." Liv folded her arms and prepared to deliver a heated setdown.

"Good. I'd prefer a cozy evening at home." He took a step

into her room. Liv's hand shot up to his chest. "Now look, Thorpe." Her palm had connected with his naked chest where the robe crossed over, and the sudden movement spread the material farther apart. Little more than dark, springy hair covered him to his waist. He continued to smile, unabashed, when she dropped her hand. "You're insufferable."

"I do my best." Lifting his hand, he twined a lock of her hair around his finger. "If you'd rather go out," he began.

"I am not going out," she repeated furiously. "And there's not going to be any cozy evening either. I want you to understand—"

"Haven't you ever heard that colleagues on foreign soil have to stick together?" His grin was suddenly boyish and impossible to resist. Liv struggled to keep her lips in a straight line.

"I'm making an exception in your case, Thorpe." She added on a note of exasperation. "Why won't you leave me alone?"

"Liv, it isn't traditional for a man to leave his fiancée alone."

His tone was so reasonable it took her a full ten seconds to react. "*Fiancée?* I am *not* your fiancée," she shouted at him. "I am *not* going to marry you."

"You want to add another hundred to the bet?"

"No!" She poked her finger into his chest. "Now you listen to me, Thorpe. Your delusions are your own business; leave me out of them. I'm not interested."

"You might be," he said pleasantly. "Some of my delusions are really fascinating."

"And I'm not going to sleep next door to a lunatic. I'm getting another room." With that she whirled away.

"Afraid?" he asked, following her as she snatched up her bag.

"Afraid?" Liv tossed the bag back down and spun back. "The day I'm afraid of you—"

"I was thinking more of yourself." He tilted his head and studied her furious face. "Maybe you're not sure you could resist—ah, tapping on my door."

Speechless, Liv stared at him. "Tapping?" she managed in

a sputter. "You think—you think I find you so irresistible, so—so . . ."

"Desirable?" he suggested helpfully.

Liv clenched her hands into fists. "I don't have any trouble resisting you, Thorpe."

"No?"

Before she could take a breath, she was in his arms. Before she could think to protest, his mouth was on hers. Pressed close—so close her body seemed to mold itself to his without her will. His mouth was firm, not impatient so much as insistent. This time, rather than tempting her surrender, he demanded it. The control, though it balanced on a fine edge, was his. With his fingers in her hair, he pulled her head back and plundered, deeper and still deeper.

"No trouble, Liv?" he murmured, lifting his mouth a whisper from hers.

Her breath was trembling. She shook her head before she attempted to speak. But he gave her no chance.

Again, his lips took hers, this time with the fire of possession. A moan of pleasure escaped her as she instinctively reached for him, tangling her fingers in his damp hair to pull him closer. Sharp, small needs began to race along her skin. He seemed to know, for his hands followed them with uncanny accuracy—a fingertip down her spine, a thumb at the sweep of her hip, his palm at the long length of her thigh.

Liv explored his face with her own hands, running her fingers over the angles and planes as if she would sculpt it. Her touch only heightened his demand, so that he crushed her to him, bending her back from the waist. Like putty, she moved to his command. Then he molded her. Under his hands, her breasts rose and fell with her quickened breathing. The nipples were taut, straining against the material of her blouse while he circled a fingertip over them.

There was no thought of resistance. She wanted the burn of his mouth, the scorch of his touch. When his lips moved to her throat, she tilted her head to give him absolute freedom. The moist heat of his tongue on her skin sent ripples of pleasure through her. She was lost in the dim, shadowed world of desires. His naked chest was pressed hard against her breasts. Caught tight, with arms that wrapped possessively around her, Liv yielded to him, to her own desire. His mouth lingered at the curve of her neck, just above the collar of her blouse; then, with deliberate leisure, he took his lips upward, lingering at the pulse in her throat, then the line of her jaw. When his mouth came back to hers, it was as though all the hunger and thirst she had ever known were concentrated in that one touch of lips.

Passion went from dark to bright. A harsh, blinding light seemed to explode in her brain. It left her limp. With a muffled cry that was half surrender, half terror, Liv leaned against him.

Unprepared for the sudden weakness, Thorpe drew her away to study her. In her eyes he could see traces of desire, hints of fear and confusion. The eyes alone were a more impenetrable defense than all her angry words or fierce denials.

Tenderness. He couldn't fight his own surge of tenderness. Taking her now would be simple, but having her physically was only part of what he wanted. When they finally made love—and he had no doubt that they would—she would come to him without fear. He would wait for it.

Smiling, he touched his lips briefly to hers. He wanted to see the flash of temper again. "In case you change your mind about resisting me, Carmichael, I'll leave my door unlocked. You don't even have to knock."

He sauntered away, shutting his connecting door with a gentle click. It took ten seconds before the heavy thud of her thrown shoe sounded against it. With a grin, Thorpe switched on the television to see what the British news had to offer.

8

With a low, monotonous buzz, the alarm woke Liv at six A.M. She reached for the button automatically, then lay staring at the bland, impersonal room without the least idea where she was. London, she remembered, and rubbed her fingers over her eyes.

She hadn't slept well. Sitting up, Liv brought her knees to her chest and rested her forehead on them. Blast Thorpe! She'd spent half the night tossing and turning with doubts and desires that hadn't existed before he had touched her. Her purpose for being in London was professional. Even if she had the time, she didn't have the inclination for anything else. She simply didn't want to be involved with him. Why couldn't he see that?

Because, she thought wearily, saying something and acting on it are two different things. How could she convince him she didn't want to be involved when she responded totally every time he took her into his arms? Yes, she had wanted him. In that flash of a moment when she had been held close, mouth on mouth, she would have given herself to him. Her will had bent to his. That frightened her.

The problem, as she saw it, had to be resolved within herself first. The most important thing to do was to change the wording: not that she didn't want to be involved, but that she refused to be involved.

Rising, Liv prepared to shower and dress. There was too

much to do that day to sit and brood about a personal dilemma. In any case, she thought it gave Thorpe too much importance to brood about him at all. How he would enjoy knowing she had done just that!

She had packed a very somber suit, charcoal gray and tailored. After doing up the final button, Liv gave herself a quick, professional study in the full-length mirror. She would do. A dab of extra makeup concealed the faint shadows under her eyes. *Thorpe again*, she thought resentfully.

The slim briefcase would carry her notes along with an extra pad and a supply of pencils. Tossing her coat over her arm, she prepared to leave. A slip of white on the floor by the connecting door caught her eye.

Liv stared at it for a moment. It looked suspiciously like a note. The best thing to do, she thought, would be to ignore it. She walked all the way to the front door before she gave up and went back. Stooping, she scooped the paper up.

"Good morning."

That was all it said. A laugh escaped her before she could stop it. He's mad, she decided again. Absolutely mad. On impulse, she ripped off a sheet of her own notepaper and scribbled a similar greeting. After slipping it under the connecting door, she left the room.

As arranged, she found her crew in a corner of the hotel's coffee shop. "Hey, Liv." Bob sent her a quick smile. "Want some breakfast?"

"Just coffee." She took the communal pot and poured. "I feel like I need a gallon of it."

"It's going to be a long day," he reminded her, and dug into his eggs.

"Starting immediately," she agreed. Absently, she shook her head at the waiter. "I want a stand-up in front of Westminster Abbey before the crowds get there, and another at 10 Downing Street. With luck, we might get some tape of Summerfield's widow. I imagine they'll start lining the streets a good hour before the funeral procession is scheduled." One of the crew tempted Liv with a piece of toast, but she smiled and shook her head. "We'll want some pans of the crowd on tape to use with a voice-over later."

"I've got to pick up some souvenirs for my wife and kids."

Bob shot Liv a grin as she picked up her coffee. "Look, Liv, I got enough grief because I took off for London without them; if I don't bring back a few goodies, I'm going to be sleeping on the sofa."

"You should be able to squeeze out a few minutes for shopping between setups," she said. As she spoke, her eyes roamed the room, skimming over the faces of other reporters.

"Looking for somebody?" Bob asked, and cut into a sausage.

"What?" Distracted, she looked back at him.

"You've been scanning the room since you sat down. Are you meeting someone else?"

"No," she said, annoyed that she had unconsciously been looking for Thorpe. "You all better hurry," she told the crew in general. "The schedule's tight."

For the next ten minutes she drank her coffee with her back to the rest of the room.

The weak sunlight brought little warmth as Liv stood across from Westminster Abbey. She waited, going over her notes for the stand-up one last time as the crew set up their equipment. She estimated the spot would take forty-five seconds. Behind her the abbey's towers rose into a murky sky. London was gray under the clouds, the air heavy with threatening rain. At the moment, she gave no thought to the city around her, but was totally focused on the forty-five seconds of tape that was to come.

"Come in on me," she instructed the cameraman. "After the intro, I'm going to turn to the side and gesture back at the abbey. I want a slow pan; then come back on me at the finish."

"Gotcha." Bob waited until his lighting man had rechecked his meter. "Okay?"

Liv took the mike, then nodded. She ran through it once. Dissatisfied, she ran through it a second time. A faint breeze tugged at her hair as she spoke of the ceremony that was to come. Thoroughly, as though she had not worked the timing to the second, she talked of the abbey's history. When the camera came back to her, she looked into the lens with direct, serious eyes.

"This is Olivia Carmichael reporting from Westminster Abbey, London."

"Well?" Bob shifted his weight to his hip.

"It's a wrap." She checked her watch. "All right. We go to Downing Street. There're two hours before the ceremonies start. That should give us enough time for a quick stand-up and a few man-on-the-streets. We'll want another briefing with Thorpe before we feed what we have back to the station."

Thorpe had time for three cups of coffee while he waited for the president. His brief meeting with Donaldson had disclosed only that the president had spent a comfortable evening and had arisen early. But Thorpe was not satisfied.

Outside, the limo waited with secret service hovering discreetly in the background. Thorpe drew on a cigarette, standing coatless, heedless of the chill spring morning. His cameraman whistled tunelessly while the rest of the crew held a mumbled conversation. Thorpe didn't pay attention. He was watching the secret service. They were quite obviously on the alert.

The moment the president stepped outside, things came to life. Thorpe heard the whirl of the camera going on. He had the mike in his hand. Almost without thought, he filed what the first lady was wearing. There would be those who would demand an exact account.

"Mr. President."

The president stopped by the door to the limo and turned to Thorpe. A brief nod kept the guards at arm's length. "T.C.," he said solemnly. "A sad day for England, and for the world."

"Yes, Mr. President. Do you feel Prime Minister Summerfield's death will have an effect on your foreign policy?"

"Eric Summerfield's death will be felt keenly by all men of peace."

A roundabout way to say nothing, Thorpe thought without rancor. It was the name of the game. He also knew protocol. He wouldn't be allowed hard-line questions on the morning of the funeral. "Mr. President," he added, changing tactics, "have you any personal memories of the prime minister?"

If he was surprised by the altered tone, he continued

smoothly. "He could walk for miles." The president smiled. "I discovered that at Camp David. Eric Summerfield liked to think on his feet."

With that, the president slipped into the limo beside his wife. Still vaguely dissatisfied, Thorpe waited for his press car.

His commentary, and the film of the funeral procession, would be broadcast via satellite. Thorpe set up less than a block away from Westminster Abbey, where the service would be conducted. His coverage promised to be a long, involved dissertation on what dignitaries had come to pay their respects, and in what order they arrived.

Thorpe announced the sighting of the royal family's limo, then others, sprinkling in tidbits of Summerfield's career and personal life. The streets were jammed with people, yet the background noise was minimal. When they spoke, onlookers spoke in hushed tones, as if they were inside the abbey.

He glimpsed Liv once, but there was no time for a personal encounter. As he talked into the mike, she was in the corner of his eye, the corner of his mind. His body tensed a split second before it happened.

A car broke through the police barricade and headed, at high speed, for the heart of the funeral procession. There was the sudden, shocking sound of gunfire. People who had lined the streets to watch scattered in a melee of fear and confusion. Cameramen raced for a better shot at the scene. Mike in hand, Liv dashed forward, reporting on the run. Thorpe was there ahead of her.

The procession was at a standstill. Bullets ripped holes in the tires of the speeding car, sending it skidding, careening out of control. The windshield cracked in a spider web of lines as the car swerved, held on course, then swerved again. It rammed into the curb and came to an abrupt halt.

Four men leaped out, rifles blazing. Bullets flew indiscriminately—toward the cavalcade, into the crowd. There were screams and a new rush of panic. People were knocked underfoot while others scrambled for safety.

Liv pushed her way through, dashing after her cameraman. She had to shove and duck as she fought against the flow of the crowd, which rushed pell-mell in the opposite direction.

Shots rang out over the shouts of anger and terror. She took a sharp blow on the arm as someone clawed his way past her. Never faltering, she continued forward, speaking into her mike.

Thorpe caught Liv's wrist as she started to brush by him. Pulling her back, he kept his body firmly planted in front of hers. He'd seen a bullet smash into the pavement no more than three feet from where he stood.

"Don't be a damn fool," he snapped before he lifted his mike again. "Four men," he continued without taking his eyes off the scene, "masked and armed with high-powered rifles . . ."

Liv jerked her wrist out of his hold. Because her way was blocked, she was forced to give her report from where she stood. Over Thorpe's shoulder, she could see the wrecked car and the gunmen. There was no need to give Bob instructions. He was down on one knee at the front of the crowd, taping the shooting as coolly as he would have taped a garden party. From whatever cover they could find, members of the world press did their job. In a medley of languages, the word of the attack went out over the airwaves.

An explosive blast of gunfire erupted. Then there was sudden and ominous silence.

Thorpe continued to report after the four men lay sprawled in the street. His voice was objective, if hurried. He had to give the facts as he saw them. He had chosen television news for just this purpose. The immediacy. It would always be the newsman's greatest challenge—to report accurately what was happening as it happened, without a script, without preparation. His adrenaline was pumping. His instincts had been right on target.

For the next fifteen minutes, he talked nonstop until the crowd was calmed and the procession continued on to the abbey. The service would go on. Inside, the London correspondent for CNC would take over. It would give Thorpe time to dig up information on the attack. He signed off and signaled his cameraman.

"You had no right," Liv began immediately.

"Shut up, Olivia." He hadn't realized until that moment just how furious he was. As he turned his mike over to the sound technician, his hand shook slightly. She could have been killed, he thought grimly. Standing right beside him, she could have been killed.

Incensed, she drew herself up straight. "Who do you think you are—" The furious question was cut off when he grabbed her arm.

"Somebody had to stop you before you ran out into the crossfire. *You damn idiot!*" He stopped, took her shoulders and shook her. "Who'd give your precious report if you walked into a bullet?"

Liv jerked away from him. "I had no intention of walking into a bullet. I knew exactly what I was doing," she said coldly.

"You weren't thinking about anything but getting on top of the action." He was shouting now, drawing the curious attention of a few of their colleagues. "Did you think you could ask politely for them to stop shooting and give you an interview?"

Almost as bewildered as she was infuriated, Liv stared at him. "I don't know what you're talking about," she said. "I didn't do anything any other reporter wouldn't have done." With a quick move of her hand, she pushed back her tousled hair. "It was exactly what you did yourself. You had no business interfering with my work."

"Interfering with your work?" he repeated incredulously. "There were four crazy men with high-powered rifles out there."

"Damn it, I know that!" Exasperated, she gestured with her mike. "That's the story. What's the matter with you?"

Thorpe stared back at her. He was overreacting and knew it. But the fury wouldn't die. To keep from shaking her again, he jammed his hands into his pockets. He wasn't able to deal with knowing she could be in any sort of danger . . . and that he could do nothing about it.

"I've got a story to cover," he said tersely, and left her there.

Placing her fists on her hips, Liv glared after him. Glancing to the side, she caught Bob's questioning stare. After blowing out a frustrated breath, she went to him. "Come on, get the rest of the crew. We've got a story to cover."

Liv interviewed officials, bystanders, police. She spoke to a pale, shocked woman who had a flesh wound in her upper arm from a stray bullet. Liv had to lean heavily on crowd reaction and speculation as the facts were still very thin: four unidentified men on what could be considered nothing less than a suicide mission.

Twenty-four people had been injured, more from crowd panic than from bullet wounds. Only six had to be hospitalized, and only two of them had serious injuries. Liv dashed down names and occupations as she worked her way through the remaining crowd.

If the terrorists had counted on aborting the prime minister's funeral service, they hadn't reckoned with British sangfroid. The ceremony went on as scheduled inside the centuries-old abbey while the press and police functioned outside.

Ambulances came and went along with official vehicles. The wrecked car was towed away. Long before the service was over, there was no sign of any disturbance on the street.

From her vantage point, Liv watched the royal family exit the abbey. If the security had been tightened, it remained discreet. She waited until the last limo had driven off. Rubbing the bruise on her arm, she watched camera crews breaking down their equipment. She'd been standing for hours.

"What now?" Bob asked her as he loaded his camera in its case.

"Scotland Yard," she said wearily, and stretched, arching her back. "I have a feeling we're going to spend most of the afternoon waiting."

She couldn't have been more right. With a pack of other reporters, print and television, she waited. They were given a bare dribble of information in an official statement and sent on their way. By six o'clock that evening, there was nothing to add to her report but a recap of the morning's events and a statement that the terrorists were as yet unidentified. Liv shot a final stand-up in front of Scotland Yard, then headed back to the hotel.

Exhausted, she soaked for an hour in the tub and let the fatigue drain. Still, when she had toweled off and slipped into her robe, she was restless. The room was too quiet, too empty, and she was still too keyed up from the events of the day. She began to regret that she had turned down the crew's offer to join them for dinner.

It was still early, she noted. Too early. She didn't want to face another night alone in a hotel room. If she chose, there were any number of reporters she could seek out for company over a drink or a meal. But Liv found she didn't want to spend her evening rehashing and speculating over the day's events. She wanted to see London. Forgetting her weariness, she began to dress.

It was cool outside, with the dampness that had threatened all day still lingering. She had a light coat thrown over her slacks and sweater. Without thinking of direction, she began to wander. Traffic clogged the streets, so that the smell of exhaust tickled her nostrils. She heard Big Ben strike eight. If she was going to have dinner, she should find a restaurant. But she kept walking.

Again, she was reminded of the trip a dozen years before. She had traveled in a Rolls then, from monument to monument. There had been a garden party at Buckingham Palace. In a pale rose organdy dress and picture hat, Melinda had curtsied to the queen. Liv remembered how badly she had wanted to visit the Tower of London. Her mother had reminded her the National Gallery would be more instructive. She had studied the paintings dutifully and thought how badly she would have liked to have seen the inside of a pub.

Once, not so many years ago, Doug had spoken of taking a trip to London. That had been in their college days, when there had still been dreams. They had never had the money to spare for the plane fare. Then, there had been no love left to spare for dreams. Liv shook herself out of the mood. She was here now, free to see the Tower of London or a pub or to ride the subway. But there was no one to share the adventure with. No one to—

"Liv."

With a gasp, she turned and collided with Thorpe. He steadied her with a hand on her arm. For a moment she stared at him, completely disoriented.

"Alone?" he asked, but didn't smile.

"Yes. I : . ." She groped around for something to say. "Yes, I thought I'd do some sight-seeing."

"You looked a little lost." After releasing her arm, he stuck his hand in his pocket.

"I was just thinking." She began to walk again, and he fell into step beside her.

"Have you been to London before?"

"Once, a long time ago. Have you?"

"In my salad days." They walked for a time in silence. The restraint she sensed in him was something new, but she said nothing, letting him choose his own time. "There's nothing new on the terrorists," he told her after a moment.

"Yes, I know. I spent the afternoon at Scotland Yard. I suppose they could have been independent."

Thorpe shrugged. "They had very sophisticated, very expensive equipment, but they didn't seem to know how to use it. They were the only fatalities."

"It was stupid," Liv murmured, thinking of the four men who had held the limelight for one brief, fleeting moment. "A senseless thing to die for."

Again, they lapsed into silence, walking in the chilly evening. The streetlamps were lit. They passed under the light, into the shadows and back into the light. Abruptly, he laid a hand on her shoulder. "Liv, there were a lot of bullets flying around out there today."

"Yes?"

"It was a miracle that none of the press or bystanders were killed."

"Yes."

She wasn't going to make it easy for him. Thorpe let out an impatient breath. "If I overreacted this morning, it was because I stopped thinking about you as a reporter. I only remembered you were a woman and I didn't want you hurt."

In silence she studied his face. "Is that an apology?" she asked him.

"No, it's an explanation."

Liv considered for a moment. "All right."

"All right what?"

"I consider it a reasonable explanation." She smiled then.

"But the next time you get in my way on a story, you're going to get a very unladylike elbow in the ribs. Understood?"

He nodded, returning the smile. "Understood."

"Have you had dinner, Thorpe?" she asked, as they began to walk again.

"No, I've been getting the runaround from Donaldson."

"Hungry?"

He glanced down at her, one brow lifted. "Is that an invitation, Olivia?"

"No, it's a question. Answer yes or no."

"Yes."

"Someone told me that colleagues on foreign soil should stick together," she commented. "What are your views on that?"

"I would be inclined to agree."

Liv took his arm. "Come on, Thorpe, I'll buy you dinner."

9

They found a noisy, crowded chophouse and squeezed into a corner table. Thorpe glanced around at the line of customers packed together at the counter. In the air was the scent of grilled meat and frying oil. Overhead were brilliant fluorescent lights.

"Very romantic," he commented. "I'm a sucker for atmosphere on a date."

"This isn't a date," Liv reminded him as she slipped out of her coat. "I'm testing a theory. You should be careful not to spoil it."

"Spoil it?" He gave her an innocent stare. "How?"

Her only answer was a narrowed look.

When they had ordered, Liv settled back in her chair to soak up the atmosphere. At the counter, two men argued heatedly over a horse race. Over the hiss and sizzle of cooking meat was a constant buzz of conversation. It was precisely the sort of place she had wanted to experience when she had been a teenager on her first trip to London.

In silence, Thorpe watched her, noting that her eyes went from person to person with no loss of fascination. Gone was the faint sadness he had seen on her face when he had first met her on the street. What had she been thinking about? he wondered. Or was it whom? There was still too much he didn't know. And, he thought, it would still be some time before she told him.

"What do you see?" he demanded.

"London." Liv smiled back at him. "A lot more of London than you can see by looking at monuments and museums."

"Apparently you like what you see."

"I only wish we weren't due to leave in the morning. I'd like another day."

"What would you do with it?"

Liv lifted her shoulders. "Oh, see everything, everyone. Ride a double-decker bus. Eat fish and chips in a newspaper."

"Go to Covent Garden?"

She shook her head. "I've been to Covent Garden. I'd rather go to the docks."

Thorpe laughed, lifting his beer. "Have you ever been to the London docks, Olivia?"

"No. Why?"

"I wouldn't advise it. At least not alone."

"You're forgetting I'm a reporter again," she reminded him.

"So would the dock workers," he said dryly.

"Well." She shrugged before leaning back in her chair. "In any case, we go back tomorrow."

"What are your plans then?"

"After I check in at the station I'm going to sleep for the rest of the weekend."

"When's the last time you saw Washington?" he asked, as grilled pork chops were set in front of them.

"What are you talking about? I see Washington every day."

"I mean for fun." He picked up his fork. "Have you ever played tourist in D.C.?"

Liv frowned as she cut into the meat. "Well, I suppose . . ."

"Ever been to the zoo?"

"Of course, I did a story on . . ." She paused and looked up. He was grinning at her "All right, what's your point?"

"That you don't relax enough."

Liv lifted a brow. "I'm relaxing now, aren't I?" she asked.

"There isn't time for me to show you London properly," Thorpe put in. "Why don't you let me show you Washington?"

Warning signals sounded immediately. Liv toyed with her

meal as she formulated a safe answer. "I don't think so," she said carefully.

Thorpe smiled and went on eating. "Why not?"

"I don't want you to get the wrong idea, Thorpe."

"What's the wrong idea?" His voice was bland and friendly. Glancing down at her hands, he remembered how her fingers had moved over his face when he kissed her.

"Look." Liv paused, wanting to choose her words carefully. "I'm not totally averse to your company, but—"

"Carmichael, you slay me with compliments."

"But," she continued, shooting him a look, "I'm not going to become involved with you, and I don't want you to think otherwise." Because the words made her feel ungracious, she unbent a little. "We can be friends . . . of a kind, I suppose."

"Of what kind?"

"Thorpe," she said impatiently. "Stop it."

"Liv, as a reporter, I need concise information." He gave her an easy smile before he sipped at his beer.

"As a reporter," she countered, "you should be intuitive enough to understand my meaning."

Leaning closer, he grinned. "I'm crazy about you, Carmichael."

"You're crazy period," she corrected, and tried to ignore the sudden increase in her pulse rate. "But I'm trying to overlook that so that we can deal together amicably. Now if you'd just agree to keep things on a friendly basis," she continued.

"What's your definition of friendly?" he inquired.

"Thorpe, you're impossible!"

"Liv, I'm just trying to understand the issue. If I don't have the facts straight, how can I reach a viable conclusion? Now, as I see it"—he took her hand—"you're willing to admit you can tolerate my company. Is that right?"

Liv drew her hand from his. "So far," she said warily.

"And you're willing to take the second step and be friends."

"Casual friends." Though she knew he was leading her, she was as yet unable to see the trick.

"Casual friends," he agreed. Lifting his beer, he toasted her. "To the third step."

"What third step?" Liv demanded, but he only smiled at her over the rim of his glass. "Thorpe . . ."

"Your dinner's getting cold," he warned, then gave her pork chops an interested glance. "Are you going to eat all that?"

Distracted from the point she had been going to make, Liv looked down at her plate. "Why?"

"I missed lunch."

Liv laughed and cut another slice. "So did I," she told him. She ate every bite.

When they stepped back outside, it was raining lightly. Liv lifted her face to it. She was glad Thorpe had found her—glad to have had his company over dinner. If it didn't make sense, it didn't matter. If it wasn't safe, she didn't care. She had needed an evening with someone who could make her laugh, make her think. Make her feel. If it was Thorpe, she wasn't going to question why tonight.

A few stolen hours was all she wanted. A few hours to forget all the promises she had once made herself. She didn't need the promises tonight. Tonight she was free of the past, free of the future.

"What are you thinking?" Thorpe turned her into his arms as she laughed.

"That I'm glad it's raining." Still laughing, she shook back her hair. Then his mouth was on hers. Liv threw her arms around his neck and gave herself totally to the moment.

He hadn't meant to kiss her. God, he hadn't meant to. He had only so much control to call upon. But at that instant, when she laughed and lifted her face to his, he couldn't resist. There was rain in her hair, on her cheeks. He could taste it on her lips.

He had never sensed this sort of abandonment in her before. It fanned his desire to a consuming fire. Couldn't she see how much he loved, how much he needed, and have pity on him if nothing else? Dear God, he thought, as he devoured her willing mouth, he was desperate enough to take pity if it was all she could give him. Crushing her to him, Thorpe buried his face against her throat.

Liv stepped back, drawing out of his arms to lean against a lamppost. Her heart was racing with a terrifying euphoria. The speed and force of her own passion left her shaken. And she had sensed something in him, a desperation that she didn't dare accept.

"Thorpe, I . . ." Swallowing, unable to admit what was happening to her, she shook her head. "I didn't mean for that—It just happened," she finished helplessly.

Still throbbing, Thorpe went to her. "Liv," he began, lifting a hand to her cheek.

"No, please." She closed her eyes. There was a tug-of-war inside her—pulling toward him, pulling away. Perhaps if she could forget everything, wipe the slate clean until that moment, then . . . But no, there was no pushing aside what had been. She wasn't yet ready to start again. "I can't," she whispered as she opened her eyes. "I just can't."

Instead of taking his hand from her cheek, he turned it over, letting his knuckles brush along her skin. It would have been impossible to have wanted her any more than he did at that moment. "Can't," he asked, "or won't?"

"I don't know," she murmured.

"What do you want, Liv?"

"Tonight . . ." She lifted her hand to his. "Just be my friend tonight, Thorpe."

There was a plea in her eyes that he couldn't ignore. "Tonight, Liv." He took her by the shoulders. "Friends tonight, but I won't make any promises about tomorrow."

"Fair enough." Some of the tension seeped out of her. After a deep breath, she smiled at him. "Buy me a drink? I've waited twelve years to see the inside of a London pub."

His hold slackened slowly. She caught a glimmer of the effort it took for him to release her. "I know a little place in Soho if it's still there."

"Let's go see." Liv linked her arm through his.

It was there—a bit more dingy than it had been seven years before. When he entered, Thorpe wondered if it were the scent of the same stale beer and tobacco that hung in the air.

"It's perfect!" Liv told him as she gazed around through the curtain of smoke. "Let's get a table."

They found one in a corner. Liv sat with her back to the wall. Customers were shoulder to shoulder at the bar. From the familiarity, she concluded most of them were regulars. Off to the side, someone played a piano with more enthusiasm than skill. Several voices joined in song.

There was talk, a constant chatter. A voice would lift now and then, so that she caught snatches of conversation. The theme ranged from the attack on the funeral procession to someone's unsympathetic boss.

"What'll ya 'ave?" The barmaid who sauntered over gave them both a suspicious stare.

"White wine for the lady," Thorpe told her. "I'll have a beer."

"Ooh, Americans." That seemed to please her. "Doing the town?"

"That's right," Thorpe told her.

With a quick laugh, she walked back to the bar. "Got us a couple Americans, Jake," she told the bartender. "Let's 'ave some service."

Liv gave a low laugh. "How did you know about this place, Thorpe?"

"I was on assignment a few years back." He flicked his lighter at the end of a cigarette. "An American attached to our embassy here had delusions of being a master spy. He picked this place for the meet."

"Cloak and dagger." Liv leaned forward, resting her elbows on the wooden table. "And what came of it?"

"Zilch."

"Oh, come on, Thorpe." Disappointed, Liv shook her head. "At least make something up."

"How about I infiltrated an international spy ring single-handedly and broke the story on the six o'clock news?"

"Much better," she approved.

"Here you go, ducks." The barmaid set the drinks in front of them. "Just whistle when you want another round."

"You know," Liv continued when they were alone again. "You just about fit the image."

"Image?"

"The tough, unflappable newsman." Liv sipped at her wine before she grinned at him. "You know, a trench coat with a few wrinkles, the world-weary face. You stand in front of a government building or a sordid pit and report the news in a drizzle. It has to be drizzling."

"I don't have a trench coat," he pointed out.

"Don't spoil it."

"Even for you," he said with a smile. "I'm not going to start doing stand-ups in a trench coat."

"I'm crushed."

"I'm fascinated."

"Are you? By what?"

"By your image of a field reporter."

"It was my image before I got into the game," she admitted. "I saw myself having meets with disreputable figures of the underworld in seamy bars and breaking world-shaking stories before breakfast. It was going to be one fast-paced story after another. Adventure, excitement, intrigue."

"No paperwork, stakeouts or time editors." Drinking his beer, he watched her. How could anyone remain so lovely after the day she had put in?

Her laugh was warm and appreciative. "That's it exactly. Reality came into focus in college, but I think I still had this image of high adventure and glamour. It stayed with me until I covered my first homicide." She gave herself a quick shake and returned to her wine. "That's the sort of thing that brings you back to earth quickly. Do you ever get used to dealing with that, Thorpe?"

"You don't get used to it," he countered. "But you deal with it."

She nodded, then pushed away the mood. The piano player had switched to a melancholy ballad. "Are you really writing a novel?"

"Did I say that?"

Over the rim of her glass, she smiled. "You did. What's it about?"

"Political corruption, naturally. What about yours?"

"I don't have one." With a spark of mischief in her eyes, she looked up at him. A dull, throbbing ache started in his stomach. "Actually," she began in lowered tones, then hesitated. "Can you be trusted, Thorpe?"

"No."

She gave a muffled laugh. "Of course not, but I'll tell you anyway. Off the record," she added.

"Off the record," he agreed.

"When I was in college and money was scarce, I did some writing on the side."

"Oh?" He wondered how money could have been scarce with her family background, but left the question unasked. "What kind of writing?"

"I did a few pieces for *My True Story*."

After choking on his beer, he stared at her. "You're kidding! The confession magazine?"

"Don't get lofty. I needed the money. Besides," she added with a touch of pride, "they were pretty good little pieces."

"Really?" Thorpe gave her a lewd grin.

"Fictional," she stated.

"I'd like to read them . . . just for educational purposes."

"Not a chance." She glanced up as the crowd at the bar grew noisier. "What did you do in your misspent youth, Thorpe?"

"I had a paper route." He cast a casual glance over his shoulder at two men who were arguing over a game of darts.

"Ah, always the journalist."

"And chased girls."

"That goes without saying." Liv watched the dart players come nose to nose over their disagreements. Customers at the bar began cheerfully choosing sides. Thorpe reached for his wallet. "We're not leaving?" she asked as he pulled out bills.

"Things are going to get rowdy in a minute."

"I know." She grinned. "I want to watch. Do you want the guy in the hat or the one with the moustache?"

"Liv," he began patiently, "when's the last time you were in on a barroom brawl?"

"Don't be stuffy, Thorpe. I'm betting on the guy in the hat. He's smaller, but he's wiry." Even as she spoke, the man with the moustache threw the first punch. With a sigh of resignation, Thorpe leaned back. She'd be safer in the corner at this point.

Those at the bar turned to watch, holding their drinks as they shouted encouragement. Liv winced as her man took a jab in the stomach. Throughout the pub, customers began to pull out bills as they wagered on the outcome. The bartender continued to dry glasses. The two men came together in a furious hug, then toppled to the floor to wrestle.

Thorpe watched them roll around on the floor. A chair was knocked over, and a man with a glass of ale set it upright, sliding it out of range. He settled on it to root for the man of his choice. There were shouts of encouragement and advice.

It appeared Liv's prediction was a sound one, Thorpe decided. The man with the hat was slippery as an eel. He had his bigger adversary in a headlock, demanding that he give. With a face reddened with frustration and lack of air, he did.

"Want another drink?" Thorpe asked Liv as things quieted down again.

"Hmm?" She brought her attention back to him, then grinned at his dry expression. "Thorpe, don't you think this is the sort of thing that makes good copy?"

"If you're going to comment on a prizefight," he agreed, but smiled. "You surprise me, Olivia."

"Why, because I didn't scream and cover my eyes?" Laughing, she signaled the waitress herself. "Thorpe, they didn't do any more than give themselves a few bruises and something to talk about. The newsroom's more violent every day before deadline."

"You're a tough lady, Carmichael," he said, toasting her.

Pleased, she touched her glass to his. "Why, thank you, Thorpe."

It was late when they walked back outside. Liv heard the hour strike one. Stubbornly, the drizzle continued to fall. Lights reflected in shallow puddles and glimmered hazily through the misting rain. Though the air was chilled, the wine had warmed Liv, so that she felt glowing and wide awake.

"Do you know," she said as they walked slowly through Soho, "the first time I was in London I went to monuments and museums, teas and theaters. I feel as though I've seen more tonight than I did in that entire week." When he took her hand in his, she made no objection. There was something natural about walking with him in the early hours of the morning in a misting rain. "When I left the hotel tonight I was tired, depressed." She moved her shoulders. "Restless. I'm glad you found me."

"I wanted to be with you," he said simply.

Cautiously, Liv skirted around his statement. "I'm glad we're getting back in the middle of the weekend," she continued. "An assignment like this drains you, especially when you get a surprise like we had this morning."

"Not much of a surprise, really," he commented.

Liv looked up sharply. "Do you mean you were expecting something like that to happen?"

"Let's say I had a hunch."

"Well, you might have shared it with the rest of us," she said with a sound of exasperation. "After all, you were the press reporter."

"And as such, I'm required to share information and facts, not hunches." He grinned as she frowned up at him. "You should have been able to put two and two together for yourself, Carmichael. You have raindrops on your lashes."

"Don't change the subject."

"And every trace of your makeup's been washed away."

"Thorpe—"

"Your hair's wet."

With a sigh, Liv gave up.

"Tired?" he asked as they walked into the lobby of the hotel.

"No." She laughed. "Lord knows I should be."

"Want to go to the lounge for a nightcap?"

"Not if I want a clear head in the morning." She headed for the elevator instead. "I have to check in with Scotland Yard before we leave. Any connections there you want to share, Thorpe?"

Smiling, he pushed the button for their floor. "You'll have to dig up your own."

"I thought your turf was Washington."

"When I'm there," he agreed, and steered her into the corridor.

"You do have a connection," she said suspiciously.

"I didn't say that. In any case, the London correspondent will take the story from here."

Knowing she faced a dead end, Liv slipped her key into the lock. "That's unfortunately true. I hate not being able to follow up on it." She turned to smile at him. "Thanks for the company."

Without speaking, he lifted her hand to his lips. When the tremor shot down from her fingertips, she started to pull away, but he kept her hand firmly in his. He turned her palm up to plant another lingering kiss.

"Thorpe." Liv backed away, but her hand was still held fast in his. "We agreed to be friends."

His eyes were fixed on hers. The husky quality of her voice stroked along his skin. "It's tomorrow, Liv," he said quietly. "I didn't make any promises about tomorrow." Putting his hands on her shoulders, he turned her toward the door, and pushed her gently in. He let go of her only to close the door behind them.

She was in his arms again. Slowly, he ran his fingertips up the slim column of her neck. With his eyes on hers, he traced the shape of her ear, her cheekbones, then her lips. They trembled open at his touch as if she would speak. But no words came. With the same slow care, he took his mouth on the journey his fingers had completed. Light, butterfly kisses roamed over her neck and face, teased her mouth. He used neither pressure nor demand, but let her own needs hold her prisoner.

When he slipped his hands under her sweater, she made no attempt to stop him. Barely touching her, he ran the back of his fingers up her sides, then down again. He felt her quiver. Still, he deepened the kiss only slightly, a gentle exploration of the moist recesses of her mouth, a tender meeting of tongues.

Liv didn't resist him. It was as if she were too steeped in a conflict of her own making to reach for him or to push him away. Her breasts were firm and taut in his hands. The rough scrape of his palm against her sensitive skin brought a moan of pleasure from her.

Somehow instinct warned him she should be treated as an innocent—with care, with patience. Yet all the while his desire for her increased. Her trembling excited him, but he needed more. He needed her to touch him, to ask for him. The passion was there; he had tasted it before. He wanted it now. His mouth pressed down on hers, drawing it, coaxing it. She was fighting herself more than him. Her breathing was ragged, her body pliant, but there was still a thin wall he had not yet broken through.

Slowly, he unhooked her slacks, and with a groan, let his fingers reach for her. Soft—the incredible softness of her took him to the edge of control. For a moment she pressed against him convulsively. Life seemed to shoot into her entire body. Under his, her mouth was suddenly avid and demanding. Then she was pulling away, backing against the door. She shook her head frantically.

"No. No, don't do this."

"Liv." Pushed to the limit, Thorpe brought her back into his arms. "I won't hurt you. What are you afraid of?"

It was too close, much too close. Her voice sharpened in defense. "I'm not afraid of anything. I want you to go; I want you to leave me alone."

With his temper straining, his grip on her tightened. "The hell you do."

His mouth came down hard on hers as fury and frustration seeped through. Even as she tried to protest, her lips were answering his.

"Now look at me," he demanded roughly, drawing her back by the shoulders. "Look at me and tell me you don't want me."

She opened her mouth to tell him but the lie wouldn't come. She could only stand and stare at him. All of her courage deserted her. She was totally without defense.

"Damn you, Liv," Thorpe muttered abruptly. Pushing her aside, he slammed out of the door.

10

When Liv walked into WWBW on Monday morning, her thoughts were calm. She had spent the remainder of her weekend assessing her relationship with Thorpe. *Relationship* was not quite the word she liked to use. It implied something personal. *Situation* was a better choice.

She had firmly decided against complications. It was true that she had found him more appealing, more enjoyable than she had thought she would. More fun. She had never considered Thorpe in the context of fun. He was an entertaining companion. And there was a quiet streak of kindness in him, which softened her.

Liv was a cautious woman; circumstances had made her so. But she was honest with herself. She knew the cool, controlled Olivia Carmichael who delivered the five-thirty news was only part of the whole woman. A great deal of herself had been in storage. She had put it there for her own survival. It was true that Thorpe had begun to pick the lock, but the years had given her strength. If she wanted to keep herself shut off, she would. It was that simple. Or so she had convinced herself.

Involvement didn't always follow a physical attraction. She had no intention of becoming involved with Thorpe. They would still work closely now and again, and perhaps she would even consider seeing him socially on occasion. Perhaps it was time to start picking up the pieces of her personal life. She couldn't mourn forever. But—she would not put herself into a position again where things could get out of hand with Thorpe. He wasn't a man to underestimate.

She had made a miscalculation when she had allowed her pride to push her into the ridiculous wager. A man like Thorpe, she mused, would only be all the more determined to have his way for the sheer devil of it. She should have simply ignored his fanciful statements about marriage.

The memory of his pleased, confident smile when she had accepted the bet still haunted her. He had looked too much like a cat who knew how to open the birdcage door.

But I'm not a canary, she reminded herself as she walked into the newsroom. And I'm not afraid of cats.

The newsroom was as it usually was. Noisy. Phones rang incessantly. Only the wall of television screens was silent. Interns bustled everywhere—college students learning the trade—running errands. The assistant director argued with a field reporter over the edited length of a segment. A crew headed out of the door with equipment and coffee cups.

"How many kittens?" she heard a reporter ask into a phone. "She had them *where*?"

"Liv." The assignment editor hailed her with an upraised hand. "The mayor's holding a press conference at two." He stuck out a piece of paper as he breezed by.

"Thanks." She wrinkled her nose at it. That might give her the time she needed to make the two million phone calls on her list.

"Who wants a kitten?" She heard the plea as she moved through the room. "My cat just had ten of them in the kitchen sink. My wife's going crazy."

"Hey, Liv." Brian caught her arm as she passed his desk. "I took two phone calls for you already this morning."

"Really?" She gave his jacket a critical glance. "New suit?"

"Yeah." He pulled a bit at the pearl-gray lapels. "What do you think?"

"Devastating," she said, knowing how Brian worried about his on-the-air image. He could agonize over the shade of his tie. "About the phone calls?"

"I was a little worried about the fit in the shoulders." He

shifted them experimentally. "The first one was from Mrs. Ditmyer's secretary. Something about setting up a lunch date. The second was from a character named Dutch Siedel. Said he had a tip for you."

"Really?" Liv frowned thoughtfully. Dutch was the one dependable source she had on Capitol Hill. He was a page with visions of a hot political career.

"Who do you know named Dutch?"

Liv gave Brian a guileless smile. "He's my bookie," she said smoothly, and started to walk away.

"Full of surprises, aren't you?" Brian commented. "Who's the dude who keeps sending you flowers?"

That stopped her. "What?"

Brian smiled and examined his nails. "There's a fresh white rose on your desk, just like the one last week. The little intern with the frizzy hair said it came from upstairs." He shot her a teasing look. "There's been a lot of buzzing about Thorpe's visit to the studio last week. Collaborating on a big story?"

"We're not collaborating on anything." Liv spun on her heel and stalked to her desk.

There it was—white and innocent with its petals gently closed. She had a mad urge to crush it in her hand.

"Nobody ever sends me flowers."

Liv turned and glared at the woman typing at the desk behind her.

"You must have hooked a romantic." She sighed. "Lucky you."

"Lucky me," Liv muttered. What was the man trying to do to her? It occurred to Liv that the room had become suspiciously quiet. A quick sweep of her eyes caught several speculative glances and too many grins. Furious, she swooped up the rose, vase and all, and plunked it down on the other reporter's desk.

"Here," she said with a broad gesture. "You can have it." She stormed out of the room. It was time, she decided, as she heard the scattered laughter behind her, to lay down the ground rules.

Liv was out of the elevator in a flash when it stopped on Thorpe's floor. Still seething, she came to a halt at the receptionist's desk.

"Is he in?" she demanded.

"Who?"

"Thorpe."

"Well, yes, he is, but he has an appointment with the chief of staff in twenty minutes. Ms. Carmichael!" She stared in exasperation at Liv's retreating back. "Oh well," she murmured, and went back to her typewriter.

"Look," Liv began before the door had slammed shut behind her. "This has got to stop."

Thorpe lifted a brow and set down the pen he'd been writing with. "All right."

Her teeth clamped together at his amiable answer. "You know what I mean."

"No." He gestured to a chair. "But I'm sure you're going to tell me. Have a seat."

"This rose business," she continued, ignoring the chair and advancing to the desk. "It's embarrassing, Thorpe. You're doing it on purpose."

"Roses embarrass you?" He smiled at her, infuriatingly. "What about carnations?"

"Will you stop!" She leaned her palms on the desk much as she had done the first time she had stormed his office. "You might fool the brass with that crooked smile and choirboy look, but not me. You know just what you're doing. It's driving me crazy!" She paused a moment for breath, and he leaned back. "You know what a rumor factory this place is. Before noon, the entire newsroom is going to think I'm involved with you."

"So?"

"I'm *not* involved with you. I never have been and I never will be involved with you. I don't want my associates thinking otherwise."

Thorpe picked up the pen and tapped on the desk top. "Do you think being involved with me damages your credibility?"

"That has nothing to do with it." She snatched the pen out of his hand and tossed it across the room. "I'm *not* involved with you."

"The hell you aren't," he countered smoothly. "Wake up, Liv."

"Listen—"

"No, you listen." He rose and came around the desk. She straightened to face him. "You were kissing me two days ago."

"That has nothing—"

"Shut up," he said mildly. "I know what you felt, and you're a fool if you think you can pretend otherwise."

"I'm not pretending anything."

"No?" He lifted his shoulder a bit, as if he thought little of her statement. "In any case, sending you a rose is hardly comparable to groping in the editing room during a coffee break. If you want something tangible to be offended about, I can oblige you." He pulled her into his arms. For the first time, Liv noticed the glint of anger in his eyes. She refused to struggle. It would be humiliating because he was stronger. She tilted her chin and glared back at him.

"I don't imagine you have to put much effort into being offensive, Thorpe."

"Not a bit," he agreed. "I'm rather pressed for time right now, or I'd demonstrate. We can hash this out over dinner tonight."

"I'm not having dinner with you tonight."

"I'll pick you up at seven-thirty," he said as he released her and picked up his jacket.

"No."

"I can't make it before seven-fifteen." He kissed her quickly. "If we have things to say to each other, they should be said in private, don't you think?"

He had a point. And her mouth was still warm from his. "You'll listen to what I have to say?" she asked cautiously.

"Of course." He smiled and brushed her lips again, lightly.

She stepped back. "And you'll behave reasonably?"

"Naturally." He slipped on his jacket. She was wary of his easy agreement, but could hardly argue with it. "I've got to go. I'll walk you to the elevator."

"All right." As she walked with him, Liv wondered if she had won or lost the argument. A draw, she decided, was the best she could make of it.

Thorpe hesitated outside of Liv's apartment. He wasn't sure why he was doing this. He wasn't accustomed to rejection, particularly rejection from a woman. He had always had success both in his personal and professional life. The professional success he had worked for. Hard. Success in his private life had always come easily. He hadn't had to devote endless hours to research, endless miles to legwork to lure a woman into his arms, into his bed.

When he had been in his early twenties, pounding Washington pavements, making contacts, reporting on faulty sewage systems, he had had his share of desirable women. Some might have said more than his share. Later, when he had done an eighteen-month stint abroad, covering the delicate and explosive Middle East, there had still been women. And as his name had become more well known, his face more widely recognized, his choices had become varied.

He knew he had only to pick up his phone and dial to insure himself an evening's companionship. He knew scores of women—interesting women, beautiful women, famous women. He had come a long way from the boy who had hung around the old Senators' clubhouse.

Still, two things had remained the same. He was determined to be the best in his field, and when he wanted something, he went after it. Thorpe thrust his hands in his pockets a moment and frowned at Liv's door. Was that why he was here? he wondered.

But it wasn't as simple as that. Even standing there alone, he could conjure up her face, her voice, her scent. There had never been another woman in his life he could see so clearly when he was alone. There hadn't been another woman who could make him ache at the thought of waiting. She was a challenge, yes, and Thorpe thrived on a challenge. But that wasn't why he was there. He loved her. He wanted her. And, he was determined he was going to have her. He pressed the doorbell and waited.

Liv had her coat over her arm when she opened the door. She had no intention of letting him in. If she was going to be with him, she preferred a restaurant where there would be no danger of making the mistake she had already made too many times.

"I'm ready," she said in her most distant tone.

"So I see." He didn't move as she shut the door at her back.

She was forced to push him out of her way or stand still. She stood still. He must have come straight from his broadcast, though Liv had no intention of admitting to him that she had watched it. He had removed his tie, however, and had loosened the first few buttons of his shirt. He looked as relaxed as she was tense.

"You're still mad." He smiled, knowing he was baiting her but unable to resist. He wasn't certain which expression he liked better: the grave sincerity in her eyes during a broadcast, or the controlled annoyance he so often saw when she looked at him.

Liv wasn't angry, but nervous—and furious with herself for being susceptible to him. She could already feel herself unbending to that smile.

"I thought we were going to thrash this out over dinner, Thorpe, not in the hall of my apartment building."

"Hungry?"

She didn't want to smile, but her lips betrayed her. "Yes."

"Like Italian food?" he asked, taking her hand as they moved toward the elevator.

"As a matter of fact, I do." She gave a slight tug to release her hand, but he ignored it. "Good. I know a little place where the spaghetti is fantastic."

"Fine."

Twenty minutes later, they pulled up in front of the little place. Liv frowned at the high white building. "What are we doing here?"

"Having dinner." Thorpe parked the car, then leaned over to unlatch her door. She slid out and waited for him.

"They don't have an Italian restaurant in the Watergate."

"No." Thorpe took her hand again and led her toward the front doors.

Her suspicions began to peak. "You said we were going to an Italian restaurant."

"No, I said we were having spaghetti." After crossing the lobby, Thorpe punched an elevator button.

Liv gave him a narrow look. "Where?"

He guided her into the elevator. "In my apartment."

"Oh, no." She felt panic as the car began its climb. "I agreed to have dinner with you so we could talk, but I—"

"It's hard to talk seriously in a noisy restaurant, don't you think?" he said easily as the doors opened. "And I have a feeling you have a lot to say." Unlocking his door, he gestured her inside.

"Yes, I do, but . . ." The thick, aromatic scent of spiced sauce drifted to her. She crossed the threshold. "Who cooked the spaghetti?"

"I did." Thorpe slipped the jacket from her shoulders, then shrugged out of his own.

"You did not." She looked at him in frank disbelief. Did a man with rough palms, intelligent eyes and casual sophistication cook spaghetti?

"Chauvinist," he accused, and kissed her before she could prevent it.

"That's not what I meant." Liv was distracted by the kiss and the enticing smell coming from the kitchen. "I know lots of men who cook, but I—"

"Didn't think I could," Thorpe finished for her. He laughed, keeping his hands on her arms. Her skin was too smooth to resist. "I like to eat; I get tired of restaurants. Besides, I learned when I was a kid. My mother worked; I fixed the meals."

His hands were gliding gently up and down her arms until she felt her skin begin to pulse. It was an erotic sensation for him, as well as for her—work-roughened palms against satin smoothness.

"Don't," she whispered, afraid she would be unable to prevent herself from taking the small step forward into his arms.

"Don't what, Liv?" Watching the suppressed desire build in her eyes, he felt his own growing.

"Don't touch me like that."

For a moment, Thorpe did nothing; then casually, he removed his hands. "Are you any good in the kitchen?"

The ground solidified under her feet. "Not really."

"Can you toss a salad?"

Why was it so easy for him? she wondered. He could smile so effortlessly, while her knees were still trembling. "Probably, if I follow directions."

"I'll write some down for you." He took her arm in a

friendly grip that still managed to shoot sparks down her spine. "Come on, give me a hand."

"Do you usually invite women to dinner, then put them to work?" It was important to match his mood and forget the moment of weakness.

"Always."

The kitchen was a surprise. Onions, garlic and potatoes hung in wire mesh baskets near the window, while copper-bottom pans dangled from hooks. There were utensils she had never seen before, all within easy reach of the stove or counter. Glass canisters stored colorful beans and different-shaped pasta. Her own kitchen was a barren desert compared to this. Here was a room of someone who not only knew how to cook, but enjoyed it.

"You really do cook," Liv marveled.

"It relaxes me—like rowing. Both take concentration and effort." Thorpe uncorked a bottle of Burgundy and set it aside to breathe. Liv was drawn to the simmering Crockpot.

"When did you have time to do this?"

He lifted the lid. "I put it on before I left for work this morning."

She narrowed her eyes at his easy smile. "You're terribly sure of yourself." It was astonishing how often he had made her angry in such a short period of time.

"Here," he said soothingly, and dipped a wooden spoon into the pot. "Taste."

Pride fell before hunger, and she opened her mouth to obey. "Oh." Liv closed her eyes as the flavor seeped through her. "It's immoral."

"The best things tend to be." Thorpe dropped the lid on the pot again. "I'll do the bread and pasta; you do the salad." He was already filling a pan with water. Liv hesitated a moment. The sauce was still tangy on her tongue. Nothing, she decided, was going to stand between her and that spaghetti. "Everything's in the fridge," he added.

She located fresh vegetables, and after filling her arms with them, took them to the sink to wash. "I'll need a salad bowl."

"Second cabinet over your head." He added a dash of salt to the water after the flame was on under it.

She rummaged for the bowl as he began to slice bread. He

watched her—as she stood on tiptoe to reach the bowl, her dress floating up then down with her movements; as she scrubbed a green pepper under a spray of water, her fingers gliding over the skin. She wore clear polish. Her nails were well shaped, carefully tended, but she never used color on them. It was something he had noticed. Her makeup was always subdued, understated, as were her clothes. Thorpe wondered if it was a purposeful contrast to her more flamboyant sister or if it was simply a matter of taste.

Liv carried the vegetables to the butcher block. She glanced up when Thorpe held a glass of wine out to her.

"Hard work deserves its rewards."

Before she could empty her hands and take the glass, he held it up to her lips. His eyes were steady on hers.

"Thanks." Her voice was as cloudy as her mind. She turned away quickly.

"Like it? You usually drink white." Thorpe lifted the glass and drank himself.

"It's good." Liv gave all her attention to choosing a knife.

Thorpe slipped one out of its slot and handed it to her. "It's sharp," he warned. "Be careful."

"I'm trying to be," she murmured, and set to work.

She could hear him moving around behind her, pouring pasta into boiling water, setting the bread under the broiler. His presence was invading her senses. By the time the salad was finished, her nerves were jangling. She took the wine he had left on the block and drank deeply. Settle down, she cautioned herself, or you'll forget what you came for.

"Ready?" His hands came down on her shoulders, and she just prevented herself from jolting.

"Yes, all done."

"Good. Let's get started."

A small smoked-glass table was set in front of a window. It was a cozy, intimate area, despite the open view of the city, raised from the living room by three steps and separated by an iron railing. There were candles of varying sizes and shapes burning through the room. The light was soft and flickering. The English bone china was another surprise. Liv tried to divorce herself from the atmosphere while Thorpe served the salad. She had come to talk. Perhaps it was best to ease into it gently.

"You have a beautiful apartment," she began. "Have you lived here long?"

"Three years."

"Did you choose it for its"—she paused and smiled—"colorful past?"

Thorpe grinned. "No. It suited my needs at the moment. I was in Israel when that went down. I've always regretted not being here to report the story." He offered her oil and vinegar. "I know an assignment editor who tossed the story out when he got the feed. No time, and he thought no one would care about some minor break-in. I think he's selling used cars now in Idaho."

Liv laughed. "How long were you in the Mideast?"

"Too long." He caught Liv's questioning glance. "Hours of tedium and moments of terror. Not a healthy way to live. War opens your eyes, maybe too much, to what a human being's capable of."

"It must be very difficult," she murmured, trying to picture it. "Reporting a war, that kind of a war, in a foreign country."

"It was an experience," he said with a move of his shoulders. "The trouble is, when you're reporting, you tend to forget you're human too. For a while, up here"—he tapped his temple—"you're indestructible. The camera's a force field. It's a dangerous delusion—one that bullets and grenades don't respect."

She understood what he meant. She herself had once walked carelessly into a government building following a bomb detection team. Her mind had been on the story. It hadn't been until later that the full impact of her action had struck her.

"It's strange, isn't it?" she mused. "And it's not just reporters. Cameramen are probably worse. Why do you suppose that is?"

"Some like to claim it's a mission, a sacred duty to let the public know. I've always considered it simply a matter of being caught up in the moment. You do it because you're focused in on the story, and the story's your job."

"Tunnel vision," she said quietly, remembering he had used the phrase before. "That's not as romantic as a mission."

He smiled, watching the candlelight flicker over her skin. "Do you look for romance in your work, Liv?"

The question startled her, bringing her back. "No. No, I don't." Now was the time, she told herself. "Which is exactly why I agreed to have dinner with you tonight."

"To keep your romance separate from your work?"

Her brows drew together. Why did that sound so different when he said it? "Yes . . . No," she amended.

"I'll get the spaghetti while you make up your mind."

Liv cursed herself and tore a piece of garlic bread in two. Why was it things never went as she planned when she was around him? And why did he always seem so on top of things? Straightening, she reached for her wine. She would simply start over.

"Here we go."

Thorpe placed a platter of thin pasta topped with the thick sauce on the table.

"Thorpe," Liv began. The aroma was irresistible, and she filled her plate as she spoke. "I really thought you understood what I said to you the other day."

"I understood perfectly, Olivia; you're very articulate." He helped himself when she had finished.

"Then you must see how difficult you're making things."

"By sending you a flower," he concluded, and offered her grated cheese.

"Well, yes." It sounded so silly when he said it. "It's very sweet, but . . ." Frowning, she rolled spaghetti onto her fork. "I don't want you or anyone else to think that it means anything."

"Of course not." He watched her sample the first bite. "How is it?"

"Fabulous. Absolutely fabulous." Liv let the pure sensual pleasure of food spread through her slowly. "I've never tasted anything better." She rolled a second forkful and tried to remember what point she had been trying to make. "In any case, it's not the sort of thing associates do, you know." The second forkful proved as satisfying as the first.

"What isn't?" It gave him a great deal of satisfaction to

watch her preoccupation with his cooking. Her tongue slid lightly over the fork.

"Send flowers," she stated. "To each other. Especially when there's rivalry as well. Local and national news are siblings. I know a bit about sibling rivalry."

"Your sister," he commented. The candlelight shot little flecks of gold into her eyes. He could almost count them.

"Mmm. With a sister like Melinda, I've had experience at being the underdog. I never minded; it makes you more inventive. The same goes for doing the local news."

"Is that how you look at it?" he asked curiously. He picked up one of her hands to examine the delicately painted nails. "As being the underdog?"

"You have the big budget," she pointed out. "The large exposure, publicity. But that doesn't mean we can't have the same quality on a smaller scale." There was a callus on his thumb. She could feel its light scrape across her knuckles. An unexpected chill shot straight down her spine. Carefully, Liv removed her hand and reached for her wine. "But that's not the point."

"What is?" Thorpe smiled at her—the slow, personal smile that scattered her wits. Liv hastily pulled herself together.

"You know how stories fly around a newsroom. Internal stories," she specified as she returned to her dinner. "It's a difficult place to have any privacy. Privacy's important to me."

"Yes, it must be. There hasn't been any mention of you in the papers or glossies since you were a teenager. The Carmichaels always make good copy."

"I didn't fit the mold." She hadn't meant to say that, and was astonished it had slipped out. "What I'm trying to say," she continued, as Thorpe kept his silence, "is that once someone in your newsroom or mine gets hold of an idea, the next minute it'll be fact. Then the sky's the limit. You know how a simple coffee date can become a torrid lunchtime affair after the third telling."

"Does it matter so much?"

Liv gave a weary sigh. "Probably not from your standpoint, but from mine, yes. I have to deal with being the new kid on the block, and a woman. It's still hard, Thorpe. Whatever progress I make is always examined more closely than anyone else's right now. Is Carmichael seeing Thorpe because she wants to jump on the national news team?"

He studied her a moment. "You don't have enough confidence in yourself."

"I'm a good reporter," she countered immediately.

"I was speaking about you as a woman." He saw the shield come up and could have sworn in frustration.

"That's none of your concern."

"Isn't that what we're talking about?" he countered. "I sent a *woman* a rose, not a reporter."

"I am a reporter."

"That's your profession, not your sex." He lifted his wine and forced back annoyance. He knew anger was no way to get through to her. "It doesn't do to have thin skin in this business, Liv. If newsroom gossip bothers you, you're going to get a lot of bruises. Look in the mirror. People talk about a woman with a face like yours. It's human nature."

"It isn't only that." Liv subsided a bit. She had wanted to talk to him. It wouldn't help if she became angry. "I don't want any personal involvement—not with you, not with anyone."

Thorpe studied her in silence over the rim of his glass. "Were you hurt that badly?"

She hadn't expected the question, or the trace of sympathy in it. It cost her a great deal to keep her eyes level and composed. "Yes."

He left it at that. That she had made the admission instead of freezing was enough. He would wait for the rest. "Why did you come to Washington?"

Liv looked at him a moment. She had been prepared for further interrogation, but not for a casual change of subject. Warily, she allowed herself to relax again. "I'd always been interested in politics. That was my beat in Austin, though most of the time I did little but read the news on the air. When WWBW made the offer, I grabbed it." She began to give her attention to the meal again. "It's an exciting city, especially from a reporter's viewpoint. I wanted the excitement. I suppose I wanted the pressure."

"Have you thought of doing national news?"

She made a vague gesture with her shoulders. "Of course; but for now, I'm happy where I am. Carl's the best news director I've ever worked with."

Thorpe grinned. "He does have a tendency to become emotional."

Liv lifted a brow as she toyed with the last of her spaghetti. "Particularly when some hotshot from upstairs steals a story. I had to step on the toes of one of your associates after the mayor's press conference this afternoon."

"Is that so? Which one?"

"Thompson. The one with the big ears and flashy ties."

"A flattering description."

"Accurate," Liv countered, but a smile tugged at her lips. "In any case, I'd gone to a lot of trouble to set up a quick interview after the conference. He tried to cash in on it."

"You set him straight, I'm sure."

Liv let the smile form. It rather pleased her to recall how she had dispatched the enterprising Thompson. "As a matter of fact, I did. I told him to do his own legwork or they'd find him hung by his tie in the basement of the Rayburn Building." She paused consideringly. "I think he believed me."

Thorpe looked into the cool blue eyes. "I think I do too. Why didn't you just sic your cameraman on him?"

Liv grinned and scooped up the last of her spaghetti. "I didn't want a vulgar scene in front of the mayor."

"Want some more?" He gestured toward her empty plate.

Liv sat back with a sigh. "You've got to be kidding."

"Dessert?"

Her eyes widened. "You didn't really make dessert?"

Leaning forward, Thorpe tipped more Burgundy into her glass. "Drink your wine," he suggested. "I'll be right back."

He took the plates away with him. Liv gave a moment's thought to giving him a hand, then sat back. She was too content to move. It was foolish to deny she enjoyed his company. Liked talking to him. Arguing with him. She had nearly forgotten how stimulating an argument could be. He made her feel alive, vital. She didn't quite feel safe with him, and even that was exciting.

Liv glanced up as she heard him come back. At the sight of

the dish of strawberries and cream he carried, she gave a low sound of pleasure.

"They look marvelous! How did you get your hands on strawberries that size this early in the season?"

"A reporter never reveals his sources."

She sighed as he set the dish on the table. "They look wonderful, Thorpe, but I don't think I can manage it."

"Try one," he insisted, dipping a berry into the fresh whipped cream.

"Just one," she agreed, and obligingly opened her mouth as he started to feed it to her. He smeared the cream along her cheek. "Thorpe!" Liv said on a laugh, and reached for her napkin.

"Sorry." He laid his hand on top of hers, preventing her from lifting the napkin. "I'll get it." Cupping her neck with his other hand, he slowly, lightly began to nibble the cream from her cheek.

Liv's laughter stilled. She didn't move, couldn't protest. Her mind and body were locked in the shock of sensation. Her skin seemed alive only where his tongue glided over it.

"Good?" he murmured, passing his lips over hers.

Liv said nothing. Her eyes were locked on his. Thorpe watched her steadily as he read the stunned passion in her eyes.

Slowly, he dipped a second berry and offered it. "Another?"

Liv shook her head, swallowing as she watched his teeth slice through the berry. Rising, she stepped down into the living room. She had to be on her feet to think, she told herself. In a moment, she would feel perfectly normal again. The trembling would stop—the heat would cool. A startled gasp escaped her when Thorpe turned her into his arms.

"I thought you'd like to dance," he murmured.

"Dance." She melted into his arms. "There isn't any music." But she was moving with him, and her head was already resting on his shoulder.

"Can't you hear it?" Her scent was teasing his senses. Her breasts yielded softly as he drew her closer.

She sighed and closed her eyes. The candlelight flickered against her lids. Her limbs felt heavy, much too comfortably so. She leaned on Thorpe. She tried to tell herself she had had too much to drink. That was what she was feeling. But she knew it was a lie. When his lips passed over her ear, she sighed again and shuddered.

I should go, she told herself. I should leave now, right now. Her fingers wandered into his hair. It's madness to stay. A slow, kindling longing was building as his body moved against hers. His hand slid up her spine and down again to settle at her waist. When she felt his lips on her neck, she gave a low sound, drugged in pleasure.

"I can't stay," she murmured, but made no effort to move from his arms.

"No," he agreed, as his mouth made a leisurely journey to hers.

"I should go." Her lips sought his.

"Yes." He slipped his tongue between her parted lips to touch hers. Liv felt her bones dissolve and her head spin.

"I have to leave."

"Mmm-hmm." Gently, he lowered the zipper at the back of her dress. She made a muffled sound as his hands ran over the thin chemise.

"I'm not going to get involved with you, Thorpe." Her mouth was moist and heated as he explored it.

"I know; you've told me."

Her dress slid to the floor.

She pressed closer and let his mouth find hers again. She was drowning, but the water was so warm, so soft. The need for him was sleepy, growing as he moved his hands over her. She was a prisoner of his touch—a touch that was gentle. She made no protest when he lifted her into his arms.

Moonlight filtered into the bedroom, shadowed light, softly white. Liv nearly broke through the surface.

"Thorpe—"

Then he kissed her again. Lost, longing, she clung to him as he lowered her to the bed. He undressed her slowly, with soft kisses and caresses. The words he murmured were quiet, stroking her nerves, arousing her body.

When his back was bare, Liv ran her hand over it. There was hard strength. She wanted him to be strong. Needed for him to be. He lowered the chemise to her waist, following the trail of his hands with his mouth.

Desire changed from dreamy to desperate in a flash. Liv moaned and pressed him closer until his mouth was hungry at her breast. Her movements under him were no longer languid, her hands no longer timid. She arched to help him strip the thin garment from her. He ran his hands up the inside of her thighs, and she felt a rush of heat engulf her. She crested on a moan, but he slid his fingers over and inside her, driving her up again.

She dug her nails into his shoulders. Nothing, no one, had ever made her feel like this—mindless, aching, glowing. Liv wanted him to take her, but he had other pleasures to give.

His tongue glided down her torso, flicking over the curve of her waist until she knew she would go mad. Wandering, he moved lower still, until on a strangled gasp, she peaked again.

Her responsiveness overwhelmed him, taking him beyond his own desire. He wanted her to experience every drop of pleasure he could give. She was sensitive to every touch, every thought. Though the moonlight gave her skin a marble hue, it felt like liquid fire under his hands. Need for her vibrated through him. Each time she moaned his name or reached for him, the shock of it rocketed straight through him. Desire pulsated from her—for him. That alone took him to the edge of reason.

His mouth crushed down on hers, and Liv answered the demand ravenously. All restraint had fled; all barriers were broken. She knew only a desperate need for fulfillment and the one man who could give it to her. She opened for him, then guided him inside of her.

Her gasp was muffled against his shoulder. She felt the muscles tense and ripple against her mouth as he took her beyond what she remembered, past what she had dreamed of. She gave herself up completely and went with him.

Thorpe lay wrapped round her, holding on to the warmth. For him, the world had whittled down to the bed—to the woman. Even in the dark he could see her, each curve of her body, each plane of her face. In all of his memory, he had never felt so involved, so totally united. Her skin was smooth against his, her nipples still taut as her breasts pressed against his chest. Her breathing was leveling slowly. He had known there was passion under her strict control, but he hadn't guessed the depth of it or what its effect on him would be. He was vulnerable, almost defenseless for the first time in his life.

Liv felt the intensity of passion drain into contentment. She had never experienced that sort of abandonment. Had that been missing all of her life? She was almost afraid to find the answer and what it would mean. One basic truth was that he had made her feel like a woman again, complete. The taste of him still lingered on her lips and tongue. She didn't want to lose it, or the warm security she now held nestled in her arms.

But who was Thorpe? she wondered. Who was he who had drawn from her what she had been unable, or unwilling, to give any man for more than five years.

"I promised myself this wouldn't happen," she murmured, and buried her face against his neck.

Her words forced Thorpe out of his dreamy state. "Regrets?" he asked carefully, and waited what seemed a lifetime for the answer.

"No." Liv gave a long sigh. "No regrets." She tilted her face back. "I never expected to be here with you, like this. But I don't regret it."

He relaxed again and held her closer. The soft, serious words stirred him. "Olivia, you're such a complicated woman."

"Am I?" She smiled a little and closed her eyes. "I've never thought so. Too simple perhaps, and singleminded, but not complicated."

"I've been working on sorting you out for a year and a half," he returned. "It isn't an easy job."

"Don't try." She let her hand roam over his shoulder again. She liked the feel of muscle, knowing he could control it into gentleness. "Thorpe, have you had many lovers?"

He gave a muffled laugh. "That's a delicate question to ask at the moment, Carmichael."

"I wasn't going to ask for names and numbers," she countered, sighing as his hand moved down her back. "It's just that I haven't really. I'm not very good at it."

"Good at what?" he asked absently. His casual explorations were teasing his own need for her.

She felt awkward suddenly, and searched for a phrase. "At—ah—pleasing a partner."

The movement of his hand stopped, and he drew back to study her face in the darkness. "Are you joking?"

"Well, no." She was embarrassed now. If she hadn't been so relaxed, she would never have put herself into such a position. She fumbled on. "I know I'm not very—exciting in bed, but—"

"Who the hell put that into your head?"

The sharp annoyance surprised her. *My husband* trembled on the edge of her mind. "It's just something I've known—"

He swore ripely and stopped her. "Do you think I was pretending just now?"

"No." She was confused suddenly, and unsure of herself. "Were you?"

He was angry, almost unreasonably so. Rolling, he pinned her beneath him. "I wanted you, from the first moment I saw your face. Did you know that?"

She shook her head, unable to speak. A fresh surge of passion raced through her at the press of his body, the grip of his hands.

"You're so cool, so aloof, and I could see all those whispers of heat. I wanted you like this, naked in my bed."

His mouth crushed down on hers, bruisingly, furiously. Her lips were eager for his, accepting the anger, the demand, matching the hunger.

"I wanted to strip away the layers," he muttered. He moved his hands over her until she was writhing mindlessly. "I was going to have you—melt all that ice." His hand slipped between her thighs and she arched, yearning for him. "But there wasn't any ice, any need for games when I held you. If you didn't please another man, it was his fault. His loss. Remember it."

She was on fire. Her hands touched, searched, stroked on their own power while her mouth roamed his neck. She could feel his pulse go wild under her tongue. She pulled at him, dragging his mouth back to hers. The taste—his taste. She was desperate for it. He trembled with her.

Then the kiss was savage, staggering her with the knowledge that she had taken him beyond the civilized. This was no pretense. He was totally lost in her—in what they made together. She felt it, marveled at it, then swirled into a mist where no thoughts could penetrate.

She was limp, utterly spent, her breath and body shuddering. His weight was on her fully, and his back was damp under her hands. There was no measuring the time they lay there, replete in each other.

"I suppose you're right." His voice was dark and husky. "That wasn't very exciting."

Liv didn't think she had the energy to laugh, but it bubbled inside her, warm and comfortable. She didn't know how he knew exactly the right thing to say, but she accepted it. It was a novel and wonderful sensation, to laugh in bed. He lifted his head and grinned at her.

"Idiot," he said softly, and kissed her. Shifting, he gathered her to his side. She was asleep in moments and lay still. He held her.

11

The alarm clock went off with a shrill. Automatically, Liv reached over to shut off the blast and rolled into Thorpe. Her eyes shot open. Disoriented, groggy, she stared into his eyes while the bell continued to peal. Part of her mind registered the shadow of beard on his chin, the sleepy heaviness of his eyes as they looked into hers.

I slept with him, she remembered. Made love with him and slept the night in his bed. The knowledge registered slowly. She could feel a trace of astonishment in the full light of day, but though she searched and wondered, there were still no regrets. She had been given passion, gentleness, caring. How could there be regrets?

Thorpe reached behind him and snapped off the alarm. Silence was abrupt and complete. Saying nothing, he gathered Liv against him. He had seen the dazed surprise in her face, then the gradual understanding and acceptance. He found it amusing, and strangely endearing. This wasn't a woman who made it a habit of waking up in a man's bed.

The quiet morning cuddle was a new sensation, and Liv drifted with it. Undemanding intimacy. Tangled with him, she explored it sleepily. She wasn't certain what she was feeling. What emotion was this? Contentment? Happiness? Simple pleasure at being close enough to touch and be touched?

Something had changed. Doors had opened. She wasn't sure whether she or Thorpe had turned the lock, but it had been done. His breath was warm on her cheek, his arms lightly possessive around her. She was no longer alone. Did she want to be? She felt the pressure of his body against her. Yesterday she had been certain that solitude was the answer for her. But now . . .

She had made love with him. Shared herself. Taken from him. Liv wasn't a casual person. Intimacy was no small gesture for her. Intimacy meant commitment. To her, the two had always, would always, walk hand in hand. And yet, she had promised herself there would be no more commitments in her life, no more one-to-one relationships. There was too much in her past to remind her of the risks. He was becoming too important. She was becoming too vulnerable. It was much too easy to stay where she was, wrapped tight, held close. If she stayed too long, she might forget how quickly disillusionment came.

She shifted, wanting to break the bond before it became too strong. "I have to get up. I have to be in by nine-thirty."

Still silent, Thorpe brought her back to him. His mouth closed gently over hers. She was so soft, so warm. And her scent still lingered. He'd waited long, too long, to wake beside her. Now he wanted to enjoy the moment. He wanted to see how she looked in the morning, fresh from sleep, her eyes still heavy. He had slept beside her, awakened beside her. He didn't intend to be without her again.

Liv responded to the gentleness and the lazy arousal. For a moment she could pretend there was no outside world that demanded their involvement and no past to inhibit her. There was only the two of them. If she closed her eyes, she could imagine it was still night and they had hours left to hold each other. But time was passing. The sun was a pale yellow light through the windows.

"We have to get up," she murmured, almost wishing he would contradict her.

"Mmm." He shifted his head slightly to see the clock. "Apparently," he agreed, and settled for a last nuzzle of her throat. "I don't suppose your conscience would allow you to come down with a sudden case of laryngitis or a convenient fever?"

"Would yours?" she countered.

He laughed and kissed her. "At the moment, I have no conscience."

"I wish I could say the same." Easing away from him, she sat up, automatically pressing the sheet to her breast. "I'm going to need a robe."

"Pity." With a groan he rolled away from her and rose. "I'll supply you with a robe. And breakfast," he added as he padded to the closet. "If you handle the coffee."

She was a little stunned to see him stand naked in front of the closet. Straightening her shoulders, she told herself not to be a fool. She had just spent the night with him. His body was no secret to her now. But to see him, Liv thought, as he pulled out the first robe for himself. He was magnificently built—hard, lean, with broad sinewy shoulders and a long torso. She had indeed often thought he seemed streamlined in his clothes. Without them, he appeared more the athlete.

"Okay?" He pulled out a short, kimono-style robe in blue terry and turned to her.

She had lost what he had been saying. Her eyes lifted to the amusement in his. "What? I'm sorry."

"Can you make coffee, Liv?" He grinned as he held out the robe.

"Have you got a jar and a spoon?"

He looked pained. "Are you joking?"

"I was afraid you wouldn't. I'll manage, I suppose," she told him doubtfully, and slipped her arms into the robe.

"The percolator's on the counter; coffee's on the second shelf over the stove," he instructed as he swung into the bath. "See what you can do."

She wrinkled her nose as he shut the door, then rose from the bed.

In the kitchen, she found things precisely where he had told her. She ran water and measured coffee. Just barely, she could hear the sound of the shower running.

She found it an odd sensation to be poking around in his kitchen, naked under his robe. *I'm having an affair,* she thought. She held the top of the percolator aloft a moment, staring into space. She had made love with Thorpe, had spent the night in his bed, and was now preparing coffee in his kitchen. In his robe, she reminded herself, running a hand down the lapel.

With a quick shake of her head, she fit the lid on top of the pot. For goodness' sake, I'm twenty-eight years old. I've been married and divorced. I'm a professional woman who's been on her own for years. Why shouldn't I have an affair? People do every day. It's a part of life. It's very simple—even casual. To make anything else out of it is foolish. We're two adults who just spent the night together. That's all there is to it.

Even as she ran the last of these cool, sensible words in her head, Thorpe came into the room. Liv turned to say something mildly sarcastic about the coffee and found herself folded into his arms.

His mouth touched hers softly at first, twice. The third time, they lingered and grew hungry. She lifted her arms to bring him closer. Everything she had just told herself was forgotten. His hair was still damp as her fingers combed through it. The scent of soap and shaving lotion brushed at her senses. Everything seemed new and fresh, like a first romance.

His hands rested at the sides of her breasts, then lowered to her hips. It wasn't a desperate kiss, but a strong one. It brought echoes of the night back to her. Thorpe drew back a little to look at her.

"I like you this way," he murmured. "Barefoot, in a robe several sizes too big for you, with your hair a little mussed." He lifted a hand to it and disordered it further. "I'll be able to picture you this way when I watch the cool Ms. Carmichael deliver the news."

"Fortunately for the ratings, the viewers won't."

"Their loss."

"Not everyone appreciates the rumpled, just-out-of-bed look, Thorpe." The coffee was perking frantically, and she drew out of his arms. There were mugs suspended from hooks under the cabinets. Liv slipped two off and poured.

"But then I appreciate the calm, sleekly groomed look too," he pointed out, offering her a small carton of cream for her coffee. "Actually, I haven't found anything about you that doesn't appeal to me."

Liv laughed and glanced up at him. "Are you always so agreeable before your coffee, Thorpe?" She handed him a mug. "I'd better shower while you drink this. It might sour your mood." He started to lift it to his lips, and she placed a hand on his arm to stop him. "Remember, before you drink it, you did promise to fix me breakfast."

She left him, taking her own mug with her.

Thorpe glanced back down at his coffee, then sipped doubtfully. It wasn't quite as bad as she had prophesied. Obviously, he thought, as he drank again, the kitchen wasn't her area. It was his, he concluded philosophically, and went to the refrigerator. He could hear the shower running. He liked knowing she was close—only a few rooms away. He took out a slab of bacon and heated a pan.

Thorpe wasn't a man to delude himself. They had made love—they would make love again—but Liv's feelings were not as defined as his. It was uncomfortable to find himself in the position of caring deeply for someone who didn't return the same depth of emotion. She could, he told himself as the bacon sizzled. She was fighting it. He was too confident a man to consider he might lose in the end.

Even in the bright sunlight of the kitchen he could remember her open giving of the night before—her initial hesitation, the gradual change to aggression and passion. Whatever she said, she was a complex woman, full of hidden corners and contradictions. He wouldn't have it any other way. Since he had fallen in love, he preferred it to be with a woman who had a few eddies and currents. Fate might have bound him to a tamer type.

Olivia Carmichael was the woman for him, and he was the man for her. He might have to be patient until he convinced her, but convince her he would. Thorpe smiled as he cracked an egg into a bowl.

As it had the night before, the scent coming from the kitchen drew Liv irresistibly. Standing in the doorway, she stared at the platter Thorpe was piling with bacon, golden eggs and lightly browned toast.

"Thorpe," she said, inhaling deeply, "you're amazing."

"You just noticed?" he countered. "Grab a couple plates," he ordered, jerking his head toward the proper cabinet. "Let's eat before it gets cold."

Liv did as he bade, plucking up the flatware as well before she followed. "I have to admit," she said as she took her chair at the table, "that I'm in deep awe of anyone who can fix a meal and consistently have everything ready at the same time."

"What do you eat at home?"

"As little as possible." She began to help herself from the platter. "Mostly I use all those little boxes that say 'Complete Meal Inside.' Sometimes there really is."

"Liv, do you have any idea what sort of things they put inside those little boxes?"

"Please, Thorpe." She shoveled a forkful of eggs into her mouth. "Not while I'm eating."

He laughed and shook his head. "Didn't you ever learn to cook?"

Liv lifted a shoulder. She remembered the meals she had fixed during her marriage. They had usually been hurried—dinners put together before she had dashed on to the evening shift at the station, a quick something after classes. She had cooked adequately, even well on sporadic occasions. But there had been so little time and so many obligations. She skipped back over that to give him the answer.

"When I was growing up, my mother didn't consider it important. In fact," she added after finishing off a slice of bacon, "she didn't care to hear about the few times I poked into the kitchen to see what was going on. That wasn't our territory."

Thorpe buttered a slice of toast and considered how remarkably diverse their backgrounds had been. He and his mother had been close, both from necessity and out of love. Liv and hers had been distant, perhaps from a simple lack of understanding.

"Do you go back to Connecticut often?"

"No."

There was a signal in the one word. *Don't press too close.* Thorpe recognized it and detoured.

"How's your schedule today?"

"Packed. The first lady's dedicating that children's center at eleven. Dell's due into National at one, though I doubt we'll be able to get near him, and I have another stakeout at the school board this afternoon." She finished off the rest of her eggs. "I'm scheduled to tape another promo. The general manager's nervous about the ratings."

"Aren't they all." He glanced at her empty plate. "Well, at least you're fortified."

"If that's your subtle way of saying I stuffed myself, I'll overlook it." Rising, Liv began to gather the plates. "Since you cooked it, I'll wash up while you dress."

"Very democratic."

She kept her eyes on the plates and platters. "I'll need to go back to my apartment to change before I go in. I'll take a cab."

"Don't be ridiculous."

Unsure of her moves, Liv lifted the stack of plates. "It's silly for you to drive halfway across town, out of your way. It would be simpler—"

He stopped her by taking the stack of plates out of her hands and setting them back on the table. Placing his hands on her shoulders, he studied her face. It was in his eyes again—the searching, the depth of intensity that was inescapable.

"Liv, last night meant something to me. Being with you means something to me." He could see the quick flicker of emotions as she digested his words. "No cabs."

"No cabs," she agreed, then slipped her arms around him to hold him tightly. The gesture surprised him, moved him. Liv closed her eyes and held on. She had been afraid he would agree without a second thought. The sensible part of herself had told her it would be best—keep it light, keep it sophisticated. Take a cab and see you later. But her heart wanted more. And her heart was beginning to outweigh everything else.

"Will you wait for me tonight?" he murmured into her hair. "Until after my broadcast?"

She tilted her face to his. "Yes." As his mouth touched hers, she thought fleetingly that the ground she was treading on might be dangerous; but she hadn't felt so alive in years.

It was five thirty-two when Thorpe stood in the control room and watched Liv through the window. He paid scant attention to her report on a robbery at a local chain store, or to the technical aspects of television that went on around him. She had, quite simply, been on his mind all day. He'd wanted to see her again before it was his turn in front of the camera.

"Punch up camera one," Carl ordered from his seat in front of the wall of monitors. She was there too, reproduced eight times in the black-and-white preview monitors and the live color ones. Her voice came through in stereo from the speakers. At his left, an engineer worked at the sound board.

"Camera two."

Brian's image replaced Liv's on the live monitor. At Carl's next order, the graphics were punched up to flash behind him.

"Thirty seconds to commercial."

Brian continued smoothly to the cut.

Carl drew hard on a cigarette and shot a glance over his shoulder at Thorpe. "See you around here more now than when you worked here," he commented.

"I've more incentive," he answered easily.

Carl studied Liv's image in the monitor and gave a grunt of agreement. He'd always liked Thorpe as a man, respected him as a reporter. He wished that he had been able to keep him on staff. Carl gave a sigh and crushed out the cigarette. He doubted he'd keep Carmichael more than a couple of years. He'd been around too long to expect anything different.

"Thirty seconds."

Thorpe looked back through the window. Liv was talking to Brian. She laughed at something and shook her head. Was it his imagination or did she seem more relaxed, more free? It would be well over an hour before he could touch her again.

Camera one was focused on her, and on cue she began the next segment of the broadcast. Thorpe left the control room with her voice still echoing in his mind.

With the show over, Liv went back to the newsroom. She had weighed the pros and cons of going upstairs to meet Thorpe, and had decided that to wait for him in her own territory would generate less speculation—and less gossip. She was not ready to put her personal life on display.

She missed him. The fact had surprised her, but there was no denying it. Her day had been hectic, at moments frantic, but somehow he had hovered on the edges of her thoughts throughout it.

Keeping to her desk, she began to go over her next day's schedule. Her eyes drifted again and again to the clock. Why, when the day had flown by, did one hour seem to be an eternity?

"This lady looks like she wants a cup of coffee."

Glancing up, Liv smiled at Bob and held out a hand. "I always knew you had great perception."

"I'd rather be irresistibly sexy," he commented, and sat on the corner of her desk.

"Of course you are." Her eyes laughed at him over the rim of the plastic cup. "I constantly have to restrain myself!"

"Yeah?" He grinned at her. "Can I tell my wife?"

"I'll leave that up to your own discretion."

"I worked with Prye today." Bob sighed into his coffee cup. "You know the little thirty-second stand-up he did in front of the Kennedy Center."

"Mmm-hmm." Liv knew what was coming, and settled back in her chair.

"Fourteen takes. You wouldn't believe how many times that guy can blow a line. He got irked when I asked him if he wanted us to make up some idiot cards for him. We should have more respect for the talent." He snorted, and gulped down more coffee. "He wouldn't know talent if it walked up and chewed on his ankle."

Liv opted to play the diplomat. She was well aware that Prye had a running battle with the crews. "The stand-up came across very well."

"Lucky for him he doesn't have to go live. If I had my choice," he said, and winked at her, "I wouldn't work with anyone who didn't have great legs. You know"—he cocked his head to study her—"you look different."

She lifted a brow. Could it be that a night of love and freedom had left some noticeable change? "If you're trying to save yourself from Prye tomorrow," she said lightly, "I've already talked to the desk about having you work with me."

He grinned again. "Thanks, but I'd rather have a wild weekend in Acapulco."

"Acapulco," she repeated, pretending to consider it.

"We could use your expense account."

"Liv's already occupied this weekend," Thorpe said mildly. Both Bob and Liv turned to look at him. He glanced down at her, then back at the cameraman. "She's going to be rowing."

"No kidding?" The information seemed to give Bob more reason to grin. "I guess I'll have to settle for Sunday dinner at my in-laws." He rose and, giving Liv a brief salute, left them.

"Thorpe." He had her arm and was already propelling her through the room. "I haven't made any plans for the weekend."

"I have," he returned amiably. "And you're included."

"I have this small idiosyncrasy," she told him when they stepped outside. "About having a voice in my own plans."

"I'm flexible." He opened the car door for her, leaned on it and smiled. "If you'd rather go to Acapulco, I can arrange it."

It was difficult to feel annoyed when he was smiling at her. She let out a small huff of a sigh. "I might consider rowing," she said, and gave in to the urge to touch his mouth with hers. "If you man the oars."

12

So much could change in a week. Liv could almost forget what it was like to be alone—truly alone. The nights no longer held absolute silence. She could almost forget what it was like to have no one but herself to depend upon. There was someone in her life again. She no longer attempted to reason out how he had gotten there.

She was growing to rely on Thorpe's companionship. She was growing to enjoy the pleasures of intimacy. Simply, she was growing to need Thorpe.

As the days passed, she found she looked forward not only to their conversations, but even to their arguments. He stimulated her, forced her to think fast if she wanted to hold her own. Intellectually, they complemented each other. There were times, she knew, he sharpened his wit on her, just as she did on him.

His strength was important to her. There was something rock solid about him. She had once looked for the solidity in someone else and had been disappointed. She wasn't looking for protection. She had been through too much to doubt her own ability to deal with whatever life tossed at her. When you had gone through the worst and survived, nothing could ever hurt you in quite the same way again. But if she chose a partner, a companion, a lover, he had to have strength.

She was still cautious. There were still guards over her emotions. But they were growing weaker.

* * *

As he had promised, Thorpe took her to a night ball game.

"I'm telling you, he should look for another profession," she stated as she stuck the key in the lock of her door. She brooded over the faults of the plate umpire as she shrugged out of her jacket. "Don't they have to go to school or something before they become umpires?"

"Or something," Thorpe agreed, not even trying to hide a grin. Liv had been indignant over the umpire's calls during the entire drive home.

"Well," she concluded, "he must have gotten dreadful marks. I wouldn't be surprised if he's a nasty person who kicks his dog."

"A sentiment probably shared by a number of ballplayers." Thorpe slipped out of his jacket and tossed it to join hers. "Maybe it's time you took over the sportscast, Liv."

She gave him an arch look. "I might do very well," she returned. "After a few more games, I could probably report a play by play as well as I do a filibuster. Would you like a brandy?"

"Fine." He smiled at her back as she fixed the drinks. "Leaving the play by play aside for the moment and concentrating on filibusters, what do you think of Donahue's chances?"

"Slim," Liv responded, and turned back with two snifters.

"I talked to him today." Taking the brandy from her, Thorpe drew Liv down on the couch beside him. "Right before he went onto the floor. He's brown-bagging it. He must have had five ham sandwiches and a half a dozen doughnuts."

Liv laughed. "Well, at least he won't go hungry. That should give him the stamina to keep his filibuster going—if his voice holds out."

"He's determined," Thorpe commented. "He told me he's going to outlast and outtalk every one of his opponents. If force of will and ham on rye can do it, Donahue's got it made." Liv settled back against his shoulder, and his arm automatically encircled her. "The gallery was packed for most of the day."

"We did some man-on-the-streets," Liv murmured, sleepy

now with contentment. "Most people were there from pure curiosity rather than any interest in the issue. But a full gallery and a filibuster make good press. That might keep Donahue going a few days longer."

"He made it through day five."

"I'd like to see him win." She sighed. How had she ever been comfortable without his arm around her? "I know it's unrealistic, and the bill will pass eventually, but still . . ."

He listened to her slow, quiet voice. There was a parallel between Donahue and himself, he thought. Thorpe had launched his own filibuster with Liv. He was just as determined as the senator to win a full victory. It wasn't enough just to be able to hold her. He wanted, needed, a lifetime. How much longer was it going to take? There were times when the need for caution frustrated him to the point of anger.

He set down his drink, and then hers. Liv lifted her face for the kiss, but it was not as she had expected. His mouth was fierce. She was pressed back against the cushions of the sofa with his body fitted to hers. He tugged at her clothes impatiently. This was something new. Always, there had been a thread of control in his lovemaking, as if he compensated for the difference in their physical strengths with gentleness. Now, she felt the urgency as he pushed open her blouse to find her.

His mouth was locked on hers, so that she couldn't speak, or even moan, as he stripped off her jeans. She fumbled with his sweater, wanting to be flesh to flesh, but the press of their bodies together hampered her. With a low, savage oath, Thorpe stripped it off himself, pulling it over his head, then letting it fall to the floor.

His mouth was suddenly everywhere—tasting, ravishing. She was pliant, fluid under his touch. She flowed wherever he took her, rising and falling to his whim. There was a wildness in him she had only glimpsed before.

He took her on the couch as if it had been years since their last joining. The desperation went on and on until she knew there could be no more either of them could want or give. Then he was pulling her to the floor with him, heating her again while her body was still humming.

She moaned his name once, half in protest, half in disbelief, as her passion mounted again.

"More," was all he said before his mouth took hers.

His hands were as avid as they had been at the first touch, and her body as receptive. There was in her now an overwhelming need to possess, to be possessed. No longer was she only guided. Her hands sought him, found him, while her mouth clung hot and fast to his.

She was shuddering without being aware of it. She heard only his labored breath in her ear when she wrapped around him. Need and fulfillment seemed to burst within her at once. Then she was once more pliant, once more limp. This time, Thorpe lay beside her and let his body rest.

Yet he couldn't prevent himself from touching her still. Her skin drew him, and the curve where waist flared to hip. His hands were gentle now. He kissed the slope of her shoulder, the delicate line of her jaw. He heard her sigh as she moved closer to him.

As fiercely as passion had whipped through him before, now love ached inside him.

"I love you." He felt her immediate stillness and realized he had spoken aloud. Cupping her chin in his hand, he lifted her face to his. "I love you," he said again. He hadn't meant to tell her in exactly this way, but now that it had been done, he kept his eyes on hers. He wanted her to understand he meant what he said.

She heard the words, saw them repeated in his eyes. Something moved inside of her like a tug-of-war, toward him and away. "No." She shook her head and the word was weak. "No, don't. I don't want you to."

"You don't have any choice." The statement was calmer than his mood. Her answer, and the anxiety in her eyes, cut at him. "And, it seems, neither do I."

"No." Pushing away, she sat up to cradle her head in her hands. Old doubts, old fears, old resolutions crowded at her. Pressure was squeezing her in a tight fist. "I can't. . . . You can't."

Love—that dangerous, dangerous word that left you naked and senseless. Accepting it was a risk, giving it a disaster. How could she let herself be caught in the web again?

Thorpe took her shoulders and turned her to face him. Her response left him hurt and angry. The pale, miserable look on her face only added to it. "But I do love you," he said curtly. "Not wanting me to doesn't change it. I love you, have loved you for quite some time. If you'd bothered to look, you'd have seen that."

"Thorpe, please . . ." She could only shake her head. How could she explain to him? What did she want to explain? She wanted him to hold her until she could think clearly again. Love. How did it feel to know she was loved? If she could have a few moments. If her heart would stop pounding.

"I'm not interested in only having your body, Olivia." She could hear the temper and frustration in his voice. She stiffened against it. No, she would not be pressured. She would not be maneuvered. She was still in charge of her own life. He could feel the change. His fingers tightened on her skin in impotent fury.

"What do you want?"

"A great deal more," he said deliberately, "than you're willing to give me. Trust, I suppose, would be a good start."

"I can't give you any more than I have." She wanted to tremble, to weep, to cling to him. She kept her eyes level. "I don't love you. I don't want you to love me."

Neither knew the extent of pain their words caused the other. She saw only a flare in his eyes that made her realize how strictly he controlled his own violence. If he had had less of a grip on himself, she felt certain he would have struck her for the cold dispassion of her words. She almost wished he would. At the moment, she would have gladly exchanged physical pain for the emotional one.

Slowly, he released her. He hadn't known he could be hurt like this. In silence, he dressed. He knew he had to leave quickly, before he did something he would detest himself for. She wouldn't drive him to that. Not by rejection, or her damn coolness or anything else. He'd leave her to herself, since that's what she wanted. The sooner she was out of his sight, the sooner he could work on forgetting her. He cursed himself for being a fool even as he shut the door behind him.

The sound of it closing brought Liv's head around. For a full minute, she stared at the panel. The silence welled up around her. Curling into a ball, she lay on the rug and wept for both of them.

The normal routine of a day was like an obstacle course. Getting up, dressing, driving through rush hour traffic. To Liv, it all seemed larger, more complicated than it ever had before. In a morning crammed with appointments, she went through the hours with a combination of nervous energy and dull fatigue. Her thoughts could never be completely centered on her objective when Thorpe was always just around the edges. She had begun to taste happiness again, and now . . .

Everything had happened so fast. Liv hadn't expected him to love her. She knew enough of him, understood enough of him to be certain he wasn't a man to love lightly. His energy and power would be bound up in it. When a man like Thorpe loved a woman, she was loved completely. Perhaps that was what frightened her most.

Yet, what she felt now as she finished up an interview wasn't fear; it was emptiness. Before Thorpe had become a part of her life, she had accepted the emptiness. The void had been filled, as nearly as possible, with her work and her ambition. It was no longer enough. During the morning, a dozen things happened that she found herself wanting to share with him. Years had passed without her feeling the need to share with anyone, and now it was inescapable. But she had pushed him away.

What should she do now? How could she make him understand that while part of her wanted to love him, to be loved by him, another part was like a rabbit under a gun. Frozen. Terrified.

How could she expect him to understand? she asked herself as she mechanically negotiated through afternoon traffic. She was no longer sure she understood herself. Put it on hold for a while, she advised herself. Have lunch with Mrs. Ditmyer, relax, and then try to think fresh again.

Hoping she could take her own advice, Liv pulled into the parking lot beside the restaurant. It was the perfect way to take her mind off things, she decided. Part business, part social. A glimpse at her watch told her she was barely five minutes late. Nothing major. It wouldn't do to keep Myra Ditmyer waiting long.

I like her, Liv thought as she entered the restaurant. She's so . . . alive. Greg was lucky to have her for an aunt, for all her matchmaking tendencies. Liv could only wish the cards had dealt her a similar relative. A woman like that would be sturdy as a boulder when the world crumbled under your feet.

Liv shook away the thought. There was also the matter of her position in Washington political and social circles. Since Myra had taken it into her head to notice her, Liv might as well take advantage of the side benefits.

"Mrs. Ditmyer's table," she told the maître d'.

"Ms. Carmichael?" He smiled when she inclined her head. "This way please." Liv followed him, amused. As a Carmichael she recognized deferential treatment. As a presswoman, she had learned not to expect it.

"Olivia!" Myra greeted her as though they were the fastest of friends. "How charming you look. And how lovely it is to have men staring again. Even if they're only speculating whether I'm your mother or your maiden aunt from Albuquerque."

Liv was laughing even as the maître d' assisted her into her chair.

"Mrs. Ditmyer, I knew having lunch with you would be the high point of my day."

"What a sweet thing to say." She beamed, pleased with herself. "Paul, do see about some sherry for Ms. Carmichael."

"Of course, Mrs. Ditmyer." The maître d' bowed away from the table.

"Now then." Myra folded her hands on the table expectantly. "You must tell what wonderfully exciting things you've been doing. I'm sure running around reporting on political corruption and world-shaking events must keep you forever in a spin."

Liv laughed. It was impossible not to be relaxed and exhilarated simultaneously in the woman's company. "It seems a crime to disappoint you, Mrs. Ditmyer, but most of the time I spend waiting at airports or outside the gate at the White House. Or," she added with an apologetic grin, "on the telephone finding out where I'm going to wait next."

"Oh, my dear, you mustn't burst my bubble." Myra sipped her own glass of sherry. "I'm perfectly content if you make something up, just so it's exciting. And call me Myra; I've decided we're going to get along famously."

"Do you know, I believe we will." Liv shook her head. "I'm sorry to say we can't all be Woodwards and Bernsteins. But I suppose all reporters run into a fat story now and again. Right now, the heat is on Senator Donahue's filibuster."

"Ah, Michael." Myra smiled, then nodded with approval as Liv's sherry was set in front of her. "Feisty old devil. I've always been fond of him. Nobody rhumbas like Michael Donahue."

Liv nearly choked on her sherry. "Is that so?"

"I shall have to introduce you next month when I give my Spring Ball. You do rhumba, don't you, dear?"

"I'll learn."

Myra smiled in her dazzling way, then crocked a finger at the waiter. "I, unfortunately, will have to make do with the fruit salad. My dressmaker's sighing horribly these days." She gave Liv a wistful glance that wasn't envious so much as reminiscent. "The scampi's exquisite here."

"Fruit salad will do nicely," Liv returned. "Being able to sit down for lunch is treat enough. I still have to thank you for asking me," Liv went on, as the waiter moved away. "It really isn't often I have the opportunity to have an hour like this in the middle of the day."

"But of course you can justify the luxury by terming it as partly business." Myra laughed at Liv's expression. "Oh, no, my dear, you mustn't think it offends me. Why not in the least. It's actually part of my intention. Now . . ." She leaned forward a bit like a general preparing to outline a plan of attack. "You must tell me what special project you have in mind. I know you must have one; it's simply in your character."

Liv sat back. Though she held the glass of sherry, she didn't drink. She was too enthralled with the woman across from her. "Myra, I believe you would have made a fabulous reporter."

A pleased pink flush spread on her cheeks. "Do you really? How marvelous. I do so love to nose around, you know."

"Yes," Liv answered faintly.

"So." Myra spread her hands, palms up. "Tell me what you have in mind."

Liv shook her head and smiled. "All right. I've been toying with trying a news special, probably slotted for late night. A personal view of women in politics. Not only women politicians, but women married to politicians. How they deal with the stress business—family, public exposure, traveling. I'd like to think I could deal with both sides of the coin that way. Women who are immersed in government for varying reasons."

"Yes . . ." Myra pouted in thought. "That might prove quite interesting. It can be the very devil on a marriage, you know. The campaigning, the staff dinners, the state dinners, the protocol. Lengthy separations, high pressure. It's a horse race, my dear. One long, never ending horse race. And the women . . ." She smiled again and swirled her sherry. "Yes, indeed, it might be interesting."

"I've been knocking it around with Carl for a couple of months. He's the news director," Liv explained. "I think he'd go for it, if and when I can give him an outline and some firm names. I suppose seeing Amelia Thaxter at the embassy started the wheels turning again."

"A remarkable woman," Myra commented. She smiled, somewhat dismally, as the fruit salad was placed in front of her. She wasn't the sort of woman who liked moderation, even gastronomically. "As dedicated as they come, and quite devoted to her constituents. Quite sincerely devoted. She made a choice between marriage and a career long ago. Some women can't mix the two." She smiled at Liv then and plunged her fork into a chunk of pineapple. "Oh, I'm not talking out of school. She'd tell you herself if asked. I believe she'll be quite interested in your project. Yes, and Margerite Lewellyn—nothing she likes better than to talk about herself. Then there's Barbara Carp . . ."

Liv listened, not touching her own lunch as Myra rattled off names of women political figures and the wives of some of Washington's top brass. This was a great deal more than she had expected. And as she spoke, Myra became more animated with the idea.

"What fun," she concluded. "I believe you'll do a marvelous job of it. I think I'll make a few phone calls when I get back."

"I appreciate it," Liv began, hardly knowing what to say. "Really I—"

"Oh, fiddle." Myra waved away the thanks with her fork. "It sounds a great deal more fun than planning another dinner party. Besides"—she gave Liv another of those blinding smiles—"I fully expect to be interviewed myself."

"That is an opportunity I wouldn't miss for the world," Liv said sincerely. "Myra," Liv said, and applied herself to her own salad, "you are amazing."

"I do try to be. Now, that's all the business nicely settled." She gave a self-satisfied sigh. She liked this girl. Oh, yes, she liked this girl very much. And when Myra Ditmyer made up her mind about someone, it was as firm as one of her husband's court decisions. "I must tell you, I had no idea when I made that little arrangement about the bridge party that you and Greg knew each other. I love being surprised."

"He was a very good friend." Liv poked at her salad. "Seeing him again was good for me."

Myra watched her carefully. "I said I was surprised. But then . . ." She saw Liv's eyes rise to hers. "It didn't take me long to put the pieces together. When he was in college, Greg had written me often about Livvy. I remember hoping he was enjoying a nice, sweet romance. He was certainly captivated by her."

"Myra, I—"

"No, no, now, let me finish. Greg was always a faithful correspondent. So refreshing in a young man. He wrote me that his Livvy was involved with his roommate."

"It was all so long ago."

"My dear." Myra placed a hand on hers. "I apologize. But Greg was very intimate in his letters. I suppose he needed a sounding board for his feelings. They were quite real to him at the time. He was desperately in love with you, and as close to Doug as a man can be to another. Being in the middle was difficult for him, and perhaps because I was removed, he talked to me through his letters. He told me everything."

The look, the press of the hand, told Liv that Myra was

being literal. There must be nothing about those years that she didn't know. Liv stared at her helplessly.

"Now, dear, have some more wine. I don't mean to upset you. We all learn to cope, don't we," she went on in an easy voice as Liv obeyed her. "To live with loss and pain and disappointment. One can't have lived to my age and not have run the gamut. It must have been dreadful for you. You probably thought you'd never live through it."

"No," Liv murmured. "No, I was sure I wouldn't."

"But you have." Myra patted her hand again, leaned back and waited.

Perhaps it was Myra's skill in dealing with people, perhaps her genuine interest in them that caused Liv to respond to Myra's silence more than she would have to a dozen well-meaning questions.

"I thought for a while it would be better to die than to have to live with the pain. There didn't seem to be anybody. . . . My family," she said on a long breath. "I suppose they tried; in their way they were sympathetic, but . . ." She stopped and let out a quiet sigh that tugged at Myra's heart. "I wanted to scream; I wanted to tear something apart. Anything. They simply never understood that kind of need. A person's grief, a person's private torment should be just that. Private. It should be handled with dignity."

"Poppycock," Myra said rudely. "When you're hurt, you cry, and the hell with anyone who doesn't like to see tears."

Liv laughed. "I believe I could have used you then. I might not have made such a botch of things."

"It's entirely your own opinion that you did," Myra said sternly. "It might be time for you to give yourself a bit more credit. But, as I've said, you've lived through it, and this is today. Tell me about you and T.C."

"Oh." Liv looked down at her salad again in fresh bewilderment. What was there to say? She'd botched things again.

"I can hardly hold any hope that you and Greg will make a match of it." She saw Liv smile at that and continued. "But as T.C.'s one of my favorite people, I've decided to be content with that."

"I'm not ever going to marry again."

"Oh, what boring nonsense," Myra said good-naturedly. "T.C. and you have been seeing each other fairly regularly now, haven't you?"

"Yes, but . . ." Liv frowned a bit. Myra really had missed her calling.

"He's entirely too intelligent a man to let you slip through his fingers. I'd bet Herbert's prize golf clubs that he's already asked you to marry him."

"Well, no. That is, he told me I was going to, but—"

"Much more in character," Myra said, pleased. "Oh, yes, that's just like him. And, of course, that got your back up."

"He was so unbearably arrogant," Liv stated, remembering.

"And he loves you so dreadfully."

That stopped her. She could only stare.

"Olivia, a blind man could have seen it that night at my little bridge game. And my eyesight's very keen. What are you doing about it?"

"I've . . ." Liv felt herself deflate like a pricked balloon. "I've ruined it. Last night."

Myra studied her in silence a moment. Really, she thought, the child was so confused. Again she reached out to pat her hand. It was such a shame to see people waste time because they thought too much and acted too little.

"You know, unlike the maxim, life isn't short, Olivia; it's really terribly long." She smiled at the serious eyes on her face. "But not nearly long enough. I've been married to Herbert for thirty-five years. If I had listened to my parents, bless them, and my own better sense, I would never have married a man who seemed too stuffy, who was too old for me and entirely too work oriented. Think of all I would have missed. Life," she said positively, "is worth a few risks. To prove it," she added and sat back, "I'm going to have some of that lemon mousse. . . ."

Even hours later, preparing for broadcast, Liv couldn't get Myra's words out of her mind. It was time to do something, she decided in the middle of the sportscaster's report. Time to stop mulling things over point by point. If she wanted to be with Thorpe, she was going to have to tell him so.

The moment her broadcast was over, Liv went upstairs. Seeing her approach, the receptionist gave a fatalistic sigh.

"He's not here," she said, as she prepared to pack up her work for the day. "He's doing his report on location."

"I'll wait in his office." Liv breezed by before the other woman could comment.

What am I going to say to him? Liv asked herself the moment she shut the door behind her. *What can I say?* Pacing the room, she tried to find words.

It seemed odd to be there without him. The room was so much his. Scattered on one wall were pictures of him with various world leaders and government officials. He looked invariably relaxed—never stiff, never overawed. He was simply Thorpe, Liv mused. And that was enough. There were scrawled notes littering his desk, and a hefty pile of papers held down by a paperweight. She went to look out at his view of the city.

She could see the dome of the Capitol. With the sun beginning to set, it had a rosy hue, almost fairylike. Traffic was thick, but the heavy glass insulated her from the sound of it. She gazed out at the lines and circles of the streets, the old, stately buildings, the cherry blossoms just coming to bloom. It didn't have the movement or urgency of New York, she decided, but was beautiful in its way. Engrossed in her study, she never heard Thorpe come in.

Seeing her surprised him. He was uncustomarily thrown off-balance. He hesitated for a moment with his hand still on the knob. Very carefully, he shut the door at his back.

"Liv?"

She whirled, and he saw her expression range from surprise to pleasure to controlled anxiety. More than he had ever wanted anything, Thorpe wanted to take her into his arms and pretend the night had never happened.

"Thorpe." At the sight of him, all her planned speeches flew out of her head. She stood rooted to the spot. "I hope you don't mind that I just came in."

He lifted a brow and she saw it—the light mockery, the easy amusement. "Of course not. Want some coffee?"

He was so casual as he strolled over to the pot, she began

to wonder if she had imagined that less than twenty-four hours before he had told her he loved her. "No, I . . . I came by to see if you'd come to dinner," she said impulsively. She could sense refusal and hurried on while his back was still to her. "Of course, I can't promise a meal like you could fix, but I won't poison you."

Thorpe abandoned the making of coffee, and turned to face her. "Liv, I don't think it's a good idea," he said quietly.

"Thorpe . . ." She turned away for a moment to gather strength. What she wanted to do was weep, and to use his shoulder to weep on. That wouldn't help either of them. She turned to face him again. "There are so many things you don't know, don't understand. But I want you to know, and to understand that I care. I care very much. Maybe more than I'm able to deal with." He could hear the nerves rushing through her voice as she took a step toward him. "I know it's a tremendous thing to ask, but if you could just give me some time."

It was costing her, he noted, to ask. Knowing her, he understood it had cost her to come to him this way. Hadn't he told himself to be patient? "I have some things to clear up here first," he said. "Would it be all right if I came by in an hour or so?"

He heard her small expulsion of breath. "Good."

An hour later, Liv was wound up tight. She tried to bank her nerves and concentrate on getting together a meal, but her eyes were forever fixing themselves on the clock.

Maybe I should change, she thought, and glanced down at her no-nonsense suit of charcoal gray. Even as she headed from the kitchen, the doorbell rang. Liv jolted. Oh, stop being ridiculous, she chided herself, but when she answered the door, her heart was thumping.

"Hi." She gave him a bright smile that was a little strained around the edges. "Your timing's good; I'll put the steaks on in a minute." She shut the door behind her and was already wondering what to do with her hands. "Steak's about the safest; I can't do too much to ruin it. Would you like a drink?"

I'm rambling, she thought. Good God. And he was looking

at her again in that calm, steady way. She went to the bar without waiting for his answer. She could use one, even if he couldn't.

"Do you want scotch?" she asked, pouring first from the vermouth decanter for herself. She felt his hands on her shoulders.

She didn't resist when he turned her, didn't lower her eyes when his looked into hers. Without speaking, he simply gathered her close and held her. With a shuddering sigh, she clung to him and felt the tension flow from her.

"Oh, Thorpe, I nearly went crazy without you. I need you." That in itself was an awesome admission. They both held on to it. Liv lifted her face to his. "Don't go," she murmured. "Don't go tonight."

She pressed her mouth to his. The world focused for her again. "Make love to me," she whispered. "Now, Thorpe. Right now."

His mouth still on hers, he lowered her to the couch. He touched her gently, feeling the shape of her through her clothes. Her body was pliant, willing to be explored. Her breath trembled on his tongue. With unbearable softness, he kissed her again and again until Liv felt the total capitulation of mind, body, spirit. She felt no aching drive, no desperation, only a warm, liquifying surrender.

He undressed her slowly, layer by layer, piece by piece, letting his fingertips linger on the point of her breast, on the curve of her hip. Liv sighed and relinquished everything. He was in command, to take her wherever he wished.

His touch was light, almost reverent as he stroked her. Even when he wandered to the heated skin of her inner thighs, he moved without hurry. She began to shudder, to arch under him, but he lingered only briefly at her moist center before roaming on.

He teased the tip of her breast with his tongue, then stopped to savor. Liv felt the passion shoot from the sensitive skin he tasted to the pit of her stomach. It pulled at her until her movements were less languid. But he wouldn't be rushed. His mouth took the same slow, aching journey his fingertips had—over and over her while her skin hummed then quivered, then flashed with heat.

She heard herself calling him in a voice that was rough with needs. Her body was no longer passive, but crying out for him. Only him. He took her, but slowly, while she clung to him mindlessly, a breath away from heaven. Then his mouth was on hers and they rocketed through space together.

13

"Hey." Thorpe nuzzled Liv's neck to wake her. "Going to sleep all day?"

She snuggled closer. "Um-hum." She kept her eyes shut. The feel of his body against her was all that she wanted at the moment. It could be night or morning or afternoon. She didn't care.

"It's after nine." He ran his hand down her back and heard her quiet sigh of pleasure. "We're going to spend the day in a boat, remember?"

Liv let her eyes open to slits. It was morning, she discovered. Saturday morning. And he was with her. With a sleepy smile, she tilted her face back to his. "Let's spend it in bed instead."

"The woman's lazy," he decided. And beautiful, he thought as he brushed the hair from her cheek. So achingly beautiful.

"Lazy?" Liv's left brow arched. "I've masses of untapped energy." Her voice was slow and heavy as she shut her eyes again. "Masses," she repeated, and yawned.

"Oh yes, I can see that. Should we go to the Mall and jog first?"

She opened her eyes again. "Oh, I've a much better idea."

He hadn't expected the kiss to be so ardent, or her move to be so quick. She was suddenly lying across his chest with her mouth on his. His sound of pleasure was muffled. Then she touched him. His pulse jumped from an easy rhythm to a racing pace in the space of seconds. His blood, cool from the night's rest, flamed headily. Her hands were urgent, unexpectedly aggressive, her mouth hungry on his skin. He was caught up in her quickly, before he could fully register that she was leading him.

His instant response seemed to fill her with power. Her mouth was greedy on his, demanding and drawing, then roaming on to his neck, his throat, his shoulders. Her tongue darted out, tracing over his chest, lingering over his nipples, and then on.

When did she become so strong? he wondered, dazed. Or was he suddenly weak? He needed to have her now. Now. He could feel the blood pounding, in his head, in his loins, in his fingertips. Pleasure was a pain clawing at his stomach.

But when he tried to roll her over, she shifted, straddling him and crushing his mouth with her own. He was suffocating, but he pulled her closer. She was in his lungs, in his pores. Her movements on top of him were driving him mad.

Then he was inside her. Sanity shattered. The world exploded. He could hear the thunder of it roaring inside his head until he thought he would never hear anything else. Then it was Liv's breathing—short, shallow. She seemed to melt onto him as the strength seeped from her. He shuddered once, then cradled the back of her head in his hand.

My woman, he thought almost fiercely as she rested against him, still trembling. He let himself lie still until the intensity passed. There was still a need to be cautious. "I suppose you want an apology."

"Hmm?" He could hear the bafflement in the sigh.

"For calling you lazy."

Liv laughed and clung to him, then shifted to his side. "It does seem to be in order," she agreed, and prepared to snuggle again. "You can give it to me when I wake up."

"Oh, no." Rising, Thorpe grabbed her and hauled her unceremoniously, unsympathetically from the bed. "Rowing," he said as she tried to scowl at him.

"You're an obsessed man."

"Absolutely." He smiled before he kissed her nose. "I'll let you have the shower first."

"Thanks."

Her gratitude seemed a trifle mordant, but he grinned at her as she shut the bathroom door behind her.

Thorpe slipped on his slacks and gave an idle thought to fixing coffee. Instead, he reached for the pack of cigarettes that lay on the table beside the bed. From there, he could hear Liv humming as she started up the water for her shower.

Picking up his lighter, Thorpe flicked it and got spark but no flame. Mildly annoyed, he glanced around for matches, then opened the narrow drawer in the table, thinking he might find some there.

The photograph caught his eye immediately. It drew his attention first because Liv's apartment was so conspicuously bare of photos or personal mementos, and second because the child smiling back at him was strikingly beautiful. Lifting it out, he studied it.

It was a small snapshot framed in silver. The boy was hardly more than a year old, full in the cheeks and grinning broadly. His thatch of black hair was thick and left to fall around his face in a style that suited the freewheeling smile. The eyes were dark, dark blue, nearly cobalt, and filled with a mixture of mischief and delight. Here was a child a stranger on the street would stop to smile at—a child aunts and uncles would have to spoil. You could almost hear the laughter that was ready to burst through the grin.

With the photo still in his hand, Thorpe sat on the bed.

"I hope I used all the hot water," Liv said from behind the door. "It would serve you right for dragging me out of bed at the crack of dawn on a Saturday." She opened the door and stood for a minute looking down as she belted her robe. "I don't smell any coffee. The least you can do when . . ."

Her voice trailed off as she looked up and saw what Thorpe held in his hand. He watched the laughter and color flow from her face.

"Liv." He started to explain the hunt for the matches, then stopped. The words would hardly matter, even if they penetrated. "Who is he?"

Thorpe could count a full ten seconds before her eyes lifted to his. He watched her swallow, saw her bottom lip tremble; but when she spoke, her voice was clear and strong. "My son."

He had known it the moment he had seen the photo. The resemblance was unmistakable. Yet he felt a thud of shock at her answer. Keeping his eyes level, he too spoke calmly. "Where is he?"

Her face was dead white now. He had never seen eyes so dark, so full of thoughts and secrets and pain. A ripple of emotion shook her. "He's dead."

Quickly, Liv turned to the closet and began pulling out clothes. She saw nothing more than a blur of colors. She chose at random with hands that were too numb to shake. Even when she felt him take her shoulders, she continued, pushing at hangers and pulling out a blouse.

"Liv." It took a firm hand to turn her.

"I have to get dressed if we're going." She shook her head, already warding off questions as she tried to break his grip.

"Stop it." The command was curt, and the shake he gave her was strong enough to draw a quick breath from her. "No, don't do that. Not now, not ever again. Not with me." Then, before she could speak, he pulled her against him and held her.

She might have withstood the command. But he was offering comfort, strength. She leaned into him, and her defenses crumbled.

"Come, sit down," he said, "and tell me about it."

With his arm still around her, Liv sat on the bed. The snapshot lay beside her. She picked it up and set it in her lap. He didn't press her further, sensing she needed a moment before she could begin.

"I was nineteen when I met Doug." Her viewers wouldn't have recognized her voice now. It was small and hesitant and threaded with emotion. "He was studying law. He had a scholarship. He was a brilliant man, very free spirited, yet intense about what he was going to do. He was going to be the best defense attorney in the country. Change the system from within the system, challenge windmills, fight dragons. That was Doug."

When he said nothing, Liv drew a deep breath and continued. Her voice grew stronger. "We were attracted to each other right away. Maybe partly because our backgrounds were so totally different and our ideals were so shiny. We sparked something in each other. And we were so young." She sighed, gathered strength and went on. "We married quickly, less than three months after we'd met. My family . . ." With a little laugh, she shook her head. "Well, leave it that they were surprised. Sometimes I'm afraid that might have been one of the reasons I married him. I don't like to think it was."

She stared off into middle distance, into her own memories. For a moment, Thorpe felt cut off from her. He shook the feeling off and continued to listen.

"It wasn't the sturdiest marriage—we were young and there were a lot of pressures. College. Doug was cramming for exams; I was interning at a local station and studying every spare minute. Money didn't matter much to either of us, luckily, because there wasn't a great deal of it. We had some good times, but Doug was . . ." She let out a long breath, as if searching for the proper words.

"He had a weakness for women. He loved me, I really believe he did in his own way, but he had a difficult time with fidelity. None of his—slips ever meant anything to him, and I wasn't very sexually experienced."

Thorpe found himself forced to choke words back. He didn't want to interrupt her now that she was talking, really talking, but the urge to curse the man she had married was almost too powerful to resist. He could remember very clearly her telling him, the first time they had made love, that she wasn't very good at pleasing a partner. Now, at least, he understood how the notion had been planted. He kept quiet and listened.

"We had Joshua within the year—hardly a year after we had first met. My family thought we were mad, starting a family so quickly and with an income far below what any of them could conceive trying to live on. But we both wanted a baby. We both wanted Josh. It seemed, for a time, he'd center our lives. He was so special." Her eyes fell to the photo in her lap. "I know all mothers think that about their babies, but he was so beautiful, so good-natured. He hardly ever cried."

She saw the tear fall onto the glass of the frame and squeezed her eyes shut. "We both adored him. It was impossible not to. For almost a year, we were happy. Really, really happy. Doug was a tremendous father. No job was too small or too demeaning. I remember once he woke me up, absolutely beside himself with pride when he had discovered Josh had cut a tooth."

Liv said nothing for nearly a full minute. Thorpe didn't want to prompt her. He understood her need to continue at her own pace. Keeping his arm around her, he waited.

"After I had graduated, we moved to New Jersey. Doug had a position with a small law firm, and I had landed a job with WTRL. I had the night desk at first. It wasn't easy on either of us. We were both just starting out, taking career crumbs, working obscene hours, raising the baby between us. I don't think Josh suffered. It certainly didn't seem so, he was such a happy baby. I was with him all day; Doug took over in the evening and put him to bed. Then, there was an incident with a law clerk Doug was attracted to. A small slip; he hadn't had one in a year. I overlooked it." She shrugged. "Tried to overlook it," she corrected herself. "He blamed himself enough for it in any case. We tried to put things back together. We had the baby to think of. Nothing was more important to either one of us than Josh.

"Finally, I got off the night shift and onto days. I started reading the weather and doing a few minor reports. We spent a lot of time finding a sitter who satisfied both of us. Even then, we disagreed. Doug wanted me to stop working and stay home with Josh. I wouldn't do it." She pressed her fingers to her eyes a moment, then laid them back in her lap. "He was so well adjusted, so content. I loved him more than anything else in the world, but it didn't seem necessary, or even wise, for me to stop work, give up my career to be with him every minute. There were financial considerations, and my own needs. And I didn't want to smother him."

Her voice lost its strength and started to waver. "It was so tempting to just stay with him, spoil him. Doug used to say if I had my way I would have kept him a baby forever. I always thought he was trying to make Josh grow up too quickly. It was really sweet the way he'd buy him a football and talk about two-wheelers when Josh was only eighteen months old. But then he bought this huge swing set on Josh's second birthday. It terrified me, all those high bars. We argued about it a bit—not seriously. He laughed and called my overprotective. Then I laughed because Doug had been the one to research car seats for three weeks before he'd bought one. If I'd . . . If I'd stuck to my instincts, everything might have been different."

Liv stared down at the picture a moment; then, she pressed it to her breast. "The sitter called me at work to tell me Josh had taken a tumble from the swing. Just a bump on the head, she said, but I dropped everything, called Doug and rushed home. He'd gotten there even before I had. Josh seemed fine, but both of us were panicked. We took him straight to the emergency room at the hospital. I remember sitting there while he was being X-rayed. This big room, with all these black plastic chairs, metal ashtrays, and overhead lights. The floor tile was black with white speckles in it. I counted them and Doug paced.

"When the doctor came out, he took us both into this little room. He had a gentle voice. It terrified me. I could see it in his eyes before he said anything, but I wouldn't believe it. It wasn't possible." She pressed her hand to her mouth to try to keep the sobs from breaking through. Every detail was flooding back over her, and with them, all the pain. "I didn't believe it when he told us Josh had thrown an embolism. He was gone. Just like that."

Liv rocked back and forth, the photo pressed close as the sobs began to tear at her throat. "I don't even know what happened then. I got hysterical; they sedated me. The next thing I remember clearly was being at home. Doug was devastated. We couldn't seem to do each other any good. Instead, we lashed out. We said terrible things. He blamed me for not staying home watching our child. Caring for him. If I had been there, then maybe . . . And I clawed back. He'd bought the swing set. The damned swing set that had killed my baby."

"Liv." He wanted to wipe it all out—the pain, the grief, even the memories. She had the photo pressed against her breast as if she would try to bring it to life with her own heartbeat. What comfort could he offer? Not words; there weren't any. He could only hold her.

She dashed at the tears in her eyes as Thorpe drew her closer. Now that it was coming out, it was far from finished.

She was functioning only on emotion now, and it had to run its course. "Greg came. He was Josh's godfather, our closest friend. God knows we needed somebody; our world had just fallen apart. He kept us from hurting each other more, but the damage was done. Josh was dead."

She gave a long sigh that rippled through her and had her shoulders trembling under his arm. "He was dead, and nothing could change it. There wasn't any blame. An accident. Just an accident."

She was silent for a long time. He could sense she was gathering her strength to continue. He wanted the pain to stop, wanted to help her close it off in the past where it had to stay. But even before he could speak, she continued.

"Greg took care of the arrangements—the funeral. I wasn't coping with it well. They were giving me something; I don't even know what it was. That first week, Doug and I were like zombies. My family came, but they didn't know me. They hadn't known Josh as I had. Every day I expected to walk by his room and hear him playing. I went back to work because I couldn't bear staying in the house waiting for him to wake up."

The tears were flowing as she spoke. Her voice was raw with grief. Whatever Thorpe had expected to find beneath the guards, it hadn't been this. She was blind with it now. He didn't think she was aware of him any longer, or the arm that kept her close.

"The marriage was over. We both knew it, but we couldn't seem to bring ourselves to say the words. It was as if we were both thinking that if we hung on, he'd come back. We were polite to each other, tiptoeing around. I wanted someone to hold on to, someone to tell me . . . I don't know what words I needed to hear, but he didn't have them. I don't suppose I had them for him. We shared the same bed and never touched each other. We lived like that for over a month. Once I—once I asked him to come into Josh's room with me to help me—help me sort through his things. I knew I couldn't do it alone, and that it had to be done. He left the house, and didn't come back all night. He couldn't face it, and I couldn't face it alone. I had to call Greg, and we . . ." She pressed the heel of her hand to her forehead and tried not to choke over the words. "Doug and I never spoke of it again.

"Then Melinda came, my sister. She'd been fond of Josh. She used to send him useless, expensive little toys. Her being there seemed to help for a while. She was a distraction. She made us get out of the house, forced us to entertain her and keep our minds off . . . everything. I think it helped me, because I began to realize that Doug and I were only hurting each other by keeping up the pretense of being married. We had to stop. I decided to ask for a divorce before one of us did something unforgivable. It wasn't easy. I thought about it for days.

"I came home early one afternoon because I wanted to have a little time to sort out what I would say. I'd made up my mind to talk to Doug that night. When I got there, Doug's car was in the drive. I thought he might have been ill and come home. When I went upstairs, I found him in bed with my sister."

Very gently, she laid the photo back in her lap. "It was the final blow. My sister, my home, my bed. I left before either of them could say anything. I didn't want to hear. I didn't want to say the horrible things that I knew I'd say if I waited. I went to a motel. That's when I made up my mind that my parents had been right all along. If you live calmly, without disturbing your life with emotional attachments, you can't be hurt. That's how I was going to live. From that moment. No one, nothing, was ever going to take me to that point again. I'd had enough pain. I filed for divorce right away. Doug asked Greg to handle it for me. I never even spoke to him again, except through Greg. After a while I began to realize that Doug had just taken the step before I had. He'd used Melinda to end something that was killing both of us. That made it easier to forgive him. And because we'd had, and lost, something extraordinary together."

On the last word, she began to weep passionately, uncontrollably. As she turned into Thorpe, his arms cradled her to hold her until the grief passed.

14

There was the faintest of breezes over the water. It rippled over the reflections in the Potomac and just stirred Liv's hair. Now that they were there, stretched out under the sky, Thorpe was glad he had persuaded Liv to come. The sun and the activity would be good for her. Another woman, he thought, would have wanted to sleep off the strain of that much weeping. Not Liv.

She was still pale. Her eyes showed traces of the tears they had spent. But there was an unmistakable aura of strength about her. Thorpe admired her for it even as he loved her for it. Now, he felt he could understand why she had iced herself over. He had seen the face of the boy in the photograph—a face full of life and undiluted joy. He ached for her, for her loss. It was difficult for him to imagine Liv married, having a son, building a life with another man. A small house in the suburbs, a fenced yard, toys under the sofa—all of that seemed a world apart from the woman who sat across from him now. And yet, that had been her life not so many years before. It could be her life again, this time with him. Thorpe wanted it for her, and for himself.

More than ever, he knew there would be a need to move slowly with her. She was strong, yes, but she had been terribly hurt.

Doug, he thought, and experienced one moment of blazing anger. He didn't forgive as easily as Liv. The man, as he saw it, had done more than lose Liv through his own weaknesses. He had scarred her. Now it was up to Thorpe to show her, convince her that he meant to stand beside her. Always.

From where Liv sat, she could watch Thorpe row. His muscles rippled. There seemed to be no effort in the skill and strength he used to guide the boat over the river. He wasn't a man who had to flex his biceps to prove he was strong or masculine. He knew himself, and his confidence came from that knowledge.

So she had told him. Years had gone by since she had opened herself like that to anyone. There was nothing he didn't know about her now. Why had she told him? Perhaps, she mused, because she had known—or hoped—he would still be there when she had finished. And he had been: no questions, no advice, only support. He had known what she needed. When had she discovered what an unusual man he was? And why had it taken her so long? She felt relaxed and safe, and more at ease with herself than she could remember. The tears and the telling had purged the pain. For a moment, she closed her eyes and let her body enjoy the cleansing of her mind.

"I haven't thanked you," she said into the quiet.

"For what?" He brought the oars up and back in a long, steady stroke.

"For being there, and for not saying all those tidy little words people say when someone falls apart."

"You were hurting." His eyes were on hers again, looking deep. "Nothing I could say can erase what happened or make it easier. But I'm here now."

"I know." Liv sighed and leaned back. "I know."

They rowed for a time in silence. There were other boats here and there, dotting the river, but they didn't come close enough to exchange waves or greetings. It might have been their own private stream in their own private world.

"It's still early enough in the spring," Thorpe said, "that the river isn't crowded. I like to come at dawn in the summer, when the light's just breaking. It's amazing how quiet all those buildings look at sunrise. You can forget there'll be throngs of tourists tramping up the monument or packing into the Smithsonian. At dawn, it's hard to think about what's going on in the Pentagon or the Capitol. They're just buildings, rather unique, sometimes beautiful. On a Saturday or Sunday, when I haven't got a story weighing me down, I can just row, and forget all the times I've climbed the stairs, ridden the elevators and opened the doors in all those buildings."

"Funny," Liv mused. "A month or two ago, I would have been surprised to hear you say that. I pictured you as a man with one driving ambition, totally focused on his job, and his job alone. I never would have imagined you needing to get away from it, to separate yourself from the pace."

He smiled and continued to stroke steadily through the water. "And now?"

"And now I know you." She sat up and let the wind catch her hair. "When did you discover that rowing was your alternative to ulcer pills?"

He laughed, both amused and pleased. "You do know me. When I got back from the Middle East. It was hard over there. It was hard coming back. I imagine most soldiers feel the same way. Adjusting to normality isn't always easy. I started working out my frustrations this way, and found it became a habit."

"It suits you," Liv decided. "The understated physicality." She grinned as he arched a brow. "I don't imagine it's as simple as you make it look."

"Want to give it a try?"

She smiled and settled back. "Oh, that's all right. I'm better at spectator sports."

"It doesn't take much coordination," he added. Her eyes, which had begun to close, opened again. "Any kid with a week at summer camp can manage it." He was baiting her purposefully. He wanted to see that gleam of competition back in her eyes.

"I'm sure I could manage it just fine."

"Come on then," he invited, and locked the oars. "Give it a try."

She wasn't at all certain she wanted to, but the challenge was difficult to avoid. "Do you really think we should switch around? I wouldn't like to capsize in the middle of the Potomac."

"The boat's well balanced," he said easily. "If you are."

She stood up at that, though warily. "All right, Thorpe, move aside."

They changed positions with a minimum of fuss. Thorpe settled down on the small cushioned seat and watched Liv grip the oars. "Don't put a lot of power into it," he advised as she struggled for a moment to unlock them. "Just keep it as smooth as you can."

"I went to summer camp," she said sweetly, then scowled as her arms refused to coordinate with each other. "But then, usually we used canoes. I'm great with a paddle. There." She managed one shaky but reasonable stroke. "Now I'll get my rhythm. Take that smirk off your face, Thorpe," she added, and put all her concentration into her task.

Liv could feel twinges from muscles she hadn't put to use in years. It was a good, cleansing feeling. She could count to eight with each stroke and feel her shoulders strain then give with the movement. The oars scraped against her palms.

Oh yes, she thought, I can see why he does it. They were moving—not as cleanly as before, but moving nonetheless through the water under her power. There was no engine, no sail, no dependence on anything but her own effort. Her body, her will and the oars. Yes she understood exactly what he meant. She believed she could have rowed for miles.

"Okay, Carmichael, time's up."

"Are you kidding? I just got started." She sent him a grim look and kept rowing.

"Ten minutes is enough the first time out. Besides"—he scooted across to her when she paused—"I don't want you to ruin your hands. I like them the way they are."

"I like yours." Taking his palm, she pressed it to her cheek.

"Liv." It was impossible to believe he could love her more at that moment than he had the moment before. Yet he did. Locking the oars, he drew her close to his side.

It was late afternoon before they walked back into Liv's apartment building. Each carried a paper sack filled with groceries.

"I know how to roast a chicken," Liv insisted, pushing the

button for her floor. "You put it in the oven and turn it on for a couple of hours. Nothing to it."

"Please." He gave her a pained look. "It might hear you." He cradled the sack that held the chicken more protectively. "There's an art to these things, Liv. Seasoning, timing, preparation. If a chicken's going to give up its life for your consumption, the least you can do is have a little respect."

"I don't think I like the tone of this conversation." She glanced dubiously at his grocery bag. "Why don't we just send out for pizza?"

"I'm going to show you what a master can do with a two-pound roaster." Thorpe waited until they had stepped out of the elevator. "And then I'm going to make love to you until Sunday morning."

"Oh." Liv gave this a moment's thought and struggled with a pleased smile. "Only till then?"

"Until very late Sunday morning," he added, stopping to kiss her before she could locate her keys. "Maybe," he murmured against her mouth, "until very early Sunday afternoon."

"I'm beginning to appreciate the idea of this cooking lesson a bit more."

He let his lips wander to her ear. "I'm beginning to appreciate the idea of sending out for pizza. Later." His mouth came back to hers. "Much, much later."

"Let's go inside and take a vote."

"Mmm, I like your thinking."

"It's the Washington influence," she told him as she slipped her key into the lock. "There's no issue that can't be resolved with a vote."

"Tell that to the senators who are waiting for Donahue and his filibuster to run out of steam."

She laughed and turned the knob. "I'll tell you something, Thorpe," she said as she closed the door behind them. "I don't want to think about senators or filibusters." She shifted the bag in her arm so that she could bring her body close to his. "I don't even want to think about that two-pound roaster you're so crazy about."

"No?" His free arm came around her. "Why don't you tell me what you do want to think about?"

With a smile, she began to undo the buttons of his shirt. "Why don't I show you instead? A good video reporter knows that action's worth a thousand words."

He felt her cool, long fingers roam down his chest. He set down his bag, then took hers and let it lean against the closed door. "I've always said, Carmichael, you're a hell of a reporter." Her laugh was smothered against his mouth.

It was late Sunday evening. Liv sat close to Thorpe on the sofa. The entire weekend, she thought, had been like a dream. She had shared with him more than she had ever intended to share with anyone. But then, he had come to mean more to her than she had intended to allow anyone to mean to her again.

Last night, they'd laughed through the cooking and eating of dinner. It was so easy to laugh with him. So easy, when she was with him, to forget all the vows she had once made. He loved her. The knowledge still staggered her. This tough, relentless man loved her. He'd shown her gentleness and understanding—traits she had needed but had never thought to find in him. How different her life would have been if she had found him all those years ago.

But no . . . Liv closed her eyes. That would be like wishing Joshua out of existence. She wouldn't give up the memory of those brief years for anything. He'd been the focus of her world. Her child.

Perhaps because her time with him had been concentrated into two short years, she could remember almost every detail of it. Loving like that was the greatest wonder a woman could know. And the greatest danger. She'd promised herself never to experience it again.

Now there was Thorpe. What sort of life would she have with him? What sort would she have without him? Both of the questions, and their answers, frightened her.

Already, she thought as her head stayed nestled on his shoulder, he's gotten close enough to frighten me. I'm not certain I can turn back now. . . . I'm not certain I can go ahead. If things could go on just as they are . . . But the time was fast approaching when she would have to make a move, one way or the other.

He knows what he wants, she mused. There isn't a doubt in his mind. I wish I could see things as clearly.

"You're quiet," he murmured.

"I know."

"Yesterday morning's catching up with you." He wanted to draw her closer, to make her forget, but forgetting wasn't the answer for either of them. "It couldn't have been easy for you, talking it all through, feeling it all again."

"No, it wasn't easy." She tilted her head to look up at him. Her face was in shadows, but her eyes were clear on his. "But I'm glad it happened. I'm glad you know. Thorpe . . ." She let out a little breath. It was becoming more and more important that he know everything. "There was a time, right after Josh died, that I wanted to die too. I didn't want to live without him; I couldn't conceive of living without him. There wasn't enough strength in me to do anything solid about it, but if I could have died, just closed my eyes and died, I would have."

"Liv." He lifted a hand to her cheek. "I can't pretend to know what it's like to lose a child. That kind of grief can't be understood by anyone who hasn't experienced it."

"I didn't die," she continued, swallowing. "I ate, I slept, I functioned. But I buried part of myself with Josh. What was left, I smothered when I divorced Doug. It seemed the only way to survive. I've lived this way a long time, without considering any changes."

"But you didn't die, Liv." His hand slipped down to cup her chin. His eyes were direct on hers. "And changes are a part of living."

"Have you ever loved someone completely?"

"Just you," he said simply.

"Oh, Thorpe." Liv pressed her face against his shoulder. Emotion squeezed her heart. The words came so easily to him, and the feelings. She wasn't certain she was strong enough yet to accept them. "I need you. It scares me to death." She lifted her face again and her eyes were eloquent. "I know what it is to lose. I'm not sure I can survive a second time."

He was so close, so close to having her. He could feel it. If he took her in his arms, if he kissed her now, he might urge the words he needed from her lips. They were in her eyes. It took every ounce of his control not to push. Not today, he told himself. She's given you enough this weekend.

"Needing someone," he said carefully, "doesn't mean you have to lose them."

"I'm trying to believe that." She took a deep breath. "For the first time in five years, I want to believe that. It matters, when I thought it never would again."

After a moment, he lifted her hand and pressed the palm to his lips. "How much time do you want?"

The tears came instantly, silently. She hadn't had to ask. He had known. He was giving her what she needed with no questions, no demands. "I don't deserve you." She shook her head. "I really don't."

"That's my risk, isn't it?" He smiled. "In my opinion, I deserve you completely, so that balances things."

"I need to do some thinking." She kissed him, then held on. "I have to be alone, because you make it hard for me to think."

"Do I?" He kissed her again. "All right," he agreed, pulling her with him as he rose. "But think fast."

"Tomorrow." She held him close for another moment. "Just until tomorrow." The arms around her had such strength. The man had so much to give. "Oh, God, am I a fool, Thorpe?"

"Yeah." He drew her back to frame her face in his hands. "I'm a hell of a catch, Carmichael; just remember that."

"I will," she murmured as he walked to the door. He paused, and turned back with his hand on the knob.

"Tomorrow."

"Tomorrow," she repeated when she was alone.

15

Things were not as clear as Liv would have liked them to be. Once before she had thought herself in love, and she had been wrong. What she had felt for Doug had been the impulses and dreams of youth. She was older now, and more cautious. Perhaps too cautious, she mused as she settled behind her desk. Yet, when she told Thorpe she loved him, she wanted to say the words without any cloud of doubt. He deserved that from her.

She didn't want to lose him. That above all was crystal clear. He had become the focal point of her life in a very short time. Dependence. No, she couldn't deny that she was dependent on him. But was that love?

Was it love when a man kept drifting into your mind? When you began to associate the tiny details of your day with thoughts of him? When you stored up the little pieces to share with him?

Liv could remember what it was like to lie beside him in the morning—the quiet, the warmth, the easy unity. She could remember how a look in his eyes could make her tremble with need even in a crowded room.

Was she in love with him? Why was she searching for another name for what she felt? The truth had been locked inside her for days. Now it was time to accept it. If she was going to ask Thorpe to take a risk, she had to be willing to take one herself. Love equaled vulnerability. He could hurt her, undoubtedly would from time to time. The shield was gone now. She would never be able to hide behind it again. Abruptly, she realized she didn't want to. What she wanted could be said in one word: Thorpe.

"Liv!"

She turned to the frantic assignment editor with a brilliant smile. "Yes, Chester." It was going to be a beautiful day.

"Take a crew. On the double. New Senate Office Building. Some guy, unidentified, is holding three hostages, including Senator Wyatt, in the senator's office."

"Good God." She was up, grabbing a pad and her purse. "Anybody hurt?"

"Not yet. As far as we know," he added, streaking toward Carl's office. "There's been some gunfire. Be careful. We want a bulletin fast."

"Twenty minutes." She was already out the door.

The Capitol Police had the building surrounded when Liv arrived. She glanced around for telltale signs of Secret Service men and FBI. When you knew what to look for, they stood out clearly. On the rooftops of neighboring buildings, she caught glimpses of sharpshooters taking position. Men armed with ugly-looking guns were going over strategy and positions on two-ways. The press area was already partitioned off and jammed with reporters and technicians. Everyone was talking at once, demanding answers, trying to sneak their way through the barricade to secure a closer position.

Liv pushed her way through and managed to get a mike out to a nearby uniformed officer. "Olivia Carmichael, WWBW. Can you give us a rundown on what's happened? Do you have an identification on the man who's holding Senator Wyatt? What are his demands?"

"He's a former aide; that's all I can tell you." That's all you *will* tell me, Liv corrected, noting the flicker in his eye. "He hasn't made any demands yet."

"How many weapons does he have? How did he get inside the building?"

"We don't know. We're only sure about the handgun. He isn't even answering the phone yet."

Liv was left with little more than nothing in the midst of a pack of hungry reporters. She had to find someone else—

with a looser tongue. She could manage a quick bulletin, but she was going to have to do a lot of digging to put anything solid on the air.

Senator Wyatt. Liv remembered him very well from the embassy party. Jovial, pink-cheeked Senator Wyatt who had joked with her and told her to dance with Thorpe. She glanced across the street and studied the dozens of windows. It didn't seem possible he was in one of those rooms with a gun held to his head.

On the edge of the crowd, Liv spotted a familiar face. It was the receptionist who had kept her cooling her heels for two hours in an office two floors below Senator Wyatt's only a few days before.

"Ms. Bingham." Liv blessed the two hours and the innumerable cups of coffee she had consumed in the woman's office. "Olivia Carmichael. WWBW."

"Oh, Ms. Carmichael, isn't it dreadful!" She stared up at the windows with her eyes wide and stunned. "They've cleared the whole building. I just can't believe it! Poor Senator Wyatt."

"Do you know who's holding him?"

"It's Ed. Ed Morrow. Who would have thought it? Why, I've ridden in the elevator with him just dozens of times." She lifted her hand to her throat at the memory. "I heard the senator had to let him go last week, but . . ."

"Why?" Liv had the mike under her arm and was scribbling quickly on her pad. The woman never seemed to notice.

"I'm not sure. Rumor is Ed got himself tangled up in gambling—something illegal. He's always so polite. Who would have thought it?"

"The senator fired him?"

"Just last week." She nodded quickly three times, and her eyes were still wide. "He was supposed to clear out his desk today. He must have gone crazy. Sally said he shot twice in the hallway."

"Sally?"

"The senator's secretary. She was just down the hall when it happened. If she had been in the office . . ." She swallowed and fixed her eyes back on the building. "He's fired twice through the window since I've been out here. Do you think the senator's going to be all right?"

"I'm sure he's going to be fine." Even as Liv said the words, the sharp report of gunfire split the air.

"Oh God!" The receptionist gripped Liv's arm. "Is he killing them? He must be killing them!"

"No, no." Liv felt the cool lick of fear. "He's just shooting out of the window. It's going to be all right." She had to corroborate the woman's identifications of the gunman before she put it on the air. That was the job—one step at a time. She couldn't think about what was happening to the people inside. Not yet. "Is the senator's secretary still here?"

"She had to go with the police. She's back there somewhere."

"All right, thank you." Quickly, Liv began to work her way through the crowd again. Spying Dutch, she headed straight for him. If anyone could give her the details, he could.

It was closer to half an hour than the twenty minutes she had promised, but Liv delivered a straightforward, detailed stand-up with pans of the police and the crowd. The building across the street was quiet—too quiet for her liking. She would almost have preferred another volley of gunfire to the silence. Terror, she realized abruptly, was always silent.

"When the hell is he going to do something?" Bob muttered beside her. The tension was seeping into them all—police, bystanders, press. Everyone was waiting for the next move. "Major league coming up," he added. "There's T.C."

"I'll be right back," Liv told him. "Make sure the engineer's ready to patch us into the station if anything goes down." She made for Thorpe like a homing pigeon heading for roost. "Thorpe."

"Liv." He touched her cheek briefly. "I figured you'd be here."

"Is there anything new?" she asked, knowing there was more than a story involved this time. They both knew the man inside.

"They've established communications with Morrow. Wyatt's not hurt; neither are the aides. Yet. He doesn't seem to be quite rational. One minute he wants a half million in cash and a plane, the next gold and an armored car. He changes his mind every time they talk to him."

"How the hell did he get in there with a gun?" she demanded.

Thorpe gave a quick, mirthless laugh. His eyes never left the building across the street. "It isn't difficult for someone security's used to seeing to pass through. He had it in his jacket, I imagine, or it was already in his desk." He shifted impatiently. Liv could tell he wanted to move, wanted to do something. "I'd feel better if he were a professional. In the state he's in, it's too easy for him to make a mistake and take the hostages down with him." He swore with a quiet urgency she rarely heard from him. "He wanted to make certain he was getting full media coverage."

"You don't really think he's doing it for the publicity, do you?" The thought appalled her.

Thorpe shook his head. "I've dealt with him several times when I've set up meetings." He took out a cigarette. "He's a taut, hungry little man. A good mind, but the nerves show."

"Gambling, I'm told."

"So the stories go." Thorpe drew on the cigarette and let out a quick stream of smoke. "Too quiet," he muttered. "Too damn quiet."

Tension was palpable. It increased, almost visibly, as the minutes dragged by. How long, she wondered, could the taut, hungry little man Thorpe had described stand up under the strain? He'd taken an irrevocable step. How much further would he go? She waited, like the others, to find out.

"Thorpe." Liv recognized the man from the Secret Service, and frowned when he singled Thorpe out. "Chief Daniels wants you."

"Sure." Thorpe crushed another cigarette under his heel. "Her too," he added with a jerked thumb at Liv. "We're a team."

Liv bit back a smile. That was quite a change. Without a word, she followed behind them.

The communications van was set up well away from the press area. She glanced briefly at the equipment, the tape recorders, two-ways, phones, the men working in shirt sleeves. What could they want with Thorpe? she wondered. This had nothing to do with the press.

Chief Daniels pushed his glasses back onto his weary face.

"T.C., Morrow's demanding to speak to you directly. You game?"

"Sure."

"The tape'll be running. Be careful what you say. If he makes any demands, don't promise, don't negotiate. Leave that to us." He spoke quickly and without inflection, but Liv caught the undercurrents. He didn't like this new twist. "You're not in a position to give him anything he wants. He's smart enough to know that. Whatever he asks for, you just tell him that you'll check and get back to him. Understood?"

"Understood."

He glanced at Liv and focused in on her press badge.

"She's with me," Thorpe told him easily.

"None of this goes on the air until I give the word." His eyes were hard, and close to hostile. "We're not going to give him a media free-for-all."

"Understood," Liv said calmly, then watched as Thorpe was handed a receiver.

"We'll ring." Daniels signaled one of his men. "Keep him talking as long as you can. If things start to get out of hand, we'll take over."

Thorpe nodded and heard Morrow pick up the phone on the first ring.

"T.C.?"

"Yeah. How you doing, Ed?"

Morrow laughed shakily. "Terrific. You going to do a report on me?"

"That's right. You want to tell me why you're up there and what it'll take to get you down?"

"You remember that day we sat in my office and talked about the Birds when Wyatt was held up in a meeting?"

"Sure." Thorpe caught a glimpse of Daniels's grim face as he held a headset to his ear. "End of last summer. The Orioles were fighting for first place." He drew out another cigarette and flicked on his lighter. "Seen any games this year?"

Liv could hear the echo of the frantic laugh come through the receiver. "I've already dropped twenty-five big ones on games this year."

"That's rough. You need money?" Thorpe's eyes were locked on Daniels's now. "Is that what you want for Wyatt's release?"

"I'll tell you all about it T.C., but just you. You come in and do one of your interviews right here. I've got an exclusive for you."

Liv could hear snatches, and what she heard was enough to have her grabbing Thorpe's arm in panic. Ignoring her, Thorpe kept his eye on Daniels.

"Too many hostages," Daniels said in an undertone.

"That'll give you one more hostage, Ed," Thorpe replied easily. "Doesn't seem like a very good deal."

"No, no, I see your point." Morrow's voice shook with nerves. "Maybe I'll send out the two aides for you. If you tell me you're coming up. You're as good as your word, aren't you, T.C.?"

"Two for one," Thorpe mused, watching Daniels steadily while Liv gripped his arm tighter and shook her head. "But then, the aides don't mean much, do they?"

There was a long pause. Liv could feel the sweat beginning to trickle down her back.

"You come up, alone, no back-up, and I'll send out Wyatt. How's that for a deal? A one-time offer, T.C. You're not going to turn down a scoop like this, are you?"

"I'll have to check back with the big shots at CNC, Ed. Give me ten minutes. I'll get back to you."

"Ten minutes," Morrow agreed, and cut the connection.

Liv grabbed Thorpe's jacket and turned him to face her. "No." She shook her head frantically while her eyes mirrored her fear. "You can't. You can't think of doing such a thing. Thorpe, you can't."

"Hold on a minute." His voice was calm and practical as he set her aside. "Well?" he said simply to Daniels.

"Number one, we can't ask you to cooperate."

"So you're not asking," Thorpe countered. "What then?"

"People I have to talk to before we consider making an exchange like his." Daniels rubbed a hand over his mouth. He didn't like the taste of it. But there was a senator involved. Touchy, he thought. Very touchy.

"Then start talking to them," Thorpe suggested.

Daniels sent him a long look. "You'd better do some thinking while I do. It's not going to be a cozy interview."

"Thorpe." Liv's voice quavered with panic. She knew that look in his eyes. "No."

Thorpe took her gently by the shoulders. "Liv," he began.

"No, no, listen to me." She gripped the front of his jacket. "It's insane. You can't just walk in there; you're not trained for this sort of thing. And who's to say he'll let Wyatt go when you do? He'll—he'll have more bargaining power then. You must see that."

"He wants to talk," Thorpe pointed out, and started to lead her away. "Wyatt can't get him national coverage; I can."

"Oh God, Thorpe, he's not stable." She was weeping now and unaware of it. "He'll kill you, and the senator too. You don't have to go. They can't make you."

"No one's making me." He signaled a member of his crew and spoke in undertones. "Call the desk. Tell them I'm going to do an interview with Morrow in exchange for the hostages. Get a camera on the building in about ten minutes; some of them should be coming out. I'll need a tape recorder."

"No!" Liv's voice rose now, in direct contrast to his. She clutched at him as if she could hold him from what he intended to do. "You can't. Please, listen to me."

"Liv." He brushed the hair back from her face. "You'd do the same thing. It's part of the job."

"Your life isn't worth a Pulitzer."

He lifted a brow. "Some might disagree with that."

"Damn it, Thorpe." She had to think fast; she had to be rational or he'd never listen. "It's probably just a trick. He can let the two aides go, and with you and Wyatt, he'll have two important people. He must realize that the network would negotiate for your release. It's just the sort of thing he's looking for."

"Maybe. Maybe not." He kissed her then to quiet her, and then because he needed to.

"Oh, please, don't go." She clung to him, knowing she had already lost and unable to accept it. "I love you." Slowly, he reached up to take her shoulders and draw her back far enough to see her face. It was tear-streaked and desperate. "I love you," she repeated. "It's tomorrow, Thorpe. Stay with me."

"God." He rested his forehead on hers and let the feeling seep through him. He pulled her close again, bruisingly close. "Your timing, Carmichael, is incredible." When he kissed her again, he felt her lips tremble under his. "We're going to talk about this later. We're going to talk about it for a long time." He drew her away and smiled at her. "You'd better give your station the latest developments or you're going to find yourself scooped."

"Why won't you listen to me?" She was angry now as well as desperate. Even her love hadn't swayed him. "You can't go in there. I need you." She didn't care if the words were unfair, as long as they prevented him from crossing the street.

"I need you too, Liv. That doesn't have anything to do with me doing my job, or with you doing yours."

She didn't want logic; she only wanted him. She clutched at him fiercely. "I'm going to marry you."

He smiled again and kissed her nose. "I've known that for months. You're just a bit slow." Glancing up, he noted the camera pointing in their direction. "And now several hundred thousand people know it too."

"I don't care." Her penchant for privacy seemed suddenly absurd. "Thorpe, you can't ask me to face losing you." She grabbed the lapels of his jacket in hands that were damp with fear. "Damn you, I can't face it! I can't face it all again. I won't."

His grip was firmer now, and his eyes intense. "You listen to me. I love you, more than anything. Don't you forget it. We live with risk every day; if we don't, we're already dead. It hurts to be alive, Liv."

Pale and calm, she faced him. "I'll never forgive you if you do this. I never wanted to love you. Now that I do, you're asking me to stand by and wait to lose you. I won't forgive you for that."

He watched her steadily. He saw the pain and the panic. He didn't want to hurt her. He would have done anything in this power to keep that look from her eyes, but he couldn't alter who he was or what he was. "Maybe you should think about who you fell in love with, Olivia. I haven't changed. I'm exactly as I was, and exactly as I'll be tomorrow. Now I've got a job to do. So do you."

"Thorpe—"

"Come on." He cut her off and began to lead her back. "Daniels should have finished talking to his people by now."

Liv stood back and watched, helpless, as Thorpe, Daniels and Morrow made the final negotiations for the exchange. There was nothing she could say, nothing she could do to stop him. He had told her she would do the same thing. She understood it, but it didn't matter. He was her love, her life. Everything that was important to her was bound up in him.

It's not fair! she thought on a fresh surge of desperation. She'd been given her second chance. Now she had to stand back and watch while it was put on the line. Myra's words played back in her head: life's not short, but it's never long enough. *Thorpe!* Her whole being cried out to him while she dug her teeth into her lip to keep silent. *Don't go! I have so much to say to you. So much time to make up for.* She wanted to tell him what he meant to her, how he had opened up everything she had closed.

Thorpe was checking the tape recorder as he listened to Daniels's instructions. Liv watched them, her eyes blinded by tears. Oh, Thorpe, she thought, I can't face the emptiness again. Not now that I know what it is to have you. I need to know you're there when I reach out. I want to love again, to hold your child in my arms. Oh, please, don't shut me off when I've just started to feel.

With a deep shuddering breath, she pressed her fingers to her eyes. She watched him again—the sharp athletic profile, the deep, intense eyes. *Is he frightened?* What's going on in his mind? Is he remembering that none of us is indestructible? But you have to be, Thorpe. For me. For us.

What does he need from me? *Not this,* she realized abruptly. He needs support, not a hysterical woman pulling at him, begging him to think of her. He needs his wits about him now. . . . If only I could go with him. But I can't. I can't *go* with him, but I can *send* something with him.

As she watched, the two aides were hustled out of the building and out of range. So Morrow had kept the first part of the bargain. There was only Wyatt now. Thorpe for Wyatt.

Drawing on all her strength, Liv stepped up to him. "Thorpe."

He turned to her. There were still tears on her cheeks, but he recognized the control.

"You always did go out of your way to scoop me on a story," she managed in a reasonably steady voice. "I hope this one's worth it. You better do a hell of a job in there. I need the copy for my broadcast."

He grinned as he kissed her. "Just don't step too close to my turf, Carmichael."

Liv clung for one last moment. "Catch my report at five-thirty."

"I've always been fond of you, T.C.," Daniels commented. "And it seems this lady is too." He gave Thorpe a long look. "You've still got time to back out."

"Thorpe walk away from an exclusive?" Liv pulled back and ordered herself not to shake. "You don't know him very well."

"You." He pulled Liv back a last time. "Think about where you want to spend your honeymoon. I lean toward Paris."

"You warned me you were a romantic." Then he was turning, preparing to cross the street. "Thorpe!" Liv couldn't prevent herself from calling out. When he turned she held back the plea and smiled at him. "If you get yourself killed, the deal's off."

He grinned. "Tonight we send out for pizza. I'll be back."

He was gone quickly, swallowed up by the building. The waiting began.

Thorpe had a pretty good idea of what he should do. The questions were already forming in his head as he rode the elevator with an armed guard. The trick would be to keep Morrow pacified, at ease. Talking. Keep him talking. He fully intended to come out in one piece. Lebanon had taught him a few things.

He'd ridden this elevator before, countless times. It was part of the routine. Hadn't Alex Haley interviewed Rockwell while the American Nazi leader had played with a gun? And that had been a hell of an interview. Reporters couldn't always choose the sane and the reasonable.

The elevator opened and he started down the hall. The tickle at the back of his neck told him there were more guns. He ignored them and knocked on Wyatt's outer office.

"T.C.?"

He heard Morrow's voice, strung out with nerves.

"Yeah. I'm alone."

"Come in slow. I've got a good view of the door."

Thorpe did as he was instructed. Morrow stood in the archway to Wyatt's inner office with his gun held to the senator's head.

"T.C." Wyatt's normally florid face was gray. "You've got to be crazy."

"How are you, Senator?"

"He's fine," Morrow snapped, his eyes darting behind Thorpe. "Shut the door and step away from it."

When Thorpe obeyed, he signaled him with a jerk of his head to come forward. He eyed the tape recorder. "Set it down and take off your jacket."

"No weapons, Ed," Thorpe said easily as he carefully stripped off his jacket. "Just the tape recorder. We made a deal." He gave Wyatt an apologetic smile. "You'll have to excuse us, Senator. Ed and I have a private interview."

"Yeah." Morrow stared at Thorpe a moment, then loosened his hold on Wyatt. "Yeah. You can go."

"T.C.—"

"I said you can go." Morrow's voice lifted. So did the gun. "He's here for me this time."

"Sorry, Senator." Thorpe's voice was calm and unruffled. His fingertips were prickling as he watched the gun hand tremble. "Ed and I have a lot to discuss. We'll set something up later."

With a nod, Wyatt started to turn.

"No." Morrow stopped him with the word. He licked his lips, then ran the back of his hand over them. "You back up, all the way out."

Thorpe waited as Wyatt followed Morrow's instructions. There was fear in the room; he could all but taste it. It didn't lessen even after the door closed behind Wyatt. Morrow stood a moment, staring at the door.

Thorpe didn't want him to start thinking too carefully. "All right," he said, and took a seat. "Let's get started." He turned on the tape recorder.

Outside, Liv watched the building steadily. Everything but her mind was numb. She couldn't feel her hands, her feet. She knew there was activity all around her—in the communications van, in the press area. Things were starting to hum. Her mind was focused on one thing. Thorpe.

Thorpe kept his questions brief. He wanted as little emotion as possible. "Ed, it might be more comfortable for both of us if you . . ." He made a gesture with his hand, palm lowered to indicate the gun. Morrow glanced at it, then shifted the revolver until it was no longer aimed at Thorpe's chest. "Thanks. Obviously, you chose Wyatt's office because you worked here," he went on. "Did you feel the senator was unjust in letting you go?"

"He's clean as a whistle, you know," Morrow answered. "Couldn't blackmail him. God I needed the money. In deep, T.C.—too damn deep. I thought about juggling some funds, but I didn't have enough time. He found out about the gambling, about the people I've been dealing with. Not the senator's kind of people." He laughed in a quick nervous giggle and shifted the gun again. It was pointed back at Thorpe, but Morrow didn't notice. "I thought I'd get some-thing for taking him hostage, but they'd never let me get away with it, would they?" The look he gave Thorpe was lost and fatalistic. "I'd be a dead man before I got my hands on the money."

Thorpe changed the line of questioning. A man with nothing to lose was the most dangerous. "How much are you in for?"

"Seventy-five thousand." The phone rang and Morrow jerked up. The gun was pointed at Thorpe's head.

"Fifteen minutes, Ed," Thorpe reminded him calmly. "We arranged for me to check in every fifteen minutes, right?"

Someone pushed a cup of coffee into Liv's hand. She never tasted it. Thorpe's voice came suddenly, low and calm, from behind her through the machines in the van. Jolting, she dropped the cup. Coffee splashed warm around her ankles. *You can't stand here and do nothing*, she told herself, steadying. Do your job. Turning, she went back to her crew to send out the next live bulletin.

* * *

Thirty minutes crawled into sixty. The office was stuffy. Thorpe knew he was dragging out the interview. All had been said. But his instincts told him Morrow wasn't ready yet. The man was slouched in his chair, his eyes filmy. There was a thin bead of sweat over his top lip, and a muscle twitched in his left cheek sporadically. But the gun was still in his hand.

"You're not married, are you, T.C.?"

"No." Carefully, Thorpe drew out a cigarette, offering one to Morrow.

Morrow shook his head. "Got a woman?"

"Yeah." Thorpe lit the cigarette and thought of Liv. Cool hands, cool voice. "Yeah, I've got a woman."

"I had a wife—kids too." The film in the eyes became tears. "She packed up and left last week. Ten years. She said ten years was long enough to wait for me to keep my promises. I swore to her I wouldn't gamble anymore." Tears rolled down to mix with the sweat. He wiped neither away. "I always swore I wouldn't gamble anymore. But I needed to get even. You know what they do to you when you can't get even." He shuddered.

"There are people who can help you, Ed. Why don't we go outside. I know some people."

"Help?" Morrow sighed on the word. Thorpe didn't like the sound of it. "No help now, T.C. I crossed the line." He looked up and stared into Thorpe's eyes. "A man should know what's going to happen when he crosses the line." He raised the gun again, and Thorpe felt his heart stop. "You make sure," Morrow sobbed, "I get my airtime." Before Thorpe could move, Morrow had turned the gun on himself.

One shot. Just one. Liv felt her legs buckle, saw the granite-faced building fade. Someone gripped her arm as she swayed.

"Liv, come on. You'd better sit down." It was Bob's voice in her ear, his hand on her arm.

"No." She shook him off. She wasn't going to faint. She wasn't going to give in. Fiercely, she began to push her way through the crowd again. She was going to be standing up when he came through the doors. When he came through them, she would be there for him.

Don't let him be hurt. Oh, God, don't let him be. . . The fear was rising in her throat. No hysterics, she warned herself as she pushed a print reporter and two cameramen out of her way. Soon he'll be striding across the street. We've got a whole lifetime to start together. Today. Risks? We'll take hundreds of risks. Together, damn you, Thorpe. Together. She shoved her way clear.

Then she saw him. Alive, whole, walking toward her. She was running, past the barricades, away from the crowd.

"Oh, damn you, Thorpe. Damn you!" Weeping, she clung to him. The more she shuddered, the more she cursed him, the tighter he held her.

Suddenly, she was laughing. It was, after all, a beautiful day. Taking his hair in her hands, Liv pulled his head back to see his face. "You bastard, you're going to beat me on the air with this, aren't you? Oh, *Thorpe*!" She pressed her mouth to his and tightened her hold. Neither of them took any note of the cameras whirling and clicking around them.

He drew her away and the grin was back, though she could see traces of horror in his eyes from whatever had happened inside. "Do you love me?" he demanded.

"Yes, damn you. Yes."

When she tried to pull him back to her, he held her off, lifting a brow. "Going to marry me?"

"The minute we get a license. We're not going to waste any time."

Briefly, his mouth touched hers. They linked arms. "By the way, Carmichael," he said, as they strolled away from the building, "you owe me two hundred dollars."

Can't get enough of Nora Roberts?
Try the #1 *New York Times* bestselling
In Death series, by Nora Roberts
writing as J. D. Robb.

Turn the page to see where it all began . . .

NAKED IN DEATH

*S*he woke in the dark. Through the slats on the window shades, the first murky hint of dawn slipped, slanting shadowy bars over the bed. It was like waking in a cell.

For a moment she simply lay there, shuddering, imprisoned, while the dream faded. After ten years on the force, Eve still had dreams.

Six hours before, she'd killed a man, had watched death creep into his eyes. It wasn't the first time she'd exercised maximum force, or dreamed. She'd learned to accept the action and the consequences.

But it was the child that haunted her. The child she hadn't been in time to save. The child whose screams had echoed in the dreams with her own.

All the blood, Eve thought, scrubbing sweat from her face with her hands. Such a small little girl to have had so much blood in her. And she knew it was vital that she push it aside.

Standard departmental procedure meant that she would spend the morning in Testing. Any officer whose discharge of weapon resulted in termination of life was required to undergo emotional and psychiatric clearance before resuming duty. Eve considered the tests a mild pain in the ass.

She would beat them, as she'd beaten them before.

When she rose, the overheads went automatically to low setting, lighting her way into the bath. She winced once at her reflection. Her eyes were swollen from lack of sleep, her skin nearly as pale as the corpses she'd delegated to the ME.

Rather than dwell on it, she stepped into the shower, yawning.

"Give me one oh one degrees, full force," she said and shifted so that the shower spray hit her straight in the face.

She let it steam, lathered listlessly while she played through the events of the night before. She wasn't due in Testing until nine, and would use the next three hours to settle and let the dream fade away completely.

Small doubts and little regrets were often detected and could mean a second and more intense round with the machines and the owl-eyed technicians who ran them.

Eve didn't intend to be off the streets longer than twenty-four hours.

After pulling on a robe, she walked into the kitchen and programmed her AutoChef for coffee, black; toast, light. Through her window she could hear the heavy hum of air traffic carrying early commuters to offices, late ones home. She'd chosen the apartment years before because it was in a heavy ground and air pattern, and she liked the noise and crowds. On another yawn, she glanced out the window, followed the rattling journey of an aging airbus hauling laborers not fortunate enough to work in the city or by home 'links.

She brought the *New York Times* up on her monitor and scanned the headlines while the faux caffeine bolstered her system. The AutoChef had burned her toast again, but she ate it anyway, with a vague thought of springing for a replacement unit.

She was frowning over an article on a mass recall of droid cocker spaniels when her telelink blipped. Eve shifted to communications and watched her commanding officer flash onto the screen.

"Commander."

"Lieutenant." He gave her a brisk nod, noted the still wet hair and sleepy eyes. "Incident at Twenty-seven West Broadway, eighteenth floor. You're primary."

Eve lifted a brow. "I'm on Testing. Subject terminated at twenty-two thirty-five."

"We have override," he said, without inflection. "Pick up

your shield and weapon on the way to the incident. Code Five, Lieutenant."

"Yes, sir." His face flashed off even as she pushed back from the screen. Code Five meant she would report directly to her commander, and there would be no unsealed interdepartmental reports and no cooperation with the press.

In essence, it meant she was on her own.

Broadway was noisy and crowded, a party that rowdy guests never left. Street, pedestrian, and sky traffic were miserable, choking the air with bodies and vehicles. In her old days in uniform she remembered it as a hot spot for wrecks and crushed tourists who were too busy gaping at the show to get out of the way.

Even at this hour steam was rising from the stationary and portable food stands that offered everything from rice noodles to soy dogs for the teeming crowds. She had to swerve to avoid an eager merchant on his smoking Glida-Grill, and took his flipped middle finger as a matter of course.

Eve double-parked and, skirting a man who smelled worse than his bottle of brew, stepped onto the sidewalk. She scanned the building first, fifty floors of gleaming metal that knifed into the sky from a hilt of concrete. She was propositioned twice before she reached the door.

Since this five-block area of West Broadway was affectionately termed Prostitute's Walk, she wasn't surprised. She flashed her badge for the uniform guarding the entrance.

"Lieutenant Dallas."

"Yes, sir." He skimmed his official CompuSeal over the door to keep out the curious, then led the way to the bank of elevators. "Eighteenth floor," he said when the doors swished shut behind them.

"Fill me in, Officer." Eve switched on her recorder and waited.

"I wasn't first on the scene, Lieutenant. Whatever happened upstairs is being kept upstairs. There's a badge inside waiting for you. We have a homicide, and a Code Five in number eighteen-oh-three."

"Who called it in?"

"I don't have that information."

He stayed where he was when the elevator opened. Eve stepped out and was alone in a narrow hallway. Security cameras tilted down at her, and her feet were almost soundless on the worn nap of the carpet as she approached 1803. Ignoring the hand plate, she announced herself, holding her badge up to eye level for the peep cam until the door opened.

"Dallas."

"Feeney." She smiled, pleased to see a familiar face. Ryan Feeney was an old friend and former partner who'd traded the street for a desk and a top-level position in the Electronics Detection Division. "So, they're sending computer pluckers these days."

"They wanted brass, and the best." His lips curved in his wide, rumpled face, but his eyes remained sober. He was a small, stubby man with small, stubby hands and rust-colored hair. "You look beat."

"Rough night."

"So I heard." He offered her one of the sugared nuts from the bag he habitually carried, studying her, and measuring if she was up to what was waiting in the bedroom beyond.

She was young for her rank, barely thirty, with wide brown eyes that had never had a chance to be naive. Her doe-brown hair was cropped short, for convenience rather than style, but, suited her triangular face with its razor-edge cheekbones and slight dent in the chin.

She was tall, rangy, with a tendency to look thin, but Feeney knew there were solid muscles beneath the leather jacket. But Eve had more—there was also a brain, and a heart.

"This one's going to be touchy, Dallas."

"I picked that up already. Who's the victim?"

"Sharon DeBlass, granddaughter of Senator DeBlass."

Neither meant anything to her. "Politics isn't my forte, Feeney."

"The gentleman from Virginia, extreme right, old money. The granddaughter took a sharp left a few years back, moved to New York and became a licensed companion."

"She was a hooker." Dallas glanced around the apartment. It was furnished in obsessive modern—glass and thin chrome, signed holograms on the walls, recessed bar in bold red. The wide mood screen behind the bar bled with mixing and merging shapes and colors in cool pastels.

Neat as a virgin, Eve mused, and cold as a whore. "No surprise, given her choice of real estate."

"Politics makes it delicate. Victim was twenty-four, Caucasian female. She bought it in bed."

Eve only lifted a brow. "Seems poetic, since she'd been bought there. How'd she die?"

"That's the next problem. I want you to see for yourself."

As they crossed the room, each took out a slim container, sprayed their hands front and back to seal in oils and fingerprints. At the doorway, Eve sprayed the bottom of her boots to slicken them so that she would pick up no fibers, stray hairs, or skin.

Eve was already wary. Under normal circumstances there would have been two other investigators on a homicide scene, with recorders for sound and pictures. Forensics would have been waiting with their usual snarly impatience to sweep the scene.

The fact that only Feeney had been assigned with her meant that there were a lot of eggshells to be walked over.

"Security cameras in the lobby, elevator, and hallways," Eve commented.

"I've already tagged the discs." Feeney opened the bedroom door and let her enter first.

It wasn't pretty. Death rarely was a peaceful, religious experience to Eve's mind. It was the nasty end, indifferent to saint and sinner. But this was shocking, like a stage deliberately set to offend.

The bed was huge, slicked with what appeared to be genuine satin sheets the color of ripe peaches. Small, soft-focused spotlights were trained on its center where the naked woman was cupped in the gentle dip of the floating mattress.

The mattress moved with obscenely graceful undulations to the rhythm of programmed music slipping through the headboard.

She was beautiful still, a cameo face with a tumbling waterfall of flaming red hair, emerald eyes that stared glassily at the mirrored ceiling, long, milk-white limbs that called to mind visions of *Swan Lake* as the motion of the bed gently rocked them.

They weren't artistically arranged now, but spread lewdly so that the dead woman formed a final X dead-center of the bed.

There was a hole in her forehead, one in her chest, another horribly gaping between the open thighs. Blood had splattered on the glossy sheets, pooled, dripped, and stained.

There were splashes of it on the lacquered walls, like lethal paintings scrawled by an evil child.

So much blood was a rare thing, and she had seen much too much of it the night before to take the scene as calmly as she would have preferred.

She had to swallow once, hard, and force herself to block out the image of a small child.

"You got the scene on record?"

"Yep."

"Then turn that damn thing off." She let out a breath after Feeney located the controls that silenced the music. The bed flowed to stillness. "The wounds," Eve murmured, stepping closer to examine them. "Too neat for a knife. Too messy for a laser." A flash came to her—old training films, old videos, old viciousness.

"Christ, Feeney, these look like bullet wounds."

Feeney reached into his pocket and drew out a sealed bag. "Whoever did it left a souvenir." He passed the bag to Eve. "An antique like this has to go for eight, ten thousand for a legal collection, twice that on the black market."

Fascinated, Eve turned the sealed revolver over in her hand. "It's heavy," she said half to herself. "Bulky."

"Thirty-eight caliber," he told her. "First one I've seen outside of a museum. This one's a Smith and Wesson, Model Ten, blue steel." He looked at it with some affection. "Real classic piece, used to be standard police issue up until the latter part of the twentieth. They stopped making them in about twenty-two, twenty-three, when the gun ban was passed."

"You're the history buff." Which explained why he was with her. "Looks new." She sniffed through the bag, caught the scent of oil and burning. "Somebody took good care of this.

Steel fired into flesh," she mused as she passed the bag back to Feeney. "Ugly way to die, and the first I've seen it in my ten years with the department."

"Second for me. About fifteen years ago, Lower East Side, party got out of hand. Guy shot five people with a twenty-two before he realized it wasn't a toy. Hell of a mess."

"Fun and games," Eve murmured. "We'll scan the collectors, see how many we can locate who own one like this. Somebody might have reported a robbery."

"Might have."

"It's more likely it came through the black market." Eve glanced back at the body. "If she's been in the business for a few years, she'd have discs, records of her clients, her trick books." She frowned. "With Code Five, I'll have to do the door-to-door myself. Not a simple sex crime," she said with a sigh. "Whoever did it set it up. The antique weapon, the wounds themselves, almost ruler straight down the body, the lights, the pose. Who called it in, Feeney?"

"The killer." He waited until her eyes came back to him. "From right here. Called the station. See how the bedside unit's aimed at her face? That's what came in. Video, no audio."

"He's into showmanship." Eve let out a breath. "Clever bastard, arrogant, cocky. He had sex with her first. I'd bet my badge on it. Then he gets up and does it." She lifted her arm, aiming, lowering it as she counted off, "One, two, three."

"That's cold," murmured Feeney.

"He's cold. He smooths down the sheets after. See how neat they are? He arranges her, spreads her open so nobody can have any doubts as to how she made her living. He does it carefully, practically measuring, so that she's perfectly aligned. Center of the bed, arms and legs equally apart. Doesn't turn off the bed 'cause it's part of the show. He leaves the gun because he wants us to know right away he's no ordinary man. He's got an ego. He doesn't want to waste time letting the body be discovered eventually. He wants it now. That instant gratification."

"She was licensed for men and women," Feeney pointed out, but Eve shook her head.

"It's not a woman. A woman wouldn't have left her looking both beautiful and obscene. No, I don't think it's a woman. Let's see what we can find. Have you gone into her computer yet?"

"No. It's your case, Dallas. I'm only authorized to assist."

"See if you can access her client files." Eve went to the dresser and began to carefully search drawers.

Expensive taste, Eve reflected. There were several items of real silk, the kind no simulation could match. The bottle of scent on the dresser was exclusive, and smelled, after a quick sniff, like expensive sex.

The contents of the drawers were meticulously ordered, lingerie folded precisely, sweaters arranged according to color and material. The closet was the same.

Obviously the victim had a love affair with clothes and a taste for the best and took scrupulous care of what she owned.

And she'd died naked.

"Kept good records," Feeney called out. "It's all here. Her client list, appointments—including her required monthly health exam and her weekly trip to the beauty salon. She used the Trident Clinic for the first and Paradise for the second."

"Both top-of-the-line. I've got a friend who saved for a year so she could have one day for the works at Paradise. Takes all kinds."

"My wife's sister went for it for her twenty-fifth anniversary. Cost damn near as much as my kid's wedding. Hello, we've got her personal address book."

"Good. Copy all of it, will you, Feeney?" At his low whistle, she looked over her shoulder, glimpsed the small gold-edged palm computer in his hand. "What?"

"We've got a lot of high-powered names in here. Politics, entertainment, money, money, money. Interesting, our girl has Roarke's private number."

"Roarke who?"

"Just Roarke, as far as I know. Big money there. Kind of guy that touches shit and turns it into gold bricks. You've got to start reading more than the sports page, Dallas."

"Hey, I read the headlines. Did you hear about the cocker spaniel recall?"

"Roarke's always big news," Feeney said patiently. "He's got one of the finest art collections in the world. Arts and antiques," he continued, noting when Eve clicked in and turned to him. "He's a licensed gun collector. Rumor is he knows how to use them."

"I'll pay him a visit."

"You'll be lucky to get within a mile of him."

"I'm feeling lucky." Eve crossed over to the body to slip her hands under the sheets.

"The man's got powerful friends, Dallas. You can't afford to so much as whisper he's linked to this until you've got something solid."

"Feeney, you know it's a mistake to tell me that." But even as she started to smile, her fingers brushed against something between cold flesh and bloody sheets. "There's something under her." Carefully, Eve lifted the shoulder, eased her fingers over.

"Paper," she murmured. "Sealed." With her protected thumb, she wiped at a smear of blood until she could read the protected sheet.

ONE OF SIX

"It looks hand-printed," she said to Feeney and held it out. "Our boy's more than clever, more than arrogant. And he isn't finished."

Eve spent the rest of the day doing what would normally have been assigned to drones: She interviewed the victim's neighbors personally, recording statements, impressions.

She managed to grab a quick sandwich from the same Glida-Grill she'd nearly smashed before, driving across town. After the night and the morning she'd put in, she could hardly blame the receptionist at Paradise for looking at her as though she'd recently scraped herself off the sidewalk.

Waterfalls played musically among the flora in the reception area of the city's most exclusive salon. Tiny cups of real coffee and slim glasses of fizzling water or champagne were served to those lounging on the cushy chairs and settees.

Headphones and discs of fashion magazines were complimentary.

The receptionist was magnificently breasted, a testament to the salon's figure-sculpting techniques. She wore a snug, short outfit is the salon's trademark red, and an incredible coif of ebony hair coiled like snakes.

Eve couldn't have been more delighted.

"I'm sorry," the woman said in a carefully modulated voice as empty of expression as a computer. "We serve by appointment only."

"That's okay." Eve smiled and was almost sorry to puncture the disdain. Almost. "This ought to get me one." She offered her badge. "Who works on Sharon DeBlass?"

The receptionist's horrified eyes darted toward the waiting area. "Our clients' needs are strictly confidential."

"I bet." Enjoying herself, Eve leaned companionably on the U-shaped counter. "I can talk nice and quiet, like this, so we understand each other—Denise?" She flicked her gaze down to the discreet studded badge on the woman's breast. "Or I can talk louder, so everyone understands. If you like the first idea better, you can take me to a nice quiet room where we won't disturb any of your clients, and you can send in Sharon De-Blass's operator. Or whatever term you use."

"Consultant," Denise said faintly. "If you'll follow me."

"My pleasure."

And it was.

Outside of movies or videos, Eve had never seen anything so lush. The carpet was a red cushion your feet could sink blissfully into. Crystal drops hung from the ceiling and spun light. The air smelled of flowers and pampered flesh.

She might not have been able to imagine herself there, spending hours having herself creamed, oiled, pummeled, and sculpted, but if she were going to waste such time on vanity, it would certainly have been interesting to do so under such civilized conditions.

The receptionist showed her into a small room with a hologram of a summer meadow dominating one wall. The quiet sound of birdsong and breezes sweetened the air.

"If you'd just wait here."

"No problem." Eve waited for the door to close then, with an indulgent sigh, she lowered herself into a deeply cushioned chair. The moment she was seated, the monitor beside her blipped on, and a friendly, indulgent face that could only be a droid's beamed smiles.

"Good afternoon. Welcome to Paradise. Your beauty needs and your comfort are our only priorities. Would you like some refreshment while you wait for your personal consultant?"

"Sure. Coffee, black, coffee."

"Of course. What sort would you prefer? Press *C* on your keyboard for the list of choices."

Smothering a chuckle, Eve followed instructions. She spent the next two minutes pondering over her options, then narrowed it down to French Riviera or Caribbean Cream.

The door opened again before she could decide. Resigned, she rose and faced an elaborately dressed scarecrow.

Over his fuchsia shirt and plum-colored slacks, he wore an open, trailing smock of Paradise red. His hair, flowing back from a painfully thin face, echoed the hue of his slacks. He offered Eve a hand, Squeezed gently, and stared at her out of soft doe eyes.

"I'm terribly sorry, Officer. I'm baffled."

"I want information on Sharon DeBlass." Again, Eve took out her badge and offered it for inspection.

"Yes, ah, Lieutenant Dallas. That was my understanding. You must know, of course, our client data is strictly confidential. Paradise has a reputation for discretion as well as excellence."

"And you must know, of course, that I can get a warrant, Mr.—?"

"Oh, Sebastian. Simply Sebastian." He waved a thin hand, sparkling with rings. "I'm not questioning your authority, Lieutenant. But if you could assist me, your motives for the inquiry?"

"I'm inquiring into the motives for the murder of DeBlass." She waited a beat, judged the shock that shot into his eyes and drained his face of color. "Other than that, my data is strictly confidential."

"Murder. My dear God, our lovely Sharon is dead? There

must be a mistake." He all but slid into a chair, letting his head fall back and his eyes close. When the monitor offered him refreshment, he waved a hand again. Light shot from his jeweled fingers. "God, yes. I need a brandy, darling. A snifter of Trevalli."

Eve sat beside him, took out her recorder. "Tell me about Sharon."

"A marvelous creature. Physically stunning, of course, but it went deeper." His brandy came into the room on a silent automated cart. Sebastian plucked the snifter and took one deep swallow. "She had flawless taste, a generous heart, rapier wit."

He turned the doe eyes on Eve again. "I saw her only two days ago."

"Professionally?"

"She had a standing weekly appointment, half day. Every other week was a full day." He whipped out a butter yellow scarf and dabbed at his eyes. "Sharon took care of herself, believed strongly in the presentation of self."

"It would be an asset in her line of work."

"Naturally. She only worked to amuse herself. Money wasn't a particular need, with her family background. She enjoyed sex."

"With you?"

His artistic face winced, the rosy lips pursing in what could have been a pout or pain. "I was her consultant, her confidant, and her friend," Sebastian said stiffly and draped the scarf with casual flare over his left shoulder. "It would have been indiscreet and unprofessional for us to become sexual partners."

"So you weren't attracted to her, sexually?"

"It was impossible for anyone not to be attracted to her sexually. She . . ." He gestured grandly. "Exuded sex as others might exude an expensive perfume. My God." He took another shaky sip of brandy. "It's all past tense. I can't believe it. Dead. Murdered." His gaze shot back to Eve. "You said murdered."

"That's right."

"That neighborhood she lived in," he said grimly. "No one could talk to her about moving to a more acceptable location.

She enjoyed living on the edge and flaunting it all under her family's aristocratic noses."

"She and her family were at odds?"

"Oh definitely. She enjoyed shocking them. She was such a free spirit, and they so . . . ordinary." He said it in a tone that indicated ordinary was more mortal a sin than murder itself. "Her grandfather continues to introduce bills that would make prostitution illegal. As if the past century hasn't proven that such matters need to be regulated for health and crime security. He also stands against procreation regulation, gender adjustment, chemical balancing, and the gun ban."

Eve's ears pricked. "The senator opposes the gun ban?"

"It's one of his pets. Sharon told me he owns a number of nasty antiques and spouts off regularly about that outdated right to bear arms business. If he had his way, we'd all be back in the twentieth century, murdering each other right and left."

"Murder still happens," Eve murmured. "Did she ever mention friends or clients who might have been dissatisfied or overly aggressive?"

"Sharon had dozens of friends. She drew people to her, like . . ." He searched for a suitable metaphor, used the corner of the scarf again. "Like an exotic and fragrant flower. And her clients, as far as I know, were all delighted with her. She screened them carefully. All of her sexual partners had to meet certain standards. Appearance, intellect, breeding, and proficiency. As I said, she enjoyed sex, in all of its many forms. She was . . . adventurous."

That fit with the toys Eve had unearthed in the apartment. The velvet handcuffs and whips, the scented oils and hallucinogens. The offerings on the two sets of colinked virtual reality headphones had been a shock even to Eve's jaded system.

"Was she involved with anyone on a personal level?"

"There were men occasionally, but she lost interest quickly. Recently she'd spoken about Roarke. She'd met him at a party and was attracted. In fact, she was seeing him for dinner the very night she came in for her consultation. She'd wanted something exotic because they were dining in Mexico."

"In Mexico. That would have been the night before last."

Yes. She was just bubbling over about him. We did her hair

in a gypsy look, gave her a bit more gold to the skin—full body work. Rascal Red on the nails, and a charming little temp tattoo of a red-winged butterfly on the left buttock. Twenty-four-hour facial cosmetics so that she wouldn't smudge, She looked spectacular," he said, tearing up. "And she kissed me and told me she just might be in love this time. 'Wish me luck, Sebastian.' She said that as she left. It was the last thing she ever said to me."

New in hardcover from
NORA ROBERTS

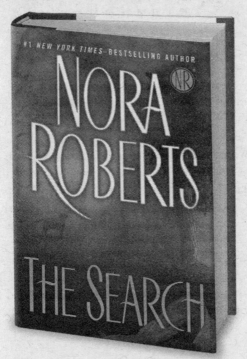

A canine search-and-rescue volunteer fights danger
and finds love in the Pacific Northwest wilderness.

NoraRoberts.com

G. P. PUTNAM'S SONS
A member of Penguin Group (USA) Inc.
www.penguin.com

M636JV0110

Now available in paperback from
#1 *New York Times* bestselling author

N o r a   R o b e r t s

BLACK HILLS

A summer at his grandparents' South Dakota ranch is not eleven-year-old Cooper Sullivan's idea of a good time. But things are a bit more bearable now that he's discovered the neighbor girl, Lil Chance. Each year, with Coop's annual summer visit, their friendship deepens from innocent games to stolen kisses, but there is one shared experience that will forever haunt them: the terrifying discovery of a hiker's body.

Twelve years after they last walked together hand in hand, fate has brought them back to the Black Hills at a time when the people and things they hold most dear need them most . . .

penguin.com